THE YEAR OF THE FRENCH

'This deserves every major literary award'

Publishers Weekly

'The finest historical novel by an American to appear in more than a decade' *Washington Post Book World*

'One of the finest epic historical novels I have ever read' *Boston Herald-American*

'His mastery of the historical material, his ear for Irish dialogue, his knowledge of the topography of Mayo and his capacity for stylistic mimicry, all combine to produce a memorable historical novel' *The Listener*

'If this book doesn't get read and esteemed then there is something dreadfully wrong with our literary world'

Financial Times

THE YEAR OF THE FRENCH

Thomas Flanagan

**THE SHERIDAN
BOOK COMPANY**

This edition published in 1993 by
The Sheridan Book Company

First published in Great Britain by Macmillan London Limited 1979

Arrow edition 1980
Random House, 20 Vauxhall Bridge Road, London SW1V 2SA

Reprinted 1981 (three times), 1982 and 1989

Printed and bound in Great Britain by
Cox & Wyman Ltd, Reading, Berkshire

ISBN 1-85501-446-7

For Jean, as always,
and for Ellen and Kate.
In memory, as always,
of Ellen Treacy of Fermanagh
and Thomas Bonner
of the Fenian Brotherhood.

COUNTY MAYO

THE YEAR OF THE FRENCH

In the year of 1798, a band of Irishmen in County Mayo
rose against British rule. The French, secure in the
success of their own revolution, were persuaded by
Wolfe Tone and others to come to their aid. Though the
French were motivated less by a concern for Ireland
than by a desire to harass the British, three ships
carrying troops broke through the British blockade and
landed in the Bay of Killala. It was the signal for the war
of liberation to begin.

Out of this historical episode, Thomas Flanagan has
written a sweeping epic novel of mesmerising power and
profound humanity. Rich, colourful and vividly alive,
The Year of the French has a memorable cast of characters: the powerfully drawn Owen MacCarthy – poet,
teacher, lover, doomed visionary; Arthur Broome, the
fair-minded English clergyman, keeping a faithful
record of the bloody drama; the aristocratic George
Moore, who watches his impetuous brother go to his
death, and sets out too late to save him; Judith Elliott,
in love with romantic Ireland, her heart eventually
broken by the reality . . . Unforgettable characters in a
story that is beautifully told, richly detailed and
memorably moving.

Prologue:

Early Summer, 1798

MacCarthy was light-headed that night when he set out
from Judy Conlon's cabin in the Acres of Killala. Not
drunk at all, but light-headed. He carried with him an
inch or two of whiskey, tight-corked in a flask of green
glass, and the image which had badgered him for a week.
Moonlight falling on a hard, flat surface, scythe or sword
or stone or spade. It was not an image from which a poem
would unwind itself, but it could be hung as a glittering,
appropriate ornament upon a poem already shaped. Problems of the craft.

Halfway to Kilcummin strand, the sullen bay hammered flat to his right, and to his left a low stone fence, he
took the flask from a back pocket of his long-tailed coat.
Within the colored glass, in the clear light of summer's
evening, the whiskey was a drowned moon. When the
flask was empty, he sent it on a high arc toward the shore.
Like moonlight's glint upon water. Or its glow upon her
rounded breast. No, the image demanded a flat surface.
Until he had the image, he would be its slave.

At Matthew Quigley's tavern, a long, low cabin across
the narrow road from the rock-strewn strand, he put his
fist to the door, knocked, and waited. Quigley opened it
for him, a short, bandy-legged man, bald, with a large
head round as the full moon.

"You are late," he said.

"I am," MacCarthy said. "I had better things to do."

"You did to be sure," Quigley said. "In the Killala
Acres."

"It is where I live," MacCarthy said. Quigley stood
back, and he entered the tavern, bending his neck to the
low door. He was a clumsily built man, tall and raw-

1

boned, with long arms reaching toward his knees from heavy, sloping shoulders. It was a plowboy's body, and a plowboy's head, thatch of coarse red hair like a beacon fire on a hill, long, thin lip.

Three men sitting by the cold fireplace looked up toward him, and one of them spoke. Malachi Duggan, a heavy bull, shoulders hunched forward. "You are late."

"So it would seem," MacCarthy said. "I don't own a watch."

But he did. A handsome gold watch as thick as a turnip, given him years before by some gentlemen of North Kerry after a poetry competition, with branches and sprays of flowers traced upon its casing. Useless now, smashed one night in Newcastle West, the casing bent, and a litter of cogs, wheels, and springs beneath the splintered white dial, a shattered moon.

"You will take a drop," Quigley said, and filled a glass for him.

"He has never been known to refuse one," Phelim O'Carroll said. "Have you, Owen?"

" 'Tis a modest boast," MacCarthy said, and sat down with them. O'Carroll the widower, with a strong farm held from the Big Lord himself; he worked it with his nephew, a harmless half-cracked creature, and a half-dozen laborers. The fourth man was Donal Hennessey; he held less land, but he had two growing sons, and a strapping handsome wife, with long legs and smooth lovely haunches. She had been shaped expressly for the purpose, but Hennessey would have little knowledge of such matters. She gave him children and that was the bargain.

Hennessey did not matter, nor O'Carroll, nor Quigley. Duggan mattered. He sat facing MacCarthy, hands on heavy knees. The eyes were pale blue, watchful; round as moons.

"We have been waiting for an hour," he said. "An hour spitting into a dead fireplace while we waited for a schoolmaster."

"Sure it couldn't have been too hard for Donal and Phelim here, with Matthew Quigley's good whiskey to keep them company. It was hard for a man like yourself who never had a thirst." MacCarthy raised his glass to Quigley.

"It is not for a joke that we asked you here," Duggan said.

2

"It is your help we want," Hennessey said, placating. "You can help us."

Whiskey, raw, burned MacCarthy's throat, and then spread its warmth through him. Light from the unglazed window fell upon the glass: imprisoned fire.

"Only a letter," Duggan said. "There is a letter that we want you to write for us in English. A letter to a landlord. You know the kind of letter we need, and there is none of us can write it."

"You cannot be serious," MacCarthy said. " 'Remorseless Tyrant beware. Long has your heel been ground into our neck.' "

"We are serious, right enough," Hennessey said.

MacCarthy spoke in English. " 'A terrible vengeance will fall upon you. Tyrant beware.' "

"By God, that must be beautiful English. You rattle that out like an agent. What did that mean, Owen?"

MacCarthy did not answer him. He spoke to the watchful bull, Duggan, heavy dark head balanced easily on thick-muscled neck.

"What is it to be, a warning to the agent of the Big Lord?" He shook his head. "He would use it as a wad to start his fire."

Matthew Quigley, greasy-aproned, leaned forward to refill their glasses, Hennessey's, O'Carroll's, MacCarthy's, his own. Duggan had no glass.

"It is no warning this time," Hennessey said. "And it will not go to the Big Lord's agent. It will go to Captain Cooper here in Kilcummin, to tell him what we have done after we have done it. We are going to hough the cattle that he has turned into the new pasture."

Slashed tendons and bloody bellowing in the night.

"Write your own letter," MacCarthy said.

"An easy thing for you to say, Owen," O'Carroll said. "You have no land to worry about. A schoolmaster has only his books, and who would take those from him?"

"You would," MacCarthy said. "You would take the fine words that are in them. Do you not think the magistrates would wonder who sent Cooper a letter in handcrafted English?" He saw himself standing before the magistrates, and his letter being passed from hand to hand. "Much better you scratched out the letter yourselves, ignorant men confessing an ignorant crime. Draw a coffin on it, is what the Whiteboys used do in the old

3

days. Cooper has enough Irish in him to understand a coffin."

"It is no crime," Quigley said, "when slaves ask for simple decency."

"Is it not? The magistrates would quarrel with you there, and so would Hussey in the Killala chapel." Whiskey lapped at the edges of his spirit. He drank again.

"A priest has no understanding of these matters," O'Carroll said.

"I know," MacCarthy said. "He has no land. If you mean to protest slavery, you might put in a word for your own. There are no worse slaves in this barony than those poor lads you bring in from the hiring fair and keep half starved on potatoes an honest man would not throw to sows."

"Now that is a hard saying, Owen," Hennessey said. "Poor Phelim does the best he can for those lads. He has the life squeezed out of him by the Big Lord's agent, and so do I. And well you know it."

MacCarthy drained the whiskey. "But you have no need to look abroad for slaves, have you, Donal? They are bred for you at home."

Puzzled. "My sons, do you mean?"

"Do you call them so? There is no great resemblance." In a corner of his imagination, the mother of Hennessey's young sons stood wide-legged by the cabin door.

"This is a letter that you will write," Duggan said. The others looked toward him. MacCarthy watched their eyes. They followed where he led, hard farmer, bully, faction fighter. Three years ago, on a fairday, he led the men of Tyrawley against those of Erris, stout stick in hand, neither pleasure nor anger shaping the creased, stolid face. Leaning against the gable end of the Belmullet tavern, MacCarthy had watched, disdainful and awed. "You will use your fine English for this letter, and it will be a long one. You will say that this will happen whenever a farm is taken for pasture by any landlord or any middleman. And there will be no other warnings. We want that known."

"You want that known," MacCarthy said. He held out his glass and Quigley refilled it. A poet's privilege. "Four men in a tavern want that known."

"There are more than four, Owen," Hennessey said. "You may be certain of that." He was a marvel. Insults dripped from him like rain from a cow's flank.

4

"The Whiteboys of Killala," Duggan said. "You will sign it that way. The Whiteboys of Killala."

"The Whiteboys of Claremorris were on public view two years ago," MacCarthy said. "Two of them, in Castlebar, outside the courthouse. Gibbeted and soaked in tar." Beyond the window, a corner of the moon. Elegant, aloof.

"Out of how many?" Hennessey asked. "The people will be with us in this.'"

"By God they will," Duggan said. For the first time he smiled.

"Not my people," MacCarthy said. "I am from Kerry." Clear water and bright cliffs; bird song.

"You are here now," Duggan said. "In the barony of Tyrawley. You would do well to remember that. It is not four men in a tavern. It is a matter for the men in all the townlands.'"

"I do not think so," MacCarthy said. "You have a grievance to pay Cooper for, because he turfed out the O'Malleys to make pastureland, and you have given yourselves a grand name, the Whiteboys of Killala."

" 'Tis a good enough name," O'Carroll said.

What did it matter? The Whiteboys of Macroom, the True Men of Bruff, the Honest Men of Tralee. For thirty years now they had been starting up in one place or another, and the end was always the same, bodies on a gibbet. But this was a strange year for Whiteboys, with every peddler and traveling man bringing stories into Mayo of the great fighting in Ulster to the north and Wexford far off to the south. They had not been Whiteboys, those United Irishmen. Now they were nothing at all. Two months ago, the armies of England had smashed them.

"It is a very good name," Duggan said. "Every landlord in Ireland knows it, and he knows what it means. There will be cattle killed and fields burned, and there is worse that could follow after. This is nothing new in Mayo. There are bodies of agents and bodies of bailiffs sunk in the bogs of Belmullet, with their eyes squeezed out of their heads and their backs cut to ribbons by thornbushes."

His voice was flat, but his lips glistened with spittle. He wants this. The thick, square fingers could fasten on bailiff's throat, tear punishing thornbush from the earth.

"Ach, there is no choice, Owen," O'Carroll said. "If the landlords turn to grazing we are done for. It is hap-

5

pening in other places. There is no argument we have but the Whiteboys' letter."

MacCarthy turned toward Quigley. "A tavernkeeper has no land. What is all this to you?"

"Well now, Owen. I have no land it is true, no more than a schoolmaster has. That is true for you." He took MacCarthy's glass and filled it again with the calm, colorless whiskey. "But a man should stand in well with his neighbors. That never hurts him, whatever his trade."

MacCarthy turned the glass around in his hand. The room was darkening. Beyond the window, the evening light had turned to the linnet-wing softness which stands at the edge of night.

"This is a foolish business you have in mind," he said to Duggan. "Great risings have now been stamped out in Ulster and in Wexford. There was a traveling man last week in Killala who said that gallows stretch from one end of the County Wexford to the other, and burned cabins. And no count will ever be made of all who were killed with musket and sword. He said that there are more English soldiers in the country now than have been here since the Boyne. They are in Tuam in their thousands, and they are in their thousands in the city of Galway."

"I heard that traveling man," O'Carroll said. "He had more to say than that. He said that for a month the army of the Gael was victorious in the County Wexford.'"

"Great comfort that was to them when they stood on the gallows," MacCarthy said.

"There are not thousands of British soldiers in Tyrawley," Duggan said. "There is only Captain Cooper and his tinpot yeomen. Protestant shopkeepers and tithe proctors. What was happening away off in Wexford or in Ulster is no matter here."

"There were thousands of them risen up in rebellion," said MacCarthy. "All of the County Wexford, and all of Carlow and all of Wicklow and parts of Kilkenny. They tried to fight their way out of Wexford. They were going to bring their rebellion to all of Ireland. They went this way and that way, but there were English soldiers on all the roads. And when they could think of nowhere else to go, they climbed a hill and waited for the English cannon to blow them to pieces."

Beyond the power of his imagination. The roads of Wexford clotted with people, their pikes a winter forest against the horizon. Priests rode in their van. Faction

6

fighters drove them against yeomen and militia. They prodded cattle before them into battle. He heard again the words of the traveling man: "There were great encampments of the people on the plains and along the rivers. They captured town after town, Camolin and Wexford and Enniscorthy. They burned Enniscorthy." Only two months ago. All over now.

"The people of Wexford were fools," Duggan said. "Captain Cooper will satisfy me. And after him, Gibson."

"Gibson is your own landlord, is he not?" MacCarthy said. "I thought that you would find time for Gibson."

"Then Gibson," Hennessey agreed. "But after him the agent for the Big Lord. By God, I hate that Creighton. He is the worst tyrant in Tyrawley."

"He does as he is bid," MacCarthy said. "The Big Lord off in London sends him a letter of instructions. That is how it is done."

"I will send him a letter, by God," Duggan said. "The Whiteboys of Killala will send him a letter."

"So that is to be the way of it," MacCarthy said, "and then a fourth and then a fifth. You have a great budget of work for me there."

"You will be safe enough, Owen," Hennessey said. "We will all be safe enough. There will be five hundred Whiteboys in Tyrawley."

"It will not stop at the bounds of this barony," Duggan said. "There are men I know in Erris, and across the Moy in Sligo."

"We are not fools," Quigley said. "We have met with this fellow and that fellow. And we have made out an oath."

"To be sure you have," MacCarthy said. "An oath is a Whiteboy's first order of business. The more mouth-filling the better." Seventeen seventy-nine, a barn close to Tralee in Kerry, and MacCarthy just turned eighteen. Frightened, boastful faces gathered around a candle. He would burn away parts of his past if he could, all the nights of the Whiteboys' moon. Fellows with blackened faces, white smocks pulled over their coarse frieze, baggy stockings peeping underneath, creeping across wet fields toward cattle. The night air a sudden jangle of bellows and shouts.

"We are not fools," Duggan said. "We know how to do this."

"You do, to be sure," MacCarthy said, draining his

7

glass again. "You are grand fellows. It was well worth my long ramble northward from Kerry to meet such grand fellows."

"Corn and oats will bring good money to the landlords," Hennessey said, "but cattle will bring better. The landlords will give farm after farm to the cattle, as Cooper gave them the farm of the O'Malleys."

The landlords had no choice and the people had no choice and the magistrates would have no choice but to hunt them down and hang them. It was like a proposition in Euclid, straight lines driving toward a point. That is what happened twenty years before, in Kerry and in West Cork. He had seen Whiteboys drink their victories in chapel yards, and he had seen them swing at the rope's end. What of me, he thought; have I a choice?

"We did not bring you here so that you could argue with us, MacCarthy," Duggan said. A question answered.

"No more do I want arguments," MacCarthy said. He took Quigley's jug of ill-tasting whiskey, and filled his glass to the brim. The parting glass.

"That is not true," Duggan said. "You would be happy to sit arguing here while there was any of that stuff left in the jug. You are a slave to it, and every man here knows it."

"We are all slaves," MacCarthy said. It tasted better now, soft and cool. "Slaves to this or slaves to that. I will write your letter for you, and I will write it with my left hand. But I will take no other action with you or for you, and I will take no oath. You will bring blood into the streets of Killala and Kilcummin, and it will not be the blood of landlords."

"Some of it will, by God," Quigley said. "If our blood is spilled, so will theirs be. We will bring the bright edge of the knife to them."

MacCarthy looked at him, despising the round, complacent face. The room was dark now. The face floated in dying afterglow, a fatuous moon. MacCarthy suddenly hurled his glass into a corner of the room; whiskey splashed across his hand.

"Listen to him," he said to Duggan. "Listen to that man. That is the kind of man you will have with you, who has never seen blood save for the blood of cows and pigs. He will be drinking his own bad whiskey and making his boasts and he will drink and boast you up the steps of the gallows."

"But you have seen blood," Duggan said, with his humorless irony.

"I was schoolmaster in Macroom when Paddy Lynch was hanged with five of his followers. I saw his feet reaching for the air and I saw his face. That brought me close enough to blood."

"By God that would take away a man's appetite," O'Carroll said to Duggan, but he smiled nervously to take the edge off his words.

Duggan shifted to face him. "If we are careful and quiet there will be no hangings in Tyrawley."

"In Castlebar," MacCarthy said. "They will load you in carts with your wrists tied behind you and take you down to Castlebar and try you there and hang you there. If you have a hundred men, you will have ten informers and if you have five hundred men you will have fifty."

"Will you listen to this man?" Duggan said to O'Carroll, his voice rough with contempt. "A man who owns nothing in this world but a sack of books and half of Judy Conlon's bed. Let you listen to him, and in two years' time there will be nothing left in Tyrawley but graziers and cowherds. And Judy Conlon."

"Be careful how you talk, Duggan." MacCarthy said, standing up. What use would I be against him, with his hands like great hams, smoked and seasoned by the blackthorn and holly of the faction fights. "By God," he said to the others, "it is once in a while a great comfort not to have land."

"It is," Matthew Quigley said. "A great comfort. If we do not forget loyalty to our neighbors."

"Owen is not the man to forget that," Hennessey said. "Sure, what life would a schoolmaster have if he did not stand in well with his neighbors?"

"None at all," Duggan said. "No life at all."

MacCarthy remained standing. "My thanks to you for the whiskey, Matthew. To which of you am I to give the letter when I have it written?"

"As well to me as to another," Quigley said. "I will walk down to the Acres for it tomorrow evening."

"Not the Acres," MacCarthy said. "Nor my schoolhouse either. I will meet you at Tobin's tavern."

"Sure don't be in such a hurry, Owen," Hennessey said. "Have you no song for us?"

"A song, is it? A pity I haven't Paddy Lynch here to teach you to dance upon air. Poor Paddy, he was a true

9

artist. He learned the mystery of that craft, but he told it to no one."

Only Quigley laughed. "You are a witty man, Owen. A witty man when you have drink taken."

"That is often enough," MacCarthy said.

"Safe home, Owen," Hennessey said.

He took a last look at them, indistinct now in the dark room. What harm will they do, four men in a tavern by Kilcummin strand? No, three men and a bullock with brains. A bullock with eyes as round as moons.

Outside the tavern, the moon mocked him. Full, perfect. It fell upon rock and strand and black bay. The night air was chill. Far to the west, Downpatrick Head, fierce-snouted peninsula, and the lonely, savage barony of Erris. To the south, the Nephin Mountains, in the softer county of Sligo. A hard land indeed, after the sweet kingdom of Kerry, and the cheerful bustle of Cork. The wildest and poorest county in Ireland, the people of Galway said of Mayo. Well were they qualified to judge such matters, poor creatures.

His path followed the line of the bay, narrow, uneven. Ahead of him, Killala, cupped by low hills. At their center, on Steeple Hill, the ancient, upthrust arm of a round tower, black against the darkened sky. What man could know the age of such towers? Far older than the Dane, some said; older than the Sons of Milesius and the coming of the Gaels. Perhaps so. It was a land where history was measured by ruins, Gaelic fort and Norman keep. Not even the round towers marked the farthest line of wrack, for were there not the dolmens, and the queer underground burial chambers, immense, as though for giants?

He entered Killala at its western end, past cabins with fishing nets hung out to dry upon their walls, and walked along narrow, winding streets. He paused by the open door of Tobin's tavern, whose sign he could make out with the moon's help: the Sign of the Wolf Dog. Even the names they gave to places of cheer were faintly ominous: stiff-bristled mastiff, lips curled back from fangs. He was Ovid, banished to wild Tomi. From the tavern, a tide of murmurs spilled out into the street. Perhaps the traveling man had more to tell them about the broken rising in Wexford. Thousands of men upon the roads of Wexford. Towns had fallen before their onslaughts; militia and yeomanry had been beaten, scattered bodies, red-uniformed, upon thick-grassed fields. Peddlers and traveling men were now their Homers and their Virgils, tales carried to distant taverns.

MacCarthy almost entered, but then walked on, past Hussey's Catholic chapel, newly built and awkward with embarrassment beside the trim shops of the Protestant merchants, Bassett, Beecher, Reeves, Stanner. Once they had been wealthy; once Killala had been a thriving town. Now the trade was all in Ballina, southward at the base of the bay, on the road to Castlebar. Poor Protestant merchants of Killala: poor Reeves, poor Stanner. Right-angled to the street, facing the market house, the Prot-estant church, and the residence of Broome, its clergy-man. In its old, flourishing days, Killala had been an episcopal see; Broome's house was still called "the Pal-ace," a large, wind-battered building of cut gray stone with tall, handsome windows. Walking beside church and bishop's palace, MacCarthy left the town, past scattered cabins, past the large, low hut where, from late autumn to spring, he held his school. All instruction offered in grammar and navigation, Euclid's *Elements*, Ovid and Virgil, bookkeeping and metaphysics. Offered but not accepted, save by a few of the brighter lads, an eye on the priesthood. The others wanted only sums and cate-chism, a smattering of English. But they loved the sonor-ities of Latin, the changelings in Ovid, the stories MacCarthy had picked up in his years of wandering across Munster. Tricked into knowledge with the honey of anecdote. He climbed a low hill to the Acres, two rows of cabins, walls of rough stone washed white, discolored thatch.

He pushed open a door. Against one wall, mattress of straw on low frame, Judy Conlon lay asleep. He lit a candle of tallow set in a clay dish, and then stood beside her. Kneeling briefly, he ran a finger gently along the line of her cheekbone. She stirred, and a small hand moved to the tangle of black hair. He put the candle on a table set against the opposite wall. Ranged across its far side, his two dozen books: the *Aeneid*, Keating's *History of Ire-land*, the *Eclogues* and the *Georgics*, some volumes of Shakespeare, *Paradise Lost*, a box which held his copies of the poems of O'Rahilly and O'Sullivan.

He opened the two boxes which contained his craft. In the larger one, his own manuscripts, poems completed, poems to be remade, his translation of the first two books of the *Metamorphoses* into Irish, his sheets of blank paper. In the other box, a small brass bottle of ink, a sharp knife, his assortment of pens, gray goose for poetry, black crow for business. He placed paper and ink before him, sharpened his quills, and dipped a black feather into the ink.

In the early morning, when he felt Judy standing beside him, he was still sitting at the table, moving a gray goose feather across the page, scratching out a word, adding one, scratching that one out. Absently, with his hand, he moved along the line of her leg, cupped her haunch. A small girl, the hand had not far to travel.

"Where were you last night?"

"That is no concern of yours."

"It might be."

"It might be, but it is not. I was at Matthew Quigley's."

"What possessed you to go out there, with three fine taverns in Killala?"

"The Sign of the Wolf Dog. That would put a thirst on a man, right enough. I felt a need for the quiet beauty of Kilcummin strand."

She ran her hand through his red hair. "You can be a terrible liar, Owen."

"I can. It is a poet's way of reaching for truth."

"There is not a sin you commit for which your poetry is not the excuse. Is it a poem that you are writing now?"

"It might be the start of one. I won't know for a while."

"That is Irish you are writing. I can tell the difference now."

"It is in Irish that all my poems are made. This will be a strange one, if it ever takes shape." He put it aside, and took a fresh sheet of paper. "I have been all the night at it. My backside is numb. There was a fine handsome moon last night. It was worth seeing."

"Did you think of me when you saw it?"

"I did, of course."

"Liar."

She cut slices of bread, buttered them, and handed him one. It was not a bad life at all, he thought. Buttered bread every day, as suited his craft and his calling. He was far above all the poor fellows who had only their potatoes, and perhaps a bit of salt fish. And he had a lovely small girl to slice it for him, and to open her bed to him. There had been better times in Munster, but there had been worse. When he finished the bread, he wiped

12

his hands carefully along the side of his breeches, out of respect for the good paper.

"Judy, in the days before I came here, used there be many evictions, the way the O'Malleys were turned out by Captain Cooper?"

"When haven't there been evictions? Wasn't my poor husband's own brother turned out, and now he is perched on the side of the mountain?"

"Who was his landlord?"

"The Big Lord himself. The Big Lord gave orders from London, and Mr. Foster who was the agent in those days turned out Hughey and his family. He must have done something that the Big Lord didn't like, and the Big Lord turned him out."

"He must hold a heavy grudge against the Big Lord."

"Sure what good would that do? But he keeps wondering what thing he did that was wrong."

Patient beasts. Like their own cows, they are moved about, uncomplaining. Of less value than the cows, for they cannot be brought to market. Like cattle, they stand motionless in the fields, fearful of rain in one season and of drought in the next. Evicted, they walk the roads or climb the hills. Duggan had his work cut out for him. Southward in distant Wexford and northward in Antrim, a bare two months before, men such as these had toppled down towns and regiments. Not here.

Lingering, regretful, his hand touched the night's work. Gray goose and black crow, maimed cattle and the virginal moon. He drew the sheet of blank paper toward him, and picked up one of the black quills.

PART
ONE

1

From *An Impartial Narrative of What Passed at Killala in the Summer of 1798,* by Arthur Vincent Broome, M.A. (Oxon.)

Some years ago, when I first took up the pastoral care of the wild and dismal region from which I write, I was prompted to begin a journal in which would be set forth, as I encountered them, the habits, customs, and manners of the several social classes, with the thought that it might someday furnish the substance of a book with some such title as *Life in the West of Ireland.* I rightly feared that time would otherwise hang heavy on my hands, and I have long been aware of a capacity for slothfulness which can reveal itself when my life lacks order and direction. And it was clear to me that few portions of His Majesty's realms are less known than this island, which might for all purposes be adrift on the South Seas, rather than at our doorstep. Before setting forth from England, I had made it my business to read Mr. Arthur Young's *Tour in Ireland,* a sage and clear-headed book, bountiful in its information, liberal and enlightened in its temper, but being nevertheless exactly what its title claims to be, the account of a tour. My work would have the advantage of a prolonged and steady contemplation of the scene, a natural history, as it were, of life in County Mayo.

Alas for good intentions! The journal did have for a time a spare existence, scattered notes set down in the excitement of my encounters with novel scenes and faces, and with a society at once picturesque and alarming. But like others of my projects, it stumbled to a halt after some months, and long lay gathering dust upon a shelf in my library. Where these notes are now I cannot say; perhaps they served to start a fire, this being a fate which locally befalls loose sheets of paper. They would have served no large purpose, however, for my early impressions were all, as I now know, misleading, this land being as treacherous as the bog which stretches across much of its surface. It is, in a most exact sense of the word, an outlandish place, inhospitable to the instructions of civilization.

My present purpose, more practical and limited, is to offer as fully and as impartially as I can, yet without idle digression, a narrative account of those events which, a few years ago, bestowed upon our remote countryside a transient celebrity. Those events, however, were given their particular shape by the collision of an extraordinary event with an extraordinary society. It is therefore necessary that I present at the outset my own halting and puzzled sense of that peculiar world which was to provide a theater and actors for my drama.

A map reveals Mayo as a county on the western extremity of what has been, for the past several years, the United Kingdom of Great Britain and Ireland. At the time of which I write, of course, Ireland was in theory a separate nation, possessing its own parliament, yet sharing with England King George as its sovereign ruler, and being much under English influence. Of its illusionary and fictitious "independence" I shall have something to say hereafter. It is more to the present point to observe that the events which I propose to unfold played their part in bringing down the much-boasted but trumpery "Kingdom of Ireland." Thus do large and stately changes have at times their origins in crude and remote circumstances.

Were I to have the coloring of that map of Ireland, Mayo would appear upon it in browns and blues, the brown of hillside and bogland, arched over by an immense sky of light blue. Save when it rains, which, alas, is often. It is raining as I write these words, steadily and copiously, and shrouding from view the bay toward which my library faces. My parish is centered upon the town of Killala in the barony of Tyrawley, once a bishop's see and a prosperous community of coastal traders, but for decades past in a state of sore decline and disrepair. There are other towns in Mayo, of course: Ballina, our successful rival to the south; Westport on the western coast, the seat of the Marquis of Sligo and graced by his elegant mansion. But there is only one town of true consequence, Castlebar, the capital of Mayo as it is grandiloquently termed, and the town toward which all the roads of Mayo lead. A Muscovite garrison placed upon the border of Siberia must have a similar appearance, although, like all the towns of Ireland, it is built entirely of stone, save for the mud cabins of the very poor. It has streets, a courthouse, a church, a gaol, a market house, a military barracks, the houses of prosperous merchants. And yet all seems provisional, gaunt, slender buildings huddled together against the immensities of sky and land. For to speak of County Mayo in terms of its towns is entirely deceptive. The impression which it first makes upon the eye and mind is that of limitless and inhospitable space, the vast, dreary expanse of bogland westward from Crossmolina, the steep and lonely headlands and peninsulas. It is its own huge and somber world, and by contrast with it, the flanking counties of Galway and Sligo present a civilized aspect which is, unfortunately, entirely spurious.

Neither is it a populous world, if we restrict our consideration to what would in England be termed "the county families." Within a morning's or a day's ride, I could then have claimed as neighbors some fifty or sixty families of the gentry and the near-gentry, these latter being locally termed "half sirs," or "half-mounted gentlemen." Close at hand, within the Killala and the Kilcummin boundaries, I had as neighbors, among others, Peter Gibson of The Rise, Captain Samuel Cooper of Mount Pleasant, George Falkiner of Rosenalis, my special friend, as these notes will reveal, and, on the Ballycastle road, Thomas Treacy of Bridge-end House. At a greater distance, involving arduous travel along wretched roads, stood the estates of George Moore of Moore Hall, Hilton Saunders of Castle Saunders, Malcolm Elliott of The Moat, and a score of others. All of them, save only Moore and Treacy, were members of my parish, for it is one of the most notorious facts of Irish life that those who own the land and those who till it are severely divided by sect, the landlords being Protestant almost to a man, and the tenants and laborers being Papists.

To speak thus of our county society is to ignore its absent center, for dominating over our barony and those adjoining it are the estates, imposing and at first sight endless, of Lord Glenthorne, the Marquis of Tyrawley, or as he is called here, in a phrase taken from the Irish, "the Big Lord." The term falls with a faint blasphemy upon the ear, and Lord Glenthorne does resemble our Creator in that, having this vast domain at his disposal, he has elected to absent himself from it. In this there is nothing unusual, for the resident Irish landlords are for the most part the smaller ones, with estates of a thousand acres or less, while the great men of property are absentees, a circumstance which many hold to be contributory to our manifold woes. Lord Glenthorne, however, has chosen never to reveal himself, not even for brief visits, and yet so vast and so eminent is his place in our scheme of things that he has achieved on peasant tongues a legendary stature, a fathomless creature, beyond good or evil. In point of fact, before taking up my present charge, I was presented to him in London, where I found him to be a small, mild man of middle years, simple and unaffected in manner, and attentive to religious duties. I was to meet him also a second time, much later, on which occasion I was to form a more distinct impression of him, perceiving then that he was in every sense a lord.

To ride from here to Ballina is to ride for mile after mile beside the walls of his principal demesne, walls so high that a man on horseback can scarcely see over them, and all of cut stone. On occasion, the road will rise, and the traveler can glimpse in the distance, beyond sheltering plantations, the lovely form of Glenthorne Castle, a vast Palladian mansion which will seem to have floated down upon these inhospitable lands by some magical feat out of the *Arabian Nights*. And this illusion will be heightened if he reflects that this palace, for it is nothing less, stands waiting, staffed and doubtless furnished with unknown splendors, for a prince who has never visited it. It was far different in the days of his father, who indeed resided there from time to time, and who has left behind him most exotic and disreputable legends. But the traveler afoot sees nothing of Glenthorne Castle. He sees only the high, endless walls, and he may be pardoned for thinking that an army labored to put them into place, or such nameless legions of slaves as built the Pyramids of Egypt.

And such legions there are. In speaking as I have done of the "society" of Mayo, I have used the word in the common but un-Christian manner which excludes all whom we do not choose to see. If we admit to view the peasants, and that multitude of laborers who are infinitely more wretched even than the peasants, ours is not at all a lonely world. It is a populous, even a teeming one. They swarm like bees from their cabins, of which the meanest are made of mud, as a child builds by a riverbank, and they are everywhere, for they fasten upon every unclaimed acre which can sustain a blade of grass or a po-

19

tato bed, and the hills are crisscrossed and crosshatched by fences made of the boulders which have been carried away by hand so as to expose every inch of arable land. Some few are prosperous, although precariously so—graziers and strong farmers and middlemen, but what of the numberless thousands of their coreligionists? It will be noted that here I have stumbled into the common Irish practice of confounding a social and a sectarian division. For beyond dispute there are here two worlds, "our" small Protestant world of property and their multitudinous Papist world of want.

I affirm most sincerely that distinctions which rest upon creed mean little to me, and yet I confess that my compassion for their misery is mingled with an abhorrence of their alien ways. Begin then with creed, but add to this that most speak a tongue not merely foreign, but as grotesque as the prattle of Sandwich Islanders, that they live and thrive in mud and squalor with dunghills piled before their windowless cabins, that their music, for all that antiquarians and fanatics can find to say in its favor, is wild and savage although touched upon occasion by a plaintive, melancholy beauty, that they combine a grave and gentle courtesy with a murderous violence that erupts without warning—pates smashed for pleasure on a fairday, cattle barbarously mutilated, bailiffs put to death with crude tortures—that they worship fetid pools as holy wells and go on pilgrimage to clumps of rock, that their eyes look toward you with an innocence behind which dances malevolence. Yet I avow my sympathy for them, and wish that I might serve them better, or at all.

How else can they live, poor creatures of the Father? The peasant has his few cows and pigs, his brief crops, but all must go to pay the landlord, every forkful of beef, every grain of oats, and he himself and his family must live on potatoes and milk. And he is fortunate, for worse there are who hold no land at all in the law's eyes, but crouch upon the mountainside or huddle near the bog. They travel with their spades to the hiring fairs, where they stand like slaves upon the block. In late winter, when the potatoes have been exhausted, they wander the roads to beg. And what of those who hold a bit of land but cannot meet the rent? A good landlord, like my dear friend Mr. Falkiner, will let it hang for a season or two, provided that he himself is solvent, but many landlords are mortgaged heavily to the Dublin banks and moneylenders and they too are pressed down by the system. Many others are not true landlords at all, but middlemen to whom the land has been set for reletting, and many of these employ the barbarous practice of the "rack rent." And there are many landlords great and small who, like Captain Cooper, when grazing proves more profitable than letting, will turn out his tenants to beg or starve upon the roads. I have myself seen families huddled in the sides of hills where they had hewn out holes, entire families, the small ones cowering and rooting beside the gaunt form of the woman.

A system more ingeniously contrived, first for the debasement, and then for the continuance in that debasement of an entire people, cannot easily be imagined. On this subject I lack both the eloquence and the lucidity of George Moore of Moore Hall, a most astonishing man to discover in such parts as these, being an historian of some note, enlightened and humane in his views, and a friend of Burke, Fox, Sheridan, and other notabilities. To attend to his acerb, sardonic voice as he discourses upon the ills of Ireland is to be confirmed in one's despair, for he has never a remedy to suggest. And yet despair is rightly held the one unforgivable sin, and I have striven mightily against it.

I have striven also to find common ground with this multitude, but with scant success. I except here Mr. Moore and also Thomas Treacy of Bridge-end House, for these are accounted gentlemen, and I have always regarded their Papistry as chivalrous adherence to a persecuted sect. And I except also, strange though this may seem, Mr. Hussey, the priest in Killala, for he is himself almost a gentleman, being the son of a prosperous grazier in the midlands. Often, it has seemed to me, he has been more dismayed than I am myself by the barbarous life and manners of those to whom he ministers. I sought, though, in my first year, to make the acquaintance of the scattering of Papist "half sirs," such men as Cornelius O'Dowd and Randall MacDonnell, but these two in particular, to speak bluntly, I found to be irreligious men, unless we account fidelity to whiskey, horses, and wanton women to be a form of devotion; and this sorry estimation of their characters was amply vindicated by the violent courses of action which they took in the events which I shall narrate. Beneath that level, of course, were farmers and servants who both understood and spoke English, indeed some who had mastered the art of writing it. But always, below the surface of our pleasant interchanges, I could feel the tremblings of the great chasm which separated us, as though we met to parley on the quaking face of a bog.

I propose to set forth in this narrative whatever I have learned of that singular and most unfortunate man, Owen Ruagh MacCarthy. He once came to me at my bidding, for I wished to dispose of some books, and believed that he might make use of them in his "classical academy," a kind of hedge school in which children were given the rudiments of an education and older boys were prepared for the seminaries. I confess that I had my misgivings, for I had often seen him in the village, a tall, wild red-haired creature with a loping stride, notoriously given to drink and bad company. His earlier reputation was equally daunting, for it was said that he had wandered, or more exactly had been swept, northward from his native Kerry to Cork and thence through Clare and Galway into Mayo, flitting from troubles with the law, some said, but according to others pursued by posses of outraged fathers and husbands and brothers, for he could keep neither his eyes nor his hands from any woman of appropriate age and here his tastes were catholic in the nondenominational meaning of the term. And yet this was a man who possessed fluent Latin and had a good knowledge of Virgil, Horace, and Ovid. More astonishing yet, I have been informed by Treacy of Bridge-end House, a fanatic upon the supposed accomplishments of his race, that MacCarthy was a poet not lacking for fame, his verses being memorized and circulated in manuscript from Donegal to Kerry. I asked Treacy to render several of these into English for me, but he replied that the rhythm and meters, if such be the proper terms, could not be accommodated to English, so that words and sounds would be quarreling together like husband and wife, an instructive view into Irish attitudes toward matrimony.

At any event, and to end this digression, MacCarthy may for all one knows have been a second Ovid, but his words are locked forever within a barbarous language, which history has sentenced to silence and the plow. Upon this occasion, I assured him that I felt keenly the unhappy lot of his fellow countrymen, and suggested that this might somehow be improved if they were able to experience more completely the safeguards of English law. He responded with the verses of some other poet, which he then put into English for me, Treacy notwithstanding: "Troy and Rome have vanished; Caesar is dead and Alexander. Perhaps someday the English too will have their day."

I challenged him as to the meaning that he derived from this dark utterance, and he replied it meant only that Greece and Rome had once been empires, and England was now in its turn summoned to greatness. I told him that I did not for a minute suppose it to mean any such thing. Rather did it express the sullen vengefulness which the Irish peasantry notoriously nurse, and which, like their superstitions, distracts them from seeking proper and rational solutions to their problems. Then I reflected: What solutions? Well-meaning Protestant clergymen write books and tracts for them, urging them to dress neatly, when in fact they are half naked; to tell the truth, when only a lie will shield them from a rapacious landlord; to be sober, when the only comfort lies drowned in a bottle.

He then smiled at me, as though he had read my thoughts, and the smile altered his coarse, heavy features, suggesting a lively if sardonic intelligence. In an obvious effort to change the subject, he picked up a small book from the pile which I had set before him, a translation of Le Sage's romance of *Gil Blas*. "It is well I know this one, Your Reverence. I had it in the tail pocket of my coat when I was on my ramblings, years ago. No better book for the task." I discovered then that he had in fact a smattering of French, as was not uncommon, apparently, among the schoolmasters of his native Kerry, where there had earlier been much traffic with France. It was from Kerry and Cork that, until some ten years before, lads were shipped off to the seminaries at Douai and Saint-Omer or as recruits for the Irish brigades in the French army, and there was also a brisk smuggling trade. Not merely the last but all three of these enterprises were forbidden by law, but this seemed not to trouble MacCarthy at all. Herein may be discovered yet another sorry consequence of those abominable penal laws by which, for a century, the Papists were kept in a condition of semi-outlawry.

I found it curious in the extreme, this conjunction of *Gil Blas* and the French language with the coarse-molded cowherd who stood before me in his long-tailed coat of rain-colored frieze. Upon this occasion and those others when I talked with MacCarthy I was most favorably impressed by his transparent love of words and of books, though doubtless he apprehended these latter in a crabbed,

23

provincial manner, and by his bearing, which was easy but at no time offensively familiar. And yet there was also about him something which did give me offense, a sly, slight mockery as though he knew, as well as I did myself, that we used the same words in quite different ways. How little we will ever know these people, locked as we are in our separate rooms. And often I have glimpsed him in another mood, stumbling drunkenly homeward, more beast than man, toward the bed he shared with some young slut of a widow. The course which he later followed saddened but did not surprise me. He dwelt deep within the world of his people, and theirs is an unpredictable and a violent world.

What most weighed down upon me in my first years in Mayo was that all seemed agreed, rich and poor alike, that the dreadful circumstances to which I have alluded were changeless, woven from a history of so thick a texture that it could never be pulled or tugged to a more acceptable shape. I am no manner of a radical. I know that the laws of human economy, like those of astronomy, are inexorable and strict. Yet I cannot escape the feeling that here these laws have been pulled awry, as comets and meteors are pulled down upon the earth. The poor we shall always have with us, but need we have them in such numbers, accounting at the very least for a simple majority of the population?

But the few remedies which have been proposed are more hideous than the disease which they affect to cure. Thus I have heard it proposed, by men no more inhumane than most, that the recurrent famines are Providential, and will in time bring down the population to a proper size, but this I hold to be blasphemy. Or, again, take the matter of the Whiteboys, which has its role to play in my narrative. For some thirty years these agrarian terrorists had been a scourge upon the land, ravaging countrysides, murdering baliffs, maiming or killing cattle, pulling down the fences which enclose pastures, inflicting crude and loathsome punishment upon enemies and informers. In some few places their ambitions were satisfied; rents were lowered, or the expansion of grazing was halted. But in most, the Whiteboys were hunted down as stags and wolves are hunted, and were then destroyed. As destroyed they had to be, for civilization cannot abide such savagery. Famine or terror: what a fearful brace of proffered remedies!

24

And of what assistance is religion itself? I shall say little about the Church of the people. Doubtless it has been deformed and brutalized by the century or more of persecution which it has endured, and doubtless too it exercises a moderating influence upon its children, and yet I cannot profess to a great sympathy. Mr. Hussey, as I have remarked, is a man of education and good manners. Few sights were more ludicrous than that of Mr. Hussey in his silver-buckled shoes, picking his way into some cabin where his presence was required, all but holding his nose against the stench. In his chapel, which had been erected with the assistance of Mr. Falkiner and other of the more liberal-minded Protestant gentry, I believe that he inveighed steadily alike against Whiteboys and against the superstitious practices of his auditors. And yet far more typical of the Roman clergy was his curate, the egregious Murphy, the son of peasants and a peasant himself, a coarse, ignorant man, red-faced, young, stout, with the voice of a bull calf. Risen from the people, he could offer no example to them. And when the crisis fell upon us, he demonstrated that he shared to the full their darkest passions. Neither was he cleanly in his habits, and of his fondness for the bottle there is abundant evidence.

But of my own Church, what can I say, save that it is the Church of a governing garrison? My Church, unlike those in many other parishes, is well attended, and here I claim some credit for my sermons, which are not empty vaporizings upon obscure Scriptural texts, but are addressed to the daily business of life. And yet when I look to the bare white walls and slender windows, to the two battleflags which Mr. Falkiner's great-great-grandfather brought home from the wars of Marlborough, to the plaques erected to those who fell serving our sovereign on the fields of France and Flanders, when I look to my parishioners, stiff and erect as turkeycocks or conquistadors, then the troubling thought occurs to me that I am less minister to Christ's people than I am priest to a military cult, as Mithra was honored by the legions of Rome. Here, I think at such truant moments, is an outpost stationed in the land by the perpetual edicts of Elizabeth and James and Cromwell and William and charged to hold this land for our lord the King.

Why else does the Protestant gentry of Ireland send forth its young men into the British army and the army of the East India Company if not from an instinct bred in

25

the bone, bred perhaps of childhoods of Sundays spent staring at battleflags? And yet one thing is certain: that if England advances upon a land with the sword, there follow soon after the arts and benefits of civilization, an orderly existence, security of person and property, education, just laws, true religion, and a hopeful view of man's lot on earth. Only here have we failed, in the very first land we entered, for reasons which were in part our fault and in part the fault of the natives. But I think it pernicious to rummage over the past, sorting out wrongs and apportioning guilts.

Perhaps I can see the more clearly for being English born and English bred and therefore not enmeshed by the ancient prides and hostilities of this land. Pride: above all else pride. For in the final quarter of the century, as the world knows, the Protestants of Ireland declared themselves to be a separate nation, owing allegiance to the King of England only in his capacity of King of Ireland. Nay, more, they had come to think themselves a separate people, neither English nor Irish, yet vowing the most utter loyalty to the British Crown, from which their rights, privileges, possessions first flowed. A prodigious and ludicrous creature it was, this "Nation of Ireland," from which the great mass of the Irish were excluded upon the open ground of religion and the covert ground of race. Its capital of Dublin was as fair a city as these islands can boast, a city of warm, wine-colored bricks and cool gray stones, dominated over by the severe, lovely lines of a parliament house in which were seated the exclusively Protestant representatives of an exclusively Protestant electorate. And yet this vaunted independence was a mockery, for the governors and administrators of the island were still appointed from London, and the Parliament itself reeked with a corruption which many of the purchased members scarcely deigned to conceal. I yield to none in my admiration for Mr. Grattan and the other "patriots" who labored to give Ireland true and honest governance, to reform Parliament, and above all, to strike the chains from their Papist fellow countrymen. And yet their efforts were as futile as their oratory was glittering and enflowered.

We knew little of such matters in Mayo, and we cared less. The interests of the landlords were well served in Parliament by Dennis Browne, Lord Sligo's brother and

High Sheriff of the county, a clever and high-spirited man, bluff and hearty when the occasion demanded, but with a mind as subtle and as insinuating as mountain mist. If in these pages I shall have much to say that is harsh in its judgment of Mr. Browne, I do indeed believe that his love of Mayo is most sincere, although it was to assume a terrible shape. I do confess that my feeble understanding of these people falters entirely when it confronts such families as the Brownes. Papists until well into the eighteenth century, they retained their property by a variety of ruses, and then, these being exhausted, they conformed to our Protestant Church of Ireland. They, and they perhaps alone, seem able to move at ease between our two worlds, great and powerful personages in our Protestant world, yet the native musicians and poets are made welcome by them, and songs and poems are composed in their honor. Or were until very recent years, for now the Brownes have a dark and somber reputation, and for reasons that my narrative will make clear. If I could but understand the Brownes, I would understand much about the tangled roots of the past, its twisted loyalties and bloody memories. But I will never come to such understanding, The meanings of this land are shrouded from the eyes of strangers. Truth, like Viking treasure, lies buried in the bogs.

Boglands and rings of mountains sealed us off in Tyrawley, and left us facing the gray ocean. But by 1797, we knew that elsewhere in Ireland events were drifting toward rebellion. The wicked and seditious Society of United Irishmen, a band of unscrupulous city radicals in Dublin and Belfast, were bent upon an insurrection, and had chosen as their instrument an unnatural alliance of the Papist peasants of the south and the Presbyterian peasants of the north. Their agent abroad, the deist and madman Wolfe Tone, had secured the assistance of regicide France: the year before a formidable invasion fleet had been beaten back from the Kerry coast only by what the peasants called "the Protestant winds." Then, in the spring of 1798, we heard, aghast, of the dreadful rebellions in Wexford and Antrim, a murderous and insensate peasantry ravishing the countryside before being put down with great brutality. There followed then a dreadful pause, for although the rebellious counties had become vast charnel houses, the networks of the hellish conspiracy survived in the midlands and in parts of Munster. A sec-

27

ond flotilla of invasion, it was said, was being assembled on the French coast, and Wolfe Tone hovered, a stormy petrel, above its masts. It is in this moment of dreadful pause that my narrative will open.

But all of this came to us as tidings from a different land. Our local corps of yeomanry, an exclusively Protestant body under the command of Captain Samuel Cooper, drilled more frequently, but less to defend our shores than to remind the Papist peasantry that the present order of things was changeless. There was first one, then several, then numerous instances of cattle maiming, by those calling themselves "the Whiteboys of Killala," but Whiteboyism was one of our old, familiar evils. The distant United Irishmen preached insurrection in the name of a desired "Republic of Ireland," but the word *republic* has no existence in the Irish tongue, and far less had the meaning of the word any existence in the minds of our peasantry. To be sure, there were some among the peasants, schoolmasters and tavernkeepers and the like, who, upon hearing of the Wexford rising, spoke in lofty terms of "the army of the Gael." And many among the Protestants, in particular those of the more narrow and ignorant sort, spoke in fear and fury of a servile insurrection. But all was far distant from Mayo.

I have once and again sought to imagine myself as present in one of the taverns frequented by the peasantry, a low, vile cabin choking with smoke and rank with odors. Someone describes for those present the Wexford insurrection, not as the butchery which in fact it was, but as a glorious hosting of "the army of the Gael," with banners and bards, like a passage in Macpherson's Ossian poems. I seek to imagine in that setting the faces which I know only from roadside or field or stable, white skin, black hair, dark eyes. With what power would not the speaker's words burst upon such an assembly, for the native Irish, as has been remarked since the days of the Elizabethan Spenser, are easily overwhelmed by high-flown rhetoric. But imagination fails me. They are an alien people.

Once, at the home of Mr. Treacy, I heard Owen Ruagh MacCarthy recite his poetry. He was visiting the servants, and Treacy, being informed of this, brought him to the dinner table, where he stood before us and spoke a poem for which he was requited most generously with silver coins and two tumblers of brandy. It was of a kind called an *aisling,* Mr. Treacy informed me, a poem of vision,

28

in which the poet, wandering in a meadow, encounters a maiden who speaks to him in cloaked and guarded terms of her present sorrows and prophesies some event of great good fortune for the Gaelic people—perhaps the Young Pretender sailing to the coast with swordsmen and casks of wine and French coins. The poem that night differed from others of its kind only in that it was not the Stuart Pretender who was invoked, but some nameless, cloudy deliverance. It is apparently a difficult and a metrically complex form, for all its conventionality, and MacCarthy's celebrity among other native poets was said to rest upon his mastery of its techniques. It was delivered with much florid vehemence of voice and body, but I do not pretend to admire what I cannot understand.

Leaving Bridge-end House some hours later, and walking toward the boy who held my horse, I passed the open door of one of the outbuildings, and again hearing MacCarthy's voice, I looked within. A number of the servants were gathered there, and MacCarthy, very drunk, was standing with one foot upon the bench. A girl was standing beside him, and his free arm was curved around her waist, his hand fondling her bosom. I needed no cicerone to explain to me the meaning of the song which he was singing. As I rode off, the song ended, but the air was then filled with the sound of a violin, playing a most engaging air, very quick and lilting, as though for a dance.

Music and dance. What I have written must surely suggest a people cursed by Heaven, men sullenly in movement beneath a lowering sky. And yet most, were they to hear my words, would deny them utterly. For if the mind's eye perceives the grinding poverty, the ear of the mind hears music. No people on earth, I am persuaded, loves music so well, nor dance, nor oratory, though the music falls strangely upon my ears, and the eloquence is either in a language I cannot understand or else in an English stiff, bombastic, and ornate. More than once I have been at Mr. Treacy's when, at close of dinner, some traveling harper would be called in, blind as often as not, his fingernails kept long and the mysteries of his art hidden in their horny ridges. The music would come to us with the sadness of a lost world, each note a messenger sent wandering among the Waterford goblets. Riding home late at night, past tavern or alehouse, I would hear harps and violins, thudding feet rising to frenzy. I have seen them dancing at evening on fairdays, in meadows decreed by

29

custom for such purposes, their bodies swift-moving, and their faces impassive but bright-eyed, intent. I have watched them in silence, reins held loosely in my hand, and have marveled at the stillness of my own body, my shoulders rigid and heavy.

Darkness hides them from me, and my sympathy is un-Christian and chill. We fear the unknown. Most earnestly do I wish to enter their lives, yet everywhere my wish is mocked, by Captain Cooper's complacent swagger, by the memory of MacCarthy's foot upon a bench, by a cabin bursting with music; by the thronging foreign faces at markets and fairdays, by dancers in a meadow, by the sounds of an alien speech. Yes, and by the very look of the land itself, the forbidding hills, the monotony of brown moorland, the small lakes set like watchful eyes upon the bog. It seems to me a land furiously guarding its meager secrets, gloating over its incomprehensibility. Whether it seems so to the people themselves, I cannot say. They are an ancient people, and possess an ancient knowledge which, because it falls short of wisdom, is frightening to a stranger.

And thus, in the narrative which I shall now commence, many of the actors come from a world which is recognizably my own, however altered by local conditions. Mr. Falkiner, my dear friend, might well be found in my native Derbyshire, arguing crops or politics with my brother. And Mr. Moore of Moore Hall would surely be more at home in London than in Mayo. Nor can England boast that it lacks such men as Captain Cooper, village Caesars and Hannibals, doughty captains of Sunday soldiers. But there my pen pauses, for one at least of Cooper's feet rests upon the bog. And when my thoughts move from him to the native Irish, to O'Dowd and to MacDonnell, to MacCarthy and above all to Ferdy O'Donnell, I feel them slipping toward the unknown, toward men whose actions and passions issue from that fearsome world of hillside and bog, choked with the petrified roots of the past. And beyond such men lies the multitudinous world of the peasantry, the dark sea which swept up upon us so suddenly that we were almost covered by its waves.

I shall nonetheless strive to present those events with such understanding of them as I have come to possess, and with an attempt at a strict impartiality. I fear in advance that I shall fail, for my knowledge of events is not matched by an understanding of their causes. But yet I

30

hold it almost sinful not to seek after causes, the black
roots of flowering passions. The rain has ceased to fall,
and beneath a sky suddenly bright and almost cloudless,
fields of a most intense green stretch northward toward
the bay.

2

Mount Pleasant, June 16

It was a long letter, closely filling three sheets of excellent
paper. Copies had been nailed by night to Cooper's door
and to the door of the Killala market house. Cooper held
the pages flat beneath one hand, while the other, elbow
propped on breakfast table, supported a head within
which brandy seemed to roll as in a half-filled jug. Across
from him sat his wife, Kate, and at his side, perched on
the chair's edge, sat Fogarty, his steward.

"It's hard to believe," he said, temporizing, while studying the wild blur of words.

"Not all of them, by no means all or even most,"
Fogarty assured him. He was a jovial man, and could not
help but bring an air of buoyancy to the least appropriate circumstances. "Only the cows we turned onto O'Malley's acres. Squint O'Malley. Do you remember the way
he kept bobbing his head when he talked to you? It was
the shut eye that did it." He imitated the gesture, and
Cooper closed his eyes against the sight.

"These are terrible times for Mayo," Kate said, "when
a man cannot use his land as he sees fit."

"Sees fit, be damned," Cooper said. "Uses it as some
bloody mortgage broker in Capel Street sees fit. I think
I might be able to take some tea." He sucked it in red and
strong, heavily sugared. He pressed small, square hands
on plump knees which strained against buff breeches, a
short-legged man with a head round and compact as a

31

cannonball. "As if the country wasn't in bad enough trouble. The Whiteboys of Killala. O Jesus, what have I ever done to deserve my troubles."

"Troubled times, Captain," Fogarty said. "Troubled times."

"I'll trouble them," Cooper said. "I'll trouble them to dance on a rope's end in Castlebar."

"To be sure you will, Captain. To be sure you will. No better man. Once we know who they are."

"My own tenants is who they are, and I haven't so many of them that their ways are mystery. And if the law can't give me satisfaction, I will take out after them with a pack of the MacCaffertys."

"Oh, to be sure, Captain."

"This isn't Dublin, you know. This is Mayo, and we settle matters in our own way here. We're Irishmen here, and Irishmen by God who stand on their own two feet."

"If you are over that now," Kate said, "maybe you will tell us what you intend to do." She was a handsome, coarse-featured woman, with a broad, humorous mouth and eyes like green agates.

He looked toward her and then away. "Fogarty, there is no need for you to sit there with an empty belly. Kate, ring the bell for Brid, and while the man is waiting pour him some tea."

"Tea would be grand," Fogarty said. "I have had my breakfast in me for two hours. I put Paddy Joe and his son to work on the fence that was knocked down."

"Well, aren't you the thoughtful hoor," Cooper said, but then said quickly, "Ach, Tim, I'm sorry. I am fair beside myself." He rubbed the palm of his hand across his eyes. "I was counting on those cattle for the market. I don't know what I will do now at all."

"No offense taken, Sam. 'Tis a sore business." He sipped at the scalding tea, and added sugar.

"And now, Sam," Kate said. "What do you intend to do?"

"I have about a fifth of the land marked out for pasturage, and 'tis the only way. The both of you know that. And I won't be the last landlord to do it here, only I had the bad luck to be the first."

"You might better have waited, then," Kate said. "Until you had some company."

"Wait wasn't in it, Kate, the sore way we are in. This

32

bitch of a barony wasn't built for farming. It is land for cattle."

The room was too small for the furniture which had been crowded in, a broad expanse of mahogany table, heavy chairs with wide arms and high, tapestried backs, a sideboard of olive wood. Two smoke-darkened portraits faced each other across the table

"You can't leave it this way," she said. "With a Whiteboy threat hanging over you if you move."

"And those Dublin leeches fastened onto my arse. Do you not think I know that?"

Across the hall, in the small office, paper bulged from his desk, lay scattered across the table. How could a man have this much land, and yet be so poor? True enough, the land was heavily mortgaged when his father died, and there was no turning back from the road of heavy mortgages. But the road had seemed pleasant once, seven or eight years ago. Those had been good years, after his father's death and before he married. Liberty Hall, you might as well have called Mount Pleasant, but without extravagance, all considered. Not a rakehelly young man of the barony but had his welcome, and not all of them Protestants by any means, he was no bigot. The two Routledges had their welcome and Tom Bellew and Corny O'Dowd, the old Catholic stock, good mounts for the chase. There were still marks on the hall floor from the time Corny O'Dowd had ridden up and through the door. All that was over now, with black hatred building up again between the creeds.

"You must stop them now," Kate said.

He spilled his tea. "You are as bad as the rest of them. Didn't my own father tell me that marrying a Papist was like building your house upon mud?" He shifted in his seat. "What in hell was the need to marry you at all, is the question I ask myself every night I can't sleep." When they had children, she would be teaching them their beads when he wasn't watching; it always went that way in this kind of marriage.

"Then you cannot have often to ask the question."

"Well, ma'am," Fogarty said, "with my best thanks for the tea."

"You will sit where you have been bid to sit," Kate said, "and you will leave when you have been excused." She leaned toward her husband. "You married this particular Papist because you were besotted by the pleasures

33

of the bed, and you knew a bargain when you saw one."

Cooper drew in his breath to answer, but then expelled it. "By God, you are right, Kate. A damned good bargain it was. But I can't let your bloody Papists—"

"*My* bloody Papists, are they? Do you think that Thomas Treacy would be safe, or George Moore? If Whiteboys are left unpunished, not a landlord will be safe against them." She rested her hand on the table. "Haven't you enough sense to puzzle things out? You have a handful of men frightened they will be turned out and maybe some ramblers with no business but mischief. And barring you find yourself an informer you will never find out who they are, not until half the men in the barony have taken the oath, and for you that will be too late. You heard no whispers of this, did you, Tim?"

"I did not, ma'am. When we turned out Squint O'Malley and flattened the cabin, there was a crowd of them standing in the road to make their moans, but that is always the way. You have the right of it there, ma'am. This is but a handful of men now, but it will grow fast."

"Do you hear that, Sam? There is no way out of this but to make them all more afraid of you than they are of the Whiteboys. And there will be no way to frighten them until you flatten cabins and send a few off to Castlebar in a cart."

"Jesus, but you are a hard woman, Kate."

"Ireland is hard. I learned how to live in it by watching my father. There was a man to take lessons from. On one side of him was the Protestants and on the other side was the Whiteboys, and all he had in this world when he commenced his progress was a lease on a few hundred acres of bad land that he let to those who could get no better. And what had he to protect it but a whip with a load of lead in the handle."

"This is no morning to hear about your father," Cooper said. Shaggy, mountainous form, hairy ears and nostrils, the loaded whip around which legends had clustered.

"You remember my father, don't you, Tim?"

"I do, ma'am," Fogarty said reverently. "I do."

Two of a kind, her father and Fogarty. Tucked somewhere in the thatch of Fogarty's cabin was a leather sack of silver shillings and gold sovereigns, a bit added to it each year, his eye on some nice bit of land, perhaps part of Cooper's own land. They hungered for land, as other men for women or whiskey. One of these years, Fogarty would be around, stroking the greasy band of his hat, ready to talk about a long-term lease, bag plump on the desk. Then he could start in business as a middleman. That is how old Mahony, Kate's father, had started forty years before, when Papists were forbidden by law to own land by outright purchase. They complain about the heretic landlords, but it is their own that sweat them worst. The worst rack-renters are the Papist middlemen. Servants make bad masters.

"There is not even need for Castlebar." Kate said. "Let the magistrates seize up a few of the likeliest rogues and throw them into Ballina gaol. And if they are too finicky about the selecting, they themselves will be the losers. It works wonders to toss a lad in gaol and hold a whip under his nose."

"It isn't forty years ago, Kate. There must be charges now."

"Are you not yourself the law in Killala now? Is not the Tyrawley Yeomanry the law? Why else did you throw away our sore needed money on red uniforms?"

"That is a different matter altogether," Cooper said, suddenly stiff. He seemed to rise taller in his chair. "The Tyrawley Yeomanry was founded to hold this barony for our lord the King."

"Whatever that means," Kate said acidly.

"Well you know what it means. It is our task to guard these shores against the French, and to protect this barony against rebels."

Kate suddenly broke into laughter. "Listen to him, Tim. Listen to him." She seized Fogarty by the arm, as though they were allied in judgment against her husband. "I declare to God that all men are children."

All save her father.

"You great fool," she said to Cooper. "What is a Whiteboy if he isn't a rebel?"

"Not against the Crown," Cooper said, making an effort at patience. "Have you no ears in your head? Have you not heard about the south of this island and the north of it? The peasants rose up in rebellion against the Crown. They destroyed Wexford. The English had to send over an army to put them down. Thanks be to God there are no United Irishmen in Mayo, there are no rebels. These are only Whiteboys."

"Only Whiteboys," Kate echoed contemptuously. "It is Whiteboys and not rebels of Wexford who can send

35

you naked and starving on the roads. It is against you that the Whiteboys are in rebellion, and you have a hundred men who owe you the red coats on their backs."

Cooper shook his head. "A Whiteboy war in the middle of a rebellion. My God, what a country!"

"Small difference," Kate said. "Whiteboys this year and rebels the next. If there was ever a rebellion in Mayo, wouldn't your Whiteboys be in the thick of it?"

"They would, by God," Cooper said.

"There you are then," Kate said. "Take your yeomen and ransack the barony. Bring the wrath of God down on them. That is what your own father would have done. He was a mean, yellow-skinned Protestant, but he knew how to deal with Whiteboys."

"Will you not listen to me when I tell you that it is not my father's time now, and much less is it the time of your own father. I hold my commission from Dublin, and I am answerable to Dublin."

"You are fearful to make use of the yeomen, is that it? Then why must I tell you what you must do? You must have a word with Dennis Browne. He is the High Sheriff for Mayo and he is the Member of Parliament for Mayo and he is brother to Lord Altamont. If there is one man who has the management of Mayo in his own two hands it is Dennis Browne."

"Dennis Browne, is it?" He laughed and turned to Fogarty, who responded with a smile. "It is little you know about the affairs of your own husband. Sure didn't Dennis Browne and I stand on the field five years ago and bang away at each other with pistols."

"Indeed I did not know that. What possessed the pair of you?"

"It was a matter closely touching a young lady's honor. Now that is enough said on that subject."

"Touching a lady's honor," Kate said. "That is the only part of a woman that Dennis Browne would not touch. He is as bad as MacCarthy below in Killala."

"There were circumstances," Cooper said. "Very delicate circumstances. It was all over and done with before I ever met you, love."

"You may depend on that," Kate said.

"Over and done with," Cooper said. "But there is little affection between us. Ach, what use has he ever had for fellows like myself or Gibson or Saunders or any of the other small landlords? He cares only for the men of great

36

property, his brother and the Big Lord and those. And his brother and himself are safe, out there in Westport."

"No one will be safe," Kate said. She bit her lip in thought. "Is there no one in these parts who has his ear?"

"One man," Cooper said. "George Moore of Moore Hall."

"A fine-looking man," Kate said. "He keeps to himself, but he is a fine-looking man. And he is a Roman Catholic."

"Sure the Brownes are half Papist themselves. They are neither fish nor fowl. And George Moore is mad. A man who sits in the middle of Mayo and writes books is mad."

"Unlike yourself," she said, "he never tried to kill Dennis Browne, and unlike yourself, he is gentry."

"Gentry, is it? By God, there is fine talk from Mick Mahony's daughter."

"I am glad you like it. I have more."

"Fogarty, why the hell are you sitting there, gawking at your betters while the affairs of the barony are being discussed? The tea is stone cold, and Paddy Joe and his son are down by the pasture fence wondering how do you put one stone on two others without it falling off."

"My own thought, Captain. My own thought. I'll be on top of them in two shakes." He stood up, and then pointed to the letter. "Mrs. Cooper is right, though, Captain. It has to be stopped now. You saw who that was written to. Not to yourself alone. 'To the Landlords and the Middlemen of this Barony,' it begins. That is the proper Whiteboy stuff, and it has to be stamped out, the way your father used do in the old days."

Cooper watched the door until it closed. Easy enough to say. Thirty, even twenty years ago, his father would have taken some brisk Protestant lads—or better, his pet Papists the MacCaffertys—and turned Tyrawley inside out. Now nothing was clear. Perhaps Cooper wasn't gentry. Perhaps he was only a farmer trying to hold his land in a hard county. Pity for himself spread, a soft sponge, in his chest. He squeezed it dry.

"Maybe I am not gentry, Kate, but I am accounted so. I have a great-grandfather's phiz to hang on the wall. It isn't your great lords who have held Mayo for the Crown from the days of Cromwell. It is men like myself and Gibson, and small thanks we ever got for it. When your great lords were off in England, it was men like my great-grandfather fought off the rapparees. It is men like ourselves took Mayo and held it."

"Let you keep your hold on it, then."

"How! What in hell is it you want me to do?"

"Go down to Ballintubber and have a word with George Moore, that he will have a word with Dennis Browne. And then turn your yeomen loose on these rogues."

"My God, what a creature you are for a woman. It is a man you should have been born."

"A strange creature that would make of me in your bed. It is a woman I am, and fine cause you have to know it. Sure what do I care, Sam, are you gentry or not. If you had grown up as I did, a Papist among Papists, you would have a full belly of such prating, with every O and Mac giving out about how grand they were in the days before Cromwell and how much land they had taken away from them. If you put all that land together, Mayo would stick out into the sea so far that you could stand on Croagh Patrick and see New York. That is all over and done with. What matters now is who has the land and who will keep it. I mean us to keep Mount Pleasant if we have to turn every perch of land into pasture."

"We shall see, Kate. We shall see. But for the moment I had best get below. It is little Fogarty knows about stonework, much less Paddy Joe."

"And Paddy Joe will have his 'Fine day, Captain' for you, and you will have your 'It is indeed' for him, and all the time Paddy Joe could be one of the lads we should be scouring out."

"Not at all, woman. Are you mad? Paddy Joe's father had his bit of land from us when my father's father died. They are not near-strangers, as the O'Malleys were."

"And do you think that the Whiteboys came from the moon? In Mayo it pays not to be soft."

"Then I am a lucky man, Kate, for you must be worth millions."

She sat on the edge of her chair, gripping its arms, her black hair falling loose about her dressing gown. He knew that he was a lucky man indeed. Small need for the excitements of gaming or the hunt when you had a woman like that at home to match tempers with, and a kind of natural genius when it came to the pleasures of the bed. It was an impressive and a frightening mixture, her hardheadedness and her lust. A solid, turbulent marriage.

Cooper opened the double doors which led off the dining room, and walked out onto the terrace, from which he could see, far off, Fogarty and the two Paddy Joes. Kate was right. She knew these people through and through—who better?—and yet, turn as he would, he could find no way to proceed. It might satisfy Kate's feminine bloodthirstiness to imagine him raging through Killala with fire and sword, at the head of the yeomanry, but this martial fancy bore little relation to the facts. In Wexford, by all reports, General Lake had loosed his troops upon the countryside, but Wexford had been in rebellion and he acted under martial law. It would have done Cooper's heart good to see these Whiteboys hanged in Castlebar, but he lacked Kate's ruthlessness. In his inarticulate way, he loved Mayo deeply.

He was not heavily burdened either with imagination or with historical information, but at times he wondered how his lands had first appeared to his great-great-something-or-other-grandfather, a sergeant who had trooped with Ireton. The Papists had risen up, as they were always doing, slaughtering hundreds of settlers and driving out thousands more to perish on the winter roads of Ulster. Cromwell, hard-pressed in England, had taken badly needed time to fall upon Ireland and crush a rebellion which had spread across the island. Shares of Irish land were sold to English companies, and smaller tracts were measured out to pay the soldiers. In this manner, Sergeant Joshua Cooper, a London locksmith, had come to Mayo, had come into possession of lands earned not by the sword of worldly conquest but by Christ's chastising sword, carried into the wilderness to avenge His slaughtered saints. Surrounded by a sullen and defeated people, sunk in savagery and hating the light, he had claimed his acres and held them.

The chain of generations bound together Sergeant Cooper of London and Captain Cooper of Mount Pleasant. But who in that chain had first come to accept the land as truly his, ratified by claims stronger than those inscribed upon legal documents? Which of them had been the first to shrug off the locksmith's shop and think himself a gentleman, no mere owner of Mount Pleasant but its master as well? Perhaps Joshua's son Jonathan, who in 1690 had raised his company to serve King Billy at the

Boyne and Aughrim and Limerick, who rode home to Mount Pleasant and defended it for five years against the sporadic sallies of the rapparees, the swordsmen, masterless now, of the defeated James Stuart. It was Jonathan who had built the present house, and who had given it its name. Heavy shutters, with loopholes for firelocks, still testified to the dangers of the rapparee times, but the name itself, Mount Pleasant, suggested that he had discovered more in Mayo than bogland and murder. Joshua and Jonathan, the successive founders of Cooper's line, faced each other from the walls of the dining room, grimfaced Roundhead and thick-necked Williamite with a dab of lace under the chin, gentility's first sign, a white rash. The Biblical sound of their names pleased Cooper; it was almost, of itself, a claim to ownership, Mayo their Canaan.

By the time of Cooper's grandfather, ivy had begun to climb the walls of what had been built as a fortified farmhouse. Within, the rooms had become cluttered with heavy sideboards and beds, purchased in Dublin and shipped around the coast to Killala. The grandfather boasted that in his boyhood, Carolan, the great blind harper, had once played in the drawing room, composing for the occasion his "Planxty Squire Cooper." Marriages had shaped Mount Pleasant as a knot in the network of Protestant proprietorship which history had cast across Mayo. There was no longer need for the loopholed shutters, and Joshua and Jonathan had become patriarchal legends. The land was Cooper's now. It owned him. Once, far off in the brown bog of the past, it had been owned by an O'Donnell family. A young hillside farmer on Cooper's land, Ferdy O'Donnell, had once shown him a valueless curiosity, a parchment which recorded the fact in faded ink the color of old, dried blood.

Moore Hall, June 17

A wide, handsome house built with blocks of pale gray limestone, it rose four stories high, facing gentle, tree-shaded Lough Carra. It was a new house, less than ten years old, and had been built by an earlier George Moore, father of the present owner, upon his return from a Spanish exile. In the 1750s, harassed by the penal laws against Catholics, he had emigrated to Spain, vowing to make or mar his fortune. He went to work in a counting house, and a few years later married the daughter of another Irish émigré. By the 1780s he was one of the powerful merchants of Alicante, the owner of vineyards and of a fleet of ships which traded between Spain and the coastal cities of Galway, Westport, and Killala. The same vessels also conducted a less open and more profitable trade, smuggling brandy and laces, satins, and silks to the lonely beaches of Connaught. Portraits of Moore and his wife, dressed for the court of Spain, hung in Moore Hall.

But he had been half-Spanicized, and from the first he planned to return to Mayo. He took care that his two sons, George and John, were educated in England, under the guidance of Catholic tutors. And he took equal care to visit Ireland in 1780, when, under the terms of the Act of Relief, Catholics were permitted to take the cath of allegiance to George III and to hold land under long leases. As he sat through the Mediterranean evenings on the terrace of his white, flat-roofed house, looking past almond trees and orange trees toward the Bay of Alicante, he remembered brown Mayo moorlands and rain-soaked fields. He had thought of Mayo as he stood on the weathered planks of Spanish wharves, watching his ships sail out to Connaught with wine and back from Connaught with the green and yellow brown kelp of Connemara. And when he had amassed his fortune, some £250,000 according to Mayo legend, he sold all his Spanish property save for the vineyards and the house in the palm-shaded street, and he returned home.

He had intended to build near Ashbrook, the house of his birth, but on his journey of inspection there he passed the low, solitary hill of Muckloon. He halted his carriage, climbed the hill, and saw Lough Carra spread before him. Here he built, having first acquired the hill and eight hundred acres by outright purchase, as a more recent law now permitted him to do. An architect named Aitken was summoned from London and built, to his specifications, a house severely proportioned but light of line, drawn upon its thickly timbered background with the exact delicacy of an engraver's pen. Three flights of limestone steps marched like regiments to a massive door which swung open to reveal a hall above which arched an Adam ceiling, blue as the Mayo sky, with oval medallions of white plasterwork. Long before the house was finished,

41

he placed his motto above the door: FORTIS CADERE, CEDERE NON POTEST. Mayo gave it a loose translation: "Scratch a Moore and you yourself will bleed." Above the four-pillared portico was a balcony, upon which the summer room opened, and here he sat in the evening, looking out toward Lough Carra, as the hammers of the stonemasons echoed below him.

He had fought his own kind of war and he had won it. The Moores had returned to Mayo wealthier and more powerful than they had been before Catholic Ireland was shattered by James's defeat at the Boyne. Lacking all sympathy for dead causes, he was a faithful if cynical subject of King George and a scrupulous though not a devout Catholic. He had built a chapel in Moore Hall, furnishing it with an altar, altar cloths which splashed crimson and gold on their surrounding whiteness, and a massive gold crucifix from Spain. He had lived to see the withering of many of the penal laws by which his youth had been oppressed, and he assumed that the others would wither. He contributed generously to the several Catholic political organizations, but took no part in their affairs. That he was forbidden by law to sit in the Dublin Parliament did not trouble him, for he had no wish to do so. It mattered far more to him that he had a voice in naming the men who did sit for Mayo, and, with the other gentlemen of Mayo, he had the satisfaction of knowing that Dennis Browne was solicitous of their interests. The Brownes and Moores came from the same world, and if the Brownes had changed faiths to hold their property, he was not inclined to criticize a choice which he had refused to make. There were other families of the Catholic gentry scattered thinly across Mayo: Blakes and Dillons, O'Dowds and Treacys and MacDonnells. He had intended that his sons should marry into them, but there he had not reckoned with the temperament of George, the older.

One night in the summer of 1795, the elder Moore sat in his chair on the balcony of Moore Hall hours past his custom, and a servant, coming to rouse him, discovered that he had died. George Moore set to work at once to dispose of his small villa on the Thames, and then shipped his papers and his considerable library to Mayo. He could give no explanation to his English friends, not because he lacked one, but because he feared they would not understand it. What Moores had, Moores held, and what they held was a hill in Mayo, facing a lake. Alicante, London, Paris were the three points by which he boxed his compass, but the needle pointed westward, to Mayo. London meant as much to him and as little as the orange groves of Alicante had meant to his father. Son and father had shared this almost subterranean love of place, a Virgilian piety.

The present George Moore was a slender man, above the average in height but with a scholar's stoop, and his face was handsome, pale, and poised. His speech was grave, but often with that courtesy which is thrown carelessly across irony. He was a writer, and would be an historian. His small book on the English Whigs and the Glorious Revolution had attracted the attention of Burke, and the two had become friends. For a year now, he had been laboring upon an experiment, an attempt to treat recent history with that meditative neutrality which other writers bestowed upon the past. He was writing a history of the rise and the destruction of the Girondist party in France, and his willingness to enter into their ideals to sympathize with their actions, their mistakes, their foolishness had darkened several of his English friendships.

In London he had been a member of the Holland House set, much to his friend Burke's displeasure, and his scholarly bent had not prevented his being involved in several love affairs which at length became scandals. One of them had issued into a duel with the husband, much to his father's displeasure. Few things about George Moore had pleased the father, who had hoped for a practical country gentleman, indistinguishable from his Protestant neighbors. And George, in his turn, had been saddened by the father's clear preference for John, the child of his old age, an unsuccessful law student but a splendid rider to hounds, a lively, high-spirited young man for whom George himself had a fondness which was almost paternal. Neither had proved the kind of heir for which the old man had hoped, but neither father nor elder son suspected that they shared a deep, irrational love for Mayo.

What had been his father's summer room he converted to a library, and there, rising very early, he worked at his history, aided by innumerable small cups of coffee prepared in the French manner. He would then go downstairs for breakfast with John, and afterward closet himself in the office with the affairs of the estate. His afternoons were spent out of doors, for the estate was still in the process of construction, and he intended, as his father

43

had, that it should be a self-sustaining community, with blacksmith's forge, laundry, bakery, stables. But one hour each day, in the late afternoon, he would sit on the balcony above the portico, looking outward toward the lake. Those hours brought him closer to his father than they had been in life. In his imagination, father and son would discuss matters together, make plans for the estate, debate John's future. The servants had learned not to disturb him then. He was sitting there when Cooper rode up the carriageway, dressed in his red uniform.

He received Cooper with quiet, distant courtesy and led him to the office, where Cooper made a brief show of admiring books which had spilled over from the library.

"You have a power of books here, Mr. Moore. I would wager that there are more books here than there are in the rest of Mayo."

"That is likely," Moore said. He measured two glasses of sherry and handed one to Cooper. Then he carefully placed the stopper back in the Waterford decanter.

Cooper sipped judiciously. "That is Spanish wine. I would know it anywhere. From your own vineyards, most likely?"

"No," Moore said. "Sherry comes from a region near Cádiz. Our vineyards are in Alicante, on the Mediterranean. Our wine is oversweet to British tastes."

"Well, this is very fine all the same. It goes down very mild."

"I am pleased by your good opinion of it," Moore said, and sat waiting.

" 'Tis wonderful," Cooper said, "to think of the wine we drink coming from such strange, far-off places."

"In Spain, of course, Mayo is thought of as far off."

"But not too far, eh? I remember my father used to buy casks from your father's ships that the exciseman never saw. They would be ashore at Kilcummin on a moonless night, and half the gentlemen of Mayo would be on the strand for their casks. You take my meaning?"

"Yes," Moore said. "I take your meaning."

" 'Tis a great pity we don't see a bit more of each other. I was remarking on that this morning with my wife Kate. You must know her, she is one of yours."

"One of mine?" Moore asked, puzzled.

"A Papist. Her father was Mick Mahony the grazier. Sure you must have known him."

"No," Moore said. "At least, I cannot remember him."

"Then you didn't know him," Cooper said flatly. "If you had known that fellow you would have remembered him." He sipped at the sherry. "A great pity we don't know each other better."

"Perhaps we are about to," Moore said.

"Yes," Cooper said. "Perhaps so. It is on official business that I am here, in a way. Yeomanry business."

"Are you certain then that your business is with me? I have understood that the Tyrawley Yeomanry is entirely Protestant."

"Well, there is little doubt of that," Cooper said. In embarrassment his thumb polished a brass button. "Largely Protestant in its composition."

"But not entirely so?"

"Well now, that is more a matter of local custom than anything. 'Tis best when the two creeds keep to themselves."

"Do not misunderstand me, Captain Cooper. I have no ambitions in that direction, no aptitude for military life."

"What I am really here about is the serious disturbance that we have had in Kilcummin. You will have heard of it, surely?"

"No," Moore said. "What disturbance is that?"

"There has been an outbreak of Whiteboyism. The Whiteboys of Killala, they call themselves. They have maimed a number of cattle. My own, in fact. And they threaten the like to any landlord who turns to grazing."

"That could be serious, of course," Moore agreed. "How did all this come about?"

He refilled their glasses.

"I started things off myself, I suppose. I had a tenant named Squint O'Malley. And a damned bad tenant he was, I can tell you. He wasn't one of ours at all. He drifted here from Achill a few years ago. He was far behind with the rent. Two weeks ago, I had my steward drive him off."

"You had no choice?"

"I had none. Do you think I like driving a man and his family onto the road? The way it is, I am fair crippled under the mortgages and the debts. In March I went down to see the worst of them in Dublin and he gave it to me straight. I am to offer proof that Mount Pleasant can be made to pay, and it is cattle that will make it pay. He is dead right about that. I have no choice."

45

"It may not be Whiteboys," Moore said. "It may only be O'Malley out for revenge."

"Not at all," Cooper said. "O'Malley is out of it. I hear he is out in Erris, on a bit of land his wife's brother has. No, it is Whiteboys, and they are out to stop all of us." He dug into his pocket, pulled out the letter, unfolded it, and handed it to Moore. Moore made room on his desk, and smoothed the letter flat with a long, pale hand. Then he took his reading glasses from their case. " 'To the Landlords and the Middlemen of this Barony. A warning take by Cooper.' " He read through the letter, glanced once toward Cooper, and then read it again more attentively. He smiled several times, but otherwise maintained his quiet seriousness of manner.

"This is a most curious document," he said. "I have never seen anything quite like it."

"Of course you have not, not in London nor any other civilized place. But they have been common enough here in the past."

"You misunderstand me," Moore said. "This is written with considerable eloquence. Listen. 'Clownish churl, you count your cows in children's lives.' "

"That is me," Cooper said. "Am I to admire insults as eloquence?"

" 'Let all churls take warning from Cooper. The people of Tyrawley have stained with their sweat the acres they till. When the sun rises up they are before it at their labors, and the white moon keeps its watch upon their poverty.' That was not written by a plowboy."

"Of course it was not," Cooper said in exasperation. "Any of twenty hedge schoolmasters in the barony could have written it. Proper bastards those schoolmasters are."

"Yes," Moore said, pleased. "That could be it. It has the stiffness of a translation."

"There used to be laws against schoolmasters, and good laws they were. What business have Papist peasants learning to read and write?"

Anger, like chips of ice, flecked Moore's mild blue eyes, then vanished.

"This could indeed be a serious matter," he said. "Am I to take it that you have ridden all the way to Ballintubber for my advice?"

"Not exactly. Or rather, yes, we would be most happy for your advice, but it is your assistance we need."

"And by 'we' I take it that you mean Gibson and Saunders and the others in your neighborhood?"

"That is it. The small landlords of Kilcummin and Killala. We have had Whiteboy trouble before, years ago, and we know how to deal with it. It is the goodwill of Dennis Browne that we need now."

Moore passed the tips of his fingers across his forehead. "I don't understand this at all, Captain Cooper. If it is Dennis Browne you need, you should be talking to him and not to me. But why do you need Browne? If there are popular disturbances in Tyrawley you should report this to General Hutchinson in Galway City."

"This is not a task for Hutchinson's soldiers. We can deal with these lads, if we are given a free hand."

"Surely that is a matter for the magistrates. You are a magistrate yourself, are you not? And Gibson?"

"We are, to be sure." Cooper was beginning to doubt the wisdom of Kate's advice. Moore was apparently a very slow-witted man, his brain bogged down in his books. "And we have no wish to act beyond what the law would allow."

"A most commendable attitude on the part of the magistrates, if I may be allowed, as a Papist, to comment on such matters."

Or that was it, perhaps. Scratch a Papist deep enough and you come upon some gnawing ambition or other. A seat in Parliament or on the bench of magistrates. Anything and everything that was forbidden to them by law.

"It isn't a sectarian matter at all," he assured Moore in what he believed to be a conciliatory manner. "This is Whiteboy trouble, and we both know what that means. Once we have a few of these rogues tied to the cart's tail, and a few ribbons cut out of their backsides, we will be close to the bottom of things. And the matter will be over before it has properly begun. That's the way."

Moore stared at him incredulously. "And that is what you mean by a free hand. Do I understand you correctly? You have come for help so that you can turn your yeomen loose upon the peasants of the barony?"

"Not your help exactly, Mr. Moore. But you stand in very well with Dennis Browne. Everyone knows that the Brownes and the Moores have been friends time out of mind."

"You foolish man," Moore said.

"Perhaps you are the foolish one, Moore," Cooper

said. He was stung less by the sudden, unexpected words than by the casual manner of their utterance. "You don't know Mayo yet."

"I know enough to be appalled," Moore said. "And so would Dennis Browne be, unless I greatly misjudge him. So would be any man of prudence and discretion. Have you discussed your ideas with George Falkiner? He seems a sensible fellow."

"You don't know Mayo," Cooper repeated stubbornly. And he had spent an entire afternoon riding here, to be insulted by a Papist ignorant of the county. Prudence and discretion in a county governed by the hounds and pistols of the gentry, the loaded whips of the middlemen, the clubs of the peasantry.

"You are a magistrate, Captain Cooper, and so are your friends, and the magistrates of this country have more power than I would once have thought possible. Use it, and keep your Tyrawley Yeomanry out of the matter. The last thing needed at this moment is the dragooning of the county by red-coated Protestants."

"Protestants, is it?" Cooper asked, seizing happily upon the word. "Now we have it out in the open at last."

Moore sighed. "I will not lecture you upon morality or law. It would be a waste of breath. You said that you would welcome my advice and you shall have it. Parts of this island have been in rebellion, and the danger is not yet past. The French may make another effort. We have been most fortunate in Mayo, and we should protect our good fortune. You must deal with these Whiteboys, of course, but it would be most unwise to inflame the countryside. I am quite certain that is the advice which Dennis Browne will give you."

"What advice?" Cooper said, the irritation squeezing him like the choker of his uniform. "To sit quietly until I go into ruin, and am swept away off my own land?"

"I am certain that your affairs are not quite so desperate," Moore said. "You have time enough to act quietly and within the law. Must this county be turned upside down in troubled times because one landlord is heavily mortgaged?"

"By God," Cooper said, stung again by Moore's insufferably cool manner, "and to think that I came here out of the goodness of my heart, to draw you in a bit into the affairs of the county."

"That was kind of you," Moore said. "I take such part in county affairs as your laws permit to me."

"Those laws," Cooper said, his anger at last bursting its dam, "are here for the very proper purpose of keeping Papists in their place."

"Just so," Moore agreed. "I am in my proper place. Moore Hall. And I wish the countryside around me to be as tranquil as possible."

Cooper puffed out his cheeks, and then expelled the air in a gesture of baffled defeat. What did this man know, with his blue ceilings decorated with naked white goddesses, of the problems a poor man faced, squeezed between the cabins and the mortgage brokers, and no place for him to turn?

"Come now," Moore said. "It is foolish of us to lose our tempers. Let us discuss this a bit more, while you sample another glass of sherry." He slipped his watch from his pocket, snapped it open, and studied the time.

" 'Tis little enough the two of us have ever had to discuss," Cooper said with dignity. "And we have less now than ever before." He rose up, and smoothed his scarlet coat. The action soothed him; authority leaked from the wool into his fingertips. "I had best be going now. It is a long ride."

Moore lifted his glass, and Spain burst upon his tongue. About one thing Cooper was right: Spain was far distant from here. He looked through the window toward the lake, and tried to picture the blazing sun upon winding streets of white walls and ochre walls. "Do nothing rash, Captain," he said, without turning his head. "Be careful."

"I shall take care," Cooper said. "You may depend on that. We have been taking care of this county for a good many years now, and we know what must be done."

Moore leaned toward him suddenly, his lips thin and the blue eyes glittering. "Do you? Has this land no other resource of governing but the whip and the cudgel, no other form of justice than a peasant's bloody back and a greasy sovereign in the hand of an informer?"

Amazed, Cooper stared at Moore.

"The whipping post and the lash and the gallows, those are your laws," Moore said, spitting out the words, "whatever may be the statutes which they enact up in Dublin. It is small wonder that your brutes of peasants murder your agents and tumble their bodies into the bog. And you have the insolence to seek my assistance in your filthy plans."

"Are you mad?" Cooper asked. He meant the question. The abrupt change from Moore's manner of icy indifference was bewildering. He had been a fool to take Kate's advice, which had provided Moore with an opportunity first to taunt him with cool ironies and then to rant at him like a Presbyterian minister.

"Perhaps I am," Moore said, regaining control of himself with an effort. "To have sat here listening to your foolishness."

"And I was foolish to have come here," Cooper said.

"You mustn't forget this," Moore said, handing him the Whiteboy letter. Clownish churl. Whoever had written that letter had a gift for phrase. A most curious document indeed. He walked Cooper to the door, as though they had exchanged only pleasantries, and bade him a polite farewell. Cooper was speechless with indignation.

Mounted on his chestnut gelding, Cooper rode glumly down the avenue. Leafy rowan trees flung dappled shadows in his path. They were all alike, Fogarty, Moore, twisting, clever men who could always get the best in words over a blunt, plain-spoken Protestant. He rehearsed speeches that he might have made, withering Moore into silence, but gave up the effort. What kind of Papist was he at all, with his elaborate manners and his English speech? What kind of a gentleman could he be, the son of a huckster who smuggled wine ashore at Kilcummin strand in the old days? It would do him good to have such words flung in his face, a man who could never sit on the bench of magistrates or hold the King's commission. Ach, much would it bother him, with his fine house and his vast acres and his quarter-million pounds. Old Joshua Cooper would have put him in his place. Cooper's spirits lifted slightly at the thought of old Joshua, and he remembered the face in the portrait, a hard, capable soldier who had beaten all the Moores to their knees, all the Papists.

Moore, standing on his balcony, watched the small, dumpy figure in its uniform of resplendent red. Exactly the kind of small man who could create large trouble, a very specimen of the type. A skeptic in spiritual matters, Moore had prided himself in London upon his indifference to sectarian divisions. It was different here. Beneath his contempt for Cooper's foolish swaggering had glowed a hot coal of anger. How dare this improvident farmer set himself above me, he had found himself thinking at one point. And now, as he watched Cooper's receding back, the coal was still warm. Ill-bred vulgarian, spawn of some Cromwellian trooper, history had given him license to crow over this dunghill of a country. Clownish churl: admirable phrase. He turned his back on Cooper and left the balcony.

But not even at dinner that night was he allowed to forget Cooper's visit. John came late to table, and still in his riding clothes, the neckband loose, and with his loose yellow hair falling about his forehead.

"In Father's day," he said as he picked up his napkin, "a man like Cooper would never have been a guest in this house."

Moore glanced up from his soup. "You are mistaken there. Father was a politic man, far more so than either of us. And when he was a young man, before Spain, he had to be very wary of such fellows. They ruled the roost. Things are a bit better now."

"They may seem better," John said.

"Whiteboys have been busy in Kilcummin. As a landlord I was grateful for the information."

"Whiteboys?" John asked, startled. "Is he certain of that?"

"Quite certain," Moore said. "He brought me their letter; it was the usual bombast, better written than most. They are not—" He broke off, and waited until Haggerty had served John's soup and had left the room. "They most certainly are not rebels, if that was the point of your question."

John said nothing. He picked up his spoon and stirred his soup. "I have been at Malcolm Elliott's," he said. "That great chestnut mare of his has foaled. It will be a lovely creature."

"Elliott is well, I trust, and Mrs. Elliott? She is also lovely, in her way. I am very fond of Mrs. Elliott."

"She is well," John said shortly.

"And Elliott and yourself found time for a long talk about political matters, no doubt?"

John put down his spoon and faced his brother. "Yes," he said, "we did. Elliott and I often discuss political matters."

"These must be depressing times for Elliott," Moore said. "The leaders of his organization imprisoned in Dublin, and the rebellion shattered."

"Have a care," John said, glancing toward the closed door.

"Oh, you are safe enough here," Moore said. "And safe enough with Malcolm Elliott in Moat House. But everywhere else, you do well to guard your tongue. This is a poor season for sedition. This wine is a bit off. Had you noticed?"

"No," John said. "If you do think it sedition, you are devilish cool about it, George."

"What I may think is not to the point," Moore said. "It is a hanging offense."

They said nothing further until Haggerty, assisted by an untidy maid, had served the meal.

"I have no wish to meddle with another man's politics," Moore said. "You spent a year in Dublin. Perhaps you joined the Society there, and perhaps Malcolm Elliott did. But as a brother I am thankful that you are safe in Mayo, and many miles away from the Society of United Irishmen."

"That is fair enough," John said. "You have never affected any sympathy for the ideals of the Society."

"For their ideals?" Moore asked. "A very large sympathy." He put down his knife. "Why can they not cook meat properly in this country? The best beef in Europe, and they burn it to cinders. One might suppose that with their long tradition of arson—"

"Not enough sympathy to take them seriously."

"I have met several of the United Irish leaders. I know Tom Emmet, and MacNevin. And I have known many men like them, in France, in the first year or two of the Revolution. Liberty, equality. They want all the proper things, all the admirable things. And it ends in butchery."

"It need not," John said.

"History is what happens," Moore said.

"Freeing one's country from oppression has usually been accounted a virtue," John said. "For the first time in the history of this country, Protestant and Catholic have united in a common purpose."

"A union of some Dublin solicitors and a handful of briefless barristers, a few Catholic physicians and merchants. But when the rising broke out in Wexford, the United Irishmen had no control over it. Do you believe that the peasants of Wexford had read Tom Paine? It was a rising up of the peasantry against the men of property, the Papists against the Protestants. 'The army of the Gael,' they called themselves."

"Surely a wish to be free does not require the reading of Tom Paine," John said.

"An excellent point," George said. "But you should make it to your friends, and not to me. Their minds are fixed upon a republic, but the peasants who do their fighting for them have their minds fixed elsewhere. When peasants respond to oppression, the response is brutal, violent. Those barristers in Dublin know nothing of the Irish peasantry. I doubt if Wolfe Tone has ever spoken with one. I doubt if he would know how."

"But you agree as to the fact of the oppression."

"Oh, I do indeed.'" Moore pushed his plate aside impatiently. "The landlords of this island, taken in the generality, are both savage and silly. A dangerous combination. Men like Cooper are intolerable. Even Dennis Browne—"

"Then what hope is there for the country, short of—"

"Alas, John. You cannot call this a country, this battered old hulk adrift on the Atlantic. You have seen France and England and Spain. You know what nations are. France is just now emerging from a convulsion, but it has remained a nation. Ireland has never been a nation. It cannot be. We have savaged each other too long, and we have cut too deep."

John laughed. "By God, if you find Ireland so complicated, how can you hope to write a history of the Revolution in France?"

"No trouble at all," George said. "The French Revolution is merely a momentous cataclysm which has changed the direction of human events. I could never write a history of Ireland."

"They are in gaol now, most of them," John said. "If I had stayed in Dublin, I might be there now myself."

"Not Tone," George said. "Tone is still in France making mischief. I wish him joy of the Directory. Not all the world's rogues are in Ireland."

"I wish him well," John said quietly.

George looked at him sharply, and with a slight smile. "You don't believe a word I've said, do you?"

"All of them," John said. "They don't matter. I know what this country needs."

"So does Cooper," Moore said. "I envy such knowledge."

By the time the fruit was served, they had managed to change the subject. John watched his brother's long, deft fingers separate an apple from its skin, the sharp silver knife twisting an even curl of red peel.

"Later this week," he said, "I may ride to Ballycastle to visit the Treacys."

"An excellent idea," Moore said. "She is a splendid, sharp, saucy girl. She is exactly what you need."

"Thomas Treacy is not a wealthy man," John said. "That doesn't bother you?"

"That is no concern of mine. I am pleased that it doesn't bother you. But I recommend you venture no political views to Thomas Treacy. There is the old Catholic stock for you with a vengeance. He is still waiting for the Stuarts, poor fellow."

"Ellen is not," John said. "She shares my sympathies."

"Then she is in love with you," Moore said. "Women have no politics, thank God. You should have more sense than to discuss politics with a woman. I did so once in London, and we had the devil of a row. Making up was most pleasant, though. I believe that she knew it would be, and thus caused the quarrel. They are very clever."

"And Judith Elliott," John said. "She is most patriotic."

"That is different," Moore said. "Mrs. Elliott is English, and they often become Irish patriots if they settle here. It has something to do with the weather. Mrs. Elliott is a romantic; it is part of her charm. She and Ellen Treacy are not at all alike, and of the two I think I prefer Ellen. Such is my own patriotism."

"But you do think Mrs. Elliott lovely. You have said so."

"Lovely indeed, and of a most loving disposition, I have no doubt. But a steady diet of high sentiments would not be to my taste. Still, Elliott thrives. I may be mistaken."

As they talked, John was remembering being a very small boy in Alicante, the air heavy with odors, the roofs below them turning purple in the evening light, their father elaborate in his Spanish clothes. He was talking of home, an unimaginable place called Mayo, thick green, warm with the memories of family. Now they were here, two brothers, restless in different ways.

MacCarthy watched the dancers.

He was standing beside the fiddler, his long, ungainly body propped against the wall of Donal Hennessey's farmhouse, one of the largest in Killala, two wide, deep rooms with a true fireplace in one of them. Nothing in the world was more tormenting to him than an image which had not yet become an image. He was like a woman giving birth to a cauled child. The moon and the surface which held its light were clotted together in his imagination, rain-shrouded.

The fiddle fought against the room's other noises, the feet upon the floor, the voices and laughter of the men and women standing against the wall, too old for dancing or too tired. The fiddle spoke to the thudding bare feet of dancers upon the mud floor, and was answered by them. There is a fine girl, he thought, watching one of the dancers. What girl is that, Maire Spellacy? A great, strapping girl, beef to the heels, as they said in Mayo, their minds always upon cattle. He watched her, prodded to a faint sensuality, but the image nagged at him. For an hour it had given him no rest. He drank half of his glass of whiskey, and raised it in salute to the fiddler, who smiled with his lips, but his eyes were turned inward toward his music. Terrible people, musicians, wedded to their wood and their catgut, caressing them like lovers. Someone filled his glass. Drinking was expected of him.

Soon it would be Saint John's Eve. Wood for the bonfire had already been piled high upon Steeple Hill, and when the night came there would be bonfires on every hill from there to Downpatrick Head. There would be dancing and games in the open air, and young men would try their bravery leaping through the flames. There would even be young girls leaping through, for it was helpful in the search for a husband to leap through a Saint John's Eve fire, the fires of midsummer. The sun was at its highest then, and the fires spoke to it, calling it down upon the crops. It was the turning point of the year, and the air was vibrant with spirits. When the fires had died down, the cattle would be driven through the embers, and hazel wands lighted from the embers would singe their backs. Ashes from the fire would be set aside to mix with next year's seed corn.

Good reason had Hussey to stand in his pulpit and give out against the bonfires, for they had little enough to do with Saint John. They were older than Christ, older than the Druids who had been driven out by Patrick. In Mac-Carthy's Kerry, on Saint John's Eve, the oldest woman in the townland would crawl three times around the fire, praying for the crops. And to bring home a burning stick was to have good luck all year. Saint John's Eve frightened MacCarthy by suggesting the antiquity of human life, the remote past casting its shadow outward from the fires, darkening the flame-reddened faces. Still, it did no harm, and this could be one of the biggest harvests in the memory of Mayo, the weather fine with soft rains and bright sunlight, the corn growing plump. It did no harm at all to keep the sun with you. O'Sullivan had a poem about Saint John's Eve, a poem too soft and easy in its construction, but not a bad poem at all. He was no man to try a contest with; at his laziest, he was better than most.

When the dance had ended, Ferdy O'Donnell, who was one of the dancers, joined MacCarthy against the wall, a jug in one hand.

"Well, Owen, it is about time we gave another try to Virgil, one of these nights. Come early, and we will have something to eat and then set to work." He had been briefly a seminarian, and had now this plan to work through six books of the *Aeneid* with MacCarthy's help.

"We will, Ferdy. I was in Kilcummin a few nights ago, and thought that soon I must call in on yourself and Maire."

"You had other business in Kilcummin, I am told," O'Donnell said, dropping his voice. He nodded toward the other room.

"I had a fool's business. Acting as secretary to a quartet of blackguards."

"It is no quartet now. There are more than forty Whiteboys now in the barony, sworn Whiteboys. They are acting under Duggan in Kilcummin, and Hennessey here in Killala."

"But not you?"

"Ach, 'tis not my style either, Owen. What have beings like the two of us to do with Whiteboys? Sure I wouldn't walk down the road to see even a faction fight. Mind you,

I'm not saying they are wrong. There may be less talk now about evictions."

"If you will not be sworn, Duggan will not weep," Mac-Carthy said. "You are a well-respected man in Kilcummin, and you did not earn that respect with a cudgel." It was not flattery. A quiet, clear-headed young man and a good farmer. They respected his learning, and they remembered that he was one of the old O'Donnells.

But their talk moved then to the *Aeneid*. O'Donnell had a decent seminarian's knowledge of Latin, but not the faintest notion of what the *Aeneid* was like as a poem. Translate thirty lines a day, and stop at the thirtieth, wherever you might find yourself. What was it that men like O'Donnell found to love in the Latin? Perhaps the sentences built like good fences, every word solidly in place, and each one giving strength to all the others. A marvelous language. Language of mystery and miracle, it brought Christ to earth, placed His body upon man's tongue.

When Hennessey came to summon him to the west room he was loath to go. What had bleeding cattle to do with the far moon, or the notes of a violin, or Aeneas cast up on Dido's shore, a kingdom burned behind him and a kingdom yet to be built, but now a queen amorous and pious. Troy flaming like the bonfires of Saint John's Eve.

"You are one of us now, Owen boy," Hennessey said, clapping him on the shoulder. "That letter had a blade to it like a knife."

"I am like hell," MacCarthy said. "I told you that I was not."

"Sure Duggan only wants you to have a drink with us. You would be wise to keep in with Malachi. He will rule the barony."

"The magistrates rule the barony," MacCarthy said. "The magistrates and the yeomen."

"Cooper has spent the last two days riding up and riding down to the other landlords," Hennessey said. "He will have them frightened out of their wits. He even went to the Papist landlords."

"Landlords have their own religion," MacCarthy said.

In the west room they were gathered around Duggan, all of them standing, Quigley and O'Carroll and nine or ten men, a few in their thirties, but most of them far younger. Some were farmers, and some were laborers. What business had spalpeens in a quarrel between farmers and landlords? The room was heavy with their smell. O'Carroll handed him a large tumbler of whiskey, and Duggan greeted him, unsmiling.

"You are a man of your word," MacCarthy said. "You have begun a Whiteboy war in this quiet corner of Mayo."

"The Whiteboys of Killala," Duggan said. The pompous title stuffed his mouth. "We will protect the people of this barony against Protestant landlords."

"A religious war, is it? You have grown more ambitious." Fine whiskey, the color of a pearl, with fire buried within.

"Sure what else has it ever been?" one of the spalpeens asked. Eighteen or nineteen, and shaped like MacCarthy himself, long arms and heavy sloping shoulders. We are a tribe of our own, MacCarthy thought, bodies shaped for the spade. He began to speak, but changed his mind.

"Well can he tell us," Duggan said, nodding to the spalpeen. "He is one of the poor people driven out of Ulster last year by the Orange Protestants. Himself and all his people, with their cabin burned behind them."

"I am sorry," MacCarthy said to the lad. "You have had a hard time of it."

"It could happen here," Duggan said. "We all know that." He rolled his bullock's eyes toward the others, and they nodded.

"Worse could happen," MacCarthy said.

"Or better," Hennessey said. "Drink up, lads." He moved his jug toward them. "These lads are just after taking the oath, Owen. You would do well to take it yourself. The schoolmaster should be with the people."

MacCarthy drained his tumbler, so that it would be empty and waiting when the jug came to him.

Quigley craned forward his bald moon of a head. "The schoolmaster in Kilcummin has taken the oath."

MacCarthy watched the whiskey fill his glass. "The Kilcummin schoolmaster is an ignorant dirty man who is a disgrace to learning. He was driven out of Ballintubber because of his ignorance, and every schoolmaster in Mayo knows that. They are not fools in Ballintubber. They are decent men with a respect for learning, but sure he is good enough for Kilcummin. They deserve no better."

"He is a man with books in his house," Quigley said hotly, "and a tremendous knowledge of the history of the Gaels from the time of Noah."

"Noah my arse," MacCarthy said. "'Tis a wonder you did not have this prodigy write your letter for you."

"'Tis more than a schoolmaster you are, Owen. You are a poet and the writer of acclaimed verses."

"And you would break my pen to your coarse plow," MacCarthy said. He felt the whiskey; his head danced.

"It makes no sense," Duggan said, "to have a fellow like this wander about without taking the oath, and him with our names in his head. He would shop us for the price of a jug."

"I am no informer," MacCarthy said. "I want no part of you."

"It would be no harm done for you to take the oath, Owen," Hennessey said. "There are good men in Kilcummin and in Killala who have taken the oath, and others will. These men here are as fine as you could wish, and they are men with friends."

"What you did the other night," MacCarthy said, "was to put the fear of God into a mean, shameless little bastard. Let it rest there."

Duggan shook his head. "If you will not take the oath, we have no need for your advice. We have our plans made."

"By God, we do," one of the farmers said. "We will rule the barony."

"You will not rule the gaolcart and the gallows," MacCarthy said. "And that is how it will end, with your black tongues lolling out and your breeches soiled."

The music began again, and the sound of feet on the floor of close-packed clay. I should be there, MacCarthy thought. Let my head be filled with music and whiskey, not argument. He drank again.

"By God, Owen MacCarthy," one of the farmers said, "you should make us a poem about the raid upon Cooper by the Whiteboys of Killala."

"I will not," MacCarthy said, furious. "My poems are not about churls crawling across fields to cut the legs of cattle. My art is noble in subject and language."

"You are too good for us, perhaps," Duggan said. "You should be spending your days and nights with Treacy at Bridge-end House, with your poems about the glory of the Gael."

The army of the Gael. In Wexford they confronted armies, seized towns, banners marched before them, and their beacon fires blazed upon the hills. In far-distant

59

France, great ships were making ready. Not here, not in this wet, muddy land beneath sullen hills.

"There is always a welcome set before me at Bridgeend House," he said, "and brandy at my hand and silver coins. Thomas Treacy knows the honor due to a poet who has mastered his craft."

" 'Tis no great honor to keep a school in Killala," Duggan said contemptuously. "You live as we do. More meanly than some of us."

"What can you know of such matters," MacCarthy said, "huddled away in a corner of Mayo? I have seen the entire world, I am a traveled man, and I have been received with honor. I have seen the great waterwheel in Clonmel, and Dunboy Castle on the Cork coast where Murtogh O'Sullivan held off the soldiers of the English King, and Dunluce Castle in Antrim amidst the black Presbyterians." Hollow, the hollow words rattled like shells in his skull. I am drunk, he thought indifferently. Notes of music cut the shells.

"You may have seen these things," Quigley said. "But you will not see them again. It is said that you would not be welcome in some of the places you have been." Moon head nodded. "Mind you, I say no word against your poetry. But Malachi has the right of it. 'Tis a queer sort of place for a man with the airs you give yourself."

"A poet always has his welcome," MacCarthy said, "in the halls of the old gentry and in the beds of the young women. Without poets, we would be a people without a voice, and who would cut out his own tongue?"

" 'Tis a wonder you waste your days teaching sums to children."

"That is my trade," MacCarthy said. "A poet has his trade and he has his craft." And a moon which music itself could not reach. "I am a poet and a MacCarthy. Before we were driven into Kerry my people were lords of Clancarty."

"And how were you driven there?" Quigley asked. "In a carriage of fine wood with the arms of the MacCarthys painted on its side in greens and gold, like the Protestant gentry?"

Duggan laughed. Rocks tumbling down a hillside. Two of the spalpeens looked at him and then at each other, then joined his laughter. Louts born of louts. MacCarthy turned upon them.

"Why should lads like you follow this man?" he asked

them, pointing to Duggan. "If his land is made safe, will life be easier for you? At the hiring fair, who sets the low price upon you, the gentry or the farmers?" Lined up like cattle or niggers while the bucks of the county rode by, pointing with their whips.

"Perhaps we will not always be selling ourselves at the fair," the lad from Ulster said.

"You will," MacCarthy said. "You were slaves on this land before Christ was crucified."

"A fine one you are to be talking about Christ," Duggan said, "when the Christians of this barony are in need of help."

MacCarthy finished off his glass. He detested the room and those in it. Music pulled at him, proclaimed his distant identity.

"Look at him," Quigley said. "Much help that one could be to anyone. He cannot even help himself to stand upright."

MacCarthy made a sudden lunge for him, missed his footing, and seized him by the jacket. The room danced.

"Pull them apart," Duggan said scornfully.

When they were standing apart, Quigley was holding his hand to a scraped lip. MacCarthy stared at it stupidly.

"Go back to your woman," Duggan said. "Much good you will be to her."

" 'Tis a disgrace to Killala," O'Carroll said. "The schoolmaster living in open sin. Half of the women will not so much as talk to Judy Conlon, and she was a decent woman once. Before your time."

" 'Tis a happy man that you would be to take my place one night a year," MacCarthy said. "No man is ever more virtuous than the envious man."

"Now, now," O'Carroll said, and took a step backward.

"Go back to your woman," Duggan said again.

"I will," MacCarthy said. "I will leave this mean, dispirited place."

"You are welcome to this jug, Owen," Hennessey said. "Go home now and sleep."

"Well said. You are a better man than the company you are in, Donal Hennessey. That handsome, long-legged wife keeps you in good spirits."

Hennessey put a hand on his shoulder. "It is an honor to have a man like yourself in the parish."

"I will put into a satire the mean, ungrateful people of Killala. Excepting only yourself, Donal. Oh Christ, I am

61

sorry for the people of Killala that they have earned Owen MacCarthy's wrath."

"Get him out of here," Duggan said.

In the other, crowded room, MacCarthy held the jug aloft and shouted, "What woman goes home with Owen MacCarthy the poet?"

He heard their giggling, hands held decorously to mouths. One girl, more reckless than the others, called out, "That girl would have the trouble of a lifetime when she walked into Judy Conlon's house."

He felt a hand on his arm. Ferdy O'Donnell.

"Would you like me to walk a bit of the way with you, Owen?"

"And why should you wish to do that?" MacCarthy asked, drawing his arm free. "I know the way. We will construe Virgil these long summer evenings, Ferdy. I am a very fine scholar."

"I know that, Owen."

"You are not. You have that low, seminary Latin. You will never see how meaning curls and curves through a line. Still, we must do our best for you. Better than nothing, Ferdy. Better than nothing."

"Much better," O'Donnell said, standing with him at the open door. "You did not quarrel with those fellows, did you?"

"Which of them deserves to quarrel with me? They are a low lot, Ferdy, a low lot. You must hold yourself apart from that lot, now mind that. Remember Virgil. That lot in there, Virgil wouldn't have given them the sweat off his balls."

O'Donnell watched him walk up the road, unsteady on his feet, drunk, a clumsy plowboy going home.

He sat on a small, grassy hill. The air was clear and cold, and the world no longer danced before him. He was disgusted with himself. He could not remember half of what he had said, and the other half he tried to forget but could not.

He was no MacCarthy of Clancarty, but a laborer's son, as his father had been before him, as the spalpeens in the cabin were. As he would be himself if his father had not found the pennies to send him to the hedge school outside Tralee. There had been an enigmatic power to the words in the foxed and battered primer, a luminous presence somewhere behind the page. He would be a laborer now had it not been for the master, a poet himself, who carefully taught him the forms and conventions. When he was older, and had himself begun to set words together, the master took him to the taverns where the poets met. MacCarthy would sit well away from the winter fire, where the poets sat, his hands wrapped around a cup of ale, an overgrown boy with long arms and legs. First one and then another of the poets would rise, speaking from memory, the bells of sound ringing across the complex nets of meter, images grouping themselves together, ring beyond bright ring. Beyond the fastened tavern door, the cold West Munster winter, with Atlantic winds cutting past Brandon and across the two bays.

Home was a hovel on the Fenit road, as bad as any in Kilcummin, the dark, windowless room across which his heavy, exhausted father fell toward sleep. Against that darkness, the splendor of shaping a poem, the sounds and images entwining. It became your own, though linked with a hundred others by poets living and long dead. It was a world of air and sunlight. Everywhere else, cabins and the smell of dung, the pigs rooting by the bed, children fighting for the potatoes at the bottom of the pot. Clownish churl, you count your cows in children's lives. But dawn would spring from blackness in a poem, a meadow in fair flower and a maiden moving across it, wondrous fair and bathed in light. The dark day of the Gael is ending, she would tell the poet, and her beauty would smite him like the power of truth. Ships are on the sea bringing the deliverer, an O'Neill or an O'Donnell, or the gallant young Scottish king, the royal blackbird. Darkness would shatter against the bright sword of that deliverer, and light would stream into windowless hovels.

In time, first as apprentice to a hedge teacher and then a master himself, MacCarthy scrambled out of the hovels, moving from village to village, posting his notices of instruction on chapel gates, meeting his winter classes in barns to which each child brought each day two sods of turf. Hens and pennies for instruction at first, then hens and shillings. It was his trade: a poet had his trade and he had his craft. His trade could be teaching, tavernkeeping, even, as with Owen Ruagh O'Sullivan, day laboring. His craft was the articulation of sound and passion. In time, still in his young twenties, MacCarthy's verses became known to other poets, spoken in taverns he had never visited by men whose poems he himself knew,

joined in the freemasonry of language. He was welcome
in the houses of the old native gentry, where Irish was
still spoken, and where beeswax candles lighted walls
upon which hung swords which a hundred years before
had gone into battle with Sarsfield. Harp and pipe would
fall silent and MacCarthy would be summoned forward
to recite his verses, and the gentry, O'Conors and
Frenches and MacDermots who had somehow kept their
land, would nod their approval. Coins of silver or of gold
for a poet who flung backward a slender bridge of words
to a world lost by Boyneside and Shannonside, buried beneath the bloody mud of Aughrim. He had his aislings
and laments for the Catholic big houses, and songs for the
taverns, courting songs and drinking songs, the loose copper change of his art. His frequent drunkenness, his loose
and wanton ways with women, his bad temper, his sardonic manner, were accepted as somehow bound into
his craft. He and his fellow poets were the survivors of
an old order, like the impoverished Catholic gentry with
their fading pedigrees and their useless, ornamental
swords.

There were times, goose feather scratching beside tallow candle, when MacCarthy lived in a cold, perfect
silence broken only by the ring of words upon his imagination. But there were other moments of chill doubt,
striking at the hand which held the pen, freezing the fingers. His poems celebrated the old earls, the O'Neills and
the O'Donnells, but what had these done in the heel of
the hunt but take ship for Spain with their families, leaving their people stuck in the mud, as stuck they were to
this day. They made fine poems about Ireland's darling,
Patrick Sarsfield, sailing off to France after Limerick
with his Irish army, but few of these spoke of their wives
who went screaming and wailing after the ships, their
babies held high above their heads. Fine poems about
King James, the Royal Stuart, but not one said what
every poet knew, that the peasants who had been
prodded and bayonet-pricked into battle called him
"Seamus the Shit," who fled so fast from the Boyne that
he outdistanced the messenger bringing southward the
news of the great defeat. Rubies in the mud, those fabled
names, O'Neill, Maguire, Sarsfield. The poets picked
them up, polished them bright, set them in a filigree of
words to comfort a people without hope.

It was true that MacCarthy had traveled widely

through his Munster and Connaught worlds, but he lied when he said that he had been to Antrim, and he had never been close to Dublin. A network of taverns lay open to a good poet, and MacCarthy had talked and drunk in Bantry and Macroom and Ballyvourney, in Limerick and Ennis and Galway. But he knew his world well enough to know that there was another world beyond it which he did not know at all. In his youth and in his father's time, and his grandfather's, and his great-grandfather's, Irish boys had slipped off to France in smugglers' ships to serve King Louis, and now the last King Louis was dead, his head rolled into a barrel, lopped off by a great engine with an immense blade in the center of it. No more songs would be written about the Irish brigades in the service of France, and there were no more toasts to King Louis in the halls of the Catholic gentry, who now were as terrified of France as the Cromwellian squires.

"Oh, the French are on the sea, says the *Sean Bhean Bhocht*," the poor old woman who personified Ireland. One way or another, the silly crone had been gibbering that for better than a century. And now the French might indeed be on the sea, but not the same French at all. These were the French who had struck off King Louis' head, and perhaps planned the same for King George. Two years before, they had brought their great invasion fleet into Bantry Bay, but had been held off from landing by the Protestant winds. MacCarthy knew that bay well, long, slender arm of the sea; men must have stood by cabin doors, staring down hillsides at tall-masted ships, a prophecy almost fulfilled. Now, with parts of the island in turmoil, there was talk that they would come again. Songs of rebellion had been drifting toward Connaught all spring, but had a way of getting drowned in the Shannon. Unimaginable, that southern rebellion, much less the Ulster rising; a hosting of thousands on the roads, peasants armed with pikes. What had this to do with O'Neill in bright saffron, his belt blazing with jewels, or Patrick Sarsfield, jacketed in white satin, sash of red silk, silver-hilted sword? And what had history itself to do with the battered strands of Mayo? Mayo moved in its own cycle, hostage to its own wide fields, stone and grass and turf.

What of MacCarthy himself, a man who would never have land, no more than his father? In the old days, it was said, poets sat at the table of chieftain and lord, but

Ireland had been thrice broken, by Elizabeth, by Cromwell, by William. All poets now were hedge poets, taking honor where they could find it. Once, in West Cork, near Macroom, walking the road in the warm afternoon, he had rounded a curve to see set before him a big house of cut Portland stone with great white porticoes and eight tall pillars soaring from the porch. There was a carriage coming down the avenue, and MacCarthy stood aside to let it pass: a gentleman in finest velvet, his linen white and shining, his face white and shining, presenting himself to the sun. Now there, MacCarthy thought, if a poet writes for lords, I should be writing for this Squire Jenkins or Colonel Bumpkin. But if he sees me at all, he sees a gawky spalpeen, tramping the roads for work. And for my part, I write of chieftains whose ruined keeps, by bog or headland, are byres for cows.

3

**From the Workbooks of George Moore, Esquire,
of Moore Hall, Ballintubber, County Mayo,
Author of "The Whig Triumph,"
"A Reply to Mr. Saurin," etc.**

Tuesday. Above all else, the Girondists prided themselves upon their oratory, and doubtless it is by their oratory that they will be remembered. Of these circumstances, the first may be said to have defined their weakness, and the second may serve as their epitaph. "Here lie, headless, certain high-minded public figures. They spoke well." But what oratory, what an appalling and insipid brew of Racine and Rousseau! Elaborate figures, formless effusions, bathetic autobiographical confidences exhibited amidst cheers. And their favorite stance, that of the austere and ancient Roman, a type most uncongenial to Rousseau's onanistic ecstasies.

I well recall Vergniaud addressing the Convention at the time of its decision that history itself was to be dated afresh, from the autumnal equinox of what we in our moribund fashion term 1792, but which to the French is now Year I. The very autumn which witnessed the appalling September Massacres, which shocked the Girondists but which they dared not denounce. There he stood, in all his tall, portly rectitude, one hand upon his bosom and the other raised aloft, felicitating himself and all within hearing that they lived within the very accouchement chamber of liberty and justice. And from that time forward, at every crisis in their affairs, they leaped into rhetoric as a fox into its covert, while their unappeasable enemies bayed and pawed the ground outside. Until, at last, their enemies caught them within the cruel trap fashioned by the issue of the King's execution. For the Girondists heartily disapproved of his death, but were by now so thoroughly frightened that they lapsed not into oratory but into silence save for the word *"mort"* by which they voted for his execution. And upon that occasion, we heard a note of more authentic eloquence, with the stuff of steel and terror in it. Here is young Saint-Just, Robespierre's Saint John, upon the matter of the King's death: "The death of the tyrant is necessary to assure those who fear that one day they will be punished for their daring, and also to terrify those who have not yet renounced the monarchy. A people cannot found liberty when it respects the memory of its chains." And here is Danton: "Let us fling down to the kings the head of a king as gage of battle." And, most eloquent of all, Danton's whisper to the Girondists: "Your party is ruined."

It is a wonder to me how my young brother John could have acquired so rich an arsenal of Girondist eloquence in the course of two Dublin terms, when he should have been studying law, or else, like a decent Irish gentleman, wenching, drinking, and gambling. Surely John is better suited by nature for such occupations, an open, manly young fellow, with a gentlemanly aversion to study and reflection, as is demonstrated by the abrupt close of his connection with the legal profession. And yet what pride it would have given Father to see his son as one of the first Papists admitted to the bar! Perhaps the spirit of Rousseau is in the very air these days, like dandelion puffballs. We were seated at breakfast the other morning, and John was discoursing to me, master to pupil, upon the tyranny of England, and the need to snap the galling

67

chains of our oppression. As he talked, I was looking through the window at a gang of our peasants whom I have set to work enclosing one of our unused fields, which I intend shall be an ornamental garden. They were carrying, with their bare hands, heavy boulders, their backs bent and straining under the effort. John did not notice them, his eyes were fixed upon our legislative wrongs, the subservience of our Parliament, the civic and social corruptions worked upon us by our imperial masters.

Wednesday. And yet it is upon these heavers of boulders, these hewers of wood and drawers of water, that the Society of United Irishmen relied. These wretches were to fight their rebellion for them. Why, they might well be living upon different planets, the Dublin barristers of the Society, and the peasants of rural Ireland. I myself, who live amongst them, have no true knowledge of their lives or their natures.

I watched their Saint John's Eve celebrations. Early in the evening, a bonfire was lighted on the low hill across the lake, and there the people gathered, talking, laughing, singing, and drinking freely. There were athletic contests of a sort, young men leaping through the flames, to the cheers of their neighbors. All was done most easily and spontaneously, and they had no notion, I am certain, that these are rituals unchanged from pagan times, a celebration and propitiation of the sun at the turning point of the year. The most powerful of all natural forces, those of fertility and generation, were being addressed. It is the custom of these people, when the ashes of the bonfire are cool, to gather them up and save them that they may be mixed with the seed corn of the following season. In this they obey not a deep natural instinct, but rather a ritual which has been carried forward, unchanged, from perhaps two thousand years in the past. And these are the men whom Tom Emmet and Wolfe Tone—and Malcolm Elliott and my young brother John here in Mayo —propose to instruct in the Rights of Man and the desirability of parliamentary reform and the virtues of a republican government.

Thursday. But in Tyrawley, northward of here, the Saint John's Eve celebrations ended with an attack upon the cattle of a Kilcummin gentleman named Gibson, a magistrate who has incurred much local displeasure by reason of his severity and perhaps also his bigoted behavior. This was more formidable than the attack on Cooper, many more cattle were injured, and a tenant who watched the attackers at work reports that there were at least forty of them. He professes to have recognized none of them, which is possible, for Whiteboys usually take care to blacken their faces.

Saturday. Tyrawley, the barony which can boast of these Whiteboys, is a long afternoon's ride northward of here, a woebegone region which straggles along the River Moy. The County Sligo borders it to the right, but to the left it merges into the waste barony of Erris, beyond which lie the almost deserted bogs and mountains of Belmullet. The great extent of its acreage is the property of Lord Glenthorne, an absentee, but there are fifteen or so fair-sized estates, most of them the possessions of Cromwellian planters. These smaller landlords are understandably beside themselves with apprehension, and one of them, Cooper, the commander of the local yeomanry, proposes that he be given a "free hand," by which he means, quite simply, that he proposes to turn, whip, and torture until he has extracted confessions.

For a time at least he will be restrained by Dennis Browne, a man of great local influence, both political and social. Browne is of course no friend to Whiteboys, but his chief present concern is to keep Mayo tranquil until the threats of rebellion and invasion have passed away. But for all the suave and splendid polish which Browne displays in the Dublin Parliament and at the Viceregal court, he is at heart a chieftain and a man of property. If these Whiteboy attacks continue, I have little doubt that he will give Cooper the "free hand" he craves. Thus has "justice" been achieved in Mayo, for as far back as runs the memory of man.

Monday. I was last night reading one of Tallien's early speeches in the Convention, a typically coarse production, although whether "cynical" or "hypocritical" is the more exact word for him I cannot say. He has the Rousseau cant down pat, and little wayside flowers of "liberty," "sacred rights of man," and "fervent love of freedom" blossom between the paving stones of brutal attacks upon his opponents. It is this man and other choice cronies who rule France today as the Directory. What a gang of rogues they are—Tallien, Rewbell, Barras, and the rest of them! They waded to power through the blood of the Terror, then turned on Robespierre lest they fell victim themselves. Nothing is left now save Power: no resounding oratory, no fine phrases, not even the sincere fanaticism which lent a baleful dignity to Robespierre. And these are the men with whom Wolfe Tone negotiates, that they may bring liberty to Ireland.

He is fit company for them. I met this young man in London, at Holland House, when he accompanied the Catholic delegation as their Protestant agent. I confess I found him a plausible, attractive rogue, all nervous energy and wit. He has a lively and audacious mind, much intellectual bravado, is a skillful musician, and has a copious appetite for whiskey and wine. Had he been born a Frenchman, or even an American, a triumphant career would assuredly have been his, for his talents are in great demand these days. But alas for him, he shares with me the misfortune of having been born an Irishman and must build with our humble bricks. And build he has done! He was in Bantry Bay two years ago, with Hoche and the French fleet, and though Hoche is dead now, the Cork coast may see Tone again. A marvelous career it may appear to some, a starveling barrister risen up to negotiate with the French Directory on behalf of a people who scarce know his name. But then, we live in marvelous times.

Ambition, brains, lack of scruples—what may these not now accomplish, in this springtime world toward which we have been guided by Rousseau's genius? I have no time for those who would argue that the authors of the Terror misunderstood their master. The Terror is implicit in Rousseau. Listen to Robespierre: "When a nation has been forced into insurrection, it returns to a state of nature, with regard to the tyrant. There is no longer any law but the safety of the people." The guillotine stands guarantor for the social contract.

Tuesday. Last evening, I walked along the path which runs beside the lake. A most mild evening, and the sky a delicate even blue, with immense billowing clouds. They were reflected in the still waters of the reed-fringed lake. Above my head, birds circled toward their nests. A feeling of almost transcendent quietude, with, inexplicably, a faint, erotic fretting at the edges. It is almost four months since I have been with a woman, and that but little Sophie M. in Dublin—taffeta, silk, and broken fingernails. Water moved gently at my feet. London, Paris, poor provincial Dublin itself are a universe distant from this lovely lake, from the hill where we settled after our wanderings. A bittern boomed, a most lonely cry, and then the lake was silent again. As I walked back toward the house a faint breeze arose, scarce stirring the heavy-leafed boughs. We possess ideas, but we are possessed by feelings. They lie too deep for understanding, astir with their own secret life and carrying us with them.

Moat House, Ballina, June 26

Late that night, Malcolm Elliott, of Moat House near Ballina, south of Killala on the Castlebar road, sat in the small writing room which he had fitted up next to the bedroom, and read again the letter which he kept hidden away in a French translation of *Gulliver's Travels*. The name of his small estate was a mystery to himself and everyone else, for although the house had been built where a Norman keep once stood, there was no evidence that there had ever been an encircling moat. The estate was bordered on one side by the River Moy, which a half-mile farther north passed through the town of Ballina, a broad, sluggish river crossed, in the town, by two wide, humpbacked bridges.

When he began reading, he sat to his desk, with lamplight falling comfortably upon what had once been his most cherished books, volumes of Helvétius, Diderot, and Holbach. When he finished however, he was pacing the floor. The lamp was weak, but he knew the letter almost by heart.

Citizen Elliott:

A provisional directory has now been established in Dublin, and has assumed the task of holding the Society in readiness.

The arrests of the Chief Directory in March, the capture and fatal wounding of Lord Edward Fitzgerald, the subsequent arrests of numerous local

71

leaders have beyond question impaired the organization, but we believe that an excellent beginning has been made upon the tasks of restoration.

Far more serious has been the suppression of the risings in Antrim and Wexford, with great loss of life. The final battle in the north has been fought and lost at the town of Ballinahinch, where the army of the United Irish withstood for hours the greatly outnumbering forces commanded by General Nugent. General Monroe, the United Commander, disputed every inch of soil, and it is claimed by the enemy that five hundred of the United Irishmen were slain. The town of Ballinahinch is now a ruin, and it is said that the forces of the Crown exacted a horrible vengeance from the defenseless townspeople. Henry Joy MacCracken, commanding the main Antrim force, had been defeated several days earlier, but not before he had captured several towns with a United army numbering six thousand.

In the south, the rising was more formidable, numbering perhaps twenty thousand, and for a time it controlled much of Wexford, winning a number of battles and occupying towns of consequence. It was impeded, alas, by the lack of proper leadership, and at last was overborne by superior numbers. One stain indeed befouled the Wexford banners. The rumors of savagery meted out in Wexford to our Protestant fellow countrymen are beyond any dispute. It was the splendor of Antrim that there Presbyterian and Papist marched, fought, and died side by side. Let Antrim be our example, and the heroes of its deep glens. The very name of the Society of United Irishmen proclaims our guiding principle: a union of Catholic and Protestant, submerging those sectarian differences which have been carefully fostered by the oppressor that we may be held in subjugation. But our army in Wexford, although holding many who at least nominally were United Irishmen, attracted great numbers who must only be termed Defenders, if indeed not outright Whiteboys, and these were fiercely and ignorantly sectarian. They fought less as United Irishmen than as a mob, shepherded by bellicose priests. Not the Republic was their ambition, but rather what they termed "the triumph of the Gael." And yet they fought most bravely, and died heroically. The peasantry of Ireland can accomplish much, nay, all, provided they have proper leadership, and provided they receive that disciplined army of French allies which we now await. The Rights of Man may be likened to a powerful sun, beneath which ancient bigotry will melt like stale wax.

When our French allies land, the United Irishmen will render to them all possible assistance. Our agents in France, Theobald Wolfe Tone and his companions, have promised them that the island shall rise up, and our task it is to fulfill that promise. In Leinster, resistance has ended with the surrender at Vinegar Hill, but in Munster our organization remains substantially intact, despite the burnings and tortures inflicted upon the counties of Waterford and Tipperary.

This letter is being sent to each of our members in Connaught, the one province which has thus far been spared the brutality of the Crown forces. We are well aware of the backwardness of that province, in whose soil our Society has never taken firm root. It is essential, however, to till that soil, so that there, as elsewhere in Ireland, the Tree of Liberty can be planted. Our cause is just, the unfettering of our native land that she may take her place among the nations of Europe. Let our energies be as firm as our hopes.

Elliott folded the letter and replaced it. It had been brought to him the week before by a man claiming to be a peddler, a scarecrow with a soiled and ill-fitting wig, riding a sorry-looking pony and leading a scrawny donkey loaded down with wares. "Are you from Dublin?" Elliott asked him. "Athlone. I am traveling to Sligo." "You were given these letters in Athlone?" "What letters?" We are well aware of the backwardness of that province. Much they knew of Connaught, those Dublin lawyers and merchants. The Provisional Directory should be marched through the streets of Ballina to judge for themselves the state of things.

He hooked his thumbs in the waistband of his trousers and walked the room again. He had the look of a Mayo squireen, a man with a jockey's slender, nervous frame.

73

and a face like a hatchet, narrow and triangular. Thick, sandy eyebrows sheltered darting eyes. He had been called to the bar, but his radical politics had incurred the hostility of the other gentlemen of the county. He was a hard-riding hunter, reckless and skillful in the Mayo fashion, and in Dublin he had been restless and dissatisfied, longing for the fields and broken fences of home. Those years, he now knew, had been the happiest in his life. His politics, he then had prided himself, were practical and unsentimental. A wave had arisen in France and was destined to sweep across Europe, destroying monarchs and ancient aristocratic privileges; it would batter down Ireland's oligarchy, sweep away hereditary corruption, cleanse government and Parliament, open up careers to honest and energetic men. There had been many such men in Dublin in the early nineties. They had formed a Society. Now they were a conspiracy, their leaders imprisoned or in French exile, and their insurrection had become a peasant uprising, with Protestants put to the sword at Wexford Bridge and on Vinegar Hill. Faint echoes reached Mayo: a note carried by a peddler; "Citizen Elliott . . ."

Taking up the lamp, he went to the bedroom, and stood looking down at his sleeping wife, Judith. A wisp of fair hair had fallen across her brow; her face was calm, oval. She was an English girl; they had met and married in London. But she was a far more ardent Irish patriot than he was himself, as though sympathy for her adopted country demanded proof. In Dublin she had become the friend of Pamela Fitzgerald, Lord Edward's earnest and vivacious French wife. At Moira House, under the benign eye of a radical peer, they had enthused together over the coming Republic of Ireland, and over their husbands, who would bring it into being. Now poor Edward was dead, of wounds suffered when resisting the soldiers who ran him to earth in a Dublin slum, sold out by an informer. And Elliott, a blunt, bitterly honest man, was back in Mayo, a man with no taste for conspiracies and useless ciphers. He was bound to the Society only by his oath and by a peddler's letter. But to Elliott, an oath was a very serious matter. He was bound in honor to the dead Fitzgerald, to men in Irish and in English prisons, to the exiled plotters in Paris. And in Mayo he was useless to them.

On their first journey to Mayo, Ireland had been an

unrolling wonder to Judith, as they left behind them the Anglified counties of the pale and crossed the Shannon into what Dublin spoke of as "the wild west." She picked up Irish turns of phrase, and used them with an impressive inaccuracy but with an eagerness to please which won the hearts of all who spoke with her. "Sure and what time of day can it be at all?" she would ask him, and he would gravely answer her, "It can be ten o'clock." A true child of her age, she traveled with her Ossian, a poet capable, in Elliott's view, of the most appalling drivel, endless bathetic windiness. She would quiz him about the mountains they passed: what heroes lay buried atop them, what ancient Fenian battles had been fought upon their slopes? Elliott knew little about Ireland's grotesque legendry. Who knows or cares, he had been tempted to reply, but clear eyes and an eager face always checked his reply.

She stirred, and in sleep turned her face toward him. Love ravished him, holding him tight by emotions which he could not name. She dwelt in a different world from his, shaped by her reading and her imagination. Once they had spent an evening at Tom Emmet's villa in Rathfarnham at the foot of the Dublin hills, in the small oval study painted in what Tom's wife believed to be the Grecian fashion, white and pale blue. Russell had been there as well, and MacNevin and Bagenal Harvey. And one other had been present there in their conversation, as they recalled Tone's quicksilver wit, his fondness for claret and the violin and flute. It had seemed to Judith, and to Elliott himself, a conspiracy of the intellect, the best and clearest minds in the kingdom, banded together against brutishness and corruption. Emmet was in prison now, and Bagenal Harvey's head was on a spike outside Wexford gaol. Prisoner rather than leader of the Wexford peasants, they called him their general, and then carried him from battle to battle. After Vinegar Hill, he hid for a week on an island off the coast, shivering and spray-stained. Where MacCracken was at that moment, Elliott did not know, perhaps waiting in some deep-walled Antrim glen for the soldiers to hunt him down. And Tone? Somewhere in France with an army that might or might not come. Elliott had not told Judith of Bagenal Harvey's fate. He could see the darkening head, lolling tongue, protruding eyes. Judith remembered wit, music, curved walls painted white and blue.

Elliott blew out the lamp, and walked downstairs in the darkness, his hand sliding along the smooth, familiar olive wood of the banister. He crossed the hall, and walked outside. It was a cool, clear night of this extraordinary summer. The air was both sweet and pungent, blending the odors of cattle and crops. To his left, the Moy moved quietly toward Ballina, where a few lighted windows still glowed.

What did it matter, here in Mayo? There was himself in Ballina and John Moore in Ballintubber, Peters the provision merchant in Castlebar, Forrest on Glenthorne's land, Burke who was steward to Lord Altamont in Westport. These were sworn United Irishmen. And John Moore had been speaking with some of the young Catholic squireens, O'Dowd and Blake and MacDonnell. With enough time, they might be persuaded to act, and perhaps could bring some of their tenants with them. Elliott knew their type, fierce, impetuous men ready to point their huge hunters toward the most daunting wall, flying over with shouts and laughter. They were capricious young bucks, ready for violence but easily bored. Put all these together and a fair showing of the tenantry and you had perhaps seventy men. Mayo was locked away from Tom Emmet's study, from Dublin-bred conspiracies. Moorland and mountain mocked all eloquence.

Across the bay, in Sligo, things were a bit better. There was a fair organization in the town, and MacTier, the Presbyterian linen merchant, was an able man, prudent and hardheaded. If MacTier had a chance to act, he would, and if no chance came to him, he would abide by that, as quiet and as calm as a man counting bolts of cloth. Papist and Presbyterian alike had been sworn into the Society by MacTier, cautious, reserved, testing each man in searching conversation. And he had managed all this from a warehouse set squarely into one of the most implacably loyalist towns in the west of Ireland, a bitter garrison town. Not here, not in Mayo. But how many could even MacTier count on? A hundred, perhaps, not more. And that had been before the collapse of the Antrim rising. Sligo looked toward the north, toward Ulster, and now the only news was from the bloody glens of Antrim. What purpose was served by a letter from Dublin ringing false with its hysterical optimism?

He walked beside the river, and heard the small night animals stirring at the sounds of his booted feet. In Dublin a few years before, he had heard a story about Danton, whether true or false he did not know. When his arrest was decided upon, Danton was at his farm in the suburbs with his new young wife. A messenger came to him with a warning from a friend. He dressed hurriedly, stuffed his pocket with a shirt and a pistol, and set off through a forest. An hour later he halted. The forest had become the landscape of a dream. He had been quietly asleep in his own house, beside a woman's warm, naked body. Now he was cold and breathless in a dark wood. He went back to his farm, and was in bed, awake and quiet, when they came for him. Elliott, walking beside the quiet Moy, understood that story. Wexford and Antrim were a thousand miles away, and the Provisional Directory was farther yet. Tone and the French fleet were across the world, phantoms. Next week perhaps, or next month, word might come that the French had landed in the south, or that Munster had risen. And perhaps, like Danton, he might dress, weigh down his own pocket with a pistol, and ride southward. But he had not ridden to Wexford, nor taken the shorter journey to Antrim. Mayo held him, stronger than dreams nurtured in a Rathfarnham villa.

Mayo was the slow, invisible river at his feet, flowing past farmland and pastureland and bog toward the distant bay. He had begun to save the hay, and soon the first crops would be ready for reaping. Each day now, he would be in the fields with his laborers, stripped to his shirt, sweat darkening its armpits. At noon, girls would bring them buttered bread and pails of cool milk. In the clear light, beneath a sky of pale blue, he could see the Ox Mountains, which sheltered Mayo from the troubling winds of Ulster. Now night pressed upon him, dark silences weightier than speech.

Ballina, July 1/Ballycastle, July 2

Very early on the first morning of July, John Moore mounted his hunter and rode northward toward the barony of Tyrawley. He made a leisurely journey of it, and did not take the shortest roads. At eleven he was in Castlebar, where he paused for two tankards of ale with Brian Peters, a provision merchant in the town. At three he was in Foxford, and engaged in a long conversation with Michael O'Hara, a strong farmer. At sundown he reached Ballina, where he stayed the night with Malcolm and Judith Elliott, at Moat House.

They had a long, quiet meal, talking of Dublin and of distant friends. After dinner, Judith sat beside her harp in the drawing room, and sang to the two men in her clear, silvery soprano. Elliott listened with his jockey's body perched on the edge of a delicate chair, his hands pressed against his knees, but John was settled deep into a sofa, his long legs stretched out before him. Judith had a small selection of French and Italian songs which, so far as John could tell, she sang most creditably, but she preferred the group of *Hibernian Airs* which had recently been published in Dublin by Miss Owenson. They sounded French to John; Elliott had no ear for music. Then Elliott and John closeted themselves in the office, where they talked late into the night, a bottle of brandy on the desk beside them.

The next morning he was again on the road. Laborers, standing in fields to his left, lifted their arms in lazy salutation to a stranger, and Moore touched his crop to the brim of his low-crowned hat. To his right, stretching toward the bay, were the high walls of the Glenthorne estate. Moore, a tall young man on a tall mount, could catch glimpses, between thick clumps of plantation, of Glenthorne Castle, white and indistinct in the morning haze.

A mile from Killala, he swung into a byroad which brought him to the Ballycastle road. Four miles farther on, he crossed over a stream, and rode through entrance gates toward Bridge-end House. It was a simple, two-story farmhouse, more modest than its ornamental gates, built with its back away from its avenue, upon the crest of a hill facing northward. As he rode toward it he could see a distant flash of bay. -

He dismounted, looped his reins to a post, and walked along a curving path of loose stone to the front of the house. A servant showed him into the parlor, where he was joined almost at once by Thomas Treacy, a tall, bent man in his fifties, with white hair falling full and loose about his neck. He seized Moore's hand in both of his.

"You are most welcome, John. Most welcome indeed."

"And I am most happy to see you, sir. I have business in Killala with Randall MacDonnell, but nothing would stop my horse turning aside to the Ballycastle road, that I might pay my respects to you."

78

"You will spend the night here," Treacy said. "I can offer you a far cleaner room than you can find at the Mac-Donnells'. 'Tis not a house they have there at all, but only stables. They are a disgrace to us all."

"I will not quarrel with that," Moore said. "And it is pleasant to look forward to a clean bed."

"They are more horse than man," Treacy said. "Like the pagan centaurs."

"They know horses," Moore said. "Better than any family in Mayo."

"Well they might," Treacy said. "But they come by it honorably. A MacDonnell commanded a squadron of King James's cavalry. He did not distinguish himself. Sit down, John. Sit down. We will have tea directly, if that lazy slut of a girl pays any attention to my orders. Is George well?"

"He is indeed. He keeps himself busy with his scribbling."

"It is an honor to the country, to have a scholar like your brother resident here. Perhaps one day he will finish his dealings with the French regicides and turn to the history of his own county."

"I doubt if George will ever be done with his Frenchmen. He is very clever about them, and cleverness delights him. He would find little to be clever about in Mayo."

"Now there you are mistaken, John. Perhaps you have been too long away, George and yourself. Your father thought so, God rest his soul. Our deepest roots are in the soil of childhood."

"But I knew Mayo from childhood on," John said. "Father spoke of it to me. He was homesick all of those years in Spain. He spoke often of your own father."

"Ah," Treacy said, smiling. "There was always a great friendship between our two families. A hard time we had of it in the black days, the old families of Mayo. There is the proper subject for George's pen, and not the base king-killers of Paris. A black century stretching forward from the disaster of Aughrim. They did their best to savage and scatter us. But we are tenacious, a tenacious people, John. Your father is a case in point."

Treacy smiled grimly, a bit complacently, proud of survival. Well might I e be, John thought. But how many other families had gone under, vanished, names lingering only as meaningless tags for townlands and hills. The

79

Brownes had survived by turning Protestant, and the Moores by exile; O'Dowds and MacDonnells had half fallen into the peasantry, uneasy hobbledehoys. And among the peasantry, families which had forgotten an early gentility, save perhaps for a battered silver teapot, a gown of frayed and shiny satin passed down from mother to daughter. Fit subject for an artist of the pathetic and the picturesque, uncongenial to his brother's pen.

"An ancient chivalry," Treacy said, warming to a familiar subject. "Destroyed by Cromwell's rabble, and by Dutch William. Mayo once was famous for its piety and learning." His hand gestured, vaguely, groping toward centuries. "Our early history. You have seen the ruins of our abbeys, our monasteries. One of the finest stands roofless upon your own land. Ballintubber."

"My brother's land," John said.

Treacy did not hear him. "We were outlaws upon our own land. Our priests were hunted down. Our sons were encouraged toward apostasy. Sergeants and corporals, the sweepings of the English cities, were set over us as magistrates. It is the stuff of epic, boy, fit subject for a Virgil. But we survived. We were not forced down into the bog."

"It has been a bad time for us," Moore said. "A sorry time. Perhaps it is changing. In Wexford—"

"Wexford! Peasants, brutal peasants hacking and killing with pikes and scythes. Drunken Whiteboys burning and butchering."

He was hopeless, Moore had known that. Celebrant of a consoling myth, counting like prayer beads the links of his bondage.

"Times may change," he said. "If the French fleet had landed two years ago—"

"With ten thousand of those ruffians and arms for fifty thousand Whiteboys? No, no, there was a time, my grandfather's time, when ships from France would have meant the Irish brigades, the return of the Wild Geese. Not now. Those bloodthirsty ruffians are as bad as the Cromwellians were. It was begun in Mayo. We have our own Whiteboys now. Six estates have been attacked."

"Six?" Moore asked, startled. "Two only, surely."

"Six," Treacy said. "And the last was the worst of all. Saunders's barns were destroyed last night, the thatch fired and the walls leveled."

"That is a serious undertaking," Moore said thoughtfully. "Six estates in two weeks. That is a small insurrection."

"Ach, sure they are Whiteboys. Cooper will hunt them down with his yeomen. It is time those little Protestant bastards did more than rattle their foolish drums."

"And all this because Cooper turned a bit of his land to grazing. This is a mysterious business."

"They don't know what they want," Treacy said. "There has been Whiteboy trouble in Killala before, thirty years ago, when I was a young man. It was tithes and high rents then, and it is grazing now. But there was a black, sullen hatred behind it; they did not know what they wanted but they knew what they hated. Pothouse poets had them stirred up, and prophecy men. There was a prophecy clear across Galway and Mayo that when the millrace in Oranmore ran red blood Ireland would be freed. And they put the prophecy in their letters."

"Their letter now is like that," Moore said. "Cooper brought it out to Ballintubber and showed it to George."

"To be sure it is," Treacy said. "They are always like that. There is always some rogue of a schoolmaster with a head stuffed with nonsense. It was a bad time for my father. We held the land on lease only in those days, and we had parts of it sublet at rents as high as any in the barony, but we were never disturbed at all, and neither were the Blakes, who are little better than rack-renters. It was the Protestants they went after, and many of the Protestants thought there was a conspiracy among all the Catholics, ourselves included. My father said one night he was thinking of burning down one of our barns as a gesture of goodwill." Remembering, Treacy laughed. "But it never came to that. There were four lads hanged in the heel of that hunt. One of them was a MacMahon, Padraic MacMahon, I knew him well, a great horse of a young fellow and the best hurler in the barony. There were no yeomen here in those days. Sam Cooper's father hunted him clear to Nephin, and rode back leading Padraic by a bit of rope. God rest the soul of poor Padraic Mac-Mahon. There was something wrong with one of his eyes, but he was the best hurler in the barony."

Imagining a past which had come and gone before his birth, John saw two figures entering Killala, a yeoman captain's father, squireen back from the hunt, red-faced and self-satisfied, behind him, led like a stray cow, a tall

81

young fellow in frieze, twisting his head this way and that.

"There is a song about him now," Treacy said. "A wretched bit of pothouse doggerel. That is the way of it, they are a leaderless people. Their heroes are Whiteboys and faction fighters and hurlers."

"Our people," Moore said. "Yours and mine."

"Ach no," Treacy said. "We are a scattered people. History put its heel on our neck. 'Tis a great pity you never knew my father, and a greater one that George did not. He was a great scholar. Mind you, he taught himself, but he was a great scholar in the two languages. He corresponded with Charles O'Conor of Belnagare, the historian and vindicator of the Catholics of Ireland. I have a packet of Charles O'Conor's letters in this house. They would be of great interest to George. Read Charles O'Conor's history, John, and you will understand the fate of the Catholic gentry of Ireland. We have been calumniated by perjurers and slanderers. King George now has no subjects more loyal, and we ask only the rights of full citizenship."

"Padraic MacMahon the hurler wanted something different, I expect," John said.

"I don't know what he wanted," Treacy said. "I know what he got."

"The end of a rope," John said.

"Yes. The end of a rope and a bad song which he never lived to hear."

The door opened, and a girl of about eighteen carried in the tea service. She was slender and for a girl extraordinarily tall, almost as tall as Moore himself.

He rose to his feet and said, "Your father told me that some lazy slut of a girl might bring tea. I hadn't known that he meant you, Ellen."

"Neither had I," Treacy said. "Neither had I. Have you no tasks to keep you busy, girl?"

She placed the tray on the long oak table and sat down before it. "I have the task of making a guest welcome, which I have been instructed takes precedence over other tasks."

"I was riding by your gates," Moore said, "and I was parched for a cup. I would otherwise have ridden on to the MacDonnells."

"The MacDonnells, is it?" she asked. "At this time of day you would be lucky at the MacDonnells to get anything but buttermilk in a bowl or whiskey in an egg-shell." Quietly, deftly, she poured the tea, sugared two of the cups heavily and handed the third one to Moore. "You will be a foreigner, John, until you have a sweet tooth like the rest of us."

"I begin to suspect that I will always be a foreigner," Moore said. "Sugar or not."

"John will be stopping the night with us," Treacy said. "If you can find time to make a bed for him."

For a moment her eye caught Moore's. "I might find time," she said. "Someday. Are you not staying with the MacDonnells then, John? With all the hospitality they can offer? Firing off pistols into the ceilings is a part of their hospitality, I understand, when they entertain young gentlemen from Ballintubber."

"They are a wild crew," Treacy said. "It comes to them in their blood. Have I told you of the reputed conduct of their Major MacDonnell on the night before the battle of Aughrim?"

"You have, Father," Ellen said. "Twice."

"I was addressing our guest."

"Sure it was John you told it to twice. I can't count the times I have heard it. Every time poor Grace MacDonnell comes to visit me, I hear it, as though she were herself some wild rapparee riding in from Aughrim."

Treacy nodded. "You would never guess that the poor mother is a Dillon, adrift as she is in that bare, drafty barn of a house. A wild crew."

"She is a very pretty young woman," John said.

"She is indeed," Ellen said. "We are most fond of one another. Grace MacDonnell has the finest forehead in Mayo and lovely green eyes."

"They are blue, I believe," John said. "Dark blue like your own."

"Are they so? Perhaps they change in the light."

"Shall we expect you for dinner?" Treacy asked.

"That would be most welcome," John said. "I will have a bit of a talk with Randall and then ride back to Bridge-end."

"Randall is a great man for the talk," Treacy said. "Especially when he has a few jars in him."

"He is," John said. "A plainspoken man."

"I met him at the market last month," Treacy said, stirring his tea. "He tells me that the two of you have talked political matters until late at night."

Moore was silent for a space, and then said, "We have. I have never kept my sentiments a secret from you, sir."

"And I have no wish to press you on the matter, if it remains a matter of sentiment and no more. I am most fond of you, John, most fond indeed, and I would grieve to see you compromised."

"Sure what can Randall MacDonnell know about politics," Ellen said quickly. "As little as myself. There is but the one thing that Randall MacDonnell knows, and that is horses."

"He is a wild rascal ready for any mischief," Treacy said, "like his father before him. They have half sunk into the peasantry."

"Not Grace," Ellen said. "I am sorry to see so fine a girl in such a disordered house."

"Her mother is a Dillon," Treacy said. "Randall and the others are children by the first wife. She was a Lally of Tuam, a very cross-tempered woman. I don't know what Aeneas Dillon was thinking of when he let a daughter of his marry into the MacDonnells of Ballycastle. A father has a heavy responsibility in such matters, does he not?"

"He does indeed," John said.

"Take myself as an example. 'Tis little enough that Ellen could ever hope to bring a man by way of dowry, but she is an only child and Bridge-end and the other bits of land would go in the course of nature and law to her husband. 'Tis a tidy little estate, although it is put to shame by one so handsome as your own, for example."

"Not mine," John said. "My brother's."

" 'Tis all one," Treacy said. "George does not seem ready or likely to marry, and if he did he is not the man to wrong a brother. But it is myself I was speaking of, of course, and not George. We are a prudent family, we have had to be prudent. 'Tis bred in our bones. I would be doing very wrong, would I not, to risk Ellen by accepting for her a rash or imprudent young man?"

"You would, of course." Moore put down his cup. "But in troubled times it is difficult to know the prudent course. In such times the bold course may also be the prudent one."

"On occasion, perhaps. On occasion. But in such times as these, the prudent course for the Catholic gentlemen

84

of Mayo, for example, is to sit quiet and pray that these winds will blow themselves out. Do you not agree, Ellen?"

"I have given little thought to such matters," she said. "They are for men to sort out. But when it comes to choosing a husband, I trust you will depend upon the common sense for which you have often praised me."

"Well, well," Treacy said. "Time enough to attend to such matters in the future."

"Was it prudent of your great-grandfather," Moore asked Treacy, "to join the Stuart army?"

"That was a hundred years ago," Treacy said. "Times change. The Catholic gentry at the Boyne and at Aughrim were fighting for their King, for their faith."

"And their country," Moore added.

"Perhaps," Treacy said. "It was a different world. They were gentlemen, John, your ancestors and mine. They would have despised these United Irishmen. We have spent too long on these matters. Is there more tea, girl?"

Ellen walked with him to his horse, and they stood to talk. He leaned toward her, but she put a hand to his shoulder. "Not here."

"He is a stubborn man," Moore said. "Polite and stubborn."

"He is a sensible man," she said. "What business is it of yours if some men in Dublin want to make trouble?"

"Make trouble?" he repeated. "They want to make a revolution, and I have taken their oath."

"And half of them are now in gaol, did you not tell me? Sure if that is what you want, you can have it with less trouble by stealing sheep or by going off with the Whiteboys to hough cattle."

Moore slapped the palm of his hand upon his horse's saddle.

"What sense is there in talking of such matters with a woman?"

"No sense whatever. Women have more important things to think about. There you stand with not enough land to your name to give grazing to a calf, and my father is willing that you should have Bridge-end. Why should he wish to see me wed to a fellow who may end in gaol at the heel of the hunt? My father has common sense. It would give great pleasure to the Protestants of Mayo to see a Moore in Castlebar gaol."

"Your father has little cause to worry. There are not

more than twenty sworn United Men in Mayo. The French will land and the battles will be fought and won and Mayo will have no part in it. This is the most backward province in Christendom."

"But you are riding off now to make a United Man out of Randall MacDonnell if you can. You would fare better by preaching to his horse."

Moore shrugged. "I promised Malcolm Elliott that I would sound out some of the Catholic squires. There have been good men sworn, in other places, Papist and Protestant alike."

"Protestant, is it? Sure what need have the Protestants of your revolution? Aren't they ruling the roost as it is?"

"Some of them. It is this accursed system which rules us all, while England bleeds us white."

"Ach," she said. "Go preach to Randall. I despair of you."

"You do not," Moore said. "You are in love with me and I with you."

"A pretty way you have to show it."

"I know a better one."

"In broad daylight beneath my father's window. When you come courting it should be for that purpose and for no other. You will drive me to tears and despair. One of these days you will say a loose word to some fellow and he will get on his horse and ride off to Westport to lay an information with Dennis Browne, and that will be the last seen of you. And all the time you could have myself and the promise of Bridge-end, as fine a farm as any young man in Mayo has ever been as good as offered. And myself with it in the bargain."

"Never fear that I will not come courting," Moore said. "It is my greatest pleasure."

"It is not," she said. "It is your greatest pleasure to talk with Malcolm Elliott and Randall MacDonnell. A queer sort of beau I found for myself. Far better would I have fared with Tom Bellew that I brushed aside in my infatuation."

Swiftly, John circled her waist and kissed her. She clung to him.

"You will fare best with me," he said. "And well you know it."

"Perhaps," she said. She brushed his lips lightly with her own, and then stood back from him. "That remains to be seen."

He mounted, and sat looking down at her. "You are too tall for beauty, Miss Treacy. Now a slight and graceful girl like Grace Nugent, who does not come up to a man's shoulder—"

"She is the pick of the MacDonnell litter," Ellen said. "I doubt is she a MacDonnell at all. She washes herself."

"You are too tall by a head," Moore said, "and you have a sharp tongue in it."

"I have," she said. "And you had best get used to it."

"I must learn Irish," he said. "It is a soft and clinging speech."

She laughed. "'Tis little you know it. Have a care what you say to Randall MacDonnell, John."

"I will," he said. "I will be as prudent as a Treacy."

On a low hill beyond the hedge of the demesne, two cottiers were digging potatoes. Ellen stood watching them, her straight, slender back to Bridge-end House. It was a firm custom that no potatoes were dug before Garland Sunday at the end of July. These fellows had begun early. It was because of the strange weather. If the weather held, it would be the fullest harvest in memory. But Paddy Lacy and his son Owen had no cause to be digging spuds before Garland Sunday. There was a time and a method for everything that had to do with sowing and reaping and gathering. The plowman in spring must turn his horses from left to right, with the sun, and when he unyokes them, they must be facing south. Friday is the day to begin the sowing, or any task which does not require iron, and Good Friday the best day of all. And the sower, as he sets forth, must say, "In the name of God," and throw some turf over the rump of each horse. There were a hundred pishogues like those ones, and the harvests depended upon them.

Much did John Moore know of such matters, or his brother for that matter, but Mayo knew them, even the Protestants. They had no head for any of the practical concerns of life. You will have no luck at the fair if the first person you meet is not fair-headed, and when you buy a horse you must put a lump of earth on his back. John Moore knew that, because she had told him, but he paid no attention to it. He did not have the luck of the beast he was riding, and it would one day do him a mis-

chance. Why had she fallen in love with a man who knew
so little?

"A lovely beast," Randall MacDonnell said, running his
hand along the flank of Moore's hunter. "A lovely beast.
Who bred her?"

"Stewart of Foxford," Moore said. They were standing
in the MacDonnell stable yard, amidst a clutter of farm
wagons and harnesses.

"A heretic lady, but she is nonetheless sound for that.
Stewart did well by you. But come over here now, John,
and you will see how a Papist lady stands." He walked
with Moore to the stalls, unlatched a door, and led out
a black mare. "This is Vixen. I am riding her next month
at the Castlebar races. Bred on this farm." He was the
right height for a rider, but he was too broad, with wide,
square shoulders and the beginning of a paunch although
he had just turned thirty. "You will be there, will you
not?"

"I will," Moore said. "Unless I have more pressing
business."

"You should never let business keep you from the
Castlebar races. Sure there will be no business done in
Mayo that week save at the races. And if you will be
guided by me, you will have a few pounds on Vixen.
There are few of them can see her run, but you can
yourself in the morning if you stay the night."

"That is kind of you," Moore said, "but I am promised
at Bridge-end House and from there I am riding out to
Tom Bellew."

"Making your stations, is it, in the name of the republic?"

"Something like that," Moore said. "I am hoping that
you will give me a word to take back to Elliott."

MacDonnell rooted in his pocket for lumps of sugar,
which he divided between his horse and Moore's.

"Elliott and I hunted together," MacDonnell said. "A
decent enough fellow."

"He is," Moore said. "A sound man. And he has been
accredited by the Society as Secretary for Mayo."

"Of course," MacDonnell said, "there was a time
when Sam Cooper and I were close, or as close as you
can get to a Protestant. He was a wild lad for a few years
after his father died. My God, the gatherings we used
have at Mount Pleasant! They would go on for days. I

88

remember riding back here to Ballycastle from Mount Pleasant with George Blake, one winter's morning, just after Christmas it was, and the two of us out of our minds with drink. We had been at it for three days. The need came upon us, and we made a wager, which one of us could piss the farther. Not the more mind you, George would have had me there, but the farther."

As he talked, he took Moore by the arm and walked with him to the house. When his tiresome anecdote had wound itself out, he gave a sudden whinny of laughter and clapped Moore on the shoulder.

"Seven years ago that was, if it was a day. By God, but has not Sam Cooper become a bloody fool. He was a bloody fool to turn out Squint O'Malley. He was looking for trouble and now he has it. And he was daft to put in for command of the yeomanry, a job every other Protestant was too busy or too lofty to take. What is it but a lot of bother and expense?"

"To keep the King's peace," Moore said, "and to guard Mayo against the French."

"Hah!" MacDonnell cried with delight. "Have you ever seen them drill? It is the drollest sight you have ever seen. Bailiffs and shopkeepers."

"You have a fine stand of barley there," Moore said. "It is the same at Ballintubber. The harvest will be prodigious if the weather holds."

"Prodigious," MacDonnell said. "There is the word for it. One of the cottiers, an old fellow named Flaherty, says there was as fine a harvest in my father's time, God rest his soul, but there has been nothing like it in my time or yours. Well sure 'tis not the crops you have in mind at all, is it, or how far can George Blake piss. Come into the house where we can talk like gentlemen, not standing with our ankles deep in stable muck."

It was what Treacy had called it, a great drafty barn of a house, a two-story farmhouse, slate-roofed and narrow-windowed, to which low, almost random rooms had been added, sprawling and graceless. MacDonnell ushered Moore in with unaffected pride, kicking a clear pathway through a litter of tackle and sacks of grain in the hall, and shouting for punch. He cleared away clutter from two chairs close to the fireplace and waved Moore toward one of them.

Ten minutes later, a dark-haired girl in red shift and bare feet brought in the punch, and placed it steaming on the hob. "There is a good girl," MacDonnell said, and as she passed him to leave he patted her casually on the buttocks. "There is a good girl, Nora. She is, by God, John, as fine a girl as has ever served in this house." He ladled punch into two cups and handed one to Moore, who noticed that the rim was smeared. The cup was greasy to his touch.

"Now I am going to give you a straight blunt answer, John."

Moore recognized this as the local preface to any tortuous circumlocution. "All right, Randall. Provided you do not lecture me upon how little I understand about Mayo. I have already had that lecture at Bridge-end House."

"From old Treacy, is it? There is a cunning old fox. You would think you were listening to a poem to hear that fellow talk about the old world that was destroyed at Aughrim, and all the while he is not doing so ill in this one, and neither did his father before him. That old fox in Ballycastle my father used call him."

"We rub together well enough," John said. "I am fond of him."

MacDonnell darted a shrewd glance at him. "There is a fine estate there at Bridge-end waiting for the right young fellow, and a fine girl standing on it. A great friend of my own sister, Grace. Mind you, the hips seem a bit narrow for children, but sure where there's a will there's a way, as the saying goes."

"It is a wife that I am looking for," Moore said. "Not a brood mare."

"Indeed? Treacy was right, you don't know Mayo. Well now, John." Moore's cup was still full, but he refilled his own. "I have been talking to some men that the two of us have discussed, Corny O'Dowd and George Blake and Tom Bellew and a few others. The old stock, if you take my meaning. And I think I can tell you that we are well disposed. Yes, that is the word. Well disposed."

"I am very glad to hear that," Moore said, "and so will Malcolm Elliott be."

"Ach," MacDonnell said, rubbing a short, blunt hand across his neck. "You keep talking about Elliott, but it is yourself that I am saying this to."

"Elliott is a member of the Connaught Directory and I am not," Moore said. "It is the directory which is in correspondence with Dublin. You have no cause to distrust Elliott."

"I doubt if it is much of a directory." MacDonnell said gently. "There are some United Men in Sligo and in Galway and a scattering of them here in Mayo. All that is common knowledge. But I doubt if there are enough to make up a good hunt. You could fill the green of Castlebar perhaps with United Irishmen but it is a small green."

"I admit that we are small in numbers now," Moore said. "That is why I have been talking with you. Elliott has recommended me for the directory, and he is prepared to recommend O'Dowd and yourself if you will take the oath."

"Would that not be the great honor. There are members of the Leinster Directory, down in Wexford, who are waiting trial at the moment, and some are already swinging from gibbets. That is altogether too high an honor for a poor Mayo squireen."

Moore shook his head. "No one is proposing action until the French have landed, and Munster has risen. All that is needed now is preparation. Men like Corny O'Dowd and yourself have a good name among the tenantry. They would listen to you and they would take the oath from you."

"They might," MacDonnell said. "They might. But would they fight is a different matter. Sure what would they fight with? Would you have me set them to work making pikes?"

"That is what Wexford did," Moore said.

"Ach, sure don't tell me about Wexford. It greatly weakens your case."

"The French will come," Moore said. "We may depend upon that. There will be a fight worth making." He sipped the punch. As he had feared, it was sweet, but he drank again, more deeply.

"By God, I like the sound of that. This country needs a fight. Drink up, John. Drink up."

"It will have one," Moore said. "And when the fight is over, it will *be* a country, and not England's granary. Will the people of Mayo fight for that?"

MacDonnell laughed, and emptied the remainder of the small bowl into their cups. "Nora," he shouted. "More punch." He waited a moment, and then shouted again. "Nora!" He nodded to Moore. "She has it ready. The secret with punch is to keep it hot. The hottest day of summer, I will take punch over cold whiskey. It clears the head."

"Will they?" Moore repeated.

"There are wilder young fellows in this county than you could find in the whole of the two kingdoms," MacDonnell said. "Jesus, in the last faction fight of the men of Ballycastle and the men of Killala, they were breaking skulls the way yourself or myself would crack open an egg. They had blackthorn cudgels, some of them, the size of a stout man's wrist. There were two men killed outright, and mind you those fellows were fighting for nothing at all but only the honor of their towns. Jesus, the honor of Killala!"

"I know about faction fights," Moore said. "They are a silly brutal business. George has forbidden them in Ballintubber."

"No sillier than a republic would seem to a faction fighter. Or a Whiteboy. They have no notion of such things. But they are fine haters. They will fight what they hate."

The girl brought in a fresh bowl of punch and placed it beside the empty one. Before she could straighten, MacDonnell encircled her waist and pulled her to the arm of his chair. "Do you have the likes of this in Ballintubber, John?" He put his hand on her rib cage, and then shoved it upwards, pressing one of her breasts toward the opening of her shift. "Study a creature like this and it will put every other thought out of your mind." She leaned against his shoulder and smiled shyly at Moore.

MacDonnell slid his hand over the breast and stroked it softly. "Get along now," he said. "We have business."

When she had left, MacDonnell looked toward the closed door. "But she is a damned lazy serving wench for all that. Her name is Nora Duggan, and she is the niece of a strong farmer named Malachi. He is one of Gibson's tenants. It is to Duggan that the men in Kilcummin look. Duggan and a fellow named Ferdy O'Donnell. A decent enough fellow Ferdy is. We are somehow related, far back. You may depend upon it that those two lads are somehow thick in this Whiteboy trouble. By God, if that trouble spreads to Ballycastle they will oblige me by sticking to Protestants."

"I have wondered," Moore said quietly, "whether it is not to these Whiteboys that we should be looking for our recruits."

92

MacDonnell nodded. "I thought we would come to that matter." He bent down and put his hand on the bowl, then drew it quickly away. "O Jesus, I'm burned. How the hell did the girl carry it? She must have hands of leather." He took a grimy handkerchief from his pocket and wrapped it around the hand. "Do you know, those fellows down in Wexford, there must have been thousands of them by all we hear, I cannot believe they were all United Men. They may have taken that oath you have, but at heart they were Whiteboys. A country lad in Wexford is much like one in Mayo, and I cannot believe he was fighting for something called a republic. He took his pike and he went out after what he hated—yeomen, militiamen, Protestant magistrates."

Moore shook his head. "I would be sorry indeed to see that here or anywhere in Ireland. The first intention of the Society has been to break down those wretched barriers of religion."

MacDonnell laughed as he ladled out the punch. "By God, it took us centuries to build them up. You have your work cut out for you. 'Tis little enough that I know about rebellions, but I know that you must work with what you have. It isn't a hundred years ago, when a lad like Corny O'Dowd could go riding out and haul his peasants after him. If there is a rebellion this time, the peasants will make it and it will be a Whiteboy war."

Moore shook his head again, his full lips compressed. "It will not. It must be controlled by the Society. The French are not sailing here to support a country rabble."

"The French! Much the French have ever cared about us. If the French come it will be to shove a thorn into England's flank. There is a bit of the Whiteboy in me, John, and if I were to ride out with you, it would be because of that bit. For a hundred years or more those Protestant bastards have been the cocks of the walk, strutting around on acres that belong by rights to the Irish, hogging all the power and all the land. There are men still living who can remember when a son could grab his father's land by turning Protestant. The priests were hunted like wild wolves with five pounds' bounty on their heads, and the people had to hear Mass in wild caves with a guard posted. Why do you think the Tyrawley Yeomanry is all Protestant? It is to keep us in our place, and to keep muskets out of our hands. I can meet Sam Cooper at the Castlebar races, and we will have a drink and a bet

93

together, but if it comes to a fight, I will gut him or he will gut me."

He spoke with what Moore found an impressive and unsettling calm, as though expressing facts so clear as to require no emphasis. Moore turned his eyes away from him, toward the bare, graceless room. On the walls hung only a few awkward portraits, the work of journeyman artists riding from county to county with canvas and paints. There were strong family resemblances, long, protuberant jaws, high, harsh cheekbones. The resentments which MacDonnell nursed had been passed on, a family inheritance, from father to son. In this room 1641 and 1691 were as young as yesterday, shaping conduct and governing passions. It was a history without triumphal arches or squares named after victories. It clung to the dour, treeless bogs and the low, abrupt hills, a history of defeats and dispossession, of smoke rising from gutted houses.

"Let the French make their landing down in Munster," MacDonnell said, "and let the people there rise up. If there is no one to guard Mayo then but the Tyrawley Yeomanry, by Jesus but we will give them a whipping. You must rest content with that, John."

"Blake, Bellew, O'Dowd," Moore said. "Are you speaking for them as well as for yourself?"

"I am," MacDonnell said. "We have talked about this, you know, one way and another. We have no objection to taking the oath of your Society, and I don't greatly care what it says. I am certain it must be a very fine oath. But your Society had damned well better understand that there is little that can be done here in Mayo."

"We know that," Moore said. "As well as you do." He smiled, a young man venturing upon deep waters. "Then my ride was not wasted. You might have begun by telling me that."

"Ach," MacDonnell said. "Here, let us finish up the punch. You don't have much—four squires and perhaps a few others that Corny and myself can find for you."

"Those two men you mentioned—Duggan and that other fellow."

"Ferdy O'Donnell. Let that rest for a bit. We are all Papists, right enough, but those fellows are peasants and we are landlords. It may be that Cooper will prove a good recruiting sergeant for us, if he turns the yeomen loose upon the barony."

94

Moore managed to down his third cup of punch with a show of pleasure. "Yes," he said thoughtfully, "he just might manage that, if he is as foolish as he would seem to be. George despises him."

"George despises all of us," MacDonnell said, and held up a hand when Moore began to speak. "All of us," he repeated, "and who can blame him? Look at me, a man my age, and I have been a dozen times to Dublin and there is the extent of my travels. I have read one book in the last six months, a trifling romance that I found in Tom Bellew's house. It was all about some English lord who was in love with the daughter of a Spanish duke and you have never read such sorry stuff. Some woman wrote it. There is no other man in Connaught with my knowledge of horses, but what is that, when all is said and done?"

As Moore walked back with MacDonnell to the stables, he felt oppressively the truth of the remark. MacDonnell was clearly an able man, for all his reckless talk, but like the hillside thorn trees he had been shaped by the winds of Mayo, and like the thorn trees, he was rooted to the land.

MacDonnell, as though to confirm this, said, "Mind now, the Castlebar races. The finest week in the year, and it will give us a good shove forward into the harvest. By God, there is nothing like a fine race."

Moore drew riding gloves from the tail pocket of his jacket. "You have agreed to join a seditious society, and all you can think of are the Castlebar races."

"Well now," MacDonnell said, leading Moore's horse from the stable, "the French won't come until after the races, surely? If they do, they will lose a few friends."

Paris, July 7

He walked with jaunty haste down the Rue Saint-Jacques, a slight, knife-faced man with a prominent nose, dressed in the uniform of a *chef de brigade* in the army of the French Republic. He was singing a snatch of opera in a harsh, high-pitched voice which attracted attention, and when a head turned toward him he saluted it with a wave of his hand. He wanted to embrace every passerby, to take all of them off to the café for toasts in French and in English. In the mirror of his pleasure he saw a young and handsomely dressed officer walking the streets of the capital of revolution on a fine summer night. He was Citizen Wolfe Tone, formerly of Ireland and shortly to return there. He was the founder of the Society of United Irishmen, its accredited representative in France, and that afternoon he had received the final decision of the Directory.

He had been in Paris almost three years, bouncing from hope to despair to hope, drafting memorials, sitting long hours in the anterooms of ministers, flattering politicians and wishing that he had the money to bribe them. Penniless and voluble in his wretched French, when they gave him his army commission he had had to beg an advance in salary so that he could buy his uniform. His proposal had been simplicity itself: he had come to Paris to secure a French invasion of Ireland. For six months he had sat at a small table in his lodging house, writing his endless memorials, accounts of the Irish political parties, how the island was governed, descriptions of the religious factions, a layman's account of the island's defenses, the aims of the Society. All written in a neat barrister's hand, the facts marshaled like regiments, logic hard and direct as curricle guns moving across an open field. The afternoons he had spent walking Paris, gawking at the sights, practicing his French on waiters and tavernkeepers. In the evening, three bottles of *vin ordinaire* and then the opera or the theater. Then the weeks of attending upon Carnot or some other minister, sitting on a hard bench beside other supplicants, cheap leather portfolio balanced on bony knees. A half-dozen nations were competing for the services of the Revolution, but Tone won the competition. He offered to the Directory a sullen and discontented island sailing on England's flank, a peasantry armed with pikes and aching for insurrection, a wide-flung revolutionary network controlled by radicals.

In December of 1796 the expedition set sail from Brest, forty-three sail carrying an army of fifteen thousand under the command of the great Hoche, the brilliant young general who had conquered the Vendée. Christmas Day saw Tone aboard the *Indomptable* in Bantry Bay, the ship buffeted by great winds. Wrapped in his greatcoat he stood frantic on deck, staring through swirling winds toward the bare Munster coast. After a week in the bay, the winds still hurling themselves down upon the ships, a British fleet prowling somewhere off the coast, the French determined to lift anchor and sail home.

Tone argued himself hoarse at their council of war in a rocking cabin, the charts and maps held down on the table with lengths of chain. Give him command of the Légion de France, a company of the *artillerie légère*, a supply of firelocks, such officers as wished to volunteer. Sail him around the coast to Sligo, clear of the buffeting winds. Or place a French officer in command, and he would serve under him as private. Anything which could get a supply of arms and a body of seasoned soldiers into Ireland, now, while the United Irishmen were strong and prepared.

The French officers were all young, sons of a revolution which had lifted them from obscurity. They listened calmly, with a cool admiration for this excitable young Irishman, so ardent, so patriotic. But only one of them volunteered to take command, a very young brigadier named Jean-Joseph Humbert, who had served with Hoche in the Vendée and understood the use of irregular troops. He joined his arguments to Tone's. With two thousand men and arms for twenty thousand rebels, he could reach the midlands in a week; the rebels could rally to him there. Hoche hesitated. It was an attractive plan, and one almost without risk to France. If it succeeded, she would have created a new ally. If it failed, she would be rid of the Légion, a choice collection of rogues and gaolbirds. If you are captured, Hoche reminded Tone, you will be hanged and disemboweled. Then hanging is not a pleasant prospect, Tone said; as for the disemboweling, *je m'en fiche*. An attractive man, this Colonel Irishman, witty, brave, and no doubt, like Humbert, his new ally, a bit unscrupulous. Hoche had the two of them leave the cabin while he made his decision.

They stood on deck, landlubber legs braced, hands gripping oak rail. Humbert had no English and could barely understand Tone's French. Ambition held them joined, stronger than language: glory enough for both of them there, faintly perceptible beyond hills, beyond snow. I can answer from the mouth of a musket all their sneers, Tone thought. That I am not the son of a bankrupt coach builder, but a bastard spawn of the Wolfes of Kildare. I can answer the Whig politicians who used my services and then flung me a few law cases as recompense. He looked at the massive, heavy-shouldered Frenchman. What of him, the same thing, perhaps? Fortune's favorites, the two

97

of us, ready for the gambler's toss. The day before, a day without snow, he had seen peasants standing on the tumble of low hills. Not one of them knew his name; not one of them could speak to him in English. Shivering in his French greatcoat, he had marveled at the west of Ireland, seen then for the first time. He had spoken in confident terms to the Directory: the western counties, untamed, fierce in their hatred of England. He hoped that this was true; he knew nothing of the west beyond a few days at Ballinasloe, within the borders of Connaught, spent cajoling cautious Papist squireens. It was wild enough, that Bantry coast, and the men upon the hills infinitely remote and alien.

Hoche summoned Tone and Humbert back into the cabin. His decision had been made. The French, and Tone with them, sailed on the morning's tide. The invasion fleet was to be dispersed. Tone stood on deck, humming tunelessly as he watched the coastline recede. Back in France, he set to work drafting fresh memorials, urging a second attempt. Above him, in the labyrinthine world of French politics, the Directory twisted and coiled. Hoche, his strongest hope, died. His memorials swelled in number and size, and his claims for Ireland grew more hectic. The new general of the hour, Buonaparte, granted him an interview, a lean, sallow man with fierce dark eyes, who heard him out impassively and then dismissed him. Other agents of the United Irishmen joined the small colony of Irish exiles, Lewines and Napper Tandy from Dublin, Bartholemew Teeling from Belfast. Edward Fitzgerald and Arthur O'Connor met with French emissaries in Hamburg. They brought stories of quarrels within the Dublin Directory. Belfast argued for a rising in the autumn of 'ninety-seven; Dublin insisted upon the following spring. Tom Emmet would not act without French help; O'Connor would act with it or without. Troops were being moved into Wicklow and Wexford, and the United Men in Belfast and Antrim were being harassed. Time was running out.

Tone persisted, pleading daily with members of the Directory. Perhaps, they told him. Perhaps a limited invasion, with French troops and Dutch ships. In the autumn of 1797, the Dutch fleet was destroyed at Camperdown. An army of England was assembled on the coast and Buonaparte was placed in command. Tone managed a second meeting with him, took out his maps and papers and unfolded them. Buonaparte again listened in silence, the dark eyes watching Tone's thin, quick hard as it flickered across the potato of an island, pointing to coastlines, bays, deep rivers. "You are a very brave man," he told Tone in a flat, tuneless voice much like Tone's own voice. A useless meeting: Buonaparte, determined upon an Egyptian expedition, was quietly draining away the regiments from the army of England. But in the face of this knowledge, Tone persisted. He had become something of a joke to the Directory, "Colonel Irishman," "the wild Irishman," but not entirely a joke, for he was speaking on behalf of a people who stood upon the edge of insurrection.

Then, early in May, word was brought to Paris that the rising had been set for the twenty-fourth of that month. There were two more messages, and then all communications failed. On the morning of the twenty-fourth, the mailcoaches leaving Dublin were seized by men armed with pistols and pikes. It was the signal. The United Men swarmed out of the northern hills of Antrim and from the small villages of Wexford in the south. Tone rode back to Paris from Rouen where he had been serving with the army, and began arguing again. But still the Directory would not move. He wore himself out with his arguments, went without sleep, drank too much wine too fast and was sick. He used every argument he could think of, and then began to lie. Every Papist and Presbyterian in Ireland was a sworn United Irishman. Every county in Ireland would rise up at the sight of a French sail. The insurrection had begun and must be supported. The Directory made no response. He visited Grouchy, Kilmaine, Humbert, at their coastal commands, and pleaded his case directly with the army. Yes, they agreed, an opportunity of this kind must be seized. At the least, it would divert a part of England's energies away from Buonaparte's expedition. Kilmaine, who was of Irish ancestry, was enthusiastic, and so too was Humbert, Tone's old ally.

Facing him across a small table, Humbert questioned him closely. Was he certain of his facts? How widespread was the United Irish organization? Could it be relied upon? Did it number leaders, men of property in its ranks? Had its preparations been thorough? With a giddy sensation that he was again risking everything upon a gambler's toss, Tone resolved to tell Humbert something like the truth. The Society of United Irishmen was a patchwork organization, an uneasy alliance of city radicals, some northern Presbyterians, some southern Papists. Tom Emmet was right, and not O'Connor and Fitzgerald: without French assistance, the insurrection was hopeless. But if France landed a sufficient force, all would change. There was everywhere in Ireland a deep, sullen resentment of English rule. It awaited only some reasonable chance of success.

When he had finished, Humbert smiled, the lazy smile of an immense, powerful cat. "Then you have been lying to the Directory. Small wonder that Buonaparte called you a brave man." Tone shook his head impatiently. His French was far better now. "I have told them that they have it in their power to free Ireland. And they do. Perhaps I exaggerated here and there. Once we have won, no one will bother about that." "Once we have won," Humbert repeated, still smiling. "My God," Tone said, "must I tell a French general that there are times when chances must be taken? It is a gamble, a good gamble." "And if we lose," Humbert said, "France will have thrown away an army." Tone shrugged. "We will not lose." "And why are you being so frank with me?" Humbert asked. "I know your reputation," Tone said; "of all the generals, we have most need for you." "Because of the Vendée?" Humbert asked; "that was a long time ago. Everything is changing." He pushed back his chair, and sat with his hands thrust in his waistband, pressing upon his heavy stomach. "Kilmaine and I have already written to Paris, to recommend an Irish expedition. What do you say to that?" "It must be a large one," Tone said at once. "Do it right, or don't bother with it. It must be as large as the expedition which sailed with Hoche. And it must be sent out at once, while Ulster and Leinster are in arms." Humbert's smile broadened. "You are a remarkable man, Colonel Irishman. You should have been born a Frenchman." "I was born an Irishman," Tone said. "Whatever that means." "We may discover what it means," Humbert said.

Now, little more than a week later, the years of pleading had ended, and he walked dazed and jubilant through the streets of Paris beside the bridges of the Seine. He barely noticed them, but in some corner of his mind they awakened thin, watery memories of the Liffey and its bridges, the Four Courts, the Custom House, the Houses of Parliament.

He entered the crowded café and squeezed past tables to the corner where Lewines and Bartholemew Teeling had been waiting for him. He shook his head at the near-empty bottle of burgundy and signaled the waiter for a fresh one. When he caught his breath, he said easily, with his playactor's love of effect, "It was settled this evening. A proper expedition. To sail by the end of the month."

"What do they mean by proper?" Lewines asked.

"A thousand men under my own darling, Humbert, five thousand under Hardy, and nine thousand under Kilmaine to follow. *Ça ira, ça ira.*"

"It is a miracle," Teeling said.

"Ah, Teeling, my old Belfast Papist, you can't get your mind off miracles. This was a miracle worked by the undeniable justice of our cause and by my own splendid self. Fierce in battle, sage in the council hall, boyish and unaffected among his intimates, Citizen Wolfe Tone of Dublin at last stormed the Directory. It is a fact, a settled fact, the orders have been written, signed, and dispatched. Colonel Tone to accompany Hardy, Colonel Teeling to accompany Humbert, Citizen Lewines to be attached to the staff of General Kilmaine. It did no harm at all that Kilmaine is Irish, no harm at all."

"Kilmaine to follow," Teeling said. "What does that mean?"

"It means that Humbert and Hardy must establish themselves and rally support. If they can do that within a week, then Kilmaine will sail. A fair arrangement. And they sail for Ulster, Bartholemew, to place themselves in aid of your friend MacCracken. The United Irish and the French will share the command equally. I insisted upon that as a citizen of the future republic, cherished and esteemed by those few who have heard my name." A corner of his eye caught his reflection in a mirror, and he winked.

"Where in Ulster?" Teeling asked. "Where do they intend to land?" Gray eyes set in a long, handsome face studied Tone carefully. His voice had the twang of Ulster.

"Lough Swilly." Tone shrugged. "Does it matter? I explained to them that we can land at any point in Ireland and the natives will leap up, their faces afire with the love of liberty."

"God send that MacCracken can still use our help," Teeling said. "It may all be over now, one way or the other."

Tone drew out a pocket map, the size of his two spread hands, and worn from much folding and refolding. "The danger is in slipping past the English fleet, somewhere off the Cork coast, so we must make a wide sweep, which will cost us a day or two. Then we cut in by Galway, take the curve here at Mayo, sail past Mayo and Sligo, and then curve north again to Lough Swilly. There was a ship's captain this evening, full of nautical terms that I didn't understand, but that is about what he was saying."

"That was a bold thing to say," Teeling said. "That the people would rise up in whatever part of the island we chose."

"Well," Tone said. "Perhaps not every part. Not Galway or Mayo, where the natives eat raw fish and worship Dennis Browne and Dick Martin."

Lewines shook his head, a dark, round man. "You may have promised them too much."

"If I had given them less, they would not have given us a corporal's guard in a longboat. I have come to know these frog-eaters. Their idea of sport is a small bet placed after the race has been won." He took the fresh bottle from the waiter. "Colonel Teeling, will you pay this man, upon instructions from the Treasurer of the Irish Republic. What do you think of that notion, Bartholemew? Shall I become Treasurer? Do you see yourself as First Lord of the Irish Admiralty?"

Teeling took out his purse. "It is a miracle that you have worked," he said counting out silver. "And we may bring it off. There are men fighting at home now with nothing in their hands but pikes. I would take any chance to bring help to them."

Tone poured wine in their glasses, and without looking up, said, "But something is worrying at you, is it not? You are too dour. All you northerners are. MacCracken is the same."

"One thousand and five thousand to sail now, and nine thousand to follow. Fifteen thousand in all. But they are sending a large army to Egypt, and they have part of a continent to guard, frontiers to protect."

"But you may depend upon it, Bartholemew." He lifted two of the glasses, and extended them to Lewines and Teeling. "In a few days' time you will be standing on a deck. It is a rare and bracing experience."

"Is the Directory of one mind about this?"

"I don't know," Tone said, "to tell you the blunt truth.

102

But it doesn't matter. It was Carnot who spoke to me, and Carnot is very firm upon the point. It has been decided, he said. That is good enough for me."

"Sure the man is right," Lewines said in excitement. "If only five thousand men land, it is that many more than we have."

"And arms for twenty thousand," Tone said. "Not pikes, either. Muskets and pistols."

Teeling smiled. It transformed the stern, pale face. "You are right indeed," he said. "I ask your pardon. And I drink your health. It has been a hard, long fight. No other man could have managed it."

"I accept the toast," Tone said, and they drank. "But I would propose a worthier one. To the Irish Republic." He refilled their glasses.

Teeling looked down at the map, shadowed as their glasses touched above it. It spread outward from its center, the towns of Leinster, the sharp indentations of Munster's coastline. Mayo was almost a blank: a few towns scattered upon an expanse of white.

4

From *An Impartial Narrative of What Passed at Killala in the Summer of 1798,* by Arthur Vincent Broome, M.A. (Oxon.)

Nothing is more abhorrent to the liberal and enlightened mind than the savage violence which at times can issue from social and sectarian animosities. And yet it became my sorry lot to witness such violences as July stretched toward August, and while the countryside was gathering to itself the transient beauty of late summer. It is that time of year when the great wheel of the husbandman's labor hangs motionless before swinging to the bustle and effort of the harvest. The pagan bonfires of the preceding month had invoked the spectral powers which once held sway over this land and which have never entirely vanished. And Mr. Hussey in his chapel and I in our church had

103

with a far greater propriety invoked the blessings of the Creator upon the ripening crops, offering our thanks that He had bestowed upon our hard-pressed people the gift of a great vegetable abundance.

But alas, other crops were also ripening beneath the sun. On the very night of the midsummer festival of Saint John, as bonfires blazed and youths and maidens danced before the flames, yet another attack was made by the self-styled Whiteboys of Killala, this time upon the property of Mr. Saunders. And this was followed in the weeks of July by other nocturnal outrages, moving at last, as such matters always do, to the shedding of human blood.

Bearing in mind that it occurred upon a festival night, I am certain that the men who attacked Saunders's estate were in a state of sodden drunkenness, a circumstance which warrents comment even at the risk of digression. In most lands, and here I do not exclude England itself, strong liquors are the cause of much social and personal unhappiness, but in Ireland this malady surpasses all belief, and I assert this not upon my own testimony alone, but that of all visitors. The peasants make use of whiskey both to ease their burdens and to exalt themselves at their frequent festivals and fairdays. The beggars expend upon it the pennies they have cadged. To walk after dark through any of the large towns is to be made distressed by the sight and sound of bawling and unsteady men. Men, and women too, lie sprawled in doors and alleys. Neither is such drunkenness limited to the poor, for the squires (if unlettered oafs may be so named) are yet more reprehensible, if only because of their more ready access to spirits. Were an account to be given of a ball or a hunt, or even an assize, which failed to remark upon this insobriety, the picture would lack verisimilitude. Strong drink, which induces first high spirits, then belligerence, then lachrymosity, then utter insensibility, is the constant attendant upon every occasion, however inappropriate. I am myself far indeed from being a canting Puritan, and derive a reasoned pleasure from wines at dinner, a brandy at night, hot punch to take off the winter's chill. With the Irish it is far different. The very atmosphere of this waterlogged island, its rain-heavy clouds and dripping tree branches, its lakes and boggy soil, is drawn off, distilled, and consumed.

Toward the end of July, an atrocity occurred, far worse

in its character than any of the offenses against property which preceded it. Sam Pryor, a bailiff, was dragged from his cabin to a neighboring bog, and there was used most barbarously by a party of masked men. His ears were cropped from his head with a shearing knife and he was then buried to the neck in a pit which had first been half filled with thorns. There he remained for a night and part of a day, until his screams attracted the attention of samaritans.

I of course visited the afflicted man as he sat disfigured and swathed with bandages in his cabin, which is little better than those of the peasants. I found myself also in the presence of six of my parishioners, shopkeepers of Killala and men with farms close by. Their mood was sorrowing and wrathful. All were members of the Tyrawley Yeomanry, and one, Bob Tompkins, was its sergeant.

It was a matter of much concern to me that they described the perpetrators of the outrage not as "the Whiteboys," but as "the Papists." I argued with all the vehemence I could muster that these "Whiteboys" were perhaps fifty in number, by most accounts, out of the many thousands of Papists in the barony, but my arguments fell weakly to the ground. These men, sitting in grave and sullen moods, hands grasping their knees, believed themselves to be surrounded by violent and superstitious enemies, and they were surprised and scandalized that I did not share their angry fears.

The history which forms the very substance of their thoughts is a series of grim tableaux, after the fashion of woodcut illustrations to Foxe's *Book of Martyrs*—the Protestants of Ulster sent naked on the roads in 1641, monks and friars preaching the massacre of heretics, drunken Papist hordes with simian faces. And they have their hagiology—brave English planters defending their homes, the Prentice Boys of Londonderry barring the gates against the besieging Jacobites, William the Protestant champion at the Boyne on his white charger, and above all Cromwell wrathful and implacable in a suit of black armor clanking across the countryside, crushing out rebellion and Popery with each tread of his metal boots. It will seem to my English readers ludicrous and pathetic that such bogeymen should instruct the fears of men gathered in a cabin to solace an outraged friend, King William and King James hovering like wraiths in the oppressive air.

I am tempted here, as I shall be in other portions of my narrative, to reproduce for my readers their exact words, or as much of them as I can recall. Nevertheless I am daunted by my lack of even the rudiments of the romance writer's art. These people, Protestant and English-speaking Papist alike, employ what we in England term the "brogue," a form of speech not unmusical but thick in texture and of course outlandish. And it but adds to the horrors of Irish life that the two communities address each other in identical accents, cursing and vilifying one another with a common tongue. My dear friend Mr. Falkiner assures me that my ear lacks the necessary training from childhood, that no Irishman would confuse Protestant and Papist speech. This may be so.

" 'Tis the start," Jack Stanner said. "Pray God that we may live to see the close."

" 'Tis a wonder to me that I am alive to see this day," poor Pryor said, "and that I did not perish in the bog in a welter of my own blood." Tompkins had brought him for solace a jug of whiskey, to which he now made sparing application. "I lay there bawling like a maimed ewe, and I would have perished had MacMahon not happened by."

"Is not MacMahon a Papist?" I asked him.

"He is," Pryor said. "A decent poor herdsman. If they were all as decent as MacMahon it would be well for us all."

"There are decent ones surely," Tompkins said. "There are some of them have debts to my shop which go back two or three years, and they come in with the odd shilling when they have it. It is the poorest ones are the most decent, the herdsmen and the laborers with the spade."

"More credit to them," Pryor said, "when Hussey stands up in their chapel and tells them they need not keep faith with heretics."

Mr. Hussey I knew to be a man of the most impeccable morality, and devout in his loyalty to the Crown. I could not say as much for Murphy, his odious curate, who was to prove by his subsequent course of action the truth of our suspicions. He was indeed an arrant rebel, lustful for the triumph of his creed and indifferent to human life. And yet the dramatic differences between these two priests were lost utterly upon the men in Sam Pryor's cabin. Their detestation of their Papist fellow countrymen was at once wholesale and capricious. Owen MacCarthy the schoolmaster was an object of their special execration, for in many places schoolmasters have been the nursemaids of disaffection, and MacCarthy was an imprudent man, brawling and boastful when drunk. They detested the Papist landlords—Bellew, Blake, Treacy, Grace, Moore, Nugent, MacDonnell, Burke. It galled them that this handful was more prosperous than themselves and affected the airs of gentlemen. Tompkins and several of the others harked back nostalgically to the days of their grandparents, when a firm Cromwellian boot had kept the necks of Papists close to the ground. And it was indeed a matter of some significance that all of these had been spared by the Whiteboys, although several had bad reputations as rack-renters.

"If it is the rents is their grievance," George Standish said, "why do they not look to William Burke of Crossmolina, who is the meanest bastard in this part of Mayo since the death of Mick Mahony? No, no. 'Tis as clear as this hand before my face. They would lift no hand against a man who is a priest's brother."

" 'Tis the start," Jack Stanner said again.

"It was this way that it started in Wexford, and see where that ended," Sam Pryor said. Hospitably, he shared his whiskey with the rest of us, and I found it prudent to accept a glass. It was wretched stuff, from some hillside distillery, and coursed like raw fire down my throat.

When I could manage speech, I said, "Surely not. That was an insurrection of the United Irishmen. These are mere Whiteboys, wretched, ignorant peasants."

"Ach, Mr. Broome," Stanner said. " 'Tis little you know them. There is not a priest in Ireland was not trained in France, and there are men like William Burke who served in King Louis' army to hunt down and massacre the poor Protestants of France."

Pryor drew his bandage away, to disclose a hideous lump of black blood where once his ear had been. "There you see it, Mr. Broome, another drop to add to the rivers of Christian blood which have flowed in this island since the days of Elizabeth. And still the loyal men of Tyrawley are bid to sit at home with their hands under their arses."

Ignoring his indelicacy of expression, as the reader will I trust ignore mine of repetition, I assured him, and the others, that to my certain knowledge the magistrates were pursuing their investigations with the utmost de-

107

termination, and I reminded them that their own yeomanry stood ready to enforce the recommendations of the magistracy.

"Ah," Stanner said. "That remains yet to see."

"There is nothing wrong with the yeomanry," Pryor said, "except that we have a captain with a Papist for his wife and with Papist friends like Randall MacDonnell."

"Come, sir! Come, sir!" I said sharply. "There is no more zealous officer in the island than Captain Cooper. He is if anything a man of too much zeal. What would you have him do?"

"Do, is it?" Pryor asked, again touching his bloody head. "Any Protestant should know what must be done."

"Easy now," Sergeant Tompkins said, with a glance toward me, the significance of which I did not then comprehend. "I will stake my word on Captain Cooper. Mr. Broome is right about him. Captain Cooper will do the proper thing."

I cannot censure them utterly. How little we in England understand their fears and loyalties! And yet for centuries we have depended upon such men. At every moment of crisis or impending violence, we in England speak brave and generous words about the loyal Protestants of Ireland, and yet at all other times we hold them in a negligent contempt, as a species of savage slightly superior to those by whom they are surrounded.

I left them with a promise that my dear Eliza would next day visit to inquire about Pryor and to bring him some small creature-comforts, and they bade me a courteous good-day, Pryor thanking me for my attention to him. And I am certain that so soon as the door was closed upon my back, they resumed conversation in a manner less restrained than that which my presence had imposed. I did not know these men well, to be sure, although they were members of my parish and attended my church each Sunday. They were not gentlemen, of course, and had no such pretensions. Indeed, they were suspicious of their own gentry, whom they regarded as lacking in zeal. Yet they and their gentry were bound together by creed and formed a single community, small in numbers and yet all-powerful.

I well remember that when I left Sam Pryor's cabin and walked back toward the town, I encountered a half-dozen or so spalpeens, wandering laborers who had perhaps drifted to Killala for the approaching harvest. They were dressed as coarsely as may be imagined, in frieze jackets so old and weathered that they might have been ripped from the landscape, and lacking hats to cover their matted or tousled hair. So might have looked the rough wood-kernes mentioned in the historical plays of the sublime Shakespeare. They were speaking most animatedly in Irish and several were laughing at the remarks of one, a wild creature taller even than Mac-Carthy. But as we passed, they broke off and greeted me most courteously, and with every show of respect, standing to one side of the road. When I had walked beyond them, they resumed talking, and reentered thus that world of theirs which was to me an entire secret, locked within their language.

It was as though I held in my hands two jagged bits of mosaic—the world of Pryor's cabin and of the Papist laborers upon the road. The pieces would not fit together, nor had I any notion of the design of which they formed parts.

Two nights later, the body of Phelim O'Carroll, a small farmer on the lands of Lord Glenthorne, was found lying naked in a shallow bog pool. He was most dreadfully mutilated, his back being no better than raw meat. O'Carroll, although a man of middle years, was a notorious faction fighter and therefore suspect as a Whiteboy. Doubtless, efforts had been made to extract information from him, but they apparently were futile. He was waked in his townland, but of this ceremony I fortunately can write nothing. The custom of the wake in peasant Ireland is nothing short of obscene, and to describe it would but excite disgust. It is sufficiently known that these wakes are not sober vigils by the body of a departed father or friend, but rather offer occasions for drink and licentiousness. But the nature of the "wake games," as they are called, is such as to lead one into despair for the fate of Christianity, so abominably do they perpetuate the pagan past. Of such games as "bout," "the bull and the cow," "hold the light," and "selling the pig," I shall say only that men and women participate, that in some the men are naked, and that in others all the activities of a nuptial night are pantomimed. There is much truth to the common saying that more marriages are made at wakes than at fairs or dances, so unbridled is the conduct of young and old alike. And yet all is done in a spirit of innocence and without the intention of irreverence, not even when the corpse itself is lifted to its lifeless feet and subjected to the travesty of an improper dance. This truly is a land sunk in the bog of an immemorial past. But I digress.

A far truer measure of the grief and passion of the people might be found at the burial of poor O'Carroll in the Killala graveyard, for the coffin was followed in silence by a long procession, which took, as is the custom, the longest route possible, making a long circle in the direction of the sun's movement. I attended the burial, standing at a respectful distance, and was much moved. When the coffin had been lowered into the earth, a group of shawled women came forward, and commenced the keen, of which so much has been written, and which, although undeniably savage, is not without musicality, and most expressive of a tempestuous grief. It is a kind of wail, and I observed that Mr. Hussey listened to it with what seemed a chilly disdain, several times glancing toward me with embarrassment, but his curate, Murphy, was most affected, and flung his arm impulsively about O'Carroll's nephew, a slack-jawed stripling. But for the most part, the large concourse of mourners listened impassively, their eyes fixed upon the rough wood of the coffin.

Into the earth which was shoveled upon the coffin was added a quantity of O'Carroll's blood, which his nephew poured out from a small flask, for there is a saying among the people that "there must be blood spilled at a funeral." If the purpose was ritualistic, then it was a wasted symbol, for the blood shed by Pryor and O'Carroll was in coming months to shower down upon us manifoldly.

On the following evening, as Mr. Gibson was returning home from an errand which had taken him into Ballina, shots were fired at him from behind a hedge which faces his entryway. Gibson is a bold man and rides armed at all times. He drew his pistol, wheeled his horse toward the hedge, and surprised into flight four men whom he was unable either to capture or to identify, although he later declared that one of them resembled Malachi Duggan, one of his tenants. Gibson was unpopular, both as landlord and as magistrate, and it was known that he had, like Cooper, been arguing for forceful action against the Whiteboys. And yet Duggan, being questioned by the magistrates, strenuously protested his innocence, and offered to bring forward twenty who would swear to it.

We had now a small war in Killala, with wounds suffered upon the one side, and death upon the other. Of rumors, born of fear and a natural suspicion, there was an abundance. Among Papists it was said that they would fare as had the peasants of Wexford under martial law in the months before the insurrection. Militia and regulars were to be brought in to lash at the triangle and to burn crops and cabins, with the Tyrawley Yeomanry to serve as their belling hounds. And many Protestants, especially among those of the lower orders, believed that a general massacre was to take place, so soon as news arrived that the French had landed. The fear and the hostility were almost palpable in the shabby streets of Killala. A peasant, bulking large and ominous in a small Protestant shop, would gesture toward the length of rope or the tin pot which he required, and the shopkeeper would hand it over in silence, tight-lipped and distant.

Men's fears having opened the gateways of their imaginations, fantasies more curious even than these gained entrance. The Irish are a most imaginative people, and have peopled the very earth and air with invisible presences, affixing to every hill and cairn some lovely or grotesque image. Yet this is but another way of saying that they are credulous and sunk in superstition, guiding their conduct by the dark utterances of old women and wandering prophecy men. This is at the best of times an impediment to their progress into civilization, and I cannot but believe, illiberal though this may seem, that the Romish faith offers shelter to the incredible. In times when great events are astir, this propensity to dream can assume dangerous forms.

So it was now. The tumults which had ravaged Ulster and Wexford had thus far left Mayo alone, but they had not passed unnoticed. Here, as everywhere in Ireland, the prophecy men, strolling entertainers and storytellers, had carried magnified and richly colored accounts of those wretched conflicts. Prophecies were carried from tavern to tavern, village to village, foretelling a great day of deliverance which would free from bondage the people of the Gael. So long as Mayo remained tranquil, scant attention was paid to such nonsense. But now, an apprehensive peasantry listened to and then repeated at the turf fire the apocalyptic poetry of ignorant men. A son with four thumbs had been born to a miller's wife in Athlone, and this miller would lead the army of the Gael. The final battle was to be fought somewhere beyond the Shannon, in the Valley of the Black Pig. Black, tall-masted ships were hurrying from France and from Spain, carrying the champions of Erin. These glorious predictions, it will be observed, did not involve Mayo: the battles were to take place at a safe, indeed a legendary distance from the Moy. And in their cloudy grandeur (should four thumbs be accounted grand) they bore little relation to our own shabby sorrows—a man killed and tossed into a bog, a man maimed and tortured.

On the first of August, the Tyrawley Yeomanry was ordered into uniform and placed on active service while the magistrates of the barony conducted an inquiry into seditious and criminal actions, with a view to the suppression of the organization styling itself the Whiteboys of Killala. The local magistrates were four in number, Captain Cooper, Mr. Gibson, Mr. Saunders, and my friend Mr. Falkiner. Of Captain Cooper I have already written, and shall have much more to say. Mr. Gibson and Mr. Saunders, although honest enough in a bluff and rough-and-ready fashion, were coarse and abrupt men. Only Mr. Falkiner at all approximated in temper what we in England understand by the word *magistrate,* which is to say an equable disposition and a respect for the rules of evidence and common sense. The magistrates proposed to examine anyone who might have knowledge of the crimes of the Whiteboys, and should answers prove unsatisfactory to bind such over for trial at the assizes. Thus far, they were of course but fulfilling their sworn responsibility. The proceedings were conducted with the most vivid display of force, those wanted for questioning being hauled out of their cabins in rough and peremptory fashion by squads of armed yeomen. There were more instances than one of extreme brutality, against which protests were unavailing. Far worse, it became clear to Mr. Falkiner that the intention of the others was that charges should be laid with or without the evidence to sustain them, on grounds of simple suspicion and to strike terror into the hearts of the peasantry. Throughout the hearings, he argued strenuously but without success against such shocking illegality, the consequences of which were, as we shall see, calamitous.

At the insistence of Mr. Falkner, I took a seat at the magistrates' bench, although of course I took no part in the questioning. It was Mr. Falkiner's belief, good and innocent man that he is, that the presence of a clergyman would place his colleagues upon their best behavior. It was a wearisome and melancholy affair. I have just now reread the minutes which were kept by Mr. Josiah Greene, the Ballina solicitor who acted as secretary, but his compounding of questions and answers into little mounds of dried oatmeal serves most imperfectly to recall for me those interminable evenings. The great number of those examined spoke no English. Cooper would put the questions in Irish to the witness and would then translate the answers for us. There is no question in my mind but that he exercised great and improper editorial discretion. A witness would respond volubly, hurling into the candle-lit room a torrent of barbaric words, gesticulating wildly, and doubtless protesting his innocence with reference to the entire calendar of saints. This would be reduced by Captain Cooper to a laconic, "He still claims he knows nothing."

I will incorporate at this point the evidence of an English-speaking witness, that the reader may sample it to the best of Mr. Greene's skill:

STATEMENT OF OWEN MACCARTHY, KILLALA, SCHOOLMASTER

I keep a classical academy in Killala where boys of all ages receive instruction. I am thirty-seven years of age. I came to this barony three years ago. I am a native of Tralee in County Kerry, and have taught school in that county, and also in Cork and in Limerick. In Kerry and in Cork I applied for and received a license to keep a school, and each time I took my allegiance to King George, whom I recognize as my lawful sovereign. I did not apply for a license in Killala because that is no longer required by law. I believe oaths are binding, and this is also the teaching of my Church. I have never heard a Papist priest say otherwise.

I have elsewhere than in this barony been arrested upon various charges, but most often for brawling or for disturbing the peace. I am not a Whiteboy or a United Irishman, and I have no knowledge of anyone who is. If I had such knowledge, I would report it to the magis-

113

trates. The United Irishmen are madmen and incendiaries. A republic is a country without a king. I have twice taken an oath of allegiance to King George. Of the plans of the Whiteboys, I know only what is common knowledge. I have been shown their so-called proclamation. They are madmen and rapparees, and the man who wrote their proclamation has need of a classical education. On the night that Sam Pryor was mistreated I was drinking in a tavern as many can attest.

The place in County Cork where I kept school was Macroom. There was much Whiteboy activity at Macroom but I had no hand in it. This would have been about twelve years ago. I never met Patrick Lynch, who was called "the Whiteboy Captain of Macroom." I saw him hanged in Macroom, as did many others.

I have never encouraged disaffection in my pupils. I am a writer of verses in Irish, and these are widely known among those who understand that language. They are all on harmless subjects such as love and the natural world. I have never broken the law when sober.

The questions which were put to MacCarthy may be inferred from his responses, as may the assumptions of his questioners. His evidence, as I recall it, has been much abridged by Mr. Greene, perhaps in the interest of common sense. Thus, both Captain Cooper and Mr. Gibson were made suspicious by the fact that MacCarthy was able to read French, and they pressed him as to whether or not he possessed revolutionary pamphlets from Paris. MacCarthy responded with patience to such imbecilities. He had been routed from his bed at the point of a bayonet, but the circumstances had quickened his wits, and he answered all the questions readily and deferentially, though with, as I thought, a faint sardonic smile. The magistrates were left unsatisfied, however, and several times called him "a plausible rogue." But for the present they took no action against him.

Seven other men, however, were bound over for trial and were taken to the gaol in Ballina. Most of the "evidence" against them was provided by a man named Paudge Nally, a small, ill-favored fellow with a humpback, who possessed a smattering of English. It was clear even to Captain Cooper that Nally was not a Whiteboy, but he professed a wide knowledge of men in the barony who had demonstrated disaffection in one way or another.

Thus, one of the men bound over was a young fellow named Gerald O'Donnell who helped his brother Ferdy work a hillside farm rented from Cooper. It was proved that in the preceding year, when Sam Pryor came there to collect the tithes, Gerald O'Donnell drove him off with curses and oaths. Nally gave evidence that since then young O'Donnell had been making threats against Pryor in the taverns, vowing once that in other counties the men knew how to deal with the ears of tithe proctors.

The testimony of Nally, who thereafter lived for safety's sake in a room in Cooper's house, I set at naught. He was the very stuff of which informers are made, retailing stale tavern gossip amidst the snuffles of a perpetually dripping nose. Mr. Falkiner suspected that his "evidence" had been forthcoming in consequence of an accommodation having been made with respect to his rent, which was badly in arrears. This assumption, however repellent, is a logical one, for surely some motive other than an abstract love of public order must have prompted him to so dangerous a course of conduct. Informers are common in Irish courts, but they seldom live into old age.

The seven prisoners were removed from Killala in two farm carts, under a guard of yeomen. The wives and mothers set up a great tumult with their wailing. They clung to the sides of the carts and sought to grasp the bound hands of the prisoners. A large number of people stood watching in the street, and, from most of these, the cries of the women drew forth a sympathetic low muttering. As the carts moved past the chapel, Murphy, the curate, rushed out and held a cross to the lips of the men, who kissed it fervently. But Ferdy O'Donnell stood leaning against the gable end of the chapel, his hands jammed into the waistband of his trousers, and his lips pressed closely together. His friend MacCarthy stood with him, and talked to him.

For a few minutes after the carts had begun to move down the Ballina road, we continued to hear the rumble of their wheels and the hoofbeats of the escort. But the town did not fall back into silence, for the women continued to wail, and the other peasants to talk among themselves. I went back into my house much troubled in spirit, and turned for guidance to our Creator, whom I addressed in language as zealous as that of any canting Methodist.

On the very next night, Paudge Nally's cabin was attacked by a large body of men. His wife and his poor innocent children were driven out onto the road. Then his cabin was destroyed and his crops burned and his few cattle slaughtered. Such an event would a scant month before have drawn upon itself the horror of the countryside, but now it had been half expected, and men spoke casually of it, as of some minor inevitability.

It is the event witnessed which has the most powerful hold upon the imagination, and I believe that the sight of the prisoners being carried off, the crying women, the creaking carts, lips pressed to crucifix, told more heavily than word of a burned thatch. I then believed, as reason prompted me to believe, that of the seven men seized up, some most likely were in fact Whiteboys and others quite possibly were not. And for the peasants of the barony the spectacle of innocent men being carted off must have been especially pitiable and enraging, a witness to them of their utter dependence upon the will and whims of their masters. In future days, when I had come to know well certain of the peasants, I was told over and over again of this incident, as though with it our troubles had begun.

This is a most sentimental and volatile society, as nearly all travelers here have reported. The bonds of friendship and of family affection are strong. Sensibilities are easily outraged. A man may be ill regarded in his community, but hang him, or even imprison him, and he becomes a popular hero, the subject of tearful or indignant tavern ballads. And should he be a man held in honor and esteem, as was young Gerald O'Donnell, this indignation waxes fierce. Perhaps our troubles did indeed begin when the carts rumbled off toward the Ballina gaol. But there is no way of knowing. The first link in the chain of human passions is often undiscoverable, lost in swirling mists of emotion.

5

The Acres, Killala, August 5

"You have made me a disgrace in my own parish," Judy Conlon said.

"Well, Judy," MacCarthy said, "I think we have worked together at that."

He was leaning against the doorpost, looking outward toward the bay.

"There was never a one to speak a word against me while my husband was alive to defend and to praise me."

"No man could go to your bed without rising up to praise your beauty and your accomplishments. I have praised you often in my heart, and in lines of verse."

"I was a married woman then, and could be married now."

"Ach, Judy, it is a chancy life a schoolmaster has, and the more so if he is a poet."

She was standing behind him in her shift, her dark hair falling about her shoulders.

" 'Tis said that you are a good poet, Owen—"

"It is the truth. By God it is."

"But you are as good a master, and there will always be need of a school in Killala."

"Not for me, Judy. I am going away onto the road. I have no stomach for what is happening here and for what will happen."

"And all because Sam Pryor got his ears clipped? Sure he looks far handsomer now, the mean old leech."

MacCarthy laughed. "You will take after me with the shears one day, you fierce woman. And pray God you will settle for my ears. No, there will be more mischief in Killala, and poets have a way of getting hurt at such times. I declare to God, I would be in Ballina gaol tonight

117

if it had not been for Mr. Falkiner and the little Protestant minister. Cooper did his best."

"Cooper had best watch out," she said, "from all the talk that I have heard. Cooper and that Paudge Nally, swearing men's liberty away from them."

"My God, Judy, what help is that to poor Gerry O'Donnell, who has never lifted his hand against any man save for the time that Pryor came with the bailiff to take two of Ferdy's cows? By now I don't know who is a Whiteboy and who is not, but I know that Ferdy is not and I will take my oath on that."

"There are those who say that a schoolmaster should stand with the people, as masters in other places have done."

"That is wonderful talk you hear."

"It is little enough that a woman knows, but only what she hears them all saying."

"Then it is little call she has to be talking about such matters. I declare to God that I did not rise up this morning to be preached at and worried by a slip of a girl."

"But you will not be leaving, will you, Owen? You said that because you were cross with me."

"No, Judy," he said, turning away from the bay to face her. "I meant that. It would be plain folly to stay here, a man like me. I would be less fortunate the next time. Do you want to see me in a cart, trussed up like a turkey? And no comfort but mad Murphy shoving a cross at me."

"O God, Owen. What would I do without you?"

"I would never leave you with an empty purse. Mr. Treacy is paying me to write out my poems for him on fine parchment, to go beside the poems of O'Rahilly and O'Sullivan. As is only proper." Not true: he had never written a poem could rival O'Rahilly.

"What good will your poetry be when you are an old man with no one to stand by you?"

"If I stay in this barony I may not live to be an old man. God, when I think of the way I have been made to drift across this island, a harmless inoffensive creature. There are vagabonds and sturdy beggars who have a more settled life."

She put her hand on his shoulder, standing on tiptoe. "You will do what you think is best."

" 'Tis little enough I know about what is best for me, or for anyone else. I sometimes look at the poor children

118

whose parents pay me for their instruction, and I wonder what am I about, flogging knowledge into their heads."

"Sure the lads have need of knowledge. You do work as honest as that of any tailor."

"Small knowledge they require to harm cattle or to ride off to Ballina in a cart."

"That is the way of it," she said.

"The army of the Gael rose up in Wexford, and there are tall-masted ships sailing from France to my own Munster. And in Mayo men fight over cows and half-acres of scrubby land that would not give grass to a goat. A sorry, mean place this is."

"I have never seen those other places where you have been. Would you not give thought to taking me with you?"

He shook his head. "Five guineas I will have from Mr. Treacy for the poems, and I will leave three with you. The two is more than I will need."

"Is it because I would not be a proper wife for a schoolmaster?"

He drew his fingers along the side of her head, touching the thick, coarse hair, the cheek.

"It is not," he said. " 'Tis that I am not a marrying sort of fellow, love. And well you know it."

"I know that," she said, and stepped backward, away from him.

He looked again toward the dull, distant bay. She was as good-hearted as any girl he had known, a fine, generous girl. But there was little else to keep him in Mayo. He had made few close friends here, for women were never friends. There was a mystery in the center of their being, a distance that was never closed, not even in the blackness of night. For friends he had only Ferdy O'Donnell up the mountain, and Sean MacKenna, the schoolmaster below in Castlebar. There was little to keep him here. The children's classes were over, and in two weeks' time he would have earned Treacy's five guineas.

Let them find a new master, some young foolish lad up from Kerry who knew no better.

Ballina, August 7

Malcolm Elliott and Randall MacDonnell met with Malachi Duggan in Ryan's alehouse, a mile outside

Ballina. MacDonnell ordered a bowl of punch, but he and Elliott had it to themselves, for Duggan drank nothing. He sat facing them, stolid but alert, his large, mild eyes looking at neither of them, but straight ahead, or, head bent, at a crack in the rough table. A gentleman, a squireen, and a peasant, they were an ill-assorted group, and, of the three, only Duggan felt no embarrassment.

"Before God, sir," he said to Elliott, "I know nothing whatever of what wild and furious rapparees do in the darkness of the night. Why, they have fired shots at Mr. Gibson, who is my own landlord and has never given me a cross word."

"Of course not," Elliott said. "But you are a man to whom the people look up, whether they are Whiteboys or not."

"Ach, sir. 'Tis only because I had a way of being first and foremost in the faction fights. But I am growing old for that now." He slapped his heavy belly. "Faction fights are frolics for young lads. There is no harm to them at all, and they bring honor to the barony." His English, although the pronunciation was thick and unpredictable, was more than serviceable.

"Jesus but you are the great one for the factions," MacDonnell said. "Three years ago I saw you swing your holly against the men of Ballycastle. Thick-headed bastards they are."

"These are bad days for the barony," Elliott said, "with the gaol in his town filling up with Killala men and Kilcummin men."

"Bad days for the entire country, sir. Every Sunday Mr. Hussey tells us of our dangers. Frenchmen on the sea who go neither to church nor to chapel. Men below in Wexford rising up against the King. And men right here about us doing evil things."

"You are a most law-abiding sort of fellow," MacDonnell said drily.

"That is the way of it," Duggan said.

"Seven men of the barony in Ballina gaol," Elliott said. "And there will be more than seven before Cooper and the other magistrates have finished."

The massive head nodded. "That was a dreadful thing to have done. Those young lads are no more Whiteboys than I am."

"I know one at least who is not," MacDonnell said, "and that is Gerry O'Donnell. When I heard that he had

120

been seized up I could not believe it. A decent, quiet lad. By God, when I heard that, I rode over to Sam Cooper and pledged my word for Gerry. I should have saved my breath to cool my porridge. He had given me a glass of whiskey, and I was that angry, I smashed the glass in the fireplace and turned my back on him and left."

"That is no fellow I would want to turn my back on," Duggan said. "Meaning no disrespect to the gentry."

"Gentry!" MacDonnell said. "Gentry, is it? That fellow is no more gentry than a tinker is. Cromwellian plunderers, the Coopers were."

"So were the Elliotts," Malcolm Elliott said.

"There is good and bad in everything," MacDonnell said quickly. "Many is the drink that Sam Cooper and I had together in the old days. And now he stood looking at me with a vain smile on his face. Poor Gerry O'Donnell has as much claim to be called gentry. The O'Donnells are the old stock."

"One thing is certain," Elliott said. "Cooper and his friends will not rest here."

"Nor those Whiteboys either," Duggan said. "They are bold, determined lads, would you not say?"

"They well may be," Elliott said. "But they are also foolish men. Perhaps they can keep the barony in turmoil for a long time, but they cannot win, because they have no clear sense of what they want. Is it to prevent evictions, or get lower rent, or to pay off old scores? Perhaps they only want violence itself."

"Ignorant men, you say," Duggan said. "Perhaps you know men of learning who would advise them, Mr. Elliott."

Elliott nodded. "Advise, that is the word. Not lead them, they have their leaders."

"And what advice would they give?"

"In Wexford," Elliott said, "the rising was made because the people there joined with the United Irishmen."

"And were they not the foolish men, those people in Wexford? When they looked around for the United Men who were to give them arms, they were nowhere to be found. I think, sir, that if a fellow was so wicked as to be a Whiteboy, he would do best to trust to himself and to darkness, and not be relying on the fine promises of gentlemen."

"The rising in Wexford was led by a gentleman," Elliott said. "It was led by Bagenal Harvey."

Poor Harvey, Elliott thought. Dragged out of Bagenal Castle by a mob of pikemen and placed, reluctant, at their head, marched bewildered up and down Wexford, half general and half prisoner, bargaining and cajoling for the lives of prisoners, quarreling with drunken and boastful peasants. It was in peasant dress that he tried at last to escape. Now his head was skewered above Wexford gaol.

"There was a traveling man who told us about that gentleman," Duggan said. "He isn't much of a recommendation." For the first time, Duggan smiled, showing broken and discolored teeth.

"Look here, Malachi," MacDonnell said suddenly. "I did not bring you together with Mr. Elliott so that you could play the fool with him."

"I have been wondering about that," Duggan said. "Not that it is not pleasant to spend the morning with two gentlemen of the barony."

"Nor with me, either. John Moore vouches for Elliott, and I will vouch for John Moore. You know very well why we are talking with you."

"Even so," Duggan said. "You tell me why, Randall."

His manner toward MacDonnell, Elliott saw, was far easier and more familiar. It went well beyond his unexpected use of a Christian name. MacDonnell was poised between the two worlds, half gentleman, half prosperous peasant. It did not bother MacDonnell, blunt, affable man, ready for a drink with anyone. But between Elliott and the sly, brutish-seeming Duggan lay a deep, unbridgeable gulf. Bagenal Harvey must have felt the same, as he wandered the Wexford roads with his pikemen.

"You are a Whiteboy," MacDonnell said. "One of the Whiteboys of Killala, you call yourself. If the magistrates were less foolish than they are, they would have sent you off to Ballina gaol. And Malcolm Elliott and I are United Irishmen. We have taken their oath. Now there is plain speaking for you."

"It is indeed," Duggan said. "It is indeed, Randall. You were ever a plainspoken man." He picked up the third, unused tumbler, and filled it with punch. "I used to be the devil for this stuff, when I was a young man. I have not tasted it in ten years." He held it to the small window's watery light. "When I got my tongue around a belt of it, there was no stopping me."

"I remember that," MacDonnell said. "You had a strong head for the spirits. Sure, used you not help my own father unload the brandy from the French ships at Kilcummin strand, and there was always a cask or two the less at the final count."

"And well your father knew it. He was a generous man without making a show of it as some do."

"There will be other ships coming below in Munster," Elliott said. "But not with brandy."

Duggan took a long swallow, and then smacked his lips. "By God, it tastes the same. I had forgotten the taste of it." He emptied the tumbler on the dirt floor, and replaced it on the table.

"And when the French land," Elliott said, "Munster will rise up."

"It may," Duggan said. "But Munster is a long way from Mayo. As far as Wexford."

"In the south and in the midlands the United Irish are strong," Elliott said. "And in Galway and Sligo there are United Men. Not as many, but they are growing. If the whole of the island rises up we can win."

"Win what, Mr. Elliott? That is what puzzles me. You are a gentleman and a landlord. What more is it that you want?"

Elliott hesitated, uncertain how best to answer him. "Freedom," he said at last.

"Freedom from what?" Duggan asked, and his puzzlement seemed genuine.

"From England," Elliott said. "From a government and a parliament that does England's bidding." Freedom from the past, he wanted to add, but that would have made no sense to Duggan.

"More power to your arm," Duggan said. "But that means nothing to Mayo. It is the landlords have their heels on our necks here. Sure you have no thought to take the landlords off us. You are landlords yourselves, the two of you."

"You can never tell," MacDonnell said. "In a rebellion you can never tell. They begin as one thing and end as something else."

Elliott looked at him sharply. MacDonnell was smiling easily. "There are landlords and there are landlords. Now you take a mean land-grabber of a landlord, like Cooper or like your own man Gibson. A fellow like that might not fare too well in the hurly-burly."

Elliott began to speak, and then checked himself. MacDonnell and Duggan were looking closely at each other.

"In a rebellion," MacDonnell said, "we would be on the one side, and men like Gibson and Cooper would be on the other. All of them would—Falkiner and Saunders and the rest of them. It would go hard with them if the men of Mayo rose up. Sure what is it the Whiteboys can do but kill cattle and burn crops, and fire off the odd shot from behind a hedge. And you will be scattered in time, make no doubt of that."

"Is that how you see it yourself, Mr. Elliott?" Duggan asked.

MacDonnell put a hand on Elliott's arm and squeezed it.

"There is a score of lads on my own land," MacDonnell said, "who have no time for the Whiteboys, but if I say the word they will take the United oath and I can lead them out. And well you know that. The men on the MacDonnell lands have always followed the MacDonnells. And the same is true with Corny O'Dowd and Tom Bellew. I have taken the United oath, and so have Corny and Tom. We will lift no hand unless the French come, but on that day we will go out onto the road. And the same is true for certain men on the coast, at Westport, whose names you would know."

Duggan rubbed a hand across his mop of stiff, wiry hair, but he said nothing.

"We want your lads, Malachi, and we want you."

"I am not a MacDonnell of Ballycastle," Duggan said. "The Whiteboys are but ignorant poor lads, and I am but one of them. Sure we don't have leaders at all. It is but a band of ignorant poor lads."

"Tell that to your grandmother," MacDonnell said.

Duggan laughed, a length of heavy chain dragged up from the deep, heavy-muscled chest.

"If you take the United oath," Elliott said, "you must take your lead from the United Men. And we have no interest in houghing cattle or cropping the ears of tithe proctors. It is this island which is our interest, and not a barony in Mayo."

"Well now, Mr. Elliott," Duggan said, "I will tell you what I might be able to do. I will keep my eye skinned for some lads that might be Whiteboys, and I will pass along to them what you have said, and I will take counsel with them."

"We ask no more, Malachi," MacDonnell said. "We ask no more." He filled their three glasses. "Now take just a sup of this, for the sake of the bargain."

124

"I will be happy to drink your healths," Elliott said. "But the oath is the bargain."

"You are a gentleman of very stiff ways," Duggan said. "Like all gentlemen."

When they were standing alone by their horses on the hot, dusty road, Elliott said, "I have little use for your Duggan. He is a sly bully."

MacDonnell smiled. "He is that. He is as bad-tempered a rogue as can be found in a day's ride. What did you expect?"

"Something a bit better than that."

MacDonnell spat, and then rubbed his boot absently over the gob. "You had best look somewhere else for it then, Malcolm. That is what we have here. And we could do worse than Duggan, and perhaps we will before this song is sung. Have you never taken a look at those wild creatures from Belmullet, who are no better than pagans? 'Christ never died for Belmullet,' is a saying they have in Erris."

Elliott smiled. "If He died for Malachi Duggan, He struck a poor bargain."

MacDonnell shouted with delight, and put his hard hand on Elliott's shoulder. "You are a terrible blasphemous Protestant, by Jesus."

"You do well enough yourself," Elliott said, still smiling.

There had been a time, seven or eight years ago, when he and MacDonnell were two of a kind, best riders in the hunt, drinking together at the races, the last two to leave a party in the streaky dawn. Before Dublin, before London. Now he saw MacDonnell as a man whose world was bounded by his horizon, bay and flat fields and distant mountains. Belmullet was the far edge of his world, like the empty white spaces on an explorer's map.

"A pair of right fools we must be," MacDonnell said. "Landlords bargaining with Whiteboys. We will be lucky to get out of this without ropes around our necks. There were landlords hanged in Wexford. Bagenal Harvey was a landlord and so was Grogan."

"You have the right of it there," Elliott said, the smile leaving his lips. "There is fair chance of hanging."

"I gave young Johnny Moore an easy answer, if you take my meaning. Neither yes nor no. But by Jesus, when they carted those lads off to Ballina it made up my mind for me. It is us or them, I said to myself, and I won't see that matter settled without a fight. The time is long past when a little shit like Sam Cooper can ride up and down the barony acting like the Grand Turk."

"Well now," Elliott said. "Whiteboys. This county has always taken a hard line with Whiteboys. Twenty years ago those lads would have accounted themselves fortunate to reach Ballina alive."

"By God, they would," MacDonnell said. "In my daddy's time, or yours. But that was long since. And there is still not enough justice in this island to fill a parson's hat. Your Frenchmen may bring us some, along with their muskets and their soldiers."

"Yes," Elliott said. "Perhaps."

"And perhaps not?" MacDonnell asked quickly. "You are a peculiar sort of a rebel, Malcolm Elliott. A reluctant rebel. It is encouragement that you should be pouring on my head and not doubt."

"Ach," Elliott said. "Pay no attention to me, Randall. I have known for three years or more that there was no hope for this country but through rebellion. No hope at all. I have no doubts on that score. But God did not build me for a rebel. It is as though I am acting against my own nature."

"You are in a sorry state, then, and you have my pity. When I stood on Steeple Hill and watched the carts moving off, and the women screeching and running down the road after them, I said to myself, By God, Randall, to hell with it, and when the Frenchmen land in the south, I will raise Mayo. And I can do that, by God. Myself and yourself and Corny O'Dowd and Tom Bellew, and Duggan with his Whiteboys if they will throw in with us. And when I thought that, it was as if I had taken a naggin of whiskey. It was as if I had won the Castlebar race. Sweet Jesus, I said to myself, and I wanted to throw my hat into the air. By the blood of Mary ever virgin, we will be the cocks of the walk. We will rule Mayo."

"Listen to yourself," Elliott said, smiling again. "You are a blaspheming, idolatrous Papist. And you understand as little about this rebellion as you do about the works of Plato."

"I understand it far better than you do, I think," MacDonnell said. He put a foot in the stirrup and swung gracefully to the saddle. "We will rule Mayo." He touched his crop to his hat, and rode off toward the north road.

But Elliott rode south, toward Ballina, where the Killala lads lay in gaol, toward Moat House. Far to his left, the distant Ox Mountains rose into blue haze. His road skirted the slow-moving Moy, a good river for salmon. He had fished it as a boy, bent pin and skewered worm dangling from string. It was his world, as much as it was MacDonnell's, but he was not at home in it any longer. In Dublin he had hungered for it, first at Trinity and then in his lodgings near King's Inn. He could remember then each bend of the river, the look of every sky, the feel of autumn paths beneath his boots. A gull wheeling gray wings in the blue and silver Dublin sky would carry him there in an instant, and he would see the river emptying into Killala Bay, smell the brackish waters of the bay. Now it was farmland, dull horizon, flat and tasteless air. To raise his spirits, he struggled without success to recapture his memories of the scene which stretched before him.

Killala, August 8

"You have the sense of it grand, Ferdy," MacCarthy said. "But it is a great poem that we have on our hands here, and not a lease or a bill of sale. Now let us go after it again."

They sat together at the low, rough table in O'Donnell's kitchen, the open book of Ovid between them, its binding loose and its leaves discolored.

"We will take it again," he said patiently. *"Inde per immensum ventis . . ."* The words echoed within his skull, sounds ripe and potent as the clanging of bells.

Inde per immensum ventis discordibus actus
nunc huc, nunc illuc exemplo nubis aquosae
fertur et ex alto seductas aethere longe
despectat terras totumque supervolat orbem.

He moved his eyes down the familiar page. The artful heathen, what man could match him! But my God, the language that had been given him, resourceful and muscular. There was no talk to which it could not be set. It stretched across the page in coils of easy power.

"Perseus is making his way through the air, through the heavens themselves, and soon the whole world will be

127

stretched out before him. He is carried through immense stretches of air, the poet tells us, first this way and then that, like the mist itself. And as he looks down, the whole world is spread before him, or what they thought was the world, the poor heathens. He didn't see this place at all. 'Tis like the seabirds as you can watch them from Downpatrick Head with their great wings, so high that with their little eyes they can see from Galway to Donegal. But free though they seem to us, the winds are their masters, and toss them about any way they choose. Keep the seabirds at Downpatrick at the back of your mind like a picture, and then have another try at it."

But O'Donnell placed his hard, heavy hand upon the page, blotting out the words. A black cloud fell upon the great southern sea.

"Ach, Owen. It was kindness itself for you to come here with your books, but I cannot put my mind to Perseus or to seabirds. Not with poor Gerry in gaol with those other fellows."

" 'Tis hard for you, Ferdy, and far harder for Gerry. But you will have a long wait of it until the assizes."

"Sure the two of us know what will happen then," O'Donnell said. He pushed away the copy of Ovid. "I am a peaceable man, but if I could get my two hands around Paudge Nally's throat, I would squeeze the life from him. I would so. He will swear Gerry's life away with that lying throat."

MacCarthy, who had no words for him, closed the book, and patted the loose pages into place. As daylight was fading, Perseus came to rest upon the border of the world, far to the west, where the sea spread out its waters, and the thousand flocks and thousand herds of Atlas wandered at their sweet will across grassy plains.

"This was the year we were to get a bit ahead of the rent," O'Donnell said, "with the harvest as fine as it will be, God willing. Maire and Gerry and I were talking of it not long ago at this table. O God, Owen, they are likely to hang him at the end of all this. Do you think that yourself?"

"Ach, sure, Ferdy, the assizes are a long way off, and God is good. A lot could happen between now and then." But there was nothing more certain, not with Paudge Nally to stand up in Castlebar court, with his hand on the Protestant Bible.

"I declare to God, Owen. If I heard this night that the

128

French had landed, I would find a pike and go join them. I would so."

"You would not be alone. I stopped at the tavern in Kilcummin and I heard that said. And the men who said it were not Whiteboys, to my best knowledge. Ach, by now they may be. That was an hour ago. Quigley is swearing them in at a great rate, and it is the same in Killala. Sam Cooper and his yeomen are great recruiting sergeants for the Whiteboys. Cooper and Duggan! A fine pair of ignorant bloody ruffians."

O'Donnell sighed. "Sam Cooper. Did you ever hear it said that Mount Pleasant was once O'Donnell land? 'Tis true. There is a great bloody parchment in the chest that says so. It goes back to the days of the Stuarts. My father was always giving out about it when he had a drop taken."

"There are parchments like that in chests across the length and breadth of Ireland," MacCarthy said, "and 'tis best to let them rot away and not think of them. It is Cromwell's crew that rule the roost, and Cromwell was a long time ago. There was an old man in Fermoy in County Cork. He had an entire oaken box of charters and deeds and the like, and he living in a hovel. He would drive you mad with his boasting, but he couldn't rub two shillings together."

" 'Tis not boasting I am at," O'Donnell said. "But it has driven me mad these past days to think of Cooper lording over us and sending off poor Gerry. It was in the middle of the night they came, and they burst in with Marie not decent. Cooper is the man. Paudge Nally is but a monkey perched on Cooper's shoulder."

MacCarthy laughed. "A good image, that. Did they school you in rhetoric, off there in Douai? 'Tis often I have envied you your sight of France and all its wonders."

"The wonders of France, is it? We lads saw as much of France as you might see from Achill Island. It wasn't to improve our knowledge of the world that we were in seminary, but to make priests of us. And it was the same in the seminary as it is here. The French priests looked down on us, they thought we were a poor class of people. The world has small regard for the Irish."

"Bugger them all," MacCarthy said.

"You are the most educated man in the barony," O'Donnell said, "barring Mr. Hussey. And they stood you before the magistrates like a spalpeen or a tinker."

129

"I slid through them," MacCarthy said. "Like a greased pig."

"Gerry will not," O'Donnell said. "He is a hot-headed young fellow and he blurts out how he feels. He will come to harm without myself to keep an eye on him."

"Education is a great advantage," MacCarthy said.

"Ach, it does us no good whatever," O'Donnell said, in a loud, strained voice. He made a violent move for the book, but MacCarthy shoved it quickly beyond his reach.

"Will you have a care, man? Grief is grief, but that book cost me three and sixpence."

O'Donnell glared at him briefly, but then smiled.

"It is time to open the jug I brought," MacCarthy said. "We will leave poor Perseus up in the sky."

O'Donnell shook his head. "Have a drink yourself, Owen, but I will not join you. Maire and I knelt down last night and I took a vow to Our Lady that I would not wet my lips with spirits until Gerry could have a drink himself in this house."

Our lives are spent upon our knees, on mud floors, the cool flags of chapels. They have courts, yeomen, gallows. They own the earth, and guard it well from us. Prayer our only recourse, soft words upon the air. It was almost ten, but the evening beyond the open door was warm and light. Too light yet for the moon. He did not want to drink in front of O'Donnell, lest it tempt him from his vow.

"Go on, man," O'Donnell said impatiently. "I have no thirst on me at all."

MacCarthy picked up the jug from the floor, uncorked it, and resting it on his crooked elbow, held the mouth to his lips.

"There now," he said, dragging the back of his hand across his lips. "That is better."

"You are right to move out of this, Owen. I cannot. I have roots growing down out of the soles of my boots. All that I know is this mountain and Kilcummin and Killala."

Roots running out from his boots into thin mountain soil. A poet's image. From Ovid perhaps, with all his people turning into plants, and flowers into people. Needing to define himself, he mints an image: his first. Without poetry, we are senseless and blind. Three languages crowded MacCarthy's skull. Irish, a nobleman in furs, trudging behind a plow. English, sober squire in broadcloth and flat, wide-brimmed hat. Latin, the queen of tongues, by which heroes were turned to stars and cast up to the heavens. He drank again.

"You are too fond of that, Owen," O'Donnell said, nodding toward the jug.

"And it of me," MacCarthy said. "We suit each other well. Like yourself and Maire. 'Tis fortunate you are to have that woman."

"She goes early to bed these nights." O'Donnell said. " 'Tis a cheerless house now and I am poor company."

"Ach, Ferdy. You never can tell. The assizes are a long way off." He had said that before. He had no other comfort.

He stood up without grace, scraping his stool across the hard-packed earth, and walked to the door. The bay was a dull, metallic gray in the soft air. A fishing smack moved toward Kilcummin strand.

"There is a man I know," he said, "who had a drink yesterday with Randall MacDonnell. There are more people than Whiteboys who are ready for trouble. By the time this summer has ended, there may not be a county in Ireland where a man can keep himself free from trouble."

O'Donnell, still seated, looked up at him. "There is another man who has spoken to me of Randall MacDonnell. Randall is a far different man from Malachi Duggan. He is a decent, pleasant fellow."

"He is that," MacCarthy said. "But he chases foxes on horseback. A comical sort of sport." He slipped his book into the tail pocket of his coat and straightened his neckcloth. "It was kind of the great warring winds that they did not drive poor Perseus to this miserable corner of the world." He smiled at O'Donnell. 'Didn't your great Prince O'Donnell come raging through here with all his kernes and gallowglasses at the time of the great rebellion, driving all before him and scattering the soldiers of the English Queen?"

O'Donnell stood up, and joined him at the door. "I don't know, to tell you the truth. I have heard it was farther to the east. But he claimed all this part of Connaught, and set up his chieftains here. It was the O'Dowds who held Tyrawley for him, Corny O'Dowd's people. My father's grandmother used say that an O'Donnell would rule Tyrawley again, when the army of the Gael rose up.'

"A wise tribe of people, grandmothers are," MacCarthy said.

" 'Tis all tinker talk," O'Donnell said. "The army of the Gael."

"Who knows that better than myself?" MacCarthy said. "Where would the poets be for their themes without the army of the Gael? We are terrible liars, the pack of us."

"Poets and grandmothers," O'Donnell agreed. "The world is spoiled between the two of you."

MacCarthy, laughing, made his way down the boreen, and then turned to wave good-bye, but O'Donnell had gone back into the cabin.

Hugh O'Donnell, greatest of all the heroes sung by the poets. Ireland a mist-choked bog to the captains of Henry and Elizabeth, treacherous chieftains and shaggy, half-naked kernes, petty princelings ready to sell cousin or brother, their armies howling mobs with matted beards, eyes like wild animals peering through thickets. To be rooted out as animals are, hunted down in their lairs, their heads lopped off. All Munster turned into a desert by Lord Grey de Wilton after the Desmond rebellion. The poet Spenser had seen it and exulted. "Out of every corner of the woodes and glennes they came crepinge forth upon their handes, for theire legs could not bear them; they looked like Anatomies of Death, they spake like ghosts crying out of theire graves." An old volume, dust-streaked, in the corner of a gentleman's library near Corofin, the type black as a death notice: *A View of the Present State of Ireland.*

MacCarthy had read his poetry, half comprehending, a young omadhaun sprawled out on the Kerry sands. Sweet Thames, run softly, till I end my song. Bower of Bliss, like a phrase in the litany to Our Lady. Flowers and flowering branches, flowers like stars. Legends and enchantments, fair women and wonder-working enchanters. Meanings, gigantic shadows, moved behind them. Later, in Cork, MacCarthy learned that the great English poem of enchantment had been written in Ireland, in Cork itself. Not strange. Soft Munster was at work within it. Near Doneraile, on the gentle Awbeg, stood the ruins of Kilcolman, his castle. Yet this same man, this Edmund Spenser, this soft and seductive enchanter, had helped butcher the Irish, turned Desmond into a wasteland, watched the starving crawl toward him, their mouths stained with nettles and shamrock. Sweet Thames, run softly, till I end my song.

O'Donnell had done for him. Puissant Gaelic prince, his lime-white mansion sung by poets. From county to county his rebellion had spread, southward from Ulster. His rebels burned Kilcolman. The poet fled, his poem unfinished, back to London and his glorious Queen. A little boy, his son, perished in the flames. Rebels, rough-clad, watched the flames leaking from the thatched roof, their faces ruddy. When O'Donnell was defeated on the southern coast, at Kinsale, a world shattered. Ruin. Now we move among ruins, peasants gawking at the broken, roofless keep of Munster and Connaught. O'Donnell, Mac-Carthy: names now for the tenant of a mountain acre, a wandering schoolmaster. The brittle pages of our parchment history turn to powder beneath the weight of our fingers. Ferdy O'Donnell moves in the dark of his cabin, distraught, blundering against table, bed upon which his wife lies sleeping. His history a father's word of mouth, a grandmother's prophecy. I walk toward a village of hovels.

Ballycastle, August 10/Ballintubber, August 14

My dearest John:

Be assured that when George approaches my father he will find him well disposed to your suit. Your family he holds in great respect, and he has a great fondness for you, cherishing your virtues and welcoming your company. He knows that you will bring me to a home comfortable and secure, well ordered and decent in every way. Indeed, a home far finer and grander than that which I will leave. (Although I am told by my father and myself know also upon instinct that our gentility stands beyond challenge.) And yet he is most concerned and worried for you at this time, as I am, and as George must surely be.

It is not alone that he opposes most severely your politics, which concern me not at all, for such is no part of a woman's proper sphere, as I am certain you will agree. Rather it is that these politics may have placed your feet upon a dangerous road. And here, dearest John, I tremble, lest his suspicions are well founded. It is being said everywhere in the barony that the disaffected poor together with reckless and misguided men who may have pretensions to family and breeding have welcomed the seductive approaches of the United Irishmen, and in the event of a French invasion will reveal their base intentions. And in such talk—most recently last evening, by Mr. Hussey and Mr. Falkiner, and at our own fireside—your name has been mentioned. All this my father stoutly denies, although in his heart he shares their misgivings.

Not only does he reprehend the seditious plans of the United Irishmen, he foresees for them nothing but bleak doom, disgrace, and death. And in this he displays to us his wisdom. Elsewhere in the kingdom, the men who involved themselves in this matter have suffered a shameful fate. Why should it be different here? And what if they were to succeed? They have stirred up the passions of ignorant men, men who are capable of the most dreadful brutalities. Surely it is no part of wisdom to administer to the patient a medicine more deadly than the disease? Thus reasons my father, and he is said by all to be a man of rare judgment and learning.

You may therefore depend upon it that he will press George upon this point, and perhaps even seek to extract from him an assurance that you have broken off your associations with men who have not at heart either your good or the good of this kingdom. No, nor the good of our Holy Church, and upon this point you may well consult Mr. Hussey, who is a saintly man and comes of a most respectable family, the Husseys being closely related to the Roches of Fermoy in Cork.

P.S. My dearest John. The lines above I have written to you after discussion with my father, and I have submitted them to his inspection. These few lines which follow are for your eyes alone. While my father may not be the wisest of men, he is far indeed from being a fool. Why in God's name do you associate yourself with such rattle-brains as Corny O'Dowd and Randall MacDonnell who less than a year ago made to me a suggestion which was as improper as it was unflattering. He may account himself a gentleman but I do assure you that he is not. He is but a faction fighter who rides well and can boast of clean linen. Malcolm Elliott is indeed a gentleman, I admit, but a more long-faced lugubrious Protestant I have never met and his wife is a perfect ninny and is English. Do you not see from my questions that the very names of your associates are known, and their intentions guessed at? It will not be long before the magistrates turn their attention beyond those barbarous Whiteboys. O the folly and wickedness of turning for help to Frenchmen who are stained with the blood of their radiant and blameless Queen. Not to mention their King, and countless others, including several Irish officers in the Royal service. My love for you is too great for us ever to part, whatever the wishes of my father. O the unspeakable stubbornness of men, and the crazed notions which tempt them away from a reasoned and sober felicity.

My dearest Ellen:

I cannot deny that there is reason for your father's concern and your own distress. What shall I say? I can at least assure you that I would not have enlisted in this cause had I judged it hopeless. On that score at least, if not on others, I am not inclined toward the romantic. I believe that an uprising of the people, if properly armed and led, and if supported by an adequate force from our French allies, stands a fair chance of success. And I am prepared to gamble on that chance, because I am entirely settled in my mind that there is no other help or remedy for this wretched island.

Yet I believe that the chance is no better than middling, and have indeed asked myself, and often, why I am prepared to put my life at risk. I believe, with both judgment and passion, that all men yearn for their own freedom. But no man can be free if his country is enslaved. Bid your father cast his eyes toward America, which fought for and won its freedom, and yet the chains that galled them were far lighter than ours. Ireland, your country and mine, is the mere creature of England, which abuses and mistreats us casually, as it serves her interests. She justly cherishes her own Parliament, and yet she has deliberately and by system corrupted ours until today it stands shamed before the world. Odious as are the religious animosities among our people, yet she has fostered and increased them, the better to keep us divided and thus weak. And our people bear, all of them, rich and servile, Protestant and Papist, some mark of this bondage

I write this without rant, as a statement of fact which few would dare to refute. Certainly George would not, for no man has so clear or so sardonic a view of our affairs.

135

Yet George, for all his estimable qualities of mind and sensibility, holds a dark and pessimistic view of human nature. For my part, I believe that every man is a locked casket of virtue, of which freedom is the key. That the great mass of our peasantry is brutish and ignorant, I shall not deny, yet what has made them so, for are they not shaped of meaner stuff than the yeomanry of England? The awful poverty of their lives has worked thus upon them, and the great cause of our national poverty is our subservience to England. It is of course dangerous to place a musket or a pike in the hands of a man inflamed with angry passion, yet with that weapon he may exchange despair for hope.

If indeed there are causes for which it is proper to risk life, is not liberty the noblest and the most necessary? Your father would not think ill of me if I took pistol in hand upon the field of honor, and wagered my life to avenge some trifling slight to my personal honor. Such is the practice of our bucks and self-proclaimed gentlemen, and I hold it in disdain.

Dearest Ellen, I pledge to you that I am seldom so solemn, and would far rather write to you of other matters, the nature of which you may judge. You speak to me of my "politics," but I am not certain that I have any. My actions are guided by an instinct which I know to be virtuous. Even as I am drawn to you by an instinct which is the most powerful and virtuous of all.

The letter signed and folded, John joined his brother in the drawing room. The curtains were closed, and George was reading by a bright lamp. A fruit knife lay upon the low walnut table.

"It is very late," George said. "I thought you were in bed."

"I was writing," John said.

"Writing, indeed. A tiring occupation."

"Only a letter," John said. "To Ellen."

"Most tiring of all," George said. "Writing to a woman is sheer hell. Every sentence is a grenade which can explode in your face. They save the letters and then fling sentences from them at you."

"Not Ellen," John said. He sat down facing his brother, and stretched his legs toward the fire. "I lack your experience with women of the world."

"A pity, perhaps," George said. With the small, sharp-bladed knife he cut open a page. "Negotiations with a clever woman is splendid training for other matters. Politics, for example."

"Or warfare," John said. "To judge by your metaphors."

"Yes," George said. "Politics or war. Dangerous matters for the inexperienced."

"Dangerous indeed," John said.

"War or politics. Or rebellion. Rebellion is the most dangerous of all. Conspiracies, informers, hot-headed companions. Exciting enough, no doubt, but a most unhealthy kind of excitement."

"Less unhealthy than courting the wife of a duelist," John said. "I have heard of such a thing."

"At least the prize was certain and specific," George said.

George pushed his spectacles high on his pale forehead.

"And was it worth the danger?"

"Oh yes," George said. "Indeed it was. I think of her often. A sweet-tempered creature and magnificent in bed. Clever as well. A damned clever woman."

"You set great store by cleverness, do you not, George? I was oppressed by that when I was younger. I am not clever at all."

"But you are, John. You are. You are just clever enough to find your way into serious trouble."

John sighed. "Very well, then. Shall we talk about it?"

"Not tonight. Time enough later on. Later on we shall have a long talk about it. It is late at night. A bad time for a quarrel."

In unsteady firelight, the portrait of a tall, straight-backed man in foreign dress faced the brothers, unnoticed.

Castlebar, August 15

"God save all here," MacCarthy said in a loud voice as he entered the alehouse.

"God save you kindly," the man of the house said, and several of the men sitting by the fireplace. Two British soldiers in their coats of lobster red looked at him incuriously and then turned away. MacCarthy put down his copper, and carried a tankard of porter the length of the room to join a bald, middle-aged man.

"You are far from Killala, Owen MacCarthy."

"I am so, Sean MacKenna, and it was to visit you that I came here. I called in at the shop, and Brid said that I would find you here. 'Tis well for you that you have both a shop and a school and can spend your evenings in the taverns."

"You are no stranger to them yourself," MacKenna said, and made room for him on the low bench.

"Ach, sure, the taverns in Killala are dirty old places. 'Tis a fine lively town you have here, with the marks of civilization upon it." The English word, *civilization*, rang like a copper on the floor of his Irish.

"You are welcome always in Castlebar," MacKenna said. His voice, like his words, was grave and quiet.

"There are a fair number of those lads in the town," MacCarthy said, jerking his head toward the two soldiers.

MacKenna nodded. "There are two regiments of them. The Prince of Wales's Fencibles one is called, and I cannot remember the other. They are in barracks now, but 'tis said that they may be put at free quarters among the people. How would you like to share your bed with those two?"

"No better than they would themselves. It is a hard life soldiers have, sent off from home to live among Irishmen and wild Indians."

"They were in the fighting in Wexford," MacKenna said, "and now they have been sent here. Strange creatures they are, and their English is very poor."

"Likely enough they will have business to attend to in Mayo." It was a question.

MacKenna answered it. "I wonder, Owen, would you not teach the Latin tongue to the Whiteboys of Killala, that they might spend their nights peacefully upon Caesar and Virgil?"

"Much use those boors would have for the Latin tongue," MacCarthy said. He buried his nose in the tankard.

"There are Whiteboys in Castlebar now," MacKenna said, "and in townlands to the east, but they have done nothing. They put a placard up on the gate of the Protestant church. The drawing of a coffin and some misspelled words."

"The Whiteboy touch," MacCarthy said. "There are lads calling themselves Whiteboys in Foxford and Swin-

138

ford as well. A carter gave me a lift from Ballina to here, and he was full of talk about them."

"What had he to say?"

"That the people in Mayo intend to rise up, as the people in Wexford did, and in the north. But he was a foolish, toothless old fellow. Words dribbled out of him and you wouldn't believe a tenth of them."

MacKenna shook his head. "You can hear the same talk in Castlebar. We are all to be set free and have fine great farms. And all the old stuff from the prophecies of Columkille and the chapbooks that prophecy men used hawk at the fairs. There has been a child with four thumbs born to a miller in Sligo, and that is a certain sign. You have never in your life heard such foolish talk."

"I have indeed," MacCarthy said. "It is a thriving trade in this country."

He picked up their empty tankards and brought them to the counter. The two red soldiers were to his left side, talking quietly together. They seemed distant from the room, encased within their coarse, vivid cloth.

"I am thinking of moving on, Sean," he said to MacKenna when he returned with fresh porter.

MacKenna nodded. " 'Tis a hard disagreeable town that you are in, beside that ugly sea."

"Ach, 'tis not that. 'Tis frightened I am. When the Whiteboys were starting up, I wrote their proclamation for them, and they are after me now for a second one. It will not be long before some little bastard of an informer whispers my name to the magistrates."

"Holy Mother of God, Owen! What possessed you to do such a mad thing? They do not care who they hang."

" 'Tis done," MacCarthy said. "Whyever I did it, 'tis done. Much choice I had. Ach, I am not sorry I did it. 'Tis a terrible life the people have, and well you know it. I declare to God, Sean, things happen in this kingdom without rhyme or reason. Some fellows hough a landlord's cattle in Killala, and a few weeks later the people in Castlebar are talking about babies with four thumbs."

"More than thumbs and babies," MacKenna said. "They say that the French are on the sea and that the army of the Gael will rise up."

Scraps from old songs floated, soundless, in the close air. He saw once again the forest of black pikes against a gray horizon.

"Perhaps they are," he said. "How would they know about a thing like that in Mayo or in Sligo?"

"You have the right of it, Owen. You should clear out of Mayo. 'Tis sorry I would be to see you at the assizes."

"I came here to see you for that reason. I thought you might know of some town to the east that had need of a master."

MacKenna drank and then nodded. "I will write tonight to Pat Dunphy in Longford. He always has great knowledge of such matters. Sure what town is there would not be proud to have Owen MacCarthy the poet for master?"

MacCarthy smiled. "More town than one, Sean. And well you know it."

"Not at all," MacKenna said quickly. "Not at all. There is not a town but should be proud. You are a fine poet, and your name is honored by men who have never seen you."

"Especially by those. I can be a great disappointment. But I keep a good school. To be sure, people must make a few allowances, but I am worth it."

"You should keep to this," MacKenna said, raising his porter. " 'Tis the hard drop makes the trouble. I will write to Pat Dunphy tonight, and to Andrew MacGennis in Mullingar. 'Tis the rich counties have the most need of masters."

"That would be kindness," MacCarthy said. "In a week or two if you have heard nothing, I may drift down that way and take my chances."

"You should, Owen. 'Tis sorry I will be to lose your company, but you should go."

"What if they are indeed upon the sea, Sean? When I was a young lad in Kerry with my head full of other men's poetry, I used walk along the cliffs, and look out across the water. They would be great, tall-masted ships, I thought, moving silently, with sails spread like clouds."

"Ach, the English could be pulled low and the French raised high, and you and I would still teach school. The cabins would be as small, and the spuds as hard. You should have more sense."

" 'Tis easy for the two of us to talk," MacCarthy said. "Yourself with the shops and the school both, and myself with the poetry. What of the thousands of poor fellows who never know will they be driven off their bit of land,

140

and who never see the inside of this alehouse because they lack the single copper to put down?"

"Sure the French wouldn't bring with them barrels of coppers for the spalpeens of Connaught. It is murder and bloodshed they would bring. I have no use for that."

"I know," MacCarthy said. "I know that."

MacKenna nodded toward the two soldiers. "Those fellows with their drums and guns and guns and drums. They mean less than a butterfly in the air or a branch in flower or a girl's voice raised in song."

"It is my sorrow that I will no longer be seeing you, Sean. There are few enough that a man can discuss serious matters with."

"What of that woman of yours, above in Killala?"

MacCarthy shrugged. "I will leave her as I found her, a small-waisted young widow who would tempt a saint."

"About some things, Owen MacCarthy, you are a careless and a selfish man."

" 'Tis far different for you, Sean, wed to a fine woman like Brid and with a fine lively little son. But that would not suit me at all. Look at poor MacGrath down in Clare, with every drop of poetry in him drained out by that shrew of a wife, and his two sons running wild. A frightful example."

"A poor example, Owen, but I would do better to save my breath. It makes little sense to preach sermons at a poet."

MacCarthy put his two hands on MacKenna's soft, sloping shoulders. "I will be back again next week and we will make a night of it."

"This next week," MacKenna said. "Brid can make us a meal, and if you have any new verses composed, it would be an honor to hear them."

"I may," MacCarthy said. "There is an image stuck in my mind, but I have no words for it. It gives me no peace. 'Tis a queer backward way of making verse, like going through a door arse first. Kiss Brid for me tonight, and give Timothy my hug."

As he was leaving, one of the soldiers called out to him. "Oy there, Paddy."

MacCarthy turned toward him. "Oy there, red soldier," he said in English.

"Where are all the pretty girls our sergeant said we would find here?"

"All locked away," MacCarthy said, "with the fathers

and husbands trembling at the thought of handsome soldiers in Castlebar."

"Would you not know where we could find a stray one or two?"

"You should ask someone else," MacCarthy said. "I am not a Castlebar man. Where are you from yourselves?"

"I am a London man, and my mate here is from Derbyshire."

"You are far from home."

MacCarthy dug in his pocket, and, having made certain that he had the coppers, bought porter for the three of them. Surprised and pleased, the Londoner raised his tankard toward MacCarthy in salutation.

"You are quiet people here, Paddy. And a great bloody relief it is. The fencibles have been in Wexford dealing with the croppies."

"Croppies?" MacCarthy asked, puzzled.

"Rebels," the Londoner said. "Down there, they call rebels 'croppies.' Haven't you heard the song, 'Croppies Lie Down'?"

"Lie down they did," MacCarthy said.

The Londoner nodded. "We slaughtered them at a place called Vinegar Hill. Fair sickened me, it did. Ordinary blokes like you and me. Spoke English too, most of them."

"Bloody savages," the man from Derbyshire said. "Rebels to the King."

He was thickset and slow of speech. The Londoner was short and wiry.

"A couple of thousand of them there were," the Londoner said, "all hunted up onto the slopes of Vinegar Hill, with nothing but pikes in their hands. We smashed them with cannon fire and musket fire, and then went after them with naked steel. And what was it all in aid of, Paddy? Can you answer me that?"

MacCarthy shook his head.

"Pikes and scythes against artillery," the Londoner said. "A great bloody way to commit suicide. Was that the plan, Paddy?"

The porter was darker than bog water.

"It makes no sense," the Londoner said patiently. "I might want to fight my mate here, but I know he could break me in two."

"Bloody fucking rebels," the man from Derbyshire said.

"Are you a fucking rebel yourself?" he asked MacCarthy.

MacCarthy nodded toward him, and said to the Londoner, "Why don't you tell your mate there to put down the drink I bought him and see can he break me in two?"

"There you are now," the Londoner said, with a delighted grin. His teeth were small and uneven. "There's your Paddy for you, always ready for a fight or a frolic. My mate don't mean nothing. Your drink was one too much for him. Don't you go messing with soldiers of the King, Paddy. There's too many of us. Look here, chum." He drained off his porter, and signaled to the tavernkeeper. "We're over here for your own good, see, not ours. You don't want a pack of Frenchies here, sleeping with your women, and you don't want mobs of bogtrotters waving pikes in your faces and insulting the King. Your King as well as ours. We've got no stomach for putting the steel to poor lads, but it's our job, see? After Vinegar Hill, I saw mates sitting on the grass puking their guts out."

"What about your friend there?" MacCarthy asked. "Did he have a weak stomach?" But he took the fresh porter from the Londoner.

"You fucking Papist whore," the man from Derbyshire said. "You are looking for trouble."

"I had not far to look. I didn't ask for your company. Your friend gave me a civil shout and I joined him. I bought you a drink and you put your big ham of a fist around it without thinking twice. You come into a tavern of quiet men and then call them out of their names. Fucking whore yourself, you great stupid turnip."

The Derbyshire man put down his porter, but the Londoner stepped quickly between them.

"You should have more sense, Joe. They're like children, laughing with you one minute, and shouting at you the next." He twisted his head to look at MacCarthy. "You'd better get back to digging your spuds, Paddy, before I lose my own temper."

MacCarthy felt Sean MacKenna's hand on his shoulder. He shook it off. "I have no quarrel with you," he said to the Londoner, "and I would drink with you any night most willingly. You are a most generous man to have come all this way to help us. Did you know that, Sean? This man came all the way from London to take care of us. First he took care of us in Wexford, and now he has come to Mayo."

143

The Londoner grinned again, at MacKenna now. "They have had a bit too much, the two of them."

" 'Tis well known to be the cause of most quarrels," MacKenna said.

The Derbyshire man was humming. "I can't remember any of the words," he said. "It's called 'Croppies Lie Down.' "

"A people gifted in music," MacCarthy said.

"Put a stopper in it, Paddy," the Londoner said.

Outside the tavern, MacKenna again put his hand on MacCarthy. "I will tell you something about yourself, Owen. You think a poet leads a charmed life. You can lie in bed when you should be in your school, and drink yourself into a stupor, and ruin a woman's name, and pick quarrels wherever you choose. You can be an ugly reckless man at times, and a danger to your friends."

MacCarthy nodded absently. "I was frightened then, Sean. The red uniforms frightened me."

"They served their purpose then," MacKenna said.

MacCarthy walked shivering from tavern to tavern, looking for the farmer who had promised him a ride back to Killala. Lobsterback soldiers wandered up the barracks in threes and fours, arms wound around the necks of comrades. Boiled lobsters, red dragons of the sea, walking upright, high helmets like briny plates of shell. At the top of Castlebar High Street, in the yard formed by the joining of barracks and gaol, three bodies hung from the gibbet, tar-coated and weighted down with chains. Worst of all deaths. A lure for the flies of summer. MacCarthy crossed himself and hurried past them.

6

Killala, August 15

Massive and intricate, Glenthorne Castle soared upward from the plain of Mayo. The central block was intransigent, declaring a solidity which would outlast bogland and pasture. Long arcs of Ionic colonnades swept outward to join wings which balanced each other with a delicate and subtle harmony. In its lightness and strength, it reproved the barbarism by which it was surrounded, the raw landscape of brown mountain and rank green fields. In sunlight, the cut stone mellowed from white to the palest of honeys.

Their vast estates in Mayo, together with the earldom of Tyrawley, had come to the Glenthornes in recognition of great though clandestine services accomplished by the third Lord Glenthorne in 1688 for the then Prince of Orange. He accompanied William to Ireland, commanding a regiment on foot. Several paintings of the battle of the Boyne display him beside his Prince, a furled map in one hand, the other outflung toward the river, saturnine face unsmiling beneath full wig, a statesman and courtier performing with competence a military task. He did not visit Mayo on that occasion; like William, he found Ireland damp and disagreeable. His son and his grandson never visited Ireland at all. They were content to enjoy their Tyrawley title and the revenues of the Tyrawley estate.

The estate was formed by the expropriation of the lands of the largest of the Mayo Jacobites, Catholic and Protestant, and a number of lesser gentry who had practiced the delusory prudence of neutrality. Its affairs were managed by agents, who had for their dwelling the fortified farmhouse of one of the expropriated Jacobites. The first two were part men of business and part centurions, for in the decades which followed the Williamite settlement, Mayo was a lawless wilderness. The Jacobite captains and colonels, returning to their confiscated acres, mustered their former tenants into gangs of reivers and highwaymen. For a time they persuaded themselves that they were maintaining the battle which in fact had ended at Limerick, but they degenerated at last into common brigands. One by one they were hunted down by packs of horsemen and hounds, and their heads fixed to the palings of the gaol in Castlebar, then a new, raw town. Those who survived turned peasant, accepting with gratitude a few acres of tillage upon their former lands.

Lacking the civilizing influence of a great resident landlord, Tyrawley became a barony dominated by squireens as wild as faction fighters, hellfire duelists, coarse, valorous, and brutal. Some farmed no land at all, but rather rented it, up to the very doors of their houses, to the drifting peasant multitudes. Others en-

145

trusted their land for renting to middlemen and submid-dlemen, thus spawning a class whose attachment to the land was more casual even than their own. Isolated even from the influences of decadence, they gave over their days to gambling and cockfighting, the abduction of heiresses and the despoilment of peasant girls.

The Glenthorne agents, managers of estates so wide and so populous as to make difficult an accurate account of either cattle or peasants, remitted quarterly revenues to a Dublin bank for transmission to England, played their parts in the social and political life of the county, and spent several months of each year in England. The handful of travelers and wandering writers who visited North Mayo over the decades invariably fell upon the Glenthorne estates as a superb instance of the evils of absenteeism. Were the Lords Glenthorne to reside in Mayo, it was argued, the lands would be better man-aged, the methods of agriculture and husbandry would improve steadily, a benign influence would be exerted upon the lawless and turbulent peasantry, the neighbor-ing squires would be given a center toward which they might look for instruction in decorum and sobriety. But the impossibility of this ideal was admitted. Glenthorne was both an English and an Irish peer, and his first duty was to his estate in Cheshire. The deplorable effects of absenteeism, therefore, were deemed part and parcel of those implacable circumstances which had set upon Ire-land the seal of a hopeless existence.

In 1759, however, the Lord Glenthorne who was father to the present earl determined to move to Mayo. The eccentricity which had secretly been nurturing itself among the Glenthornes had burst into flower in this pear-shaped original, a lover of boys and sopranos and a patron of the arts. His decision was regarded by his Cheshire neighbors as but a further instance of his frivolousness, and for once a welcome one. He had spent years flitting about the courts of Italy, trailed by portraitists, black-amoor pages in turbans, and a pathetic, hard-visaged wife. Now, so Cheshire reasoned, he had snapped the final cords and was adrift toward space. But in his mind's eye he had seen a mansion, immense, exquisite, and chaste, and placed within a natural setting of wild and picturesque grandeur.

Eight years were devoted to the creation of Glenthorne Castle. Niebuhr, the great German architect, took up residence with the agent and spent six months pacing the ground upon which he proposed to build. He held to his eye a glass of his own design, which composed into an optical symmetry the hills and bogland and estuary at which he peered. Then stonesmasons were imported from England and ornamental plasterers from Italy. Lord Glenthorne in London, with Niebuhr's detailed drawings in hand, commissioned from Parisian craftsmen the furnishings and hangings for each of the many rooms. Some thirty families were cleared from the land upon which were laid down the gardens and walks, the artificial lake and waterfall, and the two mazes.

And yet it was not the triumph for which he had hoped. It did not eclipse, in magnificence or folly, the other great mansions of the day, Santry Court near Dublin, Castletown and Carton in Kildare, Russborough in Wicklow, and a score of others. Its unique advantage was its remote location, for most of its rivals lay within the civilized pale. Travelers through the wastes of Mayo responded to it with awe and stupefaction. That it existed for the sole pleasure of one person added to its air of the uncanny, the ensorcelled. For the Countess, after enduring Mayo for eight months, returned to England, taking with her their son, the present lord. Her husband was left alone, to take his solitary walks through his ordered labyrinths, tripping, near-sighted, over his peacocks. For Glenthorne, too, the pleasures of his palace faded after a few years, and he departed for Italy to rejoin a former lover, now a youthful bishop.

The effect of Glenthorne Castle upon his hundreds of peasants was complex and profound. Song and legend had told them of their own majestic, vanquished princes and chieftains. Beyond those, more ancient still, were the kings and heroes of the sagas, and, beyond even those, rose up gigantic wraiths, the gods of the old religion, dwelling within the wealth and splendor of light itself. But Glenthorne Castle suggested to them an absolute power of existence such as no O'Neill or O'Connor had ever possessed. It was an image by which their imaginations grasped historical and political actuality. Alien and enigmatic, the absent Big Lord had at last revealed his limitless and capricious will. Of the Big Lord himself, nothing at first was known save his high walls and colonnades, his lakes and waterfall, but these sufficed. The brief years of his residence in Mayo had endowed him with the characteristics of a legendary being, exotic and remote. What in Cheshire had been judged the eccentricities of an effeminate aristocrat seemed to Mayo eyes the manners of a splendid, grotesque sovereign. Few enough saw him, but the servants carried tales.

The Big Lord now was his son, and he too remained invisible. A quiet man, evangelical in his religion and Whiggish in his politics, he divided his year between Cheshire and London. He entertained but two deep passions, a detestation of the African slave trade and a hatred of his father's memory. That Glenthorne Castle was a wonder to behold he did not doubt, but he chose not to look upon it. It had been the crowning folly of his father's life, a sybaritic life wasted upon fripperies and base sins. In nightmares he beheld it with horrid clarity, like a scene from *Vathek*, blanched towers soaring upward, naked serfs crouching by the iron gates. The very word *Irish* was repellent to him. When he heard himself described as "an Irish landlord" he was torn between embarrassment and incredulity. He chastised himself as a nabob, drawing his wealth not from brown Hindoo or black African, but from the white slaves of a neighboring island. The thought was unbearable.

The Glenthorne estates, he determined, should at least have the benefit of a wise and prudent stewardship. Toward that end, and after careful reflection and inquiry, he selected as his agent Andrew Creighton, Glasgow born but Cambridge educated. One wing of Glenthorne Castle was made into a residence for Creighton and his family, and he was given a salary suitable to his attainments. He also received two percent of the annual revenues of the estate. Lord Glenthorne's only instruction to him was that he should take as his model the good steward in the New Testament. It was his task to manage the lands and goods which had been entrusted to him, to look to the well-being of the peasants and the livestock, and to deal with all men in a candid and forthright manner. Glenthorne had chosen well, for Creighton found in the sprawling, chaotic lands a challenge both to his skill and to his conscience.

His first task was to determine the exact extent and condition of the estates, the terms upon which small portions of it had been leased away, the complex network of document, claim, and custom by which the lands had been stitched across the county. As he had anticipated, this carried him into a series of lawsuits with the smaller landlords, but all of them were settled to his satisfaction. He had next to take a census of the human and animal population, and this was no simple task, for his predecessor had fallen into the slovenly ways of the countryside. For some forty years, the remote boglands and mountain wastes had harbored squatters. His predecessor, following local custom, had exacted no rent from these wretches. Creighton was uncertain as to how they should be dealt with, but he wished at least to know their numbers and their names. He spent weeks on this task, a pale, blunt-featured man dressed in sober brown, riding broken mountain paths. Behind him rode an Irish-speaking bailiff. The squatters fled at the sound of hoofbeats, entire families scrambling up the sides of high hills.

When the task was completed, he transferred the information to a large and intricately coded map which he hung in his office. This had once been the smaller of the castle's two music rooms, and the map faced a painting of the Judgment of Paris, executed in eighteenth-century court dress, after the manner of Watteau, by one of Lord Glenthorne's protégés. For the first year of his stewardship, Creighton spent most of his time in this office, acquiring a mastery over the details of the estate as they presently existed. This task, however, was but the preliminary to a far larger one, that of bringing order out of chaos.

Creighton was a student of the new science of scientific husbandry and agriculture. He had published pamphlets on the subject and was in correspondence with the other authorities. It was for this reason, joined to his zeal and his probity of character, that Glenthorne had chosen him. His intention was to determine in what manner the estates might ideally be ordered, and then to impose that order upon them. It was clear to him from the first that the total population upon the estates was too large, and the size of the existing farms too small, for efficient farming. Moreover, little serious thought had been given to the question of what crops were best suited to particular sections. Elsewhere in Ireland, methods of reclaiming bogland were being explored, but not in Mayo.

Creighton knew that the plow of his logic was driving through hills and athwart the contours, and this troubled him deeply, for he was a humane man. Firmer and more rational principles could be imposed upon Glenthorne

149

lands by a stroke of his pen. His signature on an order of ejectment could sweep from their holdings scores of those peasants who hailed him as he rode past them, whose music floated to him, faintly, from the cabins. But this he could not quite bring himself to do, and he was troubled by his reluctance. It prevented him from performing his duty and discharging his pledge to make the estate into a model of sober and profitable industry. The life of this barbarous society offended his morals: the peasants seemed fond of filth, were lazy, drank to excess, were sunk in their superstitions, gabbled in an uncouth tongue, quarreled and fought at fairs. And yet they were a community in which men and women loved and worked, married and had children; they were bound to each and to their soil. To root them up would be a monstrous cruelty.

He temporized. He conducted business on the usual lines, but with a zeal and an intelligence lacking in his predecessors. During each year of his stewardship, the revenues rose slightly. Yet these revenues were never more than a quarter of what the lands might have been made to yield, and, knowing this, he knew that he sinned, that he served his master badly. Once a year he submitted to Lord Glenthorne an account of that stewardship, detailed and meticulously honest, together with a candid admission of his various humane inefficiencies. Glenthorne responded, each year, in a letter of civil and bland generalities, sympathetic and faintly unctuous. Creighton had hoped, each year, for a rebuke from England, a peremptory insistence that the land be forced to yield its maximum profit. The demand was never made. In time, Creighton came to regard the Big Lord much as the peasants did, as a distant, inscrutable creature whose ways were fathomless. His torn conscience gave him no peace.

In the privacy of his office he began to indulge a fantasy which claimed a greater hold upon him than he realized. It began simply enough. In a blank ledger book he began a kind of memoir describing the estates as they would flourish under proper scientific management. He went on from there to make sketches of the model farms he longed to create, the chapels and schoolhouses he hoped to build. Then, one October evening, he cleared the long library table which ran almost the length of one wall, and began the construction of the ideal Glenthorne estate in miniature, developing, over the four years of evenings which he devoted to the task, considerable ingenuity and a certain small degree of artistry. It was a plaything of the imagination, a different kind of sin. Now, the task completed, he could loom over it like Gulliver, admiring lakes made of bits of mirror.

Creighton had no notion of the figure he cut, riding the roads with dropped reins, spectacles perched on the end of his snub nose, making endless notes in a leather memorandum book, dismounting to crumble a few grains of corn between his fingers or to order the deepening of a trench. To the small landlords he was a canting, sanctimonious tradesman who had been miscast in a gentleman's role. To the peasants, he was a bloodless petty tyrant, harsh-voiced and unsmiling. The census with which he had begun his career set the seal upon his reputation. "I will have the name of every one of them," he was rumored to have said, "whether he lives in cabin, barn, or stable." When MacCarthy, newly come to Killala, heard the story he dubbed him "King Herod." And "Herod" Creighton he remained, to gentleman and peasant alike. Most would have laughed at his troubled conscience, had they known of it.

The one man in whom he could confide was Broome. He visited him one evening, to pour out his troubled feelings, and was astonished when Broome, leaping from his chair, seized his hand and wrung it. For Broome, too, felt that he had failed in his duty, that Killala had rejected his ministry. The two men sat together, late into the night, each describing the hopes which he had brought to Mayo, the agony with which he had watched them sink into the bogs. They met often after that, and at last became conspirators, for when Creighton once announced his intention to quit the agency, Broome dissuaded him, reminding him of the fate which might thereafter befall the peasants. And yet Creighton's consciousness of guilt continued to press upon him, the guilt of a man who has betrayed his talents.

On the night of August 15 he was working late in the office. He heard distant noises, a confusion of voices, the shattering of glass, and two sharp cracks like musket explosions. He leaped up, but from the office windows saw only blackness. He lit a lantern and carried it into the hall, paused to shout downstairs to the servants, and then

151

ran outside. Far off, a glow appeared in two windows of the unused right wing which balanced his. He raced along one wide sweep of colonnade, through an arcade, and then down the other colonnade. His lantern illuminated Roman statues set into niches, sculpted togas and upflung arms. As he ran, he shouted. The drapery behind two tall, shattered windows was aflame. By its light, he saw figures tumbling out the door. They paused, at some distance from the house, and yelled at him. He could not understand them. Then they disappeared into the darkness. He heard footsteps behind him, and turned to see Hendricks, the house steward, carrying a pistol.

The entrance door had been smashed in. They went inside together, cautiously, and then, walking more rapidly, went first down a long corridor and then one at a right angle to it, coming at last to an open door beyond which flames glowed. Working together, they ripped down the drapery and smothered the fire. Then they looked around them. They were in the gun room.

The previous Lord Glenthorne had been neither a sportsman nor a soldier, but he had been an avid collector of firearms, as of much else. These had lined two walls in their glass cases, muskets and fowling pieces, cases of dueling pistols of exquisite French and Swiss design. The cases had been broken open and emptied of their contents. Nothing remained save an assortment of weapons of grotesque shape and exotic origins, antique arquebuses and muskets of Turkish or Oriental shape. These lay strewn on the parquetry.

Hendricks lighted candles. The air was acrid. As they walked from case to case, still without speaking, servants came into the room, timid and curious. Shaking his head, too dazed and startled to grasp what he was seeing, Creighton gave Hendricks orders to post a guard, and to have the wreckage attended to. Then he left the room, and walked back toward his own quarters.

Once again the lantern jogged past marble togas, heads of white marble. The night air was chill. He paused. Mayo stretched away from him into the night. Close at hand, the cold, empty faces of ancient consuls and generals. Creighton shivered, caught between puzzlement and annoyance.

"This is a very bad business, sir," Hendricks said, walking toward him.

"It is worse than that," Creighton said.

"Until now," Hendricks said, "the ruffians felt no need for firearms. Putting together the muskets and the blunderbusses and the pistols, they must have made off with more than seventy."

"Yes," Creighton said. "I never counted them. Who would think to count them, outlandish weapons from the Lord knows where."

"There is something else that troubles me, sir. They went down two corridors of doors without touching a one of them." Hendricks was a merchant's younger son. He had the harsh accent of East Sligo. A faint burr reminded Creighton of his own Glasgow. "They knew what they wanted and they knew where to find it. And what that likely means is that they were told by a servant or a former servant. This is very different from the kind of deviltry they have been up to."

They stood without speaking, their faces illuminated by the flickering lantern. Then Creighton said, "We are isolated here, Hendricks. Tomorrow we must gather a score or so of the most reliable peasants and organize a patrol."

"The reliable peasants, Mr. Creighton. I wonder which ones you have in mind."

"I know," Creighton said. The fingers of his free hand pulled at his cheek.

Two of the young maids came tripping up to them, dancing with an excitement that masked itself as concern.

"Please, sir. They left a tree standing against the hall door of the main block."

It was a pine, some nine feet in height, and it stood propped against the door, as though it had left its plantation, strolled along the garden paths, and then climbed the steep flight of steps. It seemed tired now, and stood as if waiting to be let in. It was as alien, as meaningless as the Roman statues. Absently, Creighton fingered its needles.

"It must be a mark they leave," Hendricks said. "Whiteboys and Defenders are always up to that kind of nonsense."

Creighton shook his head. "Perhaps. Have one of the groundsmen attend to it in the morning. And make a note of it. I planted those firs as a windbrake."

"What else could it be if not Whiteboys?" Hendricks said.

"The tree of liberty," Creighton said. "They were everywhere in Wexford and Carlow during the insurrec-

153

tion, and now they have been appearing in Longford."

"What in God's name is a tree of liberty?" Hendricks said. " 'Tis Whiteboy nonsense."

"They carried boughs from fir trees into battle with them," Creighton said. He turned away, and carefully climbed down the stairs. "It is the emblem of the United Irishmen."

Hendricks was behind him. "You cannot be serious, sir. There are no United Men in Mayo."

"So we thought," Creighton said. "We must organize a patrol. I will ride into Killala tomorrow and talk with Cooper. But we cannot depend on those fellows. We must be prepared to defend ourselves."

"There are no weapons left on the estate but a few fowling pieces," Hendricks said. "And those heathen muskets or whatever they are. Sure matters were bad enough before in Mayo."

"It is late," Creighton said. "There is nothing to be done tonight."

"Here, sir," Hendricks said, handing him the pistol. "You had best keep this with you. It is primed."

Creighton took it awkwardly. "It is seldom indeed that I have had occasion to hold one of these," he said.

"Or myself," Hendricks said. "Good night, sir."

After they parted, Hendricks made his way back to the gun room. His fingers, in his jacket pocket, were curled around the butt of a short-barreled pistol designed by Wodgson of London. The butt was of ebony wood with inlays of silver filigree. He had long admired it, and when he entered the gun room with the other United Men he went straight to its cabinet and smashed the glass. He had barely had time to circle back in order to join Creighton.

In his office, Creighton reread a letter which he had received several days before, but had set aside as unimportant.

Westport House

My dear Mr. Creighton:

As you represent one of the largest estates in the county, I send to you information which I am sending also to Capt. Sam'l Cooper and several other gentlemen in North Mayo.

154

There is evidence in Castlebar, Westport, Killala, Swinford, and elsewhere that the United Irishmen have begun to make themselves busy here. Accordingly, I have petitioned Lord Cornwallis to post troops here for our protection. He has responded with admirable promptness. Two regiments, the Prince of Wales's Fencibles and the 67th Regiment of Foot are being sent to Castlebar. The 67th will remain in Castlebar, to strengthen the garrison there. The fencibles, Col. Montague commanding, will proceed to Ballina for the better protection of your baronies. The Tyrawley Yeomanry will place themselves under his orders. Connaught has also for its protection, of course, General Trench at Galway City, but his chief duty is the defense of this coastline against the threatened invasion.

Of the present strength in Mayo of the United Irishmen I have as yet formed no opinion, nor have I knowledge of such alliance as they may have entered into with the local Whiteboys and banditti. Should circumstances require it, I will not hesitate to recommend to Lord Cornwallis that Mayo be placed under martial law. I would however be much saddened by such a necessity. We have flattered ourselves that this remote county would be spared the harsh measures which have been imposed elsewhere. The peasantry of Mayo is ignorant and turbulent, but has thus far been remarkable for loyalty to the Crown. No section of the island, however, is these days so tranquil as to be immune to the blandishments of rebels and traitors. But the military always find it necessary to govern with a heavy hand, and many who are guiltless of any wrongdoing would doubtless suffer side by side with miscreants. Our first requirement is accurate intelligence, and I therefore ask that you inform me posthaste of any United Irish activity which comes to your attention.

We are living through a time of great danger to the realm. The embers of rebellion are still glowing in Wexford and Antrim. Wide stretches of the midlands, reaching to the borders of Connaught, await but the kindling spark. But I am determined that Mayo shall remain loyal, even should this require a gallows at every crossroads and a triangle and a whipping post in every village.

155

Should you have occasion to write to Lord Glenthorne, pray assure him that the safety of his estates is not absent from my thoughts.

Yours faithfully,
Dennis Browne

It seemed to Creighton an unsatisfactory letter, at once businesslike and ranting, moderate and furious. Mayo lay safely within the political control of Dennis Browne; who would be reluctant to surrender it, even for a time, to the army. At the same time, Browne was frightened and angry. On the few occasions when Creighton and Browne had met, the Scotsman had been unimpressed: Browne was a jovial man with a gift for blarney, and a face of smiles belied by dark eyes as hard as stones. He thrived upon the very untidiness and disorder which had driven Creighton to despair, a witty, cajoling man who knew every secret in the county, a man who could drink others under the table and then rise steady to his feet. And he was also, Creighton knew, as shrewd and as unsentimental as an Edinburgh writer to the signet. A mess of Irish contradictions. Creighton hated contradictions.

Politicians and soldiers played insignificant parts in Creighton's imagination, and rebels were creatures so lurid as to lack all substance. The grand designs of the Society of United Irishmen, so far as they could be grasped from the two pamphlets he had read, amounted to little more than a romantic fantasy. The language of the pamphlets, with their references to "the rights of man," "the obligations of patriotism," "the nobility of sacrifice," seemed to him claptrap. What did "the rights of man" matter to ragged peasants who stood in far greater need of a fair rent, a secure hold upon their little farms, guidance toward habits of thrift, cleanliness, sobriety? The tree of liberty, indeed! What meaning could the word *liberty* have for these poor wretches? Perhaps they imagined that all rents were to be swept away, that they would be allowed forever to enjoy their idleness and superstition, their existence an endless succession of fairdays. They had now a bitter lesson to learn, if the troops conducted themselves in Mayo as they had in Wexford and Antrim, placed at free quarters among the people, whipping and torturing suspected rebels, burning out cabins, rampaging drunk and licentious through the villages. Those who

156

whispered words like *liberty* in the ears of this unfortunate people were worse than wicked, they were irrational and foolish.

Creighton stood before his huge map, emblem and chart of his sprawling petty kingdom. It was speckled with dots of ink, as though flyblown, and each dot a cabin: more than four hundred of them. Fresh dots were added each month, and yet the map was never either accurate or complete. Peasants were forever subdividing their tiny holdings so that a son might marry, build his cabin, dig his lazybed of potatoes. Families from other baronies would drift onto mountain wastes and squat there for months until he became aware of their existence. If the soil proved too thin or too acid, they would drift away again. Riding his boundaries, he would discover their abandoned cabin, stone and mud, low windowless lumps. A drifting tide of people, anonymous and unknowable.

Facing the map, the Judgment of Paris: a nude hero, globed prize cupped in languorous hand; three nude goddesses, strands of long, golden hair falling over breasts, wisps of cloth floating across their loins. Surrounding them, draped in elegance across the lawn, courtiers, musicians, dressed in elaborate silks and velvets.

Creighton stared at the painting, as he had done many times before, puzzled and suspicious. What world of hedonism and soft pleasures nourished such a painting, what sensuous oils?

The Concorde, at sea, August 16

It was a clear night, with a strong easterly wind. Bartholemew Teeling walked along the deck toward the captain's cabin, elbowing his way past soldiers in undress who had come topside to drink in the air. They leaned against the gunwales, or squatted, talking quietly, with practiced indifference, bare-chested or with opened shirts. They were seasoned troops. Here, at least, the Ministry of War had not skimped. Many, like Teeling himself, had served on the Rhine; others had crossed the Alps with Buonaparte. Most of them were shorter than Teeling, their bodies wiry and dark. Teeling was a tall, solemn man, flat-chested. Even aboard ship, he walked with a springing gait.

Closely following the *Concorde*, the other frigates sailed

with full canvas, the *Franchise*, with forty guns, like the *Concorde*, and the *Medée*, with thirty-eight. The Irish coast was still a long way off, and the next dip of the horizon might bring into view the sails of Admiral Warren's squadron. Three armies, dispatched from different ports at different times, must contrive to slip past that squadron. This army of Humbert's, the smallest of the three, had been the first to sail. A miniature army, infantry of the line, two companies of grenadiers, a squadron of the Third Regiment of Chasseurs—some 1,060 men and 70 officers. They carried with them light artillery, and 5,500 stands of arms for distribution to the Irish rebels.

What most concerned Teeling, goading him beneath his sober Ulster exterior, was the urgency of getting those firelocks to Henry Joy MacCracken, the commander of rebel forces in the north. News of the insurrection had reached La Rochelle with agonizing slowness. On August 3, the day before Humbert set sail, Paris forwarded some English newspapers. MacCracken had risen up with an army of six thousand, Catholics and Presbyterians marching together in what one paper described as an unnatural and hellish combination. Antrim and Down had been captured, but a large English army was moving north along the Dublin road. But the papers were two months old. By now, MacCracken might have been defeated, or he might have fallen back into the glens of Antrim.

Those hills and steep glens were more real to Teeling than the oak planks beneath his feet or the creaking canvas or the dark waves of the Atlantic. He did not know what circumstances had forced MacCracken into rebellion without proper arms and without help from France. Perhaps he had despaired of that help. Six thousand men armed with pikes, peasants and small farmers and tradesmen from the snug townlands of Ulster. In his imagination, Teeling saw them trudging along roads which wound past valley and moorland, pikes sloped against the dull grays and duns of their jackets. An army moved against them, jackets of fiery red against the rich green of the Meath pastureland, the metallic jangle of cavalry, the snouts of cannon.

Two months ago or more, Ulster had risen in rebellion; now three ships of Frenchmen were sailing to its assistance. In those months, battles had been fought and won or fought and lost, towns taken and retaken, men piked or shot down or blown apart. His principles had forced him into flight from Ireland, into service as a French officer, had placed him among the quarreling idealists and rogues of the Irish colony in Paris. Now they carried him to an insurrection which might already have been crushed. He wore his principles like chains of iron looped across his shoulders, without pride, a burden.

In Admiral Savary's cabin he sat down beside Fontaine and Sarrizen, his fellow officers, and waited for Humbert. A map of Ireland was spread across the table, turned toward Humbert's empty chair. If Teeling reached out his hand toward the map, he could touch Antrim and Donegal. Beyond Donegal stretched the bare expanse of Mayo, white save for a chain of carets which signified mountains.

Humbert entered the cabin without fuss and seated himself, a tall, muscular man in a rumpled uniform. He unbuckled his belt, rubbed his stomach, and smiled at his officers.

"So, gentlemen. Savary informs me that the southern tip of Ireland lies to our right some fifty miles distant. If the weather holds good and Warren stays away from us, we will make a wide circle around the island and in less than a week we will see the shores of Ulster." His speech, as even Teeling knew, was rough and provincial. When the Revolution broke out, Humbert had been a small trader in the skins of goats and rabbits, tramping from village to village in the Vosges, a peasant's son who could read a bit and was able to write out his name, Jean-Joseph Humbert. Now, at thirty-one, he was one of the most celebrated of French generals. Teeling would once have thought his an exemplary career, a proof that energy and intelligence are rewarded in a revolutionary society. Two years in the France of the Directory had tempered his illusions.

By 1793, already a *maréchal de camp*, Humbert had distinguished himself by his audacity and skill, only to find his advancement blocked. For a time thereafter, he served as one of the government's numerous informers, ferreting out disloyalty among his fellow soldiers. The Revolution, a benevolent cyclone, had lifted him up from obscurity and meaningless toil; by defending it against internal enemies, he defended himself. Later, in Paris, assigned to the Directory itself for unspecified tasks, he gained the confidence of ministers and generals, and flattered their wives and mistresses. He frequented the opera

159

and the theater, large, puzzled eyes studying incomprehensible dramas, flutes and trumpets a jumble of sounds echoing in his ears. He spent his afternoons with a clerk, improving his ability to read and write. He had two ambitions, to advance himself and to defend the Revolution: he could not separate them.

At last he received his command, and was posted to the Vendée to assist Hoche in the suppression of the Chouans. It was there that he earned his fame. A master of improvisation and of irregular warfare, he moved where conventional generals never ventured, through forests and marshlands. He fought as the Chouans themselves fought, by sudden marches and night raids, by ambuscades and swift retreats. He was as ruthless as the Chouans and as fearless. He respected them. They too were peasants, simple men and brave fighters. But he was savage toward the returned *émigrés* who led them. When a nobleman was captured, Humbert hanged him without trial. He attacked and defeated the army of English and royalists at Quiberon, and then, four days later, stormed their garrison at Penthièvre. His politics were simple, and in their simplicity terrifying to moderates, who once had called him, in contempt, *marchand des peaux de lapin*. The Revolution must be preserved and extended, and England, the chief enemy of the Revolution, must be destroyed. In a time of trimmers and opportunists, Humbert was a Jacobin.

"Now, gentlemen," he said. "It is important that you should know under what orders we have set sail, and what instructions we have been given by the Directory. We constitute one of the three elements of the army of Ireland. We are to disembark on the coast of Ulster, establish a position there, and distribute arms to our Irish allies. When General Hardy's army arrives, we shall march to meet him, and shall place ourselves under his orders. He has been given latitude in his use of this combined force. He may move it to the support of the rebel army in Ulster, or he may attack in a different direction. What is essential is that he must have victories. Our army is a minute one, and his is not large. The true army of Ireland is its third element, the nine thousand men under General Kilmaine. And it will not move unless we demonstrate that we can hold a position and win victories."

"If General Hardy succeeds in reaching Ireland,"

Sarrizen said. "We do not even know if he has set sail from Brest."

"I am coming to that, Colonel Sarrizen. Have a little patience. You will learn in time that fighting battles is only a part of a soldier's task. He must first scheme to be allowed to fight them. There would be no army of Ireland at all, if it were not for the persistence of a few Frenchmen like myself and a few Irishmen like Colonel Teeling here, and his friend, Colonel Wolfe Tone. The Directory is only interested in General Buonaparte's Egyptian adventure. But they are willing—not eager, mind you, only willing—to venture a few francs on Ireland, like a cautious gambler making a side wager. Hardy and myself, we are the little wager. But if we succeed, they will plunge. They will put on the board those nine thousand men that Kilmaine had to scheme and bluster to keep away from the sands of Egypt."

"We are only a gamble, then," Fontaine said. "A small wager. That is not a comfortable thought."

Humbert, leaning back in his chair, rubbed his hands again across his stomach. He had the eyes of a cat, quick and wary, trapped within a pale, heavy face.

"A cautious gambler is likely to be a miserly one. It is a certain way to lose. As you know, we were both delayed. Hardy at Brest and ourselves at Rochefort. Supplies did not arrive, the shipments of firelocks did not arrive, we received no money with which to pay the troops. There was inefficiency perhaps. Or perhaps there were those who did not wish success for the army of Ireland. Is that possible, do you think?"

Fontaine and Sarrizen looked neither at Humbert nor at each other. Sarrizen stared intently at the map.

"That is sensible of you, gentlemen. Stay away from politics. If there was to be an invasion of Ireland, it was up to me to act. The paymaster at Rochefort was so kind as to advance me forty-seven thousand francs without a formal order from Paris. Certain friends in the army of the Rhine have lent me supplies. Even our artillery has been borrowed. I obtained the firelocks by asserting an authority which I do not in fact possess. Most important of all, I was under strict orders not to sail in advance of Hardy. I have disobeyed that order."

The lamp above the table creaked gently with the motion of the ship.

Humbert waited for their comment. "You think that I

161

have been wicked? So will the Directory. Very wicked. If I fail. But if I can hold, you will be astonished at how swiftly Hardy and Kilmaine will be sent out after me." He turned toward Teeling. "That, Colonel, if you will pardon my bluntness, is why I chose you as my *aide de camp,* and not my old companion Wolfe Tone. It is because I need a man like Wolfe Tone to stay beside Hardy, to urge him on, a man as unscrupulous as myself. You Irish, if you will forgive me for saying so, you Irish have only begun this business of revolution. You are like the fine liberal gentlemen who began our revolution in France. Revolution is a nasty, conniving trade. Wolfe Tone understands that. He has great natural talent for it. Well, gentlemen? I have no intention that you should sit there, silent and prudent. Speak up."

"I intend to, General," Sarrizen said. "You propose to land one thousand men on an island which contains, how many British troops?"

"Many more." Humbert shrugged. "British regulars, militia, and the locals . . . what are they called, Teeling?"

"The yeomanry."

"I think, then," Sarrizen said, "that you have thrown us away."

"You are wrong," Humbert said. "As you will discover. We are a thousand men who have been sent to join a people in rebellion against their oppressors. They are Chouans, like my old opponents in the Vendée. There are special ways to fight that kind of war, and I know them better than any soldier in Europe. Two days after we have landed, every one of those five thousand firelocks will be in the hands of an Irishman. And they will know how to use them, will they not, Teeling?"

Teeling smiled. "I doubt that. But they can be taught."

"Exactly," Humbert said. "Ignorant men. Men kept in ignorance by their oppressors. But they can be taught."

Sarrizen, olive skin, black, close-curled hair, traced the table edge with his forefinger. "We land, then, General. We establish a position, we distribute the weapons to the rebels, we wait for General Hardy. Is that all?"

"If the opportunity offers itself," Humbert said, "I do not intend to wait. I will take the offensive. With any luck at all, I will have an army of six thousand at least under my command."

Teeling said, "Do not misunderstand me, General. But I would remind you of the assurances which Tone obtained from the Directory. The battle is to be waged by the army of the Irish Republic. The French soldiers are to serve as their auxiliaries."

Humbert smiled and lifted his hands. "Certainly, Colonel. If such an army still exists. If this friend of yours who commands in the north—"

"MacCracken," Teeling said.

"—if he is still in the field, my force will work with him. But if the peasants must be recruited, taught to fight, taught, as you suggest, even how to use their weapons, then I will place them under my command."

"That is not Tone's understanding," Teeling said. "The Directory—"

"The Directory is in Paris," Humbert said. "We shall be in the field. And you are yourself a French officer, I must remind you, Colonel Teeling. So is Tone. You will take my orders. And so will every man to whom I issue a weapon. Naturally, the Irish will have their own leaders. We have come to liberate them, after all."

"That was our understanding," Teeling said.

"There is no need for any misunderstanding," Humbert said. "There is only need for common sense. We have the same purpose, to drive the English oppressors out of Ireland. And we shall choose the best way to do it."

"If you take the offensive before Hardy arrives," Sarrizen said, "you will again be exceeding your orders, General."

"What? What is this, gentlemen?" Humbert said, spreading out his hands, palms up. "Objections from an Irishman on one side of me, and from Frenchmen on the other side. I must be a very wicked man indeed."

He smiled, and winked broadly. *Marchand des peaux de lapin,* Teeling thought. For a moment, he was able to imagine Humbert trading his skins, leaning across tavern table to strike his bargain.

"Not objections, General," Sarrizen said quickly. "But I would like to have matters clear in my mind. You have told us yourself that we are instructed to await General Hardy's arrival."

"And so we shall, Colonel. So we shall. But we shall keep ourselves busy. We shall be ready to exploit opportunities. Orders must be interpreted in the light of circumstances. Except, of course, for such orders as I give to you."

"If you will forgive the impertinence, General Humbert," Sarrizen began, but Fontaine interrupted him.

"We are at your orders, General, of course. What may go on between yourself and the Directory is no business of ours."

"Nothing 'goes on,'" Humbert said. "Nothing improper, that is. It is true that certain events have disturbed me greatly. A short while ago, there was a formidable army assembled on the coast for the invasion of England. Now it is a shell. The men and the munitions and the supplies have all been drained away to serve General Buonaparte's Egyptian expedition. I have the greatest respect for General Buonaparte, as every soldier must. But he will make out of Egypt a catastrophe for France. The Revolution has but one enemy, England. And the place to strike England is close to her home. It was not simple slovenliness and ineptness which kept Hardy and myself without money or supplies. France has enemies within her own borders. The Revolution has always had such enemies. The guillotine could not fall fast enough to lop off all their heads."

"But surely you would not call General Buonaparte an enemy of the Revolution," Sarrizen said softly.

"Have I said that?" Humbert asked sharply. "He is a brilliant soldier of France. We have had our share of them. Hoche was as fine a soldier as we have had, and Hoche preached night and day that the British Isles must be attacked. I was with him two years ago in Bantry Bay, and so was Teeling's friend Wolfe Tone. If Hoche had landed—"

"If," Sarrizen said, and smiled, to take the edge from the word.

"These are deep waters for a colonel of infantry," Fontaine said. "I keep my mouth shut and I leave politics to the politicians."

"This is a wise policy," Humbert said. "And you will die a colonel. Unlike General Buonaparte."

"Fortune favors him," Sarrizen said. "Fortune and the Directory."

"It all depends," Humbert said. "The man who conquered Ireland could be a match for the man who did not conquer Egypt."

"That would be General Hardy, would it not?" Sarrizen asked.

Humbert smiled.

Teeling looked down at the neglected map. The ragged edge of Europe. Mists, bogs, rocky fields. What had it ever mattered, save as a pawn? An island whose natives were mutinous, and might muster to a flag and a drum roll. Of what concern to these Frenchmen was Mac-Cracken in his Antrim glen, brigand chieftain with his cluster of pikemen? Humbert had a larger map, one which stretched from Paris to Vienna And Buonaparte had the largest map of all, sweeping across the Mediterranean to Egypt, and then eastward to the plains of India.

He asked Humbert's permission to retire, and went out on deck. The Atlantic air, with its savor of salt, carried him to Cushendall on the Antrim coast. A boy, he had stood there once with his father, looking out across the water to the Mull of Kintyre, so vivid in the pellucid air that they could make out the green of mountain meadows.

Kilcummin, August 17

West of Killala, near Kilcummin on the Rathlackan road, a shebeen. Not a proper tavern at all, but the long double cabin of a widow named Doolin. Herdsmen used it, and some of the poor cottiers who lived near Downpatrick Head. MacCarthy had been there once before, and that visit had taken the edge from his thirst. Scrawny hens running loose and the floor slippery with potato peelings. Worse now. Smell of rain-soaked frieze and tobacco. Music: a fiddler in one corner, fat, his eyes mild and sightless, milky pupils turned upward.

Unknown faces, grave and self-contained, but with a disturbing look, like Nephin men. They turned toward him as he stood in the doorway, and the sound of voices died.

"Owen!" Ferdy O'Donnell shouted, and moved through the men to take him by the arm. "It is my friend Owen MacCarthy," he said in a loud voice. "The Killala schoolmaster." There was a pause, but then first one man and then another raised his hand to his shapeless hat.

"God save all here," MacCarthy said. He said in English, to O'Donnell, "They need saving by the look of them."

"You are welcome, Owen," O'Donnell said. "Come over to the fire and dry out a little."

165

"Maire said that I would find you here."

"What took you out on this dirty night?"

"I took a notion to see how you were doing, yourself and Maire."

"Here," O'Donnell said. "Sit down here where it is warm and get this inside you."

Acrid smoke from the fire of sweet-smelling turf. A lament. He knew the tune: a lament for some O'Connor or other. Smoke and music twisted themselves together in his mind. The men had begun to talk again, but quietly.

"Did she tell you why I am here?" O'Donnell asked.

MacCarthy shook his head.

"The people in Kilcummin asked would I come here and speak with the Rathlackan people. I am the leader, like, in Kilcummin."

"The leader?"

"I have joined, Owen, and so has many another in Kilcummin. We took the oath from Corny O'Dowd."

"The oath of the United Irishmen, is it?"

"To be sure. Do you think that I would take the White-boy oath?"

"Sure why need you?" MacCarthy said easily. "A man has told me that Malachi Duggan himself is in the United Men now and all his fellows with him."

"It is a good oath," O'Donnell said. "It is to free the people of Ireland from tyranny and give liberty to us."

"With the help of Corny O'Dowd? Sure that man knows as much about liberty as he does about unicorns."

They were speaking in low voices and in English.

"True for you, Owen. And Malachi Duggan is a man for whom I have little use. But small indeed would be the army of the King of England were he to pick and choose, instead of sending out press-gangs to seize poor misfortunates on the roads or in alehouses. There are United Men spread all over Mayo now. All sorts and kinds of men."

"Ferdy, would you look around this room and tell me what these omadhauns know about liberty."

"There are two men here who know better than either of us. They were in the fighting in Wexford and they have been drifting here and there ever since. In many a village they have been given sup and shelter while they tell their story."

"Which ones are they?" MacCarthy asked, his interest quickening.

166

"Over against the wall there, with the half-dozen men around them. Poor fellows, they are hard-pressed for an audience in Rathlackan, for they have only the English."

One was a burly, short man with a mat of black hair, and the other a boy not more than sixteen, thin and narrow-waisted, with long hair the color of corn.

"You should talk to them, Owen, for it is a wonderful story they have to tell, and the dark lad tells it handsomely. There is stuff for a dozen poems in his story. He says that the United Men held not Wexford alone but Carlow as well, and parts of Wicklow, and they were in Kilkenny and Kildare, and there was fighting as far to the north as Meath. There was a battle on the Hill of Tara itself. Think of that if you will. Irishmen waging battle at Tara of the Kings. Tara is right there in Meath."

"So is the Boyne," MacCarthy said. "Only a few miles away."

But it was a poem, right enough. Modern men waging battle with pikes and muskets, with their feet standing upon the ancient slumbering kings of Ireland. Not for me.

The dark man had begun a song, quietly at first, but then lifting his harsh, heavy voice. The men fell silent in courtesy, even those who could not understand him.

"O I looked behind me and I looked before,
But the yeomanry cavalry was my downfall. . . ."

They were terrible things, those songs in English, "ballads" they were called, ill-made things fitted up to old tunes or to no tunes at all, with ugly jinglejangle words in them, that a man would have to wash from his mind with clear water before he set to shaping a true line of poetry. But at least the man had no pretensions. He sang casually, to illustrate his story. The two of them had been on the move since the battle of New Ross, and once the older man had been taken up for questioning. He turned around and pulled up his jacket: his back was an ugly crisscross of new wounds.

"They tied me up to a thing called a triangle," the man said, "and set to work on me."

"Holy Mary," one of the cottiers said in Irish. "His back has been ripped off him."

167

"It is just as it says in the song I learned. 'The yeoman cavalry was my downfall.' "

"Pagan beasts," someone said.

"O but we had our day first," the man said. "At Oulart Hill and at Tuberneering, the British fencibles they ran like deer. We were over the country like a flood. We killed lords and merchants and the soldiers of the English King."

"Have you ever heard the like of that, Owen Mac-Carthy?" O'Donnell asked, in Irish now.

"Some of the men who were duck hunters from Bargy and Shelmalier had their long-barreled guns, but the rest of us had pikes or whatever we could find. We went to the houses of the gentry and took away their guns and swords."

"That has been known to happen here," a man said, smiling to his friends. "Some men went to the castle of the Big Lord and took away all the guns."

"We met their regiments in open battle and we scattered them. The Ancient Britons, the North Cork Militia. The soldiers who had burned our homes and burned the chapel at Kilcormac."

"North Cork," MacCarthy said. "Those lads are all Papists with no words in their mouth but Irish."

"God preserve us," O'Donnell said. "Why were they fighting against the army of the Gael, and destroying homes and chapels?"

"Landlords for officers," MacCarthy said. "Protestants and lickspittle Catholic squireens. Sure what more agreeable task could you give an Irishman than to kill his own kind." Plowboys dressed up in their first good suit of clothes, white breeches and blue jacket.

"By God, we scattered them," the man said. "Those hoors from Cork."

"Yes," MacCarthy said, walking forward, "but how was the end of the game played out? The massed soldiers were brought out against you, the King's soldiers from England, and you were run to ground as a huntsman runs the red fox."

"It is true," the man said. "After New Ross we did not know where to turn. But that is not a shame upon us. It is a shame upon the other men of Ireland. We strangled upon the nets cast around us, while the other men of Ireland watched their ripening crops."

There was an awkward silence in the room.

"This is what happens," MacCarthy said. "This is what happens when you run with pikes against cannons and big guns."

But militia and yeomen had been met and slaughtered. What might have happened if all the men of Ireland had swarmed from their cabins, like a muddy river spilling over its banks? Draw back from that thought. Death. Bodies festering in the summer sun. "You, boy," MacCarthy said to the man's friend. "Do you know a better song than the one we heard? A song with some music to it?" He handed the boy his glass of whiskey.

"Yes," the boy said. He smiled: a fox. His face was a sharp triangle, and his body seemed made of coils. He planted his feet firmly, looked down into the glass, and then began, in a clear effortless tenor. He had a voice.

> " 'Twas early, early all in the spring
> The birds did whistle and sweetly sing
> Changing their notes from tree to tree
> And the song they sang was of Ireland free."

The words of the song moved upon a clear thread through the smoke and coarse smells of the cabin. Castlebar, talking easily with Sean MacKenna: liberty, a word. The boy sang, "My own dear father did me deny, and the name he gave me was the croppy boy." The Irish-speakers listened in grave silence, uncomprehending. The thread hung a moment in the air, after it had been spun out. The singer turned shyly to his drink. Wexford, a place distant as Tara.

"What is it about?" someone called.

"About a boy who was hanged," MacCarthy said. Worst of all deaths, the body writhing, breeches stained with shameful death, the face blackening. The songs never told you that. Macroom: Paddy Lynch dancing on air. And the song they sang was of Ireland free. "A croppy boy. For God's sake, is there no one in this cabin has a song with some life in it?"

Before he left, O'Donnell asked him to recite his lament for O'Sullivan Beare, but he refused. It was an intricate poem and it depended upon allusions, hints, the small gestures of remembered names. These poor cowherds, matted hair, breeches streaked with the dung of cattle, would be puzzled and embarrassed. As though a velvet-coated gentleman had flung himself into the room to call for punch.

The rain had begun again and then had ended during his hour in the cabin, but the air was still heavy, and the tall grasses were drenched.

Dublin, August 18

Malcolm Elliott arrived in Dublin on the morning mail coach, took a room in a Dawson Street hotel, and breakfasted there in the company of squires, middlemen, and a few English officers.

He had spent the night in Granard, to visit with Hans Dennistoun, a member of the provincial executive, and was encouraged by what he had heard. The United Irishmen were strong in the midlands; their organization had survived harassment and the arrest of several leaders. The county executives for Longford, Westmeath, and Cavan worked closely together. More remarkable than that, the strategy of the United Irishmen, an alliance of Protestant and Catholic, had been achieved. Dennistoun, the Longford commander, was a Protestant, an affable, large-bodied farmer with a quick, decisive intelligence. Michael Tuomy, his seconder, was a Catholic apothecary in Granard. At dinner, listening to their talk, Elliott could imagine himself back in Tom Emmet's Rathfarnham villa. Why had such urban notions taken root here, in this rich pastureland? The bulky farmer and the spare, bespectacled apothecary sat perched on the edge of their chairs, amicably arguing tactics, politics, principles, as though there had never been a rebellion crushed in Wexford, as though Catholics had not been dragooned and hanged, or Protestants butchered at Wexford bridge and burned alive at Scullabogue. They lacked Elliott's bitter, unspoken belief that they were committed to a cause hopeless and tainted. Perhaps they were right.

But the road southward to Dublin offered evidence at every mile that the island had witnessed one insurrection and was preparing for a second. Mullingar, the great cattle market of the midlands, was also a garrison: The troops now stationed there had spilled from the barracks. Their neat encampments were spread beyond the edge of town, in rolling meadows. Troops were on the move south of Kinnegad, slogging past the coach in double files, followed by bored young officers. Their accents, as they shouted cheerful obscenities at the coachman, were English. Perhaps they belonged to the supplementary regiments which Cornwallis had obtained from London. There was an empty gallows and a whipping post at Kilcock cross and a row of burned cabins in the village street. But Maynooth was quiet, its single street dominated by the massive estate walls of Carton, seat of the Duke of Leinster, Edward Fitzgerald's brother. Sentries were posted along the Royal Canal, at the outskirts of Dublin.

At breakfast, Elliott shared a table with an estate agent from Mallow, a witty, choleric man, who discoursed upon cattle, fox hunting, and politics between mouthfuls of mutton chops and slabs of thickly buttered bread. Cornwallis was being too bloody lenient toward the surrendered rebels of Antrim and Wexford, he said. What the country needed was a good stiff dose of Cromwell's ghost.

"No trouble with the people on my land," he said. "Treat them fair and they'll live as quiet as a parson. A pair of these United Irish vagabonds arrived to stir them up, and one of my tenants tipped me the wink. I had my bailiff hang them up by the heels from a gable end. No need to hang them properly. Arrested, tried, convicted, and sentence executed in twenty minutes. My tenants pelted them off the land with rocks and clods."

A rough-and-ready view of matters: the national grain. Elliott found him, on the whole, a pleasant companion and they spent an agreeable hour together.

After breakfast he strolled north, across the Liffey, to Dorset Street. It was a clear, brilliant morning, and the city of cool Portland stone and warm brick seduced his senses. At College Green he paused, where the curved masses of the Parliament House faced the austere, Palladian façade of Trinity College. What was that jingle about Parliament by Swift? Wolfe Tone was forever quoting it: "Half a bow shot from the College; all the world from wit and knowledge." Tone's mind was peppered and riddled by tags of poetry and song. "A soldier's a man, and life's but a span, Why then let a soldier drink." Somewhere in Shakespeare.

Dublin was the creation of Elliott's people and Tone's, Protestant and Anglo-Irish, descendants of the Elizabethan and Cromwellian and Williamite settlers. The river was flanked by the public buildings of that nation of Protestants, the Custom House with its intricacies of design.

171

the heavy, grandiloquent dome of the Four Courts. On the streets running off the river stood the town residences of the Protestant nobility and the houses of the Protestant merchants and solicitors and barristers. Elliott was pledged to the overthrow of their oligarchy, and yet he could not walk through the streets of Dublin unreminded of the extraordinary triumphs of his caste. They had inherited a maze of mean streets huddled about the Castle. By its side they had raised up this lovely and powerful assertion of their pride. "Why then let a soldier drink." Iago: Iago's song in *Othello*. Trust Tone to quote Iago.

He paused again at the wide bridge leading to Sackville Street, and leaned over the parapet. Below him, boats and barges creaked against their moorings. The wide brown Liffey seemed to be flowing toward him, although he knew it did not, from the distant center of Ireland, bearing lake water, twigs of distant trees, the stains of black turf. A skein of arteries, roads, rivers, canals, carried the wealth of Ireland to Dublin. There it stuck, a bit of it. The rest was shipped off to England.

The door in Dorset Street was opened by Oliver Waring, a young Protestant solicitor whom Elliott knew and trusted. In a small room upstairs Patrick O'Halloran, a pamphleteer and physician, and Jack Russell, a farmer from Kildare, were seated at a round table of dark olive wood.

Elliott looked around the room and smiled. "Is this the Directory?"

"Part of it," Waring said. "And you were lucky to find us here. We are moving to the Liberties."

Elliott sat down. "Well, you have my letter, I take it. You asked for an organization of some kind in Mayo and now you have it. There are several hundred men under local leaders who say they will come out if the French land. I cannot answer for their zeal, and I am uncertain as to my authority over them."

"There is no question but that the French will land," Waring said. "But there is no way of knowing when it will be, or where, or how many men."

"Or why," Elliott said. "If they had put five thousand men into Wexford or into the north, two months ago, they would have tipped the scale."

"But they did not," O'Halloran said. "Our task now is to wait for them to come, and then to bring out as many

172

men as we can. This has gone too far. We have no choice."

"No," Elliott said. "We have no choice."

"Look here," Waring said. "We have returns from more than twelve counties, and some of them are well organized. In Longford alone—"

"I know about Longford," Eliott said. "I spent the night with Hans Dennistoun."

"Then he must have told you about Westmeath and Cavan. And we can tell you about Waterford."

"Let me instead tell you about East Mayo. There are three or four hundred Whiteboys there who think they are spoiling for a fight. The men who will bring them out are squireens and faction fighters. A few estate agents and stewards. They have some guns they picked up by raiding gentlemen's houses."

"By your orders?" Jack Russell asked.

"No," Elliott said. "After the raids, I gave my approval to them. That should give you a sense of how matters stand. A man who served with the Austrians is drilling them at night, but I don't think he will have them trained in less than a century. The only man who has any authority over the Papist squireens is John Moore of Ballintubber, and Moore is exactly twenty-two. I doubt if anyone can control the Whiteboys."

"But they have been sworn," Russell said.

"Oh, yes. Every mother's son of them is now a member of the Society of United Irishmen. What they think that means, God knows."

O'Halloran laughed. "You are not the most cheerful of delegates, Mr. Elliott."

"I am not. We had a good chance in 'ninety-six, and a fair one this spring. We have none at all now, unless the French put in a very large force and do most of the fighting."

"Are you making a suggestion, Mr. Elliott?" O'Halloran asked.

"The north is smashed," Elliott said, "and Wexford is smashed. You are going to get local risings which the British can put down at their leisure. Hundreds, probably thousands of poor bewildered peasants and artisans are going to be blown apart by cannon and strung up from gable ends."

O'Halloran rubbed a palm across his eyes. "I have spent nights saying that to myself, Mr. Elliott. I declare to God I have. And I have also told myself that if there

173

is no rising now, there will be none for fifty years. This vile system under which all of us live will be fastened upon us forever and the key cast away into the sea."

Elliott turned to Waring. "And you?"

"I have a more sanguine nature, perhaps. Those local risings could be formidable indeed. If the French make a landing and we do not take advantage of it, we will be worse than fools. And most of the delegates are agreed upon that."

"They are at the moment," Elliott said. "When it comes to the sticking point, will they take up pikes and lead peasants against regular troops?"

"We know that you will," O'Halloran said gently. "And we must hope that they will. The Directory here cannot control events. We are ten or so men of no great ability, and no claim to leadership save that we have avoided arrest. We can urge the counties to act. Order them to, if you like, but it comes to the same thing. If there is a rising, it will be a peasant insurrection, and Dublin lawyers and physicians have little power to affect such matters. By the time the French land, we will most likely be in gaol with the other Dublin men."

"In gaol or in the Liberties," Russell said.

"It is much the same," O'Halloran said. "They lifted Fitzgerald in the Liberties."

"He was stagged," Waring said. "Stagged and then lifted. Someone sold him to Higgins and Higgins sold him to Cooke at the Castle."

"Selling each other like heifers at a fair," Elliott said in disgust. "How do you know that I won't sell you? I could turn Mayo over to Dennis Browne and my fortune would be made."

"Hardly," O'Halloran said. "Not at Castle prices. I think Fitzgerald went cheap."

"Was there ever a country that deserved liberty less," Elliott said. "Four men sitting around a table in Dublin. We should be on the stage of a theater."

"An unimpressive spectacle," O'Halloran said mildly. "But the boulder has been given a shove down the hill and nothing will stop it now. If I could stop it I would not."

A short man with deep-set eyes behind spectacles and a wide expressive mouth, he had entered politics as a moderate, a member of the Catholic Committee and

174

author of pamphlets on the penal laws. Now he was implacable.

"I am no different from yourselves," Elliott said. "A Dublin solicitor stranded in the wilds of Mayo. A careless landlord and a solicitor without clients."

"You lack patrons," O'Halloran said. "Perhaps Dennis Browne is your man." He smiled to take the offense from his words.

"No," Elliott said. "For whatever good I am, you may depend upon me."

"We know that," O'Halloran said.

Elliott stood up. "This is the most misfortunate land on the face of the globe. We are like gamblers, and this is the final throw of the dice. Perhaps what's needed are swaggering playactors like Tone."

O'Halloran saw him to the door.

"I regret, Mr. Elliott, that we did not become better acquainted in your Dublin years."

"Do you see any hope in this?" Elliott asked with vehemence. "Any at all?"

"Oh, yes," O'Halloran said. "Otherwise I would not be in it. We both know that—a man like myself comes to the Directory by default, so to speak. Fitzgerald is dead. Emmet and MacNevin and Bond are in prison. Some have turned tail. Some have become government informers. But events have a momentum of their own. The French will land. Parts of the countryside will rise up. And tomorrow night I will be in a hole in the Liberties, listening to some braggart tell me how he can hold the Wicklow hills and waiting for Major Sirr to break down the door."

Elliott gave him his harsh, barking laugh, a fox in thicket. "Like a figure in Plutarch," he said.

"A clumsy Hibernian counterfeit. I am a fair physician, you know; I have a knack for it. But in my middle years I have discovered my true talent. Do you know what my talent is? Political rhetoric. I discovered it when I was writing those pamphlets. Justice, equality, the rights of man—the words fairly flowed from my pen. 'Tis little I thought then of burning cabins or unarmed men cut down by cannon fire."

"It is a common failing these days," Elliott said. "Words have a splendor for us, and so we send them off into the world to do mischief. It began for me with words. Books, pamphlets, debates."

"The words are abroad now," O'Halloran said. "And battered beyond recognition."

"Have you ever been to Mayo?" Elliott asked suddenly.

"Nor anywhere near it. I am a Limerick man."

"It is not a land hospitable to ideas," Elliott said. "Strong feelings perhaps, but not ideas. The soil isn't right for them. Perhaps someday I can show it to you." Unspoken bonds of sympathy drew him to the small, stoical man. Flies, stuck in the amber of ruined hopes.

"Perhaps," O'Halloran said. "I have always wanted to see America, but Mayo would do."

Before he opened the door they shook hands formally. A light rain had begun to fall. A rattle of drums and shrill of fifes drew Elliott to Mountjoy Square. Three companies of an English regiment were on parade, standing at stolid attention as sergeants barked orders at them. Passersby, drawn like Elliott to the spectacle, lined three sides of the square. Elliott stood watching, his hat tilted to one side. A greasy sky covered them, pressing down on the handsome red brick, the scarlet uniforms. A boy, hurrying along the footpath, paused for a moment to admire the scarlet and the music, and then went away, whistling between his teeth: "Oh, the French are on the sea, says the *Sean Bhean Bhocht;* they'll be here without delay, says the *Sean Bhean Bhocht."* Words. Words set to an errand boy's tune. Elliott turned away, and walked back toward the river of turf stains and twigs.

Dublin, August 18

A Letter, Signed "JR," Addressed To Mr. Edward Cooke Undersecretary, Dublin Castle

The Directory moves tomorrow to an address in the Liberties which I do not yet know. I passed today in Dorset Street with O'Halloran and Waring, who dispatched letters by messenger to various county delegates. They received several visitors, among them Francis Keough of Carlow and Malcolm Elliott of Mayo.

Elliott avows that Mayo holds more than a thousand sworn United Irishmen, organized and armed. He is uncertain as to his authority over them, and names John Moore of Ballintubber, the younger brother of George

Moore. Of George Moore's radical sympathies there can be no question, but doubtless he is too sly to involve himself openly, entrusting that to his brother. Elliott is gloomy and half-hearted, but a perverted sense of honor holds him to the enterprise.

I beg to repeat that a most formidable organization exists throughout the country but most particularly in the midlands. It will rise up at word of a French landing, whether or not the Directory has been arrested. Several on the Directory, O'Halloran among them, are shrewd and able men. They would not scruple at assassination. I am running a most dreadful risk in the service of my country, and my neglect of my own affairs has placed me in most embarrassing circumstances. I must have a hundred pounds in hand by the first to meet the most pressing of my creditors, and I know not where to turn. It is for love of country that I act as I do, as well you know, and I hold in scorn those base informers who for profit betray their friends and associates. I am confident that His Majesty's ministers will not see me fall into ruin.

Killala, August 20

On the night of August 20, the Tyrawley Yeomanry conducted a raid for arms and treasonable material in the town of Killala. They nerved themselves first with several rounds of whiskey, for which they crowded into the Wolf Dog in full uniform, carrying muskets with fixed bayonets. They were not soldiers at all, by training or temperament, and they were frightened. Rumors were everywhere that the Papists were drilling by night with French muskets, and that a massacre was being planned, more hideous than that of 1641, when rebels skewered babies for sport and hurled their bodies into the flames. Dublin had at last sent a regiment to Ballina, but it was an English regiment, with no notion of what Papists were like, or what they were capable of. The tavernkeeper, a Papist, served them with wary affability, his ruddy face bland and smooth, but with deep-set blue eyes moving nervously. Cooper stood treat for the whiskeys, and then mustered them in the street outside Broome's church.

"Now then," he said. "There's many a poor Papist in Killala who is as loyal as you and me. You have just seen one there in the Wolf Dog, a hard-working publican. They

177

are decent poor buggers who ask nothing better from life than a bit of peace and quiet. I don't want to hear that they have been mistreated. What we are looking for is rebels against the Crown. There are muskets in some of those cabins and there are pikes in some of them. I want those men brought here, and I want their cabins burned. We will do that by God if we have to turn tonight into Saint John's Eve, with a bonfire on every hill. You know what Papists are and so do I, and we know what the Papists did in Wexford because they were let thrive. We are like a small fort in the middle of a forest, but by God we are Protestants, and that is what has always made the difference. We stood by the good old cause in Cromwell's day and we stood by it in King Billy's day, and God saw us safely through. And every Papist who can see a flame and read its meaning will know that we still stand by the old cause."

The yeomanry band, a drum and two fifes, purchased at Cooper's expense, struck up the "Lillibulero," and the buoyant, impudent tune beat against the weathered buildings in the narrow street. Cooper rested one hand on the hilt of his dress sword, and drew the other forward and back along the line of his jaw. He was as frightened as any of his men, and yet he saw no other choice. The Papists of Killala would have to learn that the Protestants of the barony were no mere collection of agents and shopkeepers. Glenthorne and the other great landlords could spend their days in England only because men like himself, small landlords like Gibson and harness-makers like Sergeant Tompkins, were willing to stand their land and hold it. Their great-grandfathers had won the land, fighting for it and spilling blood upon it. There were two races in the island, divided by an unending quarrel, and Protestants were outnumbered four to one. But they were favored by brains, determination, and, apparently, God. But it was a dreadful act to burn a man's cabin, even in summer. Cooper's anger mounted against the Papists, who had forced cruelty upon him.

Tompkins and his squad came first to the cabin of a man named Hogan, a surly, barrel-chested man with a bad reputation as a faction fighter. Tompkins pounded on the door with his fist, and then Andrew Bludsoe, lifting his boot, kicked it open. Tom Robinson lifted his lantern and they rushed in.

Hogan and his wife were lying in the low bed, and three of their children lay athwart it. Other forms, dimly perceived, lay on the straw at the far side of the room.

"This is a search in the King's name," Tompkins said. "For treasonable material."

Hogan's wife shrieked and one of the children, hearing her, began to wail. Hogan sat up, rubbing sleep from his face.

"What the hell is this? Who are you?"

"We are here lawfully, on the King's business," Tompkins said.

"Bob Tompkins?" Hogan said. "Is that you?" He put his feet on the floor.

"Stay where you are," Tompkins said.

Hogan's wife, who did not understand English, began to weep.

"Shut up, woman," Hogan said. "And keep that child of yours quiet. Will you get out of here, the lot of you, or will I take after you with a club."

Tompkins turned to his men. "Give the place a good search. Search the thatch. That's where they keep their pikes."

"Pikes, is it?" Hogan asked. "I'll give you pikes." He lunged to his feet, and one of the yeomen, in terror, squeezed the trigger of his musket. The ball buried itself in the thatch, and the sound echoed with frightening volume. Hogan and the yeomen were shocked into a silence which was broken by the renewed wailing of the child. Its mother grabbed it tight. "Go on," Hogan growled, sinking back to the bed. "Search away."

Because of an old grudge against Malachi Duggan, he had had nothing to do with the Whiteboys or the United Men, but the next day he walked up to Randall Mac-Donnell's, and took the oath in the stable yard.

Tompkins and his men ransacked a dozen other cabins, but they discovered neither pikes nor muskets. The hills to the north and the east glowed with dull orange fires.

"Those aren't all cabins," Tompkins said. "The crops have been set afire."

"Serves them well enough," Bludsoe said. "Croppies lie down."

They stood looking at each other, half ashamed that they hadn't had better luck, half relieved that they had no cause to burn men's cabins.

"I know a pike or a musket when I see it," Robinson

said. "But would someone be good enough to tell me what treasonable material means?"

"Hogan, perhaps," Tompkins said.

"Hogan's wife," Bludsoe said.

"Evidence or not," Robinson said, "I'll take my oath that Hogan is a rebel. He used be a great one at the faction fights, do you remember?"

"Don't be a bloody fool," Tompkins said. They had found nothing in the cabins but the usual Papist filth and litter, half-naked women with squalling children hanging to their knees, red-faced men shielding their eyes against the lantern's glare.

"Spreadeagle Hogan to his doorpost back there," Robinson said, "and give him a good lashing. Then let's hear what he has to say."

"No," Tompkins said sharply. "We will have none of that. I have no stomach for this business." Another fire flared to the east. First them and now us. The other way around, they would say. The pot was on the boil now, and no way to pull it from the fire. Glaring flames burned away the familiar landscape of his childhood.

Bludsoe took a flat bottle from the tail pocket of his uniform and passed it around. Tompkins took a deep swallow.

"It was little enough we saw of your bottle when Cooper was standing the rounds," Robinson said. "You mean hoor."

"Their crops burned away," Tompkins said, "and not a wisp of thatch above their heads. By God, that's hard."

"Treasonable thatch," Bludsoe said. " 'Tis little mercy they would show to us, Bob Tompkins, and well you know it."

One of the men began to sing. After the first verse, others joined in.

> "I am a true-born Protestant,
> And I love my God and King."

Tompkins put his arm around Bludsoe's shoulder and sang with them. Where were you, when all was said and done, if you didn't stand by your own.

MacCarthy spent a day and a night at the O'Donnell's, where he helped Maire at her work. The next night he woke up in an unfamiliar room, beside an unfamiliar girl who was in service to a Rathlackan gentleman, a cheerful, empty-headed girl who said she dragged him away from a dance where he was becoming quarrelsome. He had no recollection of the dance or of the quarrel, or indeed of the girl's body. He put his hand upon her breast and it was new to him, soft and restful. "You are all the same," she said carelessly. "When you are sober you are shy and when you are drunk you are useless." "Oh, God, I feel terrible," MacCarthy said, "my guts are rolling around inside me." "When you are drunk you are useless," she said again, "you are the same the lot of you." "Thanks be to God," MacCarthy said, "I thought I was losing my memory." But he spent his days talking to men in the fields, or watching the screaming seabirds at Downpatrick Head, or talking with the fishermen on the coast. The fishermen had great sport with him, answering his ignorant questions with great patience, and bearing with his banter.

He passed a long afternoon at Randall MacDonnell's, where he arrived just as Kate Cooper, an old convent friend of Grace MacDonnell's, was leaving after a visit.

"Make way," he said, as she climbed into her cart. "Make way for the daughter of Mick Mahony of the heavy whip."

"It is your own back would feel that whip, MacCarthy, if he could hear you making sport of me."

"No sport at all, Kate. None at all. By God, you are the handsomest woman in Mayo, with the full bloom of young womanhood on you."

"You have no call to be talking that way to a married woman. 'Tis little enough time you had for me when I was a young woman, standing with the others along a wall of my father's kichen, listening to you give out with your old songs."

"You are wrong there, Kate. I could not take my eyes from you, but I was tongue-tied from shyness and in terror of your father. You were a flame in shadows."

"It has been well said that a poet cannot put his eyes on a woman without trying his luck."

"Ach, Kate," he said, resting his hand on the cart. "The thoughts that you put into a man's mind are scandalous as you sit there on a fine August afternoon."

Half smiling, she returned his stare, holding the reins in one hand, and the other resting, a loose fist, upon her hip.

"Shy, is it? You are bold enough for any two men, MacCarthy, to stand making flirtatious conversation with a married gentlewoman in the middle of the day."

"Now, Kate. I stand here drinking in every feature of you, and you call it conversation. You have been ill schooled in the use of English."

"Whatever it is, it has gone on long enough," she said, and then broke suddenly into Irish. "You are a rogue, MacCarthy, and an ill-favored one at that."

"There now," he said. "There is proper speech from you. If we start out together in Irish, there is no telling where we will end. I am almost eloquent in Irish."

"So I have heard," she said. "You are a great success with servant girls and the sisters of small farmers."

"You are a fine hot-tempered woman, Kate Mahony," he said, "with a small waist and a fine bosom. You should be very pleased with yourself."

"Cooper," she said. "I am wife to Cooper."

He stood watching her, as the cart moved down the road. By God, but the little captain had a prize for himself there. A woman like that could not rake the ashes or pare her toenails or bring water to men laboring in the fields without provoking the passion of the beholder. For hours after talking with her, MacCarthy felt randy, and the phrases of unwritten love songs tumbled in his mind.

He had a long conversation with a boy who had attended his school for a year and called him "master." They sat on a tumbled-down wall and MacCarthy taught him nonsense rhymes and riddles. "What is it can walk on the water without any feet?" "Is it a ship, master?" "It is," MacCarthy said and looked toward the bay, hidden from them by the line of low hills. "You knew that one. You have been wasting your time at conundrums."

That same afternoon he met Brid McCafferty, the old woman who was credited with second sight. The powerful swordsmen of France were coming, she told him, and the deliverance of the Gael was at hand.

"Ach, now, mother. Don't try that old one on a poet. Sure the poets have been saying that for years, and where are the ships?" They walk on the water without any feet.

" 'Tis no idle story, Owen MacCarthy. I have seen it as clearly as I see you."

"There is much loose talk to be heard here and there that could give a person ideas," MacCarthy said.

She grinned at him. Toothless. A pale, wizened apple. "Ships with great white sails, and swords shining like the moon."

"Shining like my arse," MacCarthy said. "Leave the moon to poets, would you?"

She crowed with delight, and bobbed her head.

"Tell me," he said. "Did you ever happen to see poor Owen MacCarthy sitting at his leisure in a snug school in the midlands, with obedient scholars lined up before him, and a new set of clothes on his back?"

"You, you rogue? Sure you were born to be hanged. Did no one ever tell you that?"

"The grandmother did. She was always giving out with prophecies, like some others I could name."

"I have seen it in babbies," she said. "There is a red line they have across their throats. The line is waiting for the rope."

"You are a cheerful soul," he said. "Swords and ropes."

He fixed in his mind the countryside of moorland and bare mountain, the straggling villages and isolated cabins, the taverns crowded with farmers and cowherds, the sky, barefoot girls. Bird song. Stirrings in the trees and the tall grasses, the full, heavy crops beneath the blazing sun, the slow waters of the bay. Small roads curled and twisted themselves toward larger ones, lovely for idling. The air was heavy with odors. An immense sky stretched above him, a pale and flawless blue with thin traceries of cloud.

It was late on the evening of the twenty-first, walking toward Killala, that he encountered first one, then a second of the burned cabins, roofless and with blackened walls. He walked up the boreen to the second of them and circled it, running his hand along the rough wall. When he took his hand away, it was smeared with black. He shouted, but no one answered.

He learned what had happened when he reached Killala and went into the Wolf Dog.

"There is your Tyrawley Yeomanry for you," Taidgh Dempsey said, one of Duggan's pals. "There are more than thirty families now as homeless as any of the poor people who fled from the Orangemen in the north.'"

"Who can tell me about Judy Conlon's cabin?" Mac-Carthy asked. "Or the schoolhouse?"

"They did not go into the Acres at all," Dempsey said. "They divided themselves up into squads and they went here and there, but they did not go into the Acres.'"

"That goddamned fool Cooper," MacCarthy said. "That goddamned fool."

"You would not have thought him a fool if you had seen him standing out there at the head of his yeomanry with his uniform of red and his sword buckled on and they playing the 'Lillibulero.' "

MacCarthy ordered a whiskey and drank it off fast and then ordered a second. There would now be red war in Killala.

"You should have seen the Protestant minister," Dennis Clancy said, "with his breeches pulled over his nightshirt, grabbing Cooper by the arm and begging him to call back the squads. There were fires burning on the hills like beacons."

"Much good that would do," MacCarthy said. "But it was decent of him all the same."

"Ach, they are all the same, the Protestant hoors," Dempsey said. "And well you know it, Owen MacCarthy. Is it by chance that the yeomen are all Protestant? Who is it keeps us down but the Protestants, and they have no more business in this country than a pack of Russians."

" 'Tis little enough that you know about wild Russians," MacCarthy said. "But well you know about Mr. Falkiner, who let your rent run unpaid for two years when you had the wasting sickness."

"I have said a hundred times," Michael Binchy said. "There are good Protestants and there are bad Protes-tants." Wheezed out his insipid words, puffs of flatulence.

"We know them," Dempsey said. "Well we know them. Pay them back blow for blow."

Thirty taverns in as many villages. From Kerry to Mayo. Words that passed for wisdom going from one hand to the next, pennies worn smooth with use. Not like the fresh-minted coinage of poetry, gold and silver.

He was singing when he stumbled into the cabin and smashed into the table.

"What is that?" Judy Conlon asked, sitting up in bed. "What is it?"

"Poor Owen is sick. Poor Owen is sick, Judy."

184

"How can you sing and be sick, you fool? Where have you been? The Protestants have been rampaging through Killala, burning all before them, and murdering and looting. I declare to God I thought you were the yeomen."

"The evil whiskey that is sold in this place has poisoned me. I will not get well again. I have seen men poisoned by bad whiskey."

"And was the poison all in the one glass or did they make you take two?"

"Don't be unkind, Judy. Not when you see me in this pitiable condition."' He sat down and rested his head in his arms.

"What better could you expect when you have been gone for days and God knows where."

"No harmful place at all. I was rambling here and there. Respectable. Nodding to this one and nodding to that one." He looked at the papers on the table. "Owen MacCarthy beholds his poems."

She rose up, and put her hands on his shoulders. "Come now, and I will help you to bed."

When he was on his feet, he slipped a clumsy hand over her breast, but she struck it away.

"There will be none of that when you are this way. You will not make love to me with your mind wandering off to other women."

"No other," he said, falling across the bed and forgetting about her. "No other women. Poor sick Owen."

But in the morning he felt cheerful and clear-headed. He drank several cups of water, and then carried one outside. There was a slight haze, which the morning sun was burning off. Far distant, beyond the hills which sheltered the town from the Atlantic winds, stretched the gray expanse of the bay. Beyond the bay, at the horizon's edge, were three ships in full sail.

Thomas Treacy, whose house stood upon an eminence on the Ballycastle road, was at breakfast. Beside him, addressed in a bold, florid hand lay a letter to Ellen from John Moore of Ballintubber.

When Ellen burst in, she was carrying his brass spyglass.

"Father, come at once and look. Three great ships are moving into the bay."

Treacy carefully wiped his lips with his handkerchief. "Ellen, you are more than welcome to make use of that

185

glass, but before you take it from the office you should ask my permission. It is a costly instrument, not a plaything."

"Yes, Father. Come out onto the terrace."

They stood together on the terrace. Wind ruffled his hair.

"That is a sight well worth leaving breakfast for, Ellen. Those are warships. Frigates. They must be parts of Warren's squadron."

"But why should they trouble themselves with Killala?"

"Who can say? We have a bad wind here this morning. It may be a heavy one out at sea." He handed her the glass. "On the table, Ellen, you will discover a more tempting sight. A letter from John."

She turned to go, but he caught her arm. "I have deliberated before passing it to you. You have found a fine, spirited lad in John, and I should be happy for you both. But I am not, and you know why, I believe."

"John must go his own way, Father. I have no concern with his politics."

"I do. This barony has the makings of a treasonable conspiracy, and John brought it here. There are Blakes and O'Dowds and MacDonnells playing at rebellion, and John stirred them up. I do not propose to see our house linked with such matters."

"May I go now, Father?"

"Was there ever such a stubborn girl? There was. I had forgotten your mother. You are more MacBride than Treacy, girl."

"Father, I do not care tuppence either for rebels or for the King of England. I care for John, and there is an end to it. There seems no end to the nonsense men busy themselves with."

Treacy laughed. "You may be right. Go in to your letter."

The ships were well into the bay now and they had not dropped sail.

At ten in the morning, no one had a closer view of the three frigates than Andrew Creighton, who was studying them through the telescope which the previous Lord Glenthorne had imported from London. He knew that they were warships of some sort, and he could see that they were making not for Killala but for the small bay at Kilcummin, five miles to the west. There his nautical lore ended. But he could see that they were flying British naval colors, and like Treacy he assumed that they had somehow detached themselves from Admiral Warren's squadron. He swung round the telescope on its iron base to inspect the small bridge upon which his laborers had begun to work three weeks before.

George Moore dipped his pen into the inkwell and continued:

"By reason of the very ideas which had given it birth, the Revolution was destined to move beyond the borders of France. At first, because the monarchies of Europe were massed against it, the war seemed purely a defensive one. It appeared so even to the revolutionaries themselves: 'The Republic is in danger.' But in fact they had given arms and legs and brains to a new conception of man and of human possibilities. Such conceptions are rare in history, and they never halt at boundaries drawn arbitrarily upon a map. In Poland, in Ireland, in Germany, in the Low Countries, the Revolution made enemies and friends by the simple fact that it had occurred. It is rather the rule than the exception in human affairs that the principal actors in great events lack all knowledge of the true causes by which they are propelled."

By one in the afternoon, the ships had dropped anchor in Kilcummin Bay and were putting out boats. Cooper mustered his yeomen in the Palace street and prepared to welcome them. Dressed in ranks, the men did not make too bad an appearance, but he knew that English officers would view them with condescension. He smoothed his white waistcoat over his small, hard paunch, and rested his hand on the pommel of his sword. With desperation, he cudgeled his brain for appropriate words of greeting, formal and yet hearty.

At two, after he had had his lunch, Creighton returned to the telescope, and swung it toward the anchored ships. They were no longer flying the colors. A column of men, perhaps two hundred strong, was moving along the coast road toward Killala. In their van marched three men carrying banners which he could not identify. One of them was green. On one of the ships, a different set of colors was being slowly hauled aloft.

At just that moment, a horseman rode into Killala, and wheeled to a halt in front of Cooper.

The ships were now hidden from MacCarthy's view, but he could see the town, and the column moving toward it. Their uniforms were blue, and for some reason they all seemed small. Peasants were running behind them, some carrying pikes and scythes. A sudden gust of wind pulled at the banners, and one unfurled itself. A huge square of dark green, with a large device at its center. The column moved in silence, but shouts from the mob behind it floated up to him.

Judy Conlon put her hands on his arm. "Are they the soldiers from the ships?"

"Yes," MacCarthy said. "French soldiers. The French have landed."

A century's imagining, armada of white billowing sail, bronze cannon, uniforms of white and gilt, prancing war-steeds chestnut and ebony. Now they were here, three or four score of men in blue coats, marching along a dusty road in late August. Creatures of poetry, tossed casually upon a road.

The shouting, louder now, drew women from the other cabins. They stood by the doors, children pulling at them. In the fields to the left, a man stood motionless, a forearm flung across his brow. Two or three men were running toward the Acres.

"Are those the French?" the first man to reach Mac-Carthy asked. "What are they going to do? By God, I am going down into the town."

"You might wait a bit," MacCarthy said. "I think they will have a word to say to Cooper's yeomen."

"Few enough of them, by God," the man said.

"That is the first batch only," MacCarthy said. He turned away. "Go back into the cabin, Judy, and stay there like the good girl you are."

He walked away from the row of cabins, not toward Killala, but higher up the hill. Twenty minutes brought him halfway to the top, and he turned to look down. A breeze shook the field of nettles and tall grasses. Far below him, the columns of marching men were not a mile from the town. There was no order to the shouting, gesturing crowds behind them. Sunlight glinted from a pike. The small stones by his feet were larger than the men, and the bushes larger than the shops and cabins. He stood quietly, bent forward, hugging his elbows.

PART TWO

7

From *An Impartial Narrative of What Passed at Killala in the Summer of 1798,* by Arthur Vincent Broome

Should the present work find favor with the reader, it will not do so by reason of the careful account which I have sought to render of social life in a remote corner of western Ireland. My claim upon his attention derives, alas, from the mere fact that I was an unwilling witness to those most extraordinary and romantic occurrences, the French invasion of Ireland and the rebellion by the native Irish which followed in its wake. Several popular accounts of these transactions have been published, and in these I appear by name, as the Protestant clergyman whose house was requisitioned as the rebel headquarters. In one of these, I am credited with remarks and observations which ill accord either with my character or with my sacred calling. Additionally, the Mayo rising has received brief attention in general histories of the period, as a kind of Hibernian tailpiece. It is also the case, as I am informed, that these happenings have already passed, distorted and much exaggerated, into the lore of the peasantry, who cherish rude ballads of the battles waged and won, waged and lost. Within a few years' time, the common people, in accordance with the processes of primitive poetical imagination, as these have universally been observed, have transformed into creatures of legend such most imperfect men as Randall MacDonnell, Cornelius O'Dowd, Owen MacCarthy, and Ferdy O'Donnell. And by similar processes, so ordinary and insignificant a person as Captain Samuel Cooper has become for them a kind of Homeric clown, a foil for rebel heroism, and Dennis Browne has become an ogre whose name is used to frighten children. And yet no orderly and impartial narrative has been given of those happenings upon which much depended that was of consequence to two, perhaps to three, nations.

I have no wish to offer a chronicle of picturesque exploits, some Irish equivalent of the 'Forty-five in Scotland or the wars of the Fronde. Indeed I would be ill equipped to do so, for although the insurrection swept far beyond the borders of Mayo, I know only of what happened in my own parish, and for the most part what I could observe from the windows of my own house. Of the whole of that insurrection, I believe it to be the case that it was attended by much savagery and more terror, made bright by a few patches of heroism and generosity. My canvas, however, is a far smaller one. The flamboyant and alien intrusion of the French into my parish of Killala acted as a chemical agent which brought to the point of explosion all the volatile and unstable elements of our small society. That explosion, and its aftermath, is my only subject.

As my reader knows, I had witnessed, benumbed and all but silent, events which would in England be unimaginable, men sent up for trial upon the most flimsy of concocted and perjured evidence, the King's yeomen raking over a village like so many Turkish Janissaries, whipping men at their own doorposts, burning down houses and crops. But these measures were employed to suppress an undeniable conspiracy, which daily gained new adherents. Each side to that sordid and bloody contest but added fresh hatred and fear to the imaginings of the other. From the mutilation of cattle to the torture of men and at last to their murder were easy, senseless steps into savagery.

To such a pass had we come by the twenty-second day of August. I was on that afternoon busily at work in my small library, the very room in which I write the present lines, attending to my correspondence, with my dear wife Eliza seated in a comfortable chair to one side of me, as was her habit. A servant, bringing word to us that three British frigates had dropped anchor in Kilcummin Bay, set us both into commotion, for it seemed proper that we should stand ready to offer hospitality to the ships' officers. We were not alone in this thought, for there was presently a stir and bustle in the high street, which is at a right angle to my residence, and observable from the library window. I could therefore witness Captain Cooper at his task of mustering the Tyrawley Yeomanry, who made as decent a showing as could be expected.

191

It was at two o'clock that John Sillerton, a gauger, rode into the street with the fateful news that we had all been deceived, and that the ships were now flying the French colors. I did not myself observe him, for at Eliza's insistence I was then changing into my newer coat, but I did hear shouts, and shortly thereafter was a pounding at the door of the Palace, as my house is grandiloquently termed. By the time I had come downstairs, a number of shopkeepers and their wives had entered, who beseeched me to give them safety. It was in this manner that I learned that the French soldiers had arrived and were now marching upon Killala.

I brushed past them, silently entrusting them to Eliza's ministrations, and rushed outside in my shirt to talk with Captain Cooper, whom I discovered consulting with Mr. Gibson, a fellow magistrate. Most understandably, he waved me aside. He was to conduct himself upon this unhappy occasion in a manner much to his credit, very cool and resolute, if perhaps foolhardy. He had already dispatched a rider to warn the garrison at Ballina. His task now was to decide whether or not to fight, and if to fight, then where. Outside the town, on the Kilcummin road, was a small hill called Mullaghorn. He considered advancing to hold it, but instead decided to give battle within the town itself, whose narrow streets might more easily be held against a superior force. He placed himself in front of his men, and asked if they stood ready to fight the invader. Their response was a heartwarming affirmative. Accordingly, he drew them up in line of battle. They were now, I could not but reflect, addressing themselves to a task more appropriate than that of burning the homes of their fellow countrymen. My patriotic sentiments were kindled.

At this point, I felt that I could best occupy myself within the Palace, and accordingly I walked back across the cobbled courtyard and entered the house. I discovered, to my annoyance, that all of its occupants—servants, shopkeepers, wives—had climbed upstairs to my library, and were peering out the window, as though witnessing a peepshow. I reproved them, sent them all to the kitchen for safety's sake, and then took their place.

I had some time in which to collect my thoughts, and to marvel at what had befallen us. The long-dreaded invasion of Ireland by the soldiers of revolutionary and regicide France was at last taking place, and in the most unlikely corner of the entire island. My own parish in poor, barbarous Mayo had been seized by the scruff of the neck and flung into history. I knew not whether mere accident was at work, or some preconcerted plan of hideous intent, although in a dim manner I supposed that the French had somehow been summoned here by our local rebels. It soon became known, of course, that the three warships, making for Donegal, had been forced by the winds into our bay, but at the moment, all was mystery. The village street lay before me, quiet save for the sea wind, for the yeomen did not stir in their ranks. It was a sunny day. In a gush of sentimentality, the little shops seemed dear and precious to me, the provision merchant's and the saddle-maker's.

Presently I heard a great tumult and shouting, which I now know issued from the Kilcummin rabble who had attached themselves to the advancing soldiers. It grew steadily in volume, but then for a time remained constant, and for this reason: Colonel Sarrizen had halted his force outside the town, where he divided it, sending the lesser half on an encircling movement through the fields, so as to cut off retreat along the Ballina road. Soon enough, however, we heard a noise compounded of shouts, the thudding of feet, and the clatter of hooves, for already the French officers had commandeered horses. Cooper, who could look to the far end of the street, as I could not, gave an order to his men.

Then, suddenly, a blue-uniformed man, holding a pistol in his right hand, rode down the street at full tilt, as though he intended to charge the yeomen by himself, but his purpose was to see whether soldiers with muskets had been posted in the houses. He stared upward at the windows to left and right. For a moment we looked each other in the eye. This man, as I was presently to learn, was Bartholemew Teeling, a member of the Society of United Irishmen, but holding a commission as colonel in the French army. He was a tall, graceful man, and his face, even in this moment of excitement, was pale and quiet, almost meditative. Captain Cooper gave the order to fire upon him. Bob Williams, perhaps less dumbfounded than the rest of us, raised his musket to his shoulder, and Teeling, with what seemed the utmost calmness, pointed his pistol and shot him full in the chest. Then he rode off.

Poor Williams lay on the ground, clawing the air and

screaming most dreadfully. The men broke ranks and gathered around him, until Cooper, with his sword drawn, ordered them back. But now the French were upon us, running down the street and shouting. The yeomen opened fire, which they did not pause to return. Instead they charged with their bayonets, stabbing and clubbing. The yeomen, poor fellows, held their ground briefly, but then buckled and ran. This retreat, however, brought them headlong against the second French column, so that they were caught between two waves of those seasoned and indifferent butchers. Squeezed between them, the yeomen ran screaming and howling, many of them dropping their weapons, into my courtyard, where they beat upon the door, calling out for succor. They were most horrible screams, and I shall never forget them, like pigs when the blade is pressed against the throat bone.

Thus ended the battle of Killala, a contest, some ten minutes in duration, between sixty yeomen and about two hundred Frenchmen. Derisory accounts have been given of the event, which gave no consideration to the fact that civilians, mobilized to keep order in the barony, were pitted against hardened veterans. Of Captain Cooper's personal bravery, no praise is too high, for he stood his ground, sword drawn and pistol in hand, until overborne by grenadiers. One of these, a man a head taller than Cooper, swung the butt of his musket against Cooper's skull, and then, as Cooper lay motionless in the street, struck twice more. I was appalled less by the violence of all this than by its swiftness, and the workaday conduct of the French, as though they were herding cattle. When the yeomen, those who had not fallen, were driven into the courtyard, the battle ended.

The bestial mob which followed now came into view, coarse, frieze-clad peasants and fishermen, shouting imprecations in Irish, and shaking their makeshift weapons in a menacing manner. But riding slowly through them, straight down the middle of the street, came the general himself, Humbert, not asking them to move aside, taller even than Teeling, composed and smiling. From a great distance now floated to me the sound of military music, fifes, drums, and bugles. Below me in the street lay one man in blue and more than a dozen in scarlet, motionless or writhing. Muttering a brief but not perfunctory prayer, I hurried downstairs.

On my way, I encountered Eliza, whom I instructed to

return to our guests in the kitchen. The hall and the rooms which opened onto it were crowded with yeomen and French soldiers. The yeomen, I could understand, were being herded into the dining room, brusquely yet without cruelty. Several officers, of whom one was the man who had shot poor Williams, were standing together. I was walking toward them when their general entered, as matter-of-factly as though he had strolled into his own house. He commenced a rapid conversation with the officers, and I therefore hung back, standing rather foolishly in the midst of the bustle until at last he noticed me, and beckoned me toward him.

He turned to Colonel Teeling, instructing him to inquire if I was the owner of the house, but I interposed to assure him that I commanded fluent French and identifying myself as the clergyman of the parish. This occasioned some confusion, for the general at first assumed that I was a Roman Catholic priest. He then explained to me, in a most civil manner, that my house would serve as his headquarters, but that my household need feel no concern. For the present, he had many tasks at hand, securing the town and preparing its defenses, transporting supplies from Kilcummin, and seeing to the billeting of his men. He trusted, however, that by dinnertime we would find an opportunity to become better acquainted. Until then, I was to rest tranquil in the knowledge that he had landed to aid in the liberation of my country from its English oppressors.

I replied with such dignity as I could muster that I was myself an Englishman, and as for the country, already a dozen of its sons lay dead in the street. He looked at me with some surprise, and then, giving a typically Gallic shrug, turned away.

Bartholemew Teeling then drew me aside, and in low tones informed me that General Humbert, although a man of undoubted virtues both personal and military, had a settled prejudice against the English people, which I would be wise to bear in mind. I was astonished to discover this officer in French uniform speaking excellent English, although with the unpleasant accents of the north of Ireland. When I remarked upon this, he informed me that although he was Humbert's *aide de camp*, he was also an officer in the army of the Irish Republic. Was it of interest to him, I boldly inquired, that the first Irishmen he encountered were ranged in battle against him? Not so, he replied, with a dry and faintly sardonic courtesy. The

Irish of Kilcummin had greeted him on the strand, and had followed the French into Killala. He then invited me to accompany him into the courtyard.

There all was bedlam. Reinforcements, several times the original numbers, had arrived, and also a great crowd of peasants. A large flag or banner now hung above my hall door, of a dark yet vivid green silk, with a gilt harp at its center. Above the harp was the inscription ERIN GO BRAGH, beneath it, the words IRISH LEGION. The peasants seemed drunk with excitement, and many of them were dancing, or rather capering, before two of their musicians who were working away lustily at their pipes. French soldiers, leaning on their muskets, surveyed the scene with amusement. The wounded had been carried into the courtyard, and were being attended by French medicals, whose aprons, like those of butchers, were already streaked with blood. Several of the peasants had clapped upon their heads the helmets of fallen yeomen.

"In God's name, Mr. Teeling," I cried. "What have you brought down upon us?"

"Liberty," he replied, in a neutral tone of voice.

"And is this the appearance that liberty takes?" I asked.

He did not reply. He was looking beyond the courtyard to the street, where other peasants were milling about, excited and perhaps confused, as I was.

I cannot recollect my feelings with any exactness, and cannot believe that they would be of interest to the reader. I was overwhelmed by the suddenness of the event and by its unknown proportions, by my sight of men shot down in the streets of my parish, by my fears for the safety of my parishioners and my family. I was distracted by the hubbub, and by the matter-of-fact manner in which my very house had been taken away from me. But beneath the confusion, and stronger even than my fear, lay sadness like a sodden mass in my stomach. The spirited music of the pipers, the capering peasants, the indifferent soldiers, the bloody aprons, were both the causes and the visible emblems of my grief.

Thus began the first week of the Irish Republic, as I have seen it termed in several French accounts of this adventure, or, as it has remained alive in the imagination of the countryside, *Bliadhain na bhFranncach,* the year of the French.

The Moat, Ballina, August 22

A Killala man, riding an unsaddled horse, brought the news to Malcolm Elliott, who was at work in one of his fields. Elliott listened quietly, had the man repeat several portions of his story, and then nodded.

"Go to Michael Geraghty, and tell him that this story must be taken to John Moore at Ballintubber, and then to Swinford and Foxford. John Moore will give him the names of the men who must be told at once."

"Will the men of Ballina be coming to us at Killala?"

"No," Elliott said. "The Frenchmen will be coming here to us. Tonight perhaps or tomorrow." He paused, and bit his knuckle sharply. "But I myself will go to Killala now. Tell Michael Geraghty that he is in command until he sees me again. Could you make out how many Frenchmen have come?"

"By God, Mr. Elliott, there must be thousands upon thousands of them. They have not yet all landed. They destroyed the Tyrawley Yeomanry and the streets of Killala are slippery with blood. A Frenchman gave Captain Cooper a stroke with his musket that split open his skull like a bad apple."

Elliott remembered Cooper leaning toward him across a gaming table, the cannonball head bobbing with laughter.

"Have they cannon with them?" he asked. "Did they bring cannon?"

"They brought a great green banner and hung it up from the Protestant clergyman's house. And musicians."

"Yes," Elliott said.

He rode to his house, dismounted, and calling to his wife walked quickly to his office.

When Judith joined him he had a large ebony pistol case open on his desk. He looked up.

"The French have landed at Killala."

"Our Killala? Here in Mayo?"

"Our Killala. Seven miles to the north of us."

Her hand flew to her throat, and she sank down into a chair facing him.

"Why here? Of all the places in Ireland, why here?"

"Well may you ask. They have routed the yeomen there and hold the town."

"Then they have come in strength?"

"Because they dealt with Sam Cooper and his bundle of Orangemen? The man who brought me the news was a peasant. He had no notion of numbers."

"What will you do, Malcolm?"

"Do? Why, bring out the United Men. That was to be the signal, the landing of the French."

She sat quietly, hands joined.

He took one of the matched pistols from the case. "It could become dangerous here, Judith. This is the closest garrisoned town to the French. The yeoman corps of other towns may move here and try to hold it."

"I know nothing of such matters," she said. "Garrisons, movements of men. I have never understood them."

"No more have I. Do you know Michael Geraghty, who has the big farm on the other side of the river? Geraghty is a United Man. If there is trouble here, get word to him at once. If you have trouble with either side, do you understand me?"

She felt that her mind was moving too slowly to grasp his meaning.

"I must try to reach Killala now," he said. "Very soon the fencibles will have the road closed."

"I am sorry, Malcolm," she said, shaking her head. "The French have landed, and the insurrection has begun. All over Ireland. Is that it?"

"I cannot speak for all of Ireland," he said. "It has certainly begun in Mayo." He put the pistol back in its case and closed the lid. "The hours my father spent teaching me the use of these! In his day every Mayo gentleman was a duelist. A national disease. He had a limp from a pistol ball in his thigh. Badge of honor. It was a brutish place in those days, and it is little better now."

Judith grasped the arms of her chair. "We are merchants," she said, "my father and his brother. I doubt if either of them has ever held a pistol in his hand."

Elliott smiled at her. "I will be back soon," he said. "There will be a battle for Ballina." The word echoed in his ears: *battle*, large and melodramatic.

"We must pray for its success," she said. Then she cried, in a different, shriller voice, "I don't understand any of this."

"No," Elliott said. "Few of us will understand it, now that it is here. We all talked about it." He put the pistol case under his arm, and walked to her. He shared her sense of unreality. Judith herself, the room in which he stood, the field in which the word had been brought to him, belonged to the order of actuality. He was setting out toward fantasy, a world of pistols, Frenchmen, and words like *battle*.

"What will happen, Malcolm?" she asked. "You must have some sense of what will happen?"

"I don't know," he said, and bent down to kiss her.

Two miles outside of Ballina, he encountered a carriage crowded with women. Beside them rode George Falkiner, an elderly man who sat his horse with a stiff, erect back. One of the women recognized him, an old friend of his parents.

"Mr. Elliott," she called out. "You must not go near Killala. It is in the hands of the Frenchmen and the Papists. They have murdered our yeomen."

He reined in, and touched his hand to the brim of his hat. "I must, Mrs. Saurin. I have business there."

"There are mobs in the streets, and more Papists pouring in by the hour."

"My business there is pressing."

"They will murder you," she said. "You don't understand, Mr. Elliott. They will murder you, as the innocent Christians were butchered in Wexford." She had a round, anxious face, and speaking had brought her to tears.

Falkiner called him away from the carriage, and they went together a short distance down the road.

"If I correctly understand the purpose of your journey, Mr. Elliott, I should pistol you as you sit there."

"I understand my obligations, sir, as you do yours."

"You are riding to join foreign invaders, who have come here to bring bloodshed and death. They have already slaughtered men. You intend a treason for which the only remedy is a shameful death on the gallows."

"I am not acting thoughtlessly, Mr. Falkiner. I trust and believe that I am serving our country."

"I observe that you are carrying your father's pistols. Would your father have called this service to your country?"

"He would not, sir. But I am not my father. You must excuse me. Ballina is still safe for your party, and the door of The Moat is open for you, if you wish it."

"The Moat!" Falkiner cried. "No longer, sir. No longer. I would sooner sleep in the ditch, and these poor women with me. But I have no fear of that. The houses of Ballina are loyal, all but one of them."

In the fantasy toward which he moved off, he might at such a moment expect a pistol ball between his shoulders. But he knew that Falkiner sat motionless, the reins held loosely in his white, fragile hands. Between fields of corn and barley, golden in the sun of late afternoon, Elliott rode toward Killala.

Kilcummin, August 22

On a field sloping down from Knockmany, Michael MacMahon and his son Fergus watched the French unload supplies from their boats.

"Queer small men they are," MacMahon said. "For all the talk about them."

"Ferdy O'Donnell will be bringing into Killala the men who have sworn the big oath, and I will be going with them."

"For what purpose? To make yourselves drunk in the streets of Killala?"

"Well do you know for what purpose."

"Look around you, boy, and tell me who is to give me help in those fields. Let the Frenchmen make up their army out of spalpeens and homeless men and idle, wandering fellows."

"It is often enough that I have seen you beating time with your heels when they sang about the great rising there would be when the French came, or Owen Mac-Carthy bawling out his poems. The French are here now."

"Is Owen MacCarthy with the French?"

"How would I know where Owen MacCarthy is. He is below in Killala."

"Owen MacCarthy is a scholar and a man of deep learning. You will not find him wasting his life to the rope or the cannon."

"There is no waste when an entire countryside of people rises up."

"Would you be back for the harvest?"

"Before then, sure. How long can it take? Last week the yeomen were swaggering across the countryside, burning whatever man's house they chose. Today they are dead in the streets of Killala."

" 'Tis here that the year's harvest is," MacMahon said, "and not with the dead yeomen of Killala." He rubbed his hand across his mouth. "It would be a wonderful thing to see the Protestant landlords driven off, and the English soldiers."

"It would."

MacMahon turned suddenly, flung his arms around his son, and began to weep. Fergus, taken by surprise, patted his back awkwardly.

"I don't want you killed," MacMahon said, sobbing. "It isn't the harvest at all. I don't want you to go off to the fighting and get killed."

He is an old man now, Fergus thought with surprise, holding his father close. Over the father's beefy, heavy-muscled shoulder, he saw Ferdy O'Donnell and forty men coming toward them along the road, pikes sloped.

Killala, August 22

A man wearing a helmet of the Tyrawley Yeomanry crashed into MacCarthy, who moved back a pace and held him upright. Randall MacDonnell was riding down the crowded street toward the Palace, followed by a long, straggling column of men. When he saw MacCarthy he waved, sketchy parody of a salute.

The man whom MacCarthy was holding said, "Tomorrow we will be given uniforms and firelocks, master."

"Get yourself home now and go to bed," MacCarthy said, "or tomorrow you will do yourself an injury with your firelock." He clapped the man on the back, pushing him forward.

In the Wolf Dog he found Ferdy O'Donnell, who had his uniform already, a blue coat with yellow facings, and a sword.

"Have you become a Frenchman on me, Ferdy?"

"Indeed I have not, Owen, but a captain in the Irish army, in command of the Kilcummin men."

"Will Randall MacDonnell be the general then of the Irish, or will Malcolm Elliott?"

"Not Malcolm Elliott," O'Donnell said. "He is to be on the staff of the French when he arrives, and so is John Moore. It will be Randall, or Corny O'Dowd, or George Blake of Barraclough, and the others are to be colonels. You couldn't want a better man than George Blake."

"It is true," MacCarthy said. "He is a good man. Gentleman, I should say. I observe that the rebellion is paying proper attention to social grades."

"Sure who would follow after cowherds and potboys? Owen, it has been wonderful the way men have been coming in. There are men marching in from beyond Nephin who met a party of yeomen and scattered them."

"It is wonderful indeed," MacCarthy said. "It is as if a great sackful of people had been shaken out upon Killala. The town is crowded to bursting with them."

"We will have a few jars, and then I will take you over to Bartholemew Teeling, the Irish Frenchman who made me a captain."

"I will settle for the jar, Ferdy. How many of the Frenchmen are there?"

"A thousand, and they have brought firelocks for five thousand of us. And swords and sashes for officers."

"One thousand is not many."

"In this fleet only. More are on the way, thousands more. Teeling stood on the steps of the Protestant minister's house and made a speech with the French general standing beside him."

"A speech in Irish?"

O'Donnell shrugged. "Ulster Irish, but we could make out what he was saying."

"And what is it that they intend to do?"

"I do not know for certain, except that we will first attack Ballina. In two days' time, with the help of God, my brother Gerry will be a free man."

"With God's help he will," MacCarthy said. He crossed himself and then picked up his whiskey. "I am ashamed to confess it, but my mind is all confusion. Frenchmen in their gay uniforms, Cooper's yeomen smashed to pieces, men coming in from all directions with their pikes. What in God's name do the likes of us know about armies?"

"We know as much as Cooper, and he was part of an army."

"That is not at all a comforting example. Cooper and his yeomen were make-believe soldiers, and the real soldiers smashed them like eggs. The English too have their real soldiers in this island. Thousands upon thousands of them."

O'Donnell slapped his arm. "Will you break loose out of your gloom? Your damned poems have come to life all around you."

"My poems." MacCarthy drained off his glass, and signaled for another round. "You are right there, Ferdy. Figures from my poetry are rising up all around me in the streets of Mayo, captains and colonels and generals and ships from France. And yet who is to be the leader if not Randall MacDonnell the horse dealer, with a crowd of plowboys at his back?"

"And who for a captain but only Ferdy O'Donnell from a mountainy farm near Kilcummin, why do you not add that? Well, Owen, we are what is left. There are no chieftains or proud Sarsfields, and have not been for a century. Ireland is only horse dealers and farmers."

"And peasants," MacCarthy said. "Like me. You have grown eloquent in your handsome uniform."

The innkeeper brought them their whiskeys.

"By God," O'Donnell said, "it is only a few nights ago that the Protestant yeomen were in here, putting fire in their bellies to warm themselves for their cruel tasks."

"The wheel of fortune," MacCarthy said. "'Tis oiled by whiskey."

"You have said many the time to me, Owen, that we were slaves. Will we ever see a better chance to fight?"

MacCarthy moved his glass forward and back on the rough table. "No," he said at last.

"Then come with me to the minister's house and meet Teeling. They will have need of men with learning."

"Faith, they will," MacCarthy said, "if Randall MacDonnell is to be the measure." He drank off his whiskey. "No, Ferdy," he said. "I will not go. But I wish you luck with your sword of steel." On impulse, he reached out

203

his arm, and squeezed the heavy shoulder in its unfamiliar cloth.

"Don't wait too long," O'Donnell said.

Killala, August 22

Humbert sat alone in a small room off the drawing
room. A map was spread before him on an oval table,
held flat by bound volumes of theological tracts. Until
Hardy arrived, he was in complete command. Not even
in the Vendée had he had such freedom of choice. He
looked at the whole of the island, deliberately ignoring
its details. By tomorrow, Lord Cornwallis, in Dublin,
would be sitting before such a map. A most competent
old man, it was said. An aristo, doubtless gouty and
querulous, as elderly British officers always were. What
will he have heard? That a small French force has landed
on the Connaught coast and is recruiting allies. How will
he move? To seal us off as close to the coast as possible.

He bent closer to the map. There would be a strong
English garrison in Galway, and one to the east, perhaps
less strong, at Sligo or at Enniskillen. If these commanders
had sense, they would move at once. They would move
toward this town here—he placed his finger on it—Castlebar, which controlled all the Mayo roads, and was
doubtless already garrisoned. He could move to Castlebar
himself, and perhaps knock them off balance, but to do
so he must first take Ballina, Foxford, Swinford, towns
strung like beads along the only road south to Castlebar.
If he defeated that garrison, and captured Castlebar, what
then? Cornwallis would be moving slowly toward him
from the south, his armies spread wide. By then, Humbert
would have his thousand men and perhaps five thousand
raw allies. Local uprisings would be ignited as he moved,
and would pin down the local militia. The trick then
would be to slip past the English armies, cross the
Shannon, join with the United Irish in the midlands, and
make straight for Dublin.

He had already sent off a fishing boat from Westport
with word that he had landed and had taken Killala,
and he would send a second after he had met and defeated his first force of English. That would bring out
Kilmaine. The Directory could not allow a victorious army

204

to perish for want of support. And then Euonaparte, that
power-hungry little bourgeois, would have some of the
gilt rubbed off his uniform. It was a good plan, but with
one defect: it was difficult to the point of impossibility.
The odds were heavy against even reaching Castlebar.

He stood up and walked to the window. There was still
music in the courtyard, a tall fiddler leaning against the
wall, and it was still crowded with peasants, laughing
and singing. They were a curious people, not at all what
Tone and Teeling had led him to expect. He had imagined sober, implacable men, grim, perhaps a bit bloodthirsty. The ideals of the Revolution, Tone had assured
him, formed their Bible. But these men were primitive,
with something wild and terrifying in their appearance,
like huge children. The Chouans had been lacking in
manners, God knew, but they would have fled in terror
from these fellows. All for the best, perhaps; terror had
its uses. Many of them were holding pikes, a most effective weapon against cavalry, and formidable against un-
seasoned infantry. What kind of life did they have in
this strange land of moorland wastes? Did they seek
liberty, a pikehead thrust into a tyrant's throat? Liberty,
they would discover, is elusive and problematical.

Ballintubber, August 22

Standing on the entrance porch, facing the cool dark
waters of Lough Carra, John Moore bade farewell to his
brother.

"At twenty-two, I am too old to be given orders."

"Nor do I presume to give you any. But you will
shortly be taking a great many. How many of our people
are leaving with you?"

"None. I am riding ahead to Killala. But two hundred
men from Ballinrobe will follow. About sixty of them are
ours."

"It is my intention to speak to our tenants and warn
them against this enterprise. None of them will follow
you, if I can prevent it."

"You must do what seems proper to you," John said,
shrugging. "The estate is yours."

"How many have the French landed?"

"The first messenger wasn't certain. The second said

about a thousand men, under a general called Humbert."

"Humbert!" George said, startled. "A general called Humbert. You have caught yourself a Tartar."

"Why? Is he well known?"

"He was the general of the Vendée. A Jacobin. Clever, coarse, unprincipled."

"A good general?"

"It was a special kind of war in the Vendée. Peasants and ambushes." Like Mayo, Moore thought. "I cannot imagine why so shrewd a man would allow himself to be trapped in Mayo with a thousand men."

"He has brought one part of an expedition."

"That will depend upon the winds, the British fleet, and especially the Directory, as famous a collection of rogues as has ever been collected in one city. It is useless to preach to you, but I will make one effort. Your General Humbert will never get past Castlebar. Cornwallis will scoop him up like a weasel. And the rebels who take his arms will be traitors. When you ride down that avenue, you ride straight to a gallows."

"I may. But I believe that most of the people are prepared to make a stand."

"Make a stand. Your very language comes out of penny pamphlets."

"I have never claimed to be a scholar."

"You are wise in your modesty."

They stood facing each other, motionless.

"Tell me this, George. You believe that we will not succeed. Do you hope that we will?"

"I do indeed. In that event, you will not be hanged."

"No other reason?"

George looked out toward the lake. Wind-rippled. The melancholy wind of late afternoons. "This insurrection is destined for so certain a ruin that I feel only despair. Many men will be killed or destroyed and among them my own brother. I could not be more certain."

"We are an odd pair of brothers, George. The world is full of luck and chance. Perhaps you will see me ride through the streets of Castlebar in all my glory."

George laughed. "It would become you well, John. You are a fine handsome young man, and you would look splendid in uniform."

"That would depend upon the color. Red wouldn't suit me at all, for example. Wish me luck, George."

"I wish with all my heart to see you here again. Our

father managed to get back from Spain. May you have his luck." Awkwardly, he embraced his brother.

Later, he walked along the shore of the lake. Its waters lapped against stones. If only he had been less stiff, lecturing the boy like a schoolmaster. Romantics like John had no ears for lectures. History loved them, chose them as its favored victims. It flung them, bright as new-minted coins, into the puddles of disaster. John should be courting girls, riding to hounds, gaming, writing sonnets. Instead he was involved in this trumpery melodrama, a few thousand peasants and a devious French general. The lake was clear. Rushes moved softly, faintly. A melancholy hour. Some distance away, a wild swan floated with her cygnets, elegant and calm. Her ugly feet could flail and trample, fouling the shore.

From the *Memoir of Events*, Written by Malcolm Elliott in October, 1798

In the early afternoon of August 22 I rode into Killala and presented myself as agent to County Mayo of the Society of United Irishmen. I was received most cordially by General Humbert, who seemed delighted to encounter anyone who possessed even a smattering of French, and was placed upon his staff to serve under Bartholemew Teeling, who was to act as a liaison between the French and the Irish forces. At that first meeting I gained but a shallow impression of Humbert, a slow-moving and large-bellied young man with soft, dangerous eyes. He had established his headquarters in the residence of poor Broome the clergyman, and courtyard and ground floor were crowded with men, intent upon a dozen errands, but Humbert moved quietly among them in his ill-fitting uniform, his paunch pressing against his waistcoat. All of them save for Teeling were French, and he was in French uniform. The Irish were in the outer courtyard, a mob of countrymen. They seemed leaderless and bewildered but most excited. Later in the day, the men who were appointed to command them rode in one by one, Randall MacDonnell and Cornelius O'Dowd and George Blake, but in those first few hours, they were left to themselves while the French secured the town and requisitioned horses and food.

Teeling and I had known each other for some years and had a great mutual trust and respect: I was most happy to discover him here with us. He found an early opportunity to discuss our situation. The French had been shamefully derelict in not setting sail upon the first news of the uprisings in Wexford and indeed might not have sailed at all had it not been for the persistence of Wolfe Tone and the energy of Humbert. They sailed, however, in the belief that those insurrections were still in progress, and word of their suppression came as a hard blow to Teeling, who was a close friend of the unfortunate Henry Joy MacCracken. It was a blow from which he soon began to recover. Rarely have I met a man of such calm and equable determination, nor, as events were to prove, of such swift and unreflecting courage. He seems to me now a figure from Plutarch, measured and just in his actions, stoical in adversity. There was somewhere near the center of his being a dark pool of melancholy, but this I attribute to his life in Ulster, a chill and forbidding province, as I do also his occasionally mordant and sardonic speech.

Although I then knew little of soldiers or warfare, and know little more now despite my experiences, it was at least clear to me from the first hour that we had taken up a difficult task. Peasants had been pouring for several hours into Killala. Four days later, after the battle of Ballina had been fought and won, their number had swelled to some five thousand. Far less even than myself, of course, did they have knowledge of military life or of the ways of war, save for the occasional clandestine drilling which some had received. The French sergeants began their training on the second day, but with no happy results, for each group was to the other a source of ridicule, barbarous and strange, speaking not words but an outlandish gabble. Those who were placed as their commanders knew almost as little. These for the most part were down-at-heels Catholic squireens, such as Randall MacDonnell, George Blake, and Cornelius O'Dowd, or else strong farmers and celebrated faction fighters, of whom the most notable were Ferdy O'Donnell, Malachi Duggan, and later Michael Geraghty, one of my own tenants. These men were denominated as colonels or majors of those whom they brought in with them, and in turn they appointed their subordinates. But large numbers of leaderless men also drifted in, and these were formed into companies by Teeling, and made to choose their own captains. The streets of Killala were also clotted that day by men who had come in from idle curiosity or in hopes of being given one of the French firelocks. It was in this manner that Owen MacCarthy hung about on the edges of the crowds. I saw him twice that day, once lounging in Broome's courtyard, and once holding conversation in the tavern, with his long legs thrust out, a hazard to those passing by. He seemed to me then a large-boned, hulking peasant, much given to whiskey and idle laughter, and I would not have remarked him at all save for his friendship with Ferdy O'Donnell, a virtuous and steadfast fellow.

I well remember the arrival of Corny O'Dowd. It was late at night on the first day, and the French had fixed torches along the street and in the courtyard, for they were still shifting supplies. There rose a general hubbub in the street, with wild shouts of greeting, and several muskets were fired off. I left the house, and walked toward the courtyard gate, beyond which I could see O'Dowd riding in at the head of a hundred men, mounted on a handsome mare, and wearing a broad-brimmed hat, like a preacher's, with a blackcock's feather fixed in its brim. The men behind him were farmers or laborers, clad in frieze and a number of them barefoot. Some carried pikes of straight ash. There was no attempt at order; they walked quickly but not in rank, and they shouted out to friends whom they recognized in the crowd. These were men who had taken the oath of the Society, but it was some older and deeper loyalty which brought them into Killala that night. They were a feudal band, mustered behind their chieftain. When O'Dowd came abreast of the gate he reined in, and at the same moment he saw me standing there, and greeted me with a shout. "Elliott," he called out, as he dismounted, "is Randall here?" "He is here," I told him. "In Broome's house, or in the tavern." "How many did he bring with him?" "I don't know," I said. "Damned few, I will wager," O'Dowd said; "they are a mean-spirited lot, the Ballycastle men. I have more than a hundred men from Enniscrone here, and they are spoiling for a fight. Where is the Frenchman?" He walked over to me, a tall man but bow-legged. "Take a look at them," he said; "have you ever seen the like?'

And I had not. I tried to make out their faces where the ruddy lights burned into the darkness. "Are there men here from Ballina?" he asked. "There will be," I said. "I rode on ahead of them." "Weren't you the cute whore?" he asked with a delighted crow; "commend me to the Protestants. You have us beat every time. Are you a general now?" "There is only one general that I know of," I said; "the Frenchman." "That will never do," he said. He jerked his head backward toward the Enniscrone men. "Those fellows know as much about Frenchmen as about the man in the moon." "You will need to talk to a man named Teeling," I said. Two days later, before the battle of Ballina, O'Dowd was made "General of the Army of Connaught." It was an empty title, but it delighted him, and for a time it made Blake and MacDonnell furious. There was a hat that went with the honor, black and dripping with lace. O'Dowd transferred his blackcock's feather to it.

By the time O'Dowd arrived, our headquarters were well established in poor Broome's commodious residence. Broome and his wife, together with their servants and several guests, were relegated to the second floor, but this was ample for their needs, as it contained six rooms, including the large one which faced the street and which Broome used as a library. During the time of Humbert's occupation of the house, its residents were entirely secure from harm. I am informed that such was not the case after the army moved forward from Killala, and I keenly regret such perils as Mr. Broome may have endured. He is a most humane and estimable gentleman, although knowing nothing about Ireland.

Of General Humbert my opinion was to change and modify itself constantly during the time of my service with him. This much is certain, that he was a man of most remarkable ability, seemingly bold and reckless, but in fact a calculator. There is no need for me to laud his military prowess, for the British generals who encountered him, including General Taylor and especially Lord Cornwallis, have been generous in their praise, and indeed the campaign upon which he led us is said to have had few parallels. And yet I do not believe that we ever knew more than a portion of his mind. Certainly we Irish did not, and I believe this also to be true of his French subordinates. It seemed from my conversations with them, and especially with Colonel Sarrizen, that they were bound to him by duty and by a professional admiration for his skills, rather than by trust or affection. But then trust was in short supply among the French officers, although this did not impair their efficiency. There was a touch of the playactor in him, which would explain why he and Tone got on so well. He could exhibit cheerfulness and high spirits at one moment, and the next fall into a savage rage. This perhaps was changeability, but perhaps the cheerfulness and the rage were but shows, behind which dwelt the unknowable man. This may be true of all commanders.

Late that first night, the prisoners were transferred to the market house, where they were to remain under guard for the duration of the campaign, their numbers being augmented with each passing day, and the air became more and more noxious as men were crowded in upon each other. They lived in terror, being persuaded that they were destined to be butchered by the Papists, and their defenseless families as well. Indeed, in the final days, a small number of them were brutally slaughtered, but by that time our army was far distant from Mayo, and Ferdy O'Donnell, who commanded the small garrison left behind, had despite his courage an imperfect control upon those insurgents. For Captain Cooper the imprisonment was unendurable. He had the intelligence to know that massacre was not imminent, and endeavored to reassure his men, but for the first weeks, I am told, he remained in a black, towering rage, and would sit upon the floor gnawing at his fingernails and knuckles. I did not visit him, for reasons of delicacy, but MacDonnell had no such scruples. The interview was a painful one, for the two had in earlier years been cronies, but now MacDonnell did not hesitate to mock him in his misfortune. His mind was made no easier by the actions of his wife. Mrs. Cooper, a bold, handsome woman, decisive in speech and manner, made two visits to our headquarters to demand his release, thereby arousing the admiration of the officers but serving no other purpose.

Killala remained a center of the insurrection even after our army had moved forward, being garrisoned, as I have said, by a body of Irish troops under the nominal command of Ferdy O'Donnell. Of what transpired there I have no first-hand knowledge and the stories which have been made current in recent weeks have upon them the mark of infuriated loyalists, anxious to represent themselves as the victims of Papist savagery. No one, not even among these loyalists, questions the humanity and generosity of O'Donnell himself, but I can well believe that the task of maintaining order was beyond his abilities. The rebellion drew to itself not only those willing to fight in the field, but a large mob of fellows whose only thoughts were for plunder and for vengeance against their Protestant fellow countrymen. I can well believe that without O'Donnell's firmness and popularity among the people, Mayo would have been stained by crimes such as those which have brought Wexford under an eternal disgrace.

At the outset, I had doubts that even Humbert could maintain order, but in this I was happily mistaken. The fellows who poured into Killala had but the haziest notion of our enterprise and its objectives, and many of them were bold and reckless fellows, Whiteboys and faction fighters. These were encouraged by the events of the first hours, for of course it was necessary to make requisitions upon the countryside for supplies and horses. It may well have seemed to them that this signaled a more general assault upon property. Like the peasants of most countries, they held literally to the idea of revolution, even though they had never heard the word itself. Tyrants were to be brought low, and stripped of their possessions, and their lives were held in no high account. But Humbert's discipline, and the flat of his sergeants' sabers, made short work of that notion. It is unfortunately the case that the houses of certain landlords were pillaged and set afire, both in Killala and along our line of march, but these were the works either of mobs or of bands such as those of Malachi Duggan, over which we maintained an imperfect authority. And yet taken as a whole, the conduct of the Irish forces was most creditable, as the more generous of our foes have avowed.

Just now I have read over these pages of notes, and am appalled by their falseness to my true recollections of the first days. The facts are there, without coloring or extenuation, and set down in as flat a language as I can command. But in truth what I best recall is great confusion, both in the streets of Killala and in my own feelings. Foreign troops had landed and an insurrection was being set into motion in which I had my part to play, as I did not for a moment question. And yet these were in truth my only certainties. The streets were crowded with men remote and alien to my own troubled feelings. They spoke in French and in Irish, languages of which I possess a serviceable knowledge, but not a true intimacy, and the words, familiar but foreign, were like the sounds of distant waves. Then too the French officers and their men knew what they were about, but I did not, and I was chilled by the confidence with which they shouted orders at each other. For them, it was certain, this town in Mayo was but a conquered village which may as well have been in Africa or the Carribbean. More than by the French, however, I was chilled by my own countrymen, separated from me by language, by passions which I did not share, emotions which I had no wish to express. The market house was filled with men with names like Elliott, Protestants like myself and English by blood, and I was walking the streets with their captors. Papists armed with pikes filled the streets of Killala, and I was one with them. Deeper than politics, deeper than thought, my blood stirred in sluggish protest against my belief and my actions.

The first battle of the campaign was for Ballina, my own town, which lies on the Moy, seven miles to the south of Killala. It was garrisoned by the Prince of Wales's Fencibles, some six hundred, under the command of Colonel Chapman, augmented by a detachment of carbineers and several companies of yeomen. The choice which lay before Chapman was of accepting battle or retreating southward to Foxford, thereby abandoning a considerable stretch of Mayo to his enemy yet preserving his force intact should a later attempt be made upon Castlebar. Humbert gave him the better part of two days to decide, for it was late on the twenty-fourth that he sent us forward, six hundred of the French under Sarrizen, and five hundred Irish, including MacDonnell's and O'Dowd's men, who moved through the Glenthorne estate along the old Rosserk road. MacDonnell rode at the head of the Irish, but it was Teeling who gave the orders.

I should perhaps have more vivid memories of my first military engagement, but I do not. And yet the march was sufficiently romantic. The Rosserk road is little better than a narrow, treacherous path which runs past cabins of Lord Glenthorne's tenants and issues onto the Ballina road about a mile north of the town. We moved in dark-

213

ness, and the tenants first of one, then of another cabin came outside and lighted hay and straw to show us our way. Women came from the cabins to bring us bread and bowls of milk. From that night forth, the path was called *bother-na-sop*, the road of straw. But I was possessed by a sense of the matter-of-factness of these extraordinary happenings. Men had to be organized, and formed up in lines, and they jested and grumbled, but with a white-hot wire of excitement running just beneath the surface, for like me they were moving toward their first battle, in which some would be killed in all likelihood. Yet this sense of the ordinary existed most curiously within me beside a strong feeling of unreality which had been with me from the moment that the rider brought me news of the French landing. I moved through a dream in which the landscape was known, the faces recognized.

Bother-na-sop.

Killala, August 24

On the Sunday morning of the night march upon Ballina, Mr. Hussey knelt before the altar, turned then to face his congregation, and folded his hands beneath his chasuble. Conscious of the occasion and its needs, he spoke slowly and vehemently.

"My dear people, an anxious and a dreadful time has come upon us. In the past month, it has been my sad duty to speak to you of acts of violence, beyond question committed by men of this parish. Such acts, although certainly they are black with sin, have had at least the human explanation that life in our barony is hard, and that some few of our landlords have acted in a manner which some might term un-Christian. But today I speak to you of a far greater danger to the souls of each one of you."

He was a frail, fastidious man, the son and brother of prosperous middlemen in County Meath. His previous parish of Bective in that county had been as much delight as duty, and his memory lingered upon the rich green pasturelands of the Boyne valley, the ruined Bective abbey, the graceful bridge across the river. Mayo was a place of exile, endured without pleasure or complaint.

"Several months ago, as you well know, large numbers of misguided men in the east and in the north took up

214

arms against the King. Their rebellion has been broken by the King's powerful army. But now, as the embers of that rebellion are being stamped out by the soldiers' heavy boots, Frenchmen have landed on our strand, and seek to lure you away from your homes, your families, your little farms. These Frenchmen come from the nation which murdered its king and queen and many thousands of innocent people, which has become the persecutor of all religions but in particular of our own Holy Church. These infidels and murderers now ask you to go into rebellion, . that you may be slaughtered. And it grieves me to say that certain Irishmen who have banded together with them will ask the same of you. My words are not mine alone. I declare to you the words of our Church, as they have been given to us by our bishops. To take arms from the Frenchmen or to help them in any way would be a mortal sin by which your souls would be blackened."

Uncertain of his Irish, a language toward which he felt a faint contempt, he chose his words with care, and he sought to measure their effect in the eyes of his parishioners. The church was as crowded as it was on any other Sunday, the men on one side of the aisle and the women on the other. It was the men toward whom he looked. Many, most of them perhaps, would go back to their cabins, but others would go to the French encampment. He could almost tell which were which. There were men who sat staring at the flagstone floor, or at some point to the left or right of him, shamefaced.

"Your souls would be blackened," he repeated, believing the awful words. The white lamb's wool of the soul, lamb's wool softer than cloud, smeared and sullied by black thumbprints.

"I must speak briefly of a most painful matter. Mr. Murphy, the curate of this parish, has gone to the French encampment. I have relieved Mr. Murphy of his priestly duties and will send to our bishop an account of his conduct. You may depend upon it that his lordship will deal harshly with this misfortunate man. Never believe that you are free to judge between his advice to you and mine. The judgment of the Church in these matters is clear beyond question, and our bishops have spoken with a single voice."

Fit shepherd for a barbarous flock, Hussey thought of Murphy in a spasm of sudden disgust, coarse round red face and neck sun-seamed like a farmer's, his coat snuff-stained and his breath rank with stale whiskey. Small wonder that the world scorns us, an island of cowherds and fanatics. But the spasm faded, died, and he was shamed by his feelings. He spoke more gently to those who heard him, the words floating across a space wider than that marked by the flagstones, carried to them from the trim pasturelands of the Pale, from the cloisters of Saint-Omer.

"Go back now to your homes, and stay safely within them. Remember the words of our Savior that he who lives by the sword will perish by it. Remember the duty which you owe to our Lord and to the King and to your own families, who will have need of the husband and the father, and the strong sons as well, in the harvest. I ask you to join with me now in prayer that peace will return quickly to our nation, and without the shedding of innocent blood. In the name of the Father and of the Son and of the Holy Ghost."

He made the sign of the cross, turned back toward the altar, knelt, and prayed swiftly and softly. At the close, he offered, almost in a whisper, a prayer in English, a language which, he suspected, was more suited to His ears.

After Mass, he stood on the steps of the chapel, nodding and speaking briefly to the communicants as they came out into the sunlight. This was not his custom. He was known to his parish as an austere and forbidding man, his manners and his speech formal and almost alien. But this morning they nodded in return, returned his smiles and his small talk, sensing that he was trying, in his stiff and awkward way, to plead and argue with them at a deeper level than that of word or gesture. But his words had been baffling even to those who had not the slightest intention of joining the French. The King was called King George and his head was stamped upon the coins. This ended their knowledge of him.

Hussey walked down the street to his house, a thin solemn figure in his cassock, his hands clasped behind his back. In all the barony, Thomas Treacy was the only man to whom he could talk as to an equal, a gentleman with manners and a balanced view of affairs. Who in his right mind would choose a country with a Protestant ascendancy, and yet order and stability were the first requirements of any society. King George was not a person to him, he was scarcely even a face upon a shilling. He was an emblem of order. Embarrassing that the emblem was Protestant, indeed distasteful, but at least he still had a head, unlike poor Louis.

Ballina, August 24

Colonel Sir Thomas Chapman, the Englishman who commanded the troops in Ballina, was in an embarrassing position. He was outnumbered, but not so vastly outnumbered as to make the evacuation of the town his only course of action. The Prince of Wales's Fencibles and the detachment of carbineers were the only troops upon which he could rely, however. The rest were companies of native yeomanry who had flocked into the town and who seemed to differ from the other Irish only as to the side which they had chosen. And Ballina was crowded with refugees, howling against all logic for both protection and vengeance, safety and vigorous retaliation. They were ready to believe that every Papist in Mayo was a rebel, which for all he knew was the truth. There was much to be said for falling back upon Castlebar, which was garrisoned in strength. But at worst he could delay the French here at the Moy, and with a bit of luck might throw them back upon Killala.

Early in the afternoon he had some luck of a different kind. A man named Walsh rode into town and was arrested; he was carrying a paper, signed by one B. Teeling, which declared him to be a captain in the army of the Irish Republic. Chapman held a court-martial in the open air, before the townspeople, and Walsh was sentenced to death. He was a peasant, but not of the poorest sort, for he wore a shirt of good linen. Chapman had him hanged from the crane which jutted from a wall of the market house. He was hanged in full military style, with mustered troops and muffled drums. This for a time diverted the Protestant mob. Chapman briefly surveyed, and with equal distaste, the hanged Papist and the mob of Irish Protestants. Then his thoughts returned northward, toward the invisible French.

At last he decided that there was nothing for it but to fight, and he moved out his troops at nightfall, placing the fencibles in the van. They encountered Sarrizen's French about one mile north of the town. The fighting was brisk

217

but brief, for his men fell back before the bayonet charge of the French. He ordered them to retreat toward the town and regroup, and noted with perplexity that the French, by not pressing their advantage, were allowing him to accomplish this maneuver. Then the peasant rebels emerged to fall upon his flank, shrieking like demons, firing off their muskets, and stabbing with their pikes.

Chapman discovered within minutes that he was in command not of a beaten force, but of men lost to shame and in headlong flight. Screaming themselves, they ran back toward the town, pursued by an immense mob of jabbering peasants, with the French bringing up the rear. Chapman rode through the narrow streets of Ballina, beating at his men with the flat of his sword, cursing them, urging them to turn and fight. But they ran heedless through the streets, and then made off across the fields toward Foxford. Stories that he had heard of the 'Forty-five gave him images, regulars thrown into panic by whooping, half-naked Highlanders. That, joined to cool French veterans in bayonet charge, might daunt anyone. And yet the sight of British troops scampering off into the safety of night was humiliating. In his despair, the thought of allowing himself to be captured drifted through his mind. By the French, of course, not the Irish. But that would not have been possible, for the Irish were first into the town. Why should there have been so many of them, a sea moving in darkness? Then common sense returned to him, and, with a sigh and a shrug, he rode after his men.

The battle of Ballina had been fought, a small affair when measured against the ballads which were to be written about it. In the town, the Irish gathered around the hanged body of Walsh, a Crossmolina farmer who was known to many of them. It was a sight startling in its unexpectedness, and minutes passed before anyone thought to cut him down. Humbert rode quickly into town, his swift, alert eyes studying the streets, the Irish mob, the hanging man, the buildings.

Dublin Castle, August 24

Charles, Marquis Cornwallis, both Viceroy of Ireland and Commander-in-Chief of His Majesty's forces in that realm, presided over a council of state. He was a large-bodied man of sixty, looking more a country gentleman than a soldier, mild-eyed, a broad face with humorous mouth.

"But gentlemen," he said easily, "the facts, so far as they have come to us, are merely that a small force of French have landed in the wilds of Mayo."

"More will be coming," Sir John Denham said. He was a short, choleric baronet from Roscommon. "We can be certain of that. For years they have been counting on the treason which has spread throughout this island, and they have made their plans."

"I am less certain of that," Cornwallis said. "It seems to me that the Irish project has long been the orphan child of the Directory. In any event, we have a full squadron cruising off the northwest shores. These fellows have managed to slip past us, but the others won't. What say you, Mr. Cooke?"

"They chose an unlikely place to land," Cooke said. "We do know that there is disaffection in Mayo, but it is not at all well organized. Agrarian outrage, and on a small scale at that. Most of it in a single barony. Tyrawley, as it happens. Where they landed. Dennis Browne has been complaining for weeks about stirring there. He has written for troops."

"Yes," Cornwallis said. "Well, he has them now. Wrong uniform, perhaps." He eased his gouty foot onto a chair. "I do wish we knew the name of the French commander."

"May God help the decent poor loyalists of Mayo," Denham said. "While we sit here talking, they stand naked before the fury of Papist mobs."

"It is my intention," Cornwallis told him, his voice frigid, "to meet the French forces and to defeat them, to subdue all rebels who have taken up arms, and to restore order to this kingdom. I am an old campaigner and I know my trade."

"I never intended to suggest otherwise, my lord."

"No doubt."

General Lake leaned confidently forward, across the wide table of polished walnut. "My lord, these first reports may be mistaken. It may in fact be a considerable force. Even so, it can come nowhere close to the number of men that we have under arms in this kingdom. If I receive your instructions, I will move at once against Mayo, and nip this in the bud, before their position is consolidated, before the rebels have a chance to rouse themselves up."

Cornwallis listened with a show of politeness which concealed his irritation. Lake had served under him in North America, and had proved himself an able commander. But in Ireland! Lake had been Commander-in-Chief under Camden when the Wexford rising broke out. It was his policy of whippings, torturing, and burnings which, in Cornwallis's judgment, had goaded the Wexford peasants to their frenzy. Bad soldiering, that. Inhumane as well, of course.

"I count myself fortunate, Lake, to have a soldier of your experience at my side."

"I think I know these people, sir, and I know the way they fight. That gives me an advantage, of course."

"Of course it does, General. Now then, the one thing which we must avoid is a battle which the French stand a chance of winning. The native Irish would be inflamed beyond control by the news of such a victory. With your knowledge of the people, would you not agree with that?"

"Indeed I would, sir. The skirmishes which they won in Wexford, before I took to the field, worked upon them like strong whiskey."

"And so our plan of campaign is a simple one. General Trench commands the forces eastward of the French landing. On the western coast, in Galway, is General Hutchinson. I would like you, sir, to go to Galway and take over his command."

Lake began to rise. "With your permission, sir, I will set out this night."

Cornwallis drew out his watch. "Good God, man. It is nearly eleven. Get yourself a good night's sleep, and set out refreshed in the morning."

"Now this is too much!" Denham said. "I must make my protest. I am an Irishman, as you are not, and I am a member of Ireland's Parliament. This is my country. There will be Frenchmen and murderous peasants on the loose while General Lake is getting himself a night's sleep."

"In a moment, Sir John. In a moment. By now, Lake, the enemy will most certainly have taken Ballina. From Ballina, he will move south to Foxford, unless he has orders to wait for reinforcements. Keep him contained. If he has fewer than four or five thousand men, that will be no problem. The great prize for him, of course, would be

220

Castlebar, but he will have more sense than to attempt it. Keep him contained, but don't attack unless you find a chance too good to miss. And while you are about that task, the main body of our forces will be moving toward Mayo."

"The main body?" Lake asked, in quick hurt. "And who will command those forces?"

"I will."

"You, my lord?"

"I was a soldier not so very long ago. I think I remember the art."

"Of course, my lord. I did not mean to suggest—"

Cornwallis held up his hand, and turned toward Denham. "Yes, sir. You are an Irishman, with a country and a House of Commons and a House of Lords and a Custom House and close to a hundred thousand Irishmen in your yeomanry and your militia. But the insurrections which broke out this spring in several of your counties were at last put down not by Irish but by English troops. In many of your corps of militia, the disaffection is so widespread that the officers dare not turn their backs upon their men. The pretensions and airs of your so-called Parliament are too numerous for me to list, but in the brief months that I have spent in this country, they have driven me almost to distraction. And now, sir, you propose to tell me how to fight a war. I will not have it."

Denham flushed, and he pressed his hands against the table's edge, as if to rise. "The men you malign, sir, are the Englishmen who have held this island for you since the days of Elizabeth."

"English now, are you? Irish or English as it suits your purpose. Irish when you don't need us, and English when you do. You people can't make up your minds what you are. At the moment, you do not hold this land. I do."

"By God, when I report your words to Parliament—"

"They will do nothing. Some of them have been bought outright, and would sit there smiling if they were called a pack of nanny goats. Some have been driven hysterical by their terror of rebellion. Some few are honest men, but they will know you, and will believe that you have heard what you deserve to hear. Now, sir, I shall follow my advice to General Lake and get some sleep."

Cornwallis stood alone by the window, looking down into the Castle Yard. Absurd that England, in the midst of a war against a European power, should have to expend her men and her efforts upon this wretched bog. First the risings in Wexford and Antrim, and now this. It would be difficult to say who was worst, the jabbering peasantry, the treacherous United Irishmen, the blustering Protestant landlords. Certainly the landlords were the most comical, avowing themselves British in their thick-tongued brogues.

Clearly something was wrong, or the problem would not have persisted for six hundred years. The readiest solution was union. Pitt wanted it. Sweep away that appalling little parliament, and make Ireland one country with England. The same laws, the same army. Pitt wanted it. This rebellion might make it possible. Fear would shake the landlords free of their patriotic delusions, and they could then be herded into their parliament to vote for its extinction. The unfrightened could always be bribed. Money or a meaningless title. Lord FitzBog. Sir Terrence O'Spud. Many a Connaught landlord was doubtless quaking in his boots at this moment, and with good reason. And yet the farther you moved away from Dublin, the more vivid grew the sense of something alien. And what must Mayo be like, farthest away of all, names on a map, Killala, Ballina, Castlebar? But a religious war, at this time in the world's history, Catholic against Protestant! More to it than that, of course, Protestant landlords and a Catholic peasantry. A war against property, it came to that. One thing was certain. The island could not be allowed to go its own way. A glance at the globe proved that.

What must it be like to be stranded in a far corner with a few thousand men and a rabble of Irish-speaking peasants? Perhaps the Frenchman enjoyed it. The French were fond of wild escapades and picturesque scenery.

Ballina, August 25

A great moon had risen on the Moy, where the rebels were encamped on the demesne of the Big Lord. It was like a fairday at night, with men in constant motion and heavy supply wagons lumbering in from Killala. Men were gathered there who had never seen each other before. They had come from the remote hamlets of Erris and the impoverished farms beside Lough Conn. All of the firelocks had been passed out, and now they were being issued pikes hammered upon the Ballina anvils. Most were men who had never taken the oath of the United Irishmen, had never heard of it, and would not have understood its words or their meaning. They knew that Killala and Ballina had fallen, that Westport in one direction and Swinford in another were in rebel hands, and that a great mass of the Irish were making ready to march upon Foxford.

Shortly after the fall of Ballina, the house of the Big Lord and the house of a landlord named Fortescue were plundered. Malachi Duggan led his followers and a mob of others to Glenthorne Castle. It was deserted. Hendricks, the house steward, had ridden in to Ballina to join the rebels and the servants had fled. For a time they stood silent before the steps sweeping up to the central block, ornamented on either side by the stone image of a couched, wide-mouthed lion. Then Duggan climbed the stairs and kicked open the doors.

At first they wandered, aimless and curious, down the corridors, peering through opened doors at rooms which hung in a delicate suspension of time. Dusted and polished by the castle's small army of housemaids, they held the elusive personality of the old Lord. Their hangings, carpets, and furnishings were as unimaginable to the staring peasants as the ocean's floor, or a jungle, vine-entangled and noisy with bright-plumaged birds. The peasants were seized by a conviction that they had committed something far graver than trespass, far graver indeed than armed rebellion. They had stepped from one globe to another, vast and luminous.

Then Duggan, with a roar, swung the hook of his pike into a wall hanging, a painting on watered silk, and ripped it to the floor.

They found Creighton at last, in his office, seated behind his desk, hands folded upon its surface, and square spectacles pushed up on his broad, balding forehead. He sat quietly, as though frozen, staring at them, and they at him. He did not move until one of the peasants, by accident, knocked against the table upon which lay spread out his model of the estate, to the peasant a meaningless sprawl with bits of mirror glass scattered across it. "No, no," Creighton said, and rose up from his desk, walking around it to the middle of the room. "I meant," he said, stopped, and then began again, "I meant—" Duggan drove his pike savagely into his chest, and then twisted it, tearing upward. Creighton fell against his model, and his blood spurted upon it, rivers of bright blood flowed down brown-tinted mountains of papier-mâché. "My Jesus, mercy," Donal Hennessey said. For a moment, Duggan shared his horror, then he twisted Creighton's body, and pulled out the pike. Creighton fell to the floor.

Teeling, with partial success, sought to prevent the plundering from spreading beyond Glenthorne Castle, but it was Humbert who checked it entirely by sending out squads of his grenadiers. He did not object to looting on principle, but he knew that irregular troops, operating in their own countryside, had a way of drifting home with the booty. The sight of a rebel staggering bent-backed through the encampment, a grandfather clock lashed to his shoulders, convinced him that this was a lively possibility. But of course he allowed them to keep what they had taken, and silks trailed across the pasturelands of the encampment, and paintings in their massive frames of gilded wood stood propped against trees. He was annoyed when he learned of the unauthorized murder of Creighton, although he shared their detestation of aristocrats. "He was the land agent, I have been told," Teeling said; "not an aristocrat." Humbert shrugged. "Ça me fait égal." But he issued strict orders. Looting would be punished by the whip, murder by hanging.

The French and the Irish camps were separated by the Rosserk road. Humbert visited them both, accompanied by Sarrizen and Fontaine, Teeling and Elliott. He observed with amusement that two priests in their vestments, Murphy and the Ballycastle curate, were visiting groups of men who knelt before them to receive the sacrament. Humbert, in his earlier days a spirited defiler of churches, took now a tolerant view of these priests. They confirmed his belief that he was making use of a primitive, incalculable people. No matter. He had once been a Mass-goer himself, kneeling beside his starched, black-clad grandmother.

Cows from the Big Lord's herds had been slaughtered and cooked on spits. The Irish sat on the ground working at them, joints and great gobs of charred beef. As though they had never tasted meat before. Seldom enough for most of them, poor devils.

The Revolution had once been this, peasants invading

the chateaux, doing away with the seigneurs, hauling the finery out onto the lawns and trampling gardens and setting fire to the buildings. What was it now but an ugly scramble for power—Barras and Rewbell and the rest of them. And, waiting to burst into flight, butterfly in its demure cocoon, their creature, Buonaparte. Carnot, the one honest politician, the organizer of victories, in exile since Fructidor. Hoche dead, the great general who was the true son of the Revolution. How he had hated and suspected Buonaparte! The Revolution had become a pit of coiling snakes, that Revolution which had made a general of a dealer in rabbit skins. They respected victories, though, those snakes in their pit, and this knowledge had sent Buonaparte to the sands of Egypt, and Humbert to a moorland waste.

MacCarthy too wandered about in the rebel encampment. Perhaps he had taken part in the attack on Ballina. He was not certain. The Irish, as they moved along the Rosserk road, had not marched in the French fashion, disciplined and drilled. They were a mob, formed loosely into groups, though obedient enough to the commands of O'Dowd and Teeling. MacCarthy, leaning with folded arms against the gable wall of the Wolf Dog, watched them move out of Killala, his eyes searching out the faces of men he knew, cowherds and hillside farmers, faction fighters and tavern drinkers. They seemed puzzled, some of them, and a few plainly were frightened, some joked and nudged each other with thick elbows. But the faces of most were impassive, expressionless. They carried pikes sloped awkwardly along their shoulders, unfamiliar weapons, bright, menacing heads new-forged. He watched until they were almost out of sight, pulled himself away from the wall, stood hesitant in the street, and then ran after them. He was neither welcomed nor sent away. Randall MacDonnell, preoccupied, in command of the rear column, did not recognize him. It was just as well, MacCarthy thought. He did not know whether he was there or not. Along *bother-na-sop,* the road of straw, they came from the cabins with lighted bundles of straw, flames upon the black night, and stood motionless and silent, wraiths summoned up from the past, faces wavering behind the fires.

The battle came when they emerged from the Rosserk road, at Teeling's shout, and fell upon Chapman's men, who were already in retreat. MacCarthy could not make heads or tails of it. It was all shouts and curses, a cattle fair at midnight. Most of the fighting was done by O'Dowd's column, which was in the van, and hidden from sight. "Now!" MacDonnell shouted. "Now!" His voice shot upward, shrill, on the tail of the word, and the men near MacCarthy ran forward toward the noises. Mac-Carthy ran after them, separated from them. But when he reached the Ballina road, there was nothing to see. The noises were moving along the road, toward the town. He slowed his pace, then stopped, and stood, wondering, in the road. Battle was shouting and· darkness. There was just enough light for him to see a pike, fallen or dropped. He bent down and picked it up. His free hand moved along the shaft of ash, the straight blade and the curved blade which twisted from its base. He brought the hand away, wet, and, sick with knowledge of its cause, knelt down and pawed the roadside grasses. An hour later, he found himself standing in a dog-legged Ballina street which ran at a right angle to the Moy. MacCarthy rested the pike against the bridge and left it for someone else.

Now, in bright summer sunlight, he walked among the victors of Ballina. Stretched out, at their ease, along pasturelands to the east of the town, they could see harvesters at their noontime rest, and the faces even of those whom he had never seen were familiar to him as well-worn tankards. They were the men among whom his life had been lived, the swarm of a nation, nameless. Swineherds and cowherds, they trailed their pikes across the pages of manuscript histories in Treacy's library, huddled and anonymous at the tail end of sentences that moved like pageants. "August 3, 1599. On this day perished in battle, at Abbeyleix, Sir Miles O'More, with five other gentlemen of the county, and a hundred others." "July 12, 1691. Lord Moycashel fell at Aughrim and at his side Sir Thomas Prendergast who was by marriage his kinsman. More than two hundred of the common sort died there upon the hill where he had taken his position." They were spread out before MacCarthy now, those others who had followed the beating drums, had run forward with the yelping sergeants. What drew them now? The prospect of looting the big houses, fear of massacre, vengeful hatred, simple excitement? Perhaps only a pike or a musket, and a haunch of beef to chew on, then slither off into the darkness, vomiting the rich meat on a bog road and the musket hidden in the thatch. The heavy hive had been stirred, and these had swarmed out, spilling from the cabins and the lonely huts and the stinking, fetid streets. They rallied to a meaningless banner, a square of green silk with a gilt harp on it and three words in dog-Irish.

MacCarthy, son of laborers like these, born and reared in a hut as mean as theirs, spun webs of words in which names like Moycashel and Muskerry hung like bright drops of dew, silver filaments shrouding the nameplates of defeat, Kinsale, Aughrim, Limerick. Fallen lords and colonels moved through his verses, imperious despite banishment and death. Their empty, silent houses, lime-white beneath the moon, were the landscape of his art. It was an art which could not stretch to *bother-na-sop,* a flame of straw upon the night, a woman running toward peasants with a bowl of milk. Three men from Belmullet passed him, huge, hulking men, their awkwardly held pikes spiky against the sky. Angles all askew, the pikes formed an instant's image, unraveled, vanished. Moonlight glancing from stone or metal washed across his mind, faded. That was the worst of it with poems. The meaning was right there, in the image itself, and you had no idea what it meant, but the image knew. The image was wiser than the poet. It disclosed itself when it was good and ready, casually, totally.

The Dublin-Galway Road, August 25

General Lake's carriage, with its outriders and its heavy escort of dragoons, did not pause at Athlone, at the fording of the Shannon. Heedless of Cornwallis's concern for his sleep, he had set off for the west an hour after leaving the council chamber. He had sent messengers before him. General Hutchinson, if he had not already done so, was to move the Connaught army from Galway to Castlebar, where Lake would join him and take command. When the Frenchman attempted Castlebar, as doubtless he would, he would find himself outnumbered and outgeneraled. This invasion and rebellion could be crushed while Cornwallis was making his stately, cumbersome progress to the field of action.

Lake peered through the streaky dawn at the fields of Westmeath. It wasn't merely age: Cornwallis had always been like this, first in North America, then India, now Ireland. Not a bad general at all, quite able in fact, but too cautious and too enamored of administration. And ideas! God save the realm from generals who doted on ideas. Cornwallis and Burgoyne. A soldier was a man who sought out the King's enemies and destroyed them. In Ireland they were everywhere and always had been. Cromwell had known how to deal with them, and in Wexford, Lake had taken a leaf from Cromwell's book. At Vinegar Hill he had blown them up with cannon fire, cut them down at bayonet point, hanged them from a gallows or the nearest tree. And what thanks had he received from Cornwallis a month or so later? Praise in public and a private reproof, in that gouty, offhand manner of his. But there was only one way to deal with rebels. Cornwallis would have to discover that for himself. Only one way, and it must be done as quickly as possible. Lake detested rebellion. He had the ordinary prejudices of his profession, but his detestation ran deeper than these. Rebels in arms against the King and against law itself, they had moved beyond the pale of civilization; they had cast aside their pretensions to humanity.

Castlebar would put an end to them, once and for all, trampling deep into mud the seeds which had sprouted such evil flowers in Wexford and Antrim. If this Frenchman could be forced into battle, it would be one of the classic triumphs of British arms, a textbook battle. Lake of Castlebar. Lord Lake. Some honor would certainly be owing to him, and a peerage would be the most appropriate. An obscure market town, perched upon the unvisited crossroads of Mayo, but it would not be forgotten in the histories of British arms. Castlebar.

But how rich the fields were in these days before the harvest. Rich to the point of bursting. Soon the reapers would be in the fields, as they would be in the fields of England, swinging the bright curving blades of their scythes. It might have been a landscape in England, were it not for the wretched cabins, the village streets which were straggles of mean shops and pothouses, no better than hovels. And this was one of the half-civilized counties of the Pale; beyond stretched Galway and Mayo,

228

the barbarous lands of the native Irish. At England's doorstep, yet remote and alien. Lake imagined bogland and mountain, mist-shrouded.

Castlebar, August 25

Sean MacKenna made his prudent way down Castle Street, crowded with soldiers, keeping to the inside, close to the line of shops. No one bothered him, though he was jostled once or twice, by accident. He was an unobtrusive man, short and corpulent; hatless, his bald head glistened in the evening light. Those shops which boasted shutters had them fastened shut, and he regretted that he had never made so sensible an investment. Castlebar had retreated upon itself, Catholic and Protestant alike, and had left the streets to the soldiers. It was like market day, but with soldiers crowding into the town, not drovers and black-flanked cattle.

Safe at last in his own shop, he called upstairs to his wife Brid and his small son Timothy, to say that he was there and would soon be ready for their tea. It was a word which he enjoyed saying, for it reminded him of their prosperity. Then he pushed aside several bolts of wool on the small counter, took down a heavy ledger book, and seated himself before it on his high stool. He inked his pen, read over the last entry, made a week before, stared into space as he composed his thoughts, and then began to write in Irish.

August 25. The streets of Castlebar are now filled with more soldiers than have ever been in Mayo at any time in its history. Armies there have surely been here in the past, for battles were fought here in the old days, and especially in the reign of Elizabeth and during the years of O'Donnell's uprising. But these, I suspect, were small battles, for all the extravagant words in the chronicles and the boasts of poets. There is now an army here such as those which fight upon the continent of Europe, and they have spilled out of the town and are in great encampments in the pasturelands, but they are in the town as well and have entirely filled the barracks. They have with them cavalry and cannon as well, great murderous engines. It is a sobering thought that the great nations of this world, England and France and the rest of them, can put so many thousands of men in uniform and march them where they will, flanked by their cannon and their cavalrymen, great tall fellows who have little regard for anyone save only themselves. But this is true in its way for all of these fellows, even the ones who have nothing better to do than to drive the carts. There was great fear expressed everywhere in Castlebar as they began to arrive, marching along the Galway road as though bent upon death and destruction, but it is little thought they have for us, and the reason is now known to all. They are making themselves ready to fight the army of Frenchmen and of our own people which has gathered itself to the north of us and has won a great victory in Ballina, should anything that happened in Ballina properly be termed great.

It is a wonder to me that events so prodigious should be taking place, and yet find me calmly recording them in this journal, as though I were writing of the weather, or making record of a birth or of a neighbor's death. For a century or more there has been fine talk by the poets, of France sending to us a great army for our deliverance, but I doubt whether in our hearts we believed that this would happen. Certainly I for one did not. What care about us need the French have, save that in the old days we would send them our young men to be blown apart and destroyed in their wars and thus spare the lives of their own young French boys? And if the French have indeed now sent an army here it is for their own purposes surely, and not from kindness nor from a desire to oblige our poets.

What in the name of God is this army of the Gael, of which there is now much talk? Last night in the tavern Con Horgan the farrier was making great boasts that the army of the Gael had risen up and would drive all before it, with the French trotting after them to do odd jobs and cook snails. Where has it come from, this army of the Gael, that has hidden itself for so many years? It is a crowd of Whiteboys and faction fighters, and it is to some great faction fight that they believe they are heading, but these lads here in Castlebar with their cavalry and their dark cannon have no thought of faction fights. I did not point this out to Con Horgan, a bellicose man with hands on him like rocks, and who was far gone in drink, but the truth should be plain enough to any man with common sense. He was swelled up with vainglory, as though he had himself met and vanquished a regiment of militia, and the men who were drinking with him share this delusion, clapping him on the back and calling for more whiskey. And yet true it is that Ballina was captured, miserable village that it is.

But soon enough all of Castlebar will have the opportunity to judge these matters, for it is in Castlebar that the great battle will be fought. Why else was the army of England brought here from Galway? And I for one could wish myself to be hundreds of miles from here, and Brid with me and little Timothy. At any time in the last twelve years I could have gone to Henry Rodgers, the Protestant carpenter, and for ten shillings he would have made stout shutters for the window of the shop and for the two windows above. I would by preference be in my native city of Cork, a center of civilization and polite learning, far removed from cannon and from soldiers shouting at each other as though the whole of the town were a tavern. But then if I had never come to this Godforsaken place to teach I would never have had this profitable shop, nor met my dear Brid, and there would be no Timothy, who is a great happiness to us both.

9

From the *Memoir of Events*, Written by Malcolm Elliott in October, 1798

I am told that the battle of Castlebar has attracted much interest and curiosity not only in this country and in England, but on the Continent, where exaggerated accounts of it are current. That it was an extraordinary event is certain, although, as will shortly become evident, I am no judge of such matters. Several most civil British officers have visited me in this place, and have asked for my account of the battle, and I have described it to them, much as I shall do in this memoir, but it must be remembered that my entire military career spanned a bare month or so, and that my ignorance of the craft of battle remains large. If it were a fox hunt, I could describe all that happened with energy and precision, and perhaps there are indeed resemblances between the two, but battles, if I may judge by this one, are spread across a landscape and all seems confusion, save perhaps to the two commanders.

Ballina, as I can now perceive, was a mere rout, and reflected little credit upon our arms, save for the clever manner in which Humbert made use of the Rosserk road. That town, which holds so large a meaning for me because it is my own, was a mere way station, and ill defended. The true prize, but also the source of our greatest immediate peril, was Castlebar, where General Hutchinson had moved the Connaught army at first news of the French landing. That army was known to be a large one, and although composed in part of Irish militia, it had a backbone of English soldiers. Accordingly, Sarrizen and Fontaine argued eloquently, and for me persuasively, that it must at all costs be avoided. Until the arrival of the second and larger fleet of invasion, so they argued, we should limit ourselves to holding and securing our coastal and river position. Or, as an alternative to this, we might strike eastward, toward Donegal, although this would bring us against General Trench's garrison at Sligo. Humbert, however, would hear none of this, shaking his head impatiently, and drumming his wide, soft fingers on the tabletop.

Now, at once, he said, we should knock the Castlebar army off balance, and make ourselves the masters of Connaught. We were badly outnumbered, it was true, but would be in a far worse situation if the English were given time to move up reinforcements from the south. And this argument, too, I found persuasive. Warfare, or at any rate this war, seemed to be composed of unpleasant dilemmas. But I suspected that he had an additional reason. He wanted a showy triumph, with which to impress the Irish, and still more to impress Paris. Sarrizen, indeed, came close to accusing him of this. Poor Sarrizen was like a cat on a hot griddle, second-in-command to a general who was playing his own hidden game. And Bartholemew Teeling was far from happy, for it was his concern from the first that the French should not use the Irish rebels as pawns in their own game. In this matter he was most punctilious, although his position was difficult, for he held the rank of colonel in the French army. And yet, despite his unhappiness, he agreed with Humbert as to the importance of attacking Castlebar without delay, and however great the risks. Throughout the campaign, almost to its close, Humbert and Teeling were in at least a tacit accord upon most matters, with Sarrizen and Fontaine being more often than not in opposition, although they carried out their orders most ably.

We Irish officers, O'Dowd, MacDonnell, Blake of Barraclough, Bellew, and a few others, were admitted to these counsels of war as a necessary courtesy. But there was, to begin with, a problem of language, for French was known only to myself and to John Moore, who at Humbert's insistence had been given a most curious and unmilitary position as delegate to the army from the Society of United Irishmen. But even had we all understood French, there was little that we could have added to these deliberations, because of our inexperience. This, of course, did not prevent O'Dowd and MacDonnell from swaggering out into the Irish camp as though they had helped to make great decisions. But I do not wish to make sport of them, for they were to prove most valiant and accepted every throw of the dice without complaint.

From military histories and memoirs, one readily gains the impression that generals form their battle plans after poring over maps for long, studious hours. If Humbert is typical, nothing could be farther from the case. He seemed to be everywhere, moving quickly but without the appearance of haste. Our Irish encampment must surely have astonished him, with its whiskey plundered from the taverns of Ballina, and its noise and wild music. But he smiled, clapped men on the back, several times took long pulls at jugs which were thrust toward him, and all the time kept up a rapid fire of instructions to Teeling and Sarrizen. What view he held of his allies we were presently to discover, but at any event he had no reason to query the sympathies of the Mayo peasantry. Thus, sometime after midnight there was an extraordinary sight. Down from the hill of Ardnaree, on the far side of the river, came a host of men carrying green branches. They were the men of Coolcarney and Attymass, who had heard of the victory at Ballina and had decided to join the rebellion, as one might join friends upon a holiday. And yet it was no holiday. Castlebar has always been the gateway to Mayo, for hills rise up on either side of it, an easy position to defend, a treacherous one to attack. Bloody battles were fought over it in the seventeenth century. The road, or what passes for a road in Connaught, runs southward from Ballina to Foxford, to the east of Lough Conn, and then, below the lake, runs in a southeasterly direction from Bellavary into Castlebar. Some men who came into us from Foxford told us that that town was still heavily defended, the garrison having been augmented by the troops who had fled from Ballina. They were unskilled at estimating numbers, but in Teeling's best judgment they were talking of about two thousand men. We would have to fight our way past these before ever we came face to face with the main English force.

Humbert had put aside the maps he brought with him, and instead drew one of his own, adding to it or modifying it as each crumb of information came to him. He carried it folded in his pocket, and from time to time would take it out and study it, crouched on his haunches at a campfire.

I cannot remember who brought the men from Nephin to him, but it was their arrival which determined the manner in which the battle of Castlebar was fought. I remember them standing before him, ten or twelve of them, with Teeling and Owen MacCarthy acting as interpreters. They came from a town called Coolagh, which like all of Nephin lies to the west of Lough Conn. When Humbert heard this, he put down his pencil. How did they get here, he asked, and I answered him before MacCarthy could. They followed a goat path, it was no better than that, which took them northward, to Crossmolina above the lake, and then came by the Crossmolina road into Ballina. What did we mean by a goat path, he asked, and how far did it run? It took O'Dowd, MacDonnell, and myself, racking our memories, to answer that question, although we were all Mayo men. And when we had finished, he made us question the peasants closely.

The one passable road between Ballina and Castlebar is the one which I have just described, to the east of Lough Conn. The country which stretches westward of the lake is wild even for Mayo. It is a land of mountains, dark lakes, and moorland wastes, uninhabited save by wretches who rip a miserable existence from its arable acres, or tend scrawny herds and flocks upon its melancholy slopes.

And yet there was known to be a path through it, beaten down in places by feet and hooves, in others a stubborn and treacherous morass. Southward from Crossmolina it runs past bogs and lakes, along the slopes of hills, and then begins to rise steadily and steeply through the glens of the Nephin range, trailing through the lost villages of Coolagh and Laherdane, running then over the humped crests of mountains, dropping at last into a rocky and precipitous defile called Barnageragh. Beyond Barnageragh it levels out, and then runs for two miles, straight into Castlebar.

Humbert heard us all out, interrupting us with questions, and then turned on his heels and walked away. Teeling watched him as he stood by himself, looking down into a dying fire. "Ballina is my home," I said. "I was born here. But I have never traveled that path. A cart couldn't move along that path; horses would stumble on it." Teeling nodded and shrugged his shoulders, his eyes still upon Humbert. When Humbert returned, he walked toward Sarrizen and Fontaine, but paused in front of us and said, "Tell the Irish officers that we will march south from Ballina tomorrow afternoon." "Which road?" Humbert answered in a surprised voice. "There is only one good road into Castlebar. Through Foxford. The British know that. They are already taking up their positions." "But in fact we will be going through the back door, will we not, General Humbert?" "It is a path for goats," Humbert said. "That is close to my old trade. Goat skins and rabbit skins." He struck Teeling lightly on the shoulder. "You cannot take artillery along that path," Teeling said. "We can try," Humbert said, and then walked away from us to join his French officers.

It has been said that sometime during the night a Ballina loyalist brought information to the British force in Foxford that we would be advancing upon that town the following day. It is certain that Foxford sent such a message to Castlebar, and followed it with a second.

We left at four o'clock, and I joined our column just at its point of departure, for I had spent some time at home with my wife. By my best calculations, we brought forward to the battle seven hundred French and eight hundred Irish. The remainder of our forces were left behind as garrisons in Killala and Ballina. A hundred of the

French mounted dragoons were in the van, followed by the French foot soldiers and then the Irish. We marched along the Foxford road until the first cool of evening fell upon us, and then Humbert halted the column, wheeled it around, and pointed it toward Crossmolina.

It was in Crossmolina that his intentions became clear to his soldiers and to our own men. The French were accustomed to sudden and confusing orders, and in any event they had no notion of the route which was proposed for us. With the Irish it was far otherwise, and the stir of their incredulity was so strong it could be felt. MacDonnell, O'Dowd, and Blake rode up to protest and because they did not speak French they poured out their protests to Teeling and myself. Humbert sat staring at them impassively until they had finished, then, before we could translate, he spoke to Teeling, his voice loud, and his tone harsh and vehement.

"Tell them that the British generals agree with them. They have disposed their troops and artillery and prepared their entrenchments to face an enemy advancing upon them due south along the Foxford road. But we will disappoint the British. We will make a forced march along the far shore of this great lake, and sometime tomorrow morning we will fall upon their flank. I know that it is very bad country, but we will cross it, whether we slip or slide or scramble like goats. I am a good general and I have won battles and campaigns. If they will follow my orders, I will lead them. But it is their country, not mine. If they don't want to fight for it, let them go home. Before they leave, they are to stack their muskets. The muskets are the property of the French Republic, which was born in pain and defended with blood."

It is my opinion that they grasped the meaning of his manner and tone more firmly than they did Teeling's translation, for all its fluency. The authority which an able commander exerts is mysterious. Is it some accretion from the battles he has fought, or is it some personal power, with him from the first, by virtue of which he was able to win those battles? I know that it exists, for it was present in this buyer of skins, speaking to wild squireens and peasants in a language which they did not understand. It is an ambiguous and dangerous power, as I now have reason to know, a lion watchful in the forest, but it can carry men beyond their capacities, can plunge them into dangers which any man of sense would avoid.

The Irish captains rode up and down the lines, talking to their men. My Irish is faulty and I did not grasp all of what they said, but it seemed to me a fair paraphrase of Humbert's words, cast in a homely idiom. The men, of whom many had at first been angry or frightened, grew quiet and thoughtful, or so, at least, it appeared to me. They moved me to wonder at the passions which drew men into battle, risking their lives for a wisp of cloth, a fragment of song, a flattering or a cajoling speech. Certainly it was not a risk run for the sentiments set forth in the proclamations which Teeling had brought with him, resounding affirmations of the principles of the Society of United Irishmen and of the Revolution in France. "By God," Corny O'Dowd said, jerking his head toward the French grenadiers, "those lads over there know how to fight and they have worked wonders. They have cleared all the yeomen and all the militia out of their own country, and cut off their King's head and stuck it up on a spike outside his palace." He was wearing the blue uniform of a French officer, but his own coarse breeches, and heavy boots to which still clung the muck of his farm. "And it was that lad over there who showed them how to do it. He is the most famous of the French generals, and they have sent him over here to lead us. We beat them at Killala and we beat them at Ballina and we will beat them at Castlebar, if we keep our minds to our tasks. Wasn't it always promised that the French would come over to us with men and with weapons? You know your history, and if you do not you can ask the schoolmaster." MacCarthy gave him a brief smile, half friendly and half sardonic, but said nothing. He carried neither musket nor pike, nor the pistol which had been issued to each of the Irish captains. He was the sort of fellow who can be found on any market day, propped against the gable of a shop, thumbs hitched into the band of his breeches.

It says much for Humbert that he moved us out of Crossmolina without further murmur or protest, not even from those Nephin men who knew part of the route. And Humbert himself acted as if it did not greatly matter, one way or the other, talking easily and quietly with Sarrizen and Fontaine, and several times laughing.

The people of Crossmolina watched us leave, standing quiet and observant beside their cabins.

By midnight, when Lake arrived in the drab, mean town, shops squatting on the square, courthouse, barracks, market house, and gaol, he already knew that Hutchinson had moved the Connaught forces. A messenger had reached him on the road outside Claremorris. He climbed out of the carriage and walked up and down beside it, to stretch his cramped legs, a large, imposing man who did justice to his scarlet uniform. Hutchinson was waiting for him, to explain the order in which he had disposed his troops and the instructions which he had given his officers.

"All in good time," Lake said, in a fair imitation of Cornwallis's manner. "All in good time."

There was a most singular atmosphere, turbulent and yet watchful. Castlebar was dense with army wagons; soldiers jostled each other in the narrow streets. But the shops and taverns were dark and silent.

"Do we know what he is doing?"

"He marched out of Ballina late this afternoon. About seven hundred of his French, and a like number of rebels. I have reinforced General Taylor at Foxford, and we have been waiting now for word from him."

"Taylor will never hold him," Lake said. "He will be upon us in the morning."

"He will indeed," Hutchinson said. "He seems prompt and energetic. His name is Humbert, it seems."

"His name doesn't matter," Lake said. "The names keep changing. Lose a battle and they put you to the guillotine. A bloody-minded people."

"I have begun to move out our people," Hutchinson said. "They will be in position before dawn. We are in a very strong defensive position here."

Lake nodded and looked around him. "I want the latest intelligence from Foxford. By God, this is an ugly place. The people here are all rebels, I take it?"

"I have no reason to believe that," Hutchinson said stiffly. He was an Irishman, the son of the Provost of Trinity. "The people seem quiet enough."

"Do they indeed? I've seen towns like this in Ulster and I've seen them in Wexford. You'd think butter wouldn't melt in their mouths. But give them one chance, Hutchinson. Turn your back on them just once."

They walked together into the barracks yard, where the other officers had gathered to greet him. He recognized Lord Ormonde, who commanded the Kilkennys, Lord Roden of the cavalry, Lord Granard of the Longfords. Militia regiments. Loyal enough, no doubt, but clumsy and inexperienced. Grant, the Highlander. That was more like it: the Highlanders were the real lads. Good luck that Crauford wasn't here. Cornwallis's pet Highlander, a violent, witty man, but inclined to steal every show with his cavalry flash.

Torches lit the crowded barracks yard.

"Well now, gentlemen. Well now. What is our strength, General Hutchinson?"

"Something better than seven thousand men," Hutchinson said. "Regulars and militia."

"And spoiling for a fight, I'll wager, eh Lord Ormonde?"

"They are, General Lake. If you mean the Kilkennys."

"Yes. Of course they didn't look too well a few months ago when they had their own county to defend. Things were a sorry mess down there before I took command."

"General," Grant said. "Isn't it peculiar that we have had no further word from General Taylor at Foxford?"

"Most peculiar indeed, Colonel Grant. I am looking into that. A most sensible question."

Just at dawn, Lake and his officers rode out to inspect the positions. The town was cupped by low hills, with shadowy mountains to the left. Hutchinson had chosen to hold Sion Hill, a mile outside the town. The troops were to be drawn up in three lines, protected on either flank by a lake. The cavalry would hold between the first and second lines. The artillery was placed at the north end of the hill, covering either side of the road. Lighter guns were placed at the bridge into town, and in the town itself.

Lake rode slowly over the terrain, but he could find no fault with Hutchinson's dispositions. He could hear bird song and marching feet, shrilling fifes and the rattle of drums. It would be a clear, warm morning. He turned in his saddle.

"Does this put you back in the Highlands, Grant?"

Grant shrugged and spat. Lake laughed. A textbook battle. But he would share the credit with Hutchinson. A tidy battlefield.

239

Dark moors and pools of dark water. The back of beyond. Two miles past Addergoole they were given an hour's rest, but MacCarthy could not sleep. He walked past men with their heads resting on drawn-up knees. They had reason enough to sleep, some of them. The French general had left behind him in Crossmolina all his artillery except the light curricle guns, and peasants had been yoked to these like beasts of burden. Shoulders bent, they had stumbled and staggered in the darkness, with the French sergeants bellowing at them incomprehensible oaths. What else had there ever been but men who looked like these, like himself, straggling across bogs, or through forests, with mists writhing about their legs? Our poetry, the celebrations of defeats, chieftains cut down in battle, lonely stands by fords and mountain passes, retreats. There would be no song for those who sat exhausted, chests heaving, after doing work that horses and donkeys had refused.

Moorland and rocky glen, by day the bright pale sky would stretch across their emptiness, the landscape of banishment. Here, westward of the Shannon, the Irish chieftains had been scattered after Cromwell's triumph. Here, into Connaught, the dispossessed Gaelic landowners had journeyed afoot or by cart, the "retainers" driving their herds with hazel wands. But not the peasants, hewers of wood and drawers of water. These had crept back from bogside, from slopes of rocky hill, to serve their new masters. They served newer masters now, Teeling and Elliott and Moore with their florid proclamations of fraternity and equality, this indecipherable French general, all frowns one moment and all smiles the next. Years before, MacCarthy had stood in the square of Macroom to watch the hanging of Paddy Lynch, the Whiteboy Captain, short barrel of a man, murderous and always smiling. This was a path which Lynch might have chosen, over the humps of hills, through stony defiles. A masterless people save for men like Lynch, a peasant like themselves, ignorant and brutal.

These men in loose frieze, long-lipped, black hair or red hanging loose, were held in a loop of history's long

coils. Hands hardened by the plow clutched musket or
pike. Ignorant and uncomprehending, they scrambled up
hills, walked or half ran beside starlit waters. When
colonels and chieftains had been scraped away, these men
were left.

From the *Memoir of Events*, Written
by Malcolm Elliott in October, 1798

The day, which all who have passed comment upon
these events describe as a most extraordinary one, opened
at six in the morning, when our force, after its arduous
march across that wretched country, emerged upon rising
ground, facing the British who held Sion Hill, some thousand yards distant from us. An hour earlier, they had
been brought word of our approach, and they had set to
work redressing their lines, a task which they had not yet
completed. Humbert stood for a time in contemplation of
the scene before him, as though viewing men placed on
parade for his inspection, and then moved us forward to
the shelter of a hill called Slievenagark. We were still
outside the range of the British guns.

He then ordered the Irish, under O'Dowd and Teeling,
to charge the guns. Accordingly we moved forward in a
mass, receiving, at a distance of about fifty yards, a wall
of musket fire. The Irish charged and routed the infantry
who stood lined to protect the cannon, but then the cannon, which until then had been silent, commenced bellowing explosions which battered wide holes in our ranks.
Our losses were heavy, although at the time I had no
thought of that, for the world seemed to have dissolved in
smoke and a terrifying noise. While this action had been
taking place, however, Humbert had been moving forward the rest of his forces in files, using hedges as his
cover, and then assembling them in a formation which
flanked the English. We were ordered then to charge
again, and we did, if only because we could think of
nothing else to do. The grenadiers had moved behind us,
and pressed us forward.

I can claim no distinction for myself. I remember firing
my pistol at a gunner, and I remember cutting down at
men with my sword. It was my task, I knew, to encourage
our men, but when I opened my mouth it was dry and

241

stiff. But I saw O'Dowd shouting, his hat in his hand, beating it across men's backs and shoving them forward. What I best remember are the noises, musket fire and screams. Their cavalry was left with no room in which to maneuver, for the Longford militia stumbled backward upon them, and then the Irish with their pikes fell upon them, slashing and hooking murderously at horse and rider alike.

And yet what won the battle was the flight of the enemy, as much as it was our charges upon them. When O'Dowd's men scaled their side of the hill, they ran past guns which had already been deserted. The Kilkennys and the Prince of Wales's Fencibles, it is said, were the first to buckle, and as they fled backward, they threw into panic the line behind them. The Frasers held, and fought their ground with resolute bravery, swinging their muskets like clubs. But the rest of that army, which so greatly outnumbered us, turned and fled. Humbert later confessed that he had not expected it. By throwing away the first wave of Irish as a sacrifice to draw the artillery, and then attacking from the flank, he had calculated upon a victory, but the manner of our triumph was without precedent.

I can describe but I cannot explain what is now called a most ignominious defeat for British arms, the battle of Castlebar, or, as it is derisively termed, "the Castlebar races." Humbert's night march down through Barnageragh had much to do with it, of course, for it forced the British into a new and awkward plan of defense, hastily chosen and ill considered. Perhaps Lake erred in taking command upon a field to which he had but recently arrived, but I do not believe that Hutchinson or any other officer would have fared better. Save, perhaps, Humbert himself. All of us, even the Irish-speaking peasants from Nephin, had come to share Humbert's confidence in his own abilities. It was a mysterious elixir, and we had all drunk of it. Dropped upon an alien and savage coast, commanding men whose language he could not understand, he moved and gave his orders as one persuaded that success was casual and inevitable. In the two months that have passed since then I have become far more cynical upon that point, but on the morning of the Castlebar battle, I risked my life upon his nod, as did the others. The British officers with whom I have spoken dismiss almost entirely the rebel attack, and attribute our victory to Humbert's seasoned infantry and his grenadiers. Our Irish, they say, were but a mob flung forward to create a diversion. But upon that point I am less certain. It was a mob flung forward by history, and had, perhaps, its terrifying aspect.

It is certain that the British fled. They fled toward Castlebar, abandoning their guns and dropping their muskets as they ran. In the narrow streets of the town, their cavalry rode down and trampled their infantry. Some hundreds of them were brought under control by the officers and fought a creditable action at the bridge to protect their comrades' retreat, but they were overborne. And the gunners who manned a curricle which had been placed in the town attempted to maintain a fire, which was most courageous of them. I have heard it said that one of these men was killed by Owen MacCarthy, but of this I have no knowledge. He was unarmed on our night march, but when a man named Cafferty was shot down, a peasant who served as a captain under Mac-Donnell, MacCarthy took his place, and was present during the fighting on Sion Hill. Thereafter, some in the Irish army termed him "captain," part in jest and part in earnest.

Looking over these lines, I find that I have indeed set down in most flat and perfunctory manner both my account of this signal victory and of my own first experience in battle. After the battle, I was both elated and confused. I was part of a small, desperate army which had achieved a most improbable success, through luck, skill, and the cowardice of the enemy. The English defeat was utter and entire. All was left behind them—cannons, munitions, muskets by the hundreds, battleflags. They did not pause in their headlong retreat until they reached Tuam, where they rested briefly before proceeding to Athlone to await Cornwallis, a march of sixty-three miles. And they carried with them, whence it spread throughout Ireland, word that a large and ferocious army was on the move. Three hundred of the Irish died in this encounter, the greater part of them blown to pieces in the minutes before O'Dowd began his charge upon the cannons. A few of them died at my side, and I saw British soldiers skewered and ripped open by pikes. This was the battle, now famous, of Castlebar.

MacCarthy stood dazed in Castlebar High Street. As though, a boy in Tralee, he had won a footrace, chest heaving, senses muddled. He remembered moments, held in sequence but disconnected, a night of red stars. Men shouted, smoke smeared and stained the grass of summer. A footrace past the dying. Uniforms, red and hearty, held Sion Hill, but when they turned and ran some were left to writhe upon the ground, faces contorted, eyes wild.

At the foot of Sion Hill, Cafferty stumbled and fell forward, his chest smashed in by cannon shot. The men he had been leading stopped in their tracks and stared at him, a pool of terrified quiet within the noise. The noise of the cannons was horrible, a voice given to blood, to bodies changed into butchers' meat and sodden cloth. A man beside MacCarthy stumbled, tripping upon his own awkward feet. MacCarthy seized his shoulders, held him upright, and they looked at each other without recognition. "O Jesus save me," he said, and lurched forward. The cannon exploded within MacCarthy's mind and he felt his guts loosening. Red uniforms tended them, packed death into their black, yawning mouths, opened wide to scream. "Stop them," MacCarthy shouted to Cafferty's men. He grabbed one of them and shoved him forward. "For Jesus sake, stop them." He ran forward then himself, bellowing like a bull to shut out the noise of the cannon. He paused to look backward, and saw that they were following him, about twenty of them. To his left and right were many others, running toward the Longfords, a great mass of men running up the gentle slope, their pikes held awkwardly, peasants who knew how to swing a blade against corn or downward into the turf. What would they have done had the Longfords held their ground, thin murderous bayonets grouped together? But they buckled and ran, fear spreading beyond them like a contagion. It was a message, passed in silence along the long lines of red uniforms. Turn. Run. The rebels ran toward them, courage mounting when they saw that suddenly they had no cause for fear, nothing facing them but men to be run down and butchered. Cannon abandoned, nothing filled the air but voices. The ghosts of cannon fire, wraiths of phantom sound, filled MacCarthy's ears, and he paused to press his hands against them. Then, like all the others, he ran across meadows still slippery with dew toward Castlebar, nestling in its cup of soft hills.

Now he stood in Castlebar High Street as men ran past him. He saw muskets, abandoned and kicked aside. Where the British troops had gone, he neither knew nor cared, but it was up this street that most of them had poured. At the top of the street stood a curricle gun, the gunner sprawled across it. A brave man, working his murderous engine as murder-minded men ran toward him. What would possess a man to do such a thing?

Corny O'Dowd flung an arm across his shoulder. "We beat them, Owen. We smashed them all." His eyes were mad with excitement.

MacCarthy nodded. That was what it was. A battle fought and won. He felt nothing save the dried saliva of fear upon his tongue.

"By God, 'tis a lucky stroke for you that you are here," O'Dowd said. "There will be a poem out of you about this someday."

"About this?" MacCarthy asked. Distant now, at the edge of his imagination, cannon belched noises harsher than thunder. Lines of verse by other men jumped at him, vanished, wraiths from a bog. Chieftains banished from lime-white mansions. O'Sullivan Beare retreating northward toward Leitrim, savage in his desperation. Sarsfield's night raid, small victory drowned in the red waves of Aughrim and Limerick. "About this?" he asked again, but O'Dowd was gone, jaunty rider drunk with triumph.

Men were running more slowly now, slackening to a walk, halting to stare about them, as MacCarthy had done. MacCarthy stood by a huckster's shop, exotic now as any Arab tent, separated from him by the vast distance created by what he had seen and heard on Sion Hill. He turned to look down High Street, and saw Humbert crossing the bridge which lay at its foot, the little humpbacked bridge lifting him up above his men. Teeling, the Ulsterman, rode behind him, and Elliott, the Protestant landlord. Humbert's face was difficult to make out, even when he moved closer, a face which could hide itself from other men. He was smiling, as no doubt generals always did in victory. He rode up the street of this town which he had never seen before like a squire coming in from his farm, but it was a stranger's face, dark and unknowable.

MacCarthy walked on, toward the curricle gun. The gunner's scarlet coat was a splash of color in the street of gaunt gray buildings. MacCarthy looked into his open eyes. His hair was red, MacCarthy's color, and his face was familiar. And why not? Weren't the two of them Irish, MacCarthy and the dead gunner from the Longford midlands? Racial resemblance, more certain than coat of frieze and coat of lobster red, joined gunner and schoolmaster, red hair, hard jaw, long lip. MacCarthy reached out a hand, across the gun, to touch the gunner's face, then drew it back in haste.

With angular, loping strides he left gun and gunner, pushed past the men who filled the street, and turned at the top. He watched the stream of men cross the bridge, climb the hill's easy slope, divide in two to pass the dead gunner. What poem would ever harden from that imprecise image? The loud voices were jubilant, shouting in heavy-voweled Irish across which French cut like the rattle of musket fire.

Randall MacDonnell rode up to him, blood brother to horses, no grace to him save when he sat astride one. Centaur and bumpkin. The mists had been burned away. In the clarity of flat, pale sunlight, MacDonnell reined in and leaned down toward him.

"Do you know who their general was? It was Lake himself. It was Lake and the entire army of Connaught that ran away from us."

The flat, hard monosyllable jogged MacCarthy's memory. The two United Men from Wexford, on the run in a Mayo shebeen. Cromwell come again, General Lake marching across Wexford and Carlow, in his wake an avenue of gallows and whipping posts, invincible coats of lobster red, shrill of fifes and beating drums.

"There is a poem for you in that, boy."

First O'Dowd, now him. Poems on demand. Go into a tavern and scribble it out, then hawk it through the streets of Castlebar. Make a few shillings out of it, like the jinglejangle ballads that were made in English after races. Poetry was somewhere else. Not here.

Come all you true-born Irishmen, attend unto my lay.
Of the race we won at Castlebar one gallant August day.

"Would you like a sporting poem, Randall?" he asked, throwing humor as a wall between them. "How the race was won at Castlebar?" He was hoarse. Had he been bellowing like the rest of them, an uncontrolled animal?

Puzzled. Hat pushed to the back of his head of tight black curls. Then he laughed, high-pitched, hand pressed down on short, full thigh. "By God, that is exactly what he did. Lake won the Castlebar races. He had us beat by a mile. That wouldn't do at all, though. We must have a noble poem of triumph, suitable to the occasion." They had been talking in English. He touched his whip to his cap and rode off. A jockey's whip carried into battle. But he had a great pistol strapped around him, and another in a saddle holster.

At the top of the High Street, the French soldiers turned. and moved down Castle Street, past barracks, court-house, gaol, hard, angular buildings bruising the mild air. MacCarthy stepped aside, into a cobbled alley.

Humbert rode behind a guard of grenadiers, a large man, larger than MacCarthy, his face swarthy with its private thoughts. Teeling, an even-tempered meditative man; watchful, intelligent eyes. John Moore, young and fair-skinned, full lips and delicate nose, hair yellow as corn. Young hero of a poem, claiming the conquered city. MacCarthy, hugging his elbows, leaned a shoulder against cool brown stone. The substance of poetry, young heroes and triumphant generals. Perhaps such moments had always had the look of this one, layered grains of sunlight and actuality running across passion, across myth. Men whom he knew well, and other men no different from them, walked past him, plowboys and spalpeens. They had the walk of men who lumbered at break of day across fields wet with dew. A while before, they had been screaming as they climbed Sion Hill, skewering men with their murderous pikes. A battle was an hour ripped out of the flank of existence. Sunlight soothed the wound. The commonplace, a huckster's shop, a wall of rough stone, a plowboy's lumbering gait, grew a skin over the wound and healed it.

Above the courthouse they raised the banner of green silk which had been carried from France, the harp without the crown. The officers of Humbert's staff, French and Irish, mounted the steps, and the mob which now could be called an army stood looking at them. The French band, with its drums and flutes, began to play.

When it had finished, the air was silent. Then, notes flinging themselves like coins from a pocket, a pipe. MacCarthy looked through the crowd, but could not find the
piper. One of the O'Donnell marches; he had heard it
often in Killala. Hugh O'Donnell sweeping down from
the north and laying Mayo waste. No town here in O'Donnell's day, no courthouse. Now, from the winding alleys
of cabins, townspeople were drifting toward the courthouse square.

All that shouting had given him the father and mother
of a thirst. It would be pleasant to walk down to Sean
MacKenna's shop, and take him off for a drink. Those
taverns would be open soon, one way or another. As
though nothing had happened at Killala or Ballina or here
in Castlebar. Of all the dead that he had seen that day
he remembered only the gunner with clarity. A man with
a face like his own, but with the alien eyes of the dead.

But on the way to MacKenna's he met MacDonnell
again, dismounted now, a chunky, bandy-legged man, and
went off with him to look for an open tavern. Time
enough later for a drink with Sean. A quiet man like
Sean would have no taste for wandering about in such a
scene.

"This is a great bloody morning," MacDonnell said.

"Bloody enough," MacCarthy said.

"It was," MacDonnell said. "There were three hundred
of our lads slaughtered, but by Christ the other fellows
caught the worst of it. They fled like deer with us hacking
away at them."

"I saw that," MacCarthy said.

MacDonnell smiled, small teeth with spaces between
them. "The Castlebar races."

There had been a battle and it was won and Mac-
Carthy had taken part in it. Not as a poet trailing along
to pick up the odd image, an eye out for leaders to flatter
in verse. He had climbed up Sion Hill to the militia,
raced after them across the slippery grass and weeds,
stood looking down at the dead gunner.

"By God, Owen," MacDonnell said. "Things will never
be the same again."

248

10

**From *An Impartial Narrative of What Passed at
Killala in the Summer of 1798*,
by Arthur Vincent Broome**

The appalling news of the disaster at Castlebar was at
first received with incredulity by the loyalists of Killala.
Killala, it must be remembered, was now cut off from the
rest of Mayo, and remained so until the very end. The
roads south, east, and west were held by the rebels, who
allowed no loyalist to travel upon them, and we were
therefore dependent upon the rebels for such news as
they might give to us, and this news, of course, became
increasingly alarming. Despite this, we had been confident
that the rebels and their French allies, when once they
encountered a British army in the field, would be dispersed and scattered.

My place of residence remained the headquarters for
the rebel force left behind, under the command of a most
intelligent fellow named Ferdy O'Donnell, a man of some
education and with an abundance of that rough courtesy
which can often be discovered among the Irish. I shall
have much to say hereafter concerning O'Donnell, whom
I might almost call an excellent creature, had he not
stained his soul with the dark red of rebellion. On more
occasions than one we were to owe our very lives to him,
and once at least he put his life at risk to preserve ours.
I often reflect upon the mysteries of the human soul,
wherein good and evil are so intricately intertwined that
no man has either the wisdom or the virtue to know
where the one leaves off and the other begins. For the
present, it will suffice to say that he seldom intruded upon
the privacy of the rooms which had been allotted to us
(in my own house!), and that this was one of those occasions.

He came pounding up the stairs and beat upon the

249

door to my library, which I opened with trepidation to behold him standing there and trembling with excitement. A large army under the command of General Lake himself had been defeated at Castlebar, he informed me, and all the northern part of Connaught had passed into the hands of the rebels. I endeavoured to soothe him with words while I considered the dangers now presented to us, not by his news, which not for a moment did I believe, but by the fact that he believed it. At that time, I shared the fears of other loyalists that the rebels might well choose to slaughter us either to celebrate a triumph or to avenge a defeat. The fate of the poor Protestants of Wexford was constantly in our thoughts.

I am not certain how O'Donnell expected me to respond to his words, whether with rage or with a sudden conversion to his cause. It is possible that he wished only to share with me an excitement which had brought him to the point of bursting. He was in any event unprepared for my response, for I was unable to dissemble my disbelief. At this a tumble of words fell from him which served out to heighten my skepticism. If he was to be believed, a small army, the half of it made up of rude and ignorant peasants, had defeated a large one, formed in part of British regulars and fortified by artillery. And it was no mere defeat, he claimed, but an utter and shameful rout. Faced by this band of bumpkins and French banditti, a large British army, commanding the heights, had turned tail and run, flinging away both muskets and honor. It was this wild final improbability which set the crown upon my disbelief, and I feared for our safety at the hands of men who believed so unlikely a tale.

My incredulity was shared by most other loyalists. Mr. Falkiner, who had seen service in his youth, sought with ill-concealed impatience to demonstrate the improbability of the tale which I carried to him. Not even Frenchmen, he explained, would in such fortunate circumstances turn tail; no, nor Spaniards either. And so thought we all, or rather, as I have been told, all of us save Captain Cooper. Even at his best, Cooper was after all an Irishman, and never more so than when strenuously denying the fact. Now, in his market-house prison, he seemed at times half mad, raging in impotent fury. The rumor of the Castlebar defeat he confirmed at once, shouting out that the cowards of England had always abandoned the Irish Protestants

in their hour of peril, to be slaughtered by peasants or by
God's grace to be rescued by Dutch princes. The rest of
us, however, were slow in accepting his mad wisdom.
Only after days had passed, with peasants and rebels
moving back and forth between Killala and Castlebar,
carrying with them calm and certain testimony, did we
accept the truth. Even then, we consoled ourselves for
some days with the fiction that the British army had been
evacuated southward before the battle, leaving only a garrison to defend the town.

But alas, as all the world knows British arms had
suffered a humiliating defeat, and a dangerous one. Connaught lay at the mercy of the rebels, with many of them
swaggering through the streets of Killala. These were not
O'Donnell's men alone. There was much movement between the towns in rebel hands—Killala, Ballina, Westport, Foxford, Swinford, Crossmolina, and of course
Castlebar, and each day brought news that some remote
hamlet had declared for the rebel cause. Most menacing
of all were the small bands of ruffians captained by men
akin to the brutal Malachi Duggan. These raided and
burned whenever they could move beyond the discipline
which Humbert had imposed, and a number of Protestant
houses were set afire, but none near Killala, where Ferdy
O'Donnell, "Captain" O'Donnell as he styled himself,
maintained order. The wives of the imprisoned yeomen
were especially fearful of vengeance. All of them, that is,
save Mrs. Cooper, who gathered up a band of rough and
uncouth peasants with whose help she proposed to defend
Mount Pleasant against all attack. I several times saw her
striding through the streets, an Hibernian amazon, holding in her hand a folded whip of the sort which legend
has associated with her father's name. She could easily
have been overborne, for all her truculence, but the
countryside held her in a wry respect which ill accorded
with their hatred and contempt for her unfortunate husband.

We were not long in discovering that we had become
citizens of a newborn state, the Republic of Connaught,
a pledge against that Republic of Ireland which was the
ambition of the rebellion. This was no playacting, but a
government which asserted its rights over us all, and demanded both our loyalty and our material support. Young
John Moore, brother to the justly celebrated George
Moore of Moore Hall, was appointed its President, and

251

he governed as head of a Council of Twelve. This council issued orders that all able-bodied men not otherwise serving with the rebels were to report to Castlebar. A levy of two thousand guineas was made upon the town of Castlebar and of ten thousand guineas upon the county. Additionally, assignats were issued, signed by Mr. Moore, whereby goods were requisitioned with payment promised upon the establishment of a Republic of Ireland. I have seen a number of these instruments of plunder, although by good fortune none came into my possession.

The order directing all males to report to Castlebar was not intended as a means of universal conscription. Rather, its purpose was to place those who did not comply in a position of disloyalty to the newly founded state. Almost all Protestants, and the majority of the respectable Papists, found themselves in this situation. My own position I regarded as in several ways peculiar. I suffer, although without undue pain, from the gout, and am therefore less than able-bodied. Moreover, the order clearly held only Irishmen in its contemplation, and, by what I have come to regard as one of the chief mercies granted to me by the Almighty, I am not Irish. I discussed these several points with "Captain" O'Donnell, and he readily agreed that they were well taken. Indeed, he offered it as his own opinion that my cloth alone would exempt me from what he called "this Castlebar foolishness."

A time of turbulent passions and oppressive imaginings had come upon Killala, and it was to endure for many weeks. As we shall discover, the extraordinary drama of the Mayo rebellion had not only its prologue but its epilogue here, where both the first battle and the last one were fought. But between the two, we lived upon rumors and fears. We were uncertain of our lives and our properties, and we came in time to fear for the kingdom itself. The rebels must sooner or later encounter the main body of the British army, but after the dark and sinister event at Castlebar, who could predict the outcome? To judge by our barony, Ireland may well have been in the grip of a vast servile mutiny, for the like of which one must look far past the peasant revolt of the Middle Ages to antiquity and Spartacus. Our captors, save only O'Donnell, had scant knowledge of ancient history, but to judge by their jubilant faces, they needed none.

After Castlebar, an air of carnival descended upon the

town. Many of the men, and especially the younger ones, had gone off with the rebels, but many others stayed peaceably at home, where the crops were now ready for the harvest. Yet most of these were in warm sympathy with the insurrection, despite the courageous denunciations issued each Sunday by Mr. Hussey. And had they not here the example of his curate, the repellent Murphy, who had in very fact joined the rebels and gone off with them to Castlebar, where doubtless he was celebrating Mass in ensanguined vestments. The taverns were noisy throughout the night, with shouting and drinking and singing, with the music of pipe and fiddle. Often I was fearful that not even O'Donnell would be able to restrain his people, if strong liquor should work malignantly upon their natures. During this early period of our captivity, however, they were fully occupied by their rumors of victory and triumph.

From time to time, Killala men active in the rebellion would ride in from Castlebar, and among them Owen MacCarthy, but a MacCarthy changed for the worse. He was now an avowed rebel, and had taken part in the battle. I encountered him once in my place of residence, for O'Donnell was his close friend. He had a rank of some sort, but unlike the others he was not wearing the uniform with which rebel officers had been furnished. Instead, he wore a silk shirt, and a fine coat which had once belonged to some gentleman more slightly built than he. A pistol, however, was the emblem of rank among them, and he wore one in a handsome case, strapped around him by a wide leather belt. When he saw me staring at him, he had at least the grace to look sheepish as he stood there in his plundered finery. He was at best a large, awkward man, and now he looked outlandish as well.

Because of their respect for my cloth, I was myself allowed the liberty of the town, but I seldom availed myself of this, in part because of the fears of my dear Eliza and in part because of my own timorousness. It was a saddening experience to walk through the few streets, for Killala, like MacCarthy, had changed for the worse. It had been a dour, cheerless place, its low buildings stained by the wet Atlantic winds, but it had at least been quiet. But the streets were always crowded now, and the air heavy with that menacing, incomprehensible language, so unsuited to polite or even rational discourse. Standing at the foot of the street which ran down to the pier, I felt as lonely and as abandoned as Crusoe in Defoe's romance.

And yet all these weeks, as I have told the reader to his weariness, we lived within the golden weather of late summer, and the crops now dropped their heavy heads, to signify their readiness for the scythe.

11

Castlebar, August 28

Humbert had learned late in life to read and write, and he managed these arts awkwardly. Throughout his career this had been troublesome, not because it embarrassed him, but because it forced him to rely upon aides and secretaries. His report to the Directory, written the day after the battle of Castlebar, was dictated to Bartholemew Teeling and then carried by an Irish recruit to Newport, where a fishing smack had been awaiting it. He spoke slowly, in deference to Teeling's French but also because it was an important letter.

". . . Then, after a march of seventeen hours, through a desolate and almost trackless waste, I arrived near Castlebar at six in the morning. The English position was a very strong one, and they greatly outnumbered my combined force of French soldiers and Irish . . . what shall we call those fellows, Teeling?"

"Patriots," Teeling said, unsmiling.

"Good. French soldiers and Irish patriots. Moreover, they were supported by artillery, whereas I had been obliged to leave behind in a village called . . ."

"Crossmolina."

". . . called Crossmolina all save a few light guns. Lake and Hutchinson, the English generals, had centered their defense upon a low, wide hill about a thousand yards' distance from my advance column. I decided to use the

Irish patriots for a massed attack upon the center. These troops, commanded by a brave native officer named O'Dowd, and armed with long-handled pikes, made, in all, four attacks upon the hill, and suffered heavy losses, being subjected to cannon fire. I then ordered a general attack. Sarrizen drove in the enemy's left. Fontaine compelled his right to retreat in disorder. The retreat was soon entire. In his flight, the enemy abandoned both guns and honor. An attempt was made by elements of his regiments to fight a rear-guard action in defense of the bridge which crosses into the town of Castlebar. A charge by the Third Regiment of Chasseurs dispersed them and forced them across the bridge in panic. There was some fighting within the town, but it was trifling. A brave gunner manned a curricle gun from the top of the chief street of the town. He was slain by an even braver Irish patriot. The enemy was pursued for some miles southward of the town. The defeat was utter. Arms, ammunition, even General Lake's luggage, were left behind. Do you have all that, Teeling?"

"Yes, sir." Teeling held his pen poised in respectful, faintly ironical readiness.

"There, now. That is how the report of a battle should read. Simple, no flourishes. A soldier is a blunt man but he can order his ideas with clarity."

"Especially the report of a victory."

Humbert smiled. "Just so. Have Sarrizen give you an account of the killed and wounded on both sides, a list of the cannon and equipment captured, the names of the British regiments which took part in the battle. Submit the list to me, and after I have initialed it, add it to the report."

"Will Paris be interested in the names of the peasants who were killed? It will be a long list. Men armed with pikes making four charges into cannon fire."

"How else would you have had me use them?" Humbert asked, with faint irritation. "Plowboys without training, with no experience of battle. They soaked up the cannon fire, and then my Frenchmen drove in the flanks. How else?"

Teeling did not answer. He drew a neat cross, small, in the margin of his paper.

"Also," Humbert said, "have Fontaine draw a map of the battlefield and include that. Tell him to sketch a French soldier on one side of the map, and an Irish patriot with his pike on the other side. That will look very nice. After the blunt, truthful account has been given, it is permissible to contemplate what has happened, and to suggest its importance."

He stood up, walked to the window, and looked across Lord Claremorris's sunlit acres toward a plantation of larches. Then he began to dictate again.

"The bravery and resourcefulness of my army, French soldiers who faithfully serve the Republic, Irish patriots eager to shake off the yoke of unendurable oppression, have won a most astonishing victory. A British army has been scattered, and the town which is the pivot of . . ." He turned and raised his eyebrows.

"Of Mayo, General, unless you mean Connaught."

"Explain that to me again."

"This county is Mayo, but Mayo is a part of the province of Connaught."

". . . which is the pivot of Connaught has fallen into our hands. Other, smaller towns to the west have been seized by local bands of patriots, inspired by our example. A republic has been established, and is governed by a council of patriots. The warmest bonds of affection and respect unite Irish and French. Recruits pour in to us in such numbers that we are at a loss how best to provide for them. In short, we have made a brilliant beginning, and I begin now to understand truly the praise bestowed upon his countrymen by Colonel Theobald Wolfe Tone. Like us, they are children of the Revolution. Whose lands are these?"

"A nobleman named Claremorris. He and Lord Glenthorne are the powerful magnates of East Mayo."

"Not Mr. Moore?" Humbert asked sharply. "Not the man whom we have made President? I had your assurance—"

"His brother George is a landlord of middling wealth," Teeling said. "Not a nobleman in your sense of the word, but good enough. It is a respected name."

"Our man will earn new laurels for it," Humbert said. "Continue now to write, please. My orders were to effect a landing and then await General Hardy. To secure my position, it was necessary to move inland and strike at Castlebar. Circumstances have been changed by the completeness of my victory there, and by the gratifying uprising of the people of Mayo. I now hold the initiative in this part of the island, and believe that it would be fatal not to pursue my success. I do not know if Hardy has yet set sail or if he has been intercepted by the English squadron. I intend to spend the next three days recruiting the patriot forces and securing information as to the rebellions elsewhere in the island, which will have drawn courage from Castlebar. My forces will be in readiness for General Hardy to take command of them. But if Hardy does not arrive, I intend to move forward."

The room was silent save for the scratching of Teeling's pen. "To move forward," he said.

Humbert ignored him. He had turned back toward the window and Lord Claremorris's larches.

"The fate of this island will be settled in the next ten days. There are good prospects that courage and audacity will settle it to our advantage, and France will have gained a brave and grateful comrade-in-arms. End the letter in the usual way."

Teeling put down his pen and looked over the pages of foolscap. "Shall I read it back to you?"

"No, no." Humbert walked back to the writing table. "Are you surprised that I asked you to write it out for me?"

"I was," Teeling said drily. "Not now."

Humbert smiled, and slowly settled his long, heavy body into a chair. "Explain."

"It is not my place to—"

"No," Humbert said sharply. "Explain."

"You are going well beyond the limits of your orders, on the basis of one victory, and the hope that other parts of the country will rise up. You may well wish to keep the other French officers here ignorant of the justification which you are offering to the Ministry of War."

"All right," Humbert said. "That is the size of it. And what is your own opinion? You are yourself a French officer. Of a sort."

"An Irishman," Teeling said. "Of a sort. Perhaps Tone believes in a general uprising, but I do not. Our organization was shattered months ago. Its strength was in Ulster and in Wexford. In Dublin. Perhaps in the midlands. If there is any serious rising in the next month it will be in the midlands. It is a mob of Irish-speaking peasants that we have recruited here, primitive men cut off from the rest of the island. If Hardy doesn't land, there is no hope for us."

"Hardy has not left the French coast," Humbert said.

"You may be certain of that. And he will stay there until it has been made clear and public that he is needed to complete a campaign which I have begun with great success. That old aristocrat down in Dublin, Cornwallis, is not sitting still. He is bringing a large army northward to meet me. If he finds me, there will be no second Castlebar. But if this island bestirs itself, and if I can avoid him for three weeks, Hardy will be here."

"Avoid him for three weeks?" Teeling asked incredulously. "On an island this size?"

Humbert shrugged. "It is larger than the Vendée. Much larger. I can avoid him. With luck."

"And when Hardy lands, if he does land, where will we be?"

Humbert made a curious gesture, closing his fist and then opening it over the table, fingers spread wide.

"May I ask, General, how good our chances are?"

"The odds are against us. Too many things must work properly. Local uprisings, and you are yourself doubtful of these. Hardy's prompt arrival, and after him Kilmaine. The manner in which Cornwallis disposes of his forces. The chances are that he will be able to scoop us up in the net he will throw out, and put ropes around us. I say only of my plan that it is the best one in the circumstances."

"Best for the Irish, or for France?"

"For France, of course," Humbert said. "Best for France. It was you people who came to France for help, you know, yourself and Wolfe Tone and Fitzgerald and the others. We did not seek you out, to seduce you from your loyalty to England. You needed us, to make your disloyalty effective. And here we are. With luck there will be more of us. But we are here in the service of our country, as you serve yours."

"Your country," Teeling said. "Not the Revolution."

"France is the Revolution," Humbert said, with sudden, unexpected passion. "My victory here will strengthen the Revolution, just as Buonaparte's victory in Egypt will probably destroy it."

"What meaning do you think that has for the plowboys you throw against the English cannon?"

"Ask yourself that. They are your countrymen, not mine."

"I am asking myself that question," Teeling said. "It is an ugly one."

"Yes," Humbert said gravely. "An ugly question. War

devours men. We throw our children to the cannon. It is not a question to ask in the middle of a campaign."

"I will write out a fair copy of your dispatch," Teeling said. "Will you want a copy?"

"Of course," Humbert said. "And see that it is sent off by a reliable messenger. The boat should leave on the first tide."

At the door, Teeling turned. "It is wasteful of men, is it not, General—a frontal attack across open ground, without cover?"

"It was successful," Humbert said. "This time."

From the *Memoir of Events*, Written by Malcolm Elliott in October, 1798

On the day following the battle of Castlebar, I was directed to ride eastward into Sligo to ascertain the state of the United movement there, and to learn what I could of conditions in Ulster, for Humbert regarded a juncture with what remained of the northern rebels as one of his possibilities. I was accompanied by Owen Ruagh MacCarthy, the schoolmaster. If, as seemed possible, some part of the Sligo road was held by peasants, MacCarthy stood a better chance than would I of explaining matters to them. To speak more plainly upon that point, the roads were no longer safe for anyone markedly "Protestant" in dress, manner, and speech. In the event, we did not encounter this difficulty, although parts of western Sligo have indeed gone into insurrection.

Our journey carried us through Swinford, Charlestown, and Tobercurry, and a most ill-matched pair we must have looked, for MacCarthy jounced along most painfully, although without complaint, remarking at one point that his horse, which had been requisitioned from Lord Claremorris, was clearly worth but four pounds eighteen, a reference to the old penal statute which prohibited Papists from owning horses valued at more than five pounds. He proved, however, a most intelligent and sagacious man, albeit an eccentric one, and I found fresh occasion to deplore the artificial distinctions by which the several classes in society are held separate. He was, all in all, a most excellent companion, barring only his determination to stop at every tavern we passed, thereby disclosing a prodigious head for spirits. At several of these he was known by name as a writer of verses in the old tongue. Concerning the aims and objectives of the United Irishmen he was largely uninformed, although he had read several of our pamphlets. His head was crammed with curious learning and psuedo-learning, but most of it was bounded by the four seas of Ireland, although he had a good knowledge of the classics and had read Goldsmith and Shakespeare.

"My wife," I told him, "is a great reader of Ossian."

"Who?"

"The greatest of the poets in Irish," I answered, surprised. "Ossian. Or perhaps he was Scottish. Mr. James Macpherson has made him celebrated in London."

"Usheen, is it?" he asked, after a pause. "That fellow."

When we were first married, Mrs. Elliott had me commit to memory a passage from Macpherson's eloquent translation, which I now recited for him: "Oh torrents, tumbling down upon fair Caledon, raise up your mighty spirits to murmur to the drowsy Gael. Quake not, oh slumbrous heroes, but sally forth unto the fray."

"Well now," MacCarthy said, "that is elegant indeed, and no easy task for the memory. 'Quake not, oh slumbrous heroes.' You don't come upon that sort of thing every day."

"Does it lack accuracy of sentiment or expression?" I asked him, somewhat nettled by a remark which I considered sardonic.

"Not at all," he assured me, with an almost excessive politeness. "It is grand stuff entirely. 'Slumbrous heroes,' by God. That one is worth remembering. There is a maker of verses in West Cork who would slap down shillings on the counter for the use of that one."

We had come from great distances to share at last the same road, and yet there was much which held us separate. Ireland, in my judgment, is held in check by oppressive laws and a corrupt parliament, by a government and an aristocracy which make certain of their power by fostering animosities between Protestant and Papist, by the armed might of England's alien armies. To all this, MacCarthy gave a ready assent, and yet it seemed of no great interest to him.

"My father," he said, "was what you would call landless, a laborer feeding the two of us as best he could. But his father before him had had a bit of land on Lord

Blennerhassett's estate, outside Tralee. Well, the bad years came when there were two poor harvests, the one after the other, and he couldn't pay the rent and so was driven off. Now would the United Irishmen prevent that from happening?"

"There are rents in all countries," I said, "and landlords have debts of their own which must be paid from the rents."

"When I grew up to be a young man," he went on, as if he hadn't heard me, "I was teaching school in Macroom and there the Whiteboys started up again. A man named Paddy Lynch was behind it. He was up to all kinds of deviltry. Malachi Duggan of Kilcummin is an altar boy beside Paddy Lynch. When Paddy Lynch was rampaging through West Cork the landlords went slow on the evictions. If there had been Whiteboys in Tralee in my grandfather's time he'd not have had to end his days on the road."

"It is only a beginning we are making now," I said, hearing within my head the emptiness of my words. "We must go one step at a time."

"My grandfather went one step at a time, until one winter's night he went to sleep by a ditch and in the morning they found him there, and my father beside him, crying and shivering." He bit his lips in thought, and then he said, "Sure, there is no one cares about people like my grandfather."

Swinford had been seized by the insurgents themselves, upon news of the Castlebar victory, and without help or word from the French. The village was verdant with green boughs and trees of liberty in the narrow street. They had taken the local tippling shop, although the proprietor was himself a Papist, and there was much singing and carousing in broad daylight. A corpulent young man of the sort who is foremost in faction fights had declared himself their captain, and exercised an ill-defined authority over them. When they learned from MacCarthy's boasting that we had been at the battle of Castlebar, they crowded around us for information, plying us with drinks which MacCarthy would not refuse. And it was much the same in Charlestown. In short, the line of march eastward across Mayo was open, and the villages in friendly hands. But we could learn nothing about Sligo. We were to discover as we proceeded, however, that some of the Sligo villages were in rebel hands and others were held by companies of yeomanry, but many were undeclared and living their lives as if nothing had happened. But the town of Sligo itself, a larger and more formidable town than Castlebar, was held by a strong British force which had been reinforced by troops from Enniskillen, in Ulster. Sligo to the north and Boyle to the south, in Roscommon, were the two anchors of the line by which the British hoped to hold us within Connaught until Cornwallis could move into position. If we were to reach Ulster, we would either have to fight through this line or slip through it.

The day, as we continued eastward, was splendid, and the evening long in coming. Far off on our left, toward the Atlantic, lay the Ox Mountains, blue-purple against the pale sky. We felt ourselves distant not merely from Dublin but from Castlebar. Here and there, on rises of ground or half hidden by plantations, lay the big houses of the gentry. But for the most part we had before us open rolling plains and the cabins of the peasants. We stopped at a cabin for bowls of milk, and nothing could have been farther from the minds of these than battles and insurrection. It gave my conscience a sore twinge to know that they would soon become a part of our turmoil. For what had they to do with kingdoms or republics, with equality and the rights of man? They had but their lives to live and their crops to harvest.

**From "Youthful Service: With Cornwallis
in Ireland,"
Chapter Three of *My Campaigns*,
by Major General Sir Harold Wyndham
(London, 1848)**

The city of Dublin received its northern and southern boundaries from the arcs of two canals, the Grand and the Royal, which thence stretched out across the midlands to join the capital to the Shannon and the ocean. They were, and they remain, marvels of the arts of engineering and inland navigation, bearing to the city the rich crops and herds of the luxuriant Irish meadows and fields, for shipment to England. During the years of the French and the Napoleonic wars they were lifelines indeed, binding England to Ireland, which served as her granary.

It was by the Grand Canal that Cornwallis proceeded toward Connaught. I would myself have been fuming and fretting, but he sat quietly on the deck of the barge, puffing on his long pipe and sipping innumerable small cups of chocolate. It was from Cornwallis that I received in my youth the invaluable lesson that haste and swiftness are not the same. The unfortunate General Lake reinforced the lesson by his sorry example of the consequences of haste. To be sure, as Cornwallis set out, he had not yet learned of the disaster of Castlebar.

"By the time we arrive," Cornwallis said, "Lake may have smashed the Frenchman. If not, we shall take a look around and decide what to do. This is a most peaceful countryside, is it not, Wyndham, along this stretch of the canal? It might be France or the Low Countries or even England. This is how the people of this land would live, if only they were given the chance. They are a people with a great love of justice, some old chronicler has observed. Some Englishman." As it happens, he was looking toward the great Bog of Allen, where no one at all lives, peaceful or otherwise, and yet his observation was a most sage one. The Irish people have been much maligned. They seek the blessings of a government which deals with them justly yet mercifully, save when their passions have been stirred up by demagogues. As for their belligerence and hot temper, of which so much is made by their detractors, when it is harnessed to the discipline of the British army, as it has been for the past forty years, they make the finest soldiers in the world.

It speaks well for the breadth of Cornwallis's vision, and for his humanity, that these should be his thoughts even as he moved into battle against the misguided multitude in Connaught. He had been sent to Ireland by Pitt with two missions, one avowed and the other, as yet, concealed. First to pacify the island, and then to tumble down into ruin the so-called Kingdom of Ireland, thus bringing the country at last within the full governance of the English Parliament. And yet both of these plans he discussed with me in an open and candid manner, and no lieutenant of twenty has ever received a finer education in the combined arts of war and statecraft. To pacify while at the same time laying down the foundations of a lasting social settlement is the ambition of every soldier-statesman, and Lord Cornwallis possessed the necessary largeness of vision and instinct for the wishes of humanity. At the time, however, I lacked the wisdom to profit to the full from this unparalleled opportunity.

The old man (younger, I must confess, than I am now) spoke quietly as the afternoon darkened with the wonderful gentleness of Irish summers. To either side of us stretched the red brown bogland, marked here and there by the labor of turf cutters, dark, shallow trenches crossing and recrossing the wide, level expanses. Many centuries of the past lay as yet untouched by their spades, indeed all the layered melancholy of the land's unhappy history converted by times' slow chemistry to dark, odorous fibers. I carried in a portfolio of red Russia leather Cornwallis's maps and the notes which he had dictated to me on the movements of our troops, but he found no occasion to ask for them. All these details were fixed in his mind, which looked beyond battle and sudden victory to the imposition of permanent law, of a just and fecund tranquillity.

A net was being cast over Connaught, with four sturdy nets strung along its border—Sligo, Boyle, Castlebar, Galway. The rebels would be held within this net while the main body of our troops assembled to the south. Then the net would be pulled tight. Having settled this in his mind, and having issued his orders, Cornwallis could now settle at ease in his chair, his gouty leg resting upon a small cushioned stool.

We disembarked at Tullamore, a prosperous canal town, and proceeded by coach to Athlone, which lies twenty-five miles to the northwest, on the banks of the Shannon. It guards the principal bridge across that river into Connaught. Control of Athlone, and thus of the Shannon, was bitterly contested in both the Cromwellian and the Williamite wars. In June of 1691, it was attacked by an army of twenty-one thousand Williamites, who subjected it to the most fearful bombardment in all Irish history, fifty cannon hurling ton upon ton of bombs and stones over the walls of the city. Cornwallis, whose imagination responded to history, was inspecting the battered castle and the remaining fragments of the city wall when word reached us of the disaster at Castlebar.

It was carried in the most humiliating manner possible, by light dragoons who had fled from the battlefield, scarcely pausing until they reached Athlone. They were taken before Cornwallis to make their report, but not even his stern manner and august bearing could bring them to coherence. As they would have it, overwhelming masses of the peasantry, howling like demons and spurred on by their priests, surged up and down the roads of Connaught. The principal towns between Castlebar and Athlone, including Tuam, had fallen. Cornwallis listened to them in silence, doubtless trying to strike a balance between their frenzied exaggerations and the bare fact of a defeat to the north.

Turning away from them, he resumed his inspection of the town, moved now not by historical piety but by his need to know whether Athlone could be defended against an attack in strength. He also sent a rider westward to Tuam, to discover if that crucial road junction remained in British hands. After nightfall a messenger galloped in from General Lake, bearing a dispatch couched in terms more disgraceful than any which had ever before been sent by a British officer in the field to his commander, a mixture of bluster, pity for himself, and indiscriminate condemnation of his own officers and men. British troops, he reported, had given way to abject panic, fleeing like the cowards they were from a battleground which he had prepared with care and which he had sought to defend with bravery. But the next paragraph contradicted him, placing upon General Hutchinson responsibility for the order of battle. The dispatch spoke not a word as to why panic spread so disastrously among soldiers who outnumbered the enemy and who held the high ground. Neither was there a word of generous praise for a daring and resourceful foe, whose victory had been made possible by a night march which a lesser commander would never have attempted.

I remember, with a vividness which years and age have not dimmed, Cornwallis standing on the bridge, one hand resting on the parapet to take the weight from his bad leg. The dark waters of the Shannon moved beneath it, and we faced the darker Shannon shore. In the town behind us, alarm had begun to spread, one rumor feeding upon another. He crumpled Lake's dispatch and held it over the water, but then, regaining his composure, smoothed it out and handed it to me.

"See there," he said. "If General Lake had heeded my advice and given himself a night's sleep, he would

265

have been spared all this." Then, summoning Colonel Crauford to his side, he said: "If we still hold Tuam, I propose to move there tomorrow with two regiments. Our forces, as they arrive, are to be sent forward to join me there. When I possess the strength necessary for the purpose, and not later than two days from now, I shall advance into Mayo. Draft dispatches that the road eastward must be held at Sligo and at Boyle. An urgent message must be sent to the War Office that additional forces may be required to guard the approaches to Dublin. Young Wyndham here will help you with the spelling. You dragoons can't spell worth a damn."

"Is it that grave, sir?" Crauford asked.

"We shall win, of course," Cornwallis said. "We shall win. We have been fighting wars here for several centuries, and winning has become habit with us. But we shall not win as quickly as I had hoped. And Crauford, the two regiments that I take into Tuam are to be English regiments."

"In a pinch, my lord," Crauford asked, his Scotch burr giving an angry rasp to his words, "will you accept Scottish soldiers?"

Cornwallis laughed genially and rested a hand briefly on Crauford's shoulder. "By preference, sir. By preference. Your lads are the best of all. But by God, if I had the men to spare, I would have this native yeomanry and militia sent to garrison and kept out of my way and out of my sight."

Thereafter he never referred directly to the battle of Castlebar.

It is a most extraordinary and dramatic coincidence that his request for reinforcements reached London simultaneously with the first information that a battle was under way at the mouth of the Nile, at Aboukir Bay, between the British fleet under Admiral Nelson and the French fleet which guarded Bonaparte's expeditionary army. I have often speculated, in idle moments, as to whether some occult chain bound together these two events, half a world away from each other. And yet I know that such speculation is idle indeed, for what connection could obtain between skirmishes fought beneath the leaden sky of a bogland and one of the world's decisive battles, with the fate of Europe and India hanging in the balance?

From the Manuscript Journal of Judith Elliott, Entitled, *All Dressed in Green: Memories of an Irish Patriot*

August 29. Today my brave Malcolm is somewhere eastward of Mayo, rousing the people from their slumber, as Ossian would say. Our town of Ballina lies securely within the patriot camp, although the manner in which the people are comporting themselves is not all that one might wish. Castlebar, the capital of our splendid young Republic of Connaught, is governed by a provisional executive, and all there is orderly and seemly, or so I am informed, for I have not ventured far upon the roads. But the patriots of Ballina, although spirited, conduct themselves as though liberty meant but a license for brigandage and rudeness. They are kept in order, after a fashion, by their captain, Michael Geraghty, a strong farmer who was some time ago sworn into the Society of United Irishmen by my dear husband, but his hold upon them is that of a rude chieftain who dare not assert too firm a discipline. In consequence there has been much looting of the houses of the gentry, although mercifully there has been no bloodshed. As I watch these patriots upon the road, bent under their weight of stolen furnishings, they seem far indeed from the heroes of whom Ossian wrote, those ideal creatures of flaming courage and cloudy grandeur. And yet these, as history teaches us, are the true descendants of Ossian and Oscar and Finn, though broken and crushed into the mud by the tyrannical heel which has for centuries pressed upon them. Remembering this, it is possible to forgive much, and to trust that their coming sacrifices will exalt and purify them.

I had this day a visit, kind in intention, from Mr. George Moore, of Moore Hall, elder brother of the President of our Connaught Republic. Mr. Moore had ridden to Castlebar to visit John, and returning to Ballintubber stopped at The Moat, by Malcolm's request, to make certain of my safety. It was a needless errand, for Malcolm's reputation among the country people spreads itself over me like a protecting mantle. Without his spectacles, Mr. Moore is a most handsome man, in his manner courtly yet sardonic, and with, at times, an attractive air of melancholy. I must confess to having experienced a pique upon learning that the French had chosen young John Moore, rather than my own Malcolm, to serve as our President, and must own, even now, to a suspicion, perhaps unworthy, that they were prompted by considerations of social rank and pedigree, though this would be most unseemly among the apostles of human equality. But in my heart I know that Malcolm is better placed as now he is, at the head of his troops, the sword of liberty in his hand. And yet few indeed of the gentry have rallied to the banner of freedom, John Moore and Malcolm being the notable exceptions, although there is a thick scattering of squireens and near-gentlemen, such as the boisterous and rough-mannered Randall MacDonnell. Of these latter, all are Papists. A staunch Protestant myself, and right proud of this, my soul quivers with anger and indignation that none of our kind in Mayo, save Malcolm alone, has rallied to our sacred cause, which being the cause of liberty should be also the cause of Protestantism. Twisted and snarled indeed are the roots of this unhappy though once-heroic island.

More shame then to George Moore, at once Papist and gentleman, that he holds himself aloof, heedless of the splendid example set by his brother. "Alas, ma'am," he said, "I am not as good an Irishman as yourself." "I am not Irish at all," I cried, "but English born and English bred, and yet my heart can be stirred—" "Why, so you are," he interrupted me; "and I am reproved by your love for your adopted land. I have lived too long abroad." "I know that you are making sport of me, sir," I replied with spirit, "but I believe that no cause is more sacred than that of restoring the liberty of an ancient nation." "Ancient we are, indeed," said he; "that at least is not in doubt. But do you know, I sometimes think that all sacred causes are pernicious, and a source of human sufferings." "Never think it, sir. No people can be happy if they are not free." "And is that what we are, then? A people? Myself and Captain Cooper and Malachi Duggan and Dennis Browne and Randall MacDonnell?" And yet this strange being, if all accounts are true, is not the coward he seems, but was in earlier years a notorious duelist and a courter of married women, which latter at least I am disposed to believe, for although his eye is pale and chill, his lips are full and sensual, and indeed he sat closer to me than need required and seemed conscious of my dress of soft muslin.

But his wit is an icy blast swirling within him, which has chilled and blighted his spirit, and he is too proud of his mind, which is sharp rather than lofty. Would he dare lay claim to an intellect more capacious than that of our Rousseau, that true and brave genius whose key has found and unlocked the heart of Europe? And how fares our President?" I asked him. "My brother? He fares well. As Perkin Warbeck did in his day, and Lambert Simnel and Jane Grey." His tone was one in which indifference and bitterness were strangely mingled. A difficult, remote man, but one whom many a romantic little fool might find attractive.

August 30. There was this day a most dreadful scene, when the residence of Mr. Lawrence was invaded by the mob and stripped of its furnishings before the appalled eyes of Mrs. Lawrence and her daughters. It is true that Mr. Lawrence is a fierce loyalist, now serving with the Crown forces, and most bigoted in his religious attitudes, but it is true also that he has ever been a kind landlord in a country which has lacked for these. O spirit of Finn, spirit of Ossian, spirit of Cuchulain, would you have left Mount Lawrence Hall with a tall clock strapped to your back? Yet the spirit of Ossian does live, erect and dauntless, riding now somewhere to the east.

September 2. But when I read over the lines which I have last written here, candor whispers in my ear that it is a different Malcolm whom I best remember, less heroic and more human, and my heart goes out to him. For I last saw him a week ago, after the liberation of Ballina and upon the very day when the patriot army set out upon their now celebrated march upon Castlebar. He rode up to The Moat at noon, and stayed with me until about four in the afternoon, and those brief hours I shall always hold precious in my memory, whatever the future may hold in store for us both.

I had expected, in what he doubtless would have termed in fondness my "romantic fancy," that he would be splendidly uniformed, but instead he wore the plain but decent jacket and breeches in which he had set out to meet the French at Killala, although he had now a pistol buckled about his waist. We kissed with much affection and passion, as always we do when we have been separated for some days, but when he drew away from me I saw at once that his face was drawn, and that his affection was clouded by a faint reserve. I hurried him to the dining room, and placed before him a plate of gammon and a full tankard of ale, to both of which he addressed himself heartily. I sat facing him across the table, my elbows resting upon it, and my chin in my cupped hands, and at last I said, "What is it like?"

"What is what like?" he asked, not looking up from his plate.

"A battle," I said. "There has been a battle," I said, "the first battle, and our own Ballina has been liberated. What is it like?"

His mouth was filled with gammon, and he swallowed this, and washed it down with ale before he answered. Then he put down his knife and fork, and smiled at me.

"It is like a faction fight," he said, "if I am to judge by Ballina."

"I have never seen a faction fight," I said. But I had heard of them, of course. Who that has lived in Ireland has not?

"The lads from two villages or two townlands will meet together at an appointed time," he said to me, like a schoolmaster giving a lesson to a novice, his voice dry and precise. "Who can give the cause for it, a quarrel ten years old or a generation old or perhaps no cause at all. And when the signal is given, they will set at each other with cudgels or blackthorns or rocks or whatever comes most readily to hand. You seldom know which side will win. The lads with the stoutest cudgels and the hardest pates, no doubt. Afterward, there is always much drinking, the two lots drinking together like old friends. The ones that are able to stand, that is. A battle seems to be a bit like that, but instead of cudgels, there are pikes and muskets and bayonets. And of course the two sides don't drink together when it is over."

There has always been this side to Malcolm, which I attribute to his Irishness, for they delight in self-mockery, and self-deprecation, yet there was also now a bitterness to his words which carried the ring of truth.

"There is a difference now," I said. "These lads know why they are fighting. They are fighting for liberty."

"Yes," he said. "For liberty. The French general explained that to them with great eloquence. In French, of course, but Teeling and I translated it for them. It made a great impression on them. There is no word in Irish for 'republic,' but we did the best we could." He picked up his tankard and drank off what remained of the ale. "He is a very able man, this Frenchman, so far as I can judge. His name is Humbert, and he carries a reputation with him from the Vendée. We are moving upon the English army at Castlebar tonight, and if we smash them, we will hold Mayo and most of Connaught. After that, it will be up to the rest of the country, and to reinforcements from France. As you can see, my dear, I have become most learned in such matters. Quite the soldier."

He stood up and carried his tankard to the sideboard, where he refilled it from the pitcher.

"You will smash them." I said, with quiet confidence. "The people are rising up. As you said they would."

"Yes," he said. "They are coming by every hour to our encampment. Peasants from Nephin and Ballycastle and Crossmolina. And something is waiting for them at Castlebar which they have never seen, nor heard about save in poems. The British army. 'The soldiers of the English King,' it is called in the poems. English regulars and Irish militia, infantry regiments and cavalry and dragoons and artillery. Castlebar will not be a faction fight. I don't know what it will be like. Perhaps I shall have an opportunity to describe it to you."

The quietness of his words struck sudden fear into my heart, and yet I know now that it was needless fear, for all the world now knows of our brilliant victory at Castlebar, in which Malcolm, it is certain, played his part with resolute gallantry.

He turned toward me suddenly, spilling ale in the swiftness of his movement. "You will be alone here at The Moat," he said, "save for the cook and the maids and a few lads too young to fight. I want you to remember very carefully what I told you when I left for Killala. We are leaving a garrison here in Ballina under the command of a man named Michael Geraghty. If The Moat is offered a disturbance by either side—by either side, do you understand me?—you are to send off a lad to Geraghty with word of that. Tell Geraghty that you need help and that you need it at once. He will send it to you."

"By either side?" I repeated. "I am not certain that I understand you."

"There is a gentleman named Malachi Duggan," he said. "A patriot, rather, I should say—"

"I do not know Mr. Duggan," I said.

271

"That is your good fortune," he said. "Mr. Duggan is not a reader of Tom Paine or William Godwin. You would not hit it off well together." He broke off suddenly, put the tankard on the sideboard, and walked to me. He put his two hands in mine, and raised me to my feet. Then he drew his hand gently down my cheek. His fingers brushed my lips. "I am sorry for those words, my dear. I am edgy. What you must remember is that this is not a war, but an insurrection, and those are messy affairs. It isn't always easy to sort out friend and foe. You will be safe enough here, but remember about Geraghty."

Then he bent down and kissed me, and I forgot all about Geraghty and Humbert and Duggan and the British army at Castlebar and the men from Nephin and Ballycastle. And so too, I believe, did he, for we held each other in a tight embrace, and nothing existed in The Moat or in Mayo or in Ireland, save the two of us.

We retired then to our room, where we have known so much happiness, both passionate and tranquil, though it is most indelicate of me to set down such words upon paper. But I was careful to awaken him at three in the afternoon, as he had cautioned me to do, although I did so with reluctance, for his face was quiet and at rest, and the lines which had creased them at noon were smoothed away by sleep. I touched my hand to his forehead, and his eyes opened at once, and a moment later he sat bolt upright. He remembered then the place of safety which we shared, and turning toward me he smiled. Leaning toward him, I kissed him, and he returned the kiss, softly, without passion but with much affection, and he touched my hair gently.

"We have come a far distance," he said, "from your father's house in London, and the books we read there together."

"And talked," I said. "There were times when we talked all of the evening away." And blushed, most foolishly for a married woman in bed with her husband.

"And talked," he said, with his hand still stroking my hair.

"The books are here with us," I said. "In your study. All our favorite books. I will read in them every evening while you are gone. It will be less lonely. It will be as though you had not gone."

"Yes," he said. "Almost." Then he smiled again, as

often he does, as though my words give him a secret pleasure, the nature of which he never reveals to me.

At four, he led his horse down the avenue, and I walked beside him. At the gate, he mounted, and rode off to rejoin our patriots. But when he was a short distance along the road, he turned and waved to me. I was not to see him again for many weeks, and then under very different circumstances.

From the *Memoir of Events*, Written by Malcolm Elliott in October, 1798

We had hard going the next day, with slashing rain turning the road to mud. At Tobercurry we were warned to avoid Collooney, a loyal town, and were cautioned that Sligo town was held by a strong garrison, with patrols upon the roads. We were able, with care, to move eastward between Sligo and Lough Gill, and then northward by a narrow coastal road to the village of Rosses Point, five miles from Sligo. Here an acquaintance of MacCarthy's, a verse writer named O'Hart, keeps a tavern, and through him we sent a message to Sam MacTier, the man whom I had come to meet. Poor MacTier, as everyone now knows, was on the Sligo executive of the Society of United Irishmen. It now seems to me most curious that two different free masonries, of poetry and of politics, should have brought the four of us together for a few hours.

MacTier did not arrive until late evening, and MacCarthy, O'Hart, and I sat together through a long, wet afternoon. The tavern lies close to the strand, facing Sligo Bay, at a place called Memory Harbor. The bay was but dimly visible through the rain, leaden gray and angry in appearance. Rain fell in sheets upon the thatch, and ran from it in loud rivulets. There were no other patrons, and we spent the time chiefly at a low table by the fireplace, with jugs of hot punch. MacCarthy and O'Hart had at first but little to say to each other, as is often the case when men meet who share the same trade. O'Hart had I think some faint suspicion of our errand and disapproved of it. His wife, red of face and barefoot, brought in a large bowl of boiled potatoes which we ate in peasant fashion, placing the skins in a mound on the table, and dipping the peeled potatoes in a small dish of salt.

MacCarthy was on edge, and had been since we crossed the Owenmore by the crooked bridge at Ballysadare. Twice, despite the rain, he left the tavern and walked to the small jetty, a blanket wrapped around him. When he returned, his blanket was soaked, and his thick red hair plastered to his skull. And for a full half hour he would stand by the window, his long, thick-knuckled hands wrapped around a tumbler.

It was after eight when MacTier joined us, a blunt, stocky man of middle years, with a head the shape of a hazelnut. We had met a half-dozen times before, in Dublin and Belfast. The MacTiers were County Antrim Presbyterians; I did not know what circumstances had brought him to Sligo, where he had become a linen merchant. It is said that flax is the blood of the northerners, growing it, hackling, bleaching, weaving, trading. When it is harvest time, its sweet, heavy odor fills the Ulster air. There was a commendable gravity in MacTier's manner, and a neatness to his costume. When he put aside his sodden greatcoat, you could not have guessed at the filthy weather he had been riding through, dark brown coat and waistcoat close-buttoned, clean linen with bits of plain lace at the sleeves. But the blunt-toed boots were caked with yellowy mud.

"This is a bad business," he said, glancing toward the window, but in a voice which suggested a different reference. He nodded to MacCarthy and held out his hand. His eyes were suspicious.

O'Hart served us fresh jugs, steaming and aromatic, and then left the room, closing the door carefully and pointedly. MacTier held his tumbler beneath his nose for a few moments, and then took a long, healthy sip. MacCarthy relaxed slightly, but his large eyes remained watchful.

No French ships had been sighted along the coast from Sligo to Bundoran, or from the shores of Donegal Bay. But the steep coastline of Donegal stretched northward from Killybegs, a mountainous coast indented by innumerable small bays, curving across the edge of the island, and dropping down by Lough Swilly to Londonderry. A fleet might well be riding at storm anchor off Donegal, unable to put its men ashore, as had happened when Hoche and Tone came to Bantry Bay in 1796.

"More Protestant wind and rain," MacCarthy said, giving MacTier a thin, taunting smile.

But MacTier ignored him. The Ulster rising was dead, he was certain of this. It died when Monroe's pikemen were cut to pieces in the town of Ballinahinch. There were still rebels in the glens of Antrim, but they were being hunted out and destroyed. Many of the towns up and down the Ards peninsula had been burned by the British, and scores of farms and cabins.

"Teeling's home is in the Ards," I said.

"It was."

"What if Humbert can bring our Mayo army into Ulster?"

"Into Ulster? Are you daft, man? Past Sligo and Ballyshannon, with General Taylor waiting for you in Enniskillen?"

"Lake was waiting for us in Castlebar," MacCarthy said. "But he left."

"Aye," MacTier said. "I know." He took out a pair of square-framed spectacles and settled them on his stump of a nose.

"But what if we do get through?" I asked him. "What help could we get from your fellows in the glens?"

"Ach. If you could make your way into Ulster, you would do best to bide in the Donegal hills, deep in the Derryveaghs. It would take weeks to find you, and you could wait there for the French ships."

"Too long have we waited for the ships from Spain," MacCarthy said suddenly.

"From Spain?" MacTier asked, puzzled.

"A line of poetry," MacCarthy said, with the same taunting smile.

MacTier studied him moodily, and then turned back to me. "That is my suggestion. But my other thought would be to make for the midlands. There has been talk about a rising there, and a certain man we both know has been to Belfast."

"I have visited him," I said, and told him of my talk in Longford with Hans Dennistoun.

"You people are great for knowing each other," MacCarthy said, "from one end of the island to the other."

MacTier ran a finger along the rim of his spectacles. "What people would that be, Mr. MacCarthy? The United Irishmen?"

"Perhaps," MacCarthy said. "Perhaps it was the United Irishmen."

"Perhaps," MacTier said. "And perhaps you mean Protestants, but lack the manliness to say so."

It is most curious, the effect of those words, *Protestant* and *Papist*, when used without warning and in what is termed "mixed company." Like a pistol fired into silence. MacCarthy had the stunned look of a man who finds himself murderously attacked by a small terrier.

"Because if that is your meaning," MacTier said, "I must tell you that I will not have it. I will not abide the abominable bigotries of this country, and least of all will I ride for miles through rain and muck to hear them insinuated into tavern conversation."

"Ach, that might be the rub right there," MacCarthy said. "In a Sligo tavern is one thing, and back in your Belfast home may be another."

"You may think so if you wish, sir, and be damned to you. This is a strange United Man you have brought to us, Mr. Elliott. Has he even taken the oath?"

"He has," I said. "Whether or not he accepts it is another matter."

"I have only just met this gentleman from Ulster," MacCarthy said. "And without a rudeness, 'tis little about him that I know."

"Neither is there any need for me to offer you an autobiography," MacTier said, his manner unruffled. "I know nothing at all about you, save that Mr. Elliott vouches for you and that by your accent you should be many miles to the south of Sligo."

"I should indeed," MacCarthy said. "We are of one mind in that matter, at least."

"And in others as well," I said. "I have vouched for you, MacCarthy, and I can vouch as well for Sam MacTier, who has been a United Man these four years. We have the same hopes and wishes."

"What the hell does he know about my wishes?" MacCarthy said.

"I don't have a mind to turn the country over to the Papists, if that is what you mean," MacTier said to him.

"Not when you can turn it over to the Orangemen."

"You are talking nonsense," MacTier said. "The husband of my own first cousin marched on Toome bridge with the Papists. He was hanged at Toome with a Papist, side by side on the same gallows. The last words they spoke on this earth were to each other."

"I can well believe that," MacCarthy said drily, but

then more slowly, and shaking his large head, "A Papist and a Presbyterian dying side by side."

"On the one gallows," MacTier repeated. "They were United Men, and they took the same oath that I took and that you took. Mind you, there were many of our fellows who left the cause when they heard how the Protestants were being slaughtered in Wexford, and who can blame them? But there were still enough United Men to stand together and fight together, and those are the best Irishmen of all."

"Sure they may be Irish by the relaxed standards of Sligo, but you would all of you seem outlandish people in the county of Kerry. And what were the United Men doing when the poor Papists were driven out of Ulster in their thousands?"

"That is a bitter truth," MacTier said. "That did happen."

"You are damned right it happened," MacCarthy said, "because I have seen the poor creatures in the hillside hovels of Mayo."

"But no United Man had art or part in that. You would believe me if you could but talk for an hour with Henry Joy."

MacCarthy shook his head. "I have heard of him from your friend Teeling, who came into Mayo with a French uniform and a gift for shouting out commands at people. Your Henry Joy was one man, and your Monroe makes two, and yourself may make a third. But there is little kindliness has ever been given to my people by the black Presbyterians of the north."

"Now you hold there. I am as good a Presbyterian as any man, and I will not hear them miscalled."

"You may be fighting the English, but it is yourselves you are fighting for and the devil take the hindmost, and the hindmost of all God's creatures are the Papists of Ulster."

"Talk sense, man. We have been trying to fight a rebellion, and you cannot have a rebellion in one corner of a small island. How can you have one part of Ireland free and not the other part? Look, man. I wasn't always a merchant. When I was a lad, my father was a crofter, and he was being squeezed dry by the Big Lord—"

"The Big Lord," MacCarthy said, catching up the phrase and repeating it.

"It was but a name we all had for him. He was Lord

Antrim, rightly speaking. But up and down the glen he was the Big Lord."

MacCarthy looked at me.

"There is a Big Lord in Mayo," I explained to Mac-Tier.

"And in Kerry as well," MacCarthy said. "Lord Blennerhassett and Lord Kenmare and the rest of them. And there are scores of them in County Cork. There are Big Lords in every part of Ireland that I have seen, save the western islands, which are too poor to have need of one."

He picked up a jug and refilled our tumblers.

"It was then that my brother Davey and I joined the Hearts of Oak, to force down the rents and stop the evictions, and that was years before there was any Society of United Irishmen. It was my introduction to public life, as you might say, and I was scarce nineteen then."

"Be damned if we did not do the very same thing in Munster with the Whiteboys," MacCarthy said. "The very same thing."

"And if the middleman was a Presbyterian clergyman, do you think that stopped us? It did not." MacTier held his tumbler briefly toward us, and drank off half its contents.

MacCarthy slapped the big bone of his knee and leaned forward. "There was a priest or two around Macroom who learned his manners from the Whiteboys."

MacTier removed his spectacles and rubbed his eyes. "There is bad blood between your people and mine, and too much of that blood has been spilled upon cobblestones. Peep o'Day Boys and Orangemen and Defenders butchering each other. There is scant profit to be gained by sorting out the rights and the wrongs of it. I grew up hating Papists, I'll not deny it, and do you know why? When my father was at last driven from his wee farm it was given to a Papist who could pay the high rent, and that happened in place after place. Do you mind a mountain in South Down called Slieve Gullion?"

"I have heard of it. A mountain with the graves of the ancient race on its slope, and a lake at its summit, like a blue eye staring to heaven."

"I wouldn't know of that," MacTier said. "But I know this." Now it was MacTier who refilled our tumblers. "The farms of Slieve Gullion's braes are the bonniest in Ireland, south or north. And in the seventies, when Papists were allowed to take land upon the long leases, they went after the farms and drove up the rents."

"There had been a time when Papists held all those lands," MacCarthy said, "before they were driven off by your people and sentenced to land little better than bog."

"Aye," MacTier said. "A time hundreds of years ago. But when your bit of land is taken from you, you hate those who get it. So that we hate the Papists and the Papists hate us, and the Big Lords get the best rents they can wring from the lot of us."

"It was Lord Blennerhassett who did for us," MacCarthy said. "By God, I have never seen that man but I hate him. He may be dead by now for all I know. It was a long time ago."

"There is a son," MacTier said. "They all have sons." He cleared his throat, and then, astonishingly, began to sing in a voice at once dry and moving. I remember only the last words of that song: "O the rents are getting higher and we can no longer stay, so farewell unto you bonny, bonny Slieve Gullion braes."

In the quiet that followed, MacCarthy put a large, freckled hand on his shoulder. "What savage, heretic name is it you have? Sam? Who would think to look at you that you could sing a song? All jinglejangle English words, mind you, but a proper song for all that."

There followed one of the wettest nights of my experience, and I do not write as a stranger to drink. When the jugs were empty, they were replaced by others. Presently O'Hart joined us, and he matched verses with MacCarthy for the better part of an hour. I could follow the Irish, although the references were obscure, but I have no head for poetry. It seemed to me that O'Hart greatly deferred to MacCarthy, addressing him with respect, and bringing forward his own verses with a show of diffidence. But MacCarthy was soon too befuddled to take notice of this. Tavernkeeper, schoolmaster, linen merchant, they were locked in the transient, treacherous companionship of whiskey and song.

But although I matched them drink for drink, I sat a bit apart from them, locked in a puzzle of my own making.

"It is all over in the north, is it not," I said suddenly to MacTier.

"It is," he said presently, an owl peering through whiskey. "It has been over since Ballinahinch."

"And without the French, it would not have begun in Connaught. Without the French, we would have had mobs of Whiteboys. Ask this fellow," I said, and nodded to MacCarthy.

"But you have the French now," MacTier said. "A thousand of them, and more promised. You have Castlebar."

MacCarthy sang, in English, "Oh, the French are on the sea, Says the *Sean Bhean Bhocht*."

"Because it suits them," I said. "And we have a shattered Directory in Dublin. Half of it in prison."

"Oh, the French are in the bay," MacCarthy sang. "They'll be here at break of day, and the Orange will decay, says the *Sean Bhean Bhocht*."

"It is a puzzle to me, Mr. Elliott," MacTier said, "how you have got yourself involved in such dangerous matters, a Mayo gentleman with a comfortable farm."

"I have taken the oath," I said. "And I am bound by it."

"You need never have taken it," MacTier said. "There are few enough of the gentry who did."

"A rotten parliament," I said, my tongue thick with whiskey. "The good of the country drained off to England."

"You would risk your life for an improved parliament?" he asked skeptically. "You set a slender value upon it."

"If you don't like my answers, you can go to hell," I said. "I am descended from John Elliott, who helped strike the head off Charles, and I have no love for kings." It was a braggart's swaggering answer, and in fact I have always doubted that family legend.

I had not given him a proper answer, but only a drunken boast from one tavern drinker to another. What had taken me to Castlebar and to the Sligo Coast? Was my concern for a piddling parliament indeed so great that I would sacrifice to it a good farm and a beautiful wife? The formulations of the Society, although I gave and give to them my full assent, are but abstract things less real than a blade of grass or a drop of blood. In that odd clarity which drink can give, a pale light at the center of roiling mud, I perceived that I did not know myself or my motives. Worse, that I feared to seek them out.

MacCarthy had turned to O'Hart, and was speaking or rather reciting to him, in a loud, impressive voice, heavy with incoherencies, jabbing at him with a long forefinger.

I did not recognize the words; they might have been his own, or those of another poet. They filled the room, sodden with drink. MacTier sat with folded arms, looking first at me and then at MacCarthy, parts of a puzzle which no doubt he had solved.

The rain had stopped by morning, and the ocean wind had swept the air. We stepped into a sparkling world, still wet with its scrubbing. The long grasses beneath our feet were a deep green, with drops of dew upon them, and the bay an expanse of blue stretching toward the empty sea. There was not a ship or boat in sight, save for two small fishing boats hauled up on the strand, sunlight glistening upon their skins of tarred hide. In the field beside us, separated by a low fence, cows were at pasture, brown, and red and white, and the small black cattle of the west. MacCarthy stared at the pasture with what I imagined was a poet's eye, receptive and tranquil, and then walked over to the fence, where he leaned down and vomited, a graceless, coarsely built peasant, absurdly dressed. He cleaned his teeth with a tuft of grass.

MacTier, mounted upon a serviceable, short-legged mare, shook hands with us formally. He appeared none the worse for his night's excesses, a trim, self-sufficient sort of man, his eyes mild and even behind their spectacles. "We leave by different roads," he said.

"We have long been on different roads," MacCarthy said, but he spoke now without malice. "You have a chest full of good songs, Mr. MacTier."

MacTier smiled. "If the world could be tied together by songs, it would have happened long ago. You have my good wishes, Mr. Elliott."

"We may see you in Sligo," I said.

"I doubt that," he said.

"It was doubted in Castlebar," MacCarthy said.

"Don't count too much upon Castlebar," MacTier said. "I have seen Ulster smashed."

"You were there?" I asked, surprised.

"Oh, yes," he said. "I paid a wee visit there last month. I had a great fondness for Henry Joy. It is all over in the north. All smashed."

"Farewell unto you bonny Slieve Gullion brae," MacCarthy said.

We watched MacTier ride back toward Sligo, a sedentary man jouncing along in discomfort.

"That lad will be selling linen when the rest of us are

dead and gone," MacCarthy said. "There are some fellows have a great talent for that, like a talent for dancing, or thatching." He looked around him. "A bit of cold water on our faces would do no harm at all. Do you see that strange shape of a mountain over there? It was on the side of Ben Bulben that the hero Diarmuid fought the enchanted boar, as is told to us by your wife's friend Ossian. The tumbled one over there, in the other direction, is Knocknarea. They say that Queen Maeve is buried there, where you see that knob on the top."

"A long time ago," I said.

He nodded. "Stories made up a long time ago by fellows like myself, you couldn't believe a word they said. The country people say that she can be seen at winter riding a great horse, a woman that no man could satisfy. Like Kate Cooper, unless I misjudge her greatly."

He walked to the water's edge, and dashed water over his head. "God Almighty," he said, shaking himself. "That stuff is as cold as a witch's cunt."

"We can depend upon what Sam MacTier says," I said. "He is an honest man."

"I wouldn't know about that," MacCarthy said. " 'Tis little call I have to buy linen. He has a good voice."

He spoke looking out to sea. All was empty and still in the cheerful light of morning. I would even have welcomed the sight of a fishing smack.

Galway City, August 30

The mansion of the Browne family stood facing Eyre Square, a tall, assertive town house of dark limestone, its windows intricately ornamented. Nicholas Browne, who built it in 1627, wanted a city mansion which would surpass those of the Blakes and the Martins, and the builders gave it to him. But Galway was then at the late climax of its long career as a coastal city trading with Spain and France. It was still the historical capital of Connaught, but what now was Connaught? The once-thriving city was lovely, fading, wild, and stricken. Although the mansions of the great Galway families still stood, they were only seldom used. Some had been shuttered for years, their owners gone, sunk down into the peasantry or vanished away, generations before, into the armies of France and

Spain, Austria or Russia. And the mansions of others, the clever ones, the Martins and Brownes, were rarely opened. Their owners were off in their remote big houses, or else in London. The Atlantic winds were wilder here than in Mayo or Sligo, cutting over unused quays, in winter shrieking down the narrow streets.

Two rooms only of the Browne mansion were furnished, and into these Dennis Browne had moved with a single servant, traveling from Westport by night, a bare hour or two before the rebels seized Westport House. He was dining this night at a table set before the fireplace, massive and convoluted, with the date of the house, wreath-encircled, incised upon pale, veined marble. Gammon and potatoes, with a heavy tankard of porter beside the plate.

His alert, intelligent face was at most times an amiable one, lines of laughter cut about the mouth above a fleshy chin, not quite a jowl, but tonight his eyes, moving from flame to food and back to flame, were savage. Mayo was his county, as much his possession as though he owned it, and not merely because his brother was Lord Altamont, and he himself High Sheriff and Member of Parliament. The Brownes had staked their first claims upon Mayo in 1580, when one John Browne settled at the Neale, near Kilmaine, a Sussex man, the restless, wild younger son of Sir Anthony Browne of Cowdray Castle. The Brownes were Tudor, heirs of adventurers who seized their lands with silver-hilted swords, and the land was theirs as once they were of the dispossessed Gaels, as they had never been the possessions in spirit of Cromwellian jobbers or smooth-cheeked Williamites. Mayo was Browne country, as Connemara was Martin country. Browne and Richard Martin, between them, managed West Connaught, and managed it well, in Browne's judgment. Until a few months before, there had been no Whiteboy disturbances in Connaught, the Catholic squireens had been loyal, the United Irishmen had made no inroads. But now! Mobs roving at will, burning, looting, killing, Westport House itself in rebel hands, every acre from the ocean to Sligo outside the law, an army of Jacobin frog-stickers swaggering through the province, a British army scattered, and Castlebar captured.

And for all this he held himself partly to blame. When the Whiteboys perpetrated their first outrage at Killala, when they houghed little Cooper's cattle, they should have been put down ruthlessly, as Cooper had proposed. Instead, Browne had allowed himself to be persuaded by Falkiner and Moore, the same Moore whose brother was now head of the rebel government. A Moore of Mayo, ancient allies of the Brownes in the dead days when they had all been Papists together, allied with Whiteboys and spalpeens. But at the time, George Moore had made sense. Keep Mayo quiet in a troubled time, move quietly, no need to close the heavy fist of power. But George Moore, for all his suppleness of mind, had been wrong, and Cooper had been right, little pigheaded Cooper, a jumped-up Cromwellian with dirty linen and a mortgaged estate, a tinpot captain of yeomen, married to a peasant with a trollop's body. Just brains enough to have been right. A show of force, burned cabins from Killala into Ballina, would have given them something to think about.

When this was over there would be a reckoning, or Mayo would never again know peace. The rebels and those who supported them would have to be taught an enduring lesson, and a painful one. And the task of imparting such instruction to the town of Killala would be entrusted to little Cooper, to make amends for what he was suffering now. Cornwallises came and went. British armies came and went. Lord Glenthorne and Lord Claremorris lived safe and snug in England. And someday soon the task of restoring Mayo to tranquillity would have to be taken up by the gentlemen of Mayo, with the assistance of doughty, faithful, pigheaded little Cooper.

A restless exile in his own province, Browne planned on the following day to take the Ballinasloe road to Athlone, where he was confident that he would find Cornwallis. If Cornwallis followed his practice in Wexford, the suppression of the insurrection would be followed by the hanging of the ringleaders, but an amnesty for their followers. It wouldn't do for Connaught, whose peasants learned their laws and their lessons from the lash and the triangle.

Atlantic winds shook the windows, and Browne rose to fasten the shutters. The night was black, and no candles answered his from across the square.

Selected Passages from the Diary of
Sean MacKenna, Schoolmaster in County Mayo.
Translated from the Gaelic and Edited by

Samul Forrester, Barrister at Law, B.A., University of Dublin, *Dublin University Magazine*, Volumes XVI–XVII (1848–49)

EDITOR'S INTRODUCTION

Sean MacKenna, who kept a "classical academy" in Castlebar, County Mayo, died in 1873, leaving behind him a diary in the Gaelic tongue in which he had made entries over a period of four decades. These entries, set down in a heterogeneous assortment of ledgers and copybooks, do not deserve to be termed literature, and yet translations of selected passages, chosen whether for their representative or their dramatic interest, may reward the reader's attention.

They offer an entrance into the mind of a man belonging to that race of hedge pedagogues in whose care reposed, until recently, the education of the common Irish. Such men were scattered throughout the island, and although MacKenna, who had also a drapery shop, was fairly prosperous, there were many who taught in barns and hovels. In some parts of Munster and Connaught, the language of instruction was Gaelic, although the more progressive masters, like MacKenna, employed English. His own preference in the matter, however, is revealed by the language in which his diary is composed. The government's farsighted and magnanimous Education Bill of 1831 has sounded the death knell to his picturesque tribe, and MacKenna lived long enough to record his resentment of a policy which seeks to replace bog-Latin and muddled "patriotic" history with arithmetic and the rudiments of English grammar. To enter one of the new National Schools, as the present writer has done, and to hear the children chanting together, barefooted perhaps but clean of countenance, "It is my greatest pride and joy, To know myself a British boy," is to realize that civilization is entering every part of the island, slowly yet steadily.

And yet, together with much that was lax or pernicious, much also vanished which was both picturesque and "racy of the soil." The hedge schoolmaster first made his appearance in the days of the penal laws, when harsh and unwise legislation placed obstacles against the proper education of a people once celebrated for their love of

285

learning. The typical master, like MacKenna himself, knew the ancient languages and was familiar with their principal classics. Often he was a failed, or as the county saying has it, a "spoiled" priest, and in many instances the spoiling was the consequence of intemperate habits, which were of course carried into his new calling, and therefore many were known as drunkards or libertines. But at least as many resembled MacKenna, who liked his drink, as they say, but was a peaceful and industrious man, whose rectitude shines through the pages of his diary.

Once and once only did public history touch the life of this tranquil diarist. As a resident of Castlebar, he watched the Mayo insurrection of 1798, and he was the intimate friend of Owen MacCarthy, an actor in the rebellion. Although MacKenna took no part in the outrages, one discovers traces of disloyalty even in the heart of so law-abiding a Celt. His diary entries for the late summer of 1798 are therefore of historical interest, and I have translated them without abridgment. In recent years we have witnessed a growing cult of " 'Ninety-eight," fostered by the high-minded but misguided enthusiasts of the Young Ireland party, and prompted to outright treason by the skillful but envenomed pen of Mr. Mitchel. Ballad poetry and song now abound with such titles as "The West's Awake" and "The Men of Castlebar." MacKenna gives us a truer picture of confusion, random violence, cowardice, rage, and on occasion a deluded and futile bravery. It is the more convincing by reason of his lurking sympathy for the rebels, of which he was himself not fully conscious, and his friendship with Owen MacCarthy.

MacCarthy himself kept a school at Killala, the coastal village at which the French landed. He was by birth among the lowliest of the low, the son of a seasonal laborer, or spalpeen, in County Kerry. He was a schoolmaster not of MacKenna's kind, but of the sort more frequently encountered, given over to drinking, brawling, and other kinds of mischief. Yet the extraordinary fact is that this wastrel was a most delicate and sophisticated poet in the Irish tongue, a paradox encountered in other native bards of the period; in, for example, his fellow Kerryman, Owen O'Sullivan. The present writer has been for some time engaged in the preparation of a volume which will contain most of MacCarthy's surviving verses, with faithful translations. These verses, it will be found, are at once elegant and passionate, whether they be impromptu drinking songs or his elaborate and considered elegies, of which the most affecting are three laments, one for his father, one for the ancient hero O'Sullivan Beare, and one titled most bafflingly, "Lament for a Chieftain."

It seems probable that this gifted but badly flawed man drifted into rebellion through a boisterous love of excitement fostered by his unsettled habits. Certainly he possessed little of the martial ardor attributed to him in recent ballads bawled out in Dublin pothouses—"Bold Owen MacCarthy, the Darling of Erin" and "Dauntless Owen, the Boy from Tralee." Indeed, given his distaste for what he called "jinglejangle English songs," he would surely wince could he but hear these. It would appear that at first he moped about uncertainly at the edges of the rebellion, only casting in his lot after the battle of Castlebar, emboldened, as were others, by that shameful and bewildering defeat of British arms. But by the battle of Ballinamuck he had become a full-fledged rebel, a woeful instance of the effects of a dissolute life upon a temperament all too abundantly supplied with creative energy.

And now, without further delay, I shall open to you this eccentric curiosity, the Diary of Sean MacKenna. Its style, casual and homely for the most part, often rises to an Hibernian grandiloquence or pathos. For this, I have sought to find an English equivalent, without violating the spirit of the text.

Early September, 1798. When Owen returned from Sligo, he came round to call on me with a bottle for the two of us, and three most elegant thimbles for Brid, and sweets for Timothy. He is a most thoughtful man, God spare him. But it was little enough that I could comprehend of his conversation. He has grown most knowledgeable about movements of troops and lines of advance. Let Owen but take a peep into something and he is an authority upon it when next you see him. He was as always courteous and gallant toward Brid, as if she were the rarest beauty in Connaught. Set a glass before Owen and he will drink it; set a woman there and he will make love to her. Nothing stops him. Not that I believe what I have heard about himself and old Mahony's daughter who married the Orangeman. I believe that he courts women as a duty imposed upon him by the profession of poetry.

I told him that Castlebar had become a lunatic asylum, with O'Dowd and MacDonnell and John Moore calling themselves "the Republic of Connaught," and spending their days writing proclamations. Bands of lads like the one Malachi Duggan leads rove the country, paying off old scores and carrying what can be carried. Mickey Keough of Turlough took the grandfather clock from Mount Lawrence Hall and it so high he couldn't stand it upright in his cabin, and there it lies on the dirt floor, so it is said, and everyone has to step over it when they come in. In the town itself, the French keep good order, and when some men tried to loot Jacky Craig's shop, the ringleaders got ten lashes each from a French corporal. John Moore's proclamations must be read to be believed, and for this a knowledge of English is necessary, so that the citizens of his "republic" can be observed admiring the pleasing copperplate while remaining in ignorance of the lofty sentiments. His brother, George Moore, the lord of Moore Hall, has come several times to meet with him, riding coolly and slowly up Castle Street. But once their voices drifted through an open window of the courthouse, fierce and heated in angry conversation. George Moore and I take much the same view of this republic, and although he has not consulted me, it is well known that great minds move in the same channel.

But Owen is much changed, and not for the better, with his talk of battles yet to come, and a Whiteboy glint in his eye. He had gone with Elliott to make their report to Humbert, which did not diminish his self-esteem. If the second fleet lands, he kept saying, and, if the people rise up in the midlands. "Owen," I told him, "if I had a few more hairs on my head and a few more teeth in my mouth, it is above in Killala I would be, paying my respects to Kate Cooper." I smiled at Brid to make clear that I would do nothing of the sort, and at Owen, to hint that I might. But he said nothing that would confirm what gossip reported. Then he recited to me bits of a poem he was working on, a queer misshapen thing full of moons and much else, and we fell to arguing about the forms and structures of verse.

The next day some creature from Belmullet without a word of English on him came to the shop and carried off eight bolts of unbleached linen, leaving a note behind which said, "Three pounds payable ninety days after the establishment of the Irish Republic. Cornelius O'Dowd, General." I took this remarkable document to the court-house, and asked O'Dowd what was meant by it, and when he replied, I told him to turn it over and write on the blank side, "For bolts of linen, payable to Sean Mac-Kenna in ninety days," and then to sign it. "What would be the meaning of that?" he asked. "It means that you have bought yourself eight bolts of linen, and I am ex-tending you three months' credit. You can pay from your own pocket, and then settle your accounts with the Re-public of Ireland." He dropped the paper as though I had set fire to it. "Well then, Mr. O'Dowd," said I, "there may be a republic or there may not, but in your judgment it is too risky a proposition for a three-pound wager. The way I would have it, your brother the bishop would settle the bill for you, as he has always done." "I am risking my life for Ireland," said he. "With all proper respect to your brother," said I, "your life is not worth three pounds." "It is men like yourself," said he, "who have left Ireland where she is." "With all respect to your brother," said I, "Ireland has been left where she is by swaggering gunmen with ready tongues." It was clear that there was nothing to be done, so I went back to the shop and folded the paper and put it away with the thought that it might some-day bring in a few shillings as an historical curiosity.

I draw a pained amusement from the circumstance that this was linen which I had purchased from MacTier of Sligo, now disclosed to me by Owen as an enthusiastic United Irishman. I know him as an honest merchant, but had never suspected him of cherishing hopes for my liber-ation. It was MacTier, I believe, who imparted to Owen his new-found notions about the rights of man and the rest of it. The effect upon his poetry of such windy non-sense will not be a good one. A poem must be hard and particular, and bound by stout cords to its tradition.

Into the tavern with me that night, and there is Owen holding forth to a group of wild lads who looked at him with admiration, a cut or two above Malachi Duggan's men, but not many cuts. "Owen," said I, "would you ever tell me by which of man's rights it is that Corny O'Dowd robbed me of eight bolts of linen?" One word led to the next, and, before I knew what was happening, one of the omadhauns had a hand at my throat and was calling me a gombeen. Owen had to send him away with a hard cuff to the side of his head. "Who was that," I asked, "the new Attorney General?" "'Tis lads like that we will need," said Owen; "he is a faction fighter from Nephin." "Oh, by God," said I, "Nephin Mountain, where they haven't enough knowledge to count their toes." "Time enough for that later," said Owen. Such madness I have never before encountered, although I was once in my youth to Puck Fair. These were lads who a month ago would have jeered at him, and he in a drunken state, ignorant of his reputation as a poet, but now that he has a pistol and a swagger, they are all admiration. Things in this world are never placed at their proper value.

The magnificent weather continues, the land bursting with its abundance, men working in the fields and women bringing them pails of cool water against the noonday heat. A man will pause at his work, mop a forearm across his brow, and stare at a distant smudge of smoke which signals that a big house has been set afire. Little Timothy and I walked out to Turlough on Sunday, and gained a fine view of a white-tailed plover, which Timothy entered in his book, correctly spelled. As I have several times remarked, I have encouraged him to share my delight in the many-colored wonders of nature.

How strange it is that these two worlds, a world of violence and one of harvest, can exist beneath the same bright sun, with just the first touches of slow September. A bitter September it will be for many, and I pray that it will not be so for my beloved Owen.

We are a land of ruins. Norman keeps and towers, and the queer round towers of which no man knows their antiquity, shattered manor houses of the Tudor times, the roofless abbeys and monasteries savaged by the men of Cromwell, their broken arches gaunt arms against the tumbling clouds, strongholds of O'Neills and O'Donnells, Burkes and Fitzgeralds, bashed and battered away, moss and ivy creeping over their stumps as they lie dreaming beneath the great sky of Ireland. Strangest of all, the great cairns and dolmens and fairy mounds, ruins of some race perished long before the Sons of Milesius led the people of the Gael to these shores. As though in this land all, everything, has been sentenced from the beginning to break apart, fall into pieces, powerless against our harsh divinities of rain and wind and weed and tall grasses. All in ruin, the ruin of a world, sacked and burned and smashed, by Danes and Normans and Irish and English.

While all this devastation worked its will, century after century of Coopers and Duggans hacking and slashing at each other and at all who stood in their way, did other men reap harvests in the summer sun and scatter the seeds of spring, walk hand in hand with little boys down winding roads to watch the white-tailed plover rise in flight? Who did the better work to keep for us the bit we have, the men who hacked and killed, or those who reaped and tended?

For a full week now the rebel army has hung poised in Castlebar, uncertain whether to strike eastward or north, although Owen tells me that Ulster is silent as the tomb, or as a burned hillside cabin, whereas the midlands may be in arms from Longford to Kilbeggan.

Duggan and Cooper, Gog and Magog, striding across the island in their brutal and stupid cruelty, centuries old the two of them, tearing down abbeys, burning cabins, skewering warm bodies with saber or pike. What business has my Owen with such men? He raises up cathedrals of sound, word linked to word as the stones of an arch are joined, a shaper, like those who built abbey and bridge. Poem and priory come to us from a world of quietness and order, and we stand mute before them. But he is less my Owen now, this swaggering fellow who has seen men butchered on Sion Hill, their deaths concealed behind his eyes. Often enough has he told me in better days of Patrick Lynch, the murderous Captain of Macroom, with the two of us marveling from a safe distance at that man's brutality. And now he traffics in the same wares, with song and poetry burned away from his path.

I can see him now in Castlebar High Street, plundered tailcoat tightened by belt of wide leather lifted from some slaughtered dragoon. "Owen," I long to call out to him. "Wait! Let us walk out toward Turlough down the leafy road. Let us take two hours together away from this noise, away from pikes and boastful killers." But he stalks past me, unseeing, up Castlebar High Street, not the friend who sat by my candle to speak his verses on winter nights, but a far smaller creature, the Whiteboy Captain of Castlebar, in the dark, heavy boots of Patrick Lynch.

12

A Letter from George Moore, Esquire, of Mayo,
to the Right Honorable Edward Barrett,
Member of Parliament, Westminster

Moore Hall
2 September, 1798

My Dear Barrett:

London will by now have learned that a small French
force has landed on the Mayo coast and has raised an
army of native recruits. The northern portion of the
county is in their hands, and they have for some days
been in possession of Castlebar, the county town, which
they captured after imposing an ignominious defeat upon
generals Lake and Hutchinson. Were I inclined to ped-
antry, I would inform you that we have entered upon
Year One of the provisional Republic of Connaught, of
which through no desire of my own I have become a
citizen.

Of events beyond Mayo, I have no knowledge beyond
that offered by rumor and conjecture. It is said that Lord
Cornwallis, who has himself taken the field, has crossed
the Shannon and waits at Tuam for reinforcements before
advancing upon Castlebar. Upon the assumption that this
is true and that mail coaches are free to move between
there and Dublin, I shall send this letter to Tuam by
messenger.

Much that is grievous and much that is farcical have
attended the establishment of our Connaught Republic,
but my thoughts are taken up almost entirely by a most
serious personal concern which is the occasion of my writing to you. Upon hearing of the French landing, young
John, whom you will remember with affection, rode north
and placed himself at the disposition of the rebel faction.

292

He is at present in Castlebar, where he holds a position of authority with the new "government." It speaks volumes that this youth, in his early twenties, a romantic and high-spirited boy, should be accepted by them as a weighty senator. I suspect that the French, for all their egalitarian protestations, are not free of the vanities of less advanced civilizations and have welcomed to their cause a gentleman of property and breeding. Aside from John, they have attracted only the most desperate of the peasantry, with a sprinkling of ignorant squireens, hedge schoolmasters, shopkeepers, and the like.

I have several times visited him, and although I have been unable to persuade him to return to Moore Hall, I have nevertheless discovered the following facts, upon which his future and perhaps his life may depend. He has not taken up arms, and he played no part in the battles of Ballina and Castlebar. The "government" of which he is part is a kind of civic committee, necessary to the maintenance of order in the town of Castlebar and in the countryside. He has been vigorous in protecting the lives and property of loyalists, both Protestant and Papist, as doubtless many of them will stand ready to testify at the proper time. For he will of course face grave charges and will face them very shortly. I shall do all in my power to protect him from the consequences of his folly, but this will not be an easy task. His claim to gentility will offer no shield—as witness the summary hanging of Bagenal Harvey of Bargy Castle in Wexford, who was moreover a Protestant and powerfully connected with some of the leading families. I have several thoughts upon this matter, but it will be a most worrisome and difficult business, and before we have done, I may well be calling upon you for your assistance. And thus, to be candid, the present letter.

I account it as certain that this rebellion will fail, unless it is swiftly reinforced by a second army from France, and a larger one. Wide stretches of the island remain loyal, and of those which are disaffected, all are in a state of unreadiness. It is precisely this certainty which moves me to regard our present circumstances as mysterious. Humbert, the French commander, does not have the reputation of being either a fool or an adventurer. Since his victories in the Vendée, he has been known as a shrewd and resourceful soldier, and he has threaded his way

293

cautiously through the labyrinths of the Directory. And yet here he is with a bog to roam around in until such time as Cornwallis feels inclined to cut him down. I cannot account for the reasonings in Paris which sent him forth upon so foolhardy an enterprise, nor why he agreed to so perilous an undertaking. Certain it is, however, that Ireland is playing her accustomed role of maidservant to others.

How many dramas of modern history have chosen for setting this Godforsaken bog, and always without any recompense for my unfortunate countrymen save further misery? What were the rebellions of Desmond and Tyrone but chapters in the struggle between Elizabeth and Spain, and thus of Reformation and Counterreformation? What were the wars of Cromwell here but a sideshow to the English Civil War, in which the divine right of Kings was challenged and overthrown? When James and William, the two kings, faced each other at the Boyne, the game was Europe, and Ireland but the board upon which the wagers were placed. The history of Ireland, as written by any of our local savants, reminds me of a learned and bespectacled ant, climbing laboriously across a graven tablet and discovering there deep valleys, towering mountains, broad avenues, which to a grown man contemplating the scene are but the incised names of England, Spain, France. Now the name of France appears a second time upon the table.

In my present isolation, I am perforce an ant. London must surely have but one concern at the moment—Egypt and Buonaparte. The other day, I stood upon a rise of ground, facing the road. It was early morning, chill and with a heavy autumnal air. A small band of rebels, leaderless so far as I could judge, was trudging northward, toward Castlebar, a few with muskets, and others with their long, cumbersome pikes carried at the slope. Friezeclad, they might have stepped out of history. Speak to them, and they would answer in a language unknown beyond these islands, a tongue which locks them to the past as firmly as does the sea which surrounds them. Egypt, if they know the world at all, is the land where their infant Savior was carried to avoid the wrath of Herod. For these wretches, there will be no Egypt, and General Lake will be their Herod. If I accosted them, so I thought for a moment as they moved through the mist, would they answer me with news of O'Neill, or of Cromwell, of armies gathering at Aughrim?

Killala, September 2

The men hired by Kate Cooper to guard Mount Pleasant had drifted away, intimidated by the jeers and threats of the townspeople, but for the hours before the dawn of September second she was safe and so was the house. She brushed her thick black hair with the help of a small, brass-framed mirror propped against a table in one of the bedrooms. MacCarthy watched her from the bed, a blanket of heavy, rough wool drawn about him.

"They will hang you at the end of all this," she said, pulling the brush through the unruly hair. "From a gallows in this very town."

"You never know," MacCarthy said mildly.

"And you will deserve it."

"Very likely. Owen MacCarthy, the judge will say, you have taken Kate Mahony to bed and for that you must hang. There is more woman than one would give a pull to the rope."

"My name is not Mahony," she said. " 'Tis Cooper. Have you forgotten that?"

"Well now, Kate, you did a fair job of forgetting it yourself these past two hours. Sure all Mayo knows you as Mick Mahony's daughter, and so they would call you were you married to Cooper or to me or to anyone else."

"To you? I thank you, no. Married to a hedge schoolmaster with a rope waiting for him."

"Give over that talk about ropes, would you?"

"You are frightened, are you not? And well you might be. You may play the rake, but the gallows frightens you."

"It would frighten any man. If it comes I will scream with terror but it is far distant from this room and the two of us."

She put down the brush and turned around to face him. "You are a terrible fool, MacCarthy. They will hang you or they will shoot you in the fighting, one or the other.

There are roads open to you that you could take out of Mayo."

"'I'm a rogue and you're another,'" he said in English, "'and I'll be hanged in Ballinrobe when you are hanged in Ballintubber.' There is a vile, vulgar rhyme for you. In English they have all these boasts about rhymes and what great things they are, and see there how it works."

A fine figure of a woman in her nightdress, sensuous as always, and as always a touch of the slattern, the dress hanging loose from a shoulder. Candlelight flickered on pale skin, brown-freckled. Warm beneath the blanket, MacCarthy, naked, would have rested there forever.

"A fine figure there," he said, speaking his thought. She smiled, wide, generous mouth.

"You are in grave danger yourself," he said. "Many have been hanged for consorting with rebels."

"A queer kind of consorting it is that we have been at."

"You would think differently if you knew Latin."

"All that Latin going to waste," she said. "The Latin and the poetry and the rest of it."

Soft muslin masked the wide-hipped body. In sunlight, her eyes reflected summer grasses. Now shadowed, hidden. A woman will give herself to you, belly pressed to belly, legs uplifted, wrapped, tearing fingers coiled in hair, moist open lips. Then move away, the body reclothed, hand and white arm combing with familiar skill disordered hair. And it was as though no mystery had been unlocked, no bridges crossed, no door swung back. With clothes they put on mystery again, each passionate word unsaid. And for her? What had he meant to her, unlikely stranger in a darkened room, unfamiliar form hulking above her?

"Latin and the dear knows what else," she said, "and what good has it ever done you? It will not save you now."

"Consort," he said. "To keep company with. As we now keep company."

"It has always been a wonder to me that the language of the Mass can be used to speak of matters that are best left unspoken."

"Such matters are older than the Mass," he said. "By hundreds of years. The Mass came late."

"You are a great scholar," she said. "A great scholar and poet without ten pounds to his name." She looked at herself in the cloudy mirror, and then turned her head away abruptly. What had she seen there?

"My fortune is yet to be made," MacCarthy said. "I have great hopes for it."

"You have neither fortune nor future," she said. "Not now."

"You never know," he said. "You would be more comfortable and warm under the blanket, 'tis grand in here."

" 'Twas a kind thought you had to visit Mount Pleasant and see how was I faring with no man's hand to protect me against lawless bands. You are a kindly man. That I will grant you."

"Small kindness. I came here in the hope that one thing would lead to the next, and at the end of it we would spend the night in the one bed."

"Sure I had no such thought as that," she said, scandalized. "No married woman should have such thoughts. I am not one of those sluttish wives who bring grief upon their heads. I have a husband and a home, and I am content with them."

The monumental hypocrisy of women. Sitting there before him, body still warm from his. What need would she have to brush her hair at all, had it not become entangled with their passion, damp with their passion's sweat. A woman can remember the bed without believing what she remembers. A great convenience, and man's perpetual defeat.

> "You say you will make me strong wine
> From the frothy pools of the Boyne,
> Gold from the furze, silver from ferns,
> I will die, without sense, from your words."

"And what is that supposed to mean?" she asked him.

"There was a woman, the wife of Hugh O'Rourke of Brefny, and Thomas Costello the poet was always after her. Then O'Rourke went off to fight the English, and the woman speaks this poem that he is to come back because she cannot resist Costello. To be sure, the woman didn't write it at all, but Thomas Costello."

"How do you know that—"

"How do I know it! Sure, Thomas Costello was a fine poet and what would a woman be doing, writing a poem?"

Smile, half masked by candlelight. "What, indeed. And when did all this happen, if it happened at all?"

"Ach, hundreds of years ago. In the days of the O'Neill rebellion. Come over here under the warm blanket before you freeze to death."

"Hundreds of years. Who cares about all that rubbish, save schoolmasters."

" 'Tis a fine poem, all the same. By God, it is."

"That woman didn't know the meaning of trouble. Look at myself, would you, with poor Sam locked away by the Whiteboys, and no man here to defend Mount Pleasant. They can come here when they choose, burning and screeching."

"I have a belief, Kate, that Mount Pleasant and yourself will come out of this unscratched. You are your father's daughter."

"You are not helpful, are you, when a woman turns to you in her distress?"

"I will have a word tomorrow with Ferdy O'Donnell, if you like, but 'tis little enough that Ferdy can do for one who lives this far from the town. If you are fearful, you had best go to the Palace, to Mr. Broome and his wife."

"And leave Mount Pleasant naked against the likes of Malachi Duggan? Before one of them can set a bare, dirty foot into Mount Pleasant, I will scratch the eyes out of Malachi Duggan's head."

His father could tell one bit of turf from the next, as MacCarthy could sample whiskeys, crumbling the turf in his fingers, touching his tongue to it. Landless Brian MacCarthy, son of an evicted peasant, carrying his spade from one Kerry hiring fair to the next, his own son scuffling, dirty-skinned, behind him. Mick Mahony gouging and scrambling, toe of boot to a peasant's arse, obsequious smile for landlord and magistrate. Kate Mahony, loose mouth and wild body wasted on drink-sodden Cooper, mistress of Mount Pleasant. It was land that they hungered for and not the passionate bed, but the poets spoke only of love, laments for the Stuarts, grief for the banished chieftains. He was as bad as the rest. The subjects suitable for poetry had been prescribed centuries ago.

"Gold from the furze, silver from ferns."

"Your life is wasted," she said. "You have thrown it away in your foolishness."

"I had little to throw."

"You had a school, that girl in the village, the poetry. You will have nothing now."

"By God, Kate, I am much of your opinion. What the hell am I doing at my time of life, swaggering around like some half-mounted squireen at a fair?"

"It is your question. Let you answer it."

He moved to prop himself on one elbow, and held out his other hand toward her. She shook her head.

"No more of that. It will be light soon. It was a very foolish thing I did with you tonight, Owen MacCarthy. God knows that it is my own husband should be with me now, and it is no fault of mine that he had to stuff himself into a red uniform and be captured by savages from France. It was to me that he owed his first duty, the selfish beast."

"It may have been the woman after all who wrote the poem, and not Costello at all."

"What does that matter?" she said impatiently. "A wild rover like yourself, taking the virtue from maidens and the honor from married women, you think you have the best of every bargain but you have nothing at all. No house that you can call your own, no woman's love that you can claim a year from now. A month ago, from the window of this house, I heard a man in the field singing one of your songs. The songs may be remembered, but not the man who wrote them."

"What could be better than that, for your songs to be anonymous and remembered?"

She rose suddenly and stood looking at him, loose fists pressed against hipbones. "You are a child, Owen, for all the size and the age of you and your dreadful life. God forgive me, I have gone to bed with a child." She crossed the room and sat beside him on the bed. "Owen, have you never wanted anything?"

"You," he said. He ran the back of his hand down her hair.

"Oh, to be sure. Or any other woman. That is not wanting something." But she did not draw back from him.

"I was born with nothing and I have nothing. That cannot be changed."

"That must be a terrible way to live."

"It requires practice." He touched her cheek lightly.

"Ah well," she said, "it must be wonderful all the same to live without worrying and scheming."

"Wonderful indeed," he said, drawing her head to his shoulder.

Beyond them, the candle flickered upon the empty mirror.

Ballycastle, September 2

On September second, Cornwallis moved northward from Tuam to Hollymount. A messenger from Longford brought word to Humbert from Hans Dennistoun that the midlands would rise in two days' time. And John Moore again rode past Killala to visit the Treacys on the Ballycastle road.

In the weeks which had passed, summer had begun to move toward autumn, but the morning was bronze, warm sunlight bathing fields which were turning yellow. Mayo had its own seasons, a flat land held between ocean and mountain, and was now at the turn.

At the near side of Ballina, he drew rein before the massive pillars which once had held the gates to Mount Lawrence Hall. The house, standing on a knoll and screened by a leafy plantation, had been burned. Smoke and the stench of charring clogged the nostrils of his imagination. And yet the Lawrence harvest was being reaped: he could see small figures moving in the distant fields. He rode up the straight avenue until he was abreast of them, then jumped the low wall and cantered along the narrow path until he was within hailing distance. The reapers paused and stood watching him, forearms shading their eyes.

"Where are Mrs. Lawrence and her daughters?" he called. They stood silently, watching. When no one answered he dismounted and walked toward them. "I asked you about Mrs. Lawrence."

An old man, scythe blade resting on the ground, said, "They went into Killala, to the Protestant clergyman's."

Moore looked behind him, toward the house. "Who did that?"

After a pause: "It was burned after the big battle. There is nothing left standing in there. Not so much as a chair. It has all been burned or carried off."

"By the rebels," Moore said.

The old man rubbed the back of his hand against a stubble of gray. The much younger man beside him, who might have been a son, said, "Sure who could say? They

300

came after dark, and they seemed like a small army. We stayed in the cabins until they were gone."

"But you stayed," Moore said. "Is it for Mr. Lawrence that you are saving the harvest?" Moore's Irish was very weak, and his vocabulary small.

"Mr. Lawrence may not be back, nor any of his family. 'Tis said that all of the gentry are leaving Mayo forever."

"Then you are saving it for yourselves?"

The man shrugged. "All of the cattle were driven off by the men who came at night. All but a few. And do you know what they did with those few? The gates were taken off, and those few were roasted on them, over a great fire. They took their leisure here, by God."

The old man gave a long, phlegm-choked cough, and then spat between his feet. "What is there can be done with a harvest but save it, whoever it is to be saved for? The gentry are gone out of it. Mr. Lawrence is off with the English soldiers, and the ladies are in Killala."

Moore looked from one face to the other, and then back to the fire-gutted house. He had never visited there. The Lawrences were hard Protestants.

"Are you an Englishman, sir?" the younger man asked.

Moore stared at him, puzzled, and then said quietly, "No. I am Irish."

"If you are English you should not go into Ballina. The men that are now in Ballina are very bold."

"I will be careful," Moore said gently, and then turned back toward the avenue.

The main street of Ballina, straggling off at an angle from the placid Moy, was green with trees and boughs of liberty. As Moore turned into it from the river road he was stopped by four men with pikes. One of them closed a fist upon his bridle. They did not recognize his name, but he persuaded them to lead his horse to the tavern which Michael Geraghty was using as headquarters. He found Geraghty in a small inner room, dressed in one of the French uniforms with unbuckled collar, a plate of bacon pushed to one edge of the table. Moore sat down facing him.

"What has been happening in Ballina, Captain?"

"Sure what would be happening here, with all the excitement below in Castlebar?"

"You've had your excitement. I have just seen Mount Lawrence Hall. Or what is left of it."

Geraghty nodded, and then reached toward the deal sideboard for glasses and a bottle. "A bad business."

"Is that all you have to say about it? And it was more of Malachi Duggan's work, I take it."

"It was not," Geraghty said slowly. "It is not. My own boys burned that house. The United boys."

"Your own men! What in hell are you telling me, Geraghty? If you had a hand in that business you will answer for it. Men have been whipped bloody in Castlebar for less than that."

"Then let you whip my boys and not me, for I had no part in it at all, beyond saying that they could take the cattle and the goods. And I said that only after the thing was done, to make it official, like."

"Lawrence was a decent landlord, by all that I have ever heard, and now what does he have for his pains?"

The glasses were smeared, and the whiskey raw.

"Don't I know that better than yourself? It is here in Ballina you should be and not below in Castlebar writing proclamations. It is all I can do to keep some kind of hold on my boys. They are wild boys at best, Mr. Moore, faction fighters and the like. If I didn't slack off once or twice, I'd be sitting here in Ballina by myself, and that would serve no man's profit."

"Ferdy O'Donnell in Killala has no trouble holding on to his men."

"Then let you make Ferdy O'Donnell a general. I am doing the best I can at a task for which I have little skill. There has been no Protestant killed in Ballina, nor will there be if I can prevent it. But it is landlords and not the British soldiers that these lads have spent their lives fearing and bowing down before and hating. What this rising up means to them is that the landlords will be driven out and will not come back. And that is what it means to me as well."

"Then you have scant understanding of the oath which you took, which was to an Ireland free of the English, not free of landlords. It is to a landlord that you are talking, Geraghty, or at least to the brother of one."

"Well do I know that, Mr. Moore. Yourself and Malcolm Elliott both. Do I not hold my own farm from Malcolm Elliott? But neither of you need stay as I must in Ballina and Ferdy in Killala, protecting those for whom we have no love against our own people. That is a task that might well be beyond you or beyond Malcolm Elliott or beyond your French general."

"You need not bide here much longer," Moore said. "We will be moving out of Mayo soon, and the men from the towns and villages with us. All save the garrison at Killala."

"Moving where, if that is not too much to ask?"

"Toward the midlands, I think, if we can give Cornwallis the slip. He was at Athlone a day or two ago. He must be closer than that by now."

Geraghty refilled his glass and took a deep swallow from it. "With a great army of the English?"

"Large enough," Moore said. "But not as large as the midland rising will be."

"Much midland means to me," Geraghty said. "Save that it is a word. I have never been to Athlone even, and neither have my men. We are Mayo men. And we thought that the men of all Ireland would be rising up, and not the men of Mayo carried off to fight in strange fields of which we do not even know the names. Let us bide here in Mayo, and let the Frenchmen go to the midlands."

"So you may say. But that is not how wars are fought. The French general will need all the men he can get."

"My wife is at work out there," Geraghty said, nodding toward the window, across the Moy, toward hidden fields. "Saving the harvest. And a bad job she is making of it, poor woman."

"There will be a great battle," Moore said. "In the midlands, most likely. And another one near Dublin. Then you can go back to your crops."

"I could be with my crops by a shorter way than that. I could be with my crops without leaving Mayo." He pulled the plate toward him and picked up a slice of bacon.

"You could," Moore said, "but you will not."

Geraghty grunted, and nodded toward Moore when he rose to leave. "For a man as young as yourself, you have firm ideas as to what other men will or will not do."

Riding north, beside fields and farms which he had passed on his earlier journey, Moore could find no marks of the rebellion save untended fields and a second burned house. An army had gathered in Castlebar and other armies were moving against it. Killala, like Ballina, was in

303

rebel hands. And yet the landscape was unchanged, the fields green, the trees thick with leafage, no trace of brown yet showing. He had helped to set events in motion which sent flames moving from room to room of Mount Lawrence Hall and peasants clambering up the dew-wet slopes of Sion Hill. But the quiet, sun-drenched fields asserted the inconsequentiality of his actions, of all action. The sound of a distant pheasant, leaves stirring in a mild, brief wind, hoofbeats on the road, were more actual than smoke-blackened stones, pikes, cannon, muskets, monarchies, republics.

The coldness with which Thomas Treacy received him set a seal upon this, for Treacy, as he soon made plain, regarded him less as a rebel than as the willful younger son of a neighboring family, bent upon dragging family and friends toward irretrievable disgrace. He had seen Moore riding up the short avenue and was waiting for him on the steps, his spare, elongated figure framed by the open door.

"I knew that you would wish to see us, John. Sooner or later. Or at least to see Ellen."

"To see both of you, of course, sir. But I am not certain of my welcome."

Treacy walked down the steps to face him. "It is difficult for me to say this to someone of whom I have been fond. But you are not welcome, and I cannot believe that you could have thought otherwise."

Moore sat awkwardly on his mount, fingering her reins. "And yet you knew that I would come."

"Because of Ellen. Yes, yes, I knew that. Don't sit there, boy. However brief our conversation, it had best be conducted indoors." He gave Moore a brief smile. "Or rather, I assume that that is best. I have had no experience of receiving heads of state. A most remarkable accomplishment for one of your years. Even Mr. Pitt was older when he became Prime Minister, and he has been accounted a prodigy."

He led Moore to the smaller of the two drawing rooms, sparsely furnished, two clumsily painted portraits, a heavy crucifix, a mawkish engraving of Jesus raising Lazarus from the dead. A decanter of wine stood on the sideboard, but Treacy pointedly left it untouched, although he gestured Moore to a chair.

"It is very quiet here in Ballycastle," Moore said.

"Very quiet indeed, at least between Bridge-end and

the river," Treacy said, with hostile courtesy. "As of course you must know, my friend Falkiner's house was raided."

"No," Moore said, "I did not know that."

"Oh, yes. Raided but not burned. One of your bands of ruffians was apparently driven off by a second."

"It is probable," Moore said, "that those other ruffians, as you call them, were the men under Ferdy O'Donnell's command. He has been charged with the maintenance of order in this barony. And you surely must know that he is no ruffian."

"I have known him for years, and have thought only well of him. A decent, hard-working farmer and well educated. But then, until recent months I have had a high opinion of yourself. I no longer have."

Moore did not reply. Embarrassed, he looked beyond the tall window to the flat, green meadow.

"It is being said," Treacy went on, "that I have myself been spared because of the friendship between your family and mine. Or else because I have the good fortune, as it has suddenly become, of being a Catholic."

"If you wish," Moore said, choosing his words with care, "you may give the lie to both of those rumors. The army of the Irish Republic—"

"The army of the Irish Republic," Treacy echoed derisively. "I would be amused to learn your brother's views on that subject. When I walk from room to room of this house, I am ashamed by the mere suspicion that I owe my safety to my creed, or to any connection with a rebel against the King."

"I can only repeat that you are mistaken in your suspicions."

"What else is to be thought? A dozen houses to my knowledge have been looted or burned between here and Castlebar, and all of them the houses of Protestants. When this wretched business is over, the position of Catholics in Mayo will be worse than it has been in thirty years."

"Most landlords are Protestants," Moore said, fighting a rising impatience. "And most peasants are Catholics. There is your answer. They have risen up, and their anger has spilled over upon those whom they see as their oppressors. But the Society of United Irishmen is not at war against any man's property or any man's religion."

"I have been to visit poor Falkiner's house," Treacy

305

said. "What has been done to it is dreadful." Distracted by the recollection, he drew fingers through thin white hair. "It is what may be expected when brutes are turned loose, and yet the sight shocks one—tables smashed to splinters, paintings hacked and cut. Many a pleasant evening I have spent in that befouled and violated room. George Falkiner has been all his life well disposed toward those of our faith. His was the first Protestant name on the Connaught petition for Catholic rights. Did you know that? And there is what thanks he gets. And those brutes are now your allies and your chosen companions."

"The petition failed," Moore said. "It failed because the people of Ireland do not have control of their own affairs."

"Words," Treacy said. "The facts are men killed and houses gutted. A brutal peasantry has been turned loose upon the countryside. Those are the facts."

"I have earned your displeasure," Moore said. "Let us leave it at that."

"Displeasure is the language of circulating libraries. You are a rebel in arms against your lawful King, and you are in so sore a danger that neither your brother nor any other man will be able to save you. You have disgraced your religion and your nation."

"A nation in whose Parliament I am forbidden to sit because of my religion. There also is a fact. Does it carry no weight with you?"

"I am fully conscious of the wicked burdens which have been placed upon us. That does not tempt me to turn the country over to drunken spalpeens and French brigands. I have no wish to debate the matter with you. You had hoped to marry Ellen. I have favored this intention and so has George. George has been most generous in this matter, for there is a wide distance between the fortunes of the Moores and of the Treacys. But now you can best display your affection for Ellen by forgetting that any such plans were ever considered. You can bring to her now only sorrow and misery."

"You might at least credit me with common sense, Mr. Treacy."

"That is the very last virtue which I am prepared to grant you, John."

"I am engaged in a hazardous enterprise, and like yourself I have no wish to expose Ellen to any of its dangers.

But I trust that I shall be returning to Mayo with my prospects far brighter than they may seem at present. I have ridden here today only to speak with her, and I trust that I may have your permission to do so."

"Speak with her by all means. I have no wish to prevent that. But you must accept the fact that Bridge-end House must hereafter be closed to you, and that our friendship with you has ended."

"That is a very cold statement."

"It is indeed. I am doing my best to remain calm in speaking with you, John. I have had a great fondness for you, as I am sure you must know. But I despise the course which you have taken. It is both a folly and a crime, a crime which is breeding other crimes. You will not be returning to Mayo, but the British army will, and they will very likely turn this county into a wasteland. I have lived in penal days and I have watched as the Catholics of Mayo struggled—lawfully and peacefully struggled—to establish their rights—"

"This is too much!" Moore said. "Why do you think that the United Irishmen are fighting, if not to establish the rights of all Irishmen? What have these peaceful struggles earned you save a string of miserable concessions doled out decade by decade—"

"That will do," Treacy said. "I will not debate with you, and neither will I suffer you to defend the actions of murderous peasants. Now, if you wish to have an hour's conversation with Ellen, you will find her in the sewing room, where I have asked her to remain during your visit. You and I may take our farewell of each other here, in this room." He rose, hesitated, and then suddenly held out his hand. "I am more sorry than words can express, my dear John."

"I cannot accept that my friendship with this family can end in such a manner," Moore said. Treacy shrugged.

But when Moore knocked on the door of the sewing room, he was astonished by a different reception, for Ellen flung open the door and hurled herself at him, a girl thin as her father and almost as tall as Moore himself. She twined her arms around his neck, and with her head pressed against his began to cry violently. He stood awkwardly, stroking her long, sand-colored hair and speaking quietly, until she drew back and led him into the small, sun-filled room.

For a minute she stood looking down at the litter of

silk and muslin scraps on the table, and then picked one up and held it against her eyes. She stood with her back toward him, narrow shoulders shaking, and then turned to face him with tear-swollen eyes.

"I had never thought that it would be like this."

"Like what?"

"The way you had it, there would be ship after ship coming in from France, great armadas of them. And the whole island would be rising up. Not three miserable ships and a few hundred men."

"There will be a second fleet," Moore said. "And perhaps a third."

"It will be too late."

"It will not. Your father and yourself are two of the gloomiest mortals on earth."

"We are indeed, if you mean that we are sensible. And my father says now that we are not to see each other."

"Do you accept that?"

"What else is a girl of my age to do, may I ask? I have not a choice. If you go off from Mayo with the rebels, you will not be returning here to me. You will be put to the bayonet in some ditch or else hanged at a crossroads. Your brother will not be able to get you free from this scrape."

"I have not asked my brother for his advice. I have no need of his help."

"Are you so eager to be killed?"

"My brother cares as little about Ireland as he does about a horse race."

"No more do I. Or for England or France or America. Not as you use the word. You men are forever turning ideas into things and places. Ireland is not an idea but an actual place with real people who can shed blood or swing at the rope's end. Ireland is outside that window."

"It is indeed."

"Oh," she cried impatiently. "I cannot say what I mean and you will not understand me. You are more important to me than Ireland, and so am I, and my father and the fellows out in the field and everyone that I have ever seen. When you say that you want to free Ireland, I do not know what you mean. I declare to God I do not. A young fellow like you, only a few years older than I am myself. If you said that you wanted to free a pig stuck in a fence I would know what you mean, because I know what a pig is. And a fence."

"In fact you sound very like my brother. As though you had read the same books."

"You may depend upon it that we have not. I have enough to keep me busy."

"It is late in the day for this conversation, Ellen dear. It has begun. Battles have been fought."

"Battles! There have been houses burned by ignorant faction fighters, if you mean that."

"Call them what you will. Did you know that I have been made President of the Republic in Connaught?"

"Yes," she said, and stared at him as though she wished to laugh but had not the will. "So I have heard. You are very young for such an honor."

"It is not me that they honor, but the brother of the master of Moore Hall. The French have queer notions of equality, for all their talk."

"If you were not his brother you would be a happier man."

"What do you mean?"

Her hand strayed to the remnants of bright-colored cloth, moving them forward and back.

"He is much in your thoughts," she said. "What you do is always a kind of quarrel with him."

"By God, you can talk foolishly when you want to! There are no two brothers could be more fond of each other. We differ in our politics, that is all."

"Oh, politics! I don't care tuppence for politics. They mean nothing. George is a very cool man. He can be infuriating. Do you never find him so?"

"It is not to talk about George that I rode out here, but about ourselves."

"There is nothing for us to say, John. My father has the right of it there. John, do you not know that what you have done is rebellion? That they can hang you? Oh, what good is there in talking at all? And I so much in love with you. Oh, what will I do? What will you do?"

She turned away from him, and stepped to the window. Beyond her, he saw a field's pale green, the gray stones of fences. Her shoulders moved below her quiet crying.

"I cannot, Ellen. What is done is done. I can do nothing else." But she did not reply, and he put his arms around her again, holding her without speaking.

"I would go with you anywhere," she said at last. "That is what I would wish to tell you. But I cannot. It is what they say in songs only. I will bide here, and there will be no life for us together."

"There will be," he said. "You will see."

But in that moment, though he still stared absently toward field and fence, he saw himself as clearly as in a pier glass. An open, candid face, unlined by experience, confident without cause, shock of yellow hair brighter than the girl's, a young man's face. Face of suitor or student, horseman riding full tilt toward fence or ditch. Again, as with George, with Geraghty, with her father, he felt himself shoved brutally toward a role empty of meaning, flimsy and persistent. He remembered and was mocked by the vari-colored cloths scattered on the table: patches for a clown's motley.

From "Youthful Service: With Cornwallis in Ireland," by Major General Sir Harold Wyndham

On the second of September, Cornwallis was joined at Tuam by two English regiments, the Queen's and the Twenty-ninth, which had come by forced march from Wexford. Placing these under his personal command, he moved northward at once, and set his headquarters at Hollymount, close to Ballinrobe and some thirteen miles from the rebel "capital" at Castlebar. Colonel Crauford, a Scottish officer in whom he placed a well-justified confidence, took forward a detachment of his dragoons to reconnoiter, and discovered that the rebels had begun to withdraw their outposts close to that town. On his return ride, however, he was assailed by a rebel band near the lodge gates of Mr. George Moore, whose brother was an insurgent chieftain. With their long, murderous pikes, the rebels hacked viciously at riders, horses, and bridles, and contrived to skewer two dragoons before being themselves overpowered.

Colonel Crauford summarily hanged a number of these wretches, but four of them he brought into Hollymount, stumbling along before troopers who were none too gentle with them. This was our first view of the native enemy, and a most deplorable appearance they made. They were fellows of the lowest sort, rough-dressed and roughvisaged, scowling with fear and hatred. One of our Irish sought to question them but could learn little. They were from one of the remote western baronies of Mayo, and as primitive as the tribesmen of Otaheetee, although lacking in that rude grace which Captain Cook attributes to his South Sea Islanders. The rebels had placed them there precisely to waylay and murder our outriders, but surely could not have intended that this bare score should attack so heavily mounted a force as Crauford's dragoons. And yet, pathetically faithful to their hideous instructions, they had done just that. They were either, as is the more likely case, most ignorant and stupid, or else possessed a courage worthy of a better cause.

Crauford, a lean and peppery Highlander who was to distinguish himself under the great Wellington in the Peninsular wars, was a most able and resourceful cavalryman, although his ways, it must be confessed, were rough and ready. He was still a youngish man at the time of which I write, but possessed an easy confidence which I greatly envied, joined to a dry and sardonic humor and an impatience with the more cautious temperaments of his elders. He was to earn among the peasantry of the west a reputation for unbridled cruelty second only to those enjoyed by General Lake and Dennis Browne. It is a reputation which I have no wish to challenge, for I was myself to witness deeds of his upon which memory would gladly draw a veil. I do not believe, however, that these passed beyond the harsh and stern usages of warfare, and it is certain that a time of rebellion holds no season for lenient measures.

That night, Lord Roden, on behalf of our Irish commanders, made formal protest to Lord Cornwallis against the subordinate positions in which they had been placed. Cornwallis cut him off, however, and although both his tone and his language were courteous, he made it clear that he questioned the resolve of the Irish common soldiers and the experience of their officers. And he thus taught a lesson which was to stand me in good stead throughout my career: that colonials can only be employed with confidence when they have received the stiff backbone of British regulars. It was a lesson which was to prove itself over and over, and although this may be but the prejudice of a military man, I believe it to be the lesson upon which rests the strength of our empire.

This took place at a meeting which Cornwallis had

called with his staff officers and officers in command of regiments, at which, with his customary courtesy and tact, he invited their suggestions as to how we might best proceed with the task before us. He was spending the night in the substantial dwelling place of a Protestant farmer whose name, as I best recall it, was Prendergast, and the conference was held in a commodious kitchen, at a large oak table across which had been thrown the capacious cloth of green baize which had accompanied Lord Cornwallis from his campaigning days in North America. He sipped constantly at his cups of chocolate, to which he repaired as might other men to hardier stimulants. Perhaps his habit asserted the comfort and security of an English drawing room against the savage darkness of treeless bogs.

The task before us was a clear and a simple one, but he was determined that it should be accomplished without errors on the part of his subordinates. The circumstances of the Castlebar battle were now neatly reversed. Once again a large British force would be confronting a smaller army of Frenchmen and rebels. Now, however, the enemy would be the defenders of the town, and the British on the attack. The enemy, should he manage to fight us off, could move only toward the midlands, across the Shannon, or, as an improbable alternative, eastward toward Ulster. But for him to move in either direction, it would be necessary for him to get past the British line, which extended from Sligo to Boyle. Cornwallis, however, did not repose sufficient confidence in this line. He therefore proposed to divide our forces. He would himself attack Castlebar. General Lake would join General Nugent, and move forward from Frenchpark, in Roscommon. Should Humbert manage to elude us at Castlebar, Cornwallis proposed to cross the Shannon at Carrick, thus placing the rebels between the two wings of our army, with no retreat possible, save backward toward the sea.

It was General Lake who broke the silence which followed Cornwallis's exposition.

"Lord Cornwallis, I must be more than usually slow-witted tonight. Is it not the fact that the enemy lies at this moment twelve miles distant from us, with a force that cannot exceed three thousand men?"

"Perhaps three thousand, perhaps five. It is difficult to form judgments upon the information given us by the poor frightened loyalists. And we must remember that

312

their victories will have swelled the rebel ranks. The rest of the country may be at peace for the moment, but I do not doubt that Connaught has gone into a state of general insurrection."

"Five thousand, then. Very well. Even then we outnumber him heavily. And the most of those thousands are clumsy, ignorant Irish peasants."

"Clumsy and ill armed," Cornwallis said. "Armed with pikes."

"At best," Lake said. "Pikes and scythes. Some of them are shoved into battle with scythes. I have seen them."

"You have indeed," Cornwallis said, but Lake did not feel the sting in the words.

"Then why in God's name do we not attack him as soon as the sun has risen?"

"There is a further point," Lord Roden said. "The French are not likely to have sent over a thousand men and there's an end to it. A second fleet will be following this one. We should wipe this fellow off the ground right now, before that happens."

"It will not happen before sunrise," Cornwallis said. "The main body of our reinforcements will not be here for another day. By then General Lake will have taken up his position to the east."

"We outnumber him now," Lake said, his patience wearing thin. "We outnumber him heavily, and we should engage him now."

Cornwallis smiled at him, and nodded toward the cook who was keeping his chocolate hot. "After your own unfortunate experience, General Lake, can you believe that we are dealing with some simple-minded colonel of mosstroopers? Our General Humbert is a most skillful commander, whose chief weapon is not the scythe, but the unexpected. Perhaps you can deal with the unexpected, but I must confess that it throws me into confusion. I am a most unimaginative and methodical kind of fellow, and my only weapon against the unexpected is an overwhelming superiority in numbers." Colonel Crauford's long-jawed Highland face broke into an ill-natured grin at Lake's expense.

"The Crown is in your debt, General," Cornwallis went on, in the most agreeable tone imaginable, "for your victories over the rebels in Wexford, but we must remember that you had only peasants to deal with then, blundering peasants with none to lead them save a few bloodthirsty priests. Humbert has a thousand seasoned French troops, well armed and supported by artillery. The very best artillery, cast in Sheffield by British gunsmiths. He has the cannon which you gave him as a gift when you fled from Castlebar."

It had been long in coming, that reproof for the defeat at Castlebar, and was the more devastating for coming without warning, and in the gentle manner of a man discussing a game of cards at his club. Even Crauford's mouth fell open, and poor Lake turned the color of beetroot, his cheeks and neck rivaling the scarlet of his uniform.

And yet he said, with a quiet dignity that earned our admiration, "If you believe that I am capable of taking the east wing, you will not regret it, Lord Cornwallis. Should the Frenchman get past Castlebar, you may depend upon my meeting him and destroying him."

"You will do no such thing," Cornwallis said sharply. "You will of course deny him access to Ulster, even at the risk of battle. But I prefer that you should not engage him. You will harry him constantly, by striking at him and then moving off, and by harrying him, you will drive him closer and closer to me. I want him in a vice, where we can crush him between us. No matter how enticing it may seem, you are not to engage him head on. You are of course familiar with that kind of tactic. As I recall, you marched up and down Wexford for several weeks before attacking the rebels on Vinegar Hill. I cannot imagine why." Lake began to speak, but Cornwallis held up his hand. "No need to explain, General. No need. It was a great victory."

Much later that night, Cornwallis lay abed scribbling off letters to friends in England, as was his habit, in a gown of white linen, with a lace nightcap perched atop his sparse gray hairs, looking for all the world like Sir Roger de Coverley.

He drew his pen across his lips, and then said to me, "You are wondering, Lieutenant, whether it was right of me to taunt General Lake as I did. It was. On the whole it was. Unpleasant but right. General Lake will now perform prodigies in his efforts to conform to my wishes. He will take a sullen, self-pitying pride in carrying out orders which he believes to be ill judged and craven. Nothing makes a soldier happier, especially a stupid one.

Soldiers are hired to win wars, not battles, but few of
them seem able to grasp the fact. Indeed, I believe that he
will spend the rest of his life living down Castlebar, poor
fellow. I find him a most disagreeable chap, without imagination or style. Do you not agree, Lieutenant?"

I of course made no reply, but busied myself with his
papers.

"Most disagreeable. Why, you are asking, do I return
him in command. The British army is an old, established
firm, Lieutenant, and we plan to remain in business for a
long time to come. It simply does not do to plunge a general into disgrace because he has lost a battle. Let the
Frenchies do that. They are forever shooting their generals or hanging them, now they have their guillotine,
allows them to do it wholesale, and for a time the results
are impressive. Keeps everyone on his best behavior.
But it won't do for the long haul. By the time this campaign is over, General Lake will have earned himself a
decoration. For bravery, of course, not cleverness. Now,
this Humbert is a clever man. But we never really trust
clever men, do we? Old established firms are based upon
trust."

After a time his words came more slowly, and at last
he was gently snoring. I took the pen from his hand, and,
leaving the room, summoned his servant.

Lake moved out early the next morning, and Cornwallis accompanied him to the Claremorris road, laughing
and passing pleasantries, as though harsh words had never
passed between them. They might have been two squires
riding off to the hunt. It was an overcast day, in disappointing contrast to the fine weather we had been
enjoying, a leaden sky stretched low across the flat countryside.

"Now mind," Cornwallis said, "should the enemy
choose to surrender, as any sensible man would, you need
not wait upon me, but may of course accept the surrender,
granting to his officers and men the full courtesies of war.
They have conducted themselves well."

"Not all of the men, surely?" Lake asked. "You are
speaking only of the French soldiers, I take it."

Cornwallis gave him a puzzled look. "The only soldiers
under Humbert's command are French."

"There are the rebels," Lake said. "The Irish."

"Yes, to be sure."

I wish most heartily that I had paid a more strict attention to the words which passed between them on this score, for consequences issued from them which would later bring our arms into disrepute, in the eyes of some, soiling the reputation of an otherwise splendid campaign. "Yes, to be sure," Lord Cornwallis said. "But they are not soldiers, poor devils. They are a half-armed rabble."

"Rebels in arms," Lake said.

"So they must be termed. You saw the wretches that Crauford brought in, wild, half-human creatures. I pity them. I do indeed."

"The honors of war were never meant for rebels," Lake said. "Not here, not anywhere."

"They are misfortunate creatures," Cornwallis said. "This place needs peace, an end to all this." He gestured toward the long columns which Lake would be leading eastward.

"It does indeed," Lake said grimly.

I am certain that I cannot be remembering their words with entire accuracy, although I have the general sense of them, and the offhand manner in which they were spoken. Lord Cornwallis's habit of responding to questions in a casual and unbuttoned style was an endearing one, but at times it made his wishes a matter for interpretation. And so it may have proved upon this occasion, for the fate of the rebels was not otherwise discussed until after the final engagement at Ballinamuck. For myself, knowing him as I did, and knowing well his genuine kindliness, the general drift of his remarks is quite clear. General Lake, however, may be pardoned for drawing a different conclusion.

Cornwallis watched him march off, drums beating and fifes shrilling, and then turned back to Hollymount. We heard many fifes in the course of that day, and by nightfall our complement was complete, and our plan for battle had been established. The day continued overcast, and a chill in the air told us that summer was nearing its end. By the next morning, as we moved out toward Castlebar, a light drizzle had begun to fall.

Crauford, with his light dragoons, was sent to scout the defenses outside the town, and we followed with the infantry and the heavy cavalry. We halted about two miles from the town, having encountered neither resistance nor evidence of fixed positions, and, despite the misty rain, we had a clear view, across the plain, of Crauford advancing almost to the bridge. There were two low explo-

316

sions and cannon shot fell among his men. A horse stumbled. He moved his troopers out of range. We expected to see him move back toward our lines, but instead he drew his men into formation. For a time nothing happened. There was a second salvo, but it fell short of the dragoons. After that the field was silent.

Presently we could see one of his riders coming toward us. When he reached Cornwallis, he saluted.

"Colonel Crauford requests permission to enter Castlebar."

Cornwallis shifted in the chair which had been placed for him, beneath canvas stretched across tentpoles to shelter him from the fine rain. He pursed his lips in thought, and then nodded.

"Is Colonel Crauford quite certain?"

The lieutenant resembled Crauford in appearance, but was much younger. Like Crauford, he was lean but heavy-shouldered, a cavalryman; they had the same high, thick cheekbones.

He shrugged. "Oh, yes. A few cannon, perhaps two or three. Some of their people in the town. Not many. A scattering."

Cornwallis looked toward Lord Roden, who was staring at him, puzzled, and then turned back to the lieutenant.

"Very well, then. If he is certain. If he is not, I will send forward the heavies."

While we waited, he said to me, using a pet name which he employed only when he was feeling pleased, "Well now, Prince Hal. The Frenchman has cheated you of your battle. You have yet to be blooded. Never mind. Another day."

Lord Roden shifted from one foot to the other, and Cornwallis said to him, in the tones of a schoolmaster, "The Frenchman has scampered off. Taken French leave. Good for him, and better for us."

At the end of a long period of waiting, Crauford rode back to us across the bridge, at the head of one troop of cavalry. He looked splendid, a tall cavalryman, wearing a long blue cape against the rain, which was falling more heavily now. Castlebar was once again in British hands.

During the night, as we were drawing up our plans for the battle, and assigning positions to our regiments, Humbert and his entire force had stolen from the town, leaving behind three cannon and their gunners to put up a show of resistance, and two companies of rebels and one

317

of French. If it be accounted a victory to take possession of a few streets of mud and grimy stone, of a handful of gabbling peasants, then we had achieved a victory.

"The disgrace of Castlebar has been expunged," Cornwallis said, as he climbed painfully into the saddle of his placid mount. He put one foot into its stirrup, but let his gouty leg hang free. "How pleased General Lake will be!" But his merry mood was not shared by his staff, and I must confess that I myself felt baffled and cheated.

"By the way, Crauford," he said, calling Crauford to him in his easy, negligent manner. "That was nicely executed. Nicely executed indeed."

A smile slashed Crauford's narrow jaw, a Highland face. "To take an empty town, sir?" He rode close to us. "No great problem there. A brisk canter for those lads over there, and damned little work done to earn their keep."

"But done with grace, Crauford," Cornwallis said. "Done with a bit of flair." He ran his hand slowly along the neck of his horse. "You have the right of it, though. Dragoons are active lads, lively lads. They will lack occupation here."

Crauford's smile broadened, but he said nothing.

"I think you should take your lads out of here. Take them out of here, and place yourself under General Lake's command for the next week or so."

"Under his command, sir," Crauford repeated, but with the shadow of a question in his words.

"You know my instructions to him. You heard me give them. I want the Frenchman harried but not attacked. I want him punished, and I want him kept on the move. Lake will need dragoons for that."

"He has dragoons," Crauford said. "Dragoons and cavalry."

"I intend that he should have you and those lads of yours. You will place yourself under General Lake's command, with my instructions that he is to use you as a forward column, maintaining contact with the Frenchman but not engaging him. Can you remember that, or shall I have Wyndham scribble out an order for you?"

"I can remember that well enough," Crauford said, "but I doubt it will be a source of great pleasure to General Lake. He has a great fondness for using his own troops."

"I did not haul my poor afflicted leg onto this bog in

order to give pleasure to General Lake. I came here to bag the Frenchman, and I will do it in my own way. You have no objections, I take it?"

"None, sir," Crauford said. "None whatever. But a bit of clarification might not go amiss. I will be operating forward of General Lake but under his command. Will I move at my own discretion? Sending a trooper back to Lake every hour or two might be a damned nuisance."

"I am certain that General Lake shares my own confidence in your discretion and your ability, Colonel Crauford. I anticipate no problems of that sort, and neither should you. Problems of that sort are tiresome. You had best get started, and we shall see if your lads are as active as you claim."

Crauford grinned again, and then saluted Cornwallis. Within the hour, his dragoons had left the field, and were riding eastward, toward Lake's columns, where they were to earn for their colonel a reputation for enterprise and vigor, although not, alas, for humanity or clemency.

It is to the sheer physical insignificance of Castlebar that I attribute my difficulty in remembering in any detail our entrance into the town. I do remember that we were compelled to ride past bodies which had been pushed aside in haste: Crauford's cavalry, in breaking free of the bridge, had found it necessary to cut down the defenders almost to a man. The "capital" of the republic was a sorry spectacle indeed, and for some a dangerous one, for a few of the rebels, casting aside their pikes and badges of office, sought to mingle with the townspeople, but they were hunted out most diligently by our lads. More sabers than one were bloodied in the streets of Castlebar before order was imposed. I have found, throughout all my years of campaigning, that the very butt end of an action is the bitterest. That tigerlike rage which courses through the blood of a common soldier when he is in the thick of the melee must somehow spend itself, and at times he is guilty of deeds for which later he is most heartily ashamed. Our lads were in particular enraged by the strips of green bunting with which many of the lintels were draped and by the so-called "trees of liberty." Shops or dwellings which flaunted these were made to feel their impropriety.

These final sputterings of violence died at once when Cornwallis entered the town, as dust-whirls vanish when the wind falls. There was neither dust nor wind that

morning, however, but only a steady, dispiriting rain.
When at this moment I think of Ireland, it is not the
splendid weather which I recall but the rain of Castlebar.
Few natural scenes are more desolating than those offered
by the rain-shrouded west, and the towns are grimmer
yet. Those visitors to Ireland who have been enraptured
by a summer week in Killarney, following the course of
those soft, feminine lakes and hills, lulled by the blarney-
ing voices of boatmen and guides, know nothing of this
other Ireland, dank, cold, and secretive, in which crime
and worse than crime fester beneath the sodden thatch.
Ireland loses all definition beneath the rains of autumn
—towns, hamlets, bogs, muddy road all blur together,
and memory recalls but a vast gray porridge.

On that September morning, we were at the season's
turn, in a rainy town which the enemy had abandoned to
us, and many more experienced than myself shared my
mood, a gray, damp mood, rather like the appearance of
the town. Neither the loyalists nor those rebels whom we
questioned could tell us with certainty of the direction
which the rebels had taken, whether toward Foxford or
toward Swinford. There was great need now for haste, if
Humbert was to be sealed between our army and Lake's,
for Humbert, as Cornwallis acknowledged with ungrudg-
ing admiration, was capable of moving with a rapidity
which was the more astonishing when the composition of
his force was taken into consideration. It was not until
the afternoon that Crauford returned with word that
Humbert had taken the Swinford road. And, as we were
later to learn, he had sent instructions to the rebel garrisons in Ballina and other towns, ordering them to move
eastward, over the Ox Mountains, where with luck they
might join him.

I have said that few prisoners were taken, but one of
these must be considered a prize "catch," being no less a
personage than the "President" of the "Republic of Connaught." This civic dignitary, but a few years older than I
was myself, was brought to bay outside the courthouse,
and most certainly would have been cut down had not
notice been taken of his clothing and his genteel appearance. Cornwallis, who spoke briefly with him, was con-
siderateness itself, and yet I doubt whether the poor
wretch was aware of this, for his mood seemed to move
from resignation to despair and then back to resignation.
He had been ill used by the dragoons. His left arm was

shattered above the elbow, and a heavy, swollen bruise disfigured one side of his face. Yet he retained the marks and accent of gentility, speaking in low and cultivated tones. Nor did we find this surprising, when his identity was disclosed to us as that of John Moore, younger brother of George Moore of Moore Hall, who had lived in London on terms of friendship with Burke, Fox, and others of the Whig party.

It had been intended that he should accompany the rebels on their march, but some impulse, not entirely dishonorable, had prompted him to remain in the town with the forlorn rear guard. Now, faithful to companions who had abandoned him to his fate, he professed ignorance as to their movements or plans. Cornwallis pressed him to discuss the character of Humbert, but his responses were guarded and laconic. Castlebar boasted a gaol, a gaunt, somber building, and into this he was placed, together with other miscreants. I can recall him now in his cell, his face the white of chalk where it was not livid with bruise, his eyes expressionless and staring straight into mine. I fancied that I looked into the face of a Perkin or a Simnel, a youth taken up by cynical conspirators and given a brief, derisory authority. But the face belied my fancy, so like was it to my own. What folly or what vanity had led him into the company of his King's enemy, forsaking his country and his loyalty? But then, he was Irish. I do not recall whether or not he suffered the fate which he had earned, but which I, for one, would have spared him.

By five that afternoon we were again upon the move: it was to be the first of our night marches. We were launched now upon a long campaign, which was to take us better than a hundred miles, when its twists and winding returns are taken into account.

I have seen it asserted that our progress could be followed, weeks later, by the hanged men and burned cabins along our line of march. The facts themselves give the lie to this: we were pressing forward as rapidly as possible against an enemy who, save for his stragglers and deserters, remained tantalizingly out of sight. And, again, there were frequent rains; a bundle of straw would not have caught fire, much less a cabin roof. I will not gloss over that regrettable, even terrible events took place during the week that was to come. Crauford in particular was a stern soldier, as Highlanders often are, and Lake had carried with him from Wexford a reputation for brutality. What I do say is that such events took place beyond the eyes of Lord Cornwallis, my beloved old commander, in whom wisdom and mercy were blended in equal parts. True it is that when word came to us that the long-dreaded second rising had broken out in the midlands, even Cornwallis accepted the painful necessity of driving home to the natives the folly and the wickedness of rebellion. He did so, however, with the utmost reluctance, and the rules of honorable warfare, *with respect to our French enemies*, were never breached. Rebellion against lawful authority is in all societies regarded as the most heinous offense.

13

From the Diary of Sean MacKenna

September, 1798. One of the armies left Castlebar by night, and the next morning the other one entered. I stood by the window in the front room over the shop and watched the English ride in, large reckless men they were on their heavy horses. They rode down the street at the full gallop, with their long sabers held level with their heads ready to swing downward. And on our street there was still enough to claim their blades. Most of the killing had been done at the bridge and in the streets leading to the green. But I saw them smashing down doors and dragging men out, and why they did not smash down this door I cannot imagine, nor why I was not hauled away to be thrashed or made a show of, as others were, though guiltless of wrongdoing.

It was but a fulfillment of what I had known would happen as I watched the Frenchmen and our own fellows move out the night before. The poor fellows had a stricken look, many of them, and who is to blame them, carried off at night, with rain beginning to fall, and no word given as to their destination. There are some of those fellows who don't know that the world is round, and for all they knew, they were being marched off to the edge of it. The degree of ignorance in which the men of Nephin live their sunless lives is not to be believed.

And yet they were off for a morning saunter when measured against the distance which the Frenchmen had traveled. We never knew them, for none could speak English. When I saw them mustered and ready to march out of Castlebar, they might have been creatures carried here from the moon. They had not our look at all, with their sallow faces and dark, liquid eyes. But they joked together, as our fellows did, and scuffled, and they had the same look of fear behind the joking. No doubt they too had come from farms, and once were more at home with spades than with bayonets. What France is like I cannot imagine, although I have read a few of the French tales and romances that have been put into English. But it cannot be like Ireland. All of the countries of the world are different from each other. It would be interesting to know what they think of Ireland. They can have formed no high opinion of it, poor creatures—dragged from bog to bog to gray wet town, with the country people staring at them as though they were freaks on exhibition.

But they are soldiers now, whatever they were once. They have been trained to bellow and gore like bulls, and to walk docile as cows to their own slaughter. A most curious way to live, and it is frightening to reflect how easily men can be schooled to accept it. But the songs all have it that such a life is easy and free. Foolish indeed are those who believe the words of poetry and song, as was proclaimed long before me by the lofty-minded sages of Greece. And what of our own poor fellows, lined up behind the Frenchmen, but with a few files of Frenchmen placed behind them, to prod at them with bayonets should they think of slipping off? And all this in the name of liberty and equality and this nonsense of *the rights of man,* which I must put down in English because there is no Irish for it. You could tramp the slopes of Nephin for months and before you encountered *the rights of man* you would encounter a unicorn. Of what use to them are the ideas of that misfortunate John Moore, a well-intentioned creature but fanciful and moonstruck?

My neighbor Jeremiah Dunphy saw Mr. Moore run to earth outside the courthouse, three troopers crowded around him, their pointed blades pressed against his chest. But there was something worse than fear in his eyes, Jeremiah says: they were lifeless and despairing. And indeed he is as good as lifeless, unless good birth be a sufficient safe-conduct through all the vicissitudes of existence. He cannot be altogether right in his head, but he always seemed healthy enough to me, the times I have seen him in happier months, handsomely dressed and always laughing, a most comely youth.

I can understand the deviltry that dances in men like Randall MacDonnell and Corny O'Dowd, who are the giddy scapegraces of which this country has always had an abundant supply, and I can well see them in earlier days as bold rapparees or as men riding with Sarsfield to Ballyneety. It is that sort which stakes a horse or an estate or perhaps even a woman on the turn of a card, and is forever out upon what they call their field of honor, blazing away at each other with pistols. Small loss to the world is my uncharitable opinion. The brains of children they have, rattling around in their huge skulls. And what care they how many they drag off with them to sink within the bog's brown water? There they were the other night, prancing about on their horses—chargers, perhaps I should call them—some in fine uniforms the French had brought and some in fine suits made in Galway, with silly plumes bedraggled and limp, like a man's member who has spent the night with a randy slut.

One of the last things done before they all set off was the taking down from the courthouse of the flag of green silk with the gilt harp on it. And nothing would do but that it must be carried off by one of the Wexford men who had been in all the fighting and misfortune there. It is by such seductive colors and banners that men's eyes are bedazzled and they are led off the paths of good sense and into the black bog. But are not the others worse still, with their uniforms the color of bloody death itself?

They left in silence, but an army makes a fearful noise even when it moves in silence—the sound of feet upon the road, the creaking of harness leather, the rumbling of cartwheels. I looked through the darkness for Owen, but I could not make out faces, and there were many of the fellows had his shape, clumsy, heavy-shouldered cowherds, tall and ungainly. I ask again what business my Owen has with such men?

After they had gone, I stood by the window, as I am

324

certain many others did in that street, for we were all thinking, When will the English come and what will they do? There remained but the few Frenchmen and rebels who had been left to hold the bridge for a bit, and to prevent the loyalists from leaving the town to warn the English. They patrolled until it was light. Two of them I saw across the road from my shop in the flat, damp dawn, country lads with faces like platters. One had a firelock and the other a pike, and they were standing against the poor shelter of a gable end. After a bit they left, and walked down the road. More likely than not, their bodies lay later in the morning on the footpath near the bridge.

Some there are who may take civic pride in our having housed two armies within a fortnight, not to mention our brief eminence as the capital of no less a thing than a republic. Castlebar cannot change. Low houses, mean people, as the jingle has it. We will again be drowned in our obscurity, and the windy rains will sweep away all traces of their presence—the discoloring in Castlebar High Street where the brave English gunner held his ground, the rivulets of blood on the near side of the small hump-backed bridge. And I will remember best a sight which I did not see save in the imagination—John Moore backed against the wall by the menacing riders, his eyes able to see at last beyond hope or desperation.

Later. A plowboy, who knows of my interest in such matters, tells me that some days ago he heard the clack of woodcocks in the woods beyond Sion Hill. That would have been soon after the great battle there. One would have thought that the sound of the cannon had driven away birds forever. What can they make of me, fellows like that plowboy—a man who studies the habits of birds and notes them down in a book? But it is a pleasant and an instructive pastime for me, and also, I am pleased to say, for young Timothy. Now that the two boastful armies have moved away we may perhaps be able to resume our Sunday walks.

Bellaghy, September 4

The Ox Mountains. The rain had ended hours before, and a pale moon hung from the black, endless sky. Mac-

Carthy knew the road. He had taken it with Elliott. Now circumstance had changed it beyond recognition. It was not a road now, but part of the boundaryless country through which an army moved, darkened by ignorance. They were camped upon a slope, and the mountains towered beyond them. A cluster of cabins had given a name to the slope. Bellaghy.

MacCarthy, squatting on his heels above the wet grasses, looked first at the dim mountains and then at the deserted cabins below. Three of the Ballycastle men, Lawrence's tenants, crouched near him.

"It is to wild Ulster that they are taking us," one of them said, a man named Lavelle. "And well you know it."

"To Sligo," MacCarthy said. "The road runs through Tobercurry and Collooney into the town of Sligo."

"And from Sligo northward into Ulster. More men than yourself have walked that road. If it was to the midlands they were taking us, we would not have passed Swinford."

"It is a terrible thing," Lavelle's friend Staunton said, an older man, with a small, toothless head round as an apple. "To carry us far off in the black night, with no word of our destination."

"It is no business of commanders to be telling their minds to the likes of you," MacCarthy said. And never had been. Kernes and gallowglasses, trailing their pikes down bog roads, stumbling into bloody death upon un-recognized meadows. "If you had stayed in Castlebar, you would be dead now. They got us safe out of that."

MacEvilly, the third man, said, "So that we could be killed somewhere else."

"You know no more than we do," Lavelle said, peering up at MacCarthy. "We are only a pack of poor fellows following like hounds after Frenchmen who are ignorant of any civilized language, whether Irish or English."

"And how many words of English have you?" MacCarthy said. "You have not even the English for *loy* or *spade*, which are the only words needed in your station in life."

"The word *pike* is needed in my station in life," Lavelle said, and spat between his feet. "And my two hands are needed to carry it."

"What you could do, Pat, is to get away out of all this, yourself and your two friends. Let you climb down the slope and head back toward Swinford, and into the hands of the redcoat soldiers. Let you discuss the civilized English language with them before they string you up."

"Ach, sure, Owen. What talk have we had of running away? We are better off where we are."

"You are so," MacCarthy said, walking away from them.

It was a most extraordinary sight, what there was of it beneath the pale, clouded moon. A small army stretched along either side of the narrow, twisting road, voices low and exhausted. Those were fools surely who were sitting or lying on the wet earth. It might be the death of them. He walked down the road to the village, where men had crowded into the abandoned cabins. He heard from one, suddenly, a woman's high-pitched scream, and stepped to the door. There were a half-dozen men inside, and, half lying on the floor, her back pressed against the wall, a very old woman, black-dressed, her white hair scanty and thin. One of the men, bulky and near middle age, was holding her hand in his. The turf fire cast a russet glow.

"She is terrified, poor creature," the man said. "When the people ran off they left her here. What a dreadful thing to do!"

MacCarthy knelt down beside him. The woman stared, mad, fierce eyes. A web of saliva hung from her loose mouth.

"God help her," the man said. "She doesn't know who we are or why we are here. Suddenly all the neighbors were gone and the village was filled with more people than she had ever seen together in her life."

MacCarthy took her other hand. A bird's claw. Flesh-less, yellow. "You are safe, mother. The lot of us will be gone soon, and your people will be back."

She did not turn her head toward him. Small, shapeless sack of cloth, with scarecrow head above it. When she was young, Aughrim and the Boyne were recent history. All through the dark century, she grew, weathered, shrank. Our history is here, an old woman huddled with fear in a cabin beneath mountains.

"Let her be," he said, rising and putting his hand on the man's shoulder. "She doesn't see us."

"She is not blind. She moves her eyes."

"She does not see us." But the man did not move. He rubbed the bird's claw between his heavy hands. Mac-

Carthy backed out of the cabin, bending his head beneath the low, rough doorway.

Ireland's image in the dark poetry of penal days. A crone, withered, she revealed beauty, youth, to the poet's attentive eye. Silk of the kine. *Roisin dubh.* Had any of them ever looked at an old woman, skeleton-thin, milk of sickness a film across the eye? History, unbidden, unrecognized, had entered her cabin. Kinsmen vanished. In terror, she retreated to foolishness. Spit dribbled from her slack lips. A symbol shattered on her brittle bones. Moons are far safer for poets. Remote, austere, they sustain our words, protect our images. High above now, dim and cloud-obscured. Mountains stretched away beneath it.

"There is little enough that we can do for her," someone said.

"Nothing," MacCarthy said. "Nothing at all."

At one A.M. that morning, Michael Geraghty brought in the men from the lands between Ballina and KiHala, after a march of twenty-five miles over the Ox Mountains. Humbert and Teeling had given up on them. The sentries saw them first, a moving forest on the crest of a hill, and ran shouting to the camped men, who roused themselves up and stared in wonder. A forest in winter, thin leafless branches wind-ripped, their pikes against the moonlit line of sky and hill. In silence they moved down the steep path until they reached the encampment.

Humbert, unbuttoned, bleary-eyed from an hour's sleep, came from a cabin to welcome them. Sarrizen and Teeling, standing behind him, at a distance, made a quick count. Three or four hundred men, most of them armed with pikes, a few with muskets. Some of them seemed unarmed, standing confused and useless. Geraghty bobbed his head, embarrassed and uncomprehending, before Humbert's rapid French.

Later he talked with MacCarthy. "It was an endless fucking journey, as though we were all headed for some hiring fair in China, first the rain and then a night as dirty as the back of your arse. And terrified every minute of the time that we couldn't find you, or that you would be long gone, or eaten up by the English. But we dropped down the last slope and there you were, as the man said in the note that you would be."

"Who said?"

"Teeling is his name, is it not? The Irishman in the French uniform. He said that we would find you where the path drops to meet the Sligo road, near a village. He said that that was the order of the French general. And here you are, by God. By Christ, he must be a wonderful man, the French general."

"He must indeed," MacCarthy said. "'Tis a village called Bellaghy. The people are all gone out from it. I marvel you did not find them in the mountains."

"There is nothing alive in those Ox Mountains but wild goats and owls. They are a sad excuse for land. Nothing to be seen to the left or right or up and down but the brown, dreary hills stretching away and lonely mountain lakes. I wonder that there was even the path, unless the goats beat it down. No one has ever gone that way before."

"Long ages ago," MacCarthy said. Diarmuid and Grania with Finn following after. Hugh O'Donnell from Ulster, the great prince. No path or rock or tree that lacks its legend. "We are going into O'Donnell's country, 'tis said. Into Donegal."

"God help us," Geraghty said. "The poor Donegals. Why would the French general take us into such a savage place?"

"I don't know," MacCarthy said. "But that is what is said by O'Dowd and Randall MacDonnell and some of them."

"Do they say where the English soldiers are?"

MacCarthy shook his head. "I declare to Jesus, Michael, they might be all around us. There were a hundred men we left behind us in Castlebar, and they must all of them be dead this minute by the sword or the rope or the cruel lance."

"Did you know any of them yourself, Owen?"

"I don't even know who they were. It was only an hour or so before we left that they were told to stay, and so they did. Some Frenchmen stayed with them, to work the guns. And John Moore stayed."

"May the Lord spare him," Geraghty said, making the sign of the cross.

"The Lord may," MacCarthy said, "but Cornwallis will have other ideas."

"I was talking with him in Ballina, and the two of us having a drink in Brennan's, down near the river."

"I know Brennan's," MacCarthy said. "Mr. Moore is less comfortable tonight, and so are you."

"There was a look of death in his eyes that day."

329

"Ach," MacCarthy said. "There is never a man gets into bad trouble but that someone will rise up to say that there was the look of death in his eyes."

"They were empty eyes," Geraghty said. "As empty as the sea at Downpatrick Head."

A good phrase. "We may all be in bad trouble before this is over."

"By God, we may, so. 'Twas but a short while ago that we had no thought but of the harvest and the fine weather, and see where we are now and what has been happening."

"You were a United Man yourself, were you not?" MacCarthy asked.

"I was. I took the oath from Elliott and Randall MacDonnell. But sure, what am I at all but a farmer who was a great one eight or ten years ago at the faction fighting and the hurling, before I began to lug this around with me." He slapped his heavy, sagging belly.

MacCarthy shook his head. "It is a strange business, farmers and plowboys tramping about like rapparees. I was talking about it tonight with some of the Ballycastle men."

"Ballycastle men!" Geraghty broke into unexpected laughter, and put his hand on MacCarthy's shoulder. "Sure, those poor devils would do anything to get out of Ballycastle, and who could blame them?"

" 'Tis a sorry, Godforsaken bit of land, right enough," MacCarthy said.

He left Geraghty and walked past seven or eight French soldiers huddled in a loose circle, their uniforms invisible in the night, and barely visible their dark, foreign faces. When they saw him staring at them, they fell silent, and looked up at him, impassive and uninterested. A horse whinnied. Beyond the village there was only the blackness of the night, cloud-shrouded moon. He shivered and went in search of O'Dowd, who carried a bottle in either pocket.

O'Dowd and Randall MacDonnell were together, against a cabin wall. One of the bottles was empty, but O'Dowd opened the other one and passed it to him. Officer and gentleman. Gentleman's whiskey, it poured smoothly down his throat. Small, golden explosions of warmth, promise of sun. He wiped his palm across the mouth of the bottle and held it toward O'Dowd, who shook his head.

"Keep it for a bit. 'Tis running out of me. Teeling says that we will be leaving this miserable place now."

"To the north?" MacCarthy asked.

"In Sligo town, where I was born," O'Dowd sang.

"One of the French patrols up ahead caught three British soldiers and killed them," MacDonnell said. "There are British behind us, and British ahead of us in Sligo."

"Jesus," MacCarthy said, and took another long swallow. He had not been drunk in days, and it would be pleasant now. Let the army march off and leave him to crawl into one of the cabins with his bottle. Settle down in the deserted village of Bellaghy as its sole proprietor. Sweet Bellaghy, loveliest village of the plain. Greet the farmer when he slipped down from the mountain and offer him a drink. It was a miracle, the way whiskey could give you fresh ambition.

Humbert emerged from one of the cabins, rubbing his hands briskly, then passing one of them across his eyes, like a man roused from sleep. Cool, strange Frenchman, his head packed tight as an egg with plans. He shouted out orders to Sarrizen and Fontaine, called Teeling to him. We follow. Hounds behind his horse.

From the *Memoir of Events*, Written by Malcolm Elliott in October, 1798

I am assured by British officers who have spoken to me in this place of imprisonment that the celebrated battle of Castlebar was a less impressive military accomplishment than the skill with which Humbert slipped us past the armies which were gathering against us. That may well be so, but I lack the experience and the skill needed to judge such matters. For me, and for most of those on the forced march of one hundred and thirty miles from Castlebar to Ballinamuck, the enterprise scarce merited a name, so incoherent and bewildering did it appear to us. Now, studying a map, I can perceive that our march did indeed cut a wide, bold arc across the face of Ireland, and can readily accept that to have carried us from the first of its tips to the second was a demonstration of shrewd generalship, for all that it appeared to us but senseless blundering in the dark.

We were oppressed and frightened by the knowledge

that Crown forces pressed us from the rear and were awaiting us beyond the mountains. Indeed, at two o'clock of the first morning, as we were at rest in a straggling village, a British scouting party encountered our pickets, and had they been allowed to report back to Sligo, matters might have ended then and there. The members of the party it was of course necessary to kill upon the spot, for our circumstances did not permit us to take prisoners. And they did inform us that they were indeed soldiers in General Taylor's army but that he had sent forward their Coolavin Yeomanry to the town of Tobercurry, at no great distance from us. They were Irishmen, and although it was Frenchmen who put them to the sword, the responsibility must be shared by all of us.

The close presence of this British force occasioned the first of a number of increasingly bitter arguments among our officers, the true grounds of which held me for a time deceived. Colonel Teeling argued vehemently that the British, by reason of their numbers, should on no account be engaged, but rather that we should continue to evade them, if possible, and move either toward Ulster, whither we were now headed, or else the midlands. But Sarrizen and Fontaine pressed Humbert to make an immediate attack upon the British in Tobercurry, in the hope that those elements of Taylor's army might be caught unprepared. In this manner, so they asserted, we might win a rout second only to that at Castlebar.

We were assembled in one of the cabins, a badly thatched and pestiferous hovel with an inadequate fireplace, so that the smoke from the turf fire stung our eyes.

Humbert heard us all out patiently, almost with indifference, nodding his approval of Sarrizen's impetuous eloquence, and grinning with ill-bred delight at Teeling's fluent but heavily accented French. But so far as I could judge, which was no great distance, this was not an issue which admitted of two solutions. We were, on paper as it were, a victorious army, the conquerors of Ballina and Castlebar, but in fact an ill-armed and motley force, on the run, with superior strength massing itself against us. Our one hope, so it seemed to a novice like myself, lay in moving toward safe ground, if not toward new allies. And this was the very case which Teeling argued, not with eloquence, but with a hard, flinty logic. Indeed he pressed also the case that we should march not toward his own Ulster, but rather toward the midlands, and with all haste and by whatever roads lay open, trusting that the rumors of an impending uprising there were well founded. But he was no oratorical match for the two Frenchmen, with their torrents of words that fell as thick as rain, and those accursed words *la gloire* and *la victoire* pattering like rhyming hailstones. And all this time, Humbert turned his head first to one man and then to the next, like a spectator in a playhouse following the speeches of the actors in a performance of Racine.

At last he waved his heavy, fish-white hand to silence all three of them. "I have no intention of ending this campaign in the shadow of savage mountains. What exactly we shall do I will allow circumstances to explain to us. But there will be no battle fought here if I can avoid one. Teeling's view of the situation is most obviously the correct one, and I am astonished at you, Sarrizen, astonished at your frivolous arguments. And at you, Fontaine. Like a pair of schoolboys."

To this Sarrizen said nothing, but rather turned off his eloquence as abruptly as though he had twisted a spigot in his tongue. He contented himself with folding his arms and contriving to look at once condescending and respectful, an attitude which I have found the French to be peculiarly skillful at expressing. Thus ended my first military conference, in what I supposed was a victory of the cause which I favored. Later, however, when Teeling and I were walking up and down the road to stretch our legs, I found him far from jubilant.

"Why do you think that Sarrizen is so anxious to engage the British?" he burst out passionately. "Because he loves battle? Not at all. It is because he is convinced, he and Fontaine, that it is hopeless. They want to see it all ended and make their surrender after a little flurry of arms for the sake of their reputations. Humbert is the only one of them who thinks that we have a chance." His tone, flat and sardonic, as northern speech often seems, was withering.

"And yourself?" I asked.

He hesitated, and seemed to be looking through the darkness toward the men. "We have done well enough so far," he said. "If we are reinforced in time. Or if the midlands rise. And if we can fight our way through to them."

"That is what Humbert believes?"

He shrugged. "Do you think I know what he intends

any more than Sarrizen does? Perhaps he is telling us the truth, perhaps he is trusting to luck and opportunity. That would be unfortunate. I have a suspicion that this is not a lucky campaign." He could be brisk one minute, and the next set into a cold-clay melancholy.

To lighten the mood, I said, "You have done a prodigious job of acquiring the style of these Frenchies. Did it take you long?"

"About two years," he said, taking the question seriously. "In taverns in Paris and encampments on the Rhine. Two wretched years. Humbert is a law of his own, though. He is playing his own game, and we are the pieces on his board. It seems to be our national fate." He gave me a nod then, and walked away.

It is most curious and disturbing to be moving with an army across one's own countryside. Familiar names, Killala, Ballina, Castlebar, become targets to be shot at, walls to be knocked down. I found myself envying the French, for whom the names of our towns and mountains were barbarous, places to be taken to, to fight for, to stand guard over.

The morning came clear and pale, the sky a most wonderful soft, light blue, across which stretched broken clouds, and the mountains, which had seemed so formidable behind rain or under darkness, now stretched away in their comfortable greens and browns, with dark patches of purple heather. It proved difficult to assemble the men in marching formation, for a number of bottles of whiskey had been carried out of Castlebar, and they had comforted themselves with these in the cold night. It was my task to assist Fontaine with the artillery pieces, and it was necessary to bully some of the men to their task. Add to this that they were wretchedly hungry, for they had few ready provisions save the potatoes which they had stuffed into their pockets before setting out. Whiskey and potatoes, the staples of Irish diet as depicted in hostile caricature.

Humbert seemed everywhere at once. His anger when he heard of the drinking was inordinate, and he sent his sergeants on a sweep through the camp, seizing bottles and destroying them. Two men who were too far gone in drink to march were spread-eagled and whipped. I had never before seen men lashed, and it is a most dreadful spectacle, great gouts of blood leaping from their backs as though driven forth. They were then tied, bellies down, to one of the artillery horses and were taken off with us, and although their groans were most dreadful to hear, they had reason to be grateful, for had they been left behind to the mercy of Crauford's dragoons, they would not have lasted out the day. Neither Crauford nor Lake was to show the least mercy toward any stragglers who fell into their hands, and I have heard it said that their line of march could be followed, a week later, by bodies hanging from trees or gables, which the villagers, whatever their sympathies, were too terrified to cut down. And yet we ourselves, as I have said, took no prisoners. I have become heartily cynical as to such phrases as *honorable warfare* and *the rules of war*. It is an ugly, cruel business.

When we set off, however, we made a brave enough show, and I was once again moved to admiration of the French troops, in their compact lines of dark blue, moving across the face of Sligo like a sloop cutting its path across strange waters. They were less strange to me than my own countrymen, from whom I was also cut off by faith, language, traditions. Ulster or the midlands— whichever road we took, our destination was as remote to them as Tartary. Their lives had been lived in their own baronies, beneath familiar skies. An oath, administered at night in some dilapidated barn and dimly understood, had brought them here, upon this road. That they remained sufficiently in command of themselves I attribute to the spirit of their captains, and also, I am bound to admit, to the exhortations of Murphy, the Killala curate, a bloodthirsty bigot and yet most skillful as a stoker of martial fires. Owen MacCarthy, their bard and poet, was worse than useless in that task, for of those who had recourse to whiskey courage, he was among the most assiduous, and I suspect that he escaped a lashing only because Humbert did not notice him. The peasants, of course, saw nothing wrong or harmful in his drunken condition: as a poet he was both above and below their respect. Faction fighter, jackpriest, poet and drunkard— such were their true leaders, for all that the rest of us bawled commands at them.

At ten that morning we met and defeated a body of English troops, in what newspapers, I discover with amusement, have termed the battle of Tobercurry. It was in truth little more than a skirmish. General Taylor had sent forward from Sligo town to Tobercurry the Coolavin and the Leyney cavalries, under the command of a Major Knott. These seized the town and sallied forth, to encounter Randall MacDonnell and his horsemen. There was a brisk engagement, in which MacDonnell got the better of the day, and Knott and his men were sent clattering back to Sligo, leaving a handful of their dead upon the road. And yet in Tobercurry, as we discovered to our indignation, they had taken advantage of their few hours' occupation to hang eleven of the townspeople, on the false grounds of their sympathy with the rebel cause. But in truth it was done to terrify all who might be tempted to join us or give us aid.

Their bodies we cut down, and they were laid side by side. Murphy offered prayers for the repose of their souls, and Humbert stood hat in hand before them. By this time we had all of us seen men slain in battle, and a few hours earlier had been witness to bloody floggings, but this somber spectacle was more dreadful, the fruits of a random and needless butchery. My mouth filled with the bitter taste of copper. The women of the village, their bare feet in the mud, pressed themselves against the dead, and gave voice to the fearful screams with which the dead are mourned in Ireland. Murphy began one of his atrocious harangues, holding aloft the heavy wooden crucifix which he carried with him, carved from bog oak by the piety of some peasant craftsman. His words poured out in a torrent of rude eloquence, and his listeners turned their faces toward him as though transfixed. Little knowledge of Irish was needed to follow his discourse. He saw our army, that improbable combination of bog-trotters and French conscripts, as God's hammer, forged to batter down foreigners and heretics. It was to my eyes and ears a sacrilegious scene, this coarse-voiced hedge priest bellowing forth his imprecations and exhortations, with the stiffening bodies stretched before him as text, and the voices of the women providing him with a savage choir. Men leaning upon their pikes attended to his words as they might to a preacher enlarging upon a passage from Scripture, and indeed he put me in mind of a barefoot Israelite prophet breathing destruction upon his enemies. Between myself and Murphy's makeshift congregation lay a gulf wide as the ocean.

Tobercurry is a drab village, cabins and a few hucksters' shops facing each other, a small, tidy Protestant church at one end of the street (*Protestant . . . Protes-*

tant . . . The word echoed through Murphy's harangue, drawing to itself all of his venom) and at the other the gates of a derelict estate. There must be a hundred such villages in Ireland, and what have we ever known of their people? I had a fair knowledge of my own tenants and of the country people of Ballina. But Wolfe Tone, a Dublin barrister, knew nothing of such folk, nor Thomas Emmet, a university orator. How could we have supposed a connection to exist between our ideas, city bred, and the passions of peasants? Theorems advanced in a Rathfarnham villa, beneath the cool, benign skies of a Dublin evening, are transformed by the airs of Connaught, country people hanged by indifferent dragoons, pikes piercing the horizon, an Irish-speaking priest bawling out his bloody sermons. I have sought to make this a narrative of events only setting aside reflections upon my own motives and state of mind. But I must add, for it has a bearing upon my understanding of these events, that here, in Tobercurry, I experienced a separation of being, a division between the man who acted and the man who observed. The church, its four spikes bright and sharp against the sky, the demesne gate hanging loose from its upper hinge, a cabin the color of clotted cream, the dark green of a shop door, the pocked and rutted roadway, possessed for me at that moment a reality more vivid and more strenuous than the bedlam of surrounding voices. In a half hour's time, at most, we would again be on the march, peasants inflamed by Murphy's oratory and Frenchmen who had learned to take without question whatever order was given them. Somewhere, hidden by but a single range of blue, hazy hills, lay an army waiting for us to tire—colonels and equerries and secretaries. Beyond them in time lay, most probably, prison cells, courts-martial, gallows. And there I stood, dressed as for a morning's business.

As my mind filled with this somber and troubling thought, which had somehow associated itself to the clarity with which I perceived the buildings about us, Humbert replaced his hat upon his head, and gave orders to his officers.

Tobercurry, September 4

The gates which Elliott took to be those of a derelict estate were the gates of Castle Harmony, lands which for the last fifteen years had lain beneath a winter's snow of mortgages and legal papers. The main house, a simple commodious building, had been erected by Josiah Manning, a Cromwellian settler, beside a Norman keep which now served as a byre. Richard Manning, the present proprietor, had that morning climbed the winding stair of the keep to its battlements, where he now stood with Ellen Kirwan, the countrywoman who cooked his meals and shared his bed.

He had carried with him a brass spyglass which gave him a clear view of the road which ran from Tobercurry to Sligo, and brought to him, as a clump of dense gray, the village of Tobercurry itself. He had watched Knott move forward his cavalry along that road, and, hours later, had watched their retreat.

"You had best come down and take something to eat," Ellen said.

He shook his head. "Bring up bread and meat to me here, Ellen, and a bowl of milk."

"Sure there is nothing for you to see but an old road that you know as well as you do the back of your hand."

"If you think that, you are as ignorant as you were the day God made you. There were British cavalry on that road this morning, and they went back to Sligo in great haste. If the rebels are anywhere at all in Ireland, they are in Tobercurry." He rubbed his unshaven chin. "God's curse upon them."

"God shield us from harm."

"He can if He wishes to, but I have never found Him very obliging." He held the spyglass toward the village and then lowered it again. "Of all the hundreds of roads in Ireland, they had to choose the one that runs past Dick Manning's lands."

"I will go down and get you your food. But I think you have little sense to be standing here all day. What good does it do?"

"How could I not, woman?" He beat his fist against the battlement. "If one side of them doesn't want our cows, the other will. They could end by fighting their damned battle on this farm and trampling flat the harvest. When your battles are written down in histories, devil the thought is paid to the poor bastard who provided a field for the occasion."

"Sure they will all be gone from here by evening, most likely."

338

"Is that your considered opinion, Miss Kirwan? Pray God it proves true."

"I wonder you are not out swaggering around with the yeoman cavalry, like the other gentry."

"I have all the battle I need keeping this estate out of the hands of the Dublin bankers, and keeping myself safe from your own saucy tongue. Much help was I ever given by the gentry of this country. The rebels can have it or the soldiers can have it, for all I care, provided they offer me a fair price."

"The rebels would pay naught," Ellen said. "Wild murdering creatures from Mayo. 'Tis a shambles they will make of the poor village below."

Manning grunted. "Tobercurry, the Paris of the West. Mind you, my father had great hopes for it in his day. Nothing gave him greater pleasure than to go bowling along in his carriage, with myself a little fellow beside him, past the shops and past the church and in through the gates. He was a man of great hopes and plans, my father."

"Usen't I to see him myself?" Ellen asked. "I remember him atop that chestnut mare of his, with his topboots as shiny as the mare's flank. He had the look of a lord to him, but a smile and a friendly word to every man or maid he met. Little thought had I then—" She broke off.

"That you would be sharing a bed with the master's son. No more had I, Ellen. No more had I. But here we are, the two of us, and we rattle along together well enough, the two of us."

"Dick, if there is a real danger to us from the rebels, should you not be mustering the tenants?"

"Mustering the tenants, is it? And how the hell would I do that? To my knowledge there are no arms on this estate but some old fowling pieces, and two cases of pistols below in the hall. Let them all travel away out of Tobercurry, is all I ask. And I hope that there is no man on these lands fool enough to join with them."

"Last month there was great talk in the taverns about the rising, Pat Dogherty says."

"That is the time for such talk. Before it happens, when you have a bottle before you and four or five great dollops of whiskey inside your skin. It is sick with debt that we all are upon this estate, myself and every tenant. We will not be cured by rebels or British soldiers or

339

yeoman cavalry." He stood looking beyond the plantation of larches, across the meadow toward the road. She stood beside him, not moving from the battlement wall.

"You are wondering, are you not, what would my father have done? I can tell you. He would be with the Coolavin Cavalry, and at the head of it most likely, on his mare, in a uniform of brilliant red, looking every inch the lord, with his loyal tenantry in shouting distance. Then let me tell you, Ellen, that I have not the few pounds it would take for that uniform, much less equip the tenants. Who was it, do you think, trussed us up with debts and mortgages? It is easy to live like a lord if you have an estate, and a son to stagger along under the burden of debts you have put upon him. When I sat beside him in the carriage, proud as a colt, it is little thought I had of his plans for me."

"Ach, sure, Dick, he must have meant everything for the best. You wanted for nothing."

"Indeed I did not. A gentleman scholar at Trinity, with a quarter's allowance you could choke a horse with, and a card to Daly's." He laughed suddenly, a yelp of mirth. "By God, Ellen, do you know that I was a classmate of Wolfe Tone's? I had forgotten that."

"Who is he?"

"Who is he? Well may you ask. He is your savior, and Ireland's as well. It is Wolfe Tone who has sent an army of Frenchmen and a mob of Mayo peasants into Sligo. Little thought I had for him then, myself a landlord's son, and him the son of a carriage-maker, shouting his head off in the debating society. An insignificant little scrawny fellow."

"A Catholic gentleman, was he?"

"I think he was a Mohammedan, but he called himself a Protestant. But the wheels turn and turn, and there is now a rebel army in Tobercurry, and myself stuck up here like a gargoyle with a spyglass. It is an army on the run, Ellen, with British behind them and British before them. God's curse upon the entire lot."

Mayo was red with rebellion, by all acounts, and perhaps the midlands as well. It was to the midlands that this lot should be marching, and not through Tobercurry to Sligo. Devil the Mayo harvest that would be saved this year. More Mayo gentlemen than one would have their estates go under the hammer, and off their tenants would go upon the cold winter roads of beggary. He would see

340

them at his gates, if he survived himself, the shawled
women asking for a sup for the little ones, and the men
hanging back out of pride, gaunt men with cavernous
cheeks. The pride would be suffered out of them soon
enough. And for what? In God's name, for what? For the
vanity of Wolfe Tone and the schoolmaster principles of
Tom Emmet. The loss of this harvest would do him in,
wipe him out completely. He would be a beggar himself,
and with no practice at the trade.

She put a hand on his arm. "Come on down out of this,
Dick. Let you get a hot meal inside yourself."

He shook himself free. "I am all right where I am,
Ellen. Get me the meat and bread if you've a mind to,
and let me be."

He ran his hand along the stone. When was it this
keep had been built? The fourteenth century or the fif-
teenth. The MacDermotts had held it in Cromwell's day.
There was still a MacDermott family in Tobercurry who
claimed to be lords of the manor, so to speak. On the occasional Sunday, MacDermott father and MacDermott
sons would walk up the avenue and stand before the keep,
frieze-clad and bareheaded, like the shepherds placed before castles by engravers to show scale and proportion.
History had brushed them aside. Masters one year and
servants the next. Peasants forever. When the Cromwellian army moved west from Sligo, the MacDermotts had
been blown out of their keep, quite literally. The yawning
crater in the east wall was the work of Ireton's artillery.
Small wonder that Cromwell's name still hung in the Irish
air, an invincible giant clad in black armor, clanking in
iron boots from county to county.

And here stand I, Manning thought, inheritor of that
conquest, sick at heart because other armies are moving
along the same road. Faces flushed by candleflame in
Daly's gaming rooms, children, like himself, of Cromwell's spawn, bank drafts written against the harvests of
Munster and Connaught. Ellen Kirwan taken by right
of Cromwell's conquest, peasant's daughter brought
gawky and long-legged into the big house, her legs spread
to receive that ancient conquest, Ireton's battering cannon. More wife than mistress now, fussing over him, reminding him to shave, knitting patiently by firelight as he
worked and reworked the account books. Emblems of
his father's extravagance were spread before him—empty
stables, their floors paved with flagstones from the cliffs

of Moher, a summer house, a gazebo which the curious might climb and peer toward Sligo. What could be sold was long gone—the silver plate, the blue and white china with young lovers gazing over a wooden bridge at a limpid stream. All gone, knocked down by the auctioneer's hammer to Baggot Street merchants and graziers from Roscommon.

But the carriage remained, in which his father and himself had driven through Tobercurry, proud as peacocks, the master and the young master. It stood in the carriage house, cobwebbed, satinwood finish streaked with grime. He could stand before it and hear his father's laughter, boisterous from the grave.

When Ellen climbed the winding stairs to him an hour later, tray in hand, she found him standing transfixed, the spyglass lowered. She rested the tray upon the top of the low wall and took the glass from him.

A long double column of men, some mounted but most on foot, was moving along the road. The head cf the column had just passed the keep, and the rear stretched back toward Tobercurry. There were men in blue uniforms at the head and rear, but the men in the center were clad in frieze which blended into the autumn fields on the far side of the road. Their pikes were sloped carelessly. Just as she lowered the glass to turn to Manning, a pipe began to play. She knew the tune well: O'Rorke's march. It was a wisp of dream, moving across a familiar landscape, in plain daylight, beneath a copper sun.

"They are passing us by, Ellen," he said. "Thanks be to God, they are on their way to Collooney. That's the way, lads, keep moving. There is a brisk tune for you. By God, would you listen to it? You'd think that fellow was gutting a sow."

The music floated toward them, encircled them.

"There are two thousand of them if there is one. They would have ruined us utterly. Oh, by God, Ellen, have you ever seen so desperate a crew? They will eat their way through Sligo, famished Mayo men with no bottom to their bellies."

She held up the glass again, to see more clearly the green banner they were carrying, but the glass now was filmy with a mist of water. Only then did she know that she had begun to cry. Her tears, the music of the pipes, the faint beat of horses' hooves, the forest of pikes, the long clump of moving frieze, blended together. She was filled with wonder and melancholy, and felt faint. She rested her hand on the battlement.

Out from the plantation, across the meadow, two figures came running, scythes clutched in their hands. Manning tore the glass from her and pointed it toward them. "It's the MacDermott boys," he said. "Young Conor and what do they call the other one?"

Brian, she wanted to say, but found that she could not speak.

He leaned over the battlement and shouted. "Come back out of that. You MacDermotts! Are you mad, boys? You MacDermotts, come back out of that. Conor! Do you not hear me shouting to you! My God, is there no way to stop them?"

The boys rested their scythes against the dressed stone of the demesne wall, scrambled over, then reached back and hauled over the scythes. A minute later they were indistinguishable in the sea of gray.

"These bloody young fools," he said, in a dull, even voice. "Poor MacDermott."

"Did you ever know," she began and then stopped, her voice shaking. Now he became aware of her tears, and put his arm around her shoulders.

"Young fellows like that," he said, with rough confidence. "They drift into scrapes and drift out of them. Those two may be back in a few days."

"Did you ever know," she said, "that in Tobercurry this place is never called Castle Harmony? MacDermott's, they call it."

"I know that," he said. "It is a sorry mess that history has made of the lot of us. Old wounds and old debts. God help us all." He put the heel of his hand against the spyglass and pressed it shut.

It was nightfall when they heard Crauford's dragoons. A trumpet call, silver and abrupt, floated across the demesne wall, across the meadow, through the open windows of the drawing room. Manning, stockinged feet, waistcoat hanging loose, was sitting by the cold fireplace. Nubian slaves cut from onyx black as night supported the mantlepiece of white marble, pink-veined. Ranged on shelves behind him were tall volumes of Irish parliamentary papers, their pages uncut, leather bindings unoiled. A hasty cloth had wiped clean the room's tables, but dust lay in corners, out of sight, beyond the candles' glow.

343

He sat upright when he heard the trumpet, and held his head cocked. It was not repeated. "What was it?" Ellen asked. He smiled without answering, and pulled on his mud-smeared boots.

The evening was cool. The darkening sky was broken by the distant plantation, by the spindly, absurd gazebo, by the tower to his left across a courtyard strewn with hay and dung. The hole smashed into it by Ireton's cannon was a black, yawning mouth. History clung to the tower, a disfigurement, like the ivy crawling along its flanks, the liverish splotches of lichen.

The narrow stair twisted up the full height of the tower, from room to unused room, to the door which opened onto the battlement. The steps, wedge-shaped, had centuries before been worn smooth. Halfway up, he paused to look through the fletcher window. The demesne wall bisected the narrow aperture. Beyond it, a mass of scarlet in motion. He turned away and continued to climb. Whose feet? How many?

Puffing, he rested his elbows on the wall and moved the spyglass toward the road. He had never before seen so many cavalry, the scarlet coats jogging, long sabers by horses' flanks. Faces were indistinct. Heavy thighs. Stolid, secure in their purpose, they rode without haste. Scarlet and shining steel against the darkening green of summer's long evening. A horse whinnied, a sergeant shouted. He put down the spyglass. Details vanished. Only gray wall, scarlet riders, green fields. A scarlet river flowed between wall and field.

"Those are the English?" Her voice close behind him. He had not heard her climb the stair.

"Some of them."

"Would they not be at the gallop, with the other ones hours and hours away?"

"With the task they have in mind, there is no need for haste."

Beaters moving slowly across an autumn field, knee breeches starred by thistles; behind them came the hunters, weapons cradled in crooked arms.

"There is a terrible fierce look to them," she said.

"Armies intend to be terrible," Manning said. "It is their profession. Well, there you have the end of this lot. Tomorrow the infantry will be coming by, but they won't stop, by the looks of things. Cavalry, infantry, artillery—for a proper army you need all three."

"Then the other poor fellows are no army at all," she said at once. "Country lads on the hike is more like it. God spare them from all harm."

"He will not," Manning said. He shot a sudden glance at her, understanding her emotion and yet puzzled by it. "He will not. Someday you can tell your grandnephews about this. History visits Tobercurry. Not for the first time, by God."

"There will be a terrible slaughter," she said.

"Someplace," he said. "A terrible slaughter indeed. But not here. Let them find some Godforsaken bog to do their killing in. Let us go down now. It is turning chill."

As the last of the riders passed from view, their menace ended. They became phantasms, for all their heavy-muscled thighs, hoarse sergeant's shouts. Jackets of blue or scarlet, clumsy peasants on the move—phantasms, all of them. Like this bloody tower with its open, deadly jaws. Reality was the house of choking dust, nagging account books, dunning letters from Dublin. her back curved toward him in sleep. The dust of their passing had resettled on the road. As if they had never been. A turbulence upon quiet roads, slaughter in a bog, in another man's pasture. God's curse upon them all.

"What, Dick?"

"It must be a profession free from care or strenuous labor—burning down a man's crop, or hunting peasants with the King's cavalry to serve as your beaters. They are welcome to their killings."

The air changed. Rooks cawed from the larch plantation. As a boy he had shot at them, using the special fowling piece his father had ordered from Nicholls of Exchequer Street, scrolls worked into the metal, a high polish on the dark stock. They stood side by side, the father stooping to guide his aim, steady his arm. "Pull!" his father shouted, always too soon, before he was ready. The gun exploded, pushing him back. Rooks fled from the trees, screaming. Occasionally, he would bring one down, and his father would run to pick it up. Hump of black feathers, feebly stirring wing. That same plantation, darkening now. A father and a small boy, decades ago. He had never become a good shot. He had no one to teach. The sky was dark blue now, and the thick-leafed trees a heavy green turning black against it.

The tower had been a Crusader's castle to the small boy, to be held against Saracen and Turk, the fowling piece pointed toward the road. There had been no demesne wall then. Another of his father's follies. The stone cut and dressed, set into place by masons from Sligo. His father supervised the work, leaning down from the glossy chestnut to give orders to the workmen. They would nod agreeably and then ignore him, dour and meticulous craftsmen, jaws hard as chisels. Manning, on his pony, trotted along beside his father, watching the strong, confident arm sweep arcs, settling the estate in time and order. He settled it, right enough.

With a harvest like this one, he could hold on for another year, the cabins quiet, tucked safely away from history, pikeheads, trumpet calls. The stairs black as he climbed down, spiralling. He went slowly, the woman behind him, his hand held to the uneven stones, cold to the touch. Useless. A byre for cattle. Boys, the two of them. One playing at Crusaders and Turks, the other setting out his strident, useless wall. But the father had been so confident, bobbing his plump head to mason, architect, carriage-maker. In the courtyard, sunken flagstones held a shallow pool of stagnant water.

From the *Memoir of Events*, Written by Malcolm Elliott in October, 1798

From Tobercurry the Sligo road runs northeast, through the village of Collooney, toward which we now advanced at a good pace. It was most instructive to observe the effect of our progress upon the country people, for we had now entered a fairly populous region, hilly and yet with much good farmland. Cabins lay scattered before us as though a giant had flung them forth, low, mean dwellings, many of them, such as might be seen in Mayo, but many others were substantial and pleasing, their whitened walls reflecting the sun and their thatch in good repair.

It was always known that we were approaching. Once I spied a young, bare-legged lad loping across fields to an outlying cabin: it was in some such manner, no doubt, that the news traveled before us. But perhaps the earth and the roots of trees know when an army is on the march. The people here, unlike those in Bellaghy, did not conceal themselves. They stood in the fields or beside their cabins, in a silence that could not be read. But a fair number cheered us, and shouted out greetings in hoarse Irish. And a few joined us—about fifty, I would judge—clambering down the slopes from hillside farms or walking heavily across pastures. Wordless, wonderstruck by their own foolhardiness or by the strangeness of the occasion, they fell in with the Irish troops. Several of them were among those who died a few miles farther on, at Collooney. Shaken loose from cabin and hearth fire, drawn to us by fathomless impulse, wonder or hatred or love of excitement, and then dead, after no more than stray converse with us. I hold in a more clear recollection those who stood watching us, silent, hands shielding eyes or hugging elbows.

As they would know of our approach, so did we know that Crauford's cavalry was in pursuit, a half-day's ride behind us, never closing the distance, though ready to attack should we reverse our march. Our men, mounted or afoot, would turn their heads from time to time, as though expecting to see the first dragoons upon a rise of the road. But Humbert never turned his head, neither when a peasant slipped down to join us nor when the sergeants used the flats of their swords upon stragglers. He had a curious manner of summoning his subordinates—Sarrizen or Fontaine or Teeling—by holding out his arm and crooking his finger, as a man might summon hounds. And what were these two—Humbert and Crauford—but masters of hounds, and behind them all the Lakes and Cornwallises and Hoches and Buonapartes? At the time, we did not know the name of the cavalry commander who dogged our march. But I saw him later, after Ballinamuck, a tall, sandy-haired Scotsman with an abrupt, choleric manner. He had then the look of the successful huntsman, the quarry pulled down, the hounds with bloody muzzles. Yet Humbert's expression, winning or losing, Castlebar or Ballinamuck, was stolid, large eyes stuck like raisins in his coarse, doughy face. Perhaps soldiering is merely a trade like any other, requiring only aptitude and opportunity, a calling which may provide equally for a laird's son or a dealer in skins.

We reached Collooney at eleven in the morning, and there we rested in the extensive orchards of the local landlord, who prudently kept himself barricaded within his fortified house, a somber and bellicose building of the kind favored by settler families in the early years of the century, when rapparee raids were still a danger. I felt a

347

curious kinship for this man, whose face we never saw, although he most certainly was peering at us through the musket slits in the window guards. For his people and mine were one, settlers planted upon wide, hostile acres to protect as best they could the realm and their own lives. Generation by generation, that fear had receded, but it had never vanished. It lurked in fantasy and nightmare —an army of wild Papishes, cursing and plundering, waving barbaric weapons. Now this fellow was in there with his family and with domestic servants whom doubtless he mistrusted, and as he peered through the musket slit the nightmare was made material. He could see the barnyards swept clean of every hen, goose, and turkey, cooking fires built in the pasture, could hear our men shouting to each other in their alien tongues, boisterous with the prospect of food and an hour's rest. For all he knew, this was but preface to an attack upon the house, and he may well have been cursing himself that he had not abandoned his lands for the safety of Sligo.

His people and *mine*. *Our* men. I look upon these quarreling words as they are set down in the ledger which contains this narrative. It is within my mind that this quarrel rages, an untidy battle whose frontiers I cannot measure. For in the heel of the hunt, all plans, hopes, conspiracies, ideals blown sky-high, what have I become but a turncoat settler, in arms against my own people? The man in that house was no English general or statesman, no Cornwallis or Pitt. Neither was he a Dublin Castle hack, busy upon England's work. He was, as I have since learned, a mere Mr. Oliver Adams, a simple man as blind and deaf to all politics as my father had been. At my trial I propose, if this is permitted, to make a simple and honest declaration of the principles which led me to join the Society of United Irishman and of the motives which prompted me to take up arms. Doubtless it will be accepted as either noble or impudent, in accordance with the sympathies of each auditor. But such a statement will have scant relation to my complexity of feelings that morning, on Mr. Adams's land. May not political passion be a net which holds the heart distant from all that has nourished it?

I do freely own, however, that my animal nature was happily nourished that morning by one of poor Mr. Adams's hens, and for all that it was charred and undercooked, it was more delicious than any feast. Indeed, I drew a saturnine satisfaction from the reflection that I had declined by insensible degrees from patriot to chicken thief. Not even my dear Judith's romantic enthusiasm could touch with grandeur such a progress. I stood somewhat apart from the other officers, who were attended by two French privates, a consequence of revolution which Judith's Rousseau had not anticipated, and at a considerable distance from the French and the Irish troops, who from the beginning of the campaign to its close remained separate from each other for reasons which extended well beyond language. Not that I attach blame to either party. Until a few years before, the Frenchmen had doubtless been peasants or artisans, but the machinery of warfare had transformed them into soldiers, and they wore their uniforms as though they had never had other garments upon their backs. The Irish seemed to them clumsy and ignorant barbarians, as indeed they were.

It was while we were taking our ease at Mr. Adams's expense that a small farmer rode into our encampment with word that a considerable body of British troops had advanced upon us from a northerly direction. His name, as he announced to us with a flourish, was Michael Mor Gildea, but the epithet *mor* must have been given to him in jest, for he was a diminutive creature, bald now and of middle years. His horse was a sorry creature, fitted out, after the fashion of the peasantry, with a saddle of straw, although Gildea himself seemed a cut or two above the peasant, with a fair command of English. He was puffing with excitement, and spoke first to Randall MacDonnell, perhaps attracted by MacDonnell's theatrical plume, but soon was led to Humbert and Teeling, and the rest of us drew close about them.

From the slopes of his farm, he had watched troops moving from the direction of Sligo through Carriganat, which is a half-mile distant from Collooney. They were by now in possession of that town, which lay astride our march. He was a poor hand at estimating numbers, saying first that there were "thousands upon thousands," and then "hundreds upon hundreds," although he was most specific that they had dragged with them "a great, deathdealing cannon." "Are these the soldiers who have been holding Sligo for the English King?" Teeling asked. He had to put the question a second time, for Gildea was staring with open amazement and curiosity at our encampment. And well he might, for our men had risen to

their feet and were staring at him. They knew only that
he had brought us information of some kind, but must
have sensed from his manner that it was unpleasant.
" 'Tis from Sligo they are," Gildea said; "I have told you
that." Teeling nodded, and said to Humbert, "From Sligo,
through Ballisodare." "Yes," Sarrizen said, thin-lipped,
addressing his words to Humbert, "from Sligo. And we
are caught between the two of them now, like a walnut
in a nutcracker." "It is my impression, Colonel Sarrizen,"
Teeling said, "that a French picket was posted on the
Sligo road." Humbert held out his arm, and then stood
looking at Gildea without seeing him. "It is a fierce and
savage army of heretics," Gildea said. "In blood-red uniforms." "Larger than this army?" Teeling asked. Gildea
looked about him, baffled by the question. "He has moved
out then from Sligo to meet us," Humbert said. "He feels
confident." With Humbert, the enemy was always "he,"
never, "they." We imagined a dark mass of men, noise,
violence, but he saw a commander, a man like himself
but with luck less clever, less resourceful. "No doubt he
has reason for confidence," Sarrizen said.

"Perhaps," Humbert said. "Perhaps he has. I think that
we will fight this fellow." He drew out a pocket handkerchief and wiped his large, pale hands.

But at that moment, the air was split in two by the
explosion of a cannon, whose shot came crashing down
into the leafy shelter of the orchard.

Collooney, September 5

After the rains, as clear and warm a day as you could
hope to find in September. Jacket off, he sat perched on
the orchard wall like a schoolboy, his feet touching the
tips of the tall grasses, dark green and light. The apple
balanced on his palm was the globe, ripened by sun and
dark earth. Quiet of orchards. *Poma.* Virgil, Horace, Ovid
himself, greater than either of them. Never too busy to
take time off for a few lines about apples. Devil the apple they'd ever needed to steal, swaggering around the
city of Rome. Just send the bill to my patrons. They all
had patrons. And why not? O'Rahilly had them, gentry
stranded by the receding waters of Boyne and Shannon.
I have mine: silver coins and a glass of brandy.

350

Warm sun of early September bathed the orchard. Beneath the trees, the men in their coarse shirts might have been laborers, resting from the work. Wall, leaf, rounded fruit glistened. No wind, the wall containing them. A boy in Kerry, he had gone with his father to hiring fairs. Men put up for auction like heifers or bullocks: strong legs and back, sound of wind. Landless men, no hope of land, they worked for food and shillings. Landless, they walked the harvest roads—Tralee, Killorglin, Kenmare. They stood silent for hire as farmers and graziers walked past them, boisterous in their prosperity, breath heavy with bacon and whiskey, minds clear and calculating. But at work the hired men were like these, in the orchard here, lazy and slow-moving, throats full of gossip and banter. Gallon jugs of porter passed round at midday, porter and the sun's heat working together like yeast through the afternoon's work and long into evening. Until dark; nine o'clock or ten in full summer. The cries of nesting birds attended them, corncrake and coot. Free as a bird.

Images caught by lime, by nets, as birds are caught, winging in from God knew where. Unbidden, they could not be summoned. From old books, from manuscripts of O'Rahilly and O'Sullivan, smeared at the edges for all the care you took of them. Not always. A girl's sturdy leg, rounded bosom. Harvesting images as the corn is harvested, or birds. Or the wind. In cold winter, Atlantic winds battering the wall, a room fetid with sleeping beasts, the fields of summer, flowers in full blossom. Held in the eye of memory, a flowering branch.

Geraghty put two hands upon the wall, vaulted upward to sit beside him. MacCarthy shook flowering branch and Atlantic wind from his mind.

" 'Tis well for you that you can sit on a wall eating apples and the King's dragoons riding down the road after you in full pursuit."

MacCarthy bit into the apple. The juices of summer flooded his mouth.

"Your friend Ferdy O'Donnell has the better part of it," Geraghty said. "Chieftain of all the fellows back in Killala. 'Tis what I was about myself in Ballina until the word came for me. The back room in Brennan's I had for myself. I ate bacon every day, while it lasted."

"All good things come to an end," MacCarthy said.

"Marching along like geese to the black, empty hills of Donegal, with the English soldiers behind us. I have a great mind to get out of all this at night and see can I get back to Ballina on my own."

"Why do you not, so?"

"Ach, did I not bring the Ballina men here? They have great trust in me. Malcolm Elliott thinks that he brought out the Ballina men, but 'twas myself. I was the first there to take the United oath, and the others followed after. There is no good going back to Ballina. The loyalists have it by now."

"Then you might as well take your ease on a sunny wall, as I am doing."

"I made my confession to Father Murphy, and he says that we are doing the work of Christ, fighting the heretics. He would say the same to you."

"I doubt if he has time for the list of sins I would reel out to him. I wouldn't know where to begin." Judy Conlon standing in the cabin door; through the shift, her legs sketched by the sun of evening. Kate Cooper leaning over him, her dark hair upon his chest. The red-haired gunner in Castlebar High Street, dead eyes staring into his.

"No, no, Owen. You know yourself that it is a great comfort to be without the stain of sin on your soul." A great peace, the communion wafer dissolving upon the tongue, the juice of innocence. Lighted tapers in the Tralee chapel, flames upright in the breathless air. Ovid's language. *Ad Deum qui laetificat juventutem meam.*

"Had you confessed to Mr. Hussey in Killala," he said, "or to your own priest in Ballina, you would have been given no absolution at all but the wrath of God. They would have told you that we are doing the devil's work for him."

"It was to Father Murphy I went, and he is as much a priest as they are. Sure isn't one absolution as good as another?"

MacCarthy threw away the apple's core. Apples and Eves in plenty, but no serpents: a fortunate isle. "It is," he said. "Your theology is sound."

"What counts is the intention," Geraghty said. "If you have it in mind to marry Judy—"

"Intentions," MacCarthy said. "If intentions counted, I would be a second Saint Kieran."

"You are a queer man, Owen," Geraghty said, sliding down from the wall. "But they say that much is forgiven to poets."

352

"I hope they are right," MacCarthy said.

Geraghty had left a warm bed in Ballina, snug farm beside the Moy. No absolution would bring those back to him, no haranguing sermons from Murphy. He walked solidly, strong farmer's walk, his legs were pillars. Much is forgiven to strong farmers. Not this time.

Kneel to confess, head bent. Beneath the sky, as men had knelt by Mass rocks in the penal days. Scarcely a village had not its Mass rock to be pointed out, in shame and shy pride. Small wonder the land had bred priests like Murphy, love of Christ and hatred of the Protestant landlords burning together, flames reaching toward each other. He bellows at us, spalpeens who drift upon his words. The tapers in the Tralee chapel were far different, white and virginal. A church for helots, despised by our masters. In secret, through a secret century, we hugged its secret power, dark mysteries brighter than the sun. Whose sins Thou shalt forgive, they are forgiven him. Even Murphy. A mystery of faith.

Down the road, beyond the orchard wall, a bald-headed man came riding a heavy workhorse. MacCarthy watched him talk first to MacDonnell, plumed, vain-glorious fox hunter, then dismount and walk toward Humbert and the other officers. He passed from sight, hidden by broad branches, globed fruit, clusters of leaves. Things are looking up when middle-aged farmers ride in on their own horses. Solid stock of Sligo, ready to fight for God and Ireland. Sunlight dazzled the top-most branches. No wind. A boy in Kerry, he had poached the lord's apples, climbing walls with spikes set atop them. Saint Augustine had done it. And never stopped talking about it. Without grace, the mind is bent toward sinful deeds. Sure how was poor little Augustine to know about sin, an African, ignorant, skin and mind darkened by fierce suns.

From somewhere off to the left, a cannon exploded. Its charge ripped through sunny leaves. Kerry faded. The leaves of Augustine's book drifted away. The boy who had stolen apples in Tralee shriveled, drew back within the big-boned man atop the wall. The orchard had become another trap.

Because Collooney was the last battle in which I took
part, aside of course from the shapeless catastrophe of
Ballinamuck, I shall attempt to describe it with care.

The force which had marched to engage us was under
the command of a pugnacious and resolute officer named
Vereker. The cavalry whom we had encountered in
Tobercurry had brought to him the news of our continued advance, and he well knew that his was the only
garrison which stood between ourselves and Ulster. He
was determined to deny us such access, and to check us
before we reached the town of Sligo, which was crowded
with loyalists who had fled before us. The decision speaks
well both for his enterprise and for his promptitude. I
speak here, albeit bitterly, with a certain national pride,
for Vereker was Irish, a Limerick man, and most of those
whom he commanded were members of his own regiment
of yeomen.

He planted himself athwart the road, his left being
shielded by the Owenmore River, beside which, at the
point which he had chosen, ran a high wall. His right
flank reached to the foot of a steep and rocky hill. This
placed him in a basin, with his cavalry to the rear, and,
in front of his infantry, the field gun which had announced
his presence to us. Warfare to Cornwallis and Humbert
was a form of chess which they played with bloody fingers,
but to Vereker it was a simple game of draughts. We
were advancing, and he proposed to stop us in our tracks.
And had he only simple citizens like myself to deal with,
he might well have done so, for that calling card of his,
hurled into the orchard, threw us into a panic. I remember Randall MacDonnell, a man of considerable physical
bravery, in a shouting match with twenty or so of the
Irish troops, his hat pulled low upon his head and his face
red with rage.

We lay stretched out for a half mile from the orchard,
down the road beside a pasture to the outskirts of the village. Bartholemew Teeling, on his handsome bay mare,
his saber drawn from its scabbard, and a squad of
mounted French soldiers behind him, rode to rally the
Irish troops and bring them forward. Why I speak of them

always as troops, I cannot say. Plowboys led by faction fighters and a few fox hunters would be a more accurate description, but if there is a word which encompasses this, it does not lie within my vocabulary. Indeed, I have a most clear recollection of Owen MacCarthy perched on the wall of the orchard, his long legs dangling, the very type of those yokels who may be found attached like gargoyles to every village bridge. When Teeling rode back, he was alone, having left the French horsemen to deal with the Irish and pummel them forward, should this be necessary.

During this ten minutes or so, the air was thick with noise, men shouting, the rattle of the French drums, and at least three times the crash of Vereker's cannon. Humbert, with Sarrizen and Fontaine beside him, moved forward down the road, in plain sight of the enemy, and there was joined by Teeling. They then rode slowly back, and Teeling summoned MacDonnell, O'Dowd, and myself. He dismounted, and ran his hand along the mare's neck, a long, unhurried hand, like the man himself. Teeling was always for me the most impressive, whether of the French or of the Irish. There was a time when I might have found in him the embodiment of our principles.

"General Humbert has done me the honor of asking me to lead the Irish for this engagement. He intends that the French should move up along the river, and that the Irish should engage the enemy's right flank."

"What the hell does that mean, engage his flank?" O'Dowd said. "It means that we should get ourselves blown up while the Frenchies sneak along the wall."

"Not this time, Mr. O'Dowd. Not this time. The enemy is either a valorous or an inexperienced soldier. He has put himself into a soup bowl. His flank should not be touching that hill, but holding its higher ground. As things stand, he is exposed. We shall go back through the village, circle round the hill, and attack his right."

"With that great bloody cannon blowing holes in us."

"Not in us. The cannon is formidable and the gunners seemed trained, but the French will have to take the weight of it. When we come within sight of the enemy, don't concern yourselves about keeping ranks. Those who have muskets are to blaze away, and then everyone forward with whatever they have—pikes, bayonets, scythes. Engage your enemy, hold your ground, and wait for the

French." He looked from one to another of us and smiled. "It seems simple enough."

"Well, this is the end of it," MacDonnell said ruefully, and spat between his feet. "Those bastards in front of us, and the other ones behind."

"Not at all," Teeling said impatiently. "If you will do as I have suggested, the battle is won and the road lies open."

I looked behind me at the Irish, who were staring apprehensively. The cannon exploded again, and several of them fell to the ground. I thought at first that they were slain or stunned, but it was fear which had weakened their knees. What did it matter, I thought, if the road lay open?

For the full half hour that it took us to encircle the hill, we heard but could not see the battle, the rattle of musket fire, the booming cannon. It was clear that many, perhaps most of our men were terrified. Their eyes, when I caught them, were glazed and dull, and some I saw shivering violently, as though it were a winter evening. What carried them forward? Perhaps each man hugged the secret delusion that he alone was frightened. Kilcummin, Crossmolina, Ballycastle, the men of each village walked forward huddled together.

A half hour may become a long time, with ample provision for a near-infinity of thoughts and perceptions. Thus, I observed that the birds had fallen silent: the sounds of battle claimed and filled the air. There are scores upon scores of hills like Knockbeg—"the little hill," is its English meaning—rock-strewn, its grass coarse and luxuriant. Far to our left, well out of reach of the battle, lay its twin, but with two squat cabins nestling at its foot. Cattle were pastured in a distant field. A plantation of elm half screened them from view. The noise of battle had transformed each prospect, and had drained the air of all familiar meaning.

But when we came at last into sight of the enemy, for so I must term these Irishmen from Limerick and Sligo, they seemed as fierce and strange as we must have seemed to them. Their flanks held bravely to their positions, maintaining a brisk fire against the French, who had moved up along the river, using the wall as cover, but then had halted to await our arrival. The musket fire from both sides seemed the barking of angry dogs, and yet I could

356

but wonder at the sturdiness with which they held their ground, for men had fallen and lay lifeless on the ground or else writhed in an agony which none attended. I do not regard myself as a man deficient in courage or spirit, and yet remain most puzzled that men in battle will face dangers which in other circumstances would cause them to flee for their lives. Yet I write this knowing that within a month I shall myself be dead, and were it not for my dear Judith could almost welcome it.

Our troops now spread out in a rough line at an angle to the loyalist flank. They were silent before a spectacle of which we would all shortly be a part, although for the moment we could gaze upon it as upon a pageant. Many had their eyes upon the cannon, which stood pointed toward the French. It was in truth the sovereign mistress of the battle. Several soldiers attended her, but did so under the instructions of the gunner, who for his task stood stripped to the waist. Its explosions were terrifying and deadly, and a squad of French musketeers, standing clumped together, were blazing away at her to no effect. The French had held their ground so that we could advance together, and yet I would judge, though unskilled in such matters, that the cannon would in any case have held them where they were, and it was discharged and reloaded with a professional skill and speed.

Teeling, O'Dowd, MacDonnell, and I were together, on a slight rise of ground, and we sat there, watching, for how long a time I cannot say. There was a movement beside me, and turning I saw that Teeling had taken out a pistol, not the cumbersome one which was holstered to his saddle, but a gentleman's weapon of admirable craftsmanship, its butt of dark, polished wood, and its metal engraved most elegantly. As he set to work loading it, he obtained our assurances that we understood exactly the manner in which our men should be brought into battle.

Yet clearly, I thought, whether or not they went into the engagement rested with them. I turned again in my saddle. They stood in ragged groups, with those who possessed muskets or other firearms placed in the forefront of each group. Such was the entirety of the discipline which the French sergeants had been able to impose upon them, or which their faction leaders had contrived to maintain. The men of one faction, from my own Ballina as it chanced, had fallen to their knees and were attending the maniacal exhortations of Murphy, our "chaplain," their eyes raised to the cross which he held above his head. At this distance, only the mercifully unintelligible sound of his voice reached me, rancorous and obsessed, the heavy Gaelic syllables wrenched from his throat by passion. With such men, we had fondly thought to shape a modern nation, these coarse-dressed kernes, kneeling before a zealot in shabby black.

Teeling had been observing me with a slight amusement, as though he read my thoughts. "We can but attempt it, Mr. Elliott. If all else fails, you may depend upon the French dragoons at their rear to drive them forward."

"Like cattle."

"Precisely so. Like cattle." His pistol was now primed and loaded, and he held it in his open palm as though weighing it. "How else can men be driven to this sorry trade?"

"And the ranting of that bloodthirsty priest?"

"It may be helpful. Drums, banners, rant, the edge of a sergeant's saber. How else?" He raised his voice then, so that O'Dowd and MacDonnell could hear him. "Follow along as soon as you are able."

That said, he turned his horse's head to the right, and rode off toward the loyalist line. It was a sudden and astonishing action. At that moment, the cannon shook the earth again, and the sound and movement seemed joined. He put the heavy bay mare to the canter, and shortly had moved so far from us that every one of our men had his eyes upon him, a tall, thin man in blue uniform, riding with the assurance and apparent unconcern of a fox hunter. Indeed, an image of the hunt imposed itself fleetingly upon my imagination, the air was clear and brisk, the wide sky held the mild blue of autumn, and the grassy field toward which he was riding was a dark, vivid green. A low wall lay before him: the mare cleared it easily. He was riding now at the gallop, straight toward the center of their line. The sounds of battle continued, the crack of musket fire. But many of the loyalist troops were staring at him, and I fancied, though at the distance it was too far to tell, that some of the French had lowered their muskets to stare.

Alone, held within the swift-moving circle of his intention, he rode across the field, following the soundless belling of invisible hounds. For a minute or two after he had come within range, none of the muskets were pointed in

his direction, but then the balls began to spatter the
ground before him. He rode to their lines, then wheeled,
and rode toward the gunner who stood, motionless, beside his cannon. Then, when he was almost within arm's
reach, he presented the pistol flush into the gunner's face
and fired. The gunner fell backward, as if he had been
lifted from the ground and thrown, but by the time he
reached the ground, Teeling had turned again, and now
toward the French lines. An officer was now directing fire
toward him, and two cavalrymen gave him chase, but
turned back when they came under the French guns. He
was riding at the gallop when he reached the French, and
he drove through them.

For a full minute, the field was uncannily quiet. The
scene seemed sunk within an immense jar of clear water.
Then I heard voices behind me, ragged and scattered at
first but then rising in volume, and I turned to find that
our men were shouting with excitement and something
like exultation. I had not seen them so inspirited since the
first hours after Castlebar, and I found a deep, peculiar
pleasure in the knowledge of its cause, an act of individ-
ual bravery and resourcefulness, separated cleanly out
from the deeds of packs and mobs and armies. This pleasure was so intense that I almost forgot the purpose of
Teeling's ride, although imagination could have shown
me the gunner's face, with blood exploding from the ugly
hole that had been smashed into it.

MacDonnell lifted off his hat, with its absurd, swaggering plume. "Did you see him, boys? You did. Riding past
those sods and pistoling that great bastard of a gunner.
By God, I will let no man from Ulster get the better of
me by a morning's canter. Come on out, now that they
have no gunner to batter us with the huge cannon." It
was cheap rant, I thought, but then realized that he meant
it, for he was a vain, empty, harmless creature. And he
caught their mood, for they began to run forward, first
the men of one town and then of another. When the
French saw that we were moving forward, they began
their advance upon the other loyalist flank.

It was in this manner that the loyalist garrison was
broken, and our road into Ulster opened.

After the battle, when I had an opportunity to speak
with Teeling, I remarked, in jest, that the prospect of
returning to his own province had doubtless inspired

his feat. He looked at me with his level gray eyes and smiled, but did not otherwise reply.

"You took a most dreadful risk," I said. "Your example drew the men forward, but if they had seen you dropped by a bullet, I doubt if they would have moved."

"I was not setting an example," he said coldly. "The gun could have checked the French advance, and had to be put out of action." He nodded and walked away from me toward Sarrizen and Fontaine. But he paused and said over his shoulder, "I leave examples to MacDonnell and your other squireens."

By every meaning which I know for the word *victory* we had achieved one. Vereker scrambled back to Sligo, and once there decided that the town must be left to its own fate. From Sligo, as we now know, he moved with great haste along the southern shore of Donegal Bay to Ballyshannon, where the lower Erne, emptying into the bay, forms part of the border between Connaught and Ulster. Behind him, on the field of Collooney, he left sixty dead, together with muskets and boxes of ammunition, the cannon, and, for those who value such trophies, the Limerick flag.

And we were left with our wounded, of whom some were dying. They were attended by Baudry and the two other surgeons who had come upon the expedition, first the French wounded and then the Irish. They moved with dispatch, in a brusque and almost a brutal manner, their aprons soaked with blood, less doctors than butchers, hacking away at red flesh. It was a sight which I had no stomach for, yet I forced myself to watch as Baudry sawed away the shattered leg of a young fellow whom I recognized, one of the two lads who had joined us a few miles back, in Tobercurry, clambering with their scythes over the wall of an estate. His brother, as I supposed him to be, knelt beside him, clutching his arm for dear life and weeping uncontrollably. But his solicitude was in vain, for the boy died then and there, perhaps of the shock of steel on bone and flesh. Baudry nodded, and then wiped his long, thin-bladed knife and turned his attention elsewhere.

But what purpose was served by these ministrations, such as they were? For when they had been completed, to Baudry's satisfaction, he nodded to Humbert, who ordered us thereupon to fall into marching formation. Those wounded who were able to walk were allowed to accom-

pany us, but the others were abandoned there, left to
Crauford's mercies or to make their way as best they
could into the hills. I know nothing of their fate, but
were I a religious man they would have my most heart-
felt prayers. Some of them cried, piteously, to men from
their own villages, who stood before them, irresolute and
stricken, but were then driven forward. The lad whose
brother had died beneath Baudry's knife clung dazed
to the lifeless body and was pulled roughly away. Poor
devil, he walked along with us, dazed, his face streaked
with tears, and though several attempted to speak with
him, he said nothing, but would walk along in silence
for a while and then commence again to weep. He knew
none of us. By what right did we lure children to their
deaths, caught by a glint of light on metal, a trumpery
banner? We were all of us I think—I cannot speak for
the French—shocked by Humbert's decision to leave
the wounded behind us, and many turned to look back
along the road toward them, so long as they remained
in sight, but I did not. It was that bitter taste that filled
our mouths now, and not the "victory" which we had won.

I had expected that we would march north now, upon
Sligo, to follow up our success, but instead we moved
in a direction roughly eastward, along Lough Gill, to
the small and primitive village of Dromahair, which is
dominated by a ruined and empty castle of some sort.
It was late evening when we reached it, and so here we
paused. A low hill lay beyond the castle, and there
Humbert walked, drawing Teeling, Sarrizen, and Fontaine after him. They remained there for the better part
of a half hour, holding a kind of council of war, and of
none too amicable a sort, for several times their raised
voices carried to me. Once I looked toward them, and
fancied that I caught Teeling's eye upon me, but they
were at too far a distance to be observed closely. Presently they came down with Sarrizen and Fontaine looking greatly discomfited, and Teeling told me that after
we had made camp for the night Humbert would hold
a general meeting with all of his officers. Then we set
off again, to make use of the hour of light which remained
to us. Although it may have been but my imagination,
I sensed that an uneasiness had fallen upon all of us,
perhaps because the wounded whom we had abandoned
were a burden weighing upon our backs, but for my own
part I had been made uncomfortable by the sight of the

four of them upon the hill, outlined against the evening sky, and in the foreground the shattered castle of some old defeat. The country is scattered with them, like hulks upon a strand.

Nor had I long to wait for confirmation. We had been but twenty minutes on the road before Teeling fell in beside me, and we rode in silence for a space. Then he said, "When Humbert meets with us, he will tell us of a decision he has made. I will support him in this. He would welcome your support as well. And so would I."

There was nothing I need say in reply, and after a pause, he continued. "We are not destined to see Ulster after all, it would seem. He proposes to turn southward at Manor Hamilton, and make for the midlands by forced march."

He spoke quietly, and in so easy and conversational a tone that for a moment I did not grasp the import of his words. But when I did, I said, "No," as much in incredulity as disagreement, and in a voice so loud as to startle several near us. He put his hand in caution upon my arm, and I began again, more quietly.

"We cannot do that," I said.

"We can," he said. "We can take the southern road at Manor Hamilton."

"The midlands are distant from us by a hundred miles at least. We have been moving northward and east. Away from the midlands. If that had been his plan——"

"I do not know whether it was his plan or not. Neither, to judge by their responses, do Fontaine and Sarrizen. It is his plan now, and I am most ready to support it. So should you be."

"Why, in God's name?" I asked, keeping my voice low with an effort.

"The French officers have lost whatever confidence in this enterprise they may have had. Hardy's ships have not arrived, and there is little likelihood that they will do so before Cornwallis closes with us. Sarrizen argues that they should surrender while they can still obtain honorable terms from the English."

"He can argue that a few hours after winning a victory?"

"Victory," Teeling repeated, and his tone gave the word an underscoring of contempt. "Victory over some local colonel in command of militia. That means very little. But that fellow behind us, hanging on our footsteps,

362

he is a different matter. And somewhere or other, Cornwallis is waiting for us with a great mass of troops. That is the truth of the matter. Perhaps we can slip around Sligo; perhaps, with more luck than we deserve, we can reach Donegal. Then what? It is what they expect of us. But if we cut loose suddenly, if we vanish and make for the midlands, what then? We have a hope of reinforcements there. If they join us, we can make straight for Dublin. It is worth a try."

"I have never heard so desperate a notion," I said. "It is madness itself. MacDonnell and O'Dowd have kept up the spirit of the men by telling them that soon we will all be safe in the mountains of Donegal. Now you would ask them to turn their backs on the coast and go far into the heart of the island. They will not go. And the French will not go."

"That is very likely," Teeling said. "The French are in a bad mood. There is no doubt of that. Humbert would have no choice then. He would surrender in the morning." He shrugged again. "He has made a good fight of it. Not even the Directory expects the impossible. He would go back to Paris with his credit undamaged."

It was now so dark that I had difficulty in making out his features, and sought therefore to judge him by his voice, a flat, drawling voice, with the burr of northern speech.

"It is possible," he said. "If the midlands have risen up. If they hold the roads to the south."

"If," I said. "We have heard nothing of a midland rising. And there is an army between ourselves and the midlands."

"Dennistoun is a good man," he said. "A determined man. You know him. Dennistoun is worth a gamble."

"You cannot bring them with you," I said, referring to the noises which surrounded us. "They are already terrified. They have been terrified since we left Mayo."

"Neither can they turn back," Teeling said. "Frenchmen have the choice of surrendering. But not Irish peasants in arms against their King. They should count themselves lucky for every day they stay alive."

At this, I reined in my horse, and addressed the level, maddening voice. Men moved past us in the darkness. I was whispering now. "You speak of them as dead men. Men marching under a sentence of death."

"Perhaps not," he said. "If we are very lucky indeed."
He was still speaking softly, but not whispering.

"And that is Humbert's purpose?" I asked in sarcasm.
"To keep them alive? I had not known that he possessed
so deep a well of humanity."

"Not at all," he said easily. "Humbert has always had
one purpose. To win. He will play every card in his
hand."

"And this is the last one."

"Very nearly. I cannot think of many others. He is
desperate to win, and I do not understand his desperation. Perhaps it is no concern of ours."

"What of your own desperation?" I asked him.

"The question is fairly put. I think that Humbert's plan
is in fact the best one. And I believe that we have an
obligation toward these poor fellows whom we drew away
from their homes with our promises and our fine words.
We have an obligation to the oath we both took, and
which we persuaded them to take."

"To them, certainly," I said. "But to no oath. It was
in a different world that that oath was taken."

"I asked for your support," Teeling said, in the tone
of one bringing a conversation to its close. "I have not
had your answer."

"Oh, as to that," I said. "You will have it. What choice
have we but to follow him? But he will lose his gamble."

"He has been lucky thus far," Teeling said, almost with
indifference. "Lucky and skillful."

His luck held for him that night, when he met with his
captains. They sat ranged in a semicircle around him in
the darkness, and he stood facing them, with Teeling beside him to act as translator. We could barely make him
out, a heavy, indistinct figure, and only a handful of us
could understand his words. What carried the day for
him was his tone of voice, as confident and as easy as it
had been that morning when he stood on the steps of the
Castlebar courthouse. There was incredulity at first, and
a fear which masked itself as bluster, but he painted a
picture which fanned hope in them—the midlands in
flame, and the road to Dublin open. Then he played upon
their fears, an army behind us, and another one waiting
for us somewhere ahead. He boasted shamelessly, recall-
ing what they had done, and magnifying every skirmish
into a mighty triumph. It had been all along his intention,

he told them, this long march to the northeast to mislead the English, and now this sudden swerve southward, plunging deep into the countryside. In a hundred years' time, he told them, the world would still be talking of the march which the men of Mayo and the men of France had made across Ireland. He paused then, and joined his hands loosely across his bulging paunch. "I will lead you," he said. "I led you here and I will lead you to Dublin. There are brave men waiting for you in the midlands."

"Between us and the midlands there are a great many men waiting to kill us," Randall MacDonnell said.

"If they can," Humbert said. "We all know that. Why should I deceive you? But I will not permit that. And when we join the men in the midlands, we will be unbeatable. Trust me. I know my trade. I am better at that trade than any of the English generals. You saw that today. The full garrison of Sligo came against us, and we threw them back."

"One garrison," MacDonnell said. "Cornwallis has an army."

"If we can move past that army into the midlands, it will be behind us, and the road to Dublin open."

"You can talk all you like about a midland rising," MacDonnell said, "but not a word have we heard from them."

"Malcolm Elliott has," Teeling said, and I picked up my cue.

"I was there," I said, "not two months ago. In Longford and Granard. They are better organized than we were, and there are more of them. I know Hans Dennistoun, and so does Colonel Teeling. You may depend upon it that he has raised the midlands."

"We depended on a second fleet," MacDonnell said, "but we haven't seen it."

"You can depend upon that fellow," Teeling said, pointing to the west. "He will be after us night and day if we don't shake him off. He is the beater and he has been set to drive us against the guns. We'll not play their game."

Humbert could not of course understand Teeling's words, but nevertheless placed a hand upon his shoulder to cut him off.

"I spoke to you once before, on the night before Castlebar. Do you remember that? You were reluctant to take the bad road, along the lake and then over the mountains.

But I was in the right then. We took that road and we defeated an English army and we won a famous battle which will never be forgotten. I knew then what I was doing and I know now. I cannot hold you with me. You can all run off and stay alive for a day or so or a week. A week of life is better than none. But you would be fools and cowards, as would the men whom you have brought here with you. We are an army, a small army but an army, and we have won our victories. Not once have we been defeated. Now let us in God's name march southward as an army. This is your country and you have a right to it. It is a country worth fighting for. But it is not my country. I will take you to where you should go, and I will show you how to fight. The rest is up to you."

"And what about your Frenchmen?" O'Dowd asked. "Will they fight?"

Almost before Teeling had translated the question, Humbert exploded. "My French! My French are soldiers. How dare you ask such a question? Look at them. Look at my brave Sarrizen and Fontaine. They are soldiers of the French army, the army that has challenged the kingdoms of Europe. They have fought in Italy and on the Rhine. And they have fought in Ireland. I have no need to preach sermons to French soldiers."

Fontaine and Sarrizen had reluctantly accepted Humbert's decision, and now, to do them justice, they managed to make doughty and resolute noises in the darkness. They believed that we were launched upon a hopeless enterprise, but they contrived to give no sign of this. Humbert's confidence was matched only by his duplicity.

It seems to me fitting that this most fateful conference took place in a darkness not moderated by so much as a single campfire. We had after all been moving in a kind of darkness of the spirit and the intelligence since crossing out of Sligo. Now, in the true darkness, our irresolutions and desperations seemed spread out around us, with Humbert's will and determination ranged against them. We had placed ourselves under his command, and no choice was open to us save that of remaining there. He might, for all we knew, be mad, or obsessed, or drunk with vainglory, but that was of scant account. Now that I have time to reflect, and the best of reasons for doing so, I find that his nature remains hidden from me. At present, I am informed, he enjoys a most comfortable confinement in the Mail Coach Hotel in Dawson Street, as he awaits repatriation. British officers, visiting him there, have found a soft-spoken, rather coarse-mannered fellow, of most defective education, and inclined to barracks-room humor. He talks readily and willingly of the campaign, and is especially proud, first of the attack on Castlebar, and then of the forced march into Longford, threading his way between two armies. Those of us who followed his commands saw little of this easy affability. He was a naked will—fierce, cajoling, whatever served his purpose. I would never have made a general, and have no regrets upon that score.

"Now then," he said. "It remains only for the Irish officers to explain to their men that we are moving southward, to join with our brave comrades, and to fight the last battles, as we have fought and won the earlier ones. But before we move out, we must implore our brave and good priest, who has shared our dangers, to again call upon God to bless our cause. For the men ranged against us are not only foreigners to this island, and its oppressors, they are heretics, whose eyes have not received the light of God as it shines through the powerful lamp of our sacred Church. The Church marches with us. God marches with us."

We were not to be spared even this. At the request of Humbert, to whom religion is of less account than it is to Tom Paine, the wretched Murphy delivered to us all one of those sectarian harangues which came to him so readily, setting upon us the blind seal of his bigotry. His voice, rasping and hoarse, was well suited to his discourse, and so too—though here I may display my own prejudices—was the language of its delivery, that Irish tongue which speaks to me of bogs and the rank life of the cabins. And yet it was not as a Protestant that I took the greatest offense. I had once seen in our conspiracy a union of hearts, pledged to sweep away forever the rancorous discord of creeds by which our land was disfigured. It had proved a vain hope, nursed in Dublin and Belfast by city-bred men, lawyers and merchants and physicians. Beneath the dark skies of Ireland, between bog and ocean, moorland and hill, it crumbled to dust.

I could not make out all of his harangue, for he spoke too rapidly, the words tumbling out and falling upon each other, but I had no need. The air had grown chill, though it was windless, and his voice shattered the silence. I turned away before he had done, and shouldered my way to the edge of the crowd, where I found myself standing beside MacCarthy. He was leaning forward, his hands hugging his elbows.

"An impassioned orator," I said.

MacCarthy cleared his throat and spat.

"We have a long march before us, it would seem," I said.

"I made a longer one once," he said. "All the way from Kerry. But mind you, I made it at my leisure. A night in this town, and six months in that. A more comfortable method entirely."

"The men are more ready than I had feared they would be," I said.

"What else can they do, the poor hoors? That fellow will buck them up," he said, and his voice gestured contemptuously toward Murphy. "Those were the best times I ever had, those times when I was on the road. And I didn't know it then. You never know."

"No," I said. "You never know."

That was to be my last conversation with MacCarthy, save one. I walked away from him, and stood by myself, my back to a thorn tree. Murphy's voice moved at last from scream to drone, and then fell into a silence. There was a stirring about me. We would rest here, until dawn, and men moved to the soft grass of pasturelands. I heard them talking, their voices woven together, Irish and French. I felt myself separated from all of them. There was a void at my center, devoid of thought, into which memories drifted unbidden, pale and fragmentary.

Collooney to Manor Hamilton, September 5–6

From Collooney they had marched through the day from their victory into darkness. Quiet, frightened villages lay behind them, by river bend, by crossroads. Silent cabins watched them, their windows wary eyes, dark and blank, grimy, time-darkened thatch falling like hair over low brows. Cattle watched them from the fields, lifting heavy head from sour pastureland. French drummers beat the march for them, a hollow heartbeat, feet moved to its pulse. His throat was parched for whiskey, warm milk, well water.

He remembered Teeling, a young prince of brightness, a poem fleshed and clothed, rider wedded to sunlight and

horse, blue coat against rank hillside grass, his arm cut-
stretched. Now, near the head of the column, Teeling
walked the horse, the image divided now, powerful heavy-
boned mare and beside her a tall, thin man with sloping
shoulders. He walked with leaden balls of weariness
shackling his ankles, tall farmer plodding by plow horse.
But in that moment, clearing the wall bay's head pointed
toward the Collooney cannon, he had been a figure of
legend, chieftain or prince, as powerful as verse or violin.
We followed after, caught in the snares of his courage. As
children follow a father's long stride, walking toward fair
or wake-house.

In the wake of that ride, a child writhed and screamed
on the road as knife and saw cut through bone and flesh.
A boy slipping over a wall in Tobercurry, his leg was
payment made for Teeling's bravery. Well did poets call
death the merchant. For our small victory, we walked
along a roadside of the dead and mangled. French merchant, white apron and rolled-back sleeves, blood smeared
his forearms. Through shame, we kept our eyes upon the
ground and yet we saw it all.

Near him the boy's brother walked, dazed and silent,
tearstained face beneath mop of black hair. He shook off
rough hands placed upon his arms, thin shoulders hunched
to shelter his misery. Tramping with strangers beneath the
flat afternoon sky. What brought them out, the two of
them, clambering over the wall like boys set to raid an
orchard? The excitement of armed men on the road, fifes,
a flapping banner. A sin dark as Cain is on us, to have
stolen children from familiar walls. Tomorrow's fifes will
call other children, spalpeens who see glory shining from
pikes sloped upon weary shoulders, boys weary of coarse-
voiced, bullying fathers, spades, scythes, lowing cattle,
dunghills, smoke-reeking cabins, the drip of rain from
sodden thatch. Perhaps a servant boy wearing slavery's
regalia, white stockings and buckled shoes. Standing behind high-backed chair, his master's head half hidden by
the polished wood, he hears a tumult in the road and
gives the slip to silverware and toil.

Sudden sunlight fell upon a patch of distant hill. Grass
glistened. A bright, empty world stretched toward its horizons. Brightness pulled at him from hill and field. Far off,
a mountain path ran, sketched by thin pencil, a delicate
line of brown meandering through hillside pastures held in
green haze. A silence wide as the skies. He was as voice-

less as the scene before him, his thoughts as shapeless. Was he a whit more clever than plowboy or servant, snared by the same bright lures? Far behind now, in Castlebar, MacKenna sat in the front room above the shop, his book resting between his propped elbows. Voices wreathed him: Brid, Timothy. And far beyond Castlebar, in Killala itself, his own manuscripts, sharp pens, clean white paper lay in their box in Judy Conlon's cabin. Perhaps. Or perhaps the King's soldiers had taken Killala, fired the cabins. Long strands of words, images like massy gold turned in seconds to black ash. He watched them burn. A different world.

At late evening they halted in Dromahair, by the ruined castle, and he watched Humbert climb the low hill to survey the terrain, his two French officers beside him, and Bartholemew Teeling. Unknown castle, the whole countryside unknown, beyond them, beyond bright evening, darkness waited for them. He shivered. Humbert pointed, toward the west and then toward the south his arm outstretched, a statue. Only Humbert, sly, heavy cat, was free. We follow. Where?

"If we beat them all off the way we did those fellows back there we will be safe in the hills in three days," Michael Geraghty said to him.

"We may," MacCarthy said. "But the lads we left behind us in Collooney will not."

"Ach, we will," Geraghty said. "That fellow has the lucky touch."

"I do not think he has," MacCarthy said. "I think his luck will run out before long, and ours with it."

"Jesus Christ, Owen," Geraghty said, shocked and frightened. He looked around him to see who might be listening. "That is a terrible thing to say. What makes you say such a thing?"

He shook his head. "I cannot say. I was standing here, right where we are standing now, looking at them up there on the hill, without a thought in my mind. He held out his arm, to point to something or other, and I thought, Our luck will run out. It was our death that he was pointing to."

He saw a shiver run across Geraghty's shoulders, like a hare through deep grass.

"Sure what do we know of such things?" Geraghty said in a voice that begged for reassurance. "That fellow knows. Isn't he a general from France?"

"He is indeed. And he will go back to France and leave us where Jesus left the Jews."

"It must be wonderful," Geraghty said sarcastically, "to be able to read the future from the way a man stretches out his arm."

MacCarthy grinned, and put his hand on Geraghty's shoulder. "Wonderful indeed."

But for all that, it was wonderful. Something to trust without understanding, as images came for poetry. Reason was but a plowboy doing sums on a slate, right sometimes and wrong others. Images carried their own truth, buried deep beneath appearances. An arm outstretched across an evening sky.

It stayed with him after they had resumed the march, as the air thickened, as they walked into darkness. He turned once, and could see hill and castle behind him in the western sky, held in the last light, the castle black and ominous, mute, hulking beast shouldering the horizon. The images did not lie, but a man could fail to understand them. Set them down at night upon the page, shining in the power of their truth, and in the morning they would lie there lifeless, thin and bent out of shape. One thing was certain. They were not spun out from within. They came from elsewhere, a gift to poets.

With darkness the chill came, presage of autumn. Nights now would begin to lengthen, coming earlier by a bit each day. By December, light would be bled from the air by four or five in the afternoon. A dark world. Safety in darkness. In cabins and taverns far to the south, safe beyond the Shannon, they would gather in winter's night, hot whiskey on the table, music, the disputations of poets. His world. Stretching out beyond his memories to the ensuring past. Not this. Alien darkness of bewildered men, a roadside of the dying. Distant from him by the length of a world, the sheltering winter darkness of Munster.

He loitered at the outskirt of the small semicircle gathered to hear Humbert and Teeling. Humbert's voice a rumble, deep-bellied, and Teeling's dry northern speech, harsh and unmelodious. He heard without surprise that they were moving south, toward the midlands. It gave meaning to the outstretched arm. They would blunder southward to some Godforsaken bog, red turf an ooze beneath the feet, lost in midland waste, edged by villages with unfamiliar names. "The Church marches with us,"

371

Teeling said, translating Humbert's words; "God marches with us." Centuries before, at Kinsale on the Cork coast, D'Aquila, Spanish commander, poignard beard, breast-plate of burnished steel, Christ-inspired, hammer of here-tics: "Christ never died for these people." Neither did D'Aquila. After the surrender, honors of war for the Spaniards, soldiers of Christ, and a gift of fresh fruit from Mountjoy. Not for the Irish. Fleeing the English, O'Sulli-van Beare had hacked his way across Munster and Connaught in dead winter, slaughtering his horses at Shannonside. "God marches with us." Murphy seized upon the words, embroidered them. Christ's deputy. In the darkness, MacCarthy saw him in imagination, short, bandy-legged, fringe of thick red hair around shining pate. Words tumbled from a mouth overcrowded with teeth.

He felt them listening. Drunk upon words, boiling in the blood like whiskey or music. Hedge priest, the Church his passion, Christ's wounds, he touched the springs of their passions with practiced fingers. MacCarthy felt him-self distant from the words he heard, from those who listened. Only his fear gave a form to the darkness. A bog lay before them, somewhere to the south. Humbert swung his arm round to point, the arm a curve and then held rigid. "There will be a great scattering," Murphy shouted. "The soldiers in their bloody coats will fly before us. The army of the Gael has risen up. God has blessed our mus-kets, our pikes. In Castlebar they fled before us, and on the Sligo road." Murphy could not see the bog.

MacCarthy stepped back, away from the listening men. Malcolm Elliott joined him. "An impassioned orator," Elliott said. MacCarthy cleared his throat and spat. Poor Elliott. Heretic and stranger, by Murphy's exact-ing standard. Blood of the Cromwellians in his veins, his father a magistrate, boyhood Sundays spent in the family pew, long velvet cushion and massive gilt-edged Bible, riding to hounds on autumn mornings, jaunty fox hunter's body, "View halloo" to the other squires. What brought him here amongst us? Pamphlets read in the long winter evenings, in his snug farmhouse of cut stone, windy de-clamations, the rights of man, Ireland's right to sover-eignty, the rights of Catholics, reform of Parliament. He knows now. Murphy and Humbert have explained mat-ters. "The Church marches with us. God marches with us." "We have a long march before us, it would seem,"

Elliott said. "I made a longer one once," MacCarthy said. "All the way from Kerry."

Not so long, perhaps, as Elliott's journey from big house to rebel army, but long enough. From Kerry to Macroom and the wild hills of West Cork, northward through Kanturk into Limerick, across Clare into Connaught, through Galway into Mayo. The march of an army was but a small thing measured against the driftings of his youth, the music of taverns, hawthorne in flower, bright leafy hedges, fairdays and pattern days. The thread of his youth had spun itself out upon roads twisting through valleys, over hills.

He waited for an hour, stretched out upon long, chill grasses, head resting upon elbow, until the last voices had quieted. Then he made his way, across the edge of the pasture, to the woods beyond. O Christ, he prayed, for once let me not be clumsy and trip over one of their savage sergeants. Close to the trees, he heard footsteps, the French pickets. He fell to the ground, his foot skidding as he fell across a cowpath. The sound of his body's thump upon the ground was as loud to him as roaring cannon. He lay there, lips pressed together, reciting verses, prayers, shielding his ears against the sound of footfall. Then he scrambled up and ran to the trees, expecting shouts, the crash of a musket. He did not stop then, but ran blundering on, crashing against trunks, against low branches which tore at his clothing. Beyond the woods lay another pasture, a stone fence, open fields. Free now of obstacles, he ran at full tilt, his heart pounding, his breath heavy and fast. A boy in Kerry, he had run like this, but his body was heavy now, an ungainly animal. In the distance, beyond the fields, lay a hill. He did not stop until he had reached it, clambered up its slope, and then lay flat upon the slope, head down. In the chill air he was sweating. He listened, but heard only the pounding of the blood in his ears. O Christ, he prayed, let them not know about me. O Christ, he prayed, let them not come after me. He said an Our Father and a Hail Mary, and made the sign of the cross. His face was slippery with sweat despite its stubble of beard.

He lay there until his blood had quieted, his nerves had ceased to shake his legs and hands. Presently he became aware of the hillside, of the thick damp grass, of his own body pressed upon it, a quiet weight. He rolled over and lay on his back, staring up without thought at the powdering of stars, the small, pale moon. After so long a time amongst a host of men, he felt silence as a presence upon the hill, a cool, noiseless voice, a cloak stronger than darkness. He moved his hand forward and back across the grass, then pulled up a tuft and held it, the roots wet and gritty with earth. Fear began to slacken its clawing hold upon his guts.

At last, certain now that he had got away unobserved, he stood up, and walked down the far side. He filled his lungs with air, and then sighed. Far off, there would be other hills. His back to the army, he was facing south. He set off across country, not running now, but walking quickly. A quarter-hour later, he paused and turned around to look into the darkness he had left.

In a few hours, the drummers would be setting the beat for them again. The army would march to the cross, and then turn, taking the Drumkeerin road to Lough Allen. By cowpath and loughside path, he would precede them. And at Drumshanbo, please God, he would cross the Shannon. Let them carry straight on, to the midlands and their red, unfamiliar bog. He would be on the other road, into sweet Roscommon, cross the Shannon again at Athlone, and then make straight down the length of Connaught and burrow himself as deep into his own Munster as he could get.

Let them move away from him forever. Feet, hooves, drums, passing at last into silence. Away from them now, he remembered faces, voices. Long lines upon the narrow, curving roads, pike and musket cutting the horizons of dusty summer, the smell of musket fire and sweating horses. The days that he had been with them blurred together. Rains softened the dusty roads. Skies cleared, and purple hills lightened to blue. At night, owls stirred in distant woods; badgers, weasels, moved by ditches. Randall MacDonnell rode jauntily, his black plume bobbing. Geraghty and the Ballina men trudged along in a clump, held together by remembered years, by the shards of a pattern broken by cannon fire. Humbert stood upon his hill, wrapped in the arrogance of his mystery. Outside Castlebar, men slipped upon blood-greased grass. A red-haired man lay sprawled upon his gun. A sack of broken images, he took it with him as baggage.

Far to the south another land lay waiting for him.

Fields of soft green, headlands which looked upon an ocean kindlier than Connaught's, towns which were strung beads of hospitality—Killarney, Mallow, Kanturk. Clonmel, loveliest of towns, civilized and courtly. Rivers which poets had wedded to words, Maigue, Shannon, Blackwater. An English poet as well, their greatest. The spacious Shannon, spreading like a sea. A sea at Tarbert, but not here. Here, at Drumshanbo, the Shannon flowed narrower than Maigue or Blackwater. Brief bridges, stumpy and humpbacked, crossed it. My world is bounded by river and bridge. A crossroads tavern my only fortress. Blackbird glimpsed in gap.

Frontiers of silence expanded in the darkness. Beyond their verges ran webs of roads, river crossings, loughside paths, the streets of villages, of towns banked by cabin, market house, tholsel. Young, he had tramped the roads of Munster. Schoolmaster, late of Macroom, of no fixed habitation. Blackbird called. Balls of malt in poets' tavern. By haystack's yellow shade, a girl wove legs white, tentative, around him. Candlelight fell upon the white page; his pen traced characters, black curves and arches. The land of peace. Munster.

Remembered joy, quicksilver freshet, flooded his dark pasture of fear. It surged from southern sources, far distant from armed men, blue or scarlet jackets, iron-belching cannon, lead-belching, torn flesh. Gap of brightness between hedgerows of armed men, their faces blank as those on crosses, washed flat by the rains of centuries. He discovered himself, where for weeks he had been hiding, in the silent dark. No sound but the rustling fields, stirred by faint wind. He lifted his pistol, trophy of Castlebar, and hurled it on high, invisible arc. He unbuckled the dragoon's wide belt, and let it slip to the ground. Then he walked away from the rising.

By a road which only the narrowest of carts could travel, too narrow for an army with wagons, he began to move south. Cowherd's path. Coward's? Blithe, he rubbed together two words of English, close together in sound. He shivered with the joy and fear of loneliness. In darkness he had found himself. A remembered self reclaimed his body. By first faint light, he knelt at a stream to drink and wash. Empty fields stretched across a hilly countryside. The air was pale and welcoming. The first birds stirred and began to cry, bird calling to bird. Free as a bird.

14

From *An Impartial Narrative of What Passed at Killala in the Summer of 1798,* by Arthur Vincent Broome

In the course of my desultory reading, for which my calling and my geographical situation have made ample provision, I have made the acquaintance of narratives written by some to whom has befallen the exciting misfortune of living within besieged cities or as the reluctant inmates of insurrectionary provinces. Reading these accounts of dangers bravely encountered, of turbulence, of starvation and threatened massacre, I am astonished by their uniform and constant intensity of feeling. This accords ill with my own recollections. For we were indeed aware that great dangers, both remote and immediate, threatened us, and in the final days we had cause to fear for our very lives, as shall be related in its proper place. And yet it was often the case in those weeks that the staple of our existence was a simple tedium, a fretful inactivity. The menaces which we confronted, sporadic and unpredictable, unfolded themselves within the monotony of our days. But perhaps in this I am deluded by memory, that treacherous spy upon our past.

Our circumstances were peculiar in the extreme. Castlebar had fallen to British arms, and with it the most of Mayo—Foxford, Westport, Swinford, even Ballina a scant seven miles away. It was known that General Lake with a large army, and Lord Cornwallis with a larger one, had moved across Connaught. And yet our unhappy town of Killala, at the neck of its great bay, was allowed to remain in rebel hands, together with the lands from Enniscrone to Easky on the right side of the bay, and on the left from Rathlackan outward to the wastes of Belmullet. We knew, or at least we hoped, that our swift deliverance would follow upon the destruction of Humbert's forces, and yet it was a sore trial that a few thousand men had not been spared from that mighty host for the present succor of their beleaguered fellow countrymen and coreligionists. It seemed almost that Lord Cornwallis, angered that we had permitted the rebellion to commence, was now allowing us to stew for a time in our own juices. This was a most unjust surmise, but one which found favor among some of the loyalists, whose sentiment toward their mother country was at the best of times equivocal.

Rumors reached us of an alarming sort, filtered through the wild gabble of the insurrectionaries. It was reported, for example, that the Crown forces guarding the approaches to Ulster had been smashed somewhere near the town of Sligo. And it was reported as well that the midlands had risen up, and that a great concourse of armed rebels was moving northward to Humbert's support. Most persistently, we were assured by our swaggering captors that a second and far larger fleet had set sail from France and would soon be dropping anchor in the bay. Each such rumor was celebrated in the town with drunken and clamorous demonstrations, flooding my windows with raucous noises of crude jubilation, and it is a blessing that the loyal gentlewomen who shared my captivity were ignorant of the Irish tongue, for it may be surmised that the language outstripped that of bargemen on the Thames. Standing in my library, which had mercifully been reserved for my use by "Captain" Ferdy O'Donnell, I could easily peer into the street below, and into their inflamed and clownish faces.

At first I nourished the hope that the supply of spirits in even so bibulous a town must at last exhaust itself, but in the consumption of spirits there was never a respite for the rebels had at their disposal the cellars of all the gentlemen of the countryside, together with vast quantities of spirits which had been illegally and villainously distilled. O'Donnell, perceiving in this general drunkenness a threat to his always fragile authority, made an early effort to suppress it, but with total lack of success. Late one night he sallied forth to the Wolf Dog, bristling with the sword and pistols which were his emblems of command. Toward dawn he was carried home by three of his "corporals," two of them supporting his shoulders and one carrying his feet, with O'Donnell himself bawling out some tuneless and interminable song. I was once again forcefully impressed with the impossibility of such a people governing themselves, unassisted by a callous French soldiery, or by the sly Dublin schemers of the Society of United Irishmen, atheists all.

I will not, I trust, be suspected of illiberality when I pass this judgment, seemingly harsh, upon a people capable, when left to their own resources, of courtesy, kindliness, and generous behavior. It would not be reasonable to assume that the Creator has portioned out equally all of the virtues to all of the nations of the earth, and the art of government lies as far from the native Irish as the arts of music and poetry lie close at hand. Witness in proof the spectacle of "Captain" O'Donnell, the commander of Killala, borne drunken and hilarious home by his drunken comrades. (I pass over in vexed silence the circumstance that the home to which he was borne was not his, but my own!) And yet this Ferdy O'Donnell was in most respects a superior instance of his race and class, to whom, as will be related, we may all of us have owed our lives and safety.

He was a well-favored young man, tall and slender, with a frank and manly countenance, candid in his manner, and as cheerful as circumstances permitted. Before taking over his father's acres, he had spent several years in one of the French seminaries which had, in former times, prepared Irish Papists for their priesthood and had therefore the rudiments of an education, with good Latin and a smattering of theology, though this latter was redolent of Rome and the Dark Ages. It was not education of a sort sufficient entirely to shield his mind from the superstitions, the baseless hopes and fears, the childlike fancies of the peasantry, and yet it gave to his mind a welcome elevation and to his manners a crude but engaging civility. Why a man of his virtues should have cast his lot with ignorant and murderous banditti was a question which I was never able to resolve, and I have reason to know that he himself found it puzzling.

Late one evening we discussed the matter, delicately and with circumspection on my part, while Ferdy maintained that air of polite deference which was so attractive an aspect of his being. We were seated in the library, with O'Donnell perched upon the very edge of a straight chair, his hands grasping his bony knees. It was clear that he fully realized the gravity of his situation, a rebel in arms against his sovereign, and, moreover, one in authority among rebels, for whom no mercy or pardon was likely.

378

That is, should order and true government be restored. But what if this distasteful and unnatural combination of peasants, atheists, and alien grenadiers should triumph? Wherein would life be more pleasant or more prosperous for the Ferdy O'Donnells of the island? What could justify the carnage they had wrought, the ravaged homes, the men slain on both sides? He could only answer, doggedly and repeatedly, that his younger brother had been unjustly seized up and flung into prison, an action which, as he well knew, I had myself protested most vehemently.

"Sure your protests do great credit to your cloth, Your Reverence, but what good were they to poor Gerry? If the French had not marched upon Ballina, Gerry would be in gaol there at this minute, and be as innocent of wrongdoing as yourself."

"No," I answered. "Gerry is not in gaol. He is a rebel in arms, off somewhere with the invaders. And if he isn't killed he stands a fair chance of being hanged. Hanged, it well may be, without trial."

"Without trial, is it? By God, Your Reverence, that's a good one, meaning no disrespect. If they are bound and determined to hang Gerry, it will matter little to him that the festivities are begun with a trial. Sure what has a trial ever been in this country but a way of putting red robes upon murder, and a most fitting color in my opinion."

"Would you obtain a more perfect justice by placing those robes on the shoulders of Malachi Duggan, an ignorant and brutal man?"

He shifted uneasily. "It is little that the likes of me will ever have in the naming of judges. But I believe that Mr. Elliott of Ballina would be a fair one, and he trained in the ways of courts. Or Teeling, the man who came with the French."

"A pair of sadly misguided idealists who have wandered off from their proper stations in life. Nations, Mr. O'Donnell, must be guided by the full weight of property and education, or else we are all of us plunged into the vilest anarchy. This is the teaching of your Church as much as of mine. It is the teaching of civilization itself."

"Don't I know that, Mr. Broome? Wasn't I at Douai in the seminary when the innocent blood of priests and friars was spilled upon the stones of Paris? Don't I have Mr. Hussey at me morning, noon, and night, to tell me that I am denied the Sacrament?"

"Perhaps you prefer the teaching of Mr. Murphy."

Very few figures of the rebellion are as unlovely as Hussey's egregious curate, and although not a vindictive man I cannot feign sorrow that he fell beneath a cavalryman's saber at Ballinamuck, and doubtless in his favorite posture, crucifix upheld to invoke the blessings of the Creator upon this most un-Christian of insurrections. Men such as O'Donnell had at least the excuse of believing that they made war against their oppressors, but Murphy was launched upon a Crusade, a Holy War, against the Protestant religion, being inflamed by theological passions at once rank and sulphurous, as though they had been steeping in the bogs for centuries. *Ireland* and *religion* were for him identical terms, which he shuffled with a conjurer's skill to inflame his brutish followers.

"Ach, 'tis little you would know of such men as Murphy, Your Reverence, but I saw enough of them at the seminary. Poor driven creatures so blinded by the light of faith that they can see only the light itself and not the world which faith reveals."

O'Donnell himself, it will be observed, had not spent idly his years at seminary, and had a ready tongue for those glib and silly sophistries which the Papist clergy prefer over sober and just reflection. I believe that he shared my distaste for the hideous Murphy, but could not bring himself to admit this to a heretic, as doubtless he termed me when beyond my hearing. For the word *heretic* was often on their tongues, as though the Established Church was but a cluster of Cathars or Albigensians. It is surely one of the strongest arguments for a removal of the opprobrious laws against Popery that the depraved passions which dwell in darkness would then be lanced and cauterized by the beneficent sunlight of the common day. This I shall maintain against all illiberal sentiment to the contrary. Popery has fastened its iron manacles upon this people, who are by nature spontaneous and gay, the children of our islands, as we are its gray-bearded senators.

By reason of my cloth, or perhaps merely of O'Donnell's protection, I was free to wander the town, and even, on my parole, to visit parishioners in outlying farms. A gray and oppressive town, with its mean shops, some no larger than hucksters' stalls, its malodorous taverns, no fewer than four of them, the streets greasy and fetid, straggling toward the dull and sullen waters of the bay. On days of mist or fog, the close-packed buildings seem to sweat, being covered with a cold film of moisture. Only at the water's edge, by the rude pier, can one gain a sense of openness and spaciousness, yet this too has its particular gloom. Seabirds swoop through the mist, gulls, those most baffling of birds, or so I find them, for in flight they are the very emblems of grace and freedom, bending the winds to their will, but close at hand they are greedy and raucous beggars. Gulls, kestrels, gannets, creatures wedded to wind and water, reminding us that this is but a poor raggle-sleeved island, the despised and forgotten edge of Europe.

A forcing-house of superstitions and dark conceits. Upon a small eminence within easy view of my window, Steeple Hill as it is termed, stands one of the cylindrical and grotesquely tall towers of this island, built in some unimaginable antiquity, of whose origins numerous theories exist, both learned and fantastic. That they precede the Christian dispensation is most certain, as has been demonstrated by the researches, at once erudite and ingenious, of General Vallencey and other dilettantes. The peasants, of course, have their own notions, but to rehearse these would strain the credulity of my readers. I have seen them standing in small groups beside this tower, peering outward, beyond the bay, toward the open sea. For almost to the end, they maintained their hope for the second fleet which Humbert had so confidently promised them. Poised thus between their ancient and their present delusions, they offered a tableau pregnant with meaning. Children of the mist, they live by fancies rather than ideas. Songs, prophecies, long-winded ranting poetry supply the furniture of their minds.

"There can be no denying what is written down in books," O'Donnell said. "Were there not great victories won by the people of the Gael in the days of our princes and earls, and ships coming in on every side with treasure and cannon from Spain and Italy and from the Pope himself."

"Centuries ago, my friend. All that ended at the Boyne." And I could not but be moved by the thought of the brightly colored pictures with which his mind was stocked, for these princes and earls were but ruddy-bearded barbarians prowling dark forests, glorified cattle thieves, swept easily away by history's inexorable march, which is the march also of civilization and true Christianity.

"We took Ballina and Castlebar," he said stubbornly, "and Foxford and Westport."

"Took them and lost them. My poor fellow, consider your position, I beg of you. There are more soldiers of the Crown on this island today than there were at the battle of the Boyne."

"Oh, by God, that would take some doing, Your Reverence. There were two crowns in Ireland for that battle. And the two kings, William and James." He grinned at me mischievously, in the manner of this people, with their primitive habit of unseasonable japery.

"A century ago," I said again. "The plain fact of the present is that a wily and unscrupulous French general has seduced the people of this barony from their proper allegiance. And the day is fast coming when they will pay dearly for their folly and in blood."

"Were I you, Mr. Broome," he said, sober upon the instant, "I could not take so calm a view of the matter. Desperate men take desperate measures. If the British army moves upon Killala, there are terrible things could happen in the town before they reach it. There are dreadful fellows who come in and out of Killala at their pleasure and answer no man's bidding. There is Malachi Duggan and his followers. Damn all does he care about this," O'Donnell said, flicking with a thumb his sash of office.

"Barbarians!"

"Barbarians, do you say? And what are the lobsterback soldiers, with their gibbets at every crossroads from Castlebar to Ballina? I wonder at you, the way you make every man with a pike a barbarian, and every man with a bloody English bonnet an angel of justice. There is a fierce satire that Owen MacCarthy wrote once on the soldiers, long before the trouble started. 'Tis a scrappy thing, but it has good lines in it. I asked him for a copy of it, but he said it wasn't worth the trouble of writing it out. Let me see can I remember any of it."

"Do not trouble yourself," I said in a bleak manner.

Here was this MacCarthy, a man with little to recommend him save his facility at the composition of verses in the archaic Irish language, a tardy schoolmaster, a drunkard and libertine, a brawler and a lounger in alehouses. And yet he was quoted as a sage, much as red Indians and furry Siberians are said to give reverence to fools and madmen. The spoken word, adorned with whatever ridiculous furbelows of rhetoric and artifice, has great power among primitive peoples. I have considered the possibility that poetry and song express the childhood of a race, as philosophy and history express its calm maturity.

"He knows more than many a man, Your Reverence. He is an exquisite scholar alike in Latin, English, and Irish."

"Is he indeed? And yet he spared time from his studies to ruin the name of that poor girl in the Acres."

"By God, she wasn't the first one, poor creature. He is the very devil with women, and would you not know it to look at him? Red hair and a ready tongue will always win the day."

And yet O'Donnell was a man who would defend the sanctity of his own home with utmost ardor, and several times suppressed with zeal and fury the offending conduct of his men. A primitive yet a complex people, they tease my curiosity without rewarding it. For they maintain a strict decency in sexual matters, despite the opportunities for sin which are provided by their cramped domestic arrangements, yet a man such as MacCarthy is accorded a kind of license, and his transgressions form the staple of crossroads jests. But this tolerance had most strict limits, and did not extend to the unfortunate girl. She lived in the melancholy section known as the Acres, upon land sufficient for the pasturage of a few cows, managing by herself her poor resources, for MacCarthy, into whose other vices laziness was compounded, had never lifted a hand to give her help. And if his sin was winked at hers was not, a most unjust and unChristian apportionment of blame. Poor child—for though a widow she was little more—she would slip into the village upon her errands and then return, cowled and barefoot like the other women, small, triangular face shadowed by the folds of the shawl. Nor could I accept the argument of O'Donnell that she was content with her lot, and fretted only that MacCarthy was far off and in danger for his life.

This, at least, gave her common ground with other women, for of course many hundreds of men, from this and from other baronies, were away with the French, and might as well have been upon the moon or in High Tartary. Few Irish peasants ever wander far from their country, which is for them a sufficient, even an ample

383

world. Now they were swallowed up by the blue, hazy mountains to the east, within landscapes which those who remained could scarcely imagine, an infinity of space. Dublin, Belfast, Cork, words scattered across the map of a small island, were cities more distant than Rome or Bethlehem. It must have seemed to them that the men had been spirited away, and would not return for years, or would never return.

For our other half-world, the world of my Protestant parishioners, life presented a different but an equally frightening aspect. Although our churches in Wexford had been savagely and vilely used during the rising there, the churches of Mayo were accorded respect or at least neglect, and no hindrance was placed upon my services. On the Sunday, I conducted both morning and evening services for a congregation larger and more zealous than any before or since. For the most of us, I am certain, the very walls, whitewashed and severe, carried welcome messages from that world of civility and industry from which we had been so suddenly and so violently cut off. I remember in particular allowing my eyes to dwell upon a brass plaque erected to the memory of Mr. Falkiner's grandfather, which bespoke the earnest wish of his descendants that he had now entered into "the citizenship of heaven"—a noble phrase, in its pious belief that hereafter we may enjoy a blessed state akin to the best which we have known upon this earth. Mr. Falkiner and his family, Mr. Saunders and his, took on these occasions their accustomed pews, the men past middle age but both still tall and unbent, the women becomingly dressed and tranquil, hands folded in laps about their books of prayer. I will not, I trust, be thought a ranting patriot if I declare that in such hours I grew inwardly firm and resolute in the knowledge that the people of our race, male and female alike, are fortified by adversity, and summon forth that which is hardiest and most enduring in our characters. Alas, we were not a full congregation, for Captain Cooper's yeomen still languished in the market house, and their wives, by their presence, reminded us that the parish had suffered and still was suffering. Nor did we lack, even in such sacred hours, reminders of our present peril, for once I looked up from the Book toward the window, to discover there malicious faces peering in, with broad, grinning faces and suspicious eyes.

It seemed a time suited to prudence in discourse, and

in my sermons, accordingly, I limited myself to assuring my auditors that God's will would be done, a sentiment not merely true but irreproachable. I could contrive nothing of more immediate comfort, and yet I fear that my words fell tamely upon ears familiar with the Protestant martyrology. For to these English-in-Ireland, if I may term them so, the calamity which had befallen us had the familiarity of lessons and legends learned from infancy. For several centuries now, they and their forebears had told and retold their stories of the fearful Papist uprising of 1641, when the luckless Protestants of Ulster were slaughtered or driven naked upon the winter roads, alike women and infants, of the brutal rapparees who roved the hills after Aughrim, cutthroats and brigands, of White-boys banded together against lonely and defenseless Pro-testant farms. A melancholy litany, decade after decade of hatred and brutality. It was as though our backs now smarted from the cuts of an ancient whip, a scourge de-vised to test the British spirit. The Old Testament abounded in episodes and language suited to this fierce perception of history, but I felt little inclined to roll out denunciations of Philistines and Canaanites. Far better to remind my unhappy flock of the merciful God of the New Testament, the God who forgives sinners and comforts the helpless and the afflicted. Mr. Saunders, in especial, re-ceived my news of this benignant deity almost as though I had introduced a novel heresy. And yet perhaps, I now conjecture, the God of Abraham and Isaac was better suited to their present difficulties, the God who had sus-tained his Elect People against all tribulations and wick-edness.

And yet Mr. Saunders had at least the safety and the comparative ease of the church on Sabbath, and at other times his coat beneath my roof, where he dwelled with other loyalists whose houses had been destroyed by the banditti. Far different were the circumstances of Captain Cooper and his yeomen, crowded together in the stenches of the market. Whenever in these present days I encounter Captain Cooper, I have occasion to reflect upon the re-siliency of the human spirit. For there he stands before me, buoyant and confident, busy upon the world's and his own affairs, as though the time of his imprisonment and humiliation had never been, an old scar healed over and leaving but the thinnest of lines. But I can remember, if he does not, the ravaged face with its red-rimmed eyes and rug of black beard. He and his men were fed, it is true, but fed most grudgingly, and upon occasion went for entire days without food, owing to the forgetfulness of their captors.

He had recovered most admirably from the black and wrathful despair into which he had at first been plunged, and was able now to rally the spirits of the poor fellows who shared captivity with him. Upon my visits to the market house, bearing with me such modest provisions as Eliza was able to supply from her depleted larder, he would greet me as of old, with a genial and complacent vulgarity, by which I was always deceived, thinking that he had returned entirely to his senses. He would inquire as to the health and well-being of Eliza and of the other ladies beneath my roof, and upon hearing my reply, would nod briskly, saying, "Good, good, good! Excellent!" Then he would distribute to the company my little treats, reserving for himself perhaps a single oaten cake, nibbling at it slowly so as to make it last. Only after some minutes of my visit had passed would I realize, with a sick and sudden sorrow, that all was not well with his spirit.

"And our friend Mr. Duggan," he might say, licking the crumbs from his fingers. "Has he been keeping himself busy? Slaughtering the cattle of honest men? Burning the crops in their fields?"

"No, no," I would assure him. "We have heard little of Duggan these past few days. And Ferdy O'Donnell keeps order in the town."

"Ferdy O'Donnell! It is my own Mount Pleasant that that lad has his eye on. It was O'Donnell land a century or more ago, black Papist land. Do you know how those fellows worked the land? By a plow tied to the horse's tail by a rope of straw. Connaught was dirt before we took the sword to it. Red Indians were kinder to the soil than the Papist tribes."

"A long time ago," I said, bland and foolish. For it is true that proper methods of farming and husbandry came in with the English. We brought with us from England the secrets of seed and plow, of tillage and harvest.

"Long ago, is it?" he asked sharply. "Tell that one to Duggan and to O'Donnell. By God, they are all alike. If they pass you on the road, they will take off their hats and give you a bow, but what they are thinking all the time is that we have no right to be here. No right, is it?

By God, before we are done with this, they will learn lessons about rights."

When he was on this tack, there was no turning him aside, yet I always endeavored to do so.

"Ballina has been retaken," I might tell him, "and the rebels themselves admit that to the south of us a mighty army of the Crown is advancing. Your imprisonment is galling, but deliverance is certain."

"It is worse than galling," Cooper said. "I marvel that you can endure our stench. The bloody English have left us here to stew in our own shit, while they march along at their leisure, with banners flying and fifes tootling. I declare to Christ that the Protestants of this island are the most put-upon of God's creatures, with the bare-arsed Papists on one side of us, and English thicks on the other."

"Certain it is that God has placed severe tests upon us," I said. "I pray that we may give them a proper answer."

"We know the proper answers well enough," Cooper said. "The rebels of this county are going to be given a drubbing they will not forget. The gallows and the pitch cap. Croppies lie down. There is but one weapon that can teach peace to these people, and it is a length of hempen rope."

"Peace is not taught with weapons," I said, but might as well not have spoken, for all the attention he paid to my words. Squatting there in half-darkness, his uniform soiled, his beard a coarse mat, and his head round and hard, he might have been that first ancestor of his, a Cromwellian ferocious in his piety, his sword a Scripture.

"By God, you are wrong there, Mr. Broome," he said. " 'I bring not peace but a sword.' That is in the Scriptures, is it not? The Protestant Scriptures?"

"In the Christian Scriptures," I said. "A perplexing text. So much else in the New Testament speaks with a different voice."

"Not to me it doesn't," Cooper muttered, with a quick jerk of the compact head.

" 'They that live by the sword shall perish by the sword.' Those are also the words of Our Savior."

"And He never spoke a truer word," Cooper said. "Have you not seen those fellows swaggering around with great cutlasses strapped to their waists? By God, there will be a reckoning made one of these days. If you drink the porter you must pay the tapster. This was a peaceful land a year ago, and it will be one again, please God."

"Please God," I said, overjoyed to encounter a sentiment which I could applaud without reservation. "If I am not here tomorrow, I shall be upon the day following. Mrs. Broome and I are most heartily sorry for your present circumstances. I am certain that your courageous stand in the streets of this town will be remembered by the government."

"The government!" Cooper said. "Cornwallis and his gang of clerks and parade-ground English soldiers. Don't talk to me about the government!"

It was an injunction which I was most ready to obey, and after a few meaningless civilities, I escaped from the fetid room, for as he had truly said, the air was vile-smelling and oppressive.

And yet a twenty-minute walk would take me away entirely from the gray, stony town and into the green and abundant countryside. Even in early autumn, it is a most astonishing green, unmatched in either England or France, a deep and seductive hue, and rich beyond the point of healthiness, being nurtured by the heavy rainfalls. Black cattle grazed in upland pastures, tended by women, or else by men too sensible to wander down into that disastrous village. I fell into the habit of riding the narrow roads between the fields, under the protection of my suit of black and low, broad-brimmed hat. In early morning, bird song filled the sea-washed air, and the heavy scent of wheat, corn, and barley. A most abundant crop, and its neglect may truly be called sinful. How merciful is the Creator in the simplicity of His instructions, bidding us to those tasks which lie closest to hand: the harvester's scythe, the fisherman's net, the carpenter's hammer commend us to our duties. I hold that the sin rests most heavily upon those who incited such simple men to rapine and rebellion—vainglorious squireens, tavern bards, briefless barristers drunk upon Rousseau and Tom Paine. The simple of this world are ever the prey of the clever and the unscrupulous. Most willingly and despite my cloth would I have placed the hempen noose around the neck of Mr. Theobald Wolfe Tone!

"Sure what have they to lose?" O'Donnell asked me, "those cowherds, as you call them?" It was long after midnight, with a sea wind wet against the windowpanes, and two bottles of my madeira before us. "Cowherds, spalpeens, cottiers, laboring men. A bad crop one year and they are on the winter roads, huddling in ditches with rags and bits of blanket, more naked to the rains than cows or sheep or potatoes, and of less value. You'll not frighten them with talk of hanging."

"But not you," I said. "You have fields and pastures, and you have a family. And all this you have foolishly thrown away." I would not have spoken so bleakly, almost in taunt, had I not conceived a desire somehow to extricate him from his desperate situation, for as I have said he was a young man of several estimable virtues, though mingled with vices and a foolish temper.

"I watched them take poor Gerry away to the gaol," he said. "And I knew then that I have nothing at all. Slaves we are, upon our own land and in our own country. The poor niggers in North America fare better."

But at other times he would speak of the round of peasant pleasures and pastimes with a zest and an affection which I found most moving—their feast days and patterns, even their wakes. Joy was interwoven with the harshness of their lives. Cabins bursting with music came alive for me as he spoke, the feet of the young dancers, the plaintive violins, voices thick with whiskey and song. Their lives have ever been a mystery to me, but a door will at times be briefly opened, and peering through it I can perceive essences, vivid but imprecise. Some slight distance, thin and sharp as a knife's edge, set O'Donnell too apart from those of whom he spoke, as though he spoke of a world well and richly remembered from which he had stepped aside. I thought then that this was a consequence of his years abroad, at the seminary in France. But I now believe that he realized that all had been changed for him by his fatal act of rebellion.

And all this while, as we lived with our uncertainties, the wretched affair was drawing to its predestined close. Upon that very night of sea wind and madeira, Humbert, many miles to our east, swerved from his northward path, and began his march to the south, along Lough Allen, to the midlands. Colonel Crauford, it has been said, was beside himself with rage when he entered Manor Hamilton to find the trap sprung but the quarry vanished. But to the south lay a larger trap. Lord Cornwallis had secured one side of it to the Shannon, at Carrick, and was marching eastward, to deal with the risings in Longford and Granard. Humbert's only hope now lay with the size and the success of those risings, for if the main road to Dublin lay open, he could then move upon the undefended capital. In Killala, day drifted into day, but for the two armies, time was shrinking to hours.

It has been stated that as Lord Cornwallis made ready to move he received a dispatch from Dublin which afforded him welcome amusement. The second French fleet of invasion had at last set sail, but Admiral Warren stood ready to receive them as they approached the Irish coast. And this, as my readers will surely recall, was accomplished, at which time it was discovered that aboard one of the French ships was the celebrated Theobald Wolfe Tone, who was not shielded by his French rank and uniform from the fate which he deserved. And thus all the knots of the wretched enterprise were pulled neatly together. I have not seen so much as a cheap engraving of Mr. Tone, but in my mind have formed a picture of him, an agile little fellow, sharp of nose and thin of mouth, all ambition and egotism, his head crammed with humanitarian cant, and his heart bursting with mischief. But perhaps I wrong him. It may be that he had little understanding of the bloody engines whose springs he touched. I know only what I have experienced, the men I have seen slain, the thatch in flames, the homeless upon the roads. May the Almighty show to him more mercy than I can summon up!

When I seek to recall those days and nights in which we were all locked together in Killala, prisons within prisons, it seems strange that I remember most vividly evenings spent in talk with O'Donnell. Imagine us if you will, a clergyman past middle years, balding but with a ludicrous aureole of graying hair falling to the collar's edge, plump and soft after a half-century of sedentary life, with no height to give me dignity, but round, full legs swinging back and forth as I sat facing him, the tips of black boots barely touching the polished wood. And a large-boned young peasant, a face firm yet puzzled, skin coarse and reddish of hue, great murderous pistol thrust into his belt. As we leaned toward each other across the table, we leaned from two worlds which had no knowledge the one of the other. Perhaps my face, like his, bore the marks of puzzlement, as I strained to understand him.

I can stand now, any day I choose, on the broad green at Castlebar, that green where I was one day to look upon the gibbeted bodies of the rebels, and if it is a fairday can listen to fiddler and piper, their notes jostling the lowing of cattle and the shouts of peddler and card-trickster, and all will seem but an ugly jangle, raw, brutish sound. But on another day, as I am riding, it may be, to some ailing or infirm parishioner, a voice will float to me across half a valley, or even a voice drifting from pothouse window in the gray, sea-streaked village, and I can almost read its meaning, a voice across mountain grasses or slippery cobblestone.

15

Drumkeerin, September 6

Sunlight fell in spangles through the high hedges on either side of the road, the soft sunlight of early morning, and to the south lay the warm, harvested fields. Tawny. The small hillocks of the gathered hay crouched, small submissive creatures. From cabins upon low southward hills rose plumes of smoke. He could almost smell them, warm smoke from turf fires. No wind. The plumes rose straight, unwavering. Low fences crisscrossed the fields. Well tended, they rode across the soft rolls of the countryside. The lands of peace. He twisted round, and looked behind him. Quiet fields as far north as the eye could see. A magpie in flight. Flash of black and white.

A half hour later he was in the village. At a crossroads, four houses, a huckster's shop, a tavern, a forge. Hens pecked in the dunghills. Metallic clatter from the forge. He was watched from the windows of shop, cabins. He walked to the tavern door and knocked.

An old man came at last out of the inner room. Toothless, cheeks sunken, hair grew from a brown mole on his chin.

"Could the woman boil me a few eggs and butter some bread?" MacCarthy asked. "And while I am waiting, I will have a glass."

"For God's sake, man. It is early in the morning."

"A proper time for eggs, so." He sat down on a bench facing the fire, and rested his hands on his knees.

"You are on the roads early."

"I must be, to have every face in the village peering out at me. What name has the village?"

" 'Tis Drumkeerin. You must have come a fair distance not to know the name of Drumkeerin."

He measured whiskey into a glass, carefully, and handed it to MacCarthy. "That will be twopence."

"I will pay for it with the eggs and the bread, when your woman has them ready for me."

"There is no woman. It will be twopence more for the eggs and bread. Fourpence in all."

"You are very quick at sums. You must have had good schooling."

The long, thin lips spread to a smile. "Quick at sums, slow at courting is the saying."

"Is it? I have never heard that. It must be a Drumkeerin saying."

The gold of sunlight and full harvests was in the glass. It caught the morning sun. Whiskey lay upon his tongue, familiar and comforting. Whiskey my only village. How long?

Holding the glass in his hand, he walked to the door, and resting his shoulder against the post looked out into the street. The forge had fallen silent, and the smith, a hand upon the bellows, stood facing the tavern. Two younger men were beside him. MacCarthy touched his hand to his forehead, and they returned the gesture.

He drained the glass and walked back toward the fire.

An hour later, the eggs and bread settling heavily into his stomach with four glasses on top of them, he was still sitting there, his long legs stretched toward the fire. Across from him sat the smith, whose name was Hugh Falvey, and the other men from the forge, who were Falvey's sons. The four of them had glasses in their hands, and they were moving rapidly toward friendship. Falvey had one call upon his services, but he attended to it quickly and then returned.

"You could do worse than think of Drumkeerin," he said. " 'Tis two years since there has been a schoolmaster here, and they are growing up as wild and ignorant as hares."

"Small wonder," MacCarthy said. "A priest is badly needed in a village, but it is with the schoolmaster that civilization comes. A good master to beat the love of learning into them with a stout stick."

"Oh, by Jesus," Michael Falvey said, "the master that was in it had a stout enough stick, but it was not upon the boys that he practiced with it." His brother snickered.

"There is enough of that," his father said. "You will find good masters and bad masters, as you will in any trade."

" 'Tis not a trade," MacCarthy said. "What would we be at all without the schoolmasters but a pack of bare-arsed heathens?"

" 'Twas good money the schoolmaster Scanlon got from us," Falvey said, "together with chickens for his pot and turf for his fire. Drumkeerin is not an ignorant village. Would you know him at all Mr. MacCarthy, or know his reputation? Michael Scanlon, a short, heavyset man with bandy legs. Michael Scanlon."

"That is a Limerick name, Scanlon," MacCarthy said, "and half of them are called Michael. Michael goes with Scanlon like salt with potatoes."

"There is now a wee Scanlon in Drumkeerin as well," Michael Falvey said, "but his poor bitch of a mother has no claim upon the name."

"Are you a Limerick man yourself, then, Mr. Mac-Carthy?"

"I am not," MacCarthy said, shuddering.

"But you are from Munster," Hugh Falvey said. "That is clear from your speech."

"I am from Kerry."

"Kerry, is it? They say that the best masters of all are bred in Kerry."

" 'Tis true," MacCarthy said. "The birds in the trees speak in geometrical theorems."

"Schoolmasters and poets," the tavernkeeper said. "Schoolmasters and poets. Was it not in Kerry that Owen O'Sullivan lived and wrote?"

Ignorant huckster. Say Kerry to them and they say O'Sullivan back at you, as if no other man had ever put words together. Small wonder poor Scanlon had fled their company.

"It is back to Kerry that I am traveling," he said, "and with enough experience at my back to match any master in Munster."

"By God, you have picked a poor season for it," Falvey said. "With warfare above you and warfare below, and the redcoat soldiers upon all the roads."

"Not on this road, surely? It is quiet enough here."

"And God send it remain so. Sure if you came from the north it must have been all around you."

"I came from Manor Hamilton, and it is as quiet there as it is here."

"And is it true that all of Mayo is in the hands of the people of Ireland, and the redcoat soldiers and the Englishmen driven out of it?"

"And the great landlords with them?" Michael Falvey asked.

"That is what is said in Manor Hamilton. And if that is true, the people of Ireland will not rest in Mayo. They will march down toward the south. What would Drumkeerin say to that?"

"By God, I know what I might do," Michael Falvey said. "I might go along with them, and so might Dominick here." At Tobercurry, two boys climbing over the high wall of the demesne to run after the drums and guns. One we left in the ditch at Collooney. A world's distance from Collooney.

"You would my arse," his father said. "What call has a smith's son in Drumkeerin to go off with a pack of Mayo men?"

"Mayo men and Sligo men," MacCarthy said. "And men from the midlands, if what I hear is true."

"You seem to hear a lot in Manor Hamilton," Falvey said.

"A rebellion cannot be kept a secret." It was a rebellion: the word touched MacCarthy like a finger of ice. Small wonder the soldiers were building gallows.

"It is remarkable," the tavernkeeper said. "Fighting there and fighting the other place, and here it is as quiet as a winter morning."

Wait. One day, two at the most, and it will be on top of you. Mayo men, Frenchmen, horses, artillery, and the redcoats hard on their heels. Drumkeerin will be twisted the way plantations are twisted by big winds. MacCarthy felt like an angel of doom out of the Bible, carrying destruction from town to town. But this was no city of the plain, this poor crossroads village with a tavern and a forge. The whitewashed walls hugged him; fire warmed

394

his bones. How could trouble come to this room? He drank quickly, scarcely touching the whiskey.

"Was it in Manor Hamilton you had your school, Mr. MacCarthy?"

He shook his head. "Above," he said vaguely. "In Donegal." He would never see Donegal now. Small loss. Small loss that he would not see the ugly province of Ulster. How far to Kerry, hundreds of miles, and what welcome would he find there?' A better one than the soldiers would give to Drumkeerin by Jesus. Let him but reach Killarney and he would be safe. In the town itself there were four houses in which he would be welcome, and beyond Killarney stretched all of Kerry. Lakes. The eyes of heaven. Wide and softly moving, their banks edged with ferns delicate as lace Straight, slender reeds rose from the water, softly they caught the winds. At Killorglin, Patrick O'Reardon's tavern: no bare cabin like this, but a noble and spacious room where poets and musicians drank; voices sent images, crystalline, perfect, above the smoke, contests of song, companionship. Hundreds of miles! Half the roads of Ireland between Kerry and his face.

"Sure we have a right to our own," Michael Falvey was saying. "And if the men of Mayo and Sligo are taking it back for us, more power to their arm."

His brother Dominick spoke at last. Taciturn, thin of body and face, he stood leaning against the wall. "There would be more power to their arm if the men of the other counties joined with them."

"They will have no call upon Drumkeerin men, in any event," his father said. "There will be neither rebels nor King's soldiers upon this road. Would you not agree, Mr. MacCarthy?"

He shifted uncomfortably on the bench, and then shrugged. "Ach, who can tell?" A tavern, men talking before a fire. What more was needed? A crowing cock?

"That is the way of it," Dominick said. "The men of the other counties rise up, and we bide at home hammering shoes onto horses. Like a field under water, Drumkeerin is. Dead."

" 'Tis easy talking here," the tavernkeeper said. "Let you take a scythe and run up against a company of the King's soldiers on fat horses, with lances to skewer you like a pig."

"You mind his words," Falvey said to his sons. " 'Tis

a giant that the English army is in this country, and it can walk with giant boots over those who stand up against it. It was so in Cromwell's time and it is so now."

The tavernkeeper nodded, and silently carried the bottle from one man to the next, filling their glasses. Hugh Falvey held out his glass, but avoided Dominick's eye.

They know. Blacksmiths and tavernkeepers and small farmers know. Wisdom comes to them, a slippery dust upon their shillings. Forge and tavern stand firm upon the earth, battered by futile winds and the noises of rebellion. It is the sons who slip away to join spalpeens and wandering men, and the king they rebel against may be at no greater distance than the crossroads forge.

He drank half the whiskey and then looked across at Falvey. " 'Tis well for you, Mr. Falvey, to have your forge so near the tavern. I am not so fortunate myself. I will buy a round for this pleasant company and then be off on my travels."

"Indeed you will not. If you can find enough to keep you busy through the day, you will be more than welcome to a meal in my house and a bed."

"I thank you, Mr. Falvey, but I am on my way now. Sure it is shocking the time it takes a man to eat a bowl of eggs in Drumkeerin."

"Would you not think of Drumkeerin for your school, and talk with the priest about it?"

To the north, men moved down the main road, a clumsy ship traversing dust, bristling with pikes and muskets. Here they would have me bide, in this quiet place, sheltered from history and verse. Ravagers of quiet.

He shook his head. "Fill up the parting glass, Mr. Regan, for I must go and you must bide."

"By Jesus, 'tis a lucky man you are, Owen MacCarthy," Michael Falvey said. "That you can carry the tools of your trade inside your head, and can be off on any road that pleases you."

"Oh, I was born into good fortune," MacCarthy said.

But outside the tavern, in the dusty street, the smith stood beside him. "Do you know these roads, Mr. MacCarthy?"

"I do not, but I can find my way south."

Falvey put a hand on his arm. Broad, mottled. "Keep

396

to the shore of Lough Allen for all of the afternoon, until you come to the end of the lough. The neck, you might call it. At the village of Ballintra there are two roads. There is the one road that will take you to the south. And there is the other road that will take you over a bridge across the Shannon to Drumshanbo, and beyond Drumshanbo into the midlands, to Longford and Granard, past the village of Ballinamuck."

Have you heard of the battle of Ballinamuck,
Where the oppressed people they ventured their luck.

"I will know which road of those two to take," Mac-Carthy said. "Thank you."

He looked southward, toward blue-hazed hills. Better to leave the roads at Ballintra, and travel by boreens, or across fields. Phoebus at one shoulder, beloved of poets and loving them in return.

Falvey tightened his hold upon the arm. "Which of them is it you are running from, the rebels or the soldiers?"

MacCarthy looked into his eyes, as clear and bulging as Duggan's.

" 'Tis a clever fox you are, Mr. Falvey. I should bide here in Drumkeerin and take lessons from you."

"From the rebels?"

"From all of them. I was with the rebels until last night. I slipped away. I will put the length of Ireland between themselves and me."

"And where are they?"

"They were at Manor Hamilton last night. They are closer now."

Strong fingers, shaped upon iron, bit into his arm.

"What the hell do you mean, they are closer now?"

"They were to move southward this morning, to the midlands."

"Through Drumkeerin, so?"

"By this road, perhaps."

"Then why the hell could you not have told us, man? They will be trampling through here in hours. You know that, do you not? What are they like at all?"

"Ach, sure they are men like yourself and like me.

397

Poor landless gobshites from Mayo. 'Tis little interest they will have in Drumkeerin."

"And the lobsterbacks will be here in pursuit after them, who are not at all men like you and me. They would not think twice about burning down a man's three walls and then hanging him from the fourth. In the name of Christ, what have you brought down upon us, you Kerry hoor?"

"Me, is it? Sure there is nothing I want better from life than to be free of them. Bad cess to Mayo and Sligo, and to Drumkeerin as well. Wasn't it the happy man I was before I knew the name of your stinking village."

"Then leave so, you low cunt. Are you a schoolmaster at all? Can you read and write? I have a son within there can write the best copperplate, and tomorrow he may be off with those vagabonds." He raised his voice to a sudden shout. "Why here, in the name of Jesus? Why here?"

MacCarthy pulled his arm free. "Why anywhere? Why Killala? Why Castlebar? Does bloody Drumkeerin have a safe-conduct through history?"

Farmers tilled fields at Aughrim, by Limerick, beside the Boyne. Armies swallow us, spitting out bone and gristle, savoring the flesh and blood. Plow blades at Aughrim turn over musket balls, bits of bone.

"Ach," Falvey said, and turned his head toward the blue-hazed mountains. "Are you a schoolmaster at all?"

"Good luck to you, Mr. Falvey. And to your sons there. Sure no harm may come to Drumkeerin at all. They may rush through here like skitter through a goat."

"They may," Falvey said. "We can hope for the best."

"I was kindly received here, and I am sorry to leave with your anger upon me."

Falvey, still looking away from him, shook his head, his mood shifting. "It is the strange son always that is a grief and torment to a man, and yet he is the son that is loved best. Did you see the look of him in there? A few shouts and the glint of a pike would take him from me. God's curse upon them, you are well shut of them."

Eyes watering below broad, dark forehead, the mouth a thin, downward curve. What value had speech here? Will I become a leper, bringing calamity with me from village to village? Not after Ballintra. Not if I keep to this side of the Shannon and find my way south.

"What chance have they at all?"

"I don't know. I can make neither head nor tail out of

the ways of armies. 'Tis said that the midlands have risen up, and the fellows above are coming down to join with them. But the English are everywhere."

"That is the way it has always been."

" 'Tis sick of it all that I am. I would like to take a draft and puke up the last month. Cabins burned, and men hanged and men with their throats cut like pigs."

"Sure what else is there we can do? 'Tis a terrible way we have to live, and our fathers lived that way before us and our sons will after. What justice will come but what we can take at the end of a pike?"

"By God, Mr. Falvey, your mind is as confused as my own. I no longer know what I want, save to reach Kerry with a whole skin. It was bad before but we were safe from murder. I was safe enough above in Mayo, in a snug house and a warm bed."

Falvey did not stay to see him leave; he turned and walked back into the tavern.

It was full morning. The sun hung above the cornfields. To his left, a girl carrying water crossed the field. Seeing him, she paused. The heavy pails pulled at her arms. He shaded his eyes to watch her. Vivid, delicate, her features in profile cut the sky. Beyond her, pigs rooted in a cabin yard. Ballinamuck, the place of the pig. An ugly sound. Bogwater, lifeless and brown. He waited for her to turn her head, but she avoided his glance. Deceptive early autumn covered them, the silence of morning.

From "Youthful Service: With Cornwallis in Ireland," by Major General Sir Harold Wyndham

By no means the least of Lord Cornwallis's virtues as a commander was his solid and sturdy sense of proportion. For a governor general of India and master general of the ordinance, the task of subduing a thousand Frenchmen and their native allies must have seemed a trumpery enterprise, but he addressed the task with a calm and settled seriousness which certain of his subordinates, and General Lake among them, might have studied to their profit. He was to display the merits of this attitude in the final days of the campaign, when disconcerting information came to him from several quarters.

That the second French fleet of invasion was under

sail did not disturb him unduly, for he reasoned that even should it elude Admiral Warren, which was unlikely, the present affair would be well settled before it had an opportunity to disembark. The outbreak of a second insurrection in the midlands was a more alarming matter, however, and the more so because he could not easily spare men to douse out those flames. And most grave that report from Mullingar indeed was, for several thousands of rebels were involved, having in their minds the capture of Granard and Longford. The rebellion had come to resemble that most dangerous of fires which, when the flames are put down in one wing of the building, springs to life in a second. He was in the very act of drafting orders to the Argyll Fencibles, sending them to the defense of Granard, when a rider came to us from Lake, bearing word that Humbert was moving to the south, toward the midlands.

A week or so later, I was to hear from Colonel Crauford's own lips of the anger which he experienced when, upon entering the town of Manor Hamilton, he discovered that Humbert had slipped away. He at once surmised what had happened: that Humbert, wheeling suddenly, was now marching south along the shore of Lough Allen, whence he would be able to cross the Shannon and seek a way to the midlands. He sent back a rider to Lake, and then moved south himself. Now, as throughout the campaign, he was like a wolf upon the hunt, agile and fierce, and would as surely have been a bear if on the defense—a magnificent fighting animal, resourceful and bold.

Upon the ride southward, to Lough Allen, he found the spoor of his quarry, for Humbert had abandoned his heavier guns, the prizes of Castlebar, and retained only the light curricles—the certain marks of a forced march. Drumkeerin, the first village along the new line, Crauford entered but hours after the French forces had vacated it, and here he paused to rest horses and men, and to allow Lake to move forward. And in Drumkeerin, it must be confessed, he occupied himself in his customary brusque manner, for without trial or ceremony he hanged the local United Irish leader, a blacksmith named Falvey, who had furnished one of his sons to Humbert's army. Falvey, so Crauford was to report, went to his death cursing the King, begging pardon from the Almighty, and protesting his innocence, a self-contradictory cast of mind which was common among the rebel leaders.

It was, I must confess, a distressing experience for me to learn, from Crauford's own lips, of the methods which he had so casually employed, and all interspersed with accounts of exploits and rapid decisions which won my deep and ready admiration. He was in no sense a cruel man, but he assumed that rebels had placed themselves beyond the law and were better dead. Such sentiments were of course repellent to Lord Cornwallis, as he was amply to demonstrate, yet this most humane and Christian of commanders could not withhold praise for Crauford's enterprise and dash, and such praise, being set forth in dispatches to London, put Crauford upon the high road to those honors which he was to reap under Wellington in the Peninsula. But it was unsettling to me to face Crauford as he sat at his ease, boots off and tunic unfastened, and know that those firm, square lips had ordered men lashed and hanged. My youthful mind could but too easily imagine his dragoons sweeping down into such villages as Tobercurry and Drumkeerin, their sabers at the ready. That the red passion of battle may sway the judgment and destroy the charity of any man I was myself to learn, most bitterly, upon the field of Ballinamuck, but a day or two later. And yet I believe most firmly that the finest soldier is he who wields his sword as the surgeon wields his scalpel, drawing such blood as is necessary, but not a drop more. Cornwallis was such a man, and although I have heard him condemned as a "political general," I dispute the charge.

We were spending that evening as the guests of Mr. Otway of Summerhill, a pretty house which stands upon a rise of ground above the Shannon, some two miles from Carrick. The river is most pleasant there, wide but quick-moving, and spanned by a bridge of graceful arches. A river more stained by history than the Boyne: were such stains visible, it would surely be rust-brown. For centuries, Carrick has been the town by which the upper river has been held, as we held it now, and yet it is but an Irish country town, more handsome than most, with wide and well-tended streets, and the houses of the gentry, such as Summerhill, are crisp and solid seals upon the land.

Seated in the small octagonal library, Cornwallis gave his orders and disposed of his forces with a map spread

401

before us on the table, and I observed that the campaign now moved within a constricted circle. He traced the circle with a thick-jointed forefinger. Moving southward past Lough Allen, Humbert would of course seek to cross the Shannon, but not at Carrick, which he knew we held. Accordingly, he would use the bridge at Ballintra, seven miles north of us. Cornwallis did not propose to march against him there, leaving to Lake the task of pursuit. Rather, we would move eastward early in the morning, keeping ourselves between the Frenchmen and the rebels of the midlands, and maintaining a flexibility sufficient to attack Humbert or come to the aid of the midland garrisons, as occasion demanded. The two armies, to put it briefly, would be racing for the town of Granard.

"But we shall not reach Granard, either of us," Cornwallis said, and he drew a small, neat circle around the town. "We shall intercept him at one of these villages a bit to the north—Cloone, perhaps, or Ballinamuck." He drew a second, larger circle, which impinged upon the first. Then he took off his spectacles, folded them, and placed them in their case of red leather. "The hunt is ending."

Colonel Atkinson was uneasy, a short, dumpy man but a dependable officer. "Might we not do better to move now, sir? The Frenchman is on forced march, and we know how quickly he can move."

"Not quickly enough, Atkinson. Take a look at the map. He doesn't have wings, you know. He has been on a long march, with but a few hours' rest, and he will arrive exhausted upon the field. So will Lake, poor fellow. But we shall have profited by a good night's sleep. Sleep is worth a battalion." He tapped his spectacles case against the map. "That Frenchman is very good, isn't he? My word, the things he has done, and the distance he has traveled, and all with a thousand men and a rabble of peasants. I look forward to talking with him. Don't suppose he knows any English, eh?"

"You haven't done badly yourself, my lord," Atkinson said, studying the map. "If you had taken their advice in Dublin, the city would lie open to this fellow."

"Oh, no," Cornwallis said. "That would not have done." He stretched. "He is fleet as a deer, the Frenchman, but he has nowhere left to run now, save straight into our muskets."

"He plans to use the midlands rising to slip past our flank," Atkinson said.

"He plans. Yes indeed. But we have other plans. By the time he reaches the County Longford, there will be no rising there. The impudence of those bare-arsed peasants! Much good Irishmen can do without a regiment of Frenchies to put iron in their backbones."

"Dear, dear," Atkinson said. "What can possess them, to rise up like this against all hope of success, against common sense itself." He was a kindly man. Since his arrival in Ireland, letters had been flying ceaselessly between himself and his wife in Dorsetshire. They had a boy, their eldest, with Wellington.

"Who can hope to understand these poor creatures," Cornwallis said. "They live in a different world, locked away with their superstitions and their barbarous speech. And I fear that their gentry and their nobility do precious little to bring them forward into civilization. God send that we can do better by them."

"They might at least have the sense to know that their pikes and scythes are useless against an army."

"So they might," Cornwallis agreed. "So they might. But perhaps their priests assure them that the holiness of their cause will protect them against musket and cannon-ball. Some such belief was current in Wexford. But pray remember that only a fraction of the peasantry has involved itself in this wretched business. The great bulk of them are like all poor creatures. They want only food in their bellies and a bit of quiet."

"A bit of rope more likely, for the peasants with Humbert," Atkinson said.

"They are rebels against the Crown," Cornwallis said after a pause. "They have destroyed property and they have murdered. That is the ugly part of the business." He turned toward me suddenly. "Well, young man, what do you think now of the things soldiers must do?"

I got out some kind of reply. I scarce knew what he expected of me.

"Something must be done for the wretched poor of this island," he said, "but they must also learn that rebellion is the most hideous of civil crimes. Dear God, must we teach them that lesson once a century? Can they really want it taught to them by Cromwell's methods? I shall have none of those, by God. If the landlords expect to

403

have the island policed by hangmen, let them send to the Turk."

I know now that Cornwallis, even upon the eve of battle, was turning over in his mind the plan to bring to an end the trumpery "nation" of greedy landlords and venal legislators, to unite the two kingdoms of Britain and Ireland, and thus to bring to all of the Irish, master and serf alike, the benefits and safeguards of British law, and the prosperity of British commerce. Which plan was brought to its happy fruition within two years' time. A wealthy land Ireland can never be, but she has since the Union proved herself abundantly capable of acting as England's granary, shipping to us her cattle and the produce of her fields, and thus ensuring her own modest measure of our prosperity. And so shall it continue, for so long as the potato proves able to supply her poor with a cheap and universal food. Ireland has had her continuing share of civil disturbances in this present century: she has been racked by tithe wars and new outbursts of Whiteboyism; O'Connell, the bloat-bellied demagogue, has stirred up once more her ignorant masses, but her population continues to grow. Indeed, as I pen these lines, more Irishmen stand upon her fields than at any other time in her troubled history. Long may flourish the Union and the potato, say I, and three huzzas for honest Paddy in his cabin.

Curious it is to reflect that the plans for all this were nurturing within the old man's capacious mind, as he sat in Summerhill's small library, with his back turned to Mr. Otway's Livy and his Gibbon. He insisted upon hot whiskeys for us all before sending us off to our beds, and the cup stretched to a second and a third. I was by then a bit mellow, although he was as keen-eyed as ever, discoursing upon his campaigning days in America twenty years before, and most interestingly upon the subject of Washington, whom he regarded as a most overrated commander, although a man of estimable personal qualities. I was the last to quit him, and tarried until his man had brought in his robe and his Turkey slippers. I remember him with as much affection as respect, for he was not only my commander but my father in the field, a wise Priam schooling an unlicked cub.

A wide avenue of beeches ran from the house to the river, and before turning in, I walked along it. I found it agreeable to have this half hour to myself: in the field we live atop one another, and thoughts cannot properly be called one's own. There was no wind; the heavy-leaved beeches could barely be seen by starlight. Presently I was alone with the river, which flowed invisibly before me, its quick murmurs filling my soul with a curious contentment. I have always been, after my fashion, as true a worshipper of nature as Mr. Wordsworth himself, although I am a sorry hand at finding words with which to speak of my divinity, an ability which puts to shame the drum rolls and harness-creaks of my profession.

Far off, to my left, two lanterns glowed faintly from the bridge, like fallen stars. Below the arches of the bridge, the waters of the Shannon flowed to the distant sea. But I turned my head, rather, toward their source, marveling that the two armies should now be so close, for the rebels would now be moving along Lough Allen, and would reach the river sometime in the morning. My profession, of its nature, tears landscapes to shreds, sending jagged red lightnings across them, ripping them as a drunk man might rip an engraving. Yet perhaps for this very reason, I cherish nature in her tranquillity, and have ever found in her my truest and deepest feelings. A strange avowal by an old soldier, the reader may find this.

These were feelings which would doubtless have amused Lord Cornwallis, for he was in every fiber a man of the old century. America, India, Ireland—the theaters of his career lay spread across the world, but he had discovered nothing of the romantic in them but rather spoke of them as vexing problems which had been parceled out to him. The great kingdom of the Moguls, America with its boundless forests and mighty rivers, its painted red-skinned savages, and now this misty bog, haunted by the ghosts of its hideous history—all were one to him, a soldier and statesman serving his King as best he could. He possessed, like others of his generation, a settled confidence that the world made sense. And yet, when he surrendered to Washington at Yorktown, did he not instruct the bands to play "The World Turned Upside Down"?

For a lad like myself, his sword unbloodied and his spurs yet to be won, this dark island was as large as the globe itself, and as I stood by the river I tried to imagine the army moving toward it—Humbert with his swarthy veterans and the Irish rebels. Throughout the long centuries, Ireland had hung beside us as a fireship, as a battered, black-hulled pirate craft might hang beside a man-of-war. By day, its fields were as bright and as abundant as any in England, but at night they were lonely moors stretching toward savage mountains. There was no wind, no sound save the water at my feet, the great central river of Ireland. Strongbow, Bagenal, Grey, Mountjoy, Cromwell, William—Cornwallis was but one in the series of commanders sent to reduce the island. Such were my youthful reflections, romantic, melancholy, a bit fearful, upon the evening before we marched eastward to Ballinamuck.

Drumshanbo, September 6

Lough Allen lay open before him, between folds of hills. The road swerved, and ran beside it. Reeds grew by its bank, straight, pale green. He climbed a low, grassy hill and sat down to stare across the quiet blue water to the far shore. The sounds of lake water, soft and insistent, filled his spirit. Sounds twined and entwining, he read the water's music. Dust of shattered diamonds, sunlight broke upon the surface. Water rebuked the parched roads of Mayo and Sligo. Coarse grass lay beneath his hands. Lake, foreshore, hillock were cradled safe from history. Far different from the lakes of Munster, history clinging to every rock, twining itself around root, tangling with reeds and grasses. The lake of the French, they may call this one in time, or the lake of the armed men. Not yet. A man might rest here forever, hands cupped behind his head, singing to himself or studying the clouds or lost in memory.

The foreshore of his life lay all disordered, a tumult of noises, a blaze of forms and faces, cannon shot and running men, bodies emptying their blood and bowels upon pastureland, Humbert a great cat beside a midnight fire, Duggan's bull shoulders, bloodshot his eyes. At the crest of Castlebar High Street, a red-haired soldier lay sprawled upon his gun. Images crowded his skull and beat against its sides. Let time bleach away their colors. He wanted only the whiteness of clouds, lapping of water. None was an image he could call his own; they had been thrust upon him.

His self lay hidden behind those jarring images, and he called to it as to a distant friend: footing it along the roads of Kerry and West Cork; at tavern ease, his feet propped against a bench; or a woman's long white legs beside his, her breasts open to his touch. Or, most vividly, alone at night, fingering words as bright as jewels, stronger than chain. He was invincible within the sturdy keep of his language. Now he was stripped to the bare skin of his feelings. Let them come after him, they would find him gone. He longed for Munster, a familiar old coat to cover his nakedness.

A cart rolling toward Ballintra stopped to offer him a ride, and he climbed up beside the driver. A twisted old man, the bad bone of his back curved forward, shoulders crowning his ears. They jogged along, beside the reed-fringed lake.

"If it is work at the harvest you want, you will find yourself late."

" 'Tis not."

"Sure men were being hired from all over, from God-forsaken bogs and wherever. 'Tis a fine harvest, thanks be to God."

"I can see that it is."

"But it is a laborer you are, surely."

"I am not. I am a schoolmaster."

"A schoolmaster indeed, with shoulders like those and arms like an African ape. 'Tis a laborer you must be."

"I have no responsibility for my appearance," Mac-Carthy said. "There is no statute says a schoolmaster must be a dwarf."

"Then you are a peculiar damned schoolmaster, if you will allow me to say so."

"I have no quarrel with you there."

"If it is a school you are looking for, you are on a fool's errand. They have no school in Ballintra and they want none, and there is already a fine school in Drumshanbo."

"I am looking for no school. I am going home. To Kerry."

"To Kerry!" The farmer dropped his reins and turned to look at him. "With the roads around Carrick choked with English soldiers out of their minds with vengeance and oppression? And if you cross the Shannon to go south by the Drumshanbo road you will fall into worse madness. Longford and Granard have gone mad with pikes and trees of liberty and such foolishness."

"I am not crossing the Shannon," MacCarthy said. "Under no circumstances. I am not going to Drumshanbo."

"You would have done better to bide where you were until this foolishness was ended." He picked up his reins.

MacCarthy looked across the water. The surface held its secrets. Simple and straight, the reeds ran down to their tangled roots.

"Have you come from Mayo? 'Tis common knowledge that Mayo has fallen into the hands of cowherds and blasphemous Frenchmen."

"That is it," MacCarthy said. " 'Twas no place for a man of education and piety."

"Indeed not. There is a madness fallen upon the land, 'tis far worse than the Whiteboys. Nothing will settle this but the redcoat soldiers rampaging forward and back, shooting and hanging. God's curse upon the wild fellows who brought all this down upon us."

"In Mayo they were sorely provoked," MacCarthy said. "Cabins burned down, and the yeomen making free with the lash and the triangle."

"Ach," the farmer said. "They will get their fill of the triangle before this is ended, and those mad fellows in Longford as well."

"What is this fine school they have in Drumshanbo?" MacCarthy said.

" 'Tis a well-known academy. It has attracted scholars from as far off as Mohill. There is a master in that school could out-Latin a priest. Mind you, he is not the most reputable of men."

"What name has he?"

"His name is Martin Laverty. It would not surprise me if you had heard it."

MacCarthy turned from the lake and stared at him. "By God, I do indeed know a master named Martin Laverty. Is he a tall man, with a bend in his back like your own?"

"He is a blind man."

MacCarthy shook his head. "The Martin Laverty I know is no more blind than I am."

"Well, this one is. He trains up lads for the seminary is all I know, and he used have a tinker woman, but she ran off. He was in great difficulty with the priest until that tinker woman ran off."

"A tall, broken-backed man," MacCarthy said, "and well known throughout Munster for his poetry. There is a poem of his that I would pay gold sovereigns to have

408

made. By Christ, that is a fine poem. Ach, sure what would the man who wrote that poem be doing in the County Leitrim."

"I have heard nothing of that," the farmer said. "I have not heard him spoken of in regard to poetry. But he is a bad one for the drink, I can tell you. 'Twould sicken you to see him grope his way home after the tavern has closed, and as drunk as his tinker. How can a blind man teach school, will you tell me, but he is choked with Latin."

"Merciful God, what a fate," MacCarthy said. "Blind in Drumshanbo."

"There is no finer town in Leitrim. Sure you are talking of a place you have never visited. 'Tis grateful that a blind drunkard of a schoolmaster like Martin Laverty should be that he has found a living in Drumshanbo."

"The Martin Laverty I know is a poet, and keeps a school in Ballyvourney, in West Cork. And he has made one fine poem, an aisling. If it was dark night, I would smash up your cart and set fire to it that I might read that poem. And if I could not read by the flames from your rotten wood I would burn Drumshanbo."

"Who in the name of God are you?" the farmer cried, appalled. "To use mad abusive language to me on my own cart. A vagabond that I lifted up from a ditch in the kindness of my heart."

"I am Owen MacCarthy of Tralee, you wizened little turd, and I have not sunk so deep into misfortune that I must sit atop a heap of stinking onions and hear poets vilified. You can stop your cart and let me down from it."

"I can indeed. It is some class of madman you are. Poor repayment you have given me for my kindness to you."

"Is it for courtesy itself that you would be repayed, you mean begrudger?" MacCarthy climbed down and stood facing him. "The finest town in Leitrim. By Jesus, there is a boast for you. If the dogs and cats of Kerry knew about Leitrim, they would come here to piss."

It was five mortal hours before he reached Ballintra, and there, as Falvey had told him, was the crossroads— the road south, and the road over the bridge, into Drumshanbo. He stood upon the steep hump of the bridge, and looked down. Greatest of all rivers, wreathed in legend, it flowed toward Limerick and the open sea, moving through unknown counties, opening upon lakes he had never seen, plunging southward past villages whose names he had never heard spoken. But in a week, with luck, he would be in Patrick Tubridy's tavern in Athlone, where the river flowed beneath a handsome five-spanned bridge. Safe there from all harm, the air filled with friendly voices, the jug of gold-fired whiskey within easy reach of his hand. A clear road then, south to Rathkeale, and then south again to Newcastle West. His legs had never been stronger, and he had shillings and two sovereigns in his pocket. He would be shut of it forever, the thin, hysterical beat of the French drums, the clumsy scythes and murderous pikes, the blood-soaked grasses. Beneath his feet, a twig floated southward, toward Athlone.

But it was no journey to set out upon with a dry mouth. Nor was there need for that, not if Martin Laverty indeed dwelled in Drumshanbo, blind, shunned even by tinker wenches. He turned his head and looked back toward the south road, as though to make certain that it was still there, ready for him, and he made a guess as to how many hours of sun he had left. Then, pulled like the twig by casual currents, he crossed over the bridge into Drumshanbo.

It was a pleasant town, the farmer had been right about that, at least, neat and well tended, with both church and chapel, its green protected by a low fence, huckster's shop, two taverns, a market house. He went into the nearer tavern, cut his thirst, and then bought a jug and asked the way to the schoolmaster's house.

A long, low-roofed cabin at the far end of the village, its walls streaked a dark, dirty yellow beneath the thatch. He pushed open the door, and called out, "Martin. Martin Laverty." Forms had been drawn close to the dead fire. A case of books stood against one wall. "Martin Laverty!" he called again, and waited.

Laverty came at last from the other room, a broken-backed man, holding one hand against the rough frame of the doorway. His eyes, pale blue and wide, stared past MacCarthy.

" 'Tis Owen MacCarthy, Martin. Owen MacCarthy of Tralee."

A long pause before he answered with a short bark of a laugh. " 'Tis not. Indeed 'tis not. What would Owen MacCarthy be doing in Drumshanbo? Who gave you Owen MacCarthy's name, you blackguard?"

"What is Martin Laverty doing here? By God, a man

taking a cart to Ballintra told me that you were master here, and I did not believe him."

"You believe him now. Did he tell you I was blind? Come here, and let me put my two arms around you."

MacCarthy put the jug on one of the forms and crossed the room to Laverty. He put his arms around him and embraced him. Laverty ran MacCarthy's hand roughly across his face, and then held it there for a moment.

"Oh, by God, 'tis you," Laverty said. " 'Tis either Owen MacCarthy or some great cowherd playing pranks upon me."

MacCarthy stood back, and with his hands on Laverty's shoulders recited the first lines of the aisling. He stared into Laverty's eyes, blue but with something finer than film upon them.

"Owen, Owen. 'Tis welcome you are in this house. Wait now, and I will bring us out a sup."

"Sure you cannot believe that I came to you with empty hands. I have a full jug with me. All that we need now is a pair of glasses."

They sat drinking on two of the forms, facing each other, the jug beside MacCarthy.

" 'Tis the queerest damned thing that has ever been, Owen. Four years it has been, five almost. Mind you, there has been blindness in my family. My father went blind, and my sister when she was but a wee girl. I don't know. These things go in families, they say. But at first I thought little of it. It was a cloudiness at first, and it came and it went. But what it is now—do you know, Owen, we think that a blind man lives in an eternal night, but it is not like that at all. It is as though someone flung a pan of milk into your face. I can tell the daylight from the dark, and in the daylight I can make out forms and shapes. They hover before me. There is a thin curtain between themselves and me, and for a year or more I wanted to lay hold of that curtain and tear it down."

" 'Tis surely not because of the blindness that you left Ballyvourney? No man there was held in greater respect or affection."

"Ach, 'twas not. When I knew that the curtain would be with me always, I took leave of my senses and set out upon the road. For a year I was in Buttevant and after that in Kanturk. Do you know Kanturk?"

"I do indeed. There is a great ruined castle of the Mac-Carthys there. Sure you were in good hands there."

411

"Ach, but that was it. It was neither in good nor in bad hands that I would be, and I wanted no man's pity. By God, I was the best poet in Cork, and that is no small boast. Don't be a miser with the jug, Owen."

Dust choked the air. The room had not been swept out in a month, nor the window opened.

"Sure 'twas in a far corner that I ended up myself, Martin. In a village on the wild Mayo coast."

It was as though he had not spoken. The mild eyes were turned inward.

"Until a month ago I had a tinker to look after me and attend to my wants. One of the Coffeys. But you know yourself what they are like. 'Tis a fool as well as blind she must have thought me. I waited behind the door until she came in one night, and I gave her the thumping of her life. O by God, I almost broke the stick on her ribs, and she squealing like a pig. I have been on my own since then. The lads will not be here until the harvest has been saved. No man knows what trouble is who has not opened his bed to a tinker."

" 'Twas a fine quiet girl that I had above in Mayo," MacCarthy said. "A young widow, but you could encircle her waist with your two hands."

Laverty held out his glass again. MacCarthy filled it and his own.

"Weren't we great lads, Owen? Myself and yourself and MacDermott and the rest of them. There was a brightness in the air and it put a shine upon our words. Mind you, you were the man for melancholy. Not two months ago I was remembering the poem of yours upon your father's death. That poem would drain the light from the sun."

MacCarthy shook his head. "I cannot believe that I have found you here. Martin Laverty keeping a hedge school in Leitrim."

" 'Tis no hedge school. 'Tis a classical academy, and I have most of the lads who are going on for the seminary. 'Tis a quiet life, and I have accepted quietness with this." He held his hand to his eyes. "On fine evenings I go down to the bridge, and stand listening to the Shannon. I stand there for an hour, sometimes, and then walk back to Dunphy's alehouse. I am all on my own now."

"Do the people here know at all who you are?"

"Ach, they are simple poor people. Michael O'Tuoma

412

was here with me for a week last year, and said all of his new poems for me. By God, he is an industrious man."

"He always was," MacCarthy said. "Industrious is the word for it." He looked around the dusty room. Filled at times with the noise of boys, voices stumbling over words of Latin big as boulders, the fireplace glowing with red rods of turf. It was a blind man's room now, shrunken and cheerless. "You would do well to stay clear of that bridge for the next day or two, Martin," he said. "The rebels and the Frenchmen will be coming this way, and after them the redcoat soldiers."

Laverty smacked his lips to taste the whiskey. "How is it that you know that, Owen?"

"Because I was with them. I was with them from Killala out, but I cut loose. I think their luck has run out."

"May God grant them victory," Laverty said, in the flat, smooth tone of a man saying his beads, the words hollow and rattling. "May this be the year of the Gael, and may the stranger be driven from Ireland at the point of the sword."

"Not this year," MacCarthy said.

"You were always a bold man, Owen. When you were dwelling in Macroom, it was said that you knew more than it was good to know about Paddy Lynch the Whiteboy."

"What I know about Paddy Lynch is that he was hanged in Macroom. And these fellows will be hanged, or blown apart by cannon."

"Any night that you go into Durphy's you will hear talk about pikes and such. And they have made up songs about it, such songs as you would not believe, they are dreadful stuff, and cowherds and spalpeens bawling them out at the top of their lungs. The year of liberty, they call it."

"The year is almost over," MacCarthy said. He filled their glasses again, and then shook the jug. Half empty.

"First it was Wexford," Laverty said, his two hands cupped around the glass. "And then it was Antrim and then Mayo. Now it is Longford and perhaps Cavan as well."

"Perhaps," MacCarthy said. "We went along the length of the County Sligo, and there were some people who came out to us on the roads, young lads of little judgment, and spalpeens with nothing better to do now that the harvests are in. But there were many more who stood in their

413

fields and watched us. 'Tis a pleasant life to stand in a tavern singing songs."

"If there is a God in heaven at all," Laverty said, "He must see that the people of the Gael are spilling out their blood."

"He sees it right enough," MacCarthy said. " 'Tis there to be seen. I have seen it myself and I am sick of it. 'Tis safe in Munster that I would be at this moment."

"I will tell you," Laverty said. "I have not composed a poem in three years. I will never compose another poem."

"You will indeed," MacCarthy said quickly.

Laverty shook his head. "I thought at first it was the blindness. But sure many a fine poet has been blind. I don't want to. The thing has gone out of me, whatever it was. The way a harper will feel his fingers stiffen. I can put words together, but they are like dead fishes slapped side by side. At night here I have all the time a man could want, and I say over my own poems, and·a few of yours, and MacConmara's, and one or two of O'Tuoma's. All by myself, without even the tinker to hear me, I am O'Rahilly, I am Ferriter. They make a world around me. I feast upon color and sound until I am filled. But I thank God for my good memory. I could no more make a poem now than I could shape the hull of a ship."

"The power will return to you, never fear," MacCarthy said.

But he looked with horror at the blind man. Sunken cheeks, parrot's beak, filmed eyes closed off from the splendors of the·created world, long, placid hand stroking the soiled neckcloth. For a moment he was grasped by the fear that Laverty had been struck down by an infection which lingered in the dead, dusty air. The long months between poems was a familiar misery, a sour, metallic taste in the soul. But not three years. Locked in with death, the tongue heavy, words mocking him with their shifting weights.

"It will not," Laverty said. "But no matter."

Never a man to take chances in his verse, hugging safe to the conventions, but a true poet for all that. What had his gift become, a rusted lock with the key thrown away. MacCarthy poured a heavy measure of whiskey upon the image.

"You had me bested from the start, Owen, and I never grudged it to you. You had me bested and

O'Tuoma did and O'Moran and MacConmara. The way O'Sullivan had the lot of you bested."

"Jesus, man, will you give me a chance? O'Sullivan has the work of his whole life to be judged upon." If ever I hear that name again. "You make too much of O'Sullivan. You all do."

The lips beneath the parrot's beak broke into a grin. "O'Sullivan bests you, Owen. Every poet in Munster knows that. Sure what does it matter? To be trotting after Owen Ruagh O'Sullivan is no shame. We are all of us trotting after that lad."

MacCarthy finished off his glass and poured himself another. "There is many a botched verse has O'Sullivan's name to it, and others I have heard praised that could have been written by a half-dozen fellows. It's always the great lads who are safely dead. In O'Sullivan's day it was O'Rahilly who drew the praise. I remember that."

"There you have put a name to it," Laverty said, holding out his glass. "We are all of us at the latter end of things, Owen, swaggering around the pothouses of Cork and Kerry, showing off our verses to each other like schoolchildren. But the line will drift away from us. There will be no young fellows after us to sweat blood over the shaping of a line. The world will move away from us, and will leave us gasping like fish on the strand."

"I declare to God, Martin, the loneliness of the County Leitrim has driven you mad. How could there not be poets? An ugly world it would be of dumb beasts in the field and harsh sunlight falling on the streets of mean villages. We are the tongues of Ireland, man. Drink up your drink in the name of Jesus and put your mind in order."

By noonday sun a lout wandered village streets, simple-minded, his eyes vacant, slack, white-coated tongue lolled upon his lip. The terrifying vision rose for MacCarthy behind Laverty's bent back. For a poet to speak against poetry was blasphemy: he had been punished, blinded, smashed into silence.

"Listen," he said. He leaned forward, rested his hands upon his knees, and recited Laverty's famous aisling, the poem known from Macroom to Tralee. He spoke quietly, straining several times to recall the words. His voice filled the room. Ordered intricacies of sound banished the slovenly scene. Meadows sprang from his words, spring flowers, a stream flowed between smooth banks, orchard

415

trees bore fruit, round and red. As he spoke tears welled into Laverty's eyes, slipped past the obscuring film. He ended quietly, his words sinking to stillness. Memory held them in the dusty air.

"It came to me as breathing comes," Laverty said at last. "A score of men, to my knowledge, have that poem by heart, and I made it in a single evening. Scarcely five lines in it that needed mending. I remember well when I made it, a bitter January night in Ballyvourney with frost on the fields, and the hills black as rooks. It made itself. My God, Owen, I was so happy that night that I could not contain myself. I knew so well that it was a fine poem. With every verse I knew that."

"Damned well you knew it," MacCarthy said. "So let us have an end to your dark thoughts. A man would think the world was coming to an end."

But he felt the chill of the Ballyvourney winter in the air around him, the cold that steals through cuffs and neck-cloths, the frosty silence of a lifeless world. Shivering, he turned again to the jug. Long lines of men trudged along Lough Allen, heads bent. Implacable behind them, the redcoated horsemen, their faces blurred by hatred, un-knowable. Unknown roads lay before him, villages of strangers awaited him. Misfortune had brought him to this sightless man, dweller in a dark world, a throat strangled to silence. Blithe in the fields of safety beyond Manor Hamilton, he had flung the pistol from him, had set out to find himself again upon hedgy roads. Now he was again imperiled. There would be only bad luck for him on this side of the Shannon. Laverty, sightless, crooked-spined, sat nursing his drink, his mind moving in the past, a young poet crazed with the power of creation.

MacCarthy stood up and walked to the door. Beyond the village, in the final light before darkness, the river glistened, net upon silver net. Quick-waning sunlight fell upon the square stones of the bridge. In the silence of the airless room, the ear of his imagination caught the quick-beating French drums, the heavy tread of the pikemen. A child ran out from a cabin across the road, barefoot, small face beneath a mat of brown hair. Beyond a small field, birds flew homeward, a shower of dark wings.

"You have marched with the army of the Gael." Laverty's voice came to him from the darkened room, and the conventional, grandiloquent phrase jarred him. O'Donnell's clansmen, Sarsfield's cavalry: the army of the Gael. The lime-white palaces set afire by Tyrone, array of ancient battle. Aughrim, Limerick, Kinsale—a poet's litany. Not cowherds with scythes, scrambling awkwardly to die in pastures, spalpeens giggling and sobbing, blundering into eternity.

"The army of the Gael crossing over Drumshanbo bridge," Laverty said. "You could make a poem of that."

"I make you a present of the subject," MacCarthy said. A proper poem for a blind man, who would not see the scarecrows, frieze faded by rain and weather, the baffled, frightened faces.

"You ran off from them," Laverty said. His voice whined with accusation.

"Sure 'tis little you know of it," MacCarthy said, resting his shoulder against the door. " 'Tis a throng of country people from Mayo and Sligo, shoved this way and that by Frenchmen who don't give a damn about them. The gibbets have been built for them."

"Ach, 'tis all one. There is no luck in the country. What are we but a poor misfortunate people?"

"Jesus, but were you not the foolish man to abandon poetry," MacCarthy said. "You have the stuff for a hundred weepy lamentations in you."

"There is no call for you to take amiss everything I say. I spoke the truth. We were destroyed at Aughrim and at Limerick. The old stock sailed away from us after Limerick, and since then we have been sheep without a shepherd. A black, bitter century it has been, and there is no poem can put a shine on it."

"True enough," MacCarthy said. "The whiskey in me was speaking."

The silent street of cabins and low shops was no different from the towns of his boyhood. Youth had magnified them, sent their names spinning like golden guineas across the lines of his verse. Tralee, Macroom, Kilmallock: what were they but dirty clusters of cabins, pothouses transformed into pillared palaces by whiskey and song? But the poetry was a potent magic, the bare feet of dancers moving across dirt floors, the sound of harp and violin. Alone, in the evening hour before nightfall, rising a crest of hill, a valley stretched before him, Aherlow, and Slievenaman in the distance. Shattered towers lay hidden behind hills, the delicate arches of ruined abbeys. A boy, barefoot, he had climbed their winding stairs. Winds whispered through smitten windows of a dead past.

They finished his jug, and then drank Laverty's bottle. Thirsty, they walked through the village to Dunphy's. Night had fallen. A clock in the trim, spare-spired Protestant church told him the time: nine o'clock. How far toward him had they traveled by now, drums and pikes and battered feet? Bent-backed, Laverty walked with a stick clutched in his right hand, stabbing the road. MacCarthy, drunk now, rested his back against the iron railings of the churchyard, and stretching out his arm above him seized their spikes.

"You are gloomy as an owl, Martin Laverty, but I am not. Oh, by Jesus I am not. I have my life before me to live."

"You have your own two eyes to see the daylight with," Laverty said.

Heavy-shouldered, MacCarthy held tight to the spikes and let his weight rest upon his arms.

"We are a fine pair to be washed up here in the County Leitrim. 'Tis a shabby place. Today I told a man that if the dogs and cats of Kerry knew about Leitrim they would come here to piss. They would come here to piss."

He dropped his arms, and turned around to stare at the clock. Slender, gilt in moonlight, the hands of the clock formed a right angle. Protestant spires stretched across the kingdom, snug within their railings. Dowered by their own moon, they stood apart from ruined fortresses. Welltended grass and polished gravestones shielded them from the mean cabins. English marched with the Protestant gravestones, mile by mile. SACRED TO THE MEMORY. CONFIDENT THAT THE MERCY OF THE REDEEMER. DUTIFUL SON. Language of order and power, tomorrow's language. Somewhere along the road, past the village, would be the Big House, broad avenue of crushed stone, pillars by the entranceway, surmounted by stone eagles, hard of eye, beak, claw.

"What does the clock say?" Laverty asked.

"It is late," MacCarthy said. "Time is running out."

In Dunphy's, the men were crowded around a stranger, a man from Granard. He was a fat, broad-shouldered man, a belt pulled tight against his bulging gut, and a pistol stuck in the belt.

"You would be fools not to believe me," he said. "There is not a man from the countryside around Granard and Longford who is not in arms, and the men of Cavan are rising up. If there is one man there are five thousand."

When his glass was empty, the tavernkeeper refilled it. He held it in his hand as he talked.

" 'Tis the United Men who hold all the land between there and Mullingar. By God, you have never seen such a thing in your life. There have been yeomen killed and landlords killed. By Jesus, there are yeomen cowering in Mullingar and they don't dare come out to meet us. We would slaughter them. We would cut them to tatters."

Laverty rapped on the bar, and bought glasses for MacCarthy and himself. MacCarthy drank his off quickly, and bought a second. The room was close and sweaty. He steadied himself against the bar. Weariness tugged at him.

"By God, that is a wonderful thing," one of the local men said. "First Mayo and now Longford. The people of the Gael are rising up."

"It is wonderful that the people of Leitrim have not risen up as well," the Granard man said. "It is wonderful that they are standing upon their own spittle in the taverns of Drumshanbo. Are you Irishmen at all?"

" 'Tis a quiet place," Dunphy said. "There have never been so much as Whiteboys in Drumshanbo."

"Whiteboys, is it?" The Granard man hawked up a contemptuous gob. "Fellows slipping into pastures by night to hough cattle. The United Men are the boys for the task. 'Tis not a pasture that we have seized, but the whole of the County Longford."

"By God, that is wonderful," the local man said again. "You are a United Man yourself, are you?"

"Do you not know what this is?" the Granard man asked, and put his hand on the butt of his pistol. " 'Tis a captain of the United Men I am. Hans Dennistoun made a captain of me."

"You will have another glass on the strength of that," Dunphy said, and held a bottle to his glass.

"I will," the Granard captain said affably.

"He will," MacCarthy said to Laverty. "A most courteous man."

"He is a large man by the sound of his voice," Laverty said.

"A large man," MacCarthy said. "A captain. He has a great murderous pistol the size of a cannon."

The Drumshanbo men were staring at the pistol, as

419

though the tumult of Longford had been brought into their tavern, hardened into metal. They would turn away from it, seek out each other's eyes, and then their glances would steal back to it, furtively.

"They have the towns," the Granard captain said. "They have Granard and Longford and they are sitting frightened within them, but we have all the sweet County Longford in which to roam."

"There is one of you," Dunphy said cautiously, "that has roamed as far as Drumshanbo." It was a question, and it hung in the air.

"Not roaming nor wandering," the Granard captain said. "There are some of us that have been sent to find the Mayo men and tell them what has happened in Longford. I will ride up along Lough Allen into Sligo. I would be upon the road now if darkness had not fallen."

"There is no need for that," MacCarthy said, but only Laverty heard him. He raised his voice. "There is no need to bestir yourself," he said. "The Mayo men are at Lough Allen themselves. They will be in Drumshanbo tomorrow."

They turned then to look at him. The Granard captain stared with small eyes sunk deep into his meaty face. "What in hell does that mean?"

"There is no need to find the Mayo men," MacCarthy said. "They will cross the bridge here tomorrow on their way to Longford. And the Frenchmen with them."

The Granard captain rested his glass on the counter, and said to Dunphy, "Who is this fellow?"

"A friend of mine," Laverty said quickly, turning his sightless eyes toward the sound of the voice.

"And why is he here, Martin?" Dunphy asked.

"They will cross the bridge," MacCarthy said, "and the English cavalry after them. Go back and tell that to the people in Longford."

"Jesus, Mary, and Joseph," one of the local men said.

"He was a schoolmaster with me in Munster," Laverty said. "I knew him years ago, when I had my sight. He is a most respectable man."

"He was then, perhaps," Dunphy said. "He is not now. He is drunk now."

"What would a Munster schoolmaster know about the Mayo men?" the Granard captain said to the room.

"God preserve us," another of the local men said. "The

420

Mayo men and the English cavalry. There will be slaughter here."

"Here or somewhere," MacCarthy said. "There are thousands of the English soldiers waiting for them in Carrick. They must know that in Longford, surely."

"You are the fellow that I know nothing of," the Granard captain said. "Who the hell are you?"

"I was with them," MacCarthy said. "I was with them in Mayo and in Sligo. I saw them turn south."

Laverty put a cautioning hand upon his arm.

"Is there a man in the room who believes this fellow?" the Granard captain asked. "If you were with them in Mayo, you would be with them now in their time of triumph, and not sitting drunk in Drumshanbo. Do you claim to be a United Man?"

"Time of triumph," MacCarthy repeated. "'Tis running they are, as fast as they can, with great English horsemen after them. The one hope they have is for the Longford men to keep open the road to Dublin. Get back with you to Granard and tell them that."

"Are you a United Man at all? Let you say the oath."

"You stupid great ox," MacCarthy shouted, as Laverty's hand tightened on him. "Don't talk to me about oaths."

"'May the King's skin make a drum for the United Men to beat, and may all Ireland be free from the center to the sea.' That is the oath of the United Men, and there is not a United Man in the kingdom who does not know it."

"A lovely oath," MacCarthy said, "couched in noble and stately language. I am a poet myself, and by God I envy you that oath."

"There is a drink for you here, Owen," Laverty said, and moved it toward him with his free hand.

MacCarthy picked up the glass, his hand shaking with drink and anger. Whiskey splashed upon his fingers.

"Look at that fellow," the Granard captain said. "So drunk he cannot get the drink to his mouth. If you look at that fellow you will know why we have been slaves upon our own land."

"He has the right of it there, Martin," Dunphy said. "Take your friend out of here before he does himself a hurt."

"'Tis dark night," Laverty said to MacCarthy. "Come

421

along back with me to the school and bide there until morning."

"I will go if I please or bide if I please," MacCarthy said. "And I have no wish to bide in this town. Will no one talk sense to this man, and bid him go back to Granard?"

Cautious, voice dry as thatch, Laverty said, "Let it be, then, Owen. Lead me over to the bench by the fire, and we can have a quiet drink on our own."

"You can indeed," Dunphy said. "You can have a drink without call for payment."

The Granard captain said, " 'Tis not yourself talking, but the drink. I accept that. But drink or not, you should be less quarrelsome. You have a sharp tongue in your head."

MacCarthy nodded toward his belt. "That is a handsome great weapon you have there."

"It is." The heavy, pale face broke into a sudden grin, teeth yellow, dark in flickering flame. Awkwardly, he hauled the pistol from his belt, and held it for their inspection. "Two days ago I killed a man with this pistol. Do you believe that?"

"I do indeed," MacCarthy said. "If you have been waving that engine in the air, I wonder have you any family left at all."

"I am no stranger to weapons," the Granard captain said, but he placed the pistol back in his belt. "I understand their ways."

"You do," MacCarthy said. "But you do not understand the ways of armies. No more than I do myself. And that is why we are slaves. If you would pay heed to me, you would be doing the Mayo men a good turn and yourself as well. 'Tis no concern of mine."

He turned, and walked to the bench by the fire, leaving Laverty to find his way after him with Dunphy's help.

"There now," Dunphy said, handing them their glasses. "Have a quiet drink the two of you and then clear off for Martin's school. You have had a long evening, the two of you." He nudged Laverty.

"We will so," Laverty said.

MacCarthy rested his elbows on his knees and looked up at Dunphy. The room was heavy with the smell of bodies pressed together, shapes lit weakly by candleflame. Whiskey was a sick, sweet taste in his throat.

422

"Have you believed a word of what I have been saying?"

"I don't know," Dunphy said. " 'Tis always quiet in this town. Some of those fellows you see there are full of swagger, but 'tis all talk. I don't know what to make of either of you, yourself or that big fellow from Granard. In this place we are at the latter end of things." He rubbed wet hands along the length of his apron.

"We are all of us at the latter end of things," MacCarthy said.

Ghostly, lit by pale moon, gilt clock hands swung through time.

" 'Tis prodigious," Dunphy said. "The midlands risen up and the Mayo men marching here."

"That is a terrible temper you have always had, Owen," Laverty said, after Dunphy had walked away from them. "You are too old to be brawling in taverns."

"The army of the Gael!" MacCarthy said. "They strap a belt around a faction fighter and call him a captain."

"Sure that is all we have."

"They have more. Horsemen with swords and men in uniforms who have been to the four corners of the earth. English or French—'tis all one."

Laverty twisted his glass between his fingers.

" 'Tis true," MacCarthy said. "The Frenchmen value us no more than they would the shit from a goat. They came here upon their own quarrel, and they swept up a few thousand of us to do their dirty work. We are a nation of scullions and stable boys."

" 'Tis no business of yours. 'Tis a poet you are and not a soldier. Yours is the noble calling."

"Hired boys and cowherds," MacCarthy said. "Sure when have cowherds ever been free?"

"Ach, sure we were a great people once, for all that. 'Tis in the poetry. You have written it yourself."

Stately bumpkins, wigs clapped over matted black hair, the gentlemen of Ireland rode behind James to the Boyne —Clancarty, Mountcashal, MacMahon, O'Gorman. Their levies trudged behind them, barefoot, frightened or ferocious, pike or firelock clutched in awkward hands. William did for them. Scattered them at the Boyne, leveled them into the mud at Aughrim. Behind Limerick's walls they starved. Patrick Sarsfield, Ireland's darling, sailed off for France with his bumpkins, his broad back turned against the barefoot mob on the Limerick shore. Wreathed with the bays and laurels of an intricate language, dead heroes rode through looping lines of poetry, noble and courteous, generous in defeat. Plows and cabins, stinking dunghills and the roads of beggary. Poetry shelters us.

"Oh, to be sure," he said. "A great people." Sheep without a shepherd. Dark gold in candlelight.

A far crossroads, the Drumshanbo bridge across the Shannon. He turned to look at the men gathered around the Granard captain. He brings them a miracle, the midlands risen up, mobs with sharp-edged swords attacking companies of yeomen, slashing at bridles. Scraps of verse floated down to them, the army of the Gael, sifting through tavern dust.

"Have you been in Granard, Martin?" he asked.

"Have I not! I was there two, no three years ago, when they had the famous competition of the harpers. Oh, but it was lovely, Owen! There were harpers there from all over Connaught and Munster, and they played the one against the other in competition, like stairs mounting upward. Harpers from Munster as well."

"The best harpers are from the north," MacCarthy said. "And the best poets from Munster. That is accepted knowledge."

"Wasn't Art O'Neill himself there, the finest of all harpers. But his fingers were so stiff with age that he couldn't coax the music from them, and the prize went to a man named Fallon. Was that not a shameful disgrace to fall upon a man like Art O'Neill?"

"Two days ago," the Granard captain was saying, "on the road outside Ballinalee, there were thirty or forty of us, and I was the captain. Most of us had scythes, and a few of the fellows had nothing but long poles sharpened to points on the one end."

"Mother of God," a local man said. "And you went up against the English with those?"

"There were three or four of us had proper weapons, that we had taken away from Mr. Shaw at Castlehaven. That is where I got the pistol. But the rest had but the scythes and the poles. And down upon us rode eight of the Castlepollard yeomen, from Westmeath. Lord Longford's yeomen. We made slaughter upon them. We pulled them down from their horses and killed them. There was one big fellow that was pulled from his horse and began to rise again. I put this pistol into his eye and pulled the trigger."

"Oh, Jesus," the local man said, looking at the others.

"It wouldn't fire at all. It made a tiny click that you could hardly hear. And I turned it around in my hand and beat him about the head with the butt of it until he was dead."

"I knew O'Neill," MacCarthy said.

"The age on him, Owen! And as blind as I am myself. He was ninety, I swear to God. Did you know that he was once taken to Scotland to play before the gentlemen in the Highlands?"

"I marvel you didn't hear about the time he played before Brian Boru. You could learn the history of the world by talking to Art O'Neill and with himself in the center of it."

"Well, so. I can only tell you what he told me. He told me that he had played for Murtogh Oge O'Sullivan. I don't know was that true or not."

"That was true," MacCarthy said. "I have heard that often. Murtogh's purse was always open. He was a generous man." Bonniest of the Wild Geese, quick-turning gull hovering over the coasts of France and Munster. When the English took him at last, he died hard, his body dragged at rope's end from Beare to Cork City.

"They were the great lads, were they not, himself and Art O'Leary. The last of our own gentry. After them, we had nothing left but our own muck. And they were killed, how long ago, twenty years, thirty?"

HANDSOME, GENEROUS, AND BRAVE the tombstone in Kilcreagh calls O'Leary, shot down outside Macroom because an English shoneen coveted his horse. No sword could best O'Leary's, no man could face his rages, no woman's bed was barred to him. But it was his wife who wrote his great lament.

"You have the right of it there," MacCarthy said. But perhaps they had been but squireens, like Randall Mac-Donnell, dunghill swaggerers, glorified by legend.

"That would be a story to tell," Laverty said. "To have known Murtogh O'Sullivan."

"O'Neill was the man to tell it," MacCarthy said.

"Sure I never thought you had such a dislike of poor Art O'Neill."

"Dislike, is it? He was the best musician in Ireland, and

he ended his days playing jigs in the kitchens of the big houses."

" 'Tis said he was never in Granard that he did not stop at Councillor Edgeworth's, and well received he was."

"In the kitchen," MacCarthy said. He drank off half his whiskey. "Well do I know the kitchens of the big houses. Boxty and a cup of ale."

" 'Tis true for Dunphy," Laverty said. "We are at the latter end of things."

Sudden laughter from the other end of the tavern. Greedy, they shared the boasts of the Granard captain. MacCarthy watched him spread wide his arms. Southward, at Granard and Longford, peasants had swarmed upon the bands of yeoman cavalry, pikes ripping at reins, riders pulled to the ground. At tavern ease, an Odysseus at rest, the Granard captain rehearsed his triumphs. Crowding near him, their faces were twisted with excitement.

"I went up into the house of Mr. Shaw of Castlehaven," he said, "with eight or more fellows at my back. 'Mr. Shaw,' I said, 'I am sorry to disturb your quiet evening, but we need arms for the Irish Republic, and to drive the stranger into the sea.' They were all sitting there in the drawing room, the grandest room you have ever seen, himself and his wife and their daughter Anne, a quiet and a comely maiden. She was working at her embroidery. That room was furnished as though for twenty—tables and pictures on all the walls, a great case with hundreds of books in it. 'You are making a great mistake,' he said to me. 'I don't think so, Mr. Shaw,' I said; 'I don't think so at all.' And we took away with us three fowling pieces and a musket and this pistol with which I killed the yeoman."

"There are weapons enough for an army here in Drumshanbo," a local man said. "At Mr. Forrester's house. The Rise, it is called."

"They could be put to better use," the captain said. Cowherd, belted and armed for battle. MacCarthy had seen him before, in old woodcuts from the Elizabethan wars, moldering in Munster libraries. Rude wood-kerne.

MacCarthy drained off his glass, and then put his hand on Laverty's shoulder. "I am off now, Martin. One of these fellows will see you safely home."

"Wait!" Laverty said, startled. He reached up, and put his hand on MacCarthy's. "You cannot set out now, Owen. 'Tis dark night."

"It will be light soon enough," MacCarthy said. "Mind what I told you. Stay safe in your school. In the morning the Mayo men and the Frenchmen will be here, and after them the English horsemen. They are fierce cruel men, those horsemen."

"There is no one walks the roads in the darkness," Laverty said. "I would not walk them myself and I am blind."

"I would like to reach my own country," MacCarthy said. "I would like to cross back over the Shannon, and make my way down into Kerry. And instead I will walk to Granard. 'Tis a great fool I am."

"To Granard!" Laverty said, in a sharp whisper. "You are mad indeed! That fellow there has come from Granard and you have heard his talk. There is nothing in Granard but red murder."

"There are more roads than one into Kerry," MacCarthy said. "And my luck is holding strong."

"Fools have no luck," Laverty said fiercely. " 'Tis a long road indeed that would take you to Kerry through Longford."

" 'Tis a long road I traveled here from Mayo," MacCarthy said. "I saw the first, and I may as well see the last."

"Your luck is that you have your sight and your life," Laverty said. "And you would be a fool indeed to imperil them."

"Never fear," MacCarthy said. "I will hide myself from harm, and I will one day send a note to you from Tralee."

"I will not be waiting for it," Laverty said. "And if it came I could not read it."

"You have prize scholars to do your reading for you," MacCarthy said. He lifted Laverty's hand from his and stood up.

Laverty made a lunge to hold him, but he stood back.

"He is a blackhearted hoor," a local man said to the Granard captain. "Mr. Forrester of The Rise. And well have I cause to know it. He is my own landlord. Every quarter day he has us pay the rents to him in his kitchen, and he bids us all come on the same afternoon, and stand

427

in a long row that stretches from the door down the length of the yard. One by one he summons us into the kitchen, and he sits there behind the table, and we stand, with our hats in our hands. If there is a new thatch to the cabin he knows of it, and the rent is raised accordingly."

"He is not in his kitchen tonight," the captain said. "He is sitting shivering in his drawing room. 'I am sorry to disturb you in your drawing room' is what you should say to that fellow."

"Ach, sure old Forrester," another man said. "He is not the worst. When his son came of age wasn't there a great feast day, and people came from miles around. There were barrels upon barrels of porter in the barn, and by nightfall we were all drunk. There is a folly in the park to commemorate the occasion. 'Nicholas Forrester upon the attainment of his majority,' it says. 'The pride of both parents and an object of veneration to their tenants.' "

"Object of veneration me arse," the first man said. "There are two girls or three in Drumshanbo could tell a different story."

"Stonemasons were brought over from Boyle to build the folly. Elegant craftsmen they were."

The Granard captain laughed, and put his arms around their shoulders.

"All my life I heard about Art O'Neill," MacCarthy said to Laverty. "And then one night I saw him in the Macroom tavern, putting on the airs of a lord, and so drunk that he spilled more than he swallowed." But when he took the harp from its case, he showered the room with coins of silver and gold.

" 'Twas not of Art O'Neill we were talking."

" 'Tis but a small world that has been left us to live in," MacCarthy said. "And I think it is ending."

"We have had a good night of it," Laverty said. "But I am frightened now. I can see nothing."

MacCarthy bent down and kissed him on the cheek, then walked away from him. As he made his way through the crowded room, the Granard captain caught sight of him.

"Master!" he shouted. " 'Tis over into Granard you should go. There are prodigious spectacles there. The army of the Gael has swept over Longford like a mighty wave."

"'Tis little that the men of the midlands know about waves," MacCarthy said.

A black night. He could barely make out the cabins opposite him, bridge, river, road. A light rain was falling. He walked to the bridge, and stood upon its hump. He heard water beneath him, the Shannon escaping to the sea. There were so many roads in Ireland that a man's fate was certain to be awaiting him upon one of them. What man had twisted away from his fate more cleverly than Paddy Lynch the Whiteboy, at the end of things hiding like a wolf in the caves of the Boggeraghs, raging down at night upon the outlying big houses? And all that time, fate was waiting for him in his own Macroom, feared and hated twin, a platform built upon the square beside the market house, a gallows and a bit of rope.

In that town, MacCarthy had heard Art O'Neill play, a man old as history, blind, thin white hair falling to his shoulders, bent to his harp, fingernails long and hard as talons. Prodigal with his music, he filled the silent tavern with its notes. They spilled into the streets of Macroom, sheltered town beneath hard hills, moved dark upon dark night past Lynch's gibbeted corpse, tar-coated, heavy in irons. Crafty taloned fingers swept past lamentation to jig, swift and playful as feet on earthen floor. Here, in this town, the hills of Munster rose beneath the blazing blue of MacCarthy's memory. Soft as the breasts of women, they arched toward invisible oceans. Hands pressed hard against hard stone, his fingers sensed the bridge's curve. Remembered music struck upon the ear of his imagination, mingled with the sound of water flowing beneath his feet. The sounds joined themselves within a single feeling, transient and powerful.

He pushed himself away from the low parapet, as though shoving back a powerful weight. Farewell to you, River Shannon, he said aloud, and the sound of his voice drove the notes of remembered music back into nothingness. A world vanished with them, his memories of O'Neill's gnarled fingers, the legends of O'Leary and O'Sullivan, lost princes of an impossible past, the voices of poets in a winter tavern, summer blossoming from the hard roots of language. Minute by minute, gilt hands upon the white dial of an alien, invisible church swept away his past, rich world of memory and feeling. He turned away from the bridge, and walked past the tavern. The flames of candles flickered behind its single window, uncertain and pale. Then, with his back to the south-flowing river, he set off upon the road to Granard.

16

Moore Hall, Early September

In these final days of golden summer, Moore discovered in work his only solace. His "History of the Girondists" stretched from the fourth to the fifth of the tall, cloth-bound manuscript books in which it was contained, and then into the sixth. Their rise to power, their precarious hold upon it, the utter ruin of their fall already lay sealed in the past, stuff for scholarship and speculation, and yet they had helped to usher in this new, incompre-hensible world. The ideals to which they had held were ones shared by most liberal Englishmen; their fate had been actual and devastating. One by one they mounted the steps to the guillotine,˙ actors upon the stage of events no longer. Overturners of a world, they had been destroyed by its convulsions. The glitter of their rhetoric had not saved them, nor their brief alliances with the mobs of Paris. A pageant of events—the King's flight to Varennes, the September massacres, the resplendent oratory of the Convention, the trials and executions—lay ready for the hand of the historian. But Moore was in search of mean-ings and coherences beneath this surface. Understand one part of the pattern and you would understand it all. The Terror, the fall, first of the Gironde, then of Danton, then Robespierre, the corrupt and fear-coarsened Directory, Buonaparte gaunt and hungry for glory, even Humbert and his army of Mayo peasants.

As though obsessed, but in truth deadening his mind against his own grief and worry, he plunged into the schemes and quarrels of the dead. Wanderer in thought beside the quays of Paris, seeker of its political clubs hidden in ill-lighted streets, he fled from Mayo. He opened his mind to the weight and gravity of Paris, a narcotic strong and subtle. The affairs of his estate, which he had always taken pride in conducting without the assistance of an agent, were at the moment a bewildering compound of the ordinary and the abnormal. With a wrench, furious at the necessity, he would give his occasional attention to them. There was a heavy harvest to be sent to market, along roads swollen with military traffic. Peasant women would appear at his office to explain that harvesters, their husbands and sons, were "away," and perhaps would add, " 'Tis well you know that yourself, sir." He knew it well indeed, for he had already taken the first steps in letters to Dublin and London, which might, with great luck, save John's life.

Twice a week he visited his brother, jogging along the narrow road into Castlebar, a slender man impeccably dressed, buff trousers and dark brown tailcoat, linen white as parchment at wrists and throat. Acquaintances would meet him on the road and rein in to speak, but Moore, his pale face impassive, would nod politely and touch the brim of his hat with his whip. It was a long whip of braided black leather which he carried coiled, his only concession to the troubled times. He would not speak with them, for he courted neither their sympathy nor their malice. The Moores, save for John, were a stiff and undemonstrative family. The old merchant of Alicante had governed them in silence, silence had cloaked his love for Lough Carra and his pride in the house which stood facing it. Catholic gentry of the penal days, they had made silence both shield and weapon, shaping it for their own purposes. Bred into the bone, tougher and more tenacious than London manners and Whiggish politics, the silence of the century which followed the defeat at Aughrim. But in Moore it was joined to his contempt for fools, his innate disdain.

Riding into Castlebar was a painful duty. The evidences of the battle had vanished, together with all signs of its occupation by the rebels and the French. British troops and companies of yeomen patrolled the streets, flushed with the prospect of victory and smarting under their earlier defeat. In the gray town of gaunt, ugly shops and warehouses, Protestants could once again be distinguished by their bearing and their stride. It was a garrison town. Somewhere to the south, a final battle with the rebels was shaping, but what mattered to Castlebar was that Killala and the lands around it still lay in rebel hands. Small bands of suspected rebels were each day herded into the town—five or six unshaven peasants, black hair or red hair matted above rough, harsh-boned faces. Wide eyes which had stared upon mountains and brown, empty bogland, the eyes of Belmullet, moved in sullen terror across shopfronts, courthouse, gaol. Moore, sitting impassively upon his chestnut gelding, saw one batch of them being shoved into the crowded gaol. Troopers marched before them and behind, sweating into their heavy red uniforms, obscene, cheerful men.

Seven bodies swung from the rough-timbered gibbet outside the gaol, their bodies dragging. Two soldiers stood on guard beneath them, shoulders resting against the posts. The windows of the gaol looked past the gibbet to the commons, a wide triangle of grass crisscrossed by paths. Castlebar had learned to avoid sight of the seven dark faces. Merchants and soldiers walked the paths with eyes averted. But Moore, on each of his visits to town, forced himself to stare at them. They faced the common, grotesque and hideous, masks of a shameful death.

John was imprisoned alone, in a cell whose high, barred windows looked upon the green. Prison had not changed his fair skin, the brightness of eye, but it had stilled his nervous eloquence, his impulsive gestures. He seemed feverish to his brother, but insisted that he was well in body. But he was ill in spirit, George knew.

They would spend a quarter-hour without talking, George perched upon the low, three-legged stool, John facing him upon the narrow straw bed.

"It is horrible," John said. "I cannot bear to look out upon the grass or people passing by. The bodies are always there, hanging from that monstrous gibbet."

"Did you know them?"

"Who can tell?" John shrugged. "The gaolers will not tell me. I cannot see their faces. What sort of trial had they? Who are they?"

"If you wish me to, I will find out their names."

John buried his face in his hands, then raised it again. "They may have done nothing at all. Poor country lads seized up by the yeomanry. Or perhaps they were lads to whom I spoke and gave encouragement."

"Yes," Moore said, "perhaps they were."

"There are scores of them in the cells below, penned in together like animals, quarreling over scraps of food."

"You are entitled to special consideration," Moore said. "You were President of the Republic of Connaught."

"Some nights I fall asleep," John said, "and when I wake I think for a moment that I am at my room in Moore Hall. I open my eyes to look at the shelves of books, the bright flowers of the wallpaper. Instead I see this."

"There is reason for us to hope," Moore said. "I have written to certain friends."

"They had no friends," John said, nodding toward the high, barred window.

"No," Moore agreed. "They did not."

"Is it just that they should hang and I should go free?"

"I was not speaking of freedom," Moore said. "The charges which will be brought against you will be very grave indeed. Hanging charges. Our one hope is that we can manage a sentence of banishment. But then perhaps, a few years later, when this escapade has been forgotten. . . ." He shrugged and recrossed his long legs. The waning sunlight fell upon his polished boot.

"Escapade! For God's sake, George! Men are being seized up across the province and hanged from roadside gallows. Men whose crime was taking part in an insurrection which I helped to organize."

"That is most certainly true. It would be cruel of me to come to you with false hopes. After the Wexford rising, they hanged Colclough and Bagenal Harvey, and they were both gentlemen. Gentlemen of a sort, at any rate. Protestant squireens. Harvey was a barrister and well connected. If the government lays hands on Wolfe Tone, he will certainly be hanged, and small loss to the world."

"I am no different from them," John said. "No different from Malcolm Elliott."

"You are mistaken there," Moore said. "You are different. You are my brother, and I have friends in London. Friends in high places. Our first task is to get you out of Castlebar and into some safer place of confinement. I am troubled by the atmosphere here. It is that of the drumhead court-martial. When the Protestant gentlemen of Mayo return to their estates, they will have blood in their eyes."

"No different from them," John said, nodding again toward the gibbet.

"Are you certain that you wish to join them? My influence in these parts is a trifle diminished at present, but I can readily secure a swift trial for you, and you may be certain of its outcome. Do you wish to be hanged this week?"

"That is a cruel baiting, George. It is not worthy of you." He turned his head. "No man wants to die."

"Some do," Moore said. "I am happy that you are not one of them."

"I am a fit object for your irony," John said. "It is an art which I have never cultivated."

"Even to get you out of here and into a prison in the south will be difficult. There, I think, we must rely upon the good offices of Dennis Browne, when he has returned to Mayo. I trust that will be soon."

"From Galway?"

"He went from Galway to Dublin. You may count upon Dennis to move in the direction of power. It is an instinct of the Brownes. As a family they have always been most successful."

"You are a peculiar chap, George. You preach the virtues of prudence, and yet you use the word *successful* almost as a slur. Such a man as Dennis Browne should have all your admiration."

"At the moment he has all my hope, and should have yours as well. He is High Sheriff of Mayo. If anyone can get you out of this place, it is Dennis Browne."

"Why should he? He is more likely to want me hanged. The rebels seized Westport and drove him off to Galway."

"You may be right. But I will talk to him. He is a Browne, after all, and we are Moores. We go back a long way together, the Moores and the Brownes. There are ties of blood between us."

"They will matter little to him in what will be his present mood."

"Let us see," Moore said. "I have made something of a study of Dennis Browne, and so did our father. The Brownes manage Mayo. They are an adroit family."

"Successful. Adroit. Your irony is a marvelous instrument, George." Suddenly he smiled at his brother. "Even in this wretched place we fence with one another."

Moore returned the smile. They were linked by the years, by love, by old quarrels and reconciliations.

"Have you still heard naught from Thomas Treacy?" John asked. "Or Ellen?"

"No," Moore said, more gently. "They are behind the rebel lines. But they are safe enough now, and shall be in the future. I am certain of that."

"Certain," John echoed incredulously. "What will happen, do you imagine, when the army moves upon Killala? It will be destroyed by fire and sword."

"Fire and sword, no less. Those novels you used to read have furnished you with a rich storehouse of literary phrases. Tom Treacy is a loyal subject of the Crown. No harm will befall him, or Ellen, or Bridge-end House."

"Loyal subject of the Crown is itself a fair literary term, would you not say?"

The brothers continued to smile at one another. John was neatly shaved for each visit, and the golden hair, cropped short in the republican fashion, was brushed carefully back from the high, pale forehead. Now, locking straight into the dark blue eyes, indistinct in the cell's gloom, Moore felt the mingled aches of sadness and love. More son than brother, most cherished of their father's dreams, child of his old age. Moore heard the sound of hooves, John's shout of joy as he cleared a wall. He saw John and Ellen sitting together by lamplight, John's eyes glowing, words tumbling from him. Moore Hall would one day be his. No more.

The shouts of children floated through the window. Beneath the gibbet, staring up into the blackened faces.

"Is there any news of our army?" John asked. "Have you heard anything?"

"It is your army, perhaps," Moore said. "Certainly it is not mine. I have heard many rumors, but nothing certain. It will be over in a week. You understand that, do you not? The government has thrown a net around them and the net will be pulled tight."

"Yes," John said. "It is all over now. All but the killing."

"All but that."

"That does not bother you?"

"One day it will. When I have time. After you are safely out of the country. I detest killings, whether by rebels or redcoats or Paris mobs."

In his library, the piles of notes were neatly stacked, his sources ranged on shelves close to his moving hand: speeches, journals, pamphlets. His hand, caught within a bowl of light in the dark room, moved evenly from line to line, darted outward to the ink bottle. The pen, a bird's wing, drew up black nectar.

"I am as guilty as those who will be killed," John said. "Who could be more guilty?"

"Those without friends," Moore said. "It always comes down to that, John. Power and money. Who knew that better than our father? He was most instructive on that subject."

"He loved me too much to lecture me," John said.

In late afternoon, side by side, the stiff-backed old man and the boy walked down the long avenue, hands loosely clasped. Moore, quiet and grave, watched from the window.

"He loved you," Moore agreed. "He loved us both, but you were his darling. I knew another side of him, John. He could be a hard, grasping man. He had to be. It was a bad century for us, but he flourished in it. Power is everything, he would tell me, power and money."

"He never spoke of them to me," John said. "He told me about Spain. Orange trees, the laces and stiff brocades of the women, sunlight."

Moore bent toward the floor, picked up his hat, and carefully dusted the brim.

"I will be back on Thursday," he said.

He stood up and shrugged into shape the shoulders of his coat. Then he put on the hat, settling the stiff brim evenly across his forehead. "Are they still treating you properly?"

"Yes," John said. "I have no reason to complain. To which of our friends should I be grateful for that?"

"To King George, no less. Or rather, to his head stamped upon crowns and half-crowns."

"Money and power," John said. "You should have been a schoolmaster, George. You never tire of offering me lessons."

"You have been less ready to accept them," Moore said. "Good God!" he said suddenly. "I hate to see you here, John. We will try everything. Something is bound to work."

"It did not work for me. I tried to free this unfortunate country, and now I am here."

To free his country. His mind was stuffed with phrases from novels, gestures from plays, stale secondhand rhetoric of the liberty-mongers. But Moore remembered his

436

voice, laughing, carried across a meadow, a boy on a tall horse.

"I am most truly sorry that I caused you this pain, George. We make an odd pair of brothers, but I hold you deep in my affection."

He stood stiff but uncertain, like the words he used. A splash of watery sunlight fell across his face; thin light, no motes danced in it. More son than brother. Moore ached with grief and love. He longed to fling his arms around his brother. A young colt escaped from its pasture, he had plunged down dark, twisting roads. Then, exhausted, uncomprehending, he had been brought to bay. Father and young, spoiled son, Moore had watched them from the window, unmoving. He did not move now. His legs, heavy as stone pillars, held him where he stood.

"Until Thursday," he said, and rapped on the iron door.

"The time crawls damned slow in here, George. Will you bring me some books?"

"Novels?" Moore asked.

Save for the stretch of rebel land from Killala Bay westward, the roads of northern Mayo were open. Companies of regulars and yeomen patrolled them, but displayed no wish to halt gentlemen wearing fine brown coats, brushed hats, boots of fine polished leather. Moore could ride wherever he chose. In early evening, his mind soothed by a day spent at his writing table, he would ride down the avenue and through the gates, massive stone gateposts crowned with eagles, claws clutching rough globes larger than cannonballs. Burned big houses looked down upon him from the crests of hills; their owners had not returned to claim the ruins.

He tried to imagine Moore Hall destroyed by fire, indistinct figures carrying torches through the night, flames licking from room to room, the heavy yellow draperies of the dining room afire, his books burning like kindling, flames rushing toward rosewood tables and cabinets shipped from London. On a wall, the painting of his father and mother in Spanish court dress, carried here from Alicante, the richly textured gown alien to his mother's pale northern face, background of black and sullen red. Red flame crept toward it across the buckling floor. Moore Hall, a gutted shell facing Lough Carra, great square eyes of shattered windows. In time, ivy would spread across the shell. Not yet.

At evening, herdsmen drove home their cows, lightly slapping their flanks with wands of hazelwood. Barefoot, legs daubed with dung, they walked beside their slow, patient beasts. Seeing Moore, they nodded gravely. His own herdsmen, perhaps. He knew well his tenants and subtenants, by face, name, character, size and location of farm, names and figures in an account book. But these herdsmen, mud cabin and a quarter-acre of lazybed potatoes—who knew their names, their families, their needs? No gutted shell would mark their passing. Their cabins, ill-thatched lumps of mud and stone, lay scattered across the country, by bogland and scrawny mountain. They lived below history, and there they died—Teague, Patrick, Michael.

But history, Moore's element, lay all around him, in gaol cell, on gibbets, burned houses, soldiers on the roads. A few miles from Moore Hall stood the ruined abbey of Ballintubber, unroofed and smashed by the Cromwellians. At nightfall he rode there, pushed open the crude door fastened there by piety in penal days, and walked along the broken stones to the bare altar. The slender stone windows had been marvelously carved; his fingers moved across intricate detail. He knelt beside a tomb, and by the last light studied the figures carved upon it, saints and angels, their faces battered off by troopers who detested idolatry, but their bodies still draped in long robes of medieval stone. Whose tomb did they guard? Forgotten now, unless some tattered manuscript preserved a record. They too had slipped below history.

History was not objects, mere shells of the past, hieroglyphic whorls. It was perceived relationship, patterns formed by passion and power. It dwelled with Cornwallis and Buonaparte in the field, with Pitt and Fox upon the floor of the Commons, with Saint-Simon ferreting out the secrets of Versailles, absurd courtier-pedant measuring influence by inches. His father had spoken to him of power but to John of oranges, for each the appropriate gift. Gifts refused. For John had flung away his orange, his future, and Moore was himself but a student of power, a connoisseur of action, unpracticed in the management of men, his irony a shield against experience. History was a trooper's heavy sword-hilt, smashing the carved heads of saint and angel, weighty with certainty.

He would ride back to Moore Hall, pale blocks of Portland stone raised up by an old man's remorseless will, returned exile, coffers heavy with the gold sweated from the vineyard of an alien land, from sun-splashed Spanish hills. Here in Mayo, blue lake, red bogland, the silences of meadow and pasture, he had set the seal of his will, paced out his demesne with architect and mason trotting beside him. Here at night he took his ease upon the balcony, wineglass in hand, staring across the lake. Remembering what? In the end, history was memory. History was his father.

The Moat, Ballina, Early September

But at The Moat, Malcolm Elliott's estate outside Ballina, beside the dull waters of the Moy, unharvested fields stretched toward the river. The Moat was one of several scattered estates which lay within a neutral ground between the army, garrisoned within the town, and the rebels in Killala. Cavalry patrols would sweep northward, intent, it would seem, upon some duty, clatter of hooves and sunlight glinting from saber, then return a few hours later, the riders relaxed and joking, save perhaps for the straight-backed young officer. Judith watched them from her drawing-room window, her feelings torn. In England's uniform, they were at once her kinsmen and her enemies. Somewhere, in the north or in the midlands, men in that uniform were hunting Malcolm. But at night, small groups of rebels, three or four at a time, would slip down from the hills to visit in one of the cabins. She never saw them. In the morning the cook, Mrs. Hennessey, would tell her of them.

"They should talk to me," Judith would say, standing in the cluttered, slovenly kitchen, frustrated and helpless. "Their cause is my own. I am Malcolm Elliott's wife. They must know that."

"God forbid that they should come to this house," Mrs. Hennessey would answer, resting floury hands on hipbones covered by shapeless black skirt. "A pack of frightened vagabonds looking for whiskey. When the soldiers catch them, they will be strung up by the heels."

"They are brave men fighting for their country."

"Brave men, is it? Much you know about it, ma'am. Sure they are the same cowardly skulkers who were roaming the county two weeks ago, burning people's houses down about their ears and hauling away chairs and silk gowns and plate silver. There are families sitting tonight in Ballygawley cabins to eat their spuds from bone china. Fighting for their country indeed. Fighting for their neighbors' goods is more like it."

Mrs. Hennessey had her own friends, two Ballina widows who would walk out from town two afternoons a week to sit and talk with her at the deal table by the kitchen fire, drinking endless cups of strong brown tea. The events of the day were for them an endless source of scandalized gossip. They deplored all parties equally, rebels, yeomen, redcoats. All had violated the pattern of life, all acted upon the promptings of unfathomable, primordial iniquity. The rebels were vagabonds and thieves, the soldiers brutal savages. The two old women were horrified and delighted. They left in time to be back in Ballina before dark. Once Judith encountered them on the avenue. She smiled and they made awkward curtseys, without looking into her face. She was alone.

At night, in the small office which Malcolm used as a library, she sat with head bent toward green-globed lamp, turning pages of the books which they had read together, in London and then at The Moat—*Émile* and *La Nouvelle Héloise*, Paine's *Rights of Man*, Volney's *Les Ruines*. A cargo of eloquence, crated and corded and shipped to Mayo. Watercolors of a new world, luminous and airy. But Mayo was old, dark, tenaciously holding its mysteries—three old women, like the fates, like Macbeth's witches huddled by the fire in a room otherwise without comfort, drafty, the floor paved with uneven flags and dirtied by potato peelings. She would fall asleep for an hour, the book falling from her hand. Waking, in the small room, night pressing upon the window, the fire dead, she would sit quietly, reluctant to move. Rousseau, laureate of loneliness, would be lying at her feet. Somewhere distant, Malcolm was caught up in unimaginable events, the stuff of fiction, marching armies, battles, triumphs, a republic. As though a book had swallowed him.

She carried the lamp with her to bed, resting it on the dressing table. In her loose nightdress, hair unbound, she stared at her reflection. Gray eyes, small oval face, it returned the stare from the depthless surface of the tarnished mirror. Dark land, a dark sea divided her from her London home. One night she brought with her the French translation of *Gulliver's Travels* and, opening it,

the letter to her husband from the Society of United Irishmen fell to the floor. She read it perched upon the side
of the bed, bending forward to catch the light. A summons
from the distant world of books, ideas, principles, it had
taken him from the estate, away from her. The ringing
phrases stirred her feelings now, but faintly, like music
heard across a river. She carefully folded the letter and
replaced it in the book. Little men and big men, Doctor
Johnson had said of the book, dismissing it.

To the left of The Moat and two miles distant stood
Derrybawn, Sir Talbot Parson's house. Empty, one of the
ravaged houses. Its tall, graceful windows, opening upon
an ornamental garden, had been ripped from their cas-
ings. All through a long afternoon, a small army of men
and women had carried out into the garden furnishings,
hangings, crockery, paintings, casks of whiskey and wine,
gowns and coats, chairs, tables, beds. Torn books, ripped
paintings still lay strewn in the garden, protected by an
Artemis in white marble. To the right of The Moat, at
Cloverdale, lived Mrs. Hendricks, widow of a member
for Mayo, a tall, imperious woman, red-cheeked, nose
like a cutlass. Judith, lonely for company, visited her
once but was driven away. Mrs. Hendricks's voice, mad-
dened and vindictive, followed her down the avenue.
"Rebel! Slut of a rebel's wife! Whore!" There were no
other county neighbors.

The stable boy was gone. Like Malcolm, he was off with
the rebels. She remembered him with affection. His name
was Teague, a short, stumpy-legged boy, round head balanced on thick neck, ready smile, a shock of yellow hair.
One horse remained; the others had been commandeered
by the French. She saddled it one morning, and rode
westward, toward Lough Conn. A clear September day,
puffs of cloud, a lark high in the air. Away from The
Moat, freed from her thoughts and memories, her spirits
rose.

For a woman raised in London she rode well, her slender, small-breasted body erect, hands sensitive to the
horse. The countryside, for all its desolation, was splashed
with light. Like the moors of Scotland or Yorkshire, perhaps. Landscapes of the imagination, without boundaries.
But at Garrycloona peasants surrounded her, a dozen of
them, carrying sticks and scythes. They had no English.
Their language, alien gutturals, ominous, broke across
her in a wave. Terrified, she flailed left and right with

441

her whip and rode through them. Malcolm was fighting for them, for their nation, but she could not speak their language.

He was fighting not for them but for a word. Ireland. Not moorlands and rivers, not people, but a word. The word was a bell, vibrant and thrilling, ringing through her memories of conversations. Ireland. Ireland was oppressed. Ireland must fight for its freedom. Ireland must take its place among the nations of the world. Not Derrybawn despoiled, its rooms open to the rain, nor the kitchen at The Moat with its gossiping, profane old women. It was a cold word now, thin and colorless as ice on a winter pond.

She rode back without haste, slim, straight body swaying slightly in the saddle, through Ballina town, noisy with soldiers. The green boughs of liberty had vanished from cabin lintels, and the small Protestant shops were open again, their stocks depleted, rough boards covering their shattered windows. A regimental band was at practice in the Diamond, shrill fifes and crackling drums. The music seemed to be floating to her from home, summer afternoons in London, a military review. A small girl, she stood with her father at their Jermyn Street window, as the band marched beneath them. "Slut of a rebel's wife," Mrs. Hendricks screamed down the avenue. She rode across the five-span bridge. A corporal waved his file of men against the low wall to let her pass: a lady, small, haughty face, riding habit of green velvet, black high-crowned hat.

But at The Moat, an immense map of Ireland lay spread across the table, held flat by books at its corners. Cross-hatched ranges of hills, blue silk threads of river. mouth-filling names, Clonakilty, Lisdoonvarna. Somewhere, perhaps toward the map's center, a different army, blue uniforms, dark Mediterranean faces. Peasants marched beside them, like those who had surrounded her with scythes at Garrycloona. The names all had meaning in that alien tongue. Malcolm had tried to teach her. A word had carried him away, into the map. It was not Ireland in that tongue but Eire. *Ireland* was an English word. Bold black line upon the map, the coach road westward from Dublin: Kinnegad, Mullingar, Longford. To the north of Longford, Granard, where they broke their journey for a night, a young Mayo squireen and his London bride.

442

She left the map to wander through the silent house, part farmhouse, part fortress, built in rapparee times. In the drawing room, a great-grandfather hung above the mantel, gaunt-faced beneath white, clumsy wig. Builder of The Moat, grandson of a Cromwellian trooper, sturdy colonist in an alien, savage land. A glass-fronted oak cabinet which a month before held muskets, fowling pieces, two old swords in grimy scabbards. Above it the crudely painted portrait of a stallion, raw bones and glossy flank dwarfing the conventional background of hill, trees, steeple. Beyond the window, the unharvested fields stretched toward river. Distant horizon of mountain waste. Echoes of Malcolm's voice and hers drifted from empty rooms, thin and hollow, like a spinet's music.

The black nights oppressed her. Alone, frightened by an alien land and people, she longed for London's bustle, her family's warmth, crowds in the streets, the cries of vendors. She sought nourishment from daydreams, fantasies. The patriots were entering Dublin in triumph, green banners streaming in the clear, bright air, trumpets clear of sound as silver coins upon a marble table. Malcolm in a uniform green as her riding habit, frogging of gilt and silver. A harp, gold threads woven upon green silk, unfettered by crown. A sea of people flowed toward the green from Dame Street and Sackville Street. A schoolgirl's dream, shaped from bright colored pictures, the stiff figures of storybook heroes, beneath them patriotic legends. Flimsy as gauze, the daydream shredded, vanished. Darkness and silence mocked her.

Bridge-end House, Ballycastle, Early September

It was with John in his Castlebar gaol that her mind should be filled, but the word *gaol* brought no image to her. A stone cell, straw upon the rough-paved floor, a door bolted and locked. He could not move from it, walk into the sunlight. She herself was not free: his gaol the pivot upon which her world turned and she could not imagine it, could not imagine John within it, blue eyes and hair of gold darkened by the shadows of captivity. What she could not imagine was drained of meaning for her, formless and dreadful. The foolishness of men! She had warned him that it would come to this. In the sewing room, sunlight upon scraps of bright cloth, calico, silk, muslin, velvet dark blue, sensuous. He had not listened. Her body pressed against his, she had sobbed. His hand upon her head, stroking her hair. She remembered that, shears upon the low table, blades sharp as knives. "There will be no life for us together," she had told him. "There will be," he said; "you will see." She could see nothing.

Her father could not help her, his words awkward, fumbling between comfort and unimaginable truth, the language of a remote law which held the powers of death, of restoration. "It is a capital offense," he said; "it is in every country—Spain, France, here. High treason. It is a crime darker than sedition. It cannot be argued away." But at other times he would tell her that George would manage something, he had friends in London, powerful friends. They were a clever tribe, the Moores. Spain had enriched them, vineyards and olive trees, ships from Alicante and Cádiz. Casks of wine and brandy carried in darkness to the strands of Mayo and Galway, excisemen bribed to look the other way. "Half the gentry of Connaught traded with them. A clever tribe. We stayed here and rotted. It will not help John now. They hate the Moores, all those jumped-up Cromwellian squireens. They hate George, they hate his airs. He is a cold, proud man."

"But he will manage something. You just now said so." Manage something: how were things "managed"?

"Not here. Not in Mayo. In London. Fox is his friend there, Sheridan. They are out of power now. If Burke had lived. Burke was his great friend."

"What can London do for him?" Ellen asked; "he is in a Mayo gaol. They have built a gallows there, on the green." She remembered the green, trim and well tended. On market days, squires and their wives strolled along its paths, the men shouting to each other, boisterous, pockets stuffed with pound notes, rolled and banded. She could not imagine the gallows, wooden, hideous, a noose of hemp.

"Transportation," her father said; "it is an alternative punishment. Good heavens, child! If Lord Edward Fitzgerald had not died in prison of his wounds. Do you imagine that they would have hanged like a common criminal the brother of the Duke of Leinster? These things can be managed."

Managed: it was a man's word. They were all men:

George, Fox, Sheridan, the Duke of Leinster. Smooth and opaque, a pebble plucked from the strand, the word held and hid John's life.

They were standing on the terrace from which, a few weeks before, they had watched through the brass spyglass. Three ships from France, men in blue uniforms. "Damn them," Treacy said, remembering the ships. "They have savaged the churches of their own country. Altars desecrated, tabernacles. Priests hacked to death upon the streets of Paris and in its cellars. France, the eldest child of the Church. That was once their boast. Their King slaughtered, and their radiant young Queen. Now they have brought their madness down upon us. And with what profit to us? Penned in here, waiting for the Protestants to bring their dragoons down upon us. Bands of lawless rapparees raging up and down the barony. A foolish boy awaiting his death in Castlebar gaol. Damn them!" Awaiting his death. But something would be managed for him. She was as tall as her father, slender-waisted: MacBride blood, her father said, all the MacBrides were tall. It ill became women, but her fine features atoned for this; the Treacys were a handsome race, this was agreed upon by all. She said: "They brought liberty, John said. Muskets and firelocks and soldiers trained in the wars of Europe. A chance to fight for liberty." *Liberty:* another word. Her father did not like this one: smooth pebble rejected, flung back into the bay. "The liberty of Castlebar gaol," he said.

Men lived by words, abstractions, killed and were killed by them, words impalpable as smoke, but with the power to make prison bricks, forge swords and pikes, hew and plane the wood for gallows. "Eldest daughter of the church"; what in God's name did that mean? Tabernacles smashed open, and blood on the cobbles of Paris streets. But women live within their words, powerless and uncomprehending. Liberty was a word, but love was not: love was John's hand upon her hair, stroking it. A word had taken him away from her, removed his hand.

"He was a fine boy," Treacy said. "A high-spirited boy. Like a colt. I was very fond of him, Ellen. You knew that."

"What is 'transportation'?" she said. "They would ship him off somewhere, would they not, but he would be safe?"

"With cutpurses," her father said. "Cutpurses and har-

445

lots' bullies and sheep stealers. Perhaps George might manage something better than that. If he can play for time. Spain, North America. If matters can be dragged out. He should engage Curran to manage the defense. Curran or Bushe. There was a time when Dennis Browne would have managed the affair for him, but when Dennis Browne comes to Tyrawley it will be with fire and sword. The Protestant bullies will make a fairday of their vengeance, God's curse upon them all. You don't remember the penal days, child, and neither do I, but my father did, your grandfather. Unlicensed priests hunted down like wolves with a price upon their heads. All that was winding down, but it will be back upon us now. The clever ones sailed off to France or Spain, as the Moores did. And the rogues turned their coats, swore away their faith, denied the Sacrament. We were gentry, Ellen. You must never forget that. As gently born as the Brownes or the Moores. When the Coopers and the Saunders and the Falkiners were prentice boys in London."

"None of that matters in North America, John says. Could George manage North America for him? How could that be managed?"

But he did not hear her. His mind had slipped away again into the past, more real to him than the present, the terrace upon which they stood, bright sunlight upon ungathered crops, dull waters of the distant bay, a gaol in Castlebar. Dear God, she thought, give me patience with him. The past was his life, a box of moldering parchments, cupboards of tarnished plate, his memories of her mother.

As though the thought had traveled from her mind to his, he turned suddenly toward her and smiled. Faint wind ruffled thin locks of long hair. "You should have heard your mother on the day she learned that the O'Driscolls were leaving for America. 'Mother of God,' she said, 'they will be eaten by the red Indians. Roasted alive over red hot coals and then eaten.' Your poor mother knew little of the world. She was remembering some pious book with woodcuts of the Jesuit martyrs. The O'Driscolls are thriving in America."

"John and I could thrive in America," she said. "If George could manage it. George and his friends in London."

"They have a farm somewhere on the Hudson River, north of the city. The red Indians were all driven from

446

there centuries ago. They roam the plains of the west
now. What your mother knew of the world she knew from
woodcuts and engravings—the Alhambra in Spain, and
Venice with its canals and bridges. She would sit poring
over them for hours. Novels and books of English verse.
The Seasons by Thomson was a great favorite of hers.
And Goldsmith, of course. *The Deserted Village*. She set
you the task of memorizing it, when you were far too
young for such work. Do you remember that?"

"Yes," Ellen said gently. "I remember." Sunlight
streamed into the parlor, fell upon frayed carpet and
faded damask. She sat upon the carpet, long legs folded
beneath her. Her fingers remembered the carpet's feel,
blue and red beneath her outspread hands. "I remember
bits and pieces," she said to her father; "I didn't understand it." " 'There the black gibbet glooms beside the
way,' " she said to her mother; "I don't know what gibbet
means." "That part doesn't matter," her mother said; "the
second part is very sad, but the beginning is lovely. 'These
were thy charms—but all these charms are fled.' That is
where it changes and becomes sad." "I don't like sadness," she said to her mother. "No one does," her mother
said; "but sadness is not the same when it is in a poem. It
is not really sadness then." Her mother knew the difference between words and feelings, words and things.
Perhaps this was the secret, useless wisdom of women.

"It was a good marriage," her father said. "Our families arranged it, but we were very happy together. You
saw our happiness. We were very fortunate. Many marriages are not fortunate, but people somehow manage.
Where would we all be if they did not?"

"Where indeed?" she said, drily. Families mattered,
children mattered, families and land, tight networks of
kinship and alliances. Sure why should not arranged marriages work out as well as the other kind, if not better?
But she and John had both . . . his remembered hand, his
lips upon hers. And what of her parents? You never
knew. They were very fortunate, her father said. She
remembered his grief, remembered her own. She had her
own grief now, John's fate unimaginable, North America,
or black gibbet. *Liberty* was a word, like *sadness* in books
of poetry, or the language of romance in the novels which
her mother had read in late afternoons, with half-smiles,
sighing gently. Remembering her mother, she quickly bit
her lip, turned away from her father. Perhaps the novels

had told her of unexperienced feelings, half-believed, inaccessible.

"Never fear," her father said, misunderstanding. A hand placed awkwardly upon her thin, small-boned shoulder. "George will manage something."

Manage. For him as well, it was only a word, she knew suddenly. What did he know of such matters, a farmer haunted by stories of the penal days, hugging the shadows of a lost gentility. Somewhere off in London were great men, George's friends—Fox, Sheridan, Lord Holland. Somehow, if they wished, they could turn the lock of a gaol cell in Castlebar, in the wilds of Mayo. How? Powerless for a century, the Treacys and the MacDonnells and the O'Driscolls. As powerless as women. Her father placed his hand upon her cheek, turned her head until she faced him.

"He has been very foolish," her father said softly. "You understand that, child, do you not? George warned him, and so did I. His life is at forfeit. You must learn to accept that. It is difficult, I know. I know that you loved him."

Her father knew nothing of their bodies pressed together, straining against each other, their lips touching, awareness of his flesh beneath wool. Her father knew *love*, a word. People somehow manage.

"How did you first meet?" she asked him. "Mother and yourself?"

"Why, it was at a ball," he said, surprised and pleased by the question. "At O'Conor's house, Clonalis, down in Roscommon. It took us two days of travel, your grandfather and your grandmother and your uncle and myself. We went armed, your uncle and myself, although it was against the Protestant laws for Papists to bear arms. But the roads were dangerous in those days, footpads and highwaymen and rapparees. It was at the time when the first Catholic Committee was being formed, and Charles O'Conor and Lord French were the chief men for Connaught. The ball was a most convenient excuse for the Papist gentry to meet together and discuss the petition for rights. But it was a true ball for all that, and the women were lovely, I remember their gowns and the softness of their faces by candlelight. Art O'Neill played for us that night, the greatest of all the harpers. Your mother was standing with other young women, and she was a full head taller than the ones she was with. She was the tallest young woman I have ever seen. Who is she?, I asked your grandmother, and she told me that she was one of the MacBrides. I danced twice with her that night, and would have danced a third time, but she said that this would cause comment, and she was right, of course. Your mother was a most sensible woman, as of course you know."

"But without the Catholic Committee there would have been no ball," Ellen said. Words. Abstractions. Committees and petitions.

"Why of course there would," he said, puzzled. "There were always balls in those days, and very lovely they were. And the music we had then you do not have, in these latter days. All the harpers are dead. Like the poets." He shook his head. "We were a great people, and music and poetry were held in honor among us, as they had been by our grandparents. And all that while, we were outlaws upon our own land."

"There are outlaws today," she said, turning away from him again, so that he would not see the tears of anger brimming in her eyes. "The gaols of Ballina and Castlebar are filled with outlaws awaiting sentence."

"That is very different," he said. "Rebels who had taken up arms against their lawful King. The Catholic Committee was a committee of gentlemen. We commenced our petition with a declaration of loyalty to the King. That wretched little German is our lawful King. Women cannot understand such matters. It is not their sphere."

Sphere. In her father's study stood a great sphere, a globe of the world, two feet wide and perfectly round, mounted upon a stand of wood, great oceans of blue, and continents in browns and whites and reds. Perfectly round and perfectly seamless. If you put your hand upon it and gave it a twist, it would spin upon its brass axis, within its frame of arched olive wood. Oceans and continents blurring together. But when it slowed, rested motionless again, if you looked closely, you could see that it was not seamless af all, a thin line, almost invisible, running from pole to pole, through oceans, bits of continent. Two halves, joined together by a craftsman's cunning.

"The harvest is lost," she said, when she could trust herself to speak, looking out over the yellowing fields.

"The best harvest in ten years it was," Treacy said. "And all of the spalpeens off fighting for liberty in the taverns of Killala."

"Some of them," she said. "Some are in Castlebar."

But when they turned to walk back into the house, he surprised her by putting his arms around her shoulders, and held her without speaking. "John has friends," he said at last. "You will see. We will both of us see."

Two days later, she saddled one of the two mares that the French had left to them and rode north of Ballycastle to Grace MacDonnell. On the road she passed a group of men, eight or ten of them, three with pikes, and one with a sash tied about his waist, and a pistol stuck into his belt. When they recognized her, they touched their hands to their foreheads. The year of liberty. "You are as safe upon this road as in your own house, Miss Treacy," the man with the pistol said. " 'Tis all part of the Republic from Killala to the sea." The one word of English, *republic*, fell loose and awkward from his mouth. "Is that what we have here," she asked him, "a republic?" " 'Tis what it is called," he said; "it means that we have and hold the land." "That is as good a word as any so," she said. "The whole land will soon be ours," he said, "from the center to the sea. A great army of the Gael is rising up in the midlands, and they will join with our lads who went off from Mayo and the French with their great death-dealing cannon." "That will be a grand day entirely," she said, and raised her short, braided crop to the brim of her velvet cap. "It will that," he said.

"Eight spalpeens and a farmer with a sash tied around his fat belly," she said to Grace MacDonnell. "And a new word to add to their storehouse of English. *Republic*. I declare to God they will drive me mad with their words."

"It is not a word that should come as a stranger to yourself at least," Grace said, amiably but with a faint tartness. "There is not a proclamation has been issued without the word, and John's name at the foot of it as President. President of the Republic of Connaught."

"Proclamation," Ellen said. "President. 'Tis well that the study of Latin has always been practiced in this barony."

Without its horses, the rich dungy smell of its stables, the MacDonnell farm had lost much of its character. Ellen sat with Grace in Grace's bedroom, facing each other across a small table spread with teapot, a pot of hot water, plates of buttered bread, a jampot.

"An army of the Gael is gathering in the midlands," the fellow with the sash said. "There will be a republic from the center to the sea." Some line from a tavern ballad, but he spun it out as though he had coined it upon the instant."

"He is not alone in saying that," Grace said. "You hear that said upon every side, and pray God that it is true. Poor Randall is off there somewhere in the midlands, and most of the fellows from the MacDonnell lands with him. You should have the same prayer upon your own lips. If the army of the Gael is triumphant in the midlands, the doors of the Castlebar gaol will fly open, and John will come riding back to you."

"They will be crushed in the midlands," Ellen said. She held her cup carefully in her hands and looked down at it. "The soldiers of the English King will shatter them, and then in good time they will march north upon Tyrawley. It requires but little thought to know what will happen in the weeks ahead. The English will not let this island fall from their hands for the sake of a thousand Frenchmen and a few thousand peasants with pikes. There is the truth of the matter and the rest is all words and proclamations and green banners. A child or a schoolgirl could tell you that, if she put her mind to the matter for an hour."

"I have never before heard you speak such nonsense," Grace said, "and your voice as firm as though you were reading from the catechism. I doubt not that you have learned all this from your father. 'Tis in a different world that your father lives, and ours in a new one. My own father was as bad. They are like elks from the olden times that turf cutters turn up in the bogs, great bones that would do credit to an elephant. You did not stand at the gates here as I did when Randall rode off with a hundred men behind him, and two enormous pistols strapped to him, and the sword that a MacDonnell carried at Aughrim."

Much else has been turned up from the bogs by the loys of the turf cutters, Ellen thought, brooches and bracelets of dark twisted gold, bones wedded to stiff, decayed cloth, fragments of rich raiment, swords of iron so rusted and brittle that the curved blades of the loys shattered them.

"There is no new world that is begun with a sword a

hundred years old," she said. "And from a battle that was lost."

"You will see," Grace said. "The boots of the Protestants are off our necks at last, and off they will stay. It was our country once, and it will be so again." She rested her hands upon her knees and spoke in Irish. "The people of the Gael have risen up." She was a small girl, unlike her brother, but she had his swagger, and although she spoke the words fiercely, her brother's grin was behind them, reckless with easy confidence.

"They have risen up like a wave," Ellen said quietly, "and like a wave they are falling back to the sea. The English have retaken all of Connaught from Athlone to Ballina. Castlebar lay empty before them, and they have filled its gaol with rebels. My own John is there awaiting trial. And when they have scattered our fellows in the midlands, they will march and ride into Tyrawley, and with Dennis Browne at their side. And there is your republic for you and your proclamation and your army of the Gael. It is your English that you should be practicing at now, for it is English that will give out the rules and laws and regulations in Connaught as it has done since the days of Aughrim and earlier than Aughrim."

"You have become a great little strategist of war, Ellen," Grace said in English. "I marvel that they have not made you a captain or a colonel or a general itself, in a handsome riding habit of lobster red, you are that fond of the Protestants and the English army."

"I am as good a Catholic as you are yourself, Grace MacDonnell," Ellen said, her tone cross but her voice even and quiet. "And I do not care twopence for England or for the English King. I am as Irish as you are, whatever that may mean, and well do you know it." But what did it mean? She remembered her mother reading English poetry, English novels, a wronged baronet, a noble English earl, an infant, exchanged in the cradle with a foundling, great balls in London, the great English lords and ladies at watering places, Bath and Weymouth. "They live in the great world," her mother told her, respectful and marveling. "London must be like Paris, but the people there are more like ourselves." But her father, traveling southward toward Roscommon, toward a girl he had never seen, had carried arms forbidden him by English law. Art O'Neill, last and greatest of the harpers, had flung his notes into a Roscommon farmhouse, dignified as "castle" because the once-royal O'Conors dwelled there, an old man, blind, fingernails ridged and hard as horn. "I am as Irish as you are," she said again to Grace MacDonnell. "Whatever that may mean."

" 'Tis simple enough what it means to me this summer," Grace said. "And 'tis simple enough to the O'Dowds and the Geraghtys and the Blakes of Barraclough, and to Randall off somewhere in the midlands and to your own John in Castlebar gaol, and to those fellows with pikes that you met upon the road."

"Oh, indeed yes," Ellen said. "The army of the Gael has risen up, as was foretold in the poetry of O'Brudair and O'Rahilly and O'Sullivan and MacCarthy, the schoolmaster in Killala."

Suddenly Grace grinned, and her face was lightened by an irrelevant mischief. She lowered her voice. "More has risen up in recent weeks than the army of the Gael, if there is any truth to the tale that is being told everywhere between Killala and Ballycastle. A common fellow who holds a cabin on the Cooper land has been giving out in the taverns of Killala that Owen MacCarthy has spent the night at Mount Pleasant, and with Kate Mahony and himself in the same bed. There has been a rising up indeed, if you take my meaning." For decorum's sake, she put her fingers to her lips, but they did not hide the grin.

"Grace MacDonnell," Ellen cried, suddenly shocked into the present. Her father had the right of it, the Mac-Donnells were but coarse squireens; their life a life of stables and breeding, fox hunts and beagling, and Randall with a servant girl to attend to the needs of his body. "I am shocked and surprised that you would repeat the gossip carried by some common fellow into a Killala tavern."

"But you took my meaning all the same," Grace said. "Sure what is there in what I said that should cause you surprise? There is not a woman in the barony does not know that Kate Mahony brought Sam Cooper to the altar by first climbing into his bed, and women like that do not change. It is their nature."

"That gives you no cause to repeat the story. Not even to a friend."

"Go to God," Grace said, laughing. "You will next be telling me that Owen MacCarthy has taken vows of chastity, and is walking the earth like a Franciscan. Sure there is no woman in the barony safe from that one, maid, wife, or mother."

"More nights than one he has spent at Bridge-end House, and he has treated me always with the greatest respect, and with great delicacy of language."

"And that is because of the respect he has for your father, with his cases of books and his boxes of poetry written out for him by the old ones, O'Rahilly and the others. And he has been as good as gold with me, butter would not melt in his mouth. And that is because if he so much as put a hand upon my shoulder, Randall would be after him with a whip and a cudgel. You know Owen MacCarthy's reputation as well as I do myself, and if you do not you should make inquiries of Judy Conlon in the Acres of Killala or the hired girl at Ferdy O'Donnell's. Sure MacCarthy is a poet, is he not, and they all have a name for the one vice. That and the drink."

"Even so," Ellen said uneasily. She would look a perfect fool if she denied that truth.

"And if he had Kate Mahony in Sam Cooper's bed, then more power to his arm is my final view upon that subject," Grace said.

"Another victory for the army of the Gael," Ellen said. "But for all that, it is a sin either to give scandal or to repeat it."

"It will not be the last victory," Grace said. "We will see Randall riding back in triumph to Tyrawley, and all the other fellows with him. They will be the cocks of the walk in Tyrawley, as they should be by rights in their own country. And all that mean gang of yellow-faced Protestants who have lorded it over us will be brought low into the dust."

Ellen stood up, and walked to the window. Empty stables, and a courtyard smeared with dried dung. "Perhaps that is why Randall rode off, but it is not at all what John had in mind. He wanted a free country, and all of us living together in peace, Catholic and Protestant and Dissenter." The fierceness of Grace's words echoed in her ears, and her own sounded foolish and flat, drained of John's fervor.

"Little does John know of Mayo," Grace said, "and his brother knows less. Either they will rule Mayo or we will, and that is the long and the short of it. Randall brought home one of John's proclamations, and I declare to God I have never read such windy nonsense. All about the rights of man and the end of religious animosities which have so long divided us and all the rest of it. Randall started out to read it to us, but he couldn't go on for the fit of laughter he was in, and mind you Randall has a great liking and respect for John."

She walked with John along Bridge-end House's leafy avenue, and they stood upon the bridge, the stream beneath them shallow and quick-moving. Pebbles and stones, smooth-polished, rested upon the stream's sandy bed. "I would rather talk about us," she told him. "What else have we been talking of?" he asked her; "ourselves and the kind of country in which we will be living." "Bother the country," she said; "what need that matter to us?" "It matters to me," he said; "you will see. Women take no interest in such matters." "In you," she said; "I take a great interest in you. All those words. When they have all been spoken, the country will be the same, but you will be dead or in prison." "If we lose," he said. "You will lose," she said; "it drives me to despair that you cannot see that." The words of men were polished stones upon a riverbed, opaque and lifeless. Words drown them, drag them beneath the water's surface.

Still standing by the window, she said quietly to Grace MacDonnell, "I wish with all my heart that I had given myself to John. I wish that I had given him my body."

"Ellen!" Grace cried. It was her turn now to be startled and shocked. "Whatever has possessed you to put such a wicked thought into your mind!"

"You have small need to ask such a question," Ellen said. "He is in Castlebar gaol, and he is likely enough to be hanged there, or shipped off to some place where I could not be with him for years and years. And we have never known each other."

"I should hope not!" Grace said. "A young woman who would do such a thing is lost to all honor forever. What other man would have you then if he knew of it, and if he did not you would have practiced a great deception upon him and the marriage would go wrong from the start. There is great wisdom in the laws of the Church." She added, as an afterthought, "And great virtue as well, of course."

"Much does that matter to the way I feel," Ellen said. Her tall, straight back turned toward Grace, she hugged her elbows tightly and stared down into the bare, sunlit courtyard.

"It is a natural enough thought," Grace admitted. "But none the less sinful for all that."

"My father thinks that George can somehow get him spirited away to North America or to Spain, and I could join him there, however great the distress to my father. But I have no confidence in that. When the English win, there will be a great reckoning, and 'tis small thought they will have for mercy. They will come with vengeance in their hearts, as they have always come."

Grace stood up and crossed the small room to stand beside her at the window. "Will you not give over such notions? You have not listened to a single word I have said. It is for the English that the day of reckoning has come, the English and the Cromwellians. And long overdue it is."

Ellen turned toward her, and smiled. "That will be a grand day entirely," she said, as she had said to the farmer with the sash and the pistol. What good was there in talking to any of them, her father or the men on the road or even Grace MacDonnell, who had since childhood been her closest friend? What good had there been in talking to John, his words glittering and brightly painted, like the toys of children? She was alone with her grief and her love, and her certainty that the future was there for everyone to see, but no one save herself would look at it. If men lived among words and illusions and vanities, so too did Grace MacDonnell, not to mention Judith Elliott, that lovely and exquisite little ninny to whom Malcolm Elliott was wed, and who doubtless had sent him off into battle as Grace had sent Randall, with words empty and glowing.

"It will indeed," Grace assured her. "You will see." They all told her that she would one day see, as though she were somehow blinded, but before them lay the whole world as it did to Adam and Eve in the dreary and sonorous poem of which her mother had been so fond.

"Perhaps," she said. "Perhaps I will see." But she saw only her feelings, only her feelings were real to her, grief and foreboding, and her longing for John.

Later, as she sat the short, heavy-muscled mare in the courtyard, Grace rested a hand upon her arm. "Are you not a dreadful girl," she said smiling, "that for the sake of passion you would turn yourself into a Kate Mahony and for passion's sake let John Moore give you a tumble in the hay."

"Not passion," Ellen said soberly. "I cannot give a word

to it, but that is how I feel. I regret bitterly that he has not known me."

"I have often wondered what will it be like," Grace said.

"Which of us has not," Ellen said, returning the smile. "It is one of the few questions in life that gets itself answered, one way or the other."

"And a small enough answer it must be," Grace said, "or we would hear more spoken about it by the married women."

At the gate, through which Randall had ridden with the sword from Aughrim and with the men from the MacDonnell lands behind him, Grace called out, "Remember now, the army of the Gael has risen up." But Ellen rode off without turning her head to reply.

She met no one at all on the ride home to Bridge-end House. The road was as empty and quiet as though night had fallen, but it was the bright sunlight of late afternoon, which at that season holds hill, field, and meadow in suspension beneath a film of translucent varnish, as in the old Dutch painting which hung in the parlor of the O'Dowds at Enniscrone. Her observant eye was attentive to detail, an untilled field, a pasture of small black cattle beneath low-branched trees, a lone thornbush. An empty cabin beside the road. The men perhaps were off with the rebels, but where were the women? She remembered then: a farm without women, two brothers, silent, hard-jawed men, broken into taciturnity by the thin, bitter soil. In a field beyond the cabin, a wide slab of black slate resting upon two stones: a Mass rock from the old penal days, her father had told her. On Sundays peasants had gathered there, huddled together, the women black-shawled; before their eyes a priest, half outlaw, changed bread to flesh, wine to blood. It was different now, he had explained to her, a chapel in Killala and one in Ballycastle, Mass celebrated openly by priests ordained in Ireland. History intruded upon the Dutch painting, shattered the varnish; beneath its cracked surface objects moved and changed. She hated history. History had taken John away from her.

On a rise of ground from which she could see the distant bay, she stopped and sat motionless, the reins slack in her thin, capable hands. The bay was empty, not a sail or a hull in sight, the water lifeless and gray. History had come to them upon those waters, three foreign ships riding at anchor, filled with men, muskets, cannon. History had come ashore at Kilcummin strand, watched by fishermen standing beside their huts. Poetry made actual. Not her mother's, not Goldsmith or *The Seasons* by Mr. Thomson. "Now the soft hour of walking comes for him who lonely loves to seek the distant hills." That other, older poetry inscribed on sheets of parchment in her father's study, the black letters of an alphabet remote from English, with prophecies of ships from France, gold from Spain, the deliverance of the Gael. History, poetry, abstractions, words which had transformed and shattered her world. But for all those words, the world remained, tougher and more ferocious than language. A world of bogs upon which men died, their bellies ripped open, of black gibbets, of prison doors which words lacked the power to unlock. Erect, thin-shouldered, wiser than her years, wiser than her father or her lover, she stared at the bay as at an enemy which she lacked the power to fight or to resist.

But of that wisdom, she had no notion. Every voice in her society assured her that she knew nothing of the affairs of men, of nations, of armies moving across landscapes more vast than the boundaries of her proper world. Her sphere. In that other, larger world, matters were "managed" by men, farms sold and bought, committees formed, men left cabin and big house to follow words written upon proclamations, a banner of green silk. Her small world was bounded by a sewing room, scraps of bright brocade and calico, her mother lost in the sounds of murmurous verse, improbable romances. Wisdom rested within her father's rheumy voice, his prudence fortified by knowledge of the past, or John's eager voice, his new, bright-coined words, his talk of the future. Wisdom was farmers bargaining on market days, a grazier, pen in hand, bent over his ledgers. She took no pride in her quick, alert intelligence, the shrewdness of her judgments, her firm grasp upon the practical. These were virtues which she did not know that she possessed. She knew only that she was puzzled, and angry, but at what she did not know, and in anguish at the loss of John.

She rode on to Bridge-end House, to her father, who could assure her once again that George would manage something, that John would have a fate more fortunate than the black gibbet in Goldsmith's poem.

Late that night, alone in her room, she did something which surprised and shocked her even as she did it. Carefully, she lit the two candles which stood on either side of the pier glass which had once been her mother's. Then, facing herself in the mirror, she took off her modest nightdress of white muslin, and stood motionless, staring at her naked body. She had so rarely studied herself that it was almost the body of a stranger, a young, wild woman, an intruder upon her privacy. When the shock had quieted itself and she was able to accept the stranger as herself, she looked at her face, indistinct within the tarnished mirror, the wan light from the candles, a thoughtful face which had learned to conceal feeling. It was a handsome face, she had been told that often enough. But it was too hard-boned for beauty: her mother had told her that, softly and almost in apology. The cheekbones were too high for beauty, and the small chin too determined, the mouth thin-lipped and too wide. There were fashions in beauty, of course, as in everything else, and she had been born out of fashion. But her eyes were lovely, her mother had told her; they were her best feature, and she should make the most of them. Blue eyes, ill served by candlelight, studied the stranger's body which was her own: too tall for a girl, as everyone told her. I am myself, her mother had told her, all the Mac-Bride women are, and there is nothing to be done but to stand up straight and make the best of it. The stranger's breasts were small, pointed. She raised her hand to touch one of them, and then, guilty and ashamed, dropped it to her side. The body was shadowed, slim flanks and long legs. She turned and the stranger's body that was her own turned with her. Sudden light caught her flank in the mirror's dark, depthless surface. She raised both arms, and put her hands upon her cheeks, but continued to look, motionless now.

Then, as carefully as before, she took up her nightdress from the chair and put it on again, blew out each of the candles. Odor of candle lingered briefly in the air and then was gone. In darkness, she crossed the familiar room to her bed. Beyond the window, field and pasture lay in darkness, the moonlight too faint for vision.

She lay motionless in bed, her hands by her sides, staring upward into darkness. Presently, silently, she began to cry. Tears filled her eyes and, then moved down her cheeks. She did not raise her hand to brush them away. She cried for John, in his dark, unimaginable gaol, who had never known the stranger's body which was her own; for her mother, sitting half asleep as sunlight streamed upon the foolish book which lay in her lap; for Randall MacDonnell, riding boisterous and confident between the gateposts; for the Tyrawley men stumbling somewhere in the darkness of the midlands armed with pikes and scythes; for her father standing beside her on the terrace, comforting and puzzled, the wind ruffling his hair. She cried for her own grief, for the anguish and knowledge which were locked within her, incommunicable. Then, much later, her hands still resting by her sides, the tears drying upon her cheeks, she fell asleep.

The Granard Road, September 7

A fairy fort. Tall grasses stirred upon its earthen mound in the faint wind. Cattle grazed near it. Lucky the man who owned them, sleek glossy flanks and haunches. Powers of the air rode out from it, if you believed old men, a powerful host thronging the air like storm clouds. Fairy forts and fairy mounds, dolmens and cromlechs, their habitations hugged the land, a network of the *sidhe*. Thorn trees were sacred to them: never cut the lone thorn. Devil the help or harm they had ever been to him, but you never knew.

His father had believed in them. "It is a fool would put his blade against the lone thorn. Sure everyone knows that." Hoarse voice heavy with phlegm. In the mud cabin they sat together, rotten thatch over their heads. Weariness hung like chains from his father, pulling down the heavy shoulders. The father sat upon strewn straw, the boy beside him, solemn face and matted red hair. "Oh, by Jesus, no. Fear would stay my hand. If you cut the lone thorn, harm will surely befall you." The father nursed the jug of whiskey as you would a baby. Whiskey would battle against the weariness. "There is more work to be had now than there are lads to do it. Tomorrow we will rise up early and walk to Squire Coghill's. No beggary for us, boy. Leave that to the scruff." But one winter they had begged, across Kerry and into Limerick, standing in yards pleading with farmwives, or at crosses, running up to men on horseback. "Please, your honor, a couple of coppers for the little man here. Take a look at him would you, sir?" Remembering, shame crawled in his belly. In the cold nights, his father would wrap his arms around him. In the stolen shelter of a barn, he would talk the boy to sleep: loose, rambling stories, parts forgotten or told twice. A boy like himself, poor and ragged, but a great lady would love him, take him to her palace. Everything would be laid out there for his pleasure, ham and boiled chicken. In sleep his father's heavy muscles heaved and tightened.

Owen MacCarthy, poet and schoolmaster, remembered his childhood, an improbable misery. He was two miles outside Drumlish: the sea of his life lay between himself and his father. Affection pulled him like the strong tides. Winds of Kerry battered the lone thorn, sacred to his father's memory. He recited a poem to the empty air, driving away his childhood. A foreign countryside, bogland and wet pastures.

Drumlish had been burned. The air stank with the smell of charred thatch. Empty. Cabins with smashed doors glared at him. Cyclopes. Spirits had swarmed from the fairy mound and carried off the people. The chill of winter seized him and he shivered. Fourteen, twenty cabins, two shops, a tavern. Loneliness lay all around him, stretching toward the bogs. Empty. Village of the dead. Swiftly, mechanically he made the sign of the cross. He was terrified and did not know where to run.

He walked to one of the shops and pushed open the door. The stench became part of his mind. He thought in dirty smoke. On the floor by the low counter a man lay stretched out at his ease. He grinned at MacCarthy, his mild blue eyes fixed upon the door. His throat was a mop of blood, torn flesh, bone. Dead. MacCarthy stepped backward, grabbed the door with both hands. "O Jesus, Mary, and Joseph. O save me, Holy Mary Mother of God." He heard himself speak, like the voice of a man standing beside him. He backed out of the shop.

He stood again in the street and shouted. "Where are you?" In the flat light, the cabins mocked him. He walked down the road to the tavern, a large cabin, windows set on either side of the broken door. He hesitated and then stepped inside.

Behind the counter stood a short, bald-headed man, a pistol in his hand. He raised the pistol and pointed it at

MacCarthy, black, heavy, the mouth wide as the door to hell.

"Who are you?"

"In the name of God, point that engine somewhere else. You could blow a hole into me."

"Who are you? Where have you come from?"

"My name is MacCarthy. I am on my way to Granard."

"To Granard, is it?" He placed the pistol on the counter, beside a bottle. Dark, cool, the corners of the room lay in silence. "You can spare yourself that trip."

MacCarthy took a step forward, and the man put his hand in warning on the butt of the pistol.

"You can sell me some whiskey," MacCarthy said.

Long lips parted in a grin. Dark, uneven teeth. "You can take all you want. That is what I have been doing." He reached below the counter for a second glass. Carefully, his eye on the pistol, MacCarthy filled his glass and raised it to his lips. Familiar taste, it brought him comfort.

"I heard you clattering about out there, shouting to rouse the dead."

"There is a dead man in the shop."

"I saw him. By Jesus, they did for him. He owns the town now. He owns Drumlish."

MacCarthy took another sip. " 'Tis a curious sort of tavernkeeper you are."

The grin widened. "I am not a tavernkeeper. I came here an hour before you did yourself. We have the tavern to ourselves."

"What in the name of God has happened here?"

"The army happened. They must have moved through here after the fighting at Granard. Or before it. They killed the shopkeeper and fired the cabins. The people are off there somewhere. They will be coming back. Devil the copper will I pay for this whiskey."

MacCarthy shook his head. "The army could not have been here. I was at Drumshanbo last night, and I have been keeping ahead of them."

"Drumshanbo has nothing to do with it. The British army has moved out of Carrick, and they are stretched across the country from there to Granard and beyond. This morning they smashed the rebels at Granard and now they are moving north to fight the Frenchman. They are everywhere. I don't understand how you can fit so many soldiers into one county."

MacCarthy took his glass to a bench and sat down.

"The rebels at Granard have been beaten? Do you know that for certain?"

"By God, no man has better reason to. I was there with them. Are you a United Man yourself?"

"I don't know what I am."

"I was a captain with the United Men."

"I can believe that," MacCarthy said. "I have yet to meet a United Man who wasn't at least a captain. I met one last night in Drumshanbo."

"I am a famous United Man. Captain Francis Reagan." He put the pistol in his waistband and, taking the bottle and his glass, went over to sit by MacCarthy. "I am famous in Granard and Ballinalee. 'Tis all one now. They gave us a thorough drubbing and destroyed us utterly."

MacCarthy shook his head. "But there were thousands of you. That is what I have heard everywhere."

"We were. There must have been eight thousand of us. But they bested us. At Mullingar and then at Longford and then Granard. But we put up a fight for it at Granard. There are bodies strewn across the meadows of Granard."

"'Tis over then," MacCarthy said. "There is no hope left." Saying it, he felt an unexpected relief. "Were there many of the English?"

"English and yeomen," Reagan said. "They were as thick as blackberries in the hedges. A thousand of them, fifteen hundred perhaps. With cavalry and sergeants and artillery. They went after us piecemeal. First Longford and then Granard."

MacCarthy drank off his whiskey. Nausea lay like a stone in his belly. "You were bested by a thousand men." Clowns and cowherds.

"Sure there could be no standing against those fellows. We stood for a half hour at Granard and then we turned and ran. The cavalry rode down upon us, slashing with their sabers."

They ran in terror, arms above their heads. Heavy legs indentured to plow and spade, they ran across pasturelands. Familiar hills looked down upon their deaths. Ripe harvests behind them, the sweet, heavy air of late summer.

"It was a slaughter," Reagan said, "Outside Granard I hid behind a hedge with my hands over my ears but I could hear them screaming. For a long time there was no quarter given. There would be a man running along screaming and a trooper would ride up and cut him down.

463

One of them was so close to me that I could hear the swipe of his saber cutting down upon the fellow. But after a time they gave quarter, and the ones that were left were taken off. And all of that time I hugged myself in the hedge, and not a man saw me."

"And that is the end of it," MacCarthy said.

"Oh, by God, you never know. I met twenty or more of the fellows on my way there. They were going north, by the boreens, to see can they meet the Frenchmen. There are thousands upon thousands of Frenchmen marching here, with cannon and cavalry. There will be a great battle between the Frenchmen and the English army."

"The Frenchmen are running themselves," MacCarthy said. "With another English army behind them."

Reagan shot him a sudden, startled glance. It changed his face, marking lines of shrewdness around his eyes.

"Is that the truth?"

"It is. By now they will have crossed the Shannon. They were counting upon you fellows. And there are not as many of them as you might think. About a thousand Frenchmen and the like number of our own fellows."

Regan shook his head. "By Jesus, we are done for, then. Every road to the south is choked with English soldiers. I stood upon the rise of a hill, and I could see them in the distance. 'Twas only a regiment or two that they sent to Granard to deal with us. The English have caught us up into a sack."

"I will take your word for that," MacCarthy said. "You are a captain, after all."

"Ach." Reagan cleared his throat and spat on the dirt floor. "I am a soldier. A real one. I was twenty years in the French army, in Dillon's regiment. After the regiment was broken up I made my way back home to Longford, to my sister's house. That is why the United Men made so much of me. I taught them their drilling, months ago. The English will have my name by now and there will be a rope waiting for me."

"They will have my own name as well," MacCarthy said. "I was the schoolmaster at Killala, and I joined up there with the Frenchmen."

Reagan nodded, and almost absently refilled their glasses. He held the bottle toward the sunlight from the doorway. "Do you know these roads?"

"I do not," MacCarthy said. "But only the one road here from Drumshanbo."

"They could move down this road, or by the road through Cloone. But the English will have the two roads covered, and they will be moving up their artillery. I don't know which way to turn and that is the truth of it. We are as safe here as we would be on the roads. The hills might be safest if we crossed over the bogs to them. Afterward they will be beating the hills looking for fellows like ourselves, but that will take time."

MacCarthy walked behind the counter, and found a loaf of bread and a round of cheese. The cheese was dry and tough. He tore it into two pieces, and handed one to Reagan, who thanked him and filled his mouth.

When he could speak again he said, "Twenty fucking years with Dillon's regiment and I never rose above the rank of private. I never had any wish to. They told me to go there and I went there, and to do that and I did that. But I can tell when there is to be a slaughter. You can feel it in the air, the way you can feel rain before it comes."

"Neither hills nor roads will be safe," MacCarthy said. "Here we stand with a man lying murdered in his shop. Holy Mother of God, what have they done to this village, the bloody-handed butchers."

"What a French army would have done," Reagan said. "Or any other army. I have seen worse than this. They will be thick upon every road now, and they will kill any creature with two legs inside a pair of breeches."

" 'Tis a band of butchers they are," MacCarthy said. "Burning and killing for the sport of it, the way you would chase a badger."

"I have seen worse," Reagan said. "God send we don't see worse ourselves before the day is out."

The cheese was wretched stuff. MacCarthy chewed it without pleasure.

"What was it that possessed you," he said, "to go off with the Brigades?"

Reagan washed down the last of his cheese. " 'Tis so long ago that I can scarcely remember. I was a young lad then. A fellow came along recruiting. A major he was, Major Nugent, the Nugents are one of the old families here. He had a sergeant with him. He took a room in his brother's house in Castlepollard, and passed out the word that he was looking for likely lads to take service with the

Irish Brigades in France. There was little recruiting in these counties before him, or after him either for all that I know. They got most of the fellows for the Brigades from Cork and Kerry."

"Yes," MacCarthy said. "I know that."

He had watched one night, from a hill above Carhen. A dozen lads crowding into the two boats, jingle of francs in their ears, a rough voyage facing them and an unknown land. Recruiting officers in taverns, spry, confident men, hats cocked to one side, shrewd as graziers. Stuff of poetry: the Wild Geese. Ireland's glory, names blown backward on the wind. Dillon, Lally, O'Brien, periwigged commanders, their chargers carried them above the battle, faces stern and exultant. At Fontenoy they turned the tide, defeat certain for the French, and then Clare's dragoons swept down the field of war. We wrote their praises, hugging their triumphs, hiding their defeats. They would return someday, terrible their vengeance, overturning Aughrim and the Boyne. Here they were. Frightened veteran of France and Granard, drinking his fill in a dead town.

"Spalpeens and tinkers is what we had at Granard," Reagan said, as though reading his thoughts. "How could that lot stand up to a real army? I carried my musket in the army of King Louis. Twenty years of it."

" 'Tis all one now," MacCarthy said. He lifted an unopened flask of whiskey and slipped it into the tail pocket of his coat.

"Here now," Reagan said, startled. "Where are you going?"

"I don't know," MacCarthy said. "Away out of this place."

"We would be safer if we stayed together," Reagan said. "An armed man and a great strapping lad like yourself."

MacCarthy walked to the door, and looked out into the empty street. " 'Tis past noon," he said. "Time is running out."

"In the hills," Reagan said. "If we bide in the hills we will be safe enough."

MacCarthy caught a note of sudden pleading in his voice. He is an old man. Twenty years with the French and now this. He turned his head to look at him. Reagan had risen from the bench and stood facing MacCarthy, holding the glass in his shaking hand. Alone he would

466

never reach the hills. They would find him in this tavern, drink-stupid, his breeches damp with piss. Perhaps not. He might wander until he found a cabin, swagger in with his pistol cocked, demanding food and drink, boasting of Granard. Dull pity rose in MacCarthy and ebbed away. He shook his head.

Red face flushed, Reagan said, "Very well so. Go off and let yourself be butchered upon the roads. I will be better off on my own. I have been in bad scrapes before."

"Good luck to you," MacCarthy said.

" 'Tis yourself will need the luck," Reagan said.

The empty cabins frightened him, silence and smoldering thatch. A flat countryside, with low hills about ten miles distant from the village. A dog yelped at him, useless sentinel. Soft, faint rain was falling. A mist, with a pale sun behind it. Beyond the hills lay Cloone and Ballinamuck, the place of the pig.

From "Youthful Service: With Cornwallis in Ireland," by Major General Sir Harold Wyndham

In the annals of modern warfare the encirclement and destruction of the French army in Ireland is but the briefest of footnotes, and in truth it deserves but scant attention. At the very hour, great events were shaping themselves far off in the Mediterranean, as two great commanders, Nelson and Buonaparte, took each one the measure of the other. In the decade which followed, half the known world was to become a theater of war, from Egypt to Spain to Russia. Upon the scale of that mighty conflict, our little affair in Ireland was a paltry matter, a scuffle in a pasture.

It did not seem so to me at the time. Carrick was astir that morning with the loveliest and most exciting of spectacles, an army preparing to meet the enemy. The shouts of sergeants echoed from the low gray walls of the sleepy Shannonside town, and gun carriages rumbled down the narrow road. Highlanders, Irish militia and yeomanry, regiments of regulars jostled and banged against each other. But it was the cavalry which won my heart. Down the road they moved, past Otway's entrance gate, heavy, long-legged men, thighs bulging their breeches. Wisps of music

467

floated toward me through the misty air, shrill fifes and rattling drums.

A keen emotion held me captive. I wanted to run toward them, to cry out something, I knew not what. It was the finest army in the world, and it was moving into battle. I was very young, it must be recalled. Other men of my age were still in university, heads crammed with Horace and Livy. What would they have for memories but fagging and treats shared in drafty rooms? Fife and drum attended us, our colors a scarlet river coursing through a brown countryside, glints of light from steel and silver.

"Worth remembering," Cornwallis said to me suddenly. "But it isn't like that at all, you know. Hacking away with those sabers, horses with bellies ripped open. By God, I wouldn't like to be Monsieur Frenchman this time tomorrow." Early though it was, he had arisen to see them off, clear-eyed and freshly shaved. "He will never reach Granard, our Monsieur Humbert. He may pass Cloone, but he won't reach Granard. We'll be waiting for him. A nasty little battle he can make of it, if he's angry enough."

It was a cold morning, with a haze on the stubble fields.

"Why will he fight," I asked, "if he has no chance of winning?"

"Why?" Cornwallis looked at me over the tops of his spectacles. "Why, for the glory of la belle France, of course. Generals do that. Two parts of being a general is simple childishness. A general must put up a decent fight, get a decent number of his men killed. Then he can surrender with honor. If a shopkeeper conducted his affairs upon such a principle he would go smash. It is high time that you and I had some breakfast, young man."

But in the avenue he stopped and turned toward me. "The rebels will be the losers from all this. Rebels against the Crown. Much they know of the Crown, the wretched creatures. I watched them in Wexford, going up to the gallows. Great dark eyes. No help for it."

Peasants stumbling to a gallows. It was indeed a soldier's duty, but it lacked chivalry and gallantry, which in those days were of great consequence to me. Cornwallis read my expression.

"Chasing French generals and passing in review is only a part of this business, young man. We clean up messes, like scullery maids. We serve as common hangmen. And more often than not we make a poor job of it."

But his saturnine wisdom could make little impression upon me that morning, for my eyes were dazzled by color, and my ears filled with martial music. And this I believe he perceived and respected, for we had a most pleasant breakfast with tea for myself and for him his innumerable cups of chocolate.

When we had finished, he called for his writing equipment, and scrawled out a short letter in his impatient hand, which he then sanded and gave to me.

"Now then, Prince Hal," he said. "I want you to get yourself an escort of cavalry, and take this to General Lake. You will most likely fall upon him this side of Cloone. You may read the letter if you wish. I have informed him that the enemy's lines forward have been sealed off, and that I am moving to the attack. If he himself finds an earlier opportunity to give battle, he may do so."

I was of course surprised and flattered that he should have entrusted to me so important an errand, and I attempted to thank him but he waved me quiet with a negligent hand.

"You are carrying a letter for me, that is all. But it will give you a part in your first battle. You want that, do you not? You do, of course. After tomorrow, you will not be the same person. You will know that this is a trade, like any other. But a dangerous trade. Mind yourself."

His geniality gave me confidence. "It is a trade which has held your interest for a long time, milord."

He glanced at me sharply, but then smiled. "It has its attractions. Few soldiers ever tire of it. I have read an essay by some scribbler upon this fellow Washington. He was a farmer at heart, it would seem, happiest on his plantation, among his slaves. Stern duty called him into the field. I don't believe a word of it. Mind you, you will not be seeing a true battle—a handful of French and a rabble of peasants. It will be an ugly business. It is best that you should see it."

"But if the outcome is certain . . ." I began.

"The Frenchmen are soldiers, of course," he said, as though he had not heard me. "But the Irish are common rebels. That is the ugly part of it. We must do our best. Needless cruelty serves no purpose." He seemed to be struggling in his mind with some unvoiced concern. "General Lake has never learned that lesson. He is a blunt, coarse fellow, and a damned poor soldier. I tell you this in confidence."

"Of course, sir," I assured him.

"We have had a close shave, I can tell you. If the French had landed in force, if the peasants throughout the country had rallied to them. The Irish must be taught a lesson. London will expect that. We are schoolmasters as well, you see. Scullery maids and hangmen and schoolmasters. The lessons taught by armies are hard ones."

"We will give them a sound drubbing," I said in my innocence.

He smiled at me, but it was a distant smile, without humor. "Yes indeed, Mr. Wyndham. We will do just that. We will give them a sound drubbing." My words, as he echoed them, seemed those of a schoolboy, as doubtless he intended. He measured out another cup of chocolate. He had a service which accompanied him in the field, narrow cups of china, red-glazed, with a design of flowers worked upon the surface.

But his words could cast no chill upon my morning. The task of selecting a cavalry escort and the importance of my errand exalted me, but before I addressed myself to the task, I paused again at the entrance gate to watch the army moving past me out of Carrick. I lack literary skill to suggest the splendor of that morning, or my own excitement. Words are but poor things, dull blocks of wood or iron hammered clumsily into place. What would I not now give to recover that excitement, or the glamor which youth casts upon events. And yet it is all vivid in my mind, the wide gray river, the rolling countryside, the lines of marching men, their music and bright colors. I would not exchange a year of my life for my memory of that morning. The scenes which I was to witness in the next two days sought to stain that memory, a stain of blood moving across the margins of a page. The stain is old and faded now, a dull faint brown, but the picture is vivid and bright. It was the last morning of my youth. Presently, as a huntsman might say, I was to be blooded.

From the *Memoir of Events*, Written by Malcolm Elliott in October, 1798

Toward evening, we entered the village of Cloone, a mean village straggling up a steep hill, and dominated

by its church, a spare building with a spindly steeple.
We made camp in the churchyard, although this is perhaps too formal a term, for we were at the point of
exhaustion, and sank down gratefully beside the gravestones. I remember the inscription upon one, the florid
lettering subdued by rains and weather. THY FAITH HATH
SAVED THEE; GO IN PEACE. French grenadiers or Irish
rebels, I doubt if one in fifty of them could read it, and
it seemed standing there expressly for my instruction. We
had moved by forced march, not pausing for food or rest,
along the gloomy length of Lough Allen, and crossed the
Shannon at Drumshanbo, where an attempt was made by
our rear guard to destroy the bridge. This was, however,
prevented by the promptness of Colonel Crauford, and in
the skirmish Sarrizen and some sixty of the French
were killed or taken prisoner. Between Humbert and Fontaine, who thus became his principal commander, there
now existed an extreme hostility, and they barely spoke
to each other.

A somber fatalism had descended upon the French
troops, matched perfectly by the bleak and inhospitable
land, the scattered farms, the sedge-choked lakes. Yet
I again felt closer to them than to the Irish, my own countrymen, in whose faces I could read only exhaustion and
bewilderment. One of them, a strong, heavy-shouldered
farm lad, still carried the flag of rich green silk. In the
windless air, it hung limp from its standard. O'Dowd
and his squireens rode together, staring absently upon
the dark lake.

To be sure, we believed that we were marching to join
our forces with those that had risen up in the midlands,
but Longford, although at most thirty miles distant, must
have seemed to those fellows more remote than Mayo. In
Drumshanbo we heard much talk of the rising, and were
even told that a captain of the United Men had been
sent out to meet us, but of this man we heard nothing
further. We knew only that Crauford was close behind
us, and that the main body of the British would be waiting for us somewhere to the south. I believe that in some
dim, inchoate fashion the Irish did trust that in the midlands, or if not there then somewhere in Ireland, a
mighty force had raised itself up, "the army of the Gael,"
and to this shadowy host they had entrusted their salvation.

We did not pause until we reached Cloone, and Hum-

471

bert rested us there only because we could go no farther. The men spread themselves out from the door of the church to the foot of the grassy hill, stretching out at full length or sitting with hands clasped about their drawn-up knees. They looked at each other or, more covertly, at Humbert, who was tireless, his large dark eyes studying the countryside. Teeling was now his only confidant, and they stood together close to the narrow, unglazed windows of the church. It was very like the church in Ballina, homely and familiar.

THY FAITH HATH SAVED THEE; GO IN PEACE. It was the gravestone of a man named Thomas Ticknell, who had died in 1701 at the prodigious age of eighty-one. He may have crossed over with Cromwell, his head stuffed with cannon fire and the Bible, claimed his acres here, settled in like a colonist amidst red Indians. His people were mine. I read our signatures in gaunt steeple and tombstone text. Inside the church, stone tablets set upon whitewashed walls, I could have found our kinsmen—Harvey, Greene, Atkinson, Benson, Elliott. Fragments of a world, they held me in mute argument. Why have you come here with these murderous pikemen, our ancient enemies, Papists gabbling in Irish? In the weed-choked churchyard, I was reproved by the decencies of my childhood. Steeples like pointing fingers stretched across the island, each one offering assurance that we were bound together, that we had come to stay. I remembered my father, tall and sententious, pacing our pastures as I ran to keep up with him. Biblical phrases, an inheritance of words, laced his language. At Ballina, a gravestone like this one stood above his head.

Such reflections are proper to my present habitation, a chill gray prison on the far outskirts of Dublin, where I await execution of the sentence which has been passed upon me. But the human mind, capacious and prodigal, can flood memories upon us in a single unbidden moment, rich in sights and odors. I was amidst an alien people, separated from them by race and creed, by the very words upon our lips. And yet in those bright and optimistic Dublin days we had formed ourselves into a Society of United Irishmen, believing that such differences must melt beneath the mild sun of reason.

As though in confirmation of my thoughts, Murphy, their odious priest, rose to address them, tireless as Humbert, dressed like a crow in rusty black. My Irish is so faulty that I could make out but a third of what he said, but he spoke with his face and squat body, his hands clasped to his chest. *Heretic, Protestant, Englishman,* the words were graceless rocks around which the torrents of his speech swirled and eddied. Unforgiving and long-memoried, he might well have been a hunted cleric from Cromwell's time, exhorting a band of wood-kernes. But his listeners, though respectful, were now too tired to heed them. Beyond them, the French listened with weary contempt.

We rooted out bones from the shallow hillside graves to make fires for our cookpots. The fires were beacons for Crauford, but he knew well enough where we were, fox hunter riding to the kill. I crouched beside two of the Crossmolina men. One of them plunged his knife into the pot and then held it toward me and I took the hot potato with both hands. "It is a sorry business for a gentleman like yourself," he said in English. A deep ravine divided us, spanned by his courtesy.

"Is it far that we have yet to go?" he asked.

"Not far," I said. "We are less than a day's march from Granard."

"There is a great gathering of the Gaels at Granard," he said.

"That is what we believe," I said, but he caught the hesitation in my voice, and his eyes, wild as a mountain hare's, turned away from me.

I thought again of Judith, whose mild eyes grew bright with passion. Landscape, music, poetry, moonlight upon a flowering hedge—they stirred her heart, and I was stirred by her. Mayo, which to me was but the hard, exacting business of the estate, flowered beneath her fancy. Often I would be at work in the room which I used for the business of the estate, heavy black-bound ledger books from my father's time stacked upon the floor, and she would burst in, talking as she moved, her eyes luminous and soft. It would be a trifle, or what I then thought a trifle, although now I know that we were bound in love by such moments. Suddenly I knew that I would not see her again. My mind was upon her, though I watched the lad from Crossmolina cramming his mouth, and the knowledge came to me with the flat certainty of noon. In the event I was mistaken, for she was permitted to visit me before the trial and twice since then, for which I stand indebted to the humanity of the Attorney General.

Thus, my thoughts upon that final night were a jumble. I beheld my life as a bright, small room at the end of a dark corridor. The room was crowded—Judith, my parents, Tone and Emmet gesticulating like Punch and Judy, the auctioneer at Castlebar from whom I had bought a gelding, a London girl whom I had courted before meeting Judith. My memories were fragments of glass, sharp as razors. I held them tight, although they cut and brought the blood.

At some time in the night, one or two o'clock I would judge it, twenty men from Granard arrived, stumbling in the darkness up the steep hill, and we learned from them that the midlands rising had been crushed and the trap sprung. Although they had been searching for us, they came into Cloone by chance, and the sentries fired upon them, fortunately without result. We were as great a shock to them as they were to us, for the rumor had taken hold that we were a mighty army—thousands upon thousands of French and a like number of rebels, with cavalry and monstrous, terrifying cannon. Instead, they found another band of fugitives, sheltering in a graveyard.

They had a leader, a "captain" or "colonel" of some sort. He peered through the darkness at us, as though not believing that he had found us, and Teeling got answers to his questions only by taking his arms and shaking him. He spoke in long-winded braggadocio of how they had seized a building at Edgeworthstown and of how they had defeated companies of yeomen, and, over and over, he spoke of a battle near Granard. His words were those of pothouse ballads, empty and swaggering. It was as though he was rehearsing a song about himself which other men would sing. "We drove our pikes against the yeoman cavalry," he said. "King George's regiments we put to flight." He was reshaping what had happened, peopling with heroes the landscape of a disaster.

For such it was, and at last we got the truth from him. The rebels had been slain or put to flight, and the British were drawn across the roads in a tight, heavy knot. The defeat had been utter. At least a thousand men, making full allowance for his hyperbolé, lay dead in the fields outside Granard. "They fought like wild wolves," he told Teeling, "and with bursting hearts." "They have been smashed," Teeling said in French to Humbert. "These are survivors." Humbert, who must have understood as much, nodded but continued to stare at the Granard man.

"Holy Mother of God," Randall MacDonnell said to me. "Did you hear him? We are as good as dead. Did you hear that man? There will be no way out of this place."

But I could find nothing to say to him, and we stood silently together until Teeling joined us. By the faint starlight I could make out his long pale face, but his voice startled me, calm and harsh.

"It will end tomorrow," he said "We will move out in the morning, but they will be upon us before noon. General Humbert proposes to take us into Ballinamuck, a village that this local fellow knows of. There is a good hill there and a bog to protect our flank. It will not be much of a battle."

"Fight, is it?" MacDonnell asked, indignation fighting with fear. "What good will that do?'

"If we remain in good order we can put up a fight for an hour or two. That will end matters."

"Sure an hour's fight will have us all killed," MacDonnell said. "And what sense is there in that? 'Tis a few men with white flags that we should send out, and surrender now, before we are blown apart by their bloody cannon."

"It will be more difficult to surrender than you believe. For us, that is. It will be a different matter for the French."

"They wouldn't murder us in cold blood," MacDonnell said.

"Murder?" Teeling asked, as though weighing the word. "It is not called murder, Mr. MacDonnell. We are rebels in arms against the Crown. The British are not obliged to give us quarter. I doubt if they will wish to."

There was a long pause before MacDonnell replied in a low, spiritless voice. "I call it murder."

"And so do I. So does Mr. Elliott here. General Humbert would not. He gave no quarter to the peasants in the Vendée. We are not protected by the rules of war."

"The rules of war permit the slaughter of unarmed men?" I asked. "Men who have surrendered? Yes, I would indeed call that murder." I am astonished now that we should have spoken so calmly of our own deaths, and yet we did. The human disposition to argue against calamity is relentless.

475

"My God," MacDonnell said. "Oh, my Jesus." Whether as prayer or curse I could not tell.

But as we spoke together, all about us was commotion. The Irish, dragging themselves wearily awake, grasped but slowly, through ripples of rumor and talk, that no help awaited us to the south. Fear grappled them then, like iron chains, made more terrible by the darkness and confusion. I joined the Ballina men, to explain to them as best I could what had happened, but my words were wasted upon them. They had come so devoutly to believe that an army of the Gael awaited them that nothing would persuade them to the contrary. Yet at the same time they accepted that some catastrophe had occurred in the south. It was useless to reason with them, and after a time I walked away.

Humbert stood facing the south, his arms clasped behind his back. I could not read his face. Nothing had served his purpose. The country had not risen up, the fleet from France had not arrived, the Dublin road was blocked. Spread out all around him were the men whom he had led and dragged across Ireland, foreign and remote as Laplanders. He was thinking, perhaps, that at last he had been trapped. *He* was trapped. Not an army of two thousand men, but one commander, so great is the vanity of generals. In a village called Cloone, an ugly name on a map. As I stood watching him, he suddenly shrugged and straightened his shoulders.

He saw me watching him and stepped toward me. "Your Irish down here were useless," he said, in a grating, angry voice. "Worse than useless. They have dragged me down into this dark bog. They will deserve what happens to them."

"They trusted in us," I said. "And already they have begun to pay. They were killed in their hundreds at Granard."

"They will be killed in their hundreds out there," he said, waving his arm toward the dark south. "I once wondered why the English had such contempt for the Irish. Now I understand."

He jerked his head toward the men invisible on the slopes below us. "You wanted to make a revolution with those. You are a fool." He turned then and walked away from me.

Toward morning, with the first streaky light, we were assembled to march, but only with difficulty. The French

476

troops had no stomach for battle, and the sergeants were compelled to thwack them with sabers. As for the Irish, bewilderment had settled so deeply upon them that they moved as they were bid, but slowly, as though not fully awakened. We were no longer an army, so much was clear even to my unpracticed eye, but we went through the motions of an army, squaring ourselves off into columns. MacDonnell had managed somehow to recover his spirits, or at least his style, for he behaved as though saddled for a morning's hunt, bantering with the men and cajoling them with coarse pleasantries. Vanity and recklessness had brought him out with us, a roaring horseman with a foolish plume stuck in his hat, but he was now to prove his merits. I watched him with a mild envy. For myself, I had before this lost confidence in our enterprise, and awaited with dull heart its predestined end.

In the dawn hours before we set forth, other men from the Granard fighting joined us, men who had moved northward because no other path lay open to them, or else men who had believed the rumors that we were advancing with a powerful host. More than half of them still carried pikes or weapons of some sort, and these Teeling formed up into a company. Their familiarity with the countryside seemed but to make more intense their bewilderment and fear. And also, about an hour before we left Cloone, we were joined by Owen MacCarthy, the Killala schoolmaster, who had deserted from us outside Manor Hamilton.

More even than the rest of us, he appeared exhausted, his eyes, beneath the mat of red hair, sunk into their sockets. He stood irresolute upon the path which led down the hill, and then walked toward my own Ballina men, with one of whom, Michael Geraghty, he had struck up a friendship.

Randall MacDonnell leaned down from his saddle and shouted to him. "Owen MacCarthy! You were lonely for our company."

MacCarthy looked over toward him. "There is no way out of here. I have been within a mile of Mohill, and the road is thick with British soldiers."

Teeling walked over to him and said, "Speak in English. Where else have you been?"

"I began in Drumlish. It has been burned and a man killed in his shop. Then I walked toward Mohill, but when I caught sight of the soldiers I turned off onto this road. I spent part of the night in a cave, hugging my knees with my clasped hands."

"You would have been wise had you stayed in the cave."

"Sure I am not a fox or badger. I had a bottle with me, and when it was done I set forth into the darkness. The English have covered the entire world. They burned Drumlish, the great brutes. Would you not think that men hurrying to a battle had no time to burn a village."

"They are in no hurry," Teeling said. "They have the day before them."

At exactly six, by my father's heavy gold watch, we began our march, two long, straggling columns. Humbert, mounted, lingered on the hill, holding a spyglass to his eye. Perhaps he could see the first of the English moving in their southerly direction from Mohill.

As we marched out, I turned round to look at the church. Prim and disdainful, it held itself aloof from our tumult. It was so like the Ballina church that they might have been built from the same set of plans. And again my memory stirred within me. Spare, undecorated, it stood guard over Thomas Ticknell, Cromwell's slumbering trooper.

17

From "Youthful Service: With Cornwallis in Ireland," by Major General Sir Harold Wyndham

I set out with my small escort, feeling myself a most important personage to be carrying the order for battle, and riding, if only for an hour, at the head of a body of horse. I was now making my own jingle and flash of scarlet, like the dragoons whom I had envied. Cornwallis must have derived amusement from the spectacle which I presented, for the color of war had long since been bleached from

478

his thoughts, and it remained for him only a duty to be scrupulously performed.

The countryside, after we had left behind us the pleasant river, was somewhat somber in appearance, farmlands divided and redivided by rocky walls, yellowing fields, low hills. But the morning itself was splendid, and the air as fine a tonic as claret. Birds, starlings and rooks, were surprising in their numbers, breaking suddenly from trees like bursts of grapeshot. Far from the road, down narrow lanes, stood the cabins of the natives. I saw no one stirring near them, and it was most curious to see them washed clear of their usual swarms of shouting children. It was in truth a silent scene, save for the thud of our hooves, and bird cries, the abrupt whir of wings.

It was only when we drew near to Mohill, which stands midway between Carrick and Cloone, that we began to encounter the burned cabins. The village itself had been left untouched, so far as I could judge, but the outlying cabins had been fired, and the stench from those which stood near the road carried to us. It seemed a poor way to begin a battle, and I turned to observe its effect upon my escort, but their stolid faces told me nothing.

A mile beyond the village we encountered a most unexpected sight, a body of some fifty French prisoners marching along under guard in the direction of Carrick. The officer in command, a Captain Milett as it proved, rode up to greet me. He explained that this was the rear guard of Humbert's army, captured by Crauford as they attempted to destroy the bridge over the Shannon at Drumshanbo.

"Did you help capture them?" I asked.

But he laughed and said, "I am only a poor officer of militia. Crauford commands dragoons. He caught one of their generals, with a droll French name." He scratched his chin. "Can you speak any French? Give a shout and ask their general's name."

I called out to the prisoners, and several of them answered, "Sarrizen."

"Saracen, that's it. Like a bloody Turk. The Saracen's Head, like the signpost on the tavern."

"Is he not with them?"

"He is with Billy Lake, and bloody glad to be with him. Ten minutes after Crauford fell upon him he was riding up and down with his hat stuck on the end of his sword in token of surrender. And this lot are bloody glad to be walking down a country road, swinging their arms in the sunlight. I wouldn't like to be on the sharp end of Crauford's saber."

They did not seem either glad or sorry, but only exhausted. I thought of the extraordinary march they had made, from Mayo into Longford. A few were swarthy southerners, but most could have exchanged coats with Millett's men. The difference lay in their eyes, round and dark with fatigue.

"Where is Lake?" I asked. "I have orders for him from Lord Cornwallis."

Millett stroked the neck of his horse. "You had best move quickly then, or you won't be in for the kill. Crauford has been keeping a grip on the Frenchman's tail, and now Lake has moved to close the gap. Infantry, cannon, the lot."

"But where should I go?" I was beginning to see that battles are less tidy than a morning room in Carrick.

"Toward Cloone. Keep to this road and don't turn at the cross. You should be able to see all of them from there; the town is on a hill. The enemy camped there last night. In the churchyard." He looked toward one of his soldiers, a gangling boy who stood leaning on his musket. "Do you know what the savages did? They pulled up the bones from the graves."

"What?" I asked. The grotesque words leaped at me from nowhere.

"The natives. The rebels. They used the bones of the dead for firewood. There are bones scattered across the churchyard, between the stones."

An ugly incoherent image sought to shape itself in my mind.

"Savages," Millett said. "Do you have another word for them? Damme if I do."

I did not reply. Like animals in their den, I thought, the earth strewn with bones.

"That is my quarrel with this lot," he said, nodding toward the French. "Putting muskets in the hands of those savages. I trust I am as tolerant as the next man, but I draw the line when it comes to savages. I was in Wexford. I saw what happened to the poor Protestants there."

"What will happen to them now?" I asked, nodding toward the French, as he had done.

"These lads? They'll be exchanged. Back they go to

480

la belle France. They won't be eager to visit this damned place again."

"No," I said. The air was cool, despite the autumn sun.

"I have all day to get them to Carrick," he said, "but you'd best not waste any time."

"No," I said. "I have never seen a battle."

"No more have I," he said. "But I can live without the sight. Not that it will be much of a battle. According to Sarrizen, they are about ready to drop from fatigue."

From beyond the hill, faint and fragile, came a sound like furniture being pulled across the floor of a distant room. We looked at each other.

"Yes," he said. "That could be the artillery." He half raised his hand and then lowered it. "Good luck to you, Mr. Wyndham."

"And to you as well."

"None needed here," he said. "I shall be snug in Carrick, watching these lads eat their frogs."

I never saw Millett again. His company was one of those which took part in the final operation in Killala and along the Belmullet road, earning there an unenviable reputation for severity toward the inhabitants. When I had gained the rise of the road I turned round to wave to him, but he did not see me.

Cloone, as he had told me, stands upon a high hill. As we rode toward it, the bursts of sound grew more frequent, and even my unpracticed ear could now recognize it as cannon fire.

Although Lake had moved forward, Cloone was held by a regiment. The churchyard was crowded with uniformed men. I had to dismount to make my way past them to the church, where a knot of officers stood facing south. I attempted to introduce myself and explain my erand, but they paid not the slightest attention. One of the officers, a major, held a brass spyglass to his eye.

In the very far distance, great masses of men were spread out in a manner which made no sense to me at all. Some were in motion, clumps of horsemen and infantry moving forward in straggling lines. A dense, solid body of men stood motionless on the slopes of a hill. The cannon looked no larger than slivers of black wood. As I stared at them they spoke again. Smoke hung about them. To the left of the hill, distant from it by a mile, lay clumped together the cabins of a village, like children's toys. The cannon spoke again, and before the noise had quite died away a body of horsemen rode toward the hill. Beyond hill and village, red bog stretched away toward the horizon.

One of the officers was a young man of my own age, with a smooth, pale face and features delicate as a girl's. I seized him by the arm and asked him what was happening. He turned toward me impatiently, his eyes so full of the scene that he scarce saw me. But I kept my grip upon his arm and repeated the question. I think that when he understood me at last he welcomed the chance to display his superior knowledge.

"That's Humbert down there," he said, pointing to the base of the hill. "He contrived to seize the hill before we forced him to turn and fight us. A few minutes ago he shifted his main strength to the eastern slope so that he could meet our cavalry." The cannon spoke again, this time a more ragged sound. "That will be the last barrage, unless we want to blow off Crauford's head."

"Then those are Crauford's dragoons?" I asked.

"Crauford's or Lord Roden's. Who can tell at this distance?"

Now a body of our infantry also moved forward toward the hill, at a kind of slow trot, on a line at right angles to the village.

"And the rebels? Where are they?"

"Why, with Humbert, I should think. Down there, perhaps, holding the road that leads from the hill to the village. I believe that General Lake is in the village. He rode off in that direction."

"Rebels perched upon a slope," the major said without lowering his glass. "Lake must think he's back in Wexford. At Vinegar Hill."

"I wonder if this one will take him as long," my lieutenant said, and the major laughed.

"He should have more confidence now," the major said. "Since then he has won the races at Castlebar."

"Perhaps Lord Cornwallis has confidence in him," I said. "I am carrying his dispatch."

The major turned toward me. "Who the devil are you?"

"Lord Cornwallis's aide," I said, feeling unaccountably prim. "I am carrying a dispatch for General Lake. Requesting him to engage the enemy."

"Are you indeed? Lake has anticipated his orders. Today will not be a second Castlebar. Cornwallis doesn't lose battles. The cavalry he sent up from Carrick are behind those hills, holding the Granard road."

"Perhaps I should ride down into the village," I said.

"By all means, young man. It is safe enough from all that I can tell. Matters will be settled between the hill and the bog."

"What is the name of the village?" I asked.

He paused for a moment, screwing his eyes half shut. "Damme if I know. Does anyone know what it's called? The Irish must know. That is a Longford regiment over there," he said, pointing with his glass.

A battle fought upon British soil, and we did not then know what name to give it. Ballinamuck. Years later, in India, I asked an Irish officer serving with the company what the word meant. He was insulted by the suggestion that he might understand the language.

"He lost one battle," I said.

"What?"

"Lord Cornwallis. At Yorktown. He lost the American colonies. He has described it to me. When he sent his sword to Washington, he had the bands play 'The World Turned Upside Down.'"

"That was different," the major said and resumed his inspection of the battle. It was amazing how closely the scene resembled those engravings of battle plans, which had always seemed to me improbably neat and spruce, with their lines and arcs to indicate the positions of infantry and cavalry, and triangles to represent parks of artillery. Our cavalry and infantry were still at the advance, and now a second regiment of horse moved forward from the village. Its line of attack was upon the right flank of our infantry, as Crauford was placed upon the left, and if the lieutenant was correct in his surmise it would drive against the rebels holding the road. There were no lines of retreat open to Humbert unless he chose to scramble up the hill or fall back onto the soft, wet bogland. It was as though a map had been unfurled before me, the colors blurred and indistinct, but the lines and contours sharp. The excitement which I had felt earlier in the day rose within me again. No one, I believe, has ever witnessed his first battle under more agreeable circumstances, and it was therefore with feelings of sharp and pleasurable anticipation that I bade farewell to my new-found friends at Cloone and rode down toward the village of Ballinamuck.

From the *Memoir of Events*, Written by Malcolm Elliott in October, 1798

Of that wretched half hour at Ballinamuck I propose to say little. I am told that Humbert and the other French discussed it at length in Dublin, where they were entertained, and doubtless their account has been recorded for posterity. Even if I wished to describe the disaster I could not, for it was swift, and my recollection of it fragmentary and confused. I marvel at the clarity and precision which military historians command, for my experience of battle is of a bloody tumult in which men butcher each other like beasts, and minds are distracted by their screams and by the hideous objects into which, dying, they are transformed.

We were midway between Cloone and Ballinamuck when they fell upon us, and our march became a rout, lacking in all order. We turned and stood at Ballinamuck because we had no choice, and because Humbert welcomed the advantage given to him by the hill. It is a point of pride with generals that they obey the precepts of their trade, taking advantage of high ground and the rest of it. The French and perhaps a third of the Irish, myself among them, he placed upon the gentle slope of the hill, and the other Irish, under Teeling's command, he placed athwart the road which led from the hill to the village. He made a brave show of barking out orders, and telling us what we should do and where we should stand, but his mood seemed to me one of savage despair. Of artillery we had now but two small curricle guns, and these he left upon the road to be worked by gunners named Magee and Casey. I think it likely that he intended that the Irish should take the first shock of the British as they moved upon us from the direction of the village. His fury, for I can call it nothing less, was directed not toward the British but toward his allies, and even Teeling he addressed with a brusque contempt.

In fact, however, we were attacked first by Crauford's dragoons, coming down upon us in a line lying at an angle to the village, and riding up the slopes with fearful shouts,

484

their long sabers slashing the air. Humbert had barely time to turn about before they were upon us. They were driven off a short distance, however, by MacDonnell and his pikemen. I could see MacDonnell among the English riders, his theatrical plume flapping. And yet I drew no pride from his courage. I felt only fear, a thin nerve beating against the numbness of my brain. By this time we had already taken losses from their artillery. *Taken losses:* a fine gray phrase. Grapeshot and chain shot ripped chests and bellies open, chests sodden with blood, and bowels spilled open from bellies. A man knelt beside me on the grass, his spread hands holding bowels which oozed between his red fingers.

Humbert ordered me to move the Ballina men to the support of MacDonnell, who had now fallen back. Patches of grass were already slippery with blood, and in our haste we stepped over wounded men, who clawed at our knees. MacDonnell turned to look at me: his eyes were wide and staring and his mouth slack. I had supposed from the vigor of his defense that his fox hunter's bravado was sustaining him, thinking him childish to the last, but saw now that he was terrified. "Holy Mary Mother of God pray for me," he said, and then, his voice twisting to a scream, he shouted out a string of obscenities in Irish.

The British infantry had begun their advance upon us, walking steadily through the long grasses, their muskets held out before them. I turned my head to look at Crauford's cavalry, which stood poised ready to sweep forward a second time. Magee fired off our two curricle guns, and I saw several of the British stumble and fall. Teeling was sitting his horse beside the guns, his drawn sword in his hand. He now made a gesture with the sword, as if asking whether he should move his men up from the road to join us upon the hill. Humbert motioned him to remain in position. Humbert had dismounted, and was standing with his legs spread wide apart, his hands on his hips. He moved his head constantly, as though looking for something which he could not find. As if in answer to the curricles, the English now let off a volley of musket fire which was answered by the French. Of the Irish, not one in ten had a musket. The others were armed with pikes, and thus far had done nothing but wait upon our ground for the grapeshot and the musket balls. Some were retching, leaning forward with hand pressed to knee.

Crauford was taking no more chances. He held his dragoons as the infantry came toward us, reloading as they walked, and then a second body of cavalry rode up from the village. Now the infantry paused again and fired another volley. Crauford moved his saber in a downward arc, and came forward at the gallop.

I told my men to hold their pikes at the ready, and if I should fall to take their orders from MacDonnell. But they no longer heard me. They gripped their pikes and waited, not because I had told them to, but because there was nothing else to do. Behind us, the bog stretched for several miles to a line of low hills. There was no battle beyond the hills. Cows stood in their pastures. Perhaps in farmhouses like mine at The Moat men were sitting to their morning tea.

Crauford cut through us like a man wading through a litter of puppies. He was looking not for us but for the French behind us. A dragoon cut down at me and missed, then rode past without giving me a second glance. But MacDonnell took a saber full in the throat; the blood gushed out as though the blade had opened a fountain. When Crauford found the French there was a bloody scuffle, but it lasted no more than five minutes. Humbert, as though he had at last discovered what his darting eyes had been seeking, put his hat upon the point of his sword and held it high above his head in token of surrender. The momentum of Crauford's charge could not be stayed, however, and his men smashed into the French, who held their muskets like swords to ward off the blows. But in a minute or two the charge had ended. The French officers were imitating Humbert's signal, and the men were laying down their muskets upon the slippery grass. The second body of cavalry had now reined in and stood looking at Teeling's Irish, but the infantry continued to advance. Crauford's trumpeter sent them a signal. It meant, doubtless, that resistance on the hill had ended. But I saw that Teeling had not told his men to drop their weapons.

I turned back from Teeling toward Humbert. He handed his sword to Crauford, who touched his fingers to his hat and then accepted it. He held it a few inches from the hilt, as though weighing it, and then passed it to a dragoon. Then he looked straight into my eyes. He had a long, high-cheekboned face, the face of a hunter, and although his eyes were calm and chill, his shoulders were heaving.

From "Youthful Service: With Cornwallis in Ireland," by Major General Sir Harold Wyndham

It might well be argued that I was not present at the battle of Ballinamuck, for I witnessed its opening from Cloone, and it had come to its close before I reached the village. For several miles beyond Cloone the road is thickly wooded and I saw nothing as I rode toward the roaring cannon and pattering musket fire, but before I was clear of the trees I had begun to hear, faintly at first, the shouts of screaming men. It was as though I were passing through a tunnel from one world to another.

But beyond the trees, fields, hill, and bog lay beneath the even light of morning, a bright clarity which revealed the vivid uniforms, the splendid horses, the cannon. The scene, so orderly when I had viewed it from Cloone, was a confusion of movements and sounds, hooves, rumbling wheels, muskets, shouts, puffs of smoke, rattling drums. I paused upon a slight rise of ground, like generals in the old military prints who sit mounted, above the battle, gesturing with furled battle map, and I had a clear sight of the action which ended the battle, Crauford's second assault upon the hill. It was an immensely exciting moment, scarlet horsemen and their black and chestnut mounts sweeping forward irresistibly, clattering past the pikemen and pointed straight as arrows toward the French. I spurred forward, but before I had reached the village the charge had ended and the battle with it. The sudden close astonished me.

And yet Ballinamuck was in sober truth but a bloody scuffle, and so great was our superiority in men and arms that it scarce merits the name of battle. I had seen the pikemen swinging forward and back their fearsome weapons and the sabers cutting down, and from my distance it seemed the bloodless sport of children at play in a garden. But an hour or so later, as I walked amidst the fallen bodies, stepping several times upon the pikes which lay beside them, I knew that the sport had been bloody indeed. The Irish pike is a singular instrument to encounter upon a modern field of war—a long straight shaft of ash, and a three-pointed head, a broad blade at the center and curving away from its base two shorter prongs for

487

seizing or ripping. It was a weapon from an earlier century and so too was the wretch who carried it, lumbering forward from the bog of the past. They lay together upon the field, weapon and man, broken upon the wheel of history.

By the time I had reached the village—the usual narrow, filthy street of mean cabins—the echoes of cannon and musket had faded from the air. The street was crowded: I narrowly avoided a wagon loaded with heavy canvas sacks of grapeshot. Lake had brought to his battle enough musket balls, grapeshot, chain shot to scatter an army, but his ordnance was sloppy and the village was a scene of frantic, ill-directed activity presided over by gesticulating captains and bellowing sergeants. At the time I could not judge such matters and believed that the bedlam was necessary to the proper disposition of his forces. But I could judge correctly the temper of his men. A tiresome and disagreeable campaign was ending, and for all the angry orders which were being shouted at them, they were cheerful and good-natured.

Lake had taken up his own position in a pasture beyond the village, commanding a view of the long, narrow plain which stretched toward the enemy. He was standing with his long, heavy legs spread wide apart, a soft, tall man whose plump face was bullied by a fierce, beaklike nose. He dominated over the officers who stood near him, as much by height as by rank. Despite the hubbub he caught sight of me at once and called out cheerily, "Almost in time, Mr. Wyndham. Almost in time."

I dismounted and saluted. "Lord Cornwallis sent me forward with instructions that you may engage the enemy."

"Instructions which I have carried out to the letter," he said. "To the letter. Look over there."

The scene on Shanmullah Hill—as yet of course we did not know its name—was extraordinary. The French had drawn themselves apart into a compact body and stood as quietly as men waiting for a horse race to commence. Near the western base of the hill stood the rebels through whom Crauford had cut. A second and far larger group of Irish had been placed athwart the road which led from the village to the hill and there they still stood. They had not dropped their arms but held them clutched at every angle. A French officer sat mounted among them, or so from his uniform I judged him to be, although in fact this was Bartholemew Teeling, a notorious United Irishman. He was one of those later taken to Dublin, as was one of the men on the hill, a Mayo squire named Elliott, and there they suffered the fates appropriate to their crimes. Stretched out in a series of lines at the foot of the hill stood our massed infantry, flanked on either side by Crauford's dragoons and Roden's horse.

The air must surely have been noisy with shouts, and yet I remember it as a quietness which troubled the mind, like the sky after thunder.

"It might be best to march the prisoners down here," a colonel said to Lake. "Keep them out of harm's way."

Lake bit his lip and then nodded. "It would," he said. "It's a mess there on the hill, everyone crowded together."

It was a clear, windless morning. The wide Irish sky, a small island but the greatest of the world's skies, stretched bright soft blue over us. The sky made one with the quiet, an immense blue silence.

Lake turned to his aide. "Ride down and tell Colonel Crauford that I wish all the French prisoners to be moved toward the village. And remind him that they have made honorable surrender."

"Crauford understands the rules of war as well as we do," the colonel said in a stiff manner. He was Irish, with a faint but unmistakable brogue. "He took the Frenchman's sword."

The aide was midway to the hill and about even with the infantry when Crauford moved, sending his men down upon the hillside rebels with sabers raised to shoulder level. They rode with a most ferocious shout, which soon was joined by the screams of the Irish. The aide reined in and looked back toward Lake. Crauford limited his killing to the men on the hill, and he had given orders that Elliott and any others with officer's insignia were to be spared. It seemed an endless time. The troopers kept shouting, to keep up their ardor, perhaps, or to fill their minds with their own voices, but I believe from what I now know of the necessities of war that they were then as mindless as men at work in an abattoir. An hour later they may have been suffused with shame at the recollection of what they had done. And a few years later, in tavern talk, each would have his tale of the man he had spared or the villain who had tried to pike a comrade in the back. For many of the rebels indeed seized their weapons and sought to defend themselves, but they had

489

been taken by surprise. I could not tear my eyes from the hill, and I was astonished that the skies were not raining blood. But they remained clear and bright, and still the figures on the hill were scuffling children at war. The French stood quietly to one side, their backs turned to the slaughter.

Crauford moved his troopers forward and back, their hooves indifferent to the fallen bodies. Then he rallied them and led them toward us across the field. As he passed the infantry they set off a great shout and raised their helmets. He rode past them without turning his head, but Lake listened to them, vexed, gnawing his lower lip.

Crauford had done his own share of the work, for his sword when he brought it to the salute was red and wet. I almost puked. This was the first blood I had seen shed in battle, deep red and shiny, not yet turned thick. He had carried it to us from the hillside.

"A brisk ride," he said to Lake. He was panting from his exertions, but struggling to keep his composure. He looked from one of us to the next.

"I had sent young Boxhill to you to give you your orders," Lake said in a strained voice.

"But I did not wait for them," Crauford said, and, glancing toward me, winked. "Any more than you waited for Lord Cornwallis's."

"Unlike yourself," Lake said, "I was empowered to act at my discretion. You most certainly had no orders to ride down upon unarmed men."

"Unarmed," Crauford said. "That is very much a matter of definition. Those people there could not be called unarmed." He gestured to the Irish upon the road, who at Teeling's instructions stood prepared for our assault. "With your permission, sir, I will give those people a taste of steel."

"You will not have the permission, sir. The infantry can deal with them."

Although they held their pikes at the ready the rebels stood as quietly as the French who looked down upon them from the slope, as the cavalrymen who stood guard over Elliott's handful of survivors. They were a sea of mist-colored freize.

"General," the Irish colonel said, "I might suggest that they be given the chance to surrender."

"Surrender, do you say?" Lake said angrily. "Rebels

against the Crown, standing with weapons in hand? No, by God!" He thrust his hands flat into the pockets of his trousers. "We shall drive them to the bogs, and bring back those who can make it. Give them a taste of steel, as Crauford says. They are still in arms," he said plaintively. "You can see that for yourself."

He needed bayonets as bloody as Crauford's sabers, I thought suddenly, or else the honors would all go to Crauford. He had to wipe out the disgrace of Castlebar.

The colonel had made his point. Now he shrugged. "Into the bog, then. Or until they throw down their arms. Perhaps you have no choice."

"None at all," Lake said briskly. "No choice at all."

He gestured to his orderly, who brought forward his horse. For a man of his size and weight, he climbed up nimbly, as though setting off for a gala. His staff turned, more slowly, toward their own mounts, with the manner of men who have accepted a disagreeable duty.

Lake spied me then, and said, "Your first whiff of action, isn't it, boy? Come along then. No need for you to be left out."

I took a deep breath and screwed up my courage. "Of course, sir, if you so wish. But Lord Cornwallis instructed me only to deliver his dispatch and then return to Carrick."

He glared at me with lips pursed. "You are not under my orders," he said angrily. "Stay or not as you please." Fierceness and irresolution were at war behind his watery blue eyes.

I watched them ride across the long pasture. As they approached the infantry, several of its officers rode out to meet them and then sat parlaying. I was aware now of the smell of battle, the air stained by smoke. Lake was not much liked by the men but they cheered him now, lifting their helmets above their heads. Answering, he drew his sword and held it at arm's length, pointing toward the ground. He looked across the field toward the Irish. The drummers, upon a command which I could not hear, commenced a steady, dry rattle.

By a general agreement, to which even Crauford gave his indifferent assent, the rebels displayed considerable bravery, harried as they were and driven back into the bog, where they were cut down with as much system as might be employed by butchers' apprentices in a shambles.

They struggled at the uncertain verge between pasture and bog, but then turned and sought to flee, with the infantry following closely, the bayonet-tipped muskets moving up and down, forward and back. I watched them die. To have turned my back upon them would have been callous and inhuman. I was weak with shock and my belly was twisted.

An hour later, when such prisoners as had been taken were herded into the village, I had my first glimpse of these unhappy wretches. They were emissaries from a baser world, long-jawed or rock-faced, coarse hair matted over their ears; fatigue and terror had sunk their eyes deep into foreheads, the eyes of stupid and uncomprehending animals. Their jackets, stained and shapeless, were more skins than garments, hanging loosely from them, streaked with mud. They stood packed together, filling the narrow street. A squad of soldiers sufficed to guard them. Here and there among them, a vivid face, an absurdity of dress would catch the eye. A man named Cornelius O'Dowd was one such, a Mayo squireen decked out with epaulets pinned to a dark blue coat, and a hangdog look like some village ruffian who has misbehaved himself at a wedding. And a tall, raw-boned peasant with flaming red hair who had somehow managed to ram himself into a gentleman's tailcoat several times too small for his hulking shoulders. He stood, whistling tunelessly, beside a companion whose arm, shattered at the elbow, hung useless and grotesquely bent. Some were boys, fourteen or sixteen, and perhaps spared on that account, but I cannot believe that in the heat of butchery upon the bog there was time for such consideration. This was but a remnant, saved upon no principle save that of chance, and herded down into the village by curse and bayonet prick and musket blow.

Bartholemew Teeling and Malcolm Elliott I saw for but a minute: they were taken to Lake for questioning. Elliott was an insignificant fellow, with a coarse, disagreeable face, but Teeling, I must confess, was an impressive being, tall and self-contained and bearing himself almost with dignity. I thought the less of him for that. These two were educated men with some pretensions to breeding, and to them and men like them must fall the full responsibility for the calamity which had befallen their country. But for them, the peasants killed by Crauford's dragoons or battered to death upon the bogs might have lived out their lives upon the friendly acres of their native Mayo.

Between our own lads and the French private soldiers a rough-and-ready goodwill quickly established itself, for both knew that the danger had passed, and the French knew that nothing now awaited them more arduous than a choppy voyage home. And they were united in their attitude toward the rebels, for whom the French too had come to entertain a large contempt, as for unwashed savages. And yet for my own part I pitied them as they stood huddled together, forlorn and terrified. It became the chivalrous fashion in the weeks which followed to praise Humbert's audacity and skill, his soldierly conduct of a desperate enterprise, but it would have been better for all, and not least for the rebels, had he been smashed at Killala as his men were wading ashore. For he surely had come to his predestined conclusion, but he had dragged with him the simple peasants who heeded his exhortations, seduced by the trumpery banner which he brought to them.

The banner of course survived the battle, for such trifles are immortal. It was discovered on the bog by a soldier who sold it to an officer in Longford's regiment for five shillings and it was carried into Ballinamuck and then to Carrick, where it excited some derisory interest. It was a large square of good green silk with a gilt harp embroidered upon it. There was much bantering speculation as to which regiment best deserved it as a trophy to hang among more worthy ones and by a general agreement it was offered to Crauford's dragoons, but he laughingly refused it. In the end it passed into the keeping of Dennis Browne of Mayo, and for aught I know may still be stored away somewhere in Westport House.

I returned to Carrick with General Lake's staff, the general riding boot by boot with Humbert, who was silent. He was a grumpy, sad-faced creature, heavy-jowled, and the skin beneath his pouchy eyes was the color of hay. We left behind the prisoners, both French and rebel, to be brought forward the next day. As we rode out of the village and past the field one of the bands of the Irish militia, drums and flutes, struck up the "Lillibulero," and Lake turned round in his saddle to wave to them. I had not before this heard that spirited song of Protestant triumph, older than the Boyne, an impudent, rollicking tune which seemed to swagger through the village. "Well done, brave Irish lads!" he called to them, and in answer the drums rattled more loudly and the flutes shrilled more merrily.

Ballinamuck, September 10

Two days after the battle, Richard Lovell Edgeworth, the learned and eccentric squire of Edgeworthstown, rode to the battlefield in an open carriage, accompanied by his daughter Maria, who was later to gain celebrity as the authoress of *Castle Rackrent*. He was an angular, nervous man, a collection of wheels, springs, and coils across which skin had been stretched. He was dressed carelessly, his cravat loosely knotted and his hat perched on the back of his head of sandy, close-cropped hair. Maria's gown of flowered muslin and the shawl across her narrow shoulders suggested an afternoon's drive to a neighboring estate. Down the village street of Ballinamuck they rode, looking neither to left nor right, and out upon the narrow road toward Shanmullah Hill, where the Irish had made their last stand.

Tents had been pitched upon the pastureland, and far-off figures moved among the bordering thickets. "Who are they?" he asked, in a rasping, high-pitched voice. "What are those people about?"

Maria too was near-sighted, but the motions of the distant figures, as she studied them, grew familiar. "Berrying," she said decisively. "Those must be blackberry thickets."

"Are they indeed? A fine task for soldiers." He drummed his long fingers upon his kneecaps. "A county gone to ruin, houses burned, men slit from belly to gullet at their own doors. And now they turn to berry picking."

"It would be foolish indeed to let the berries waste upon their bushes."

It was a splendid day. Fields, pastures, hill lay beneath a warm sky of intense blue, flecked with clouds the exact color of angelica. The bell-shaped tents lent an air of carnival. As they drove nearer, she saw that the soldiers were using their tall helmets to hold the berries. Beyond them, the reddish bog stretched toward the horizon of low hills. But her father pointed to the hill which lay near them.

494

"That is Shanmullah," he said. "The French turned here and made their stand. Climb a hill is the first thing a soldier thinks to do. Cornwallis's troops swarmed around them. A cheap sort of victory, but doubtless we shall hear it described as a great triumph."

"What matter?" Maria said. "The rebellion is ended. We must be thankful for that."

"Waste," Edgeworth said. "Waste and mismanagement for years. I have sought by all means at my disposal to improve matters. I have spoken upon the floor of the Commons, I have published pamphlets, I have conducted a voluminous correspondence with men of learning and influence. No one heeded me."

"Would that they had, Father," Maria said. "You are the cleverest man in the kingdom."

"Not the cleverest," Edgeworth said. "Many are more clever. But I am the most thoughtful, the most thorough. No one heeded me. I have explained and explained at length how the children of the Irish might be educated into habits of thrift and sobriety. I have explained how this island might be transformed into a flowering garden through the reclamation of the bogs. Arthur Young himself has praised me. You have read his letters."

It was all true, she knew. She acted as his secretary. In the long evenings he dictated to her, pacing up and down in the drawing room, pausing from time to time to consult the tables of statistics which lay spread upon the long table. The dry voice, cogwheels with an engine, spun out facts, evidences, proofs, arguments, theories. Each pamphlet addressed a problem, wasteland, education, the reform of Parliament, the suppression of local superstitions, the excise, imports and exports, a more efficient system of canals. They would go out by post to English savants, learned societies, amateurs of political economy. Letters would come to Edgeworthstown in reply, flattering and deferential, "an astonishing wealth of convincing and detailed evidence," "a trenchant mind brought to bear upon the manifold problems of an ill-governed island," "a true apostle of science and rationality." Nothing happened. All waste.

At the first line of tents he halted, and shouted to three soldiers crouched about a pot hung over a low fire. One of the men looked up and answered, but he could not understand the words. "What?" he shouted again, and the man repeated his reply, but now with a faint, derisive smile.

"What did he say, child? What did he say?"

"I doubt if he has English, Father. They are Highlanders."

"Highlanders!" Edgeworth echoed. "Highland Scots. Set a savage to catch a savage. Wild bare-bottomed clansmen in their first sets of trousers. I will have a seizure of the heart before this month is out and you can lay the blame before Lord Cornwallis."

He folded his long arms across his chest and sat waiting. Presently, from the far row of tents, a young officer rode out toward the village and paused by their carriage.

"Are these your ruffians?" Edgeworth asked.

The officer looked over at the three grinning Highlanders and then back at Edgeworth. "They are, sir. They are indeed. My ruffians. My name is Sinclair, sir."

"I am Edgeworth of Edgeworthstown. I am a Member of Parliament and of the board of magistrates for this county."

"An honor." Sinclair touched his hand to his hat.

"The devil take your honor. It is your commanding officer I am looking for."

"That would be Colonel Grant. He rode in to Carrick this morning. Perhaps I can help you."

"Perhaps," Edgeworth said doubtfully. "My bailiff is a man named Hugh Laffan. He was seized up as a United Irishman and his cabin burned down around the heads of his wife and his children. He is no more a United Irishman than either of us. I want him found and I want him delivered over to me as quickly as possible."

"You won't find him here," Sinclair said, puzzled. "This is a battlefield. Or it was."

"I have been to Granard," Edgeworth said. "He is not there. The officer in command suggested that I try your people. I have no time to ride back and forth across the countryside."

Sinclair shook his head. "We had only the prisoners who were taken after the battle. They are being held in Carrick. You won't find your man with that lot. If I were you, I should try Mullingar and Longford."

Edgeworth turned to Maria. "Do you hear that? A man is taken up at his own door, and he may be anywhere. Longford, Mullingar, Carrick. And half a county burned down." He turned back to Sinclair. "The rebels burn the houses of the gentry and you burn the cabins. Between one lot of you and the other you have sought to reduce the county to a smoldering ruin."

"I am sorry for that," Sinclair said. "It is what happens in a time of rebellion."

"You are sorry for it. That is pleasant news to hear. How would you like it if I took a torch to your own shabby mountain and then told you that I was sorry."

"I come from no shabby mountain," Sinclair said stiffly. "My father is a minister of God in Edinburgh."

"Do you hear that, Maria? Mark it well. Edinburgh, the Athens of the North. And their clergymen produce cubs who go about ravaging the countryside of Ireland."

Sinclair was becoming dimly aware that he had entered upon a conversation for which he was unprepared. "I have never before heard of you, sir, until you just now gave me your name—"

"Then you are an ignorant young man, and not simply a vicious one."

"Mr. Edgeworth, complaints as to the conduct of His Majesty's forces should be taken to Lord Cornwallis. It ill becomes you to give a tongue-lashing to a lieutenant who has never to his knowledge set eyes upon your estate. No cabins have been burned by this regiment, I can assure you."

"No doubt, no doubt," Edgeworth said testily. "I ask your pardon in that case. What has happened in this county is a disgrace to our common humanity and it has disturbed me greatly."

"I can understand that, sir. I took part in the battle here and it was a messy business. War is an ugly business, I am discovering. To speak plainly, I believe that I have not selected a calling suited to my nature."

Edgeworth peered at him closely and then nodded. "I spoke too sharply, Mr. Sinclair. It is a failing of mine. I acknowledge that. I am a just man, I trust."

"Were many taken prisoner here?" Maria asked suddenly.

Sinclair took a long time in answering her. "Very few," he said at last. "About eighty." He shifted in his saddle. "About .eighty natives. Close to nine hundred of the French."

"I don't understand," she said. She was a sharp-featured young woman, and she sat stiff and erect in the carriage.

Sinclair stretched out his arm and pointed. "The rebels fell back, past that hill—"

"Yes, yes," Edgeworth said. "Shanmullah Hill. Things have names, Mr. Sinclair, even in this county."

"They fell back from there to the bog."

"And there they surrendered?" Maria asked. She leaned forward now, and her near-sighted brown eyes studied him closely.

She anticipates my reply, Sinclair thought. He wished himself far away from Ballinamuck, far away from Ireland. The three Highlanders were watching them, uncomprehending.

"They were rebels," he said. "They were in arms against the sovereign."

"They were indeed," Edgeworth said. "That is the definition of a rebel."

"And there they surrendered?" she asked again.

Sinclair took a deep breath and expelled it slowly. "Their surrender was not accepted. They were cut down. I—we—cut them down."

Maria clambered to her feet, a small, graceless woman, and stretched her neck forward, toward the bog.

"I cannot see that far," she said. "I cannot see."

"Oh, my dear God," Edgeworth said softly.

"It is as well that you cannot, Miss Edgeworth. Their bodies are scattered across the bog, beyond the hedges."

Edgeworth took off his spectacles and held them poised in the air. "You killed them all? You took the Frenchmen prisoners but you killed the rebels?"

"Not all. Most were killed upon the bog, but some were hanged in the village. They drew lots for it. The short straws were hanged. And seventy of them were taken to Carrick. I have been sick to nausea for two days, but I helped to kill them. I took those fellows there out to the bog."

Maria was still standing, motionless in the carriage. Her father said, "They have been lying there for two days, like the carcasses of sheep."

"They died rebels," Sinclair said doggedly, his eyes upon his horse's neck. "They died with pikes in their hands. They were a murderous crew, you know."

"They were," Maria said, with contemptuous irony. *"They* were murderous."

498

Edgeworth's eyes, which had been alert and quick-moving, held bewilderment and shock. "I will not believe this," he said. "I will not believe that Lord Cornwallis gave such an order."

"General Lake's order," Sinclair said. "General Lake was commander in the field."

"An island cursed by God," Edgeworth said. The brisk, grating voice was half strangled.

"Talk to Lake," Sinclair shouted in torment. "Talk to Cornwallis. What good is there in talking to me?" The Highlanders were standing now, attentive to alien words, moving their eyes from Sinclair to Edgeworth and then back again.

"They are to be an example, are they?" Edgeworth asked. "A warning to rebels. They are an example that we are as barbarous as any pikeman from Mayo or Wexford."

"If my eyes were keener I could see them," Maria said. "But I can see only the bog."

"I can see them," Sinclair said.

"All these ancient hatreds," Edgeworth said. "And the people have never learned proper habits. Drinking themselves into a stupor. Groveling before their priests."

"I know little about them," Sinclair said. "We came here six weeks ago. They are rather like Highlanders, I think."

"If the bogs could be reclaimed there would be land enough for all of them," Edgeworth said. He gestured loosely with his spectacles. Sudden sunlight glinted from the lenses. "My pamphlets upon the matter earned the praise of Arthur Young."

"You should look in Longford for your bailiff," Sinclair said. "First Longford and then Mullingar."

Maria put her hand upon her father's arm.

"I tried to raise a company of yeomen," Edgeworth said, "but I admitted Papists to their ranks and the government would not supply me with arms. Neighbors wrote to Dublin, warning them against me."

"There are many Papists in the militia," Sinclair said. "The North Cork."

"I know these people," Edgeworth said. "They are not governed by reason. All the laws and pamphlets ever written mean less to them than a poem. I have written against the dangers of poetry in this country. It is their only academy, wild words sung in taverns. Hatred breeding hatred. I have tried. No one listened to me."

Maria sat down and took the reins from him. "I wish you a safe return to Scotland," she said to Sinclair.

"Not yet," Sinclair said. "The rebels still hold part of Mayo."

"Hatred and intolerance," Edgeworth said. "Elsewhere they have been banished."

"Not here," Sinclair said.

Maria looked again toward the bogs. The soldiers were returning from the thickets, swinging from the straps their helmets filled with berries. She flicked the reins against the horse's rump, and the Edgeworths turned away from the bog, and rode back through the village of Ballinamuck toward the Longford road.

PART
THREE

18

From *An Impartial Narrative of What Passed at Killala in the Summer of 1798,* by Arthur Vincent Broome

If memory serves, there is an essay by Oliver Goldsmith or some familiar writer which in a spirit of capricious paradox argues that the freest existence is that enjoyed by the prisoner. It has ever been the practice of impecunious scribblers to devise derangements of common sense and thereby to gain the admiration of thoughtless readers, who imagine themselves in the presence of some novel profundity. If I recall Goldsmith as the perpetrator of this folly, it is only, perhaps, in contrast to his massive and sagacious friend Doctor Johnson, whose writings shine the more brightly for their soundness of judgment. But then Goldsmith, I cannot forebear to mention, was an Irishman and the product of a hedge school, wherein fancy was doubtless commended to him as equal in worth to reason and deliberation. And yet, without that touch of fancy could he ever have offered us so affecting or so memorable a poem as his *Deserted Village?* Who that has read that poem does not cherish it, and who has not read it?

Had the gentle and sentimental spirit of Goldsmith visited Killala in September of 1798, it would, we may be certain, have fled aghast. It had been for many days now the capital and center of our topsy-turvy world, given a fragile semblance of order by the humane conduct of Ferdy O'Donnell and yet managed by lawless bands who chafed beneath the weight of his discipline. My own house and others in the town were crammed to overflowing with loyalists whose residences had been assaulted and who had now the doubtful pleasure of peeping through curtained windows upon those who had worked their ruin. In the market house still languished our yeomanry, hos-

tages to fortune, as indeed we all were. For bearing down
upon me with special heaviness was a melancholy paradox. I never doubted that British arms would triumph,
yet saw in this our greatest danger. For the defeat of
French and rebels arms to the south would expose us to
the fury of desperate and vengeful insurrectionaries.

Do not seek to sketch for yourself our circumstances
from what you may have read of the Terror in Paris. That
was the work of city mobs, inflamed by ruthless pedants
in the service of an ideal social order. The Killala rebels
were peasants, moved by deep and long-nurtured passions
which imparted to their actions a primordial brutality.
That our throats might be sliced by rural rather than
city ruffians may seem an overly nice distinction, and yet
as I looked upon them, I felt that I was staring into a
deep and deforming past, as the spade may turn up
from the bog the artifacts of a lost world, pickled in the
briny past. Several accounts of the rebellion have recently
been published by loyalist pamphleteers, with the work
of such skilled artists as Mr. Rowlandson furnishing
the imaginary portraits of its leaders—long, simian lips,
low brutish foreheads, bits of clay pipe and the rest of it.
I do not recognize in these the features of Ferdy O'Donnell or the despicable Malachi Duggan, or even that
coarse and malignant ruffian who styled himself "Captain" O'Kane. The veritable Irish bear little resemblance
to such caricatures.

Imagine if you will a pleasant evening at the very end
of summer, the sky still bright, a faint wind drifting from
the Atlantic through the small town, an evening suited
to tea and conversation, or perhaps the reading of a novel
in a quiet garden, soft sunlight scattered upon the grass.
Before you lies the prospect of dinner with the faces of
friends about the table, news and innocent gossip, the
affairs of the parish and of the great world which lies
beyond it. Such, to my way of thinking, is an image not
merely of a decently ordered society but of civilization
itself. For a time, in my first weeks in Killala, I thought
that Ireland, as much as England, offered the prospects
of such a life. Most assuredly my dear Eliza and I did
all in our power to bring it into being, and in this we were
cheerfully assisted by such new friends as Mr. Falkiner.
But almost from the first, as I have hinted in earlier
portions of my narrative, there lurked my suspicion that

503

something ancient in Ireland resists such attempts at moral cultivation.

Shall I call "Captain" O'Kane an emissary from that dark world? What shall I say of such a creature but that he emerged from the mists, driven by a mysterious energy? He was no native of Mayo, although he had for some years held land in Belmullet, close by the surly, leaden ocean. A persistent rumor held that he had once been a priest, deprived of his office for riotous and sinful behavior. This rumor he would not deny, but rather allowed to accumulate about his name the awe which the Irish peasantry accord to even the most unworthy of their clergy. Clearly he possessed education of a sort, for he had a storehouse of mouth-filling phrases, which he rolled out easily to the delight of his followers and the fearful disgust of the loyalists, trumpery references to "the army of the Gael," and to the pleasures of wading knee-deep in "Saxon gore." He was in person a short, plump man, bandy-legged, with a beet-red face and a vulgar mouth.

He came one day swaggering into my residence, knowing full well that O'Donnell was away in Crossmolina, and assured me that all our lives were subject to the whim of the rebel army.

" 'Tis a great flock of cuckoo birds you all are," he told me, leaning against one of my cabinets of books. "All over Ireland you have settled yourselves into the nests of others. 'Tis time now for the people of the Gael to be rid of the lot of you. Do for you as you did for us over the long centuries." He may have been drinking, for he swayed as he stood before me, with Jeremy Taylor and Lancelot Andrewes forming a kind of halo behind his bald head. " 'Tis sweep you into the sea is what we should do with the pack of you." And how may cuckoo birds be swept into the sea, I thought.

"That would be an ill-service to your cause," I said in as even a tone as I could muster. "Your army will hold you responsible for the safety of the civilian population."

He made a hawking noise, as though he were about to spit upon my Turkey carpet. "You would long ago have killed us all, man, wife, and child, but that you needed us to till your fields and tend your cattle."

"I hold it a grievous sin to mistreat the helpless," I said, "and so must every Christian."

"Helpless," he mocked me. "Well do you think of that

504

now, when 'tis yourself that is helpless. The boot is on the other foot."

I did not answer him, finding it prudent not to add fresh coals to the fires of his wrath. Often in these past weeks I had had occasion to reflect upon the stories which had come to us out of Wexford, of men and women piked upon Wexford bridge and flung into the river for no better reason than that they were Protestants.

"I declare to God," he said, "when I look at your little dunce-cap steeples and when I hear your language spoken, the gorge half strangles me."

"You are no stranger to that language," I said. "You express your feelings most vividly."

His pale blue eyes seemed to bulge out of his head, and his red face darkened. " 'Tis not by my own wish that I learned your language. 'Tis in your language that money is counted out and fields measured. A man would be a fool not to learn English." He turned suddenly around, and, grasping books in his two hands, flung them to the floor. They spilled over his boots, solid, stored with the world's knowledge, the fate of empires, mysteries of the human soul.

"They were written for you," I said. "As much for you as for me or anyone else."

"They were not," he said. "You would keep us as ignorant as the beasts in the fields."

He wore one of the blue coats which the French had distributed, but his breeches were of coarse homespun. Two pistols were jammed into his wide belt, cannon and artillery of whatever war he fought. I let the books lie where they had fallen, although the sight of them distressed me, for the spine of at least one had been smashed.

He stood before me, at once furious and irresolute, as though contemplating a violence which prudence held in check. Nor could I find words that I was willing to risk. I caught a glimpse of myself in the gilt-framed mirror above the cherrywood table. We were both of us short, corpulent men.

"Have a care then," he said at last, in an anticlimax which made him appear almost sheepish. " 'Tis heretics you all are, and tyrants."

But how different was his appearance when he harangued his followers. The harsh gray street was his pulpit. The cords of his neck strained like taut ropes, and his voice was a bull's bellow; his Irish swept over them in a torrent at whose meaning I could but make conjecture. They drank in his words like thirsty men and were intoxicated.

I described this menacing visit to O'Donnell upon his return from Crossmolina, and showing no surprise he nodded and sank down into a chair.

"That fellow is half mad," he said, "and the whiskey always rolling around in his head."

"You should tell that to the wretches who listen to him."

"That lousy crowd of tavern sweepings? They need not concern us for a bit longer. 'Tis my own men who are beginning to get nervous. We are sealed off here, and no word from beyond."

"I have told you before, Captain O'Donnell," I said. "You should ride down into Ballina and make terms with the commander there."

"Would he so? That would be most obliging of him. The redcoats in Ballina are commanded by Ellison, a right Orange bastard. A fine conversation the two of us would have." He shook his head. "I pledged my word that I would hold Killala for the United Men, and hold it I will."

"What use is that now?" I asked. "The French are off somewhere to the south, and the soldiers are in possession of Mayo from Westport to Ballinrobe. All but this Godforsaken waste."

He shook his head again but did not reply.

"It is not only the safety of the loyalists that you must consider, but your own people as well."

"I would serve them ill if I turned Ellison upon them. He is but a tinpot version of Dennis Browne, beyond in Westport."

"Mr. Hussey, your own clergyman, is in agreement with me."

"Mr. Hussey is the son of a big grazier in Westmeath and he is back there every year to eat red meat and drink wine from Spain. 'Tis easy for him to preach submission to drifting men and to men with farms hanging from the sides of Mayo hills. If the lot of us were hanged, Mr. Hussey would call it the working of God's will and preach a sermon against lawlessness. When poor Gerry was carted off to Ballina gaol there wasn't a peep from Mr. Hussey."

We were speaking in the long evening, the air clean after a brief shower. Soft light fell upon my poor bruised books. Despite my own sharp anxieties, I could not withhold sympathy from this perplexed young man, in whom a most evident goodness of heart warred against less worthy resentments and fears. He sat with his legs spread apart and rough farmer's hands cupping his knees. From the window I could look beyond the mean streets toward the sullen Atlantic, which had brought to us this cargo of ruin and murder. Rebel and loyalist alike, we were locked within a common misery.

With such delicacy and tact as I could muster, I pressed home to him the desperateness of his situation, but he himself knew it well.

"We have heard no word of the French," he said, "but 'tis plain that the country has not risen up. There is scant hope for us unless the French send their second fleet, and for that they may have need of Killala. What has me puzzled is why the English have not moved against us. What have we to defend ourselves with but pikes and a few hundred muskets and three cannon that we don't know how to work properly. That and a market house full of yeomen."

It was a moment before I took the meaning of his words and then my expression must have spoken for me.

"Oh, to be sure," he said. "I will not let O'Kane be butchering the loyalists of Killala while I can use them to bargain with."

Being sorely afflicted by these words, I knew not what reply to make, and looked for inspiration to window, to mirror, to books.

"I will so," he repeated, speaking, I felt, as much to himself as to me. "I will so."

"I will not believe what I have heard you say, Captain O'Donnell. You would never give over yourself or your people to the slaughter of unarmed men."

He jerked his head contemptuously toward the market house. "One of these days I may have to save my own neck and the necks of the fellows with me. And you may depend upon it that I will make use of that crowd. They are the ones who have tyrannized over us for a hundred years and held down our necks beneath their boots."

"That is nonsense," I said, "and well you know it. There are no landlords there save poor Cooper with his mortgages. They are hucksters. Coopers and carpenters.

507

A miller. A few men with farms smaller than your own. They do not differ from you at all, save that you are Papist and they Protestant."

" 'Tis amazing," he said, "how little you know of this country, Your Reverence." And with this his mood brightened, in the mercurial manner of his race. "Sure it need never come to that. Did we not both see a strong army marching out with cannon and soldiers from France? They drove the English headlong from Castlebar, stumbling over each other in their haste to escape."

"Do you believe," I asked him, "that the British government will permit Ireland to be overrun? You are a man of good judgment, Captain O'Donnell. I implore you to make use of it."

"Ach," he said, "what use is there in talk? I put my plow to the furrow and I cannot turn back. How often used I to sit in my own house and listen to Owen Mac-Carthy saying his poems about the ships that would come from France and the deliverance of the Gael. The ships have come right enough, and see where they have left us."

"You might have found better entertainment for yourself than the words of a tavern bard."

"Tavern bard, is it?" he said fiercely. " 'Tis little you know about us, or have ever troubled yourselves to learn." He might for that moment have been the abominable O'Kane, but his language, unlike O'Kane's, displayed no anger toward me. It was as though he hated history itself. "Our life has been a house with the door bolted and the shutters fastened tight."

And saying this, he left me without a word of farewell, and I was once more alone with my room of books, which now seemed to me more precious than ever before.

In such a precarious manner we lived our lives. Upon rare occasions, word would reach us from the world which stretched beyond Ballina, brought by some peddler or wandering fellow who had drifted through the British lines. Each had his sack of wild tales gathered in tavern or crossroads. From such tales it was possible for the credulous to accept that the rebels, a mighty host, with the French mere auxiliaries who worked the great-mouthed cannon, had swept across Connaught, gaining victory after victory, and then had vanished, perhaps into Ulster, perhaps into the midlands. These fables were made much of in the taverns of Killala, and each such messenger was applauded and drink poured down his gullet. We loyalists set but slight store by such braggart claims, and yet it was most unpleasant to hear them made and to witness the scenes of drunkenness which followed upon them.

But one afternoon in early September, a fellow of a different sort appeared, a prophecy man called Anthony Duignan, a middle-aged scarecrow with an enormous, ugly-colored wen, who spoke in both English and Irish, moving from one to the other with scant regard for the needs of his auditors. I cannot recall whether, when enumerating the types of Ireland's floating population, I made mention of prophecy men. Like pipers, fiddlers, poets, tinkers, dancing masters, they drift from village to village. As their name implies, they deal in prophecies, mixed with storytelling and a bit of simple magic, and are regarded by the country people as odd fellows indeed, unreliable and prevaricating, and yet gifted with occult and preternatural power. They could only flourish, I regret to say, among a primitive and credulous people, whose minds have already been weakened by the ceremonies and mumbo jumbo of the Papist creed.

I stood by the window looking down at him, and at the mass of men and women who gathered around him. A light rain was falling and all the world seemed gray—buildings, road, sky, and air itself. But his voice, a melodious chant, was a thread of bright, invisible color. He had seized like a magpie upon old rumors, snatches of song, faded prophecies, and had stitched them to the soiled and frayed fabric of Gaelic fable, that tissue of incomprehensible wonders. The present, the future, and the fabulous past were all one to him, and he was beside himself with excitement, as though he had wandered into one of the grotesque epics of his race. The mob listened to him at times with laughter, poking each other in the ribs and once shoving him with good-natured contempt against the wall of my residence. But at other times they seemed beneath his spell, listening in slack-jawed wonder. But whether they scoffed or wondered, they kept him well supplied with malt liquor, which of course made him more loquacious and which he drank until it dribbled down his unshaven chin. Looking down into his mild, mad eyes, watching his lips fumble for words, I believed that I had been pitched backward into an abysm of time, a dark world which my own ancestors had abandoned centuries before.

"Mad Duignan," O'Donnell said as he stood beside me at the window.

"If he is mad, why listen to him?" I asked. "A man like that should be chased from the town as you would chase a beggar."

"He is on to the black pig again," he said. "He was at that two nights ago in Ballycastle and he had the tavern roaring with terror and excitement."

"Black pig indeed," I said. Nothing now surprised me.

"The prophecy men have been giving out about it for as long as I can remember," O'Donnell said. "It was a terrible magical creature that came raging across Ulster rooting up a great ditch, and at last it disappeared."

Mad, it occurred to me, was too gentle a term. A man stood talking about supernatural swine and other men stood listening to him. O'Donnell listened with a superior smile, but his eyes revealed that a corner of his mind attended the swirling words.

"In the Valley of the Black Pig Ireland will be lost and won," O'Donnell said. "It is a valley somewhere in Ulster, but no one knows where. Dead heroes will rise up out of the earth." His heavy shoulders gave a slight shudder which he sought to suppress.

Duignan was speaking in Irish now, to the relief of his listeners. They had fallen silent.

"He has it all confused in his mind with what is happening now," O'Donnell said. "That is how those fellows work upon simple people. Would you look at them standing there with their gobs hanging open? He knows how to play upon them. By God, we are a simple people. He says that a terrible battle has been fought at the place of the pig and the ground is dyed red with the blood of the people. Ballinamuck, that is, in Irish. The place of the pig."

The word now bristled with intelligibility in the fool's torrent of Irish. It came again and again—Ballinamuck—Ballinamuck.

"Is that in Ulster?" I asked.

"I don't know. There must be a score of places with that name."

One of the men seized Duignan by the shoulder and shouted at him and Duignan shouted back.

O'Donnell laughed. "The clever rogue. They want to know if the battle was won, and Duignan says he doesn't know. What he knows came to him . . . in . . ." He hesitated for a word.

"In a dream?"

"A dream or a vision. Something like that." O'Donnell drew the drapery across the window. "There will be a battle fought somewhere," he said, "and that fellow will be able to turn it to account. They will keep him in drink for weeks."

In this extraordinary and inexplicable manner the news first came to us of the battle at Ballinamuck. I have cudgeled my brain to recall the exact date, for I reason thusly: Somewhere to the south, Duignan had learned of the battle, and cleverly stitched it to the rambling old tale of the black pig. That tale is, as I have learned, a very old one, being part of the body of Fenian lore that stretches back into the dark ages. And yet Ballinamuck is but a hamlet, and so for weeks afterward it was to be spoken of throughout Ireland as the battle of Longford. And I have also a strange, persistent thought that Duignan came to Killala and spoke outside my window before ever that battle had been fought. This surely cannot have been the case, and I regret that I did not keep a journal during those days. My mind no doubt is playing tricks upon me, and small wonder, with the many grievous weights which had been placed upon it. Yet if these answers fail, what others remain? There are times even now when I look out from the same window upon a village street once again slumbering in its quiet decay and remember the mad prophecy man. In my imagination his voice breaks the silence . . . Ballinamuck . . . Ballinamuck. And I am touched by that icy hand which the occult can fasten upon us.

"He may have been a schoolmaster once, poor devil," O'Donnell said. "He has the marks of learning upon him."

Carrick, Mid-September

About seventy rebels survived the slaughter at Ballinamuck, but the numbers in prison increased each day as patrols brought suspects into Carrick. All were housed in a large grain warehouse at the river's edge with circular barred windows, set high against thieves. A few of the new arrivals were indeed rebels who had escaped across the bog or who had contrived to desert on the night march to Cloone. But the greater number had been seized upon suspicion or the accusations of loyalists—shebeen braggarts and faction fighters, a half-mad singer who nursed a smashed fiddle, a doctor and a grazier who held "advanced" notions, a squireen with a stock of quotations from Tom Paine and a Papist wife.

At first the squireen, Dominick Vesey of Carrick House, demanded legal counsel, but he gave that up and now sat dispirited with the doctor and the grazier, a small circle of gentility. What would be done with them or with the survivors of Ballinamuck, no one knew, neither the prisoners nor the Irish militiamen who guarded them. MacCarthy and Geraghty had been marked for return to Mayo when the army moved north, and this gave them a distinction which was almost enviable. The others hung in limbo, innocent and guilty alike. Innocence was battered like a twig in a rapid stream. All were conscious of being imprisoned, a stain accidental and deep.

It was an airy prison. A tall man, stretching to his full height, could look out upon the river and the wooded fields on the far shore. Often a gentleman rode down the path which followed the riverbank, hat cocked to one side, coattails falling away from the saddle. He could ride where he chose, that gentleman, to fairdays and market days, walk into a tavern and rap his shilling on the oak. As far distant as Chinamen, or black, barefoot Africans.

Geraghty's arm had been shattered at Ballinamuck. MacCarthy ripped laths from the walls and bullied the doctor into setting it.

"I have had no traffic with treason," Doctor Cumiskey said. "I would be a free man walking the streets of Carrick but for the spite of my neighbors."

"You have traffic with it now," MacCarthy said. "And you should keep your hand in at your profession. You never can tell."

Geraghty sat patiently as Cumiskey wound strips of shirting around his arm.

"This fellow here," Cumiskey said. "Does he have any English at all?"

"He does not. 'Tis as dark a mystery as the language of the ancient Egyptians."

"I had the misfortune to serve as secretary in Leitrim for the Catholic Committee. An entirely lawful engagement. And after that I took no part in public affairs. I was never a member of the United Irishmen. I spoke out against them."

"You've persuaded me," MacCarthy said. "When you have the arm set, rap on the door and tell them to let you go."

"It is a different matter for you. I have a wife and two little girls, one of them just learning to read. They came to my surgery and hammered on the door. I thought they had come for help with their own wounded."

"I know," MacCarthy said.

"What in the name of God have I in common with a wild omadhaun like this one, ravaging and killing out of the wastes of Mayo?"

"Think about that one. The answer may come to you."

Cumiskey gave a practiced tug to the cloth and then knotted it. "My God, Mr. MacCarthy, my home is in this very town. I could walk to it in ten minutes. It is as though Hell had opened up and dropped me into it."

MacCarthy looked into Geraghty's stolid face. "It will mend as good as new now," he said in Irish. Geraghty shrugged. MacCarthy stood up. Bitter to be penned here and think of a daughter learning to read, her fingers moving over the letters, symbols that held wonder, mystery. The power of beauty was locked in them.

"We brought this upon you," he said to Cumiskey. "It was none of your making."

"Indeed it was not. Nor of anyone I know." He had been neat when he came to the warehouse; now gray stubble covered his cheeks, and his coat was streaked with dirt.

"This began at the edge of the world," MacCarthy said, "with men wild from cruel treatment and tall-masted ships from France."

He walked away, picking his path between men sitting with slack shoulders on the flagstone floor. Cumiskey followed him.

"The Catholic Committee were loyal subjects of the Crown. We were drawn from the most respectable classes, solicitors and doctors. Merchants with a stake in the community. We sought only a redress of our many grievances, in a peaceable and constitutional manner. Our address to the Crown spoke cheerfully of our loyalty to King George."

"Excellent," MacCarthy said. "The King will not forget you in your time of trouble." He shrugged himself against the wall.

"You hedge schoolmasters will have much to answer

for," Cumiskey said. "Teaching bog-Latin and sedition. You call that education, do you not?"

"I don't know what I call it. It is what I have."

"Stuck in the past like a calf in a bog. Some of us were proving ourselves as civilized as any Protestant. And then you bring wild peasants down upon us from mountainy wastes."

"Good God, man. There is no special virtue in living on flat land. It wasn't these lads turned the militia on you, it was your civilized Protestant neighbors. 'Tis tired I am of your reproaches, and I begin to think that they are too high a price to pay for the setting of Michael Geraghty's arm." He drew up his own arm suddenly, and rubbed the back of his hand along his cheek.

Cumiskey leaped back a pace. "Go on so. Strike me. What other argument has a hedge master when his store of tags is empty."

"I have no wish to strike you, Dr. Cumiskey, but I wish to Jesus you would get back where you belong, with Mr. Vesey and your friend the grazier. It is sick at heart I am, and I need no terrier to pull at my stockings."

Suddenly Cumiskey's anger collapsed. "I am sick at heart myself, Mr. MacCarthy, and frightened as well."

"We are all frightened," MacCarthy said. "The room stinks with our fear."

"What was it for, Mr. MacCarthy? Can you tell me that, at least? Peasants and Frenchmen cutting Ireland open like a knife wound."

MacCarthy shrugged. "It was all written out in a proclamation. The French brought it with them, together with a green flag."

Last seen on the bog, a body half hiding it, the color of hope.

After that Cumiskey and Vesey and the grazier, Hickey, made a place for MacCarthy in their conversations, but they were always aware of his guilt and of their own innocence. They would not be long imprisoned. Placed there by hate and hysteria, they would in time be released. "The King," "Lord Cornwallis," "Mr. Grattan," "Counsellor Curran," vague, beneficent deities filled their speech, guardians destined to discover the wrongs they had suffered. But at times, in bold whispers, they would praise the rebels.

"Jesus, boy," Vesey said, "you gave it to them at Castlebar. I have no use for your cause, but you gave it to them at Castlebar."

"I have no cause," MacCarthy said.

Geraghty was interested in the life of the prison, learning the name of each arrival and the circumstances of his arrest.

"I declare to God, Owen, they will not rest until they have every man in Ireland inside a gaol."

Edmund Spenser's plan.

"This could be worse," MacCarthy said. " 'Tis a terrible gaol they have in Clonmel, and the gaoler is a brute. I spent a month there and I came out half dead."

"What in God's name ever landed you there?"

"Mischief. 'Twas years ago and I a young lad. There was a lad there not much older than myself that they took out and hanged. I made a song for him."

"When we are back in Mayo they might let my wife come to the gaol."

"Yes," MacCarthy said. "They might."

"If she has let the harvest waste I will take a stick to her. I declare to God I will."

Vesey the squireen was turned loose, upon the intercession of friends, and left the warehouse much subdued, not a swagger left in him. Prison had wrung out his quotations from *The Rights of Man.* His place was taken by a wild-eyed lad who had drifted south from Roscommon, a boaster in taverns that he had done wicked deeds with the rebels. Geraghty despised him.

"He chose a poor time for his boasts," MacCarthy said. "Let you wait a few years. You won't strike a road in Connaught without some rambler on it telling you he was with the Whiteboys or the United Irishmen."

"Before this thing I was never ten miles beyond the baronies," Geraghty said.

Nightfall, and the dip of the road into an unknown village, a tavern waiting with tumblers of whiskey and men to hear his songs. Unfamiliar hills dark against the sky.

"You had the best of it," MacCarthy said. "Your own fields waiting for you in the morning."

"I do," Geraghty said. "I do have the best of it."

The round window with its rusted bars drew MacCarthy to it for hours at a time. Down along the river road laborers would walk at evening, without haste, the evening air cooling sweat-soaked shirts. Or that gentleman whose hat was always cocked to one side, saying "Damn you" to the world, "I have a horse and a well-brushed hat and a gold watch." The river which separated him from them flowed toward Munster. The spacious Shannon, spreading like a sea: Edmund Spenser, exterminator and poet.

Cumiskey joined him at the window, precise and fussy, no brushing could keep the prison grime from his trim brown coat. Local savant, organizer of petitions, civilized as any Protestant.

"You are not a Mayo man yourself, Mr. MacCarthy. Your accent speaks to that."

"Kerry," MacCarthy said. "I was born near Tralee."

"The classical kingdom. A great nursery for schoolmasters."

"And poets," MacCarthy said.

"All of the island breeds poets," Cumiskey said. "Oliver Goldsmith. 'Sweet Auburn! loveliest village of the plain.' *The Deserted Village*. You must know it."

"Yes," MacCarthy said. "I have a better knowledge of poetry in Irish."

"You have the better of me there." Had he snuff left, he would have taken a sniff of it, brown flecks resting on downturned wrist. "It is still being composed in the rural areas. Very beautiful, some of it."

Beyond the river, a magpie rose, black and white, low-flying.

"Some of it," MacCarthy said.

"Have you ever thought of producing English versions of the best of it? So that it might become better known to the educated public."

Where was the second magpie? One for sorrow, two for joy. A small boy sat beside his father on a Kerry ditch and studied the flight of birds. I heard that said by my father, boy, your grandfather, and he was as full of wisdom as an egg is full of meat. Wonderful that wild creatures of the air should carry messages to men, warn them of changing fortune.

"My grandfather could rattle away in Irish whenever he chose," Cumiskey said. "His English was perfect, of course. He needed Irish to deal with the laborers."

"Of course," MacCarthy said.

Words wedded to spade and furrow, intricacies of sound tethered to the dark soil.

Lying at night near the Killala men, he heard their voices speak in the cadences which had shaped his world.

516

To speak in English was to wear another man's coat, stiff against shoulders and back. Doctors spoke it, middlemen, shopkeepers, lawyers. Someday soon, in Castlebar, they would use it to sentence him. English did the world's work, set broken bones, made laws and books. Sweet Auburn! loveliest village of the plain. English shattered us. We live in a pool of darkness at the edge of the world. A poem by O'Rahilly leaped into his mind, austere, sardonic. A world flowered within its turnings. Laborers used it. Lying in darkness, he recited poetry in soft whispers, unheard, O'Brudair, O'Rahilly. Beyond them he saw taverns, valleys, massive keeps on Kerry headlands, the swift feet of dancers.

Martin Brady, the singer with the broken fiddle, was a poor misfortunate creature, not right in his head. The yeomen found him singing rebel songs in a crossroads tavern, but he might as easily have been singing "Bumpers, Squire Jones," or "The Loyal Briton." His luck had run out. Whatever the company desired, he had it for them, and a clear, light tenor voice to sing it with. He was a scrawny man, with a frame built for more flesh than he carried, long, gesticulating arms, and narrow feet that were never at rest. Lank black hair matted his face and fell beneath his collar. A musket butt had smashed in the fiddle, but he held on to it, swearing that he knew a man in Athlone who could repair it. At night or in the long afternoons, motes dancing in beams from the windows, he would sing quietly. Few heeded him.

"I have songs of yours," he told MacCarthy. " 'But when I'm drinking, I'm always thinking—' "

"I did it in Irish and then in English," MacCarthy said, "to see could I catch how the sounds moved. A foolish notion it was."

Brady's songs were a patchwork of English and Irish, like an old coat. MacCarthy could see him by tavern hearth, black eyes darting beneath matted hair. "Come on now, boys, what will you have? 'The Coolin,' is it?" Or in the kitchen of big house or strong farm. "Not a song you can name that I haven't it locked in this fiddle. Name it and I'll turn the key." Had they escaped from the smashed fiddle, battalions and regiments of sound rushing out from the shattered wood? There was magic in a fiddle. It had a life of its own.

"Listen to this one," he whispered to MacCarthy.

517

"There has no one heard it yet. I have carried it all over this county." He leaned back his head and closed his eyes. Adam's apple bobbed to his prefatory swallow.

"Have you heard of the battle of Ballinamuck,
Where the oppressed people they ventured their
luck. . . ."

"Good man," MacCarthy said. Running in blind terror across the treacherous bog. Everywhere the down-slashing blades of the cavalry. The screams of butchered pigs. Ballinamuck: the place of the pig.

"I can make a song the way another man would turn over turf with a loy. As easy as that."

" 'Tis a gift, surely," MacCarthy said politely.

" 'Tis my misfortune I was seized up when I was. There were half the men in Grogan's spoke English. Bargemen on the big canal. I was singing 'Monaseed.' Do you know that song?"

"Yes," MacCarthy said. He didn't want to know it. Sweet Auburn! loveliest village of the plain.

"There is the world of difference between yourself and me," Brady told him. "They will call me a liar in Athlone when I tell them Owen Ruagh MacCarthy heard my songs. Isn't that a good one, though? 'Have you heard of the battle of Ballinamuck, Where the oppressed people they ventured their luck?' "

" 'Tis a good rhyme," MacCarthy said. "You could not best it for a rhyme."

"I can go into a town where a word of English would be as rare as a golden guinea, and I will be as welcome as a bishop. Listen."

Roisin Dubh. Who wrote it? Older than O'Rahilly. Word and sound yoked together like man and wife. Behind it lay a world for which MacCarthy ached in the ugly, stinking room. Brady's memory was a magpie's nest, silver rings and tin thimbles buried in the twigs.

"They had no cause to seize me up and smash my fiddle. I know delightful songs of loyalty in English, that are much admired by the yeomen and the militia. I could have set their feet tapping." His own feet twitched. Road-battered brogues, mud-caked.

518

> "O ye bright sons of Mars,
> Who defend our green isle. . . ."

MacCarthy took the fiddle from Brady's lap and balanced it in his hand.

"That's a yeoman's song for you," Brady said. "I sang
it to the yeomen in Mullingar last month and they poured
whiskey into me until it ran out my nose."

A jagged splinter of dark, polished wood hung almost
free. Carefully, MacCarthy removed it and dropped it into
the gaping wound. No fiddle-maker in Athlone could repair it, however great his skill.

"Ye bright sons of Mars," he said.

"Whoever he might be," the singer said.

"A god of battles," MacCarthy said. "In the Roman
times. With a breastplate dazzling like the sun and a bolt
of lightning in his naked hand."

"There now," Brady said. "There is the scholar for you.
What am I beside you?"

"We are neither of us much," MacCarthy said. "Sacks
of old words." He handed back the fiddle and stood up.

A slack smile from Brady. Gaps between his yellow
teeth. "There is a song you have about a woman."

"Oh, by Jesus there is. A dozen of them." In meadows,
strong legs spread wide, wild, shy bodies pressed beneath
him. "Women, drinking, rambling. There is not a mischief
in Ireland that I have not put a song to it." The small
change of my craft. The true poems were slow, mysterious, fresh light flashed from the smooth sides of their ritual.

Days passed. The warehouse was a backwater of war,
its heavy door a weir. Odd fish flopped in. The men from
Mayo, pilgrims to Ballinamuck, were quiet in their knowledge of an earned vengeance; men with pikes, all of them,
and some had set fire to big houses. They remembered
buildings red against an evening sky. The others were
carried in by the tides, mouths slack with incredulity and
fear. If they had read a pamphlet by the United Irishmen they were suspect, or if they had signed the wrong
petition. There was a great scouring of the midlands, sedition was being scrubbed out as you would scrub burned
porridge from a pot.

Cumiskey was released. Fair to him, he saw to the
wounded one last time. He knelt beside O'Murtha, one

of the men from Belmullet, and they seemed to MacCarthy creatures from two different planets, O'Murtha a heavy-boned spalpeen, his arms long and heavy-muscled.

Cumiskey pointed to the darkening wound which ran from knee to ankle, exposing tendon and bone. "Nothing to be done," he said. "It has mortified. I am as useless to this fellow as an old woman with her sack of herbs."

"It is a great comfort to him all the same," MacCarthy said. "Yourself a doctor from the town of Carrick."

"It is a criminal neglect of helpless prisoners," Cumiskey said. "I refuse to believe that Lord Cornwallis knows of it. A man with his reputation for humanity." He resettled his spectacles on the bridge of his small, soft nose. Curved glass, gold-encircled, they ordered his world.

"A great comfort," MacCarthy said.

Cumiskey stood ill-at-ease. Already, in imagination, he had left the fetid, crowded room, was trotting down the riverside street to his house, his surgery of sharp knives, his small daughter tracing the letters of the alphabet. Embarrassment held him.

"It is most unfortunate that you involved yourself so deeply in this dreadful adventure. Violence boiling beneath the crust in those barbarous counties."

"A misfortune indeed," MacCarthy agreed.

MacCarthy watched him walk into the sunlight. Militiamen, briefly glimpsed, stared with indifference. North Cork Militia. English books awaited him, words marched across their pages, trim as platoons, busy with the world's business. English sent wheels spinning, sent out ships from harbors, regiments moved at its command. Sweet Auburn! loveliest village of the plain. Goldsmith, shy Longford stammerer. He found his place among the London poets, their words resonant with power, empire of iambs. Great ocean waves hold us locked.

Shards of language lay about his feet; broken echoes filled the room. He heard his voice bellowing in Munster taverns, saw MacKenna bending near-sighted head over manuscripts copied and recopied. A language for rent days and pothouse bawlers. Taverns deep-valleyed beneath Kerry hills. Who speaks it but ourselves, to wind and bog? Merriman teaching school in Limerick. English, their parents want for them. Far from Kerry they will fit the knot under my jaw. On the butt end of this century I will choke, and my poems will become curiosities.

"Trench will deal with the rebels holding north Mayo," Cornwallis said. "An English regiment or two and some Irish militia. Good for appearances. Irish rebels scattered by loyal Irish militia."

"Break them up," Dennis Browne said. "After order has been restored, the magistrates of Mayo and Galway can deal with them. You may depend upon that."

"Oh, I do, Mr. Browne. I do indeed," Cornwallis said. Along the dark, polished table, heads wagged at him. The gentlemen of Connaught. Members of Parliament. Magistrates. The misgovernors of this bog. Impatient to let loose their yeomanry. "I have a more serious task in hand. A second French fleet has set sail. If it contrives to slip past Admiral Warren, I propose to smash the Frenchmen on the beach. Wherever they land."

"Bloody damned Frenchmen," John Broderick said. "Turn a province upside down and then wind up as guests of the state at the Mail Coach Hotel."

"It is what we would expect for British officers should they be so unfortunate as to be captured on French soil."

"Ladies sauntering down Dawson Street to peer at them the way they would at a pack of the royal princes," Broderick said. "What are they but banditti? Forty houses burned to their foundations from Mayo to Longford."

"Not by the French," Cornwallis said patiently. "Our friend Humbert is a most remarkable rogue. He will have a worse time when he gets back to France. They have become damned uncivil in their treatment of defeated generals." He smiled down the table. "It is a sore point with me. I have been a defeated general in my time."

The gentlemen of Connaught politely studied their sleeves. Uniform sleeves, some of them. Militia. Yeomanry. A warty little squire leaned forward. What was his name? Master of reclaimed bog and a few hundred bare-arsed peasants. "Browne has the right of it. Don't trouble yourself about Connaught. We'll settle those lads for you."

"Yes," Cornwallis said drily. "After the British army has smashed them for you." He gestured to Wyndham, who leaned forward to hand him an order book. "The President of their precious republic was a young landlord named Moore. He is in Castlebar gaol."

"The brother of one," Broderick said. "He is the brother of George Moore of Moore Hall. A Papist, with a headful of strange notions."

"George Moore?" Cornwallis asked. "Not at all. We have friends in common. He dabbles in history. I am damned sorry that this misfortune has befallen him. The brother must be a harum-scarum sort."

"He is," Dennis Browne said. "I know them well, the two of them. Our families are connected, in a manner of speaking. It goes back a long way, to the times when the Brownes were Papists as well." He stared straight at Broderick and smiled.

"Whatever about that," Cornwallis said, "the real instigator seems to have been a solicitor named Elliott. There is no doubt that he was a member of the Directory of the United Irishmen. A crony of Tone and Emmet and the rest of them. We will try him here in Dublin, together with Bartholemew Teeling. State trials. Some of the local leaders go back to Castlebar—a schoolmaster and a few other ruffians."

"There is enough rope for them in Castlebar, by God," another magistrate said. Cornwallis knew that one. Gingery little man from beside one of their lakes. Lake Cong.

Cornwallis turned to Wyndham. "Make certain that the prisoners in Carrick have been seen to. Some of them may be wounded. We will hold them there for a few weeks, until Killala has been settled. I have seen them. Ignorant and pitiable wretches."

"Those are the men who fired houses and carried the pike into Longford," Warty said. "If they can stand up to the rope, it should be given to them."

A bloody-minded people. We spurred them on. From the days of Elizabeth. Here in this castle. So much for a rebel's head. Delivered in a sack, and the gold coins counted out to them. My God, how these people hate each other! Blind men, fighting with daggers in a hogshead.

"How you restore order—civil order—to Mayo is your own affair," he said, "but I will deal in my own way with military prisoners."

"Never fear, Lord Cornwallis," Dennis Browne said. "Never fear. Give us a month, and Mayo will be as peaceful as Yorkshire. It is our own county, after all. A poor enough place, to be sure, but we wouldn't trade it for all of India." He swept his eyes over the others, as though drawing their weight into his words. "We will give you order, I promise you that."

He would keep his word. To landlords, viceroys, henchmen. The true Irishman, affable, obliging, clever as a weasel. The others were bumpkins, but this was a very clever gentleman indeed. Cornwallis would not trust him ten yards beyond the room. Crooked as a ram's horn, unprincipled, charming. The power of the Crown in Ireland rested upon Dennis Browne and a handful of men like him. My God, what a country! Cornwallis sighed.

When the others had left, Browne lingered, leaning forward over the table, humming.

"You have the right of it there," he said. "All this killing and tying up country lads at the triangle. It is order and justice we want, not random cruelty."

"I am much of your mind, Mr. Browne."

"One lad in particular I was thinking of. The one you mentioned. John Moore. You yourself found the right word for him, harum-scarum. You could no more keep that lad from mischief than you could keep yourself from high treason."

"The charge against him is not mischief but high treason."

"Treason is but a word," Browne said. "Like any other. John Moore would be a captain of militia today, had there been no Malcolm Elliott to pour poison into his ear. Elliott was the instigator, you said that yourself. It is a marvel to me, the firm grasp you have of these matters."

"It is not a word," Cornwallis said. "It is a crime, punishable by hanging. Young Mr. Moore was President of the Republic of Connaught."

Browne laughed, as though at a sally of wit. "Sure they could as well have called him a Roman emperor. There you have it. George should have kept a firmer rein upon him, but his head is always in his history books. As you said yourself."

"I am not certain of your drift, Mr. Browne. Are you suggesting that the nominal head of the rebellion should not be brought to trial?"

"Indeed I am not!" Browne held up strong white hands in deprecation. He smiled at Cornwallis, and thought,

Don't play the dull, stolid Englishman with me, you bastard. "Indeed not."

"What then?"

"Those fellows we were just now talking with. Good-hearted lads, every last one of them. But I would never call them a brainy lot. Would you? Returning Mayo to the ways of peace will take more than Johnny Broderick stumping across Tyrawley with a company of yeomen and a portable gallows. Mayo is like any part of the world, it is a sort of tissue of power—Lord Glenthorne and my brother Altamont and myself. The big landlords. And I would put George Moore there. Papist or not. It would do the Crown no harm at all to place George Moore under an obligation."

Before speaking, Cornwallis paused to study him. An attractive man, not one of your red-faced squireens. Pale, composed face, brown eyes soft and watchful, ready, flickering smile. A witty man, with a gift for irony. A selfish man, too fond of his own cleverness.

"And if he were under an obligation to yourself as well," Cornwallis said. "You would not object to that?"

The smile was quick as spring rain. "I would not. George's friends in England are well placed. And I have a suspicion that in the future most of Ireland's business will be transacted in London. The days of our little Parliament here in Dublin are numbered, I think. But of course you would know more of that than I do. Much more. No, you are quite right. I would welcome a chance to be of service to George."

"And at such a cheap price," Cornwallis said. "We have only to turn loose a traitor."

"Not turn him loose," Browne said sharply. "Not hang him. There are other punishments. Transportation is a bleak enough fate for a young man. George would be most grateful to settle for that. And I have not lied tõ you about John. I know him well. He is not a traitor but a spoiled boy. Spoiled first by his father and then by George. He is a high-spirited young fellow. You would take to him, I think."

"I doubt that," Cornwallis said. "He is old enough to know right from wrong, and it was sinfully wrong of him to seduce from their loyalty poor peasant lads who unlike him have no friends at court. It is time that the people of this country, high and low, rich and poor, learn that the law is more powerful than their willful passions and follies."

"But you are not saying, are you," Browne asked, "that poor young John must hang? Sure that would break more hearts than George's."

"I haven't said that," Cornwallis said. "We must talk a bit more about the changes which will be taking place in Ireland in the next few years. You are a most able man, Mr. Browne, and your advice is always welcome. But please don't let that brogue which you affect creep back into your speech. You are much more persuasive when you sound like an Englishman."

"By God," Browne said, "there are damned few Englishmen who have your sense of the country. Are you certain you don't have a drop of Irish?"

"I intend no discourtesy, Mr. Browne, when I say most fervently that I do not."

Browne smiled again, this time a wide, genuine smile of delight. "Let us talk a bit about Ireland then, if you have the time. There is no subject closer to my heart."

An hour later, Cornwallis stood looking down from the state apartments into the upper Castle Yard. Spitting rain fell upon the cobbles, and the two soldiers who stood sentry at the gate, beneath the statue of blindfolded Justice, were soaked. Better for England if the entire island sank without a trace. Half water already: rain, bogs, rivers, reedy lakes. A brown-coated figure answered the sentries' query and then dashed through the yard, hat held down with both hands against the blustery wind. A clerk? Perhaps an informer. Ireland nurtured them: go a bit of the way toward treason, then turn in panic and run to government. We bargain with them here, in this sprawling castle, modern brick joined to Tudor towers. Elizabeth bought heads from them, chieftain's head dripping with gore, sightless eyes, hauled by lank hair from the sack.

The others were as bad, the gentry of Ireland—Anglo-Irish or English-in-Ireland, whatever they chose to call themselves. Trailing their brogues around London, then going back to shiver in their mortgaged manor houses. Country magnates scheming for office, a kind word from the Castle, their wives warmed by the candles of Viceregal balls. Dennis Browne was their prime specimen, mouth stuffed with affable japes, but the brown eyes watchful and treacherous. What need had he for the life of a foolish young squire unless it served some unnamed scheme? As well deal with Mogul prince or red Indian sachem. Not for much longer. Only for as long as it took to sweep away their doll's-house parliament of silver-tongued orators and bribed placemen.

"Sir?"

Cornwallis turned toward Wyndham.

"Dispatches from the packet boat," Wyndham said. "They will keep until morning."

"No word of Nelson, then," Cornwallis said. "Or Buonaparte. Europe is at stake out there—Egypt, the Mediterranean—and we are stuck in this bog. No matter. I have had a good run—forty years, almost. Settle the affairs of this damned place once and for all, and then a squire's life, eh? Not much older than yourself, Monsieur Buonaparte. And there he is, a new Alexander. Bad luck you weren't born a Frenchman, Mr. Wyndham."

"Yes, sir."

"Have you ever thought, Mr. Wyndham, that in a year or so you will be serving in a new century?"

"It will be the same army."

"Now there is a point which you should discuss with Monsieur Buonaparte. He has different notions. Bold as brass and smart as paint. Give that fellow his head and he will turn the world upside down. Mustn't let that happen, eh? Eh?"

"No, sir," Wyndham said. He centered the dispatches neatly on Cornwallis's bare, massive desk.

"They are new men," Cornwallis said, "Buonaparte and Humbert both, and the whole pack of them there in Paris. A most remarkable man, poor Humbert. Do you know that he can barely put his signature to a piece of paper? A most remarkable man."

"He showed to no great advantage at Ballinamuck," Wyndham said.

"Ah, Ballinamuck. More reputations than his have been lost in Ireland—Essex, Raleigh, Lauzun, that Spaniard. Pity Lake's battle didn't have a loftier name— Ramillies, Malplaquet, Yorktown. I intend to bring my own reputation out of here in one piece. Ireland is going to be changed, Mr. Wyndham, and changed now. Too many half measures for too many centuries. We can no longer afford that. Not with the Frenchies on the march. Make Ireland British. Smash up their wretched little

526

parliament, and bind her to us with bands of steel. Pitt wants that, and I want it."

"A tall order, sir."

"Is it, Mr. Wyndham? Perhaps so. Perhaps we aren't clever enough to contrive a new Ireland, but at least we can smash the old one. All we need for that is enough gallows and enough men like Dennis Browne."

Carrick to Castlebar, September 17

Dennis Browne traveled back to Mayo with General Trench's army, and Trench, a less exacting judge than Cornwallis, found him a most likable man, every inch an Irishman of course, as good-humored as the day is long, full of wit both droll and dry, but with flashes of shrewd common sense. His language was a delight, so like that of Sir Lucius O'Trigger in *The Rivals*, but of course Sheridan himself was Irish and was said to have the very devil of a brogue.

He put the question to Browne as they rode along in the open carriage. Behind them and before, the cavalry clattered northward along a straight coach road. Far behind them tramped the infantry, and behind them the baggage, which included five prisoners in a cart, being brought to Castlebar for trial.

"Sheridan?" Browne said. "Not that one. Wasn't he schooled at Whyte's Academy in Grafton Street, where every bit of brogue is flogged out of you, the way you would take a crop to a stupid servant? Where we are going is where you will hear proper speech, with the shamrocks growing out of it."

"Shamrocks growing out of it," Trench repeated. "You have a good mastery of Irish speech yourself, Mr. Browne." The Honorable Dennis Browne, Member of the Irish Parliament, Sheriff of Mayo, Lord Altamont's brother.

"And why shouldn't I have? It is my own country, Mayo. We have been there since the days of Elizabeth."

"More Irish than the Irish themselves now?"

"That is it, General. There you have it." He thrust out a short, muscular arm, pointed with short forefinger to a fortified house on the hillside, half hidden by plantation. "That fellow over there, Geoffrey Rodgers of Rodgers

527

Hall. His people came over with William, a hundred years ago. They're only trotting along behind the Brownes. Give us another century and we'll have made good Irishmen of them." Dennis Browne, Master of Arts of Oxford University, Greek scholar, author of several florid, graceful essays in support of Catholic Emancipation.

"I freely confess, Mr. Browne, that I find you a delightful but baffling people."

"Why shouldn't you, then? Sure we baffle ourselves. We are the puzzle and perplexity of the world."

"So much warmth and generosity, a cheerful and deferential peasantry, and then this black, murderous affair."

"Ah, but that is a different matter, General, a different matter entirely. There is an ugly and murderous side to us as well. You are a clever man to have spotted it." He glanced sideways at Trench. Had he gone too far? No. You couldn't go too far with this one. "It works its way through our bodies, like poison, and breaks out upon our skin in great ugly boils."

"Perhaps a surgeon should take a lancet to you."

"Isn't that what you are doing yourself? Surgeon General of Ireland and the best since William."

"Surgeons cure very little," Trench said. Thoughtful: the wise soldier. "A physician is required, who heals with medicines. Bloodletting is a sorry cure at best."

"True for you, General. True for you." The underlying causes of Irish discontent: a general with a pamphlet in him. Why not? Burgoyne wrote a play.

"What are your own thoughts upon the subject, Mr. Browne? Here you have been letting a stranger dogmatize to you upon your own people."

"Devil the stranger, General, devil the stranger. You are as welcome as the first spring flowers." Browne reached a hand outside the carriage. Fingers strayed across dark, glossy wood. "A few weeks ago, I was beyond in Galway, shivering beneath the Atlantic winds, and Mayo naked to the rebels. Without the British army, you would have had a bloodbath in this country. Much good would yeomen and militia have done. The Parliament in Dublin can spout and orate as it pleases, but it is always the British army that sets matters to rights here. In the heel of the hunt."

"You are a member of that parliament, Mr. Browne?"

"I am indeed. And my brother as well." Different doors: House of Lords, House of Commons. Great gray

528

building of massive and graceful curves, facing Trinity College. "Half a bow shot from the College, Half the world from wit and knowledge." Jonathan Swift. Ambitious and poor, a shadowy connection with Sir William Temple, pride gnawing at him like the Spartan's fox. England offered power, influence, friends. In the end they ditched him, sent him back here to molder in Saint Patrick's. Fit punishment.

"An answer, Mr. Browne," Trench demanded cheerfully. "Unriddle your country for a poor benighted Englishman."

"He would be a wise man who could do that," Browne said. "Lord Cornwallis fancies he has the solution, I suspect. A union with England."

"Indeed!" Trench said. "I have heard that rumored. Has he told you that?"

"A hint or two," Browne said. "No more. A downy bird, Lord Cornwallis."

Trench nodded judiciously. "It seems the best solution, does it not? A union of our sister kingdoms. It worked once before—it was the salvation of Scotland."

A master of irony, perhaps. Browne stared at him, speechless.

"Not an easy task, though," Trench said. "Not all of your countrymen take your own large view of the subject. There are hotheads in that parliament of yours."

"Hotheads with empty pockets," Browne said.

Let him puzzle that one out. It had taken Cornwallis no time at all. Cornwallis has a good mind in that large skull of his. He plays the bluff country gentleman, Uncle Toby, but he is as wily as they come, and steel beneath the broadcloth. He knows what he wants and how to get it: the permanent pacification of Ireland. And he knows whose help he requires. This one is a child when his mind moves beyond the sound of his beating drums, the crack of his muskets.

"Bribe them?" Trench asked. "Can a parliament be bribed?"

"Cheap at the price," Browne said. "They will come cheap. Pensions, profitable office, a few titles."

"To put an end to their own parliament! To vote the extinction of their very country!"

"By God, a few of them will be sorry that they have but the one country to sell." Dick Martin above at Ballinahinch, in wildest Connemara, master of thirty miles of

529

bogland and a population of pheasants and woodcocks. Stables floored with green Connemara marble, deep as the ocean, but staggering under a dozen mortgages tucked away in Capel Street offices. He could tumble tomorrow into ruin, two bad harvests finish him off. Martin would stand hat in hand for a chance to sell his vote, and so would a hundred others. Not this year, though. Not with a harvest like this one, haystacks yellow beneath the mild sun, mellow land ripening to autumn. The finest in twenty years, and the Mayo men had left it to follow a French banner and ranting hedge priests. And rhapsodical schoolmasters, like the fellow we are carting back to Castlebar with us. By Jesus, they will pay for it.

"Of course, if it is in the best interests of the country," Trench said, pouring fatuity upon his conscience. "Our two countries."

"My very thought," Browne said. "You reached your fist into my mouth and pulled out the words."

Pulled out the words: a delightful people. We will be the richer for them, all that imagination, and a wit racy as a mountain stream. Union will not solve all their problems, though. This appalling poverty, beggars by the roadside, entire families of them, barefoot, their clothes tattered beyond the point of decency. Cabins in which an English farmer would not stable his horse, stones with mud daubed over them, leaking thatch. Within the cabins, unimaginable evils, no doubt, parents and children huddled together in sleep. No, something here was abominably wrong. Putting it right was not a soldier's task, thank God. Clear them out of Killala and the little campaign is over. Who comes out of it well? Not Lake, certainly; not after the debacle at Castlebar. Not Humbert, not really. Sly but reckless, like all Frenchmen. Cornwallis, no doubt, but what glory is there in amassing a powerful army to defeat a few thousand Frenchmen and natives?

"Such a rich countryside," he said. "Such a splendid harvest. Proper government and laws, security of life and person—it could become the garden of Europe."

"It could indeed," Browne said, "but devil the much we know about such things. We must look to England."

"To the future," Trench said. "England can offer you a future."

"It can indeed," Browne said.

"But you must not look slavishly. Each nation has its peculiar genius. The world would be the poorer without

Irish gaiety and wit. Music, poetry. You have given us so much—Swift, Goldsmith, Sheridan, Macklin. Our finest model of the pathetic—'Sweet Auburn loveliest village of the plain.' "

"That is well said, sir. A point well made. Are you certain you have no drop of Hibernian blood yourself, General?"

Trench laughed, delighted. "They never told me about it. It would be an honor, I assure you."

An honor. Happy the land that can afford lads like this one.

"A great pity it is that you will not be seeing the Mayo that I know. Before it was overtaken by this madness."

"Never fear," Trench assured him. "I will hand Mayo back to you safe and sound."

"I have never doubted that," Browne said. "Never for a moment. And if there are any awkward odds and ends left over, you may depend upon the gentlemen of Mayo to attend to them."

"Odds and ends?" Puzzled again.

"It is a queer, tricksy sort of country up there," Browne said. "The way we have been cut off from history. We are our own small world, you might say. Putting us to rights again will not be easy. Lord Cornwallis will need old Mayo foxes like myself for that. We had a long talk about it. At the Castle."

"Ah." Wise, Trench nodded. The Castle. "Your poor country is going to need men like yourself."

"I will be there," Browne promised him. "It is difficult to know what a country like this needs. All that an honest man can do is look into his own heart."

Honest men, they rode side by side toward Mayo. At their ease, leaning back against sun-warmed leather, each with an arm stretched out along the backrest, hands pointing in opposite directions.

Carrick to Castlebar, September 17

MacCarthy had a last good look at the Shannon. He was moved north with Trench's army, in one of the provision wagons, himself, Geraghty, and three others, trussed up like turkeys. It flowed beneath them as they creaked over the Carrick bridge, busy upon its southward journey.

531

" 'Tis toward home that they are taking us," Geraghty said. "All of us but you."

Merchants' houses of claret brick, spacious and trim. He had stood upon the bridge at Drumshanbo, watching a leaf drift by. How many bridges arched across the Shannon? Greatest of rivers. At Limerick so wide that you could shout and a man at the other side would not understand your words.

"Let them hang us here and be done with it," Patrick Tubridy said. A faction fighter from Enniscrone, hamfaced, murderous in his brutal rages. "They will make a show of us in Castlebar with tinkers and fiddlers. They will make a holiday of it, the hoors."

"Will you give over that?" Geraghty said. "They have finished with their hangings."

"You are a fool," Tubridy said.

" 'Tis a queer thing," MacCarthy said, "that a river can look one way at one place and one way at another and it will be the same river."

Tubridy spat on the floorboards. Ugly bullock, tethered now, his horns sawed off. " 'Tis sorry I am that I didn't get my pike into more of them." Heavy eyes rolled toward the militiamen who walked beside them, scarlet jackets gay in the warm morning.

"You did your best," Geraghty said. "Angels could do no more."

Brown eyes moved back toward him, sullen anger.

"Sure no one has any fear of you now," Geraghty said, "with your arms pulled back and tied together with Limerick rope. A child could poke a stick at you."

In places meaner than Carrick I have spent the gold coins of my youth. A life like Sean MacKenna of Castlebar I could have had, the same schoolroom from one year to the next, deferential to priests with hat pulled off and ready smile, wed to the one woman and never an eye to the others, her legs and belly soft from breeding and my own piece as rambunctious as a cock. At night, punctual as the striking clock, I would set paper before me and a bottle of the best ink.

Lovely in the morning light, across the river now, the houses of Carrick. Perhaps in one of them the little doctor fussed over his bottles and the daughter bent to her book of English letters. Sweet Auburn! loveliest village of the plain. You will end my world, small book for children.

532

"God's curse upon that town," one of the men said. "And God's curse upon that black bog."

"He will curse it surely," another one said. "A place where men were ripped open with their arms flung above their heads. There will nothing ever grow above the place where they are buried."

MacCarthy looked at them with distant interest. Ballinamuck lay distant from bridge, road, sun-sparkling river.

The road twisted between pasturelands, hedged with hawthornes. A landscape for poets, meadows moving toward a river. A maiden, brighter than Aurora, would appear upon green meadow, blinding the eye into vision. The meadow would live within the poem, never touched by winter, never a bitter wind to batter the hawthornes.

Beyond the pasturelands, the road climbed a steep hill. MacCarthy clambered to his feet to see the river.

"Get down out of that," a militiaman shouted nervously, in Irish.

"I will," MacCarthy said. "Just in a minute now."

River and town lay spread before him, quick-moving river past the neat, handsome town. Nowhere in Ireland so fair a river, a man might live out his life beside it with no thought of wandering off.

"Sit down there in the cart, croppy, and don't make me take the butt of my musket to you."

"'Tis a Kerryman you are," MacCarthy said in surprise.

"I am."

"That is my own country," MacCarthy said. "I was born and reared outside Tralee."

"Well enough I know who you are. Owen MacCarthy, and it is a great disgrace you have brought upon yourself and upon Kerry."

Awkwardly, arms pinioned, MacCarthy got himself back onto the floor of the cart.

Kerry head beneath stiff tricorne and lobsterback coat.

"'Tis far we are now from Kerry, the two of us," MacCarthy said.

But the Kerryman, thin-lipped, looked at the road before them.

"'By Killarney's fair lakes where I oftentimes strayed,'" MacCarthy said. "Do you know that one?"

"I know that one," the militiaman said, and then fell back to let the wagon rumble past him.

What harm was there in a fellow like that, doing his landlord's bidding, proud of his red coat? Never again would he have a coat so fine, the cloth smooth and rich.

Beside pastures rich in the September sun, autumn a subtle presence in the air, the wagon moved north toward Mayo. Norman keeps guarded distant hills, fairy mounds kept silent sentinel. Laborers watched them, motionless as mountain hares, by nightfall a tavern tale. Provisions and sacks of grapeshot traveled with them, soldiers and militiamen thick as blackberries on the bush, wide-mouthed cannon. Edmund Spenser and Oliver Goldsmith traveled with them, and great bulging libraries of books and statutes printed in English, bills of lading and proclamations, John Milton and Richard Steele, white-wigged orators and a new alphabet. An image filled MacCarthy's mind: General Trench's army carried northward into Mayo a great handsome clock, the wood of its casing shining and polished, its delicate strong springs ticking off the final hours of his world.

19

From the Diary of Sean MacKenna, September, 1798

Thursday. On this day, General Trench brought into Castlebar from the south a great army for the war against the Killala rebels. They marched past the common, past courthouse and gaol, down Castlebar High Street, up Stoball Hill and down it, and then pitched their tents in the very fields where Lake's soldiers had broken and run. I stood outside my shop with young Timothy.

We heard them long before we saw them, for there were altogether five regimental bands with fifes and flutes and cornets and drums, and the musicians were vying the one band against the next to test which would make the most able and splendid sound as they swung into High

Street. No man who lived in Castlebar but was out to watch them, whatever his religion or his political sentiment. This is a power that armies have upon the human mind and there is no use in denying it—the bright colors of the uniforms, the banners and flags and standards, the black cannon, the cavalrymen looking down at us like the watchful heroes of ancient Troy and the officers like minor deities, with a knowledge of deaths and battles masked by pale imperious faces. They looked as proud as men swinging out of a tavern with a few good pints inside them and the knowledge that a holiday was beginning. The Castlebar loyalists cheered them and so did some of our own kind from excitement at their gay sound and appearance. As one of the regiments moved past the shop, Timothy began to stamp his feet up and down in time with the music, imaging himself a handsome hero with deadly musket. I put a hand on his shoulder to quiet him, but he did not understand my signal, and looked up puzzled toward me. And so he marched along as we stood together there, our hands linked, his feet alive with the jinglejangle nonsense of the "Lillibulero." Well it is for children that they have the sights and colors of the visible world spread out before them, unshadowed by dark knowledge. That regiment, as I have learned this evening, was Fraser's Fencibles, from Scotland, with a terrible reputation for cruelty. And yet when one of the soldiers caught sight of Timothy, he winked at him, and Timothy waved his free hand, then looked up to see if I had noticed.

After the soldiers and the cavalrymen with their long swords and the cannon came a chain of wagons with cannonballs and sacks of shot and musket balls and provisions, and then, at the rear, guarded by two files of soldiers, a cart with five men sitting in it. When first we saw them we did not know what we were seeing, but then we took notice that their hands were bound behind them with rope. It was Michael Geraghty, a strong farmer from Ballina that I first recognized, and only after that did I find myself looking straight at Owen, who sat at the back of the wagon, resting against the board and with his knees drawn up. He was still wearing the gentleman's fine coat which he had found for himself, but it was in ruins now, smeared with mud and dirt, and with one lapel ripped away to show a filthy shirt. His eyes were puffed and swollen, and one cheek carried a discolored bruise.

"Owen," I shouted. But he did not look toward the sound of my voice, although several did. It was then that Timothy saw him and shouted out in puzzlement, "It is Owen. Look at Owen." But Owen did not look toward him either. And before I knew what he was doing, Timothy had pulled his hand free from mine and was running toward the cart. He and Owen were great friends, and there would always be some trifling gift for him when Owen came back from one of his rambles, were it only a peach pit carved into the shape of a basket. Before he could reach the cart, one of the soldiers scooped him up and thrust him back toward me, but not in an unkind or brutal manner. "Owen," I called to him again. "Can you not hear me? It is Sean MacKenna." Timothy began to cry then, bewildered sobs which racked his body as he arched against my embracing arm. Owen's eyes moved toward me but they were the eyes of a stranger and held no glint of recognition. At last the cart moved past us, and turning Timothy around so that he faced me, I kissed his two wet cheeks. The town grew quiet, men looking at each other, many of them not speaking at all. The alehouses began to fill. Timothy and I went back into the shop.

Westport, Late September

When he learned that Dennis Browne had returned to Westport, his brother's great house at Cahenamart, Moore rode there, setting out in the very early morning and arriving at clear, warm noon.

The road rose up to crest a steep hill, and Moore, reining in, sat facing farmlands and pasturelands which declined, hill by soft low hill, to Clew Bay with its numberless small islands. On the horizon the glittering Atlantic was an enameled ocean on which rested, distant, two mother-of-pearl sails. To his left lay the town, set out by Wyatt twenty years before. Beyond the town, demesne walls of cut stone encircled ornamental gardens, a river arched by charming, florid bridges. And Westport House, finest of the houses created in Ireland by Cassel, heavy German master of Palladian façades and massive black marble. Compared with it, Moore Hall was a crude, unfinished sketch and Glenthorne Castle an exotic fantasy. Seventy years old now, it had weathered well, a seal of power set between hills and bay. Back set to the mountains of Mayo, the windows of its nine-bay façade glinting toward water, stone eagles with outstretched wings soaring from its cornices, in the pediment, richly carved, baroque, the arms of the Altamont earldom, guarded by wolf dog and stallion. Altamont, Sligo, Westport, Mount Eagle—peel away the titles, one by one, and you came at last to the Brownes of Mayo.

At this distance, in the windless, pellucid noon, house, town, river, pastures, bay, formed a painted panorama, each with its emblematic value. Distant, on the pediment, invisible from hill crest, stone scroll beneath stone shield, SUIVEZ RAISON. Mixed blood in the Brownes, O'Malley, Bourke, Bermingham—Gaelic pirate, Norman knight, Tudor adventurer. In the early years of the penal century, John Browne, outlawed Papist and Jacobite, soldier under Sarsfield, survivor of Aughrim's great disaster, bankrupt, had turned smuggler, sheltered by this ring of hills. Black-hulled ships from France and Spain dropped anchor here with wines, lace, brandy, bolts of silk. Profits, but never enough. A hundred thousand acres sold off at six shillings the acre. In 1705 he had himself declared dead, but lived another seven years, in hiding, a wraith, to watch his son restore the fortunes of the Brownes. Peter it was, adroit and determined, who made the fateful trip to Dublin, swore his allegiance to King George and renounced all claims upon his loyalty by Pope and Pretender, abjured the errors of Rome and was received into the Protestant Church as by law established. SUIVEZ RAISON.

Who had trusted him? Like the *marrano* grandees of Spain, those Jacobite colonels who turned Protestant in the decades after Aughrim. Aughrim had been a watershed, a black line drawn across history, separating old and new. Ratified at Limerick by treaty and surrender, signed by "Patrick Sarsfield Earl of Lucan, Pierce Viscount Galmoy, Colonel Nicholas Purcell, Colonel Nicholas Cusack, Sir Toby Butler, Colonel Garret Dillon, Colonel John Browne of Mayo." Sarsfield and Dillon sailed off for France to serve an alien, Catholic king. John Browne had returned to Mayo, smuggler in hiding, dead man who watched his son change kings and church, moving from old world to new. Shamefaced, sullen beneath the reproachful eye of pious wife, the son sends away the chaplain, nails shut the chapel door. Dust slowly smears chalice and pyx. Fish aswim in strange waters, he attends Sunday service with his Protestant neighbors. Bored but uncomplaining, he moves his eye across the plain, white-washed walls unmarred by effigy or idol. No Mass: no mumbo jumbo changing wine to blood, bread to flesh. Safe at last from the "discoverers," the property safe, the right to bequeath and to inherit it safe. And the son's son in due course, ear unsullied by Papist ritual, knowing only whitewashed walls, the Book of Common Prayer, marries a Protestant, is anointed as lawyer, magistrate, gentleman. Thus, as the old chroniclers might have put it, perished the old nobility. But the chroniclers had perished as well, and the poets and the harpers.

But not the Brownes of Mayo. Stepping nimbly from old world to new: Jacobite into Hanoverian, Tory into Whig, Papist into Protestant. Study their faces on the walls of Westport House: crafty old colonel clad in the sober brown of peace; politic son in silk and periwig, small fleshy jowl above the lace; grandson, full figure against panorama, architect's plans in one hand, the other gesturing toward a mansion rising up beside the ocean; great-grandson, father of Dennis Browne, martial figure in King George's lobster red, behind him, past drawing-room windows, a glimpse of terraces and formal walks. SUIVEZ RAISON. "Mr. Browne's house is very pleasantly situated on the south side of the rivulet over which he has built two handsome bridges, and has form'd Cascades in the river which were seen from the front of the house; which is built of Hewen Stone, a coarse marble they have here. It is an exceeding fine house and well-finished, the design and execution of Mr. Castels. Mr. Browne designs to re-move the village and make it a Park improvement all round; there are fine low hills everywhere which are planted and improved, and the trees grow exceedingly well. The tide comes just up to the house; the Cascades are fine salmon leaps. In the house are handsome chim-ney pieces of the Castle Bar marble, which are a good black without any white in them like the Touchstone, which the Italians call Paragone and value very much." Thus Bishop Pococke in 1752, indefatigable traveler, garrulous graceless author, Anglican bishop upon visit to Anglican magnate. Only Mayo remembered what the Brownes had been—managers, go-betweens, adroit negotiators. If you have an affair that needs managing, take it to Dennis Browne. Now Moore had come.

Motionless astride his glossy-flanked chestnut, Moore studied the scene as he might study an historical document. The great house an assertion of power, the new prosperous town its illustration, the farms and distant wharf its corroborative footnotes. Like those medieval paintings which required explanations from scholars, their beasts not legendary but emblematic. Pococke could not have read the painting, eccentric cleric jouncing in closed carriage along narrow deep-rutted roads. Nor poor Mr. Broome of Killala, his head stuffed with ignorant benevolence from black shovel hat to white collarbands.

No portraits faced them in the dining room. Walls of white and blue, the ornate plasterwork of Ducart, the Sardinian master, summoned to Mayo by Lord Glenthorne and lingering for three years to adorn the walls of lesser lords. Intricate, stiff-bodied, allegory stretched across the ceiling: Time rescuing Truth from the assaults of Discord and Envy. Dennis Browne could read allegory, more ably than Altamont, his absent brother, master of the house.

He placed a walnut between the jaws of a cracker. A small brown world shattered and he picked meat from it.

"It is no good, Moore. A messy *jacquerie*. Peasants swarming across the entire countryside burning and killing. By God, if Altamont had been here he would have been skewered in his bed. I have had ample time in Galway City to reflect upon our Mayo peasants, with my butt frozen blue by Atlantic winds."

"We were not speaking of peasants," Moore said. "We were speaking of John."

"Far worse." He brushed walnut shell away from him, across stiff linen. "Far worse. I can understand the little half sirs, the O'Dowds and MacDonnells. What are they but peasants with airs? Horse pistols, and a scrap of Jacobite parchment in the west room. But your brother and Malcolm Elliott are men of education. They knew what they were about."

"I doubt that. Elliott certainly, but not John. He is a boy. He is also a Moore, and the Moores have claims upon the friendship of the Brownes."

"Would I ever deny that? Though, mind you, your father never sought out mine in friendship."

"They are claims older than our fathers. They go back a century or more."

"What was it that your father called mine? The turncoat's son?"

"He was an old-fashioned man," Moore said.

"Yours was," Browne said. "Not mine. After Aughrim we all had to find our way in a new world. Your father went to Spain. The Brownes turned their coats inside out. What matter? They were men of pluck, the two lots of them. I drink to them."

The coat hung in the hall, encased in glass and black walnut, scarlet coat with gilt epaulets and facings.

"What else were we to do?" Browne asked. "Sink down into the peasantry, like the Treacys and the MacDonnells? Not bloody likely. The Protestants had won, and they had us by the balls. They would have bled us white, stripped us of every acre. We are the old Mayo stock, George, strong trees that hold firm against the winds."

"John is the old Mayo stock," Moore said, "and he is in Castlebar gaol with a gallows for a view."

"He may have a closer view of that gallows before his race is run."

Bareheaded, John took his mount over the high stone fence, then waved his hat toward Moore Hall. Their father, standing by his chair above the portico, returned the salute.

"He will if he is tried here," Moore said. "By the gentry of Mayo. Cooper would fasten the knot with his own hands."

"What does it matter where he is tried?" Browne asked. "My God, George, he was the President of their bloody republic."

"Just so. And took no part in the fighting. Tuck him away in some gaol in the south and wait for quieter times."

Browne turned shrewd eyes toward Moore. "Wait until your friends in London have pulled a few strings."

"If I can persuade them. And with your help. I must have your help, Dennis, you are Sheriff of Mayo. There is no need for us to fence. I propose to save John's life if I can. Hanging John will not restore tranquillity to Mayo. The Crown can afford it."

"O'Dowd will hang, you know, and Elliott and the rest of them. For doing no more than John has done. Less perhaps."

"I accept that," Moore said. "I am not here to argue the justice of the matter. John is my brother, and I want him saved."

Browne laughed and drew the stopper from the decanter of brandy. "By God, you are a cool one, George. I have never seen this side of you before. Elliott swings and John goes off to Hamburg or America."

"Or Spain. He was born a Spanish subject. I do not pretend to be arguing upon principle."

"This brandy was born in Spain," Browne said, "but it is Mayo brandy now." He filled their glasses.

"By reason of broken laws," Moore said. "The coast guard never saw the ship that brought it into Clew Bay, and the excise man never saw the cask. You have hit upon an excellent instance."

"A bottle of brandy is one thing," Browne said, "and a rebel in arms against his sovereign is another."

They sat quietly, sipping the brandy. The warmth of Spain was a faint, plaintive echo in Moore's glass.

"What did they expect," Browne asked, "himself and Elliott? Stirring up a rabble and bringing in Frenchmen."

"They were United Irishmen. You know as well as I do what they wanted. A republic, a written constitution, total separation from England."

"A constitution," Browne said. "Randall MacDonnell would not have known a constitution if it came up and bit him. He was killed, you know. In Longford."

"John is alive."

"There has been no better friend in Parliament to Catholic Emancipation than myself. I have written for it and argued for it. Turncoat or not, I am half a Papist myself."

"They wanted a bit more than that."

"Did they not! A gang of jumped-up merchants. Whatever they wanted, it has no place in Mayo."

"So it would seem."

"It will not be enough to bring this rebellion to a close," Browne said. "The fear of God and the fear of the Crown must be beaten into these people. They are fools to be frightened of the British army. Let them fear Dennis Browne."

"You have a policy?"

"I do. I intend to whip loyalty into them. A hundred years from now the cabins of Mayo will still be using Dennis Browne as a curse."

"Well now," Moore said, "of all the ambitions that have ever been unveiled to me, that is the most curious."

From wall and ceiling, antiquity counseled them. Discord and Envy drew back. Time raised from the ground the languid form of Truth. Figures in white plaster, delicately molded against blue medallions.

"End it," Moore said. "Dragoons hacking away at frightened men, crops burned, husbandless women turned out upon the roads with winter setting in. End it. I shall never believe that you want that."

"Everything is ending, George. Cornwallis and Pitt intend to press through a union with England. Cornwallis sat in the Castle and explained it all to me. It will be public knowledge soon. He is going to take each Member of Parliament by the shoulder and bully or cajole or bribe him into voting the extinction of the kingdom. How does that strike you?"

Moore shrugged. "He can for all I care. I am no patriot. It isn't England that has humiliated me and kept me deprived of civil rights and liberties. Why should I care a damn about a parliament in which I am forbidden to sit? Until a decade ago, I didn't have a vote. This nation is governed by a gang of Protestant bullies, and corrupt bullies at that. I have no tears to shed for them."

"There you have it, George. And it matters as little to me. Mayo matters."

"Yes," Moore said. "Mayo matters. I take it, then, that Castlereagh and Lord Cornwallis will have your vote without going to the trouble of a threat or the expense of a bribe."

"To be sure, they can. And I will have more than my vote to deliver to them. I will give them Mayo wrapped in cloth, and tied with red ribbon and a dab of sealing wax. I look forward to serving in the London Parliament, George. A larger stage for my talents."

"I doubt that you will find it there," Moore said. "Irishmen in London will find that they are country cousins, like the bonnet lairds of Scotland. England will feast at the table and toss the scraps to Ireland."

"Perhaps," Browne said. "And perhaps you underestimate my resourcefulness. But I will need backing, all the help I can get. I would welcome your own support, George."

"Mine!" Moore exclaimed, as though in surprise, al-

542

though he had been expecting it. "What use could you make of a poor Papist farmer?"

"Come now, George. You are a well-connected man indeed. You are thick with that London crowd."

"With Fox, Sheridan, Lord Holland. My friends are Whigs. They are out of office now, and out of favor with the King. They are out of favor these days. They oppose the war with France."

Browne shrugged. "And there is a matter nearer at hand. Your word has more weight than mine does with the Catholic gentry. If you were to argue the case for a union, they would listen to you."

"Persuade them that they have no need for a country," Moore said with distaste.

"What country have they now? You have said that yourself. I ask you only to make public your views on the matter. They are a stubborn lot, the Catholic gentry. They are likely to cling to a nation which has abused them for a century."

"They are likely, that is, to believe that a poor nation is better than no nation at all."

Browne nodded. "I think that they will put it in exactly those terms. But you could argue the case for a union most effectively to them, and without doing violence to your own feelings. They would fare better under the union, George. Catholic Emancipation is far more likely to come from London than from those fellows in Dublin. It is a matter which you should discuss with Cornwallis. He is a most enlightened fellow in that regard."

"I think," Moore said after a pause, "that I would welcome another drop of your brandy."

"I am sorry!" Browne cried. "I am an inattentive host." When he had poured, he held the decanter of sharp-cut glass and studied its contents. "God be with the days when this brandy was a bond between your family and mine. Before our time. Your father shipping it up from Alicante, and my grandfather on the beach at Clew Bay to receive the casks. And the excise man bribed and drunk. We were hand-in-glove in those days. 'Spanish' Moore and the turncoat. The Moores and the Brownes. The old Mayo stock."

"They were good bargainers," Moore said. "I have never mastered the art."

"You never had the need," Browne said. "Your father left you a rich man. But we all come to it, sooner or later.

We all must bargain, it is the way of the world. Not always for money."

Moore drank off the brandy at a single pull. His throat burned. Body of boneless plaster, Truth rested in the arms of Time.

"We have drifted off the subject," he said.

"We have," Browne said. "But not far. The Brownes and the Moores. We go back together a long way. They thought they had us whipped after Aughrim, but we rose again, one in one way, one in another. John's business is a tricky matter, but we can manage it, I think. There is a gaol in Clonmel that he might find more to his liking than the one in Castlebar. And after a while, a month or so, a gaol in Waterford that he might like even better." He filled their glasses again. "Waterford is on the coast. A great town for shipping—Hamburg, Barcelona. You have a good head for politics, George. You should discuss your ideas with Cornwallis. He is very open in his dealings with Irishmen. Of the right sort."

"Then we have made a bargain, I take it."

"What bargain?" Browne asked, puzzlement in his voice. "I don't understand you. John is a harum-scarum sort, but he is a good lad. I will help him any way I can. What else are friends for?"

The following evening, Moore stood where once his father had spent his evenings, on the balcony above the portico. His hands rested upon the smooth, cool stone of the parapet. Motionless after rain, the waters of Lough Carra were green beneath the sky. A flight of rooks circled above it, flocks of black. From elsewhere upon the estate, populous as a village, noises floated toward him, the shouts of herdsmen, from the forge the beat of hammer upon iron. In other months, at this time of day, he had heard song lingering in the distance, cadences wedded to soft, moist air. He heard none now. The flames of August had burned away song. Shout and dull hammer-blow merged into the silence.

He had paid a cheap price for a brother's life. His father would have thought it a fine bargain. Not a shilling to pay out, but only his pledge to serve the interests of England and of Dennis Browne. Never again would he survey the world from his balcony of cool and superior amusement, judging, appraising, condemning. His irony, in which he had taken pride as a function of his intelligence, would become a shell, each year more brittle and more thin, a mannerism, a gesture. John's reckless folly had bound him hand and foot, delivering him into a world which he had learned to despise. What a simpleton he had been, to believe that he could escape history, whose sources were as close to hand as a brother's passion, a neighbor's ambition. History was Dennis Browne at ease in a dining room, glass in hand, and feet stretched out full length, or John unshaven in the stink of Castlebar gaol.

Where had the chain begun, of which his bargain with Dennis Browne was the final link? In some mountainside shebeen, Whiteboys nursing their grievous burden of evictions, their grotesque, invented history. Or in Dublin, solicitors and merchants' sons, their heads crammed with Tom Paine; city-bred, they thought in pamphlets. Or in Paris, Wolfe Tone, fertile-witted mountebank, doubtless making sweeping, empty gestures, promising an island in turmoil to the Directory, that gang of swindlers and opportunists. Or as a dangerous notion in Humbert's head, quick island glory with Buonaparte half the world away. Moore's mind drifted toward possible ties, world stacked upon world, motives, probabilities, pantomime actors gesticulating in the theater of his imagination. Abstractions beside a green lake. He was at home. Harsh-throated, the rooks settled noisily in the beech trees.

20

From *An Impartial Narrative of What Passed at Killala in the Summer of 1798,* by Arthur Vincent Broome

September 23, the final day of the "Republic of Connaught," as it styled itself, was one of those days which have earned for our barony its cheerless and unenviable reputation, with ocean, coast, and town alike lying gray and dour beneath a blanket of dirty cloud. From dawn and through the early hours of the morning, a rain fell, soft as mist, a rain so soft that it seemed a portion of the air itself. The ancient watchtower atop Steeple Hill served the rebels as sentinel, for men had clambered up its bowels and leaned from its shattered top looking toward the south, perched there like gargoyles. We could see them through the streaky, pallid light, their clothing as colorless as stone and rain. The town dogs, a band of scrawny curs, had been awake with the dawn, snapping and yelping at the bands of men who passed beneath my bedroom window. From what I could make out of the waters of the bay, there was not a sail upon it, as there had not been for several weeks. It was a great bowl of vile water.

Few within my residence had slept that night. The loyalists gathered upon the upper floor were in great fright, comforted as best they could be by my tireless Eliza. I led them several times in prayer, seeking to instill in them a humble confidence in Providence. In those hours, I felt myself drawn closer to them than ever before. All their lives, from the first stories told to them by mothers or nurses or school-fellows, they had been instructed that the Papists were a dark and mutinous race, wedded to violence as though to a witch. Not even so generous and large-minded a man as my dear friend Mr. Falkiner was entirely free of this brooding suspicion, which for many amounted to a mania. It serves no purpose to expostulate against mania, and had I done so I would have been thought demented, for events had assuredly arranged themselves in accordance with loyalist belief and Protestant piety. For there we sat, prisoners within the very house of the Protestant clergyman, which clergyman I was, as shouts and curses floated to us through plank and plaster.

For below us, in the principal rooms, there had all night been ceaseless noise and chatter, voices raised in fierce and unintelligible disputation. Once, at perhaps three or four in the morning, the tread of a number· of men fell upon the stairs, and the prospect of a dreadful and immediate fate rushed into our minds, but before our landing had been reached, the feet turned and retreated.

I thrust resolutely from my mind all conjecture as to the nature of these arguments. The rebels awaited a certain retribution, with only its hour in doubt, and desperation and fear guided their councils. Throughout the night reports brought to them by patrols told them of soldiers advancing from all directions, these reports being often in such conflict with one another that reliance could not be placed upon them. Near midnight, O'Donnell sent out his cousin, Roger Maguire, with a dozen horsemen, and within a few hours they had come back to report their encounter with a small detachment of British soldiers. Maguire (he was among those slain later in the morning) was a resolute and intelligent young man, whose word could be relied upon. Terror, mingled with savage and un-Christian rage, now filled the rebels, and it was at this point that a final discussion was held, if that be the proper term, as to the disposition of the loyalist prisoners, and not only the yeomen in the market house, but those unoffending men and women, and their children who had taken refuge beneath my roof.

My knowledge of their council is not direct, of course, but comes from several rebel sources, and in particular from the dying declaration of "Colonel" Patrick Barrett. This declaration, which I myself watched him make, must be taken *cum grano salis,* for in the two hours which elapsed between his condemnation and his execution he was eager if not to exculpate, then at least to show himself in a favorable light. Thus he represents himself as a steadfast supporter of O'Donnell's efforts to maintain a semblance of humanity, and by the same token a resolute foe of O'Kane and of Malachi Duggan, whose quite simple plan it was to slaughter us all before sallying forth into battle. It was for this hideous purpose that feet had come clattering up the stairs, but at the last moment they were called back by O'Donnell's loaded pistols. It is a wonder to me that O'Donnell's mind did not crumble before the task of preventing a massacre while at the same time preparing for a hopeless battle. Preparation, it must be remembered, for which he was utterly without experience, so that he blundered constantly, sending out patrols of men upon foolish errands and thus weakening his defenses.

For Barrett himself I cannot vouch. Both of his legs had been smashed by cannon, and he lay with other men on the filthy floor of a cabin in the Acres. He made his statement at night, and a subaltern took down his halting English by the light of a guttering candle, with a half-dozen of us gathered around. He was desperately eager to speak with a minister of his own creed, but Murphy lay dead at Ballinamuck, and Mr. Hussey had fled to a place of

547

safety, lest the misplaced vengeance of the soldiers fall upon him. I offered to pray with him, but he smiled, making no other reply. I am most uncertain as to his true feelings, for he seemed at some points eager to set matters straight in his mind, but at others he was clearly concerned to enlist our sympathy, although he must surely have known that there was no possibility of mercy, for his guilt was beyond question.

He was a well-favored man in his middle thirties, about O'Donnell's age, with yellow hair and ruddy face, and a broad, deep chest. He was in great pain which minute by minute contorted his face, and words were dragged out from him.

"He was like a bull gone mad," he said, speaking of O'Kane, "and he bellowed at Ferdy that the heretics should all be slaughtered, and the more he bellowed the whiter Ferdy's face would get. They had both been drinking, as the others had."

"O'Donnell was drunk?" the subaltern asked.

"Not drunk, but he had been drinking. I had a few good drinks myself from O'Donnell's jug."

"But there were rebels who wanted to murder the women and the other prisoners," the subaltern said.

"There were," Barrett said. "A crowd of them did."

"And this matter was then discussed."

"Discussed, is it?" I am not certain that he understood the word. "There would be three or four things happening at once, and men would come in to make reports, and Ferdy and O'Kane would set to arguing. Then there would be an hour when nothing happened at all, and the room was full of men standing around. But most of the time Ferdy was sitting at the big black table." He meant my mahogany dining table, which still bears scars of the rebel occupation.

The subaltern had stopped writing. "O'Kane is dead," he said. "So is O'Donnell. So is a man named Maguire who held rank among the rebels. If anyone is left who is answerable for the conduct of the people here, it is yourself. Were you not styled a colonel?"

"Ach," Barrett said. He endured a spasm of pain. "Devil the meaning those words had. I brought in a hundred men from Crossmolina, so the French clapped a comical hat on my head and called me a colonel. There were majors and captains and colonels. We had a few generals but they went off with the army."

"We know about the generals," the subaltern said.

"But everyone knew that Ferdy O'Donnell was the commander here. He was the man that most of us followed, and I was myself his follower. O'Donnell is a great name here."

"And O'Donnell, you claim, prevented the murder of the people who had taken shelter with Mr. Broome here."

"I know this to be true," I said, interrupting them. "Without excusing Mr. O'Donnell's conduct in the rebellion."

The subaltern looked toward me impatiently. "So I understand, Mr. Broome."

"Prevented it?" Barrett said. "By God, he did. I heard him threaten to put a pistol ball into O'Kane. And so he would, by God. He was very excited."

"And the yeomen," the subaltern said. "The prisoners in the market house. Did O'Donnell have the same care for their safety?"

Barrett took his time in answering. "The yeomen," he said. "Well now, they were our prisoners the same as I am yours, and see what is happening to me."

He turned his eyes away from the subaltern toward me, and then from me to a dark corner of the cabin, beyond the light of the candle.

At the first good light, the watchers in the tower gave a shout which brought a number of rebels swarming up Steeple Hill. These were presently joined by the leaders, including Maguire, O'Donnell, O'Kane, and Barrett. All stood looking across the estuary toward Tyrawley's Sligo flank. It was certain to me that they were observing a troop movement of some kind, although I could not guess as to its nature. After a time O'Donnell turned and walked back to my house. The other "officers" followed him, but many rebels remained upon Steeple Hill and they were joined by more. They remained there for an hour and from time to time gave vent to shouts of the most terrifying description. O'Donnell, by himself, went out to them a second time, and they shouted now at him, as he stood looking across the estuary. Presently he walked back, but this time he climbed the stairs and rapped at my door.

His face was drawn and as white as parchment, and his

eyes leaden and puffy from lack of sleep. "Mr. Broome, there is something which you should see. The people want you to see it, and I believe that they are right."

I settled my hat and left the room with him, but at the landing Eliza ran after us and flung herself upon me.

"There is no need for concern," I said, patting her shoulder. "I am going out now with Mr. O'Donnell but I will soon be back."

"He will indeed, ma'am," O'Donnell said.

Eliza looked at him uncertainly. Under my tutelage, she had come to give O'Donnell a measure of trust, but he was not a reassuring figure, with his distracted air, and his huge pistols and French sword.

"What is happening?" she asked in a tremulous voice.

"I do not know," I said truthfully.

"I will have him back with you shortly, ma'am," O'Donnell said, "and he can tell your friends what is happening. What I am doing is for the best. There are very angry people below, and they are beside themselves in their anger."

It was not the most tactful of reassurances, but he spoke with but part of his mind, his attention wandering.

The morning air was chill, and the fine rain coated my face where the hat's broad brim did not protect it. We climbed the narrow footpath up Steeple Hill, with knots of men staring at us, to the very top, beside the tower, and turned eastward. A man grabbed my arm and shouted something at me in Irish, which of course I did not understand. What I saw was well worthy of their attention.

Stretching as far as the eye could see a line of fires burned fiercely, like beacons set at irregular intervals, and at first I thought they were exactly that. I marveled that they could burn in the rain, but then saw, from the sky above the blazes, that the rain had not spread into Sligo.

"Is that the army?" I asked. "Are those the campfires of the army?"

O'Donnell turned on me fiercely, as though I had made an insulting jest.

"I do not understand," I said. "What need have they of fires?"

"What need have they, is it?" he cried. "What need? Are you blind, man? They are troubling themselves to burn every cabin they can find, and God knows what they are inflicting upon the people."

550

I knew at once that he was right. The straggling line of fires took pattern and meaning. My ear held the echo of his stilted word, *inflicting*, which perhaps was used in the prayers of his creed.

The man who had seized my arm shouted at me again. "He says that this will happen in Killala in a few hours, and worse than that. By God, he is right. Do you doubt that he is right?"

"Thirty," I said. "There must be at least thirty fires."

"Small trouble it is," O'Donnell said, "to set fire to a bit of thatch. There is an army coming upon us from the south and one from the east." He scrubbed his face with his two fists. "And I declare to God I don't know what to do. Have you ever heard the like of that, Mr. Broome?" He shook his head. "There is not a ditch for us to hide in but they can scour us out of it."

"There is but one thing for you to do, Mr. O'Donnell," I said.

"Surrender, is it?" he pointed to the fires. "Do you think those people were let surrender?"

"You must make the attempt," I said. "How can you hope to withstand an army?"

He shook his head, turned upon his heel, and made his way down the hill. I followed close behind, although I turned my head once, upon hearing a roar from the men, and following their gaze could see that another cabin had been set afire. There seemed a mixture of rage and terror in the air itself, that wet, clinging air which had nothing in it of life or freshness.

"By noon," Barrett told the subaltern, "the two armies were in plain view, the one coming toward us from Castlebar, and the other from the direction of Sligo. If there was one redcoat, there were ten thousand. And if there was any place for us to run or hide it was the waters of the bay itself."

"So you have told us," the subaltern said. His hand was weary from scribbling, and perhaps he saw little purpose in the task to which he had been set. But General Trench required an account of the rebel intentions and actions, to round out his dispatch. "And it was O'Donnell's decision to send out the white flag?"

"It was," Barrett said. "He sent out Maguire and six horsemen, and he compelled Captain Cooper of the yeomen to accompany them."

"What were Maguire's instructions?"

"He was to tell the English soldiers that we wanted to surrender and be let live, and if we did not have that promise, then we would kill all of the yeomen."

"That was your intention, then? To kill the yeomen?"

Barrett hesitated. "There were some said one thing and some another. Myself, I thought it would be dreadful to cut down men with empty hands."

"Indeed," the subaltern said drily. "And what did O'Donnell think?"

A soldier held a leather flask to his lips.

"Did O'Donnell intend to kill the yeomen?" the subaltern asked.

I bent forward anxiously, for the question had been much upon my mind. The movement caught Barrett's attention, and it was to me that he spoke.

"We were all of us talking about what Maguire would say to the soldiers, and not what we would do afterward."

"But General Trench would not accept their surrender," I said to the subaltern, as a question. "Is that what happened?"

"How should I know?" the subaltern said testily. "What do I know of such things? What does it matter now? Maguire was shot down and that was the end of the matter."

"Shot down carrying a white flag," I said.

"When O'Donnell saw Maguire fall from his horse he let out a terrible wail," Barrett said. "We were standing on Steeple Hill, not three fields away from where it happened. Maguire was shot and one of the men with him, and then Cooper broke away from them and rode to the English, shouting who he was. After that we knew there would be no more talk about surrender. There would be no—what is that word they have for mercy?"

"Quarter," the subaltern said. "There would be no quarter for rebels."

"That is it," Barrett agreed. "When we knew that, even O'Kane turned pale. Then he pulled out his sword and shouted, 'By God, we will do those bastards now.'"

"By which he meant the yeomen prisoners?"

"Yes. The yeomen." Barrett lowered his hands to his knees, and then held them up to the candle, wet and gleaming. "My poor legs are destroyed," he said. Once again I urged that we join our hands and humbly seek from the Redeemer forgiveness for our transgressions.

Embarrassed, the subaltern lowered his pen again and looked away from us. Barrett drew a deep, sighing breath.

"Ferdy told me to get my men in good order and to take them a mile down the road and there wait for the others. And that did not take me long, because they were angry, although many were frightened. I was frightened myself. We left the town so, and I don't know anything more about the prisoners. I saw nothing of that."

"But O'Donnell and O'Kane went back into the village, did they not? They went to the market house and ordered out the prisoners."

"Have I not told you that I do not know where they went or what they did?" In the flickering light, his eyes were dark and evasive.

"He went first to my house," I said. "I talked with him there."

"You did?" the subaltern asked, surprised. "Can you remember what he said?"

"Oh, yes," I said. "I remember."

He stood before me, swaying. There was a bottle of my brandy on the table, and he had a tumbler of it in his hand.

"Avoid needless killing, did you say?" he asked me. "Sure it was to kill us that they came here, and they will do so."

I could find nothing to say to him.

"The way you would go after badgers or foxes," he said. "They have destroyed the most of us in Longford or wherever, and now they have come back to finish matters."

I could not understand why he stood there talking to me while his men were preparing to do battle.

"It is a mad business," he said, "and it has been from the start. Owen MacCarthy said so, and he was as mad as any of us. I cannot remember when it started, but it was long before the French came. The French lit the fuse, but the powder was there waiting for it."

"There is nothing I can tell you," I said. "You should have been given your chance to surrender. The unfortunate Maguire—an accident—I would most readily go forward myself with a flag. . . ."

He shook his head. "The fighting will not last long," he said, "and then the town will be yours again."

It had never been mine. Neither its people nor the fields

553

and hills which stretched away from it. It is not mine now.

He raised the tumbler and drained it off, choking on it.

"I doubt will I be back again," he said. "Unless they bring me back to hang me. There is a mad thing to say."

"Mr. O'Donnell," I said, "I am—all of us in this house are most thankful to you for your humanity, of which we have all been witnesses. And you may depend upon us to make this known to the army."

He smiled without humor. "That would be most kind of you." He turned to leave, but then paused and took one of the pistols from his belt. "I will leave this here for you. You may be safer so." He put the deadly looking engine on the table and then left the room.

For a moment I stood looking at the door and then moved my eyes downward to the table. I had never held a pistol, and had no idea of its operation, beyond pointing it and pulling the trigger. I picked it up and held it in my open hand, surprised by its weight. Then I carefully replaced it, and walked to the window.

It was then I discovered that a group of prisoners had been dragged from the market house, some fifteen or twenty of them, wearing the scarlet coats and white breeches of the yeomanry, although much befouled. A mass of men and women swarmed around them, and they stood huddled together, not knowing where to look. It was raining more heavily now. Then, as I watched, a man rushed forward from the crowd, his pike held like a spear at the level of his waist, and thrust it with a quick, upward motion into the belly of a yeoman. For a shocked moment the crowd fell silent: the one sound was the yeoman's agonized screech. His weight hung upon the pike, dragging it downward, and the rebel holding it took a step forward. They stood thus, joined together by the pikeshaft, men of similar build, corpulent and tall. Then the yeoman crashed to the ground, in his fall ripping the pike from his assailant's hands.

From my height I could see the fallen figure more plainly than those who stood on the fringes of the crowd. I pressed my head against the window and closed my eyes, as if in the childishness of my panic I hoped that the scene might be obliterated, lost forever, somewhere within the blackness of my skull. With my eyes squeezed shut, I heard the shouts begin anew, which, being in Irish and therefore unknown to me, were the more frightening. Then there was a second scream, more pro-

554

tracted than the first, but like it high and inhuman, as
when an animal is slaughtered. With a great effort of
will, I opened my eyes. There was a commotion in the
room next to mine, and I knew that there, too, appalled
faces pressed to the window. How can I describe the
feelings which now overwhelmed me? Least of all did I
think myself at that moment a servant of the Almighty.
Human life had been taken, and two of God's creatures
wantonly destroyed. Most strange of all, the rain washed
across my thoughts. They would be slaughtered in this
mean rain, a drizzle of nothingness, and their blood would
flow past dung and over wet cobbles. My window
sheltered me, glass upon which the rain pattered. I saw
O'Donnell now, moving through the crowd, grabbing men
by the shoulders and thrusting them roughly aside. But at
the crowd's center, two men had seized yet another yeoman, forcing him to his knees in a travesty of prayer.

His life hung by but a thread, and the knowledge was
too terrible for me to endure it. I turned away from the
window and ran out of the room. On the landing I
collided with Mr. Gardiner and Mr. Sammons, who endeavored most strenuously to restrain me, but I struggled
free of them and rushed down the stairs. Then I seized up
the pistol from the dining-room table and ran out into the
street, waving the heavy, foolish weapon above my head.
"Stop, stop," I shouted. "Blood! Murder!" Then I ran
down the street, past a straggle of men.

I never reached the yeomen or their tormentors. Halfway down the street, a man took me by the shoulders and
flung me against a shuttered shop, where he wrested the
pistol from my grasp. We looked for a moment into each
other's eyes, and I remember his face as a fragment of
nightmare floating in blackness, a fleshy face, the eyes
protruding. He held the pistol as one holds a club, by its
barrel, and swung it high. Then, as I came to know later,
he smashed it against my head, above the ear. I fell to
the ground, against the door, and lay there as one dead,
for how long I cannot say, for I next remember Mr.
Gardiner bending over me, and with him a woman who
was then a stranger to me, a Methodist. By that time the
rebels had moved outside the town to make their stand
against the oncoming army, and the street was now, for a
brief time, in the possession of the helpless.

My head reeled with pain and giddiness, and leaning
over I retched upon the cobbles, although I also befouled

my coat. The street was a jumble of sensations, noises, faces, moving figures. Rain fell upon my senses. I put a hand against the pain, but Mr. Gardiner drew it away; my fingers were sticky with blood. "We cannot leave him here," I heard Mr. Gardiner say, but the woman argued with him, saying that worse would befall should I be moved. Presently Gardiner knocked on the shop door, and then, when there was no response, tried it and found it unlocked. How they carried me inside I cannot recall. Mr. Gardiner was a dry stick of a man, all elbows and knees, and the woman, though sturdy, was but a woman. They rested me on the floor, where I again lost consciousness.

Two hours later, Ferdy O'Donnell died in the streets of Killala, not ten yards from the shop where I lay injured. The "battle" of Killala was a rout, in which the rebels briefly held their ground, with the doggedness of men who know themselves doomed, as General Trench's men pummeled them with grapeshot and canister, and then swept forward with saber and bayonet. When at last they broke, they fell back upon the town, there being no other line of retreat. That road down which they rushed, closely followed by Trench's cavalry, is known now among the country people as *casan an air*, which is to say, the road, or way, of slaughter. How many were slain upon it I cannot say, but it is the appalling fact that six hundred were killed in the narrow streets of Killala.

I was awake to hear them perish. Beyond the door of the shop all was Bedlam, shouts, screams, the sounds of hooves and booted feet. It was a shabby death which our troops dealt out, a kind of butchery. I remind myself that this is the way of war, which does not greatly resemble our romantic notions, and yet this reminder does not persuade me. I bear witness that the streets ran red with blood, and this as no figure of speech but as simple fact. A sizable number of rebels, perhaps seventy or eighty, scrambled up Steeple Hill and there stood massed to await the deaths which soon fell upon them. Later, their bodies lay at the foot of the watchtower. Most had been bayoneted. A hundred or more made their way past the town itself to the Acres, and there perished, together with a score of cabin dwellers. Others fled toward Rathfran, on the very coast, where some drowned, the tide being then at the full, and others fell beneath the musket fire which was brought to play upon them. But all these made up the lesser part. Most were killed in the streets, and all this I heard, although mercifully I did not see it. When today I walk those streets, I am at times surprised that the cries of the dying have not lingered in the air.

By the afternoon, Mr. Gardiner and I felt sufficiently emboldened to leave the shop and venture back up the street to my house. I dared not look to left or right lest horror overwhelm me, but we were forced to slip past the soldiers as unobtrusively as possible, relying upon my cloth for safe conduct, and to pick our way through the scene of slaughter. So many lay upon the cobbles that death had lost all dignity. Once I foolishly glanced up toward Steeple Hill, and saw the bodies scattered there, and several Highland soldiers standing idly, their weights resting upon their muskets. And I found also, nay almost stumbled upon, the unfortunate Ferdy O'Donnell.

He was not quite dead. His saber lay beside him, that blade hammered in France which had brought this violent madness upon us. I knelt beside him, fighting back nausea. His chest had been shattered and upon it lay a mat of darkening blood. Mr. Gardiner tugged urgently at my arm, but I knelt down, speaking my name and then his own in the hope that he might recognize me. Every romance must have its ogre, and O'Donnell has been pressed into this service by government pens and in the accounts of such loyalist historians as Sir Richard Musgrave. In the houses of some Mayo Protestants, children are cautioned toward their best behavior "lest Ferdy O'Donnell get them." It would be more to the point were they to be frightened by the brutish Duggan or the half-mad O'Kane, who also perished, but time has given these names no resonance. I do not recognize O'Donnell in these accounts, nor in the wretched pothouse ballad which praises him as "the darling of Erin." He was speaking, in a voice which croaked like a raven's, and I bent my head to listen to his words. But he spoke in Irish, and I could not understand him. Presently I rose to my feet and left him to die. I remember his body sprawled in the street, his last words spoken to the rain.

Thence we made our way home, like London gentlemen picking their way along a filthy thoroughfare, and I was welcomed with rejoicing by my dear Eliza and by the loyalist families who had sheltered with us. About an hour later, a Colonel Timmins called upon us, doubtless in time snatched from more sinister tasks, to assure us that we had indeed been rescued, and I thanked him with such courtesy and presence of mind as I could muster. A most ludicrous figure I must have appeared, sitting in a high-backed chair with linen wrapped around my head in the fashion of an India turban. He advised us not to venture out into the streets, where an occasional musket shot reminded us that the process of "scouring" was not yet completed.

Nor did I move from that chair until evening, for I continued giddy and nauseous, and there was a maddening pressure within my skull and considerable pain. Eliza brought me a bowl of porridge, but I could do no more than look upon it and then wave it away. Presently, however, I felt sufficiently recovered to rise and walk to the window, but at once regretted that I had done so. The rain had stopped and the air was clear. The sky had a faint greenish cast, with a few ragged strips of cloud. I looked down the street to the market house. An iron rod, hooked at the end, projects from its wall, about two feet above a tall man's head. This rod had been pressed into service as a gallows, and a man's body was hanging from it by a short length of rope. I turned away from the window, and went out into the street, despite Eliza's alarmed protests. She seized me by the arm but I pulled myself free.

The bodies still lay in the street, but had been shoved to both sides, against the walls of the shops and cabins. At the street's end, the hanged man was a dark mass pressed against the green sky. I walked toward it, with hesitant steps, but before I could reach it I encountered Stanner, one of our Killala yeomen, a man of middle years who keeps a provision shop. He carried a month's growth of beard, and his uniform was filthy beyond description.

"We are a free people, Mr. Broome," he shouted. "We are a free people again. Praised be the name of the Lord."

"Death," I said. "Bloodshed and death. It is all around us."

"Have you seen my shop, Mr. Broome? Have you seen how my shop has been used this past month? We have been held in the jaws of iniquity but we have been delivered by God's mercy."

"End," I said. "It must be ended or we will be forever soaked in blood." I must in truth have been enduring a fever, for I felt that the very walls of the town oozed blood. It lay in pools upon the street, and ran between the cobbles.

"They are savages," Stanner said. "We were losing the power of our eyes in that pesthouse. When we came out into the light it burned our eyes. As much sunlight as could come to us through rain, mind you. They would have piked us in the street, ripped out our bowels."

"You have suffered grievously," I said, and turned away from him. Down the street I ran, pushing my way past soldiers and gawking townspeople. The man they had hanged was Duignan, the prophecy man. I had never seen a man hanged. His face was dark red, his tongue hung loose from his slack jaws. His thin trousers were stained in an unseemly and disgusting manner. What had this witless and wretched fellow done? Perhaps he had run toward the soldiers, shrieking his unintelligible gibberish. Or perhaps he had done nothing, had stood staring at them with round mooncalf eyes.

A fresh wave of nausea swept over me, and I stood against the wall. Perhaps my senses took leave of me again, for I next remember an arm across my shoulders, and I opened my eyes to find myself looking into those of Captain Cooper.

"Come away out of this, Mr. Broome," he said. "Let me take you home." He had a heavy mat of beard, like Stanner, and his eyes were red-rimmed.

"Men hanged," I said. "Dead everywhere upon the streets, and now a man hanged."

"More than this fellow," Cooper said. "They have put up a gallows on the wharf, and they are court-martialing men and then hanging them. It is madness itself. They have all gone mad. I am leaving this place, by Jesus. I am going back to Kate at Mount Pleasant. But first I will take you to your house."

"They have no authority to do that," I said.

He gave a kind of yelp of humorless laughter, and took my arm. "No, sir," I said, and would not budge. "This is my parish. I will not hide in my bed. I will demand to know what is happening in my parish."

"Look around you, man, and you will see what is happening. There is no need to ask. I am sick of all this. Blood and death." He echoed my words, and suddenly, despite my own unbalanced state, I saw that he too was distracted and upon the verge of hysteria and tears. "My

559

own men will not listen to me," he said, "much less the English soldiers. The Highlanders are the worst. I saw them smash a man's skull. There has been a stop put to that, at least. There are court-martials now."

"And the gallows," I said.

"Stay in this charnel house if you will," he shouted in sudden anger. "I will have no part of it. I am going home, and if they want this bloody uniform they can send for it." He dropped my arm then, and walked away from me.

I ran down the street in the opposite direction, toward the wharf, but stopped by the body of Ferdy O'Donnell. Death had diminished him. He lay with his head lolling toward the street. I began to weep. Great tears squeezed from my eyes and coursed down my cheeks. Perhaps he would have killed the yeomen. I will never know what went through his mind in that last hour. I took his hand in mine and held it against my tears.

"Can you think of anything you want to add to this?" the subaltern asked.

"I cannot remember what I have said or what I have not said," Barrett answered. "What does it matter?"

"You must compose your thoughts now," I said. "You must pray."

"Can you write?" the subaltern asked. "Can you put your name to this?"

I put my hand on his arm. "Leave him alone, young man, leave him some time alone."

"How much time have I?" Barrett asked.

"Until the first light."

"It is almost the first light now," someone said.

But there was no light in the cabin save for the weak light from the candle.

"I will be with you," I promised Barrett.

"I would give much for a priest," Barrett said. "It is a black, dirty soul I will be bringing to judgment."

"You must pray," I said. " 'Where there is true repentance.' Ours is a merciful God."

Suddenly Barrett smiled at me. "It was a queer kind of confession," he said. "To a Protestant clergyman and an English officer. It will have to do."

"All right, then," the subaltern said. "We will give you some time to yourself." He stood up, and his body obscured the candle's flame.

560

"I will be with you," I promised him again. "At the end. You will not be alone."

Barrett did not reply.

Outside the cabin, the subaltern and I stood together in darkness through which the first light had begun to creep.

"I am sorry the poor devil could not have his priest," he said. "They believe that their priests have powers to forgive sins, do they not?"

"Something like that," I said. " 'Where there is true repentance.' "

"Is this the truth, do you think?" he asked.

"Part of the truth," I said. "Part of it is true."

"Is this what he would have told his priest?"

"I do not know," I said.

21

Weymouth, England, Late September

The King was taking the waters at Weymouth, which he had been visiting regularly since 1789. Two days earlier, the officers of the frigate *Argus* had presented him with pikes taken up from the bog of Ballinamuck. His Majesty held one of them, marveling at its crudity, a length of ash and then, hammered crudely out at some Mayo forge, the flat spear with the short, deadly hook curving outward from its base. Savages on the African coast must carry such weapons as these. His Majesty shook his head, and consigned the pikes to his collection of curios.

The King was strolling on the esplanade when the messenger brought him the dispatch from Nelson, having covered the hundred and thirty miles in seventeen hours. London already knew. The news had come yesterday, and the bells of Saint Paul's pealed, then those of a second church, and a third, until the whole of the city was clanging. That night the city was illuminated, and the guns at the Tower fired salute after salute. His Majesty read the dispatch twice, once almost hysterically, after seeing the first three words, and then a second time, more slowly. To the astonishment of the crowd on the esplanade, he began to cry. Great tears rolled down his cheeks and his heavy body shook. They thought that he had been brought the news of a disaster. Then, almost as astonishingly, he began to read aloud to them, his voice, at once coarse and soft, carrying a thin, nervous edge of relief.

"Admiral Lord Nelson begs leave to report to His Majesty and to their Lordships of the Admiralty that the French Fleet in the Mediterranean has been destroyed at Aboukir Bay at the mouth of the Nile. General Buonaparte's army is now cut off in Egypt, without hope of reinforcement. The Mediterranean is now a British sea and shall remain so. The destruction of the French Fleet was achieved without loss of British ships."

"It is a most wonderful and miraculous victory, Your Majesty," Lord Stanley said. "Within a single month, rebellion defeated in Ireland and the enemy in Egypt. The two ends of the world."

But the King scarcely heard him. Holding the rolled dispatch in his hands, he walked the length of the esplanade. Unimaginative and untraveled, his mind shuffled vague landscapes, green plans, the sandy desert, deep blue waters. British infantry, at the run, stormed enemy positions, a blur of scarlet. Officers led them forward, pointing toward the foe with drawn swords. On still waters, beneath the blue and white sky of a colored engraving, British ships pummeled the enemy, black cannon protruding from the gunports, puffballs of white smoke. The British ensign floated, defying logic, in a windless sky. Grandson and great-grandson of German princelings, his heart expanded in patriotic fervor. Providence had come once again to the side of England, not rushing, but with measured step, across moorland, desert waste, the broad expanse of ocean. Truly a people blessed by Heaven.

That evening His Majesty attended the theater, which displayed an illumination, hastily contrived. *Britannia Treading Anarchy and Rebellion under Her Feet*. Aboukir. The King pronounced the unfamiliar word, mouthing its syllables with pleasure. Britannia, her breasts swelling with triumphant indignation, held down rebellion with firm, sandal-clad feet. Anarchy crouched beside them,

562

looking fearfully toward her. It was a vigorous scene, and the King applauded it heartily. He tried to remember the name of the Irish county where the French had landed. It had all ended well.

Dublin, Late September

Humbert and his officers were lodged in the Mail Coach Hotel, south of the Liffey in Dawson Street. It had become a fashionable district some decades before, when the Marquis of Kildare built his great town mansion. "Where I go," he told his critics, "the rest will follow." And follow they did, peers, Members of Parliament, solicitors, bankers, merchants. Their houses faced leafy squares and gardens, or else faced each other across wide, dusty streets. A pleasant, easy society, conscious of its modernity, dwelling in buildings without a past, without history, undarkened by the shadows which hung north of the Liffey, a Dublin which remembered footpads and ruffians, sedan chairs, torchlight falling upon narrow alleys. Here the city was spruce and new, bricks and stonework fresh. Wind from the mountains drew off the pungent smoke of turf fires, sudden showers cleansed the streets. From Stephen's Green to College Green was a pleasant walk, ten minutes or so, nods for acquaintances, chat with a friend, and, at the foot of Grafton Street, Trinity College and the Houses of Parliament facing each other, far from rebellions and the bogs of Mayo. An equestrian statue of King William commanded College Green, Protestant emblem for a Protestant city. Turn right, stroll down Nassau Street beside the railings of Trinity, turn right again, and you are in Dawson Street.

In these weeks, many Dubliners took the stroll, in the hope of catching a glimpse of the French officers, who were often to be seen at the windows. Fontaine, in particular, was gallant by nature, and would occasionally blow a kiss to a young lady or to a pair of young ladies walking with arms linked, peering shyly toward the window from under lowered lids. They would hurry past, then pause at the Anne Street corner, and each would describe what she had seen. The French officers were a great success with the Dubliners, who now felt, all danger past, that theirs had been a most romantic adventure. They had expected to see desperate, hardened Jacobins, but these fellows, despite their hard-worn uniforms, were more like dandies. It became the fashion for British officers to visit them, and hear at first hand an account of their plans and exploits, and the more astute could detect the tension between Sarrizen and Fontaine. None could miss the contempt and detestation with which they spoke of their Irish allies.

Humbert himself, however, did not receive visitors. He had taken, by preference, a large room in the rear of the hotel, on the first floor, and he remained behind its closed door. The one exception which he made was for Cornwallis, who visited him late on a September morning.

Cornwallis was in uniform, scarlet against the pale Dublin sky as he climbed down from his coach. Leaning on a stick, he walked slowly up the steps, with a few dozen citizens watching. When they recognized him they set up a cheer, which, turning briefly, he acknowledged with a wave. " 'Cornwallis, he's our darling, he saved us from the foe,' " someone shouted, quoting a street ballad. Cornwallis, his back turned, grunted and stumped into the hotel.

Humbert stood up to receive him. He had been sitting behind a small dining table, with a bottle of brandy in front of him. His uniform was rumpled, and there was a glaze of dark beard on his cheeks.

Cornwallis waved his hand. "Sit down, General. Sit down." He sat down himself, but first drew up a third chair. With great care, gently, he rested his left foot on it. "Gout," he said. "A damned painful disease. Like a hundred small daggers sticking into you." He spoke idiomatic French, but with a wretched accent.

"In my country," Humbert said, "it is called the aristocrat's illness."

"It isn't true. I knew a footman with gout once. Perhaps he'd been eating too well. That will do it, that and wine."

"We are in your debt," Humbert said stiffly, "for the courtesy which has been shown to us."

"Not at all, my dear fellow. You will be home soon. Your passage is being arranged. By way of Hamburg." He folded his hands across his belly and smiled. "You must be very eager to see Paris again,"

"Very eager," Humbert said drily.

"By God, sir, your government will have no cause to fault you. A brilliant campaign, sir, if I may say so."

"My government prefers victories to brilliant campaigns."

"All governments do," Cornwallis said. "All governments. We are in the business of winning battles, we generals. And if we drop one—I speak from experience, as you must know. You failed here, on this wretched island. But as for me, I lost an entire continent. There's carelessness for you. What the devil, you could not possibly have succeeded. Not in a thousand years. You were outmanned and outgunned, with no allies save those poor wretched peasants. You did splendidly at Castlebar, but after that you were in a cleft stick. You couldn't stay and you couldn't move."

"If the second fleet had arrived while I was in control of Castlebar . . ."

"If," Cornwallis repeated, and shrugged in sympathy. "It has now arrived. I thought I should drop by and tell you. A ship of the line, eight frigates, a schooner. Warren intercepted them off the Donegal coast."

Humbert sat quietly. "What ship of the line? Do you know?"

"The *Hoche*. She put up a good fight. Didn't strike her colors for four hours. That fellow Wolfe Tone was aboard her. He is coming down to Dublin. In chains."

"So. It began with Hoche and it ends with his name. Hoche and Tone. What a pair!"

"Mr. Tone claims the rights and privileges of an adjutant-general in the French army."

"So he is. And Bartholemew Teeling is a colonel in the French army. He should be with me here, and not in some prison awaiting trial. I have written strong words to you on that subject."

"It won't do, old fellow. Mr. Tone and Mr. Teeling are subjects of the British Crown and they have committed treason. They will hang for it."

"That is unjust," Humbert said. "As a soldier you must feel its injustice. Teeling was the bravest of my officers. A chivalrous man. He protected the persons and the property of your loyalists."

"I am sorry," Cornwallis said. "I cannot judge this matter as a soldier. Treason is a most damnable offense. Especially when it is unsuccessful."

565

It was Humbert's turn to smile. He studied Cornwallis through half-opened eyes, a large, sleepy cat. "Perhaps," he said. "I have made my protest. I will miss Colonel Teeling."

"And Tone?"

"Teeling is a most serious man, a formidable man. I could never understand Tone, with his jokes and snatches of song. Hoche adored him."

"A damned nuisance," Cornwallis said. "A traitor and a nuisance. I have been told that General Buonaparte mistrusted him."

The cat turned its dark head away from Cornwallis and looked toward the window. "So I have heard."

"Now there is a remarkable man," Cornwallis said. "Your General Buonaparte. He is in desperate straits now, is he not? Stranded off there in Egypt with his army. He could have made his mark in the world. That Italian campaign, eh? The fortunes of war. They make us or mar us."

"He is a most remarkable soldier," Humbert said.

"You must know him well," Cornwallis said.

"Not well," Humbert said. "Not well enough to discuss him with a British general."

"Your point is taken," Cornwallis said. "But I must confess that I am curious to know about him. Who is not?"

"You will know about him soon enough," Humbert said. "I think we all will know about him."

"There is little left to know," Cornwallis said. "He will rot out there in Egypt. Ah, but that Italian campaign! He made his mark. Great energy you French fellows have! Buonaparte invades Egypt, you invade Ireland. An ambitious people, spreading the gospel of the Revolution to left and to right, as you might say."

"We intend to defend the Revolution, if that is what you mean to say. We defended it against the monarchs of Europe and we will defend it against the British Empire. We shall not let ourselves be strangled."

"Is that the way of it?" Cornwallis asked. "Well now. But from the first I have had a different notion. Only a notion, mind you." He leaned forward. "It has occurred to me that the liberation of Ireland was not your true goal, General Humbert. It has occurred to me that you wished to return to Paris as a victorious general, while Buonaparte was safely away in Egypt."

566

Humbert's eyes flew open. "For what possible purpose?"

"Why, to defend your revolution, of course. Not against the British Empire, but against General Buonaparte."

Humbert smiled, but the dark, heavy eyes remained wide and watchful. "You British develop peculiar notions indeed about other peoples. France is a nation, General, a great nation. It is not a gang of—of bandits."

"Of Corsican bandits, you were about to say. I may be entirely mistaken. No doubt I am. In the event, it does not matter, does it? The two of you have been shipwrecked, poor fellows. Yourself and Buonaparte."

"You have—you must excuse me for saying this—you have too much self-satisfaction, you British. We will manage our affairs, we French, and we will defend ourselves against you. You are welcome to Ireland. It is a most unhealthy country."

"You have found it so," Cornwallis said. "But the Irish people are charming, are they not?"

"They are a rabble," Humbert said, with sudden ferocity. "They are the most backward race in Europe."

Cornwallis nodded. "Best leave them to us. Damned if I know what we would do without them. It is like having an invalid wife or an idiot daughter." He lifted his gouty leg to the floor and stood up. "Perhaps we will have another opportunity to talk before you leave."

"That would be pleasant," Humbert said, and added, with faint sarcasm, "it is interesting to exchange confidences in this manner."

At the door, Cornwallis paused. "I have received a letter from the clergyman at Killala. A man named Broome."

Humbert smiled broadly. "I shall not forget Mr. Broome. A good little man. A bit foolish, perhaps, but good-hearted."

"Yes, he would appear so. He is concerned about the behavior of our troops there—my own people, you understand. And he praises the young fellow whom you left in command of the rebels. Name of O'Donnell. Do you remember him?"

Humbert thought and then shook his head. "I should. If I placed him in command I should remember him. There were so many of them. We gave them muskets and they wasted the balls firing at crows."

"It doesn't matter. He was killed in the fighting. Broome

seems to have taken quite a fancy to him, but Trench calls him a murderous ruffian."

"Trench is probably right," Humbert said. "Most of them were ruffians."

Cornwallis's coach, with its escort, rattled down Dawson Street and Nassau Street, then into College Green and down Dame Street to the Castle. In Dame Street, handsome and well proportioned, soldiers and merchants paused to stare at it, peered inside for a glimpse of the Viceroy. Near Cork Hill, a group of urchins set up a cheer. Cornwallis leaned forward and raised his hand. A ballad singer leaned against the red brick of the theater. A coat reached to his ankles; beneath a slouch hat, black hair hung lank.

"In the County of Longford one September morn,
Lake roused himself early and blew on his horn.
The rebels they scattered, the French had a fright,
And the Crown was triumphant before it was night."

He held a broadsheet to passersby. The balls of his eyes were turned inward. A month ago, that fellow would have been singing "The French Are on the Sea." By God, if they intend to turn Lake into a hero, they have their work cut out for them. Now Humbert! Give that fellow a proper army and God help us all. He will never get one. Perhaps, with luck, some minor command in the provinces or the West Indies. That other fellow, off in Egypt, was a different matter. He wants to contrive his own fate, that fellow does. One of the new men. The world turned upside down.

The coach swung into the lower Castle Yard, clattered across cobbles.

That night, for the first time since Paris, Humbert got drunk. Sitting by himself in the dark room, he finished the bottle of brandy and sent for another. Even Cornwallis, the fat, indolent English aristo, knew what had happened. He "had a notion." Paris had been lost in the bog of Ballinamuck. All his boasts and promises had sunk there, and now he would be shipped home, courtesy of the enemy, a defeated general. A ridiculous defeat, blundering across Ireland in the company of savage pikemen. Tone

568

had led him on with his glib, lying talk of an island ripe
for revolution. Eyes closed, he saw Tone again, dandified
in his French uniform, long hook of saber nose, soft feminine mouth, striding up and down the room, gesticulating
as he talked, jokes and passion, shrill cockatoo voice.
Playactor. He lit the candle and poured another glass.

More pleasant to think of the night march upon Castlebar, along the dark lake, peasants dragging cannon like
beasts of burden, strawlight from distant cabins guided
them forward. The tactics of the Vendée, Quiberon, sudden, unexpected. If the second fleet had come in time. He
waited a week for them. What had held them at Brest?
Intrigue, bungling, bad weather? It did not matter. All
the skill in the world was useless without luck. Once he
had had them both. Dealer in rabbit skins flung upward
by revolution. *Ci-devant* gentlemen obeyed him, Sarrizen,
Fontaine; resentful, supercilious, they obeyed him. Now
his luck had run out. "I make my own luck." Buonaparte's boast. No longer, perhaps. Night on the hill of
Cloone. In the churchyard, by morning light, he saw the
English spread out, the net pulled tight. Someday, perhaps,
peasants would point out the hill to their grandchildren.
The French camped here. All night their fires burned.
Among the gravestones. Meaningless.

Dublin Castle, Late September

"Whereas it appears that during the late Invasion many
of the inhabitants of the County of Mayo, and counties
adjacent, did join the French forces and did recieve from
them arms and ammunition; and whereas it may be ex-
pedient to admit such persons to Mercy who may have
been instigated thereto by designing men, We do hereby
offer our pardon to any person who has joined the Enemy, provided he surrenders himself to any of His Majesty's officers in the country, and delivers up a French
Firelock and Bayonet, and all ammunition in his possession; and provided that he has not served in any higher
capacity than that of Private; and provided that he will
fully inform the authorities as to the names and actions of
those who served in a capacity higher than that of Private
and may thereby be adjudged guilty of high treason.

CORNWALLIS"

Dublin Castle, Late September

"Whereas I have received information upon oath that the persons undernamed have been guilty of high treason, in aiding and assisting the French in their late Invasion of this country, I do offer a reward of one hundred pounds sterling for the apprehension of, or for such information as may cause to be apprehended, any and each of the persons undernamed: Christopher Crump, Esq., M.D., of Oury; Valentine Jordan, Esq., of Forkfield; John Gibbons of Westport; Rev. Myles Prendergast, Friar, of Westport; Rev. Michael Gannon of Louisburgh, Priest; Rev. Manus Sweeney of Newport, Priest; Mr. Peter Gibbons of Westport, Agent to Lord Altamont; Mr. Peter Cleary of Newport, Merchant; James MacDonnell, Esq., of Newport; Thomas Gibbons of Croc, Farmer; Austin O'Malley of Borrisool; Thomas Fergus of Murrisk, Farmer; James MacGreal of Kilguever; Hugh Macguire of Crossmolina, Farmer; Edmond Macguire of Crossmolina, Farmer; Hugh Macguire, jnr. of Crossmolina; Patrick Dunphy of the town of Ballina, Joiner; Michael Canavan of the town of Ballina, Painter; Thomas Rigney of Ballymanagh; Pat MacHale of Crossmolina, Farmer; James Toole, late of County Tyrone; Pat Loughney of Raheskin, Farmer; Martin Harkan of Cloongullane; John Heuston of Castlebar, Chandler; Malachi Duggan of Kilcummin, Farmer.

"All who offer aid or shelter to those here named or to any others who shall hereafter be so named shall be adjudged guilty of the capital crime of abetting high treason.

"The inhabitants of the County of Mayo are again put upon warning that no person who joined the French forces in any capacity shall be admitted to the King's Mercy until he has first made surrender either to one of His Majesty's officers or to Mr. Dennis Browne of Browne Hall, High Sheriff of the County. Until such time, he shall be considered a fugitive outlaw, subject to the rigors and penalties of martial law.

CORNWALLIS"

My Dear Trench:

My thanks to you for your letter informing me that Mr.
John Moore, Prisoner, has been sent under guard to the
gaol in Waterford. I believe, as you know, that his removal from this county well serves both the general interests of the Crown and, more particularly, the
restoration of social stability to this county. I have in the
meanwhile been most vigorous in my pursuit of Lord
Cornwallis's firm yet humane policy. I have established in
the western part of the county a system of informants, by
which means I expect shortly to have in hand a complete
list or inventory of those who took part in this wretched
and accursed rebellion, and I support ardently the view
that those who served in a capacity higher than private
should be tried for high treason and if found guilty should
suffer the appropriate punishment, viz, death by hanging.
The chief agents of the conspiracy were most certainly
Malcolm Elliott, Randall MacDonnell, and Cornelius
O'Dowd. Of these, two were slain in Longford and the
first-named awaits State Trial in Dublin. It is therefore
the more important that trials and executions of other
principals be held in Castlebar that the folly and wickedness of rebellion be impressed upon the populace.

Of those at present held for trial in Castlebar gaol, I
would single out three above others. Peter Gibbons of
Westport was agent to my own brother and admitted the
rebels to Westport House; he was the chief rebel on the
western coast of the county. Malachi Duggan, whom I
seized and sent forward to you on Tuesday, is a notorious
and brutal leader of banditti. He it was who formed and
led the "Whiteboys of Killala," by which title the United
Irishmen at first masked their purposes, and in the weeks
of the rebellion killed many harmless loyalists and destroyed much property. The third name, that of Owen
MacCarthy, I set down in sorrow, for he is a gifted poet
in the Gaelic tongue, whose verses have for years afforded to me and to others fond of the ancient tongue
much pleasure. And yet he is one of that rascally tribe of
hedge schoolmasters who have for centuries kept sedition
alive in this island. Of his participation in the rebellion

there can be no question, and I am persuaded that his public execution will offer vivid evidence to the populace of our intentions.

I am certain that Lord Cornwallis, for all his magnanimity and liberality of spirit is in agreement with us both, that this country must once and for all be scoured clean of disaffection.

Dennis Browne

Dublin, October 22

FROM LEONARD MACNALLY, ESQ., BARRISTER-AT-LAW, TO EDWARD COOKE, ESQ., UNDERSECRETARY OF STATE FOR IRELAND, DUBLIN CASTLE. UNSIGNED. MARKED *Most Urgent. Most Confidential.*

As counsel to the late Malcolm Elliott, I spent much time with him both before his trial and in the two days which preceded his execution. I talked also with his widow, a most handsome young Englishwoman, who has returned with his body to Mayo. Elliott, it is true, was a member of the Provincial Executive for Connaught, but his discussions with me added nothing to what we already know. The events of the past two months destroyed all of his illusions, and his mood was sullen and despairing. His attitude reminded me much of Bagenal Harvey of Wexford fame, like him a gentleman of advanced republican sentiments who found himself caught up in the miseries of a servile insurrection and lost thereby his taste for sedition. I found him, I must confess, a much more attractive specimen, for he was a man of considerable intelligence, and his disgust was directed chiefly toward himself rather than his confederates.

There could be dealings more profitable with Cornelius O'Grady of Limerick, a member of the Munster Provincial, also a prisoner in Kilmainham, although on a lesser charge. Here also I am counsel for the defense, being junior to Mr. Curran. He is a man far different from Elliott or Teeling, being a grain merchant large and jovial in manner, although much dashed down by present

572

circumstances. Should he be offered terms by the Crown, dependent upon his disclosure of the names and state of his Provincial, I am confident that they would be accepted, and I would encourage him to that end. But I must insist, as always, that the Crown keep its part of the engagement, for I will not be party to shabby dealings.

I must now, and yet again, remind you, at whatever embarrassment to myself and to you, that with me you have not to do with some common informer, some Samuel T———or Thomas R———. Much less am I one of Higgins's band of spies and turncoats, basely and for profit betraying men who are their superiors in rank, spirit, and aspiration. As you well know, and as others at the Castle know, I joined the Society of United Irishmen from a wish, sincere though misguided, to better the lot of my unfortunate fellow countrymen and to strengthen their just liberties. Only when I had become convinced that their enterprise was destined to serve far different purposes did I offer my services to the Crown. And for the Crown I have labored in the most odious of ways, by tampering with the sacred relationship which should exist between a defendant and his advocate. For this I have received as recompense a pension of three hundred pounds upon the Secret List, together with some trifling additional sums tossed to me as to the conscienceless wretches who slink into the Lower Castle Yard, and the vague promises of honorable employment at some future time. I received promises fairer than these when first I engaged with Lord Castlereagh and yourself.

You may depend upon it that my services to this realm are of incalculable value. Dangerous conspirators remain undetected, especially in the southern counties, and of these you will not make discovery by turning loose upon the peasantry such bullies as Lord Carhampton and Mr. Dennis Browne, nor by placing a gallows at every cross-roads. For that you require the services of someone as public-spirited as myself, and with an earned reputation for patriotism among the advanced elements of the population.

We live in evil times. As I sat with Malcolm Elliott in his narrow cell, I could not escape the reflection that many gifted and honorable men have been dragged down to ruin by this wretched affair. And I recalled, with an ache for which there is no remedy, words spoken by one of the great orators of antiquity to the effect that no duty is

573

higher or more painful than that which obliges us to deliver friends to the punishment of the state.

From the Reminiscences Appended by Judith Elliott to Her Manuscript, *All Dressed in Green: Memories of an Irish Patriot*

I took Malcolm back to Ballina and buried him there, where his ancestors lay buried, and placed above his head a simple stone on which are inscribed the dates of his birth and death (1798, that fatal year!) and the words DULCE ET DECORUM EST PRO PATRIA MORI.

For several years I attempted the management of the estate, although I understood little of such matters, until at last the loneliness of Mayo became too oppressive. The first months were bitter to endure, for even as I nursed my deep grief at my own loss, I was painfully conscious of the *dragonnade* of the county by forces of the Crown under the command of General Trench, most brutally assisted by Mr. Dennis Browne, High Sheriff and brother to Lord Altamont. Many hamlets were put to the torch, especially in the outlying lands beyond Belmullet and many a peasant or small huckster was strung to the triangle and his back lashed into bloody ribbons. Hangings were an almost daily occurrence at Castlebar and the gibbets bore their dread cargo of bodies coated with tar and caged in iron. Michael Geraghty, a tenant farmer upon the Elliott lands, was among those hanged, having been transported for that purpose from the battlefield at Ballinamuck, and I sought to offer sisterly comfort to his widow, but with scant success, for she had scarce a hundred words of English to her credit, a tall, heavyset woman old before her years, barefoot and slovenly. From the families of all those whom Malcolm had led into battle I was cut off by deep trenches of class and language, and, indeed, of nationality itself, for deprived of Malcolm's companionship I grew increasingly aware that his people were not mine, and had never been.

The county families, need I say, treated me with a cold and almost contemptuous incivility as the widow of a hanged rebel who made no secret of her patriotic sentiments, for I lost no occasion to speak of Colonel Elliott and of the brave fight which he had waged for Irish liberty. Some few, it is true, Mr. and Mrs. Broome in particular, and Mr. Falkiner, showed to me an unfailing sympathy and courtesy, but this too I found unendurable in its way. They saw in me, I am certain, a lost and bewildered young Englishwoman, taxed beyond her capabilities by a sprawling and near-bankrupt estate, and mourning a husband who had fallen in what was to them an unworthy cause. I remember an evening at Mr. Broome's, in Killala, when I found myself speaking yet again in glowing words of Malcolm's chivalry, and of the selflessness which had placed him at the head of a daring and forlorn enterprise. Between the candles, Mr. Broome's head bobbed in sympathy, his hair a fuzzy gray aureole about his bald pate. Behind him, beyond the high window, stretched the dull waters of the bay, sullen and lifeless. I felt myself alone and frightened.

And yet within two years, wonderful to relate, the rising had begun to fade from Mayo memory, or rather to recede into that past, compounded of legend and fact, which lies as an almost palpable presence upon the heavy Irish landscape. *Bliadhain na bhFranncach,* the peasantry now called it, which is to say, the year of the French, and they spoke of it as an event remote in time, equal in its distance from the present to a horse race run a decade before or to the wars of Elizabeth. Songs were sung, the most in Irish but a few in English, and these celebrated chiefly young Ferdy O'Donnell, a Mayo youth, or Malachi Duggan, described to me by Malcolm as a most fearful ruffian but transformed by folk imagination into a Robin Hood. No song of those that I heard enshrined the memory of Malcolm Elliott, their gallant leader. He has left no memorial upon the land save the simple tombstone in the Ballina churchyard. A mountain path leading into Castlebar became known as the "road of straw," for along it the rebels had been guided in dark of night by the blazing straw brands of the cabin dwellers. And Ballinamuck, far off in Longford, was spoken of as a place of terror and destruction yet mercifully remote from the here and now of things. English-speaking children had a rhyme they would shout to one another, "Be a good boy, And I'll buy you a book, And I'll send you to school at Ballinamuck." The burned cabins were rethatched, and there is about the Irish a savage and unfeeling ability to link sorrow and pleasure, to wash a river of easy sentiment over cruelty and bloodshed. But surely the blame for this rests not with them but with the harsh facts of their dreadful history.

But it was the landscape itself which I came in time to find unbearably oppressive, that very landscape which once had seemed to me endowed with a magical power and beauty. The River Moy, which formed one boundary of the estate, flowed dull and sluggish toward Killala and the sea, and the red bog which stretched westward was desolate and somber. The low hills, upon which cottiers crouched in their misery, were formless and mute of meaning. And above all arched the immense Irish sky, at times bright as porcelain, but often sunless and heavy, terrifying in its ability to drain all human definition from the earth and water beneath it. It was a landscape which hugged dark and unfathomable secrets before which I stood alien and unprotected.

In 1804, I resolved to return to England, leaving the estate in the capable hands of Mr. Robert MacAdoo, a Scottish agriculturist who has since then tended my Irish interests in a most able and diligent manner. I have become, in short, an absentee, a class of landlord toward whom Malcolm was always most unsparing in his scorn, and yet I am confident that he would not have wished me to remain in Mayo, lonely and burdened by unhappy memories. On my journey home I paused in Dublin for a visit with Mr. Leonard MacNally, the advocate who so courageously defended Malcolm at his trial. There at least, in Mr. MacNally's bosom, the memory of Malcolm Elliott is green, and the cause for which he fought is honored and cherished. He held my hand in his two. "Do not think harshly of us," he implored me. "We are a confused and divided people, but we have our memories of the dead, and someday, God willing, the tree of liberty will flower from those memories." I pray that this will be so, and yet I lack his serene and affecting confidence. We strolled together through the streets of the city, and he pointed out to me scenes which he knew would claim my interest— the house where poor Lord Edward was run to earth, and the one in which Malcolm paid his fateful visit to the Directory in the month before the rising. It was a sunny day, and beyond the rows of brick and stone the Dublin hills glistened in the distance. His voice brought back the past to me, and yet it was a past compounded only of that voice and of shadows moving across the screen of imagination. All about us was the bustle of a city indifferent to that noble enterprise to which Malcolm had given his hope, his energies, and, at last, his life.

Time has been kind to me. In 1811 I married Mark Matthews, who is not without celebrity both as a water-colorist and as the author of several delightful books on the hill towns of Italy. Much of our life together has been spent in that fragrant and sun-drenched countryside, for Mr. Matthews serves as British Consul in Florence, and we have many friends in the large British colony here. The story of Malcolm Elliott, his share in the Mayo rebellion and his tragic death, is for them among the most romantic of legends. The English are gallant and chivalrous toward those who oppose them in a manly and straightforward spirit, and in no other people does a respect for high enterprise glow more ardently. Lord Edward and his Pamela, Robert Emmet and his Sarah, Malcolm Elliott and poor me—we will be forever touched by the pale light of an old romance.

No shadow of a needless jealousy has clouded Mr. Matthews's sentiments. Indeed, he has painted for me from my descriptions a portrait of Malcolm which he presented to me upon the occasion of my thirty-eighth birthday and which now hangs in our drawing room. In the year of 'ninety-eight, Mr. Matthews was serving with the Somersetshire Militia and it was only by chance that he was not sent to Ireland. Strange are the workings of Providence! Often, in jest, he will remind me that "the year of 'ninety-eight" has a different signification. It was the year which saw the publication of the *Lyrical Ballads* by Mr. Wordsworth and Mr. Coleridge. "And which will history deem the more important," he will ask me playfully, " 'The Ancient Mariner' or an obscure uprising in Mayo? To my best knowledge, there were no poets among the Mayo rebels?"

It was all poetry, I think to myself. It was all a dream.

22

Waterford to Moore Hall, Early October

In October John Moore of Moore Hall, prisoner, was transported, under a guard of Hompesch's cavalry, to the gaol at Waterford, in the south of Ireland. Waterford is a coastal town, and the window of his cell faced south, toward Spain. He was never well enough to rise from his cot and look out across the town, across the wide wharfs, toward the sea. He carried with him from Castlebar a draft for a thousand pounds upon his brother's Dublin bankers and a case of gaol fever, two spots of hectic red upon his cheeks. After a week, his condition had so worsened that he was removed to the Royal Oak Tavern, where, on the nineteenth, he died.

George Moore rode to Waterford upon receiving word of his brother's dangerous condition, but he arrived too late. He stood beside the body. The skin was drawn tight over the bones of the face and was covered by a bristle of yellow beard. The eyes had been closed, but the mouth was half open, giving the face a dull, vacant appearance. George sat for a time before the body, and then walked downstairs to the taproom, where the commander of the Waterford garrison, Colonel Harrison, had been waiting for him.

"It is a great misfortune, Mr. Moore. He was made comfortable here at the inn, and of course he was properly attended, by my own regimental surgeon. He was bled regularly. There was never a hope for him."

Moore nodded. "Was he sensible?"

"Not at the end. Not when I visited him. It was a fever, you understand."

"Yes," Moore said. "A long fever."

"It was very difficult," Harrison said. "Poor fellow. We did not think of him as a prisoner."

"You have been most considerate," Moore said. "I am indebted to you."

"Mayo," Harrison said. "You will have a long journey with him. Poor roads, there, are they not?"

"He will be buried here," Moore said. "In Waterford."

Harrison cleared his throat. An awkward man to deal with, this Moore, cold and aloof. He had expected a Connaught squireen, all brogue and tears.

"He is not the only gentleman to have been caught up in this wretched business," he said. "There were a number of gentlemen in Wexford. Men of substance."

"So I have heard," Moore said.

"You will want to speak with the parson, then."

"With the priest," Moore said. "The Moores of Mayo are Catholic."

"We didn't know that," Harrison said, in quick apology. "We could have brought a priest. He was delirious. Does that make a difference?"

"I believe it does," Moore said. "I will arrange for his burial. You have been most considerate. Very kind indeed." He settled his hat and pulled on his gloves.

Harrison walked with him into the street. "If I can be of any assistance to you. . . ."

Moore turned toward him. Winter smiled from his long, pale face. "We have already made too many impositions on your courtesy."

Harrison looked away from winter, from the cold, blue eyes. Damned awkward business, a gentleman's brother being gaoled for treason, carted from Castlebar to Waterford like a common criminal. This fellow here had no wish to make it less awkward. London manners like a slap in the face.

"There were no effects," he said. "Not even a pocket watch. But there was a bank draft—"

"I know about that," Moore said. "I will attend to it."

The street ended at the quay, where a ship rode gently at its moorings.

"British," Harrison said. "Bound for Santander. In Spain."

"We were born in Spain," Moore said. "My brother and myself. I had hoped that perhaps—" He shook his head. "Good day to you, Colonel."

Peculiar fellow.

Moore spent the night in Athy, on the Barrow, and then pushed on to Mayo. It was a dreary, windless day, a landscape of pastureland, low hill. He studied it for lack of anything better to do. He had brought no books or paper with him. Near Edgeworthstown the weather changed. Drops of rain fell into the carriage. Silly man, Edgeworth, fussy little pedant with clockwork brains. Left no effects; not even a pocket watch. He sat with crossed legs, folded hands resting on his knees. Time later for bringing John home. Not now, a local curiosity, landlord's son who mingled with rebel cowherds and sickened in prison.

Rain thickened. Mist hid the hills. Some curse has held us here, distant from the live warmth of Spain, the book-crowded villa on the Thames. A summer room faced the river, copper bowls choked with chrysanthemums.

"You should meet them, George. They are splendid fellows. Tom Emmet is a musician. Would you believe that? He has a small house out in Rathfarnham, by the Dublin hills. He and Tone play duets. Spinet and flute. Tone plays the flute with great spirit."

"Does he indeed? A most talented gentleman."

"He is a most affectionate man. He has taken Russell and myself to dine with Mrs. Tone and their children, of whom he is prodigious fond."

"I have been told of his large affections by his friend Knox. Mrs. Tone cannot satisfy them, it would seem. He requires also Dick Martin's wife."

"That is untrue," John said. "And at all odds, you should be the last man in the world to be critical in such matters. I know your London reputation. Father knew it. Come now, George. We are men of the world, the two of us." How old was he then, nineteen, twenty? Men of the world.

"I cannot hope to compete with him on that score. Mr. Tone's affections are so large as to embrace an entire nation. And Ireland at that. He shows poor taste."

"You are Irish yourself, George. We both are."

"Are we? What are we? Irish? English? Spanish? I have never been certain. More English than not, I would think. I am happiest in London. My friends are there."

"Burke? Sheridan? Do they think themselves English? The English know better."

"What does it matter?"

"It mattered to Father. He brought us home from Spain."

"Not to Ireland. To Mayo."

John laughed suddenly. Sweet bell of a hound at nightfall. "You are as mad as the rest of us, George. Sobersides, Father called you. You believed him. You are not like that at all. I know you."

I buried him in the nearest churchyard, alien dirt flung upon the coffin. A fat, nervous priest gabbled Latin over him. British soldiers watched from beyond the wall, a handful of country people. Not there forever. Bring him back to Mayo. I loved him. He knew.

At Longford, he sent the coachman in to order him a meal, and stood bareheaded in the wide, rainswept street of the ugly town.

"Will we be staying here the night, sir?" Walsh asked.

"Not at all. I don't like leaving the Hall without a master. See to the horses and get yourself some food." He turned and walked into the inn.

A queer, cold man, with a brother just buried in Waterford. At Ballintubber, Father Lavelle would have leaped upon the Mass rock to speak the panegyric. Walsh could see him: in Longford of the heavy-shouldered cattle dealers he could see Lavelle's stumpy body balanced on the flat, broad rock, his arm outstretched, behind him the skies swept clean by the Atlantic winds. "A young man of the Moores has parted from us, and has gone from the beauty of Mayo and from the sad suffering of this sinful world. There is no man standing here who does not remember John Moore astride his horse on such a morning as this, his scarlet coat bright as the sun. . . ." Trust Lavelle for that, not a word that would not brim with praise, not a word about the shameful death in prison. Black-cloaked women fringed the crowd. And before that a proper wake, with whiskey and barrels of porter. The old man would have known what to do, for all that he was half a Spaniard.

Flat, sweetish ale, cold ham, potatoes boiled in their skins. Moore pushed the plate aside and called for a bottle of brandy.

"It was less quiet here a month ago," the innkeeper said. "The rebels came at the town from all four sides. There must have been a thousand of them. Thank God this is a garrison town. The soldiers beat them off."

"Your news is stale," Moore said. "Like your ham."

Aggrieved and obsequious, the innkeeper backed away, but stood facing him. "You would do well to pass the night here, sir. You are a gentleman from England, are you not?"

Moore smiled without looking up from his glass. "I was just now discussing that point with my brother. My brother is Irish. He can prove it." Unshaven and shivering in the moist-walled cell. He proved it. "My father is Spanish, my brother is Irish. What am I?"

"Is the brandy to your liking?" the innkeeper asked nervously.

"That depends," Moore said. "Is it Irish brandy?"

"Sure, it could be, sir. It could be. There are Irish people named Lynch who ship brandy from Spain. Often enough in the bad times Irishmen went off to Spain and entered the wine trade. And they never came home again. Devil the one of them."

"No," Moore said. "Devil the one."

He carried the brandy and the glass into the coach with him, and flung a shilling to Walsh. "Go back and buy yourself a drink. You will have a cold journey up there."

"Jesus, Mr. Moore. We will be traveling the roads of Christendom in the pitch black."

"If you call this Christendom you have much to learn."

Moore settled himself in the seat and opened the pistols which rested beside him. Dueling pistols. Another sport of this fool's island. Another fine sport of this bloody-minded country. Bumpkins drawing up dueling codes that would have put Froissart to shame. No party can be allowed to bend his knee or cover his side with his left hand; but may present at any level from the hip to the eye. Starve the poor and shoot each other. Small need they have for invading armies. He primed the pistols.

By post roads westward and north, they crossed Ireland in darkness. A few bands of soldiers, drunkards wandering homeward from hillside shebeens, cattle strayed from broken-fence pastures interrupted the journey. Nothing more. Twice Walsh lost the road, and knocked at frightened cabins to ask the way. In the early night, lights from big houses gleamed from the branches of their sheltering plantations, far back from walls of cut stone.

Moore drank quietly and steadily from the heavy bottle of brandy, sipping it like a cordial, his hand unshaken by the jolting carriage. The rain eased off, making the roads passable. At the bridge across the Shannon, sentries stopped him, and held a lantern to the window.

English militiamen. Yorkshire accents. Moore blinked at the sudden light. He handed out his pass. Signatures of Dennis Browne, High Sheriff; Trench, General commanding. The pass was refolded and handed back. George Moore, Esquire, of Moore Hall, County Mayo.

"You have a long journey before you, sir."

"I was seeing my brother aboard ship," Moore said. "He has left for Spain. From Waterford."

"The roads get worse beyond the bridge," the sentry said. "You must know that, sir."

Moore replaced the pass.

"Was he an Irishman at all?" one of the privates said to the corporal. "He talked like a gentleman."

"He was a gentleman," the corporal said. "It said so on Trench's safe-conduct. But he was Irish, right enough. Did you get a whiff in there? It stank of brandy."

"I wish I did," the private said, hugging himself against the night's chill.

West of the Shannon. Where Cromwell had herded whatever Catholic gentry he had left alive. Not the Moores: we have always been in Mayo. We were waiting for them when they drifted there in the winter, long trains of wives and children, herdsmen, droves of cattle. Provision carts loaded with furnishings from houses abandoned in Meath and Carlow. No swordsmen to guard them: no Papist will travel in arms through the kingdom. Hunting out whatever acres had been allotted to them, thin-soiled farmland fringed by bog and mountain. No worse than elsewhere, other countries. Our history. Woe to the vanquished.

The glass slipped from his fingers. Searching, his heel crushed it. He drank from the neck of the bottle. Jews and Moors hunted down in Spain, Huguenots in France, red Indians in America. One man armed with whip and pistol more powerful than ten men naked in their shirts. Rough justice. Brandy coated parts of his mind, flared other parts to fitful thought, will-o'-the-wisps of drunken wisdom. How happy could I be with either, were t'other dear charmer away. Sheridan's song. Which was Sheridan? Irish? English? John rode down graveled paths, beyond demesne walls of smooth gray stone, cool to the touch, joined peasants jabbering in Irish. Banner spun from French silk, dyed green to catch fools in its web.

583

John caught. The harp without the crown. Grief. John dead. Violence. Bodies torn apart. Me. Last of the Moores. Cheap novel. Much to John's taste. Box of pistols on the seat beside me. Fool.

Invisible, bogland stretched away from him toward distant mountains. Bog lakes chill in the rain-soaked autumn air of Connaught. In the black cold, Moore shivered and drank again. English lady remembered. Mrs. Sophie Germain. London and Wiltshire. White skin stained pink at cheek and bosom. A week's long afternoons in country inns. Black, disordered hair on white pillow, wide brown eyes. Afternoon sun streaming through unfastened curtains. Its memory cannot warm me. "Are there many Irish like you?" "I cannot say. I do not know many Irish." "What is it like there?" "Like anywhere. Lakes, roads, houses, people." "Like Spain?" "No. Not like Spain." "It has put a streak of strangeness into you. It is most becoming." "Spain has?" "No. Ireland." "Do I sound Irish?" "You do. Mine now. My Irishman. Life is very gay there, I have been told." "Fools find it so. It is splendid country for fools." "My Irishman." Her fingers moved across his chest. Melancholy scraped at the edges of his lust. Her Irishman.

She vanished from the mind locked within the rattling coach. Querulous and harsh, his father paced the grounds beside the unfinished house, and Moore walked beside him. Sunday. No sounds save those of evening birds. Flights of rooks circled toward their nests. Beyond the young plantation, the waters of Lough Carra stretched cool and green, the color of a banner whose silk would not be spun for years. "John will marry," his father said; "he will not grow up to waste his substance and his body upon the whores of London." "No more do I. I have never found whores to my liking." "And books. Books and strumpets. By God, there is a pretty combination. You are as pagan as any Protestant." "You misjudge me, Father. You have always misjudged me. I love this place. The lake. As you do." "They stripped away our land. Sent me off penniless to a distant country." "Now we are back. Times change." "This man with whom you fought the duel in London. It was in the Dublin papers, spread out for every Protestant to read. What was his name?" "Germain." "You fought over a woman, no doubt?" "Certainly not. Over cards. We had been gaming late, and drinking." Very proper, very English. Her Irishman.

In this country, the woman would have come in her coach to watch. "John will be different." "John has always been different. You have always been at pains to point that out to me." "I have loved you both. As the Blessed Virgin is my judge, I have loved you both." Stretched dead in a Waterford inn, tight skin and yellow-stubbled cheeks. Different now.

Fell into sleep. Woke up. Still night. He sang snatches of verse, song, scattered, senseless. "O, the French are on the sea, Says the *Sean Bhean Bhocht*." Great wave, tumbling past Downpatrick Head, and sweeping a broken brother to Waterford. "O, the French are in the Bay, They'll be here at break of day." History drowns us, mutinous, formless waves. "Did you hear that one?" he shouted to the unhearing coachman. "I know that song, by God. John listened to that one." Filthy, rain-soaked island. Cannot leave now.

By the time they had reached Ballyhaunis he was noisy and quarrelsome. The empty bottle rolled at his feet. He insisted upon stopping at the inn, waking up the innkeeper, and buying a second bottle. One drink from it finished him. He sat sprawled beside the long table, wild eyes and flushed cheeks, shirt and waistcoat stained. My Irishman. White hand crept toward his belly. He held the glass in both hands and lowered his head toward it, drank off half its contents, then choked and spewed it out. "All done for the best," he said, his head lolling on his chest. "Got him out of the country. Safe now." Walsh had never seen Moore drunk and he was terrified. It was as if a different soul had taken possession of the body, shouting wild nonsense and contorting the face. "I also loved him, Father," he said, looking directly into Walsh's eyes. "Loved you too. Told you once. Gone now."

"Jesus, Mary, and Joseph," the innkeeper's wife said. "What can we do with him?"

"Can he not hold his drink?" the innkeeper asked.

"Not this much," Walsh said. "No one could."

"Who is he?"

"A Mayo gentleman," Walsh said. "Help me get him to bed."

"By God, he is, and a rare one at that. Will you take a look at him there?"

"He can hear us," Walsh said.

But by early afternoon, when they reached Castlebar, he was himself again, fresh-shaven, fresh clothes, fresh linen. The clear Mayo sky found reflection in the long, poised face with its alert pale eyes. No bottle rolling at his feet, the case of pistols closed. Only the wineglass, crushed to powder by his boots, remained from the long night.

At Castlebar High Street the coach was blocked by a crowd.

"Get away out of that now," Walsh shouted at them and raised his whip.

Moore leaned out the window. "No." He opened the door and stepped down into the street.

British soldiers, militia, farmers, townspeople. He turned to talk to a young officer, but felt a hand on his shoulder. Yeoman's uniform, short pudgy body, round head and small, full face. Cooper. The man who had come to him about the Whiteboys. Speak a word to Dennis Browne for us. Disturbances in Killala. Before all this started.

"By God, you came in on a good day, Moore. But Friday next will be a better one. You should be here then. The company is on duty in Killala, but I am here today and I will be here again on Friday. I wouldn't miss a day of this. By Christ I wouldn't."

"A day of what?" Moore asked. Absently, coldly, he looked at the small hand on his sleeve. Cooper withdrew the hand, and then rubbed it along the length of his buff breeches.

"I spent a starving month as a prisoner waiting for this, and by God it is what kept me alive. By God, your Dennis Browne is a busy man when he sets his back to it. But the afternoons are no good, and by evening everyone is drunk. Get here in the morning. A good brisk morning as this one was. It has put years on me."

"What has?" Moore asked.

"Why, the court-martials, of course. The hangings. What else have we been talking about, man?"

"I am not your man." Master of Moore Hall to Killala farmer. What difference does it make?

"We have been topping them in batches. Three or four a week."

Mean garrison town—courthouse, prison, shops, taverns. The capital of Mayo. Moore looked down the street to where it straggled away in cabins, and upward, where it rose to the courtyard, beyond the crowd.

586

"I have never been able to draw much pleasure from hangings," he said.

"Well now," Cooper conceded. "I am not a bloody-minded man myself. But this is a different matter. They are beaten now and we will put the fear of God into them. Take a look around the county. See what they have done."

"You call freely upon God," Moore said, and then said, in the same flat, casual tones, "you would have hanged my brother, you know. John, my younger brother."

"Oh, Jesus," Cooper said, startled and abashed. "I had forgotten John, I had forgotten your brother. I ask your pardon. You did well to get him away out of this. Where is the poor fellow now? In Clonmel is it not, or Waterford?"

"Waterford," Moore said. "His difficulties are being sorted out. I expect that shortly he will be permitted to leave for Spain. We have commercial interests there, as you know."

Cooper knew. Moores, Brownes, Martins, Glenthornes. Nothing could touch them. Gentry. Everything arranged over a glass of sherry—marriages, bonds, the hunt, even a case of high treason. But John was a decent fellow, high-spirited. Cooper did not begrudge him Spain. Not like this glass of cold water.

"That is welcome news," he said.

"These fellows whom you are topping in batches," Moore said. "They should have had commercial interests in Spain. They were short-sighted."

Cooper looked sharply at the impassive face, pale eyes. Cold, sardonic bastard. Eyes like arctic ice.

"I have my own cause for joy," he said.

"I am certain of that," Moore said. "A length of hemp and a trapdoor."

Puzzled, Cooper drew his hand across his round chin. A vulgar man.

"You must have mistaken my meaning. The fact is, Moore, that all the while I was wearing my heart out in that prison, near mad with rage, my wife Kate was carrying our child. She had the news waiting for me when I got back to Mount Pleasant."

"My congratulations to you, sir. And to Mrs. Cooper. We have never met, I believe."

"You would have known her father, Mick Mahory the

587

grazier. He held lands near Ballycastle and near Cross-molina."

"I have heard the name," Moore said. "You have a worthier cause for happiness than a hanging, and I do indeed wish you joy."

"A great beauty she was in the county. And still is. A black-haired woman."

"Black-haired women are often beautiful," Moore said.

"But a most dutiful wife," Cooper said hastily. Moore lived quietly in Mayo, but his reputation had followed him from London. "A most dutiful woman. She is one of yours."

"One of mine?"

"A Papist. I have never tried to change her. She says her confessions and goes to Mass, the same as you do."

"More frequently, I trust. You mentioned Friday. Why is Friday a special day?"

"Friday?" Cooper blinked. "Oh, to be sure. Friday. They will be hanging Owen MacCarthy on Friday."

"Who is he?"

"Well may you ask." Cooper spat, and ground the gob into the dirt with the toe of his boot. "He was the school-master at Killala, and he was one of the ringleaders of the Whiteboys. He wrote that bloody proclamation that started the whole business. The one I brought to you at Moore Hall." Clownish churl, you count your cows in children's lives.

"I remember it," Moore said. "A most peculiar paper. It had a touch of the poet, I thought."

"He is a poet," Cooper said, "and a damned good one, Kate tells me. They often are, those schoolmasters. And they are often the greatest ruffians left unhanged."

"And you will remedy that omission on Friday."

"He has admitted it all," Cooper said. "The proclama-tion and the rest of it. A few brisk lads of the Killala Yeomanry visited him in Castlebar gaol one evening. He took little persuasion, though. He is a beaten cur. Bal-linamuck took the fight out of him, and the poetry as well."

A dusty street, the houses gray and drab in the even sun of afternoon. In a side street, invisible, a dog yelped in pain.

"God damn you," Moore said mildly. "God damn us all. God damn this country."

588

Cooper, legs spread wide apart, fists planted on hips, watched the coach roll away, toward Ballintubber. Moore had placed a touch of winter upon his pleasure, English accent strained through his long, arrogant nose, his Papist creed flaunted like a decoration. Mayo was settling back into place, thanks to the tough fiber of its loyal Protestants, a touch of the whip, a touch of the rope. But nothing could touch Moore, not even a brother's disgrace. The great families were all alike—Browne or Moore, Protestant or Papist. They lived within a conspiracy of kinships and secret alliances, spoke a secret language which was a rebuff to ordinary men like himself who were the backbone and sinew of Ireland. I declare to Jesus, Cooper thought, I had more that I could share with Mick Mahony than I have with these bastards.

But by nightfall he was himself again, sitting in the Wolf's Head with two officers of the Kerry Militia, and describing to them the arrival of the French and his defense of Killala.

"It could as easily have happened to us," Captain Stack said. "In 'ninety-six when Hoche's fleet was beaten into Bantry Bay at Christmas, with Wolfe Tone aboard the flagship. It was only that miracle of a storm that prevented them from landing in Kerry. They would have burned Tralee, the bastards."

"What the people there call that storm," Lieutenant Hassett said, "is the Protestant wind."

"We have been lucky with our winds," Cooper said, "and we have been since the days of the Armada."

"It is more than luck," Stack said. "I believe that. I believe that it is Providence. We are a people placed under God's protection. How else could we have survived, a small garrison surrounded by that great mass of ignorance and idolatry?"

But Cooper was less certain. Winds came and went. There were terrible winds off the Mayo coast and Kerry was even worse. But it was comforting to think of the Protestants of Ireland as a people protected by Providence, a spare, taciturn people, the heirs of Cromwell, resolute in adversity, forthright in their dealings with themselves and others, God-fearing, shunning idolatry and superstition. The people of an unbroken tradition of courage and respectability. On the strength of that feeling, he ordered another round of porter.

"Mind you," Stack said, half smiling, half taunting, "I

can only speak for the Protestants of Kerry. The Mayo Protestants may be another lot entirely. Sure, the Mayo Protestants may be half Papist for all I know 'Turned rotten' is the word we have in Kerry for a Protestant when that happens to him. First he will find himself a Papist wife, and after that the rot sets in. When the children begin to arrive."

Over his tankard, Cooper peered at him. Was this an unlucky hit, or had Stack been talking to people?

"There is nothing wrong with their women," Cooper said. "Some of them. Bed them down with good Protestant farmers and you have the best stock in Europe. In such matters, it is the man that rules. And Protestant men are bred up from birth to rule. It is our special skill."

"Best to stay with your own," Hassett said.

"Best indeed," Stack said.

"It is said in other parts of the kingdom that Kerry is a nursery for treason," Cooper said. "The lad who is going to swing on Friday is a Kerry man."

"Driven out from there," Hassett said. "With his tail between his legs. Sure, I know all about that lad. He was born in Tralee and his father worked as a laborer for my own grandfather. It was the people of Mayo who took up that lad and let him have his own school. Kerry knows how to deal with wild lads."

" 'Wild' is the word," Stack said. "Sure how many years is it since he left Kerry, and they haven't done talking about him? Didn't the priests themselves denounce him from their altars?"

"One of them did," Hassett said. His mouth softened to a reminiscent smile. "Away to the east, at Castleisland. There were two lassies big with child at the same time, and each of them claiming MacCarthy as the lucky man, so to speak. The Papists still say that he couldn't be left alone with any woman be she maid, wife, or mother."

But Stack's mouth remained firm. "The Papists can have little enough to boast of, if they keep a thing like that in memory."

"Ach, now fair is fair," Hassett said. "He could write a lovely song. It is the songs that will keep him in memory, and not the other thing."

"Much good that will do him on Friday," Cooper said.

"I know the sort," Stack said. "Kerry spawns them. You have the right of it there. Get drunk and take a man's daughter to bed with you, and the next day off to confession and write a hymn to the Blessed Virgin."

"Or a Whiteboy proclamation," Cooper said. Clownish churl, you count your cows in children's lives.

"Their religion suits them," Stack said. "Spend your shilling on drink and never a thought about tomorrow. Confession works the same way."

"He was the same here," Cooper said. "He lived in a cabin with a wild young widow. Be a very pretty little piece if you gave her a good wash. And God knows what other women."

"When he was pitched out of Kerry," Hassett said, "he landed in Macroom, and there is a story about him there that I have from a Macroom grazier of my acquaintance. It seems that MacCarthy and a priest were interested in the same lassie, a servant girl at one of the big houses."

"Their priests are the worst," Stack said. "Whitened sepulchres."

"Get on with your story," Cooper said, leaning forward.

This was more like it, a pleasant tavern with lads like these two, scarlet-clothed elbows leaning on table, jests and stories given salt and savor by shared loyalties. Up the dogleg road to the gaolhouse, where the man sat waiting to be hanged, was distant by a thousand miles, a remote arctic far removed from the warmth of the tavern.

When Moore's carriage drove back between the gates of Moore Hall, one half of his life ended. The other half, a slow movement toward an acceptance of his character and fate, did not reveal itself to him for several years.

The first months of 1799 were given over to a fulfillment of the promise which he had made to Dennis Browne in exchange for John's removal from Castlebar gaol. In a series of pamphlets, five in all, he argued the case for the abolition of the Irish Parliament and the union of the two kingdoms of Great Britain and Ireland. It was the great issue of the moment, over-shadowing even Buonaparte's failure to capture Acre—"that miserable hole which came between me and my destiny." The first two pamphlets, which set forth the general considerations, were couched in terms too lofty to be of consequence, but the other three set forth with great persuasiveness the grounds upon which the Catholic nobility and middle classes should support union as best calculated to secure the restoration of their civil and

591

political rights. These pamphlets were an immediate success, and they led to an extensive correspondence with Archbishop Troy and with Lord Kenmare. He traveled several times to Dublin to present his views to the Catholic Association, and it has been accepted by historians that his was one of the chief voices by which the Catholic community was led to endorse the policy of Pitt and Cornwallis. He received a cordial letter from Pitt, in which the Prime Minister hinted that Catholic Emancipation would indeed receive the early consideration of a united parliament.

Moore cared nothing for either Pitt's gratitude or Archbishop Troy's admiration. He had expressed his actual political convictions. The "Protestant Nation," as it was now being called, seemed to him hopelessly venal and corrupt, and its parliament an assembly of placemen leavened by a handful of patriotic but ineffectual rhetoricians. Any hope for reform or for the removal of Catholic disabilities lay with London. His own instincts and preferences were English rather than Irish, and he relied upon England to drag his country forward into the modern world. It was a most tentative and conditional reliance, for he did not expect England to act upon any motives other than those of selfishness and the need to protect itself. This too he presented in the pamphlets with a candor which lent weight to his arguments. And his cynicism seemed justified as the country watched the ill-concealed process by which Cornwallis and Castlereagh set to work bribing the legislators in Dublin with pensions, titles, and promises of sinecures. The "Protestant Nation," so he insisted, did not deserve to survive, and was proving the point by being bribed out of existence.

And yet his brief adventure into practical politics filled him with disgust and self-loathing. He had written what he believed to be the truth, but he had done so in payment of a debt to Dennis Browne, who had devoted months to a remorseless dragooning of Mayo. At Browne's instigation, companies of militia and yeomanry had crossed and recrossed the county, burning hamlets which had sheltered rebels, lashing suspects at the cabin door, dragging them at the rope's end to the gaols in Castlebar and Ballina. Informers, working under the direction of Paudge Dineen, one of Browne's creatures, brought word to him of rebels who had taken refuge in remote villages, and these were hunted down upon the bogs or the hillsides, frightened men in stained and damp clothing. A whipping triangle was set up at the cross of Ballintubber, upon Moore's land, and remained there until he tore it down with his own hands. And as he wrote his pamphlets, as he conducted his correspondence with clerics and gentry, with the Catholic bankers and merchants of Dublin and Limerick, he had always before him, in a corner of his imagination, the memory of Dennis Browne at Westport House, leaning forward toward him across the table, bland and insinuating. Moore felt himself soiled beyond the possibility of cleansing.

He was visited once by Thomas Treacy of Bridge-end House, on his way to Dublin. In the cool evening they sat together on the balcony.

"Your father sat here often," Treacy said. "Do you remember?"

"Yes," Moore said. "I remember."

"Would that he could see you now," Treacy said. "Taking your place among us at last. He had great respect for your abilities of mind, George. Great respect. He felt that you were wasting yourself over there in London. You were the clever one, and John was—" He paused.

"He loved John," Moore said. "We both did."

"And so did I." Treacy looked away from him, toward the dark green of the evening lake. "I should tell you about Ellen. She is becoming interested, I believe, in a young man. You know him, perhaps, Dominick O'Conor of Roscommon. A good family. His father is a cousin of O'Conor of Clonalis. Nothing has been settled, of course. It is too early for that."

"That is welcome news," Moore said without irony. "I am most fond of Ellen. She has wit, and spirit."

"I had wished a different life for her," Treacy said, his eyes still upon the lake. "They were very much in love. Herself and John. She was heartbroken. You can well imagine how she felt."

"Yes," Moore said.

"My God, what a waste," Treacy said. "But his motives were generous. You must remember that, George."

"History does not judge us by our motives," Moore said.

"History does not judge us at all," Treacy said. "God judges us."

"God does," Moore said.

"I was reflecting upon that as I read your latest paper.

It was most kind of you to send it to me. It is the judgment of God upon this Protestant nation of theirs that it is perishing at last in squalor. They have lorded it over us since the Boyne, since Cromwell. Moss-troopers and jumped-up joiners' apprentices, and their sons and grandsons and great-grandsons. The judgment of God. You might well have made that point."

"And so they will in the future," Moore said. "The property and commerce of this island are firmly in the hands of the Protestants. That will not change. But with a London parliament there is a chance that we will have our liberties restored to us. A chance only. That is all that I have argued."

"A most lucid argument," Treacy said. "If only your father—He would have been most proud of you."

"We may gain our liberties," Moore said. "The Papists may. But the country will lose whatever independence it has enjoyed. John would not have been proud."

"John was a boy," Treacy said. "What liberty could we have been given by the French? Cutthroats and blasphemers."

"Yes," Moore said. "I know." He passed his hand over his eyes, rubbing them. "I made a bargain with Dennis Browne," he said. "Browne got John out of here, to a safe gaol in the south. In time we would have got him out of the country. To America, perhaps. Or Spain. And in exchange I agreed to argue on behalf of the Union. I was bribed. As those wretched timeservers in Dublin are being bribed with ribbons and pensions. I had my price."

Treacy turned to look at him. He paused, puzzled, before he spoke. "But you believe what you have written?"

"Oh, yes," Moore said. "Every word of it. But I would not have written save for that bargain. I gave Browne his pound of flesh."

"That is a disagreeable way to put it, surely," Treacy said. "It was for John's life that you bargained. God Almighty! Dennis Browne is a man beneath contempt. I would not have thought it of him."

"He kept his part of the bargain and I have kept mine. It was a worthless bargain. John is dead."

"Not useless," Treacy said gently. "It was for John that you made it. To save John."

"I would have made any promise. Strung lies together, given him money. Whatever."

"But you did not. You promised only to make public

your true opinions. You are troubled by a scruple of conscience which any intelligent priest could resolve for you. Speak to Hussey. I can assure you that he admires what you have written."

"Oh, that!" Moore smiled. "I am something of an expert upon scruples of conscience. I have no need to consult Mr. Hussey." He shook his head impatiently. "Let us speak of something else. It is too pleasant an evening to waste."

But Treacy persisted. "Even if you had bribed him, if you had written what you do not believe . . ."

"I despise bargaining," Moore said. "And bargainers."

"Our Savior did not," Treacy said. "He bargained with the Father for our redemption."

"A blasphemous analogy," Moore said. "Mr. Hussey would not welcome it."

How could he explain himself to someone like Treacy, a conventional man, rustic and pious? He did not attempt it. His integrity had been soiled by the soot of circumstance. History, society had existed for him as networks of power, intricate webs of cause and effect, weakness and strength, authority and subservience. But his mind, the power of his intellect, had held him free of those webs. Cool and deliberate, his thoughts dipped in preserving liquor of irony, he had tested, weighed, evaluated, judged. His independence had been vested in the freedom of his mind to move among possibilities, uncommitted. His thoughts were birds, circling the earth, swooping low and then darting up again. Browne had limed the nets, his very thoughts fluttered helpless in their folds. To save John he had given more than gold. He had sent his ideas to do Browne's bidding. It was a fitting irony. His father would have approved and would have been delighted to see his affected pride brought low. Damn him.

Treacy was right, of course. It was a scruple of conscience, but not in his Christian meaning of the term. If Moore was anything, he was an historian, or so he believed, and historians did not sell the truth to politicians, not for gold or power or the lives of brothers. This was Moore's only piety, and history suggests that it was a mistaken one.

In the event, of course, the Act of Union was passed in 1800, but Catholic Emancipation was not achieved for another thirty years, and by then Moore was dead. He had taken no further part in public affairs, although he was several times urged to accept a position of leadership in the Catholic Association. He published nothing, and it was generally believed that he was continuing his researches into the history of the French Revolution. In Mayo he was accounted a learned, indeed a profound scholar, but in London his very name was forgotten, save as the author of his short, early treatise on the Whigs.

In 1805 he married, and the nature of the union prompted much comment and gossip in Mayo, for he married Sarah Browne, Dennis's niece, who had returned to Ireland upon the dissolution of her scandalous relationship with Lord Galmoy, a notorious rake. Moore had met her three years earlier, when the business of his estate carried him to Woodlands, Browne's house.

It was a modest house, far smaller than Westport House, the residence of his brother. The brother was Lord Altamont no longer; with the passage of the Act of Union he had been created Marquis of Sligo, in partial recompense for Dennis's services to the government. Dennis had been repaid in other ways as well: he was Member of Parliament in London now, and the most powerful man in Connaught. Among the peasants, his actions in 'ninety-eight had earned him a reputation as an ogre which would last long decades after his death, but this bothered him little. He had promised to pacify Mayo, and it was indeed at peace. The last of the hanged men had rotted beneath their overcoats of tar and they had been cut down from the gibbets. Songs were sung against him in shebeens, but he took no notice of these. In Ireland, power was seldom accompanied by popular approbation.

The proportioning of Woodlands was clumsy. Stables and kennels stood close to it: their odors filled the air in the cramped courtyard, and droppings of horse and dog were smeared across the uneven cobbles. The sounds of men shouting drifted to Moore from the outbuildings, the good-humored banter of grooms and stable boys.

"We have the simple life here," Browne said, welcoming him. "None of the brother's music rooms and artificial lakes and Chinese wallpaper. Did you ever see the like of that wallpaper? Pagodas and Ming horsemen and the dear knows what else stuck upon the walls of Mayo." He placed a hand upon Moore's shoulder. "Come inside, man. Come inside."

"I am here only to discuss the grand jury assessments," Moore said stiffly. "You understand that, do you not? I made it clear in my letter. It is good of you to receive me."

"To be sure," Browne said. "To be sure. You are a sight for sore eyes. It has been years now."

The entrance hall was dark. Portraits hung upon the walls, dim and indistinct, white faces glimmering beneath varnish and dust.

"Poor daubs they are," Browne said. "Westport House has the good ones, of course. The old man and Peter after him and then the grandfather. These are the scruffs—cousins and the like. All but one. Take a look here, would you?" He led Moore to the portrait of a man in seventeenth-century military dress, florid coloring, high arched nose. "There he is in all his glory, Colonel John in his regimentals, ready to ride off with King James and bash a few Protestant skulls. Small wonder brother Sligo doesn't want that one on his walls. Sure we were all Papists then—Moores and Brownes and Treacys."

"A resourceful-looking fellow," Moore said.

"Not a bad bit of canvas," Browne said. "A London artist named Turville."

They settled down to their talk in Browne's study, a small pleasant room, with a turf fire built against the chill of early evening. Bookshelves rose toward the ceiling along two walls. Tall double windows opened upon a meadow. Haze clung to the yellowing grass, a herd of black cattle grazed in the distance, beneath trees. One picture, bright against firelight: Westport House seen from a distant hill, with Clew Bay spread beyond it. A formal, awkward painting, as much chart as landscape, plantations and avenues laid out in meticulous detail.

"By God, the lad who did that was determined to give value for money," Browne said. "He would have stuck in every tree if he'd had room."

"It is a handsome house," Moore said.

"It is that," Browne said. "And built to last. There is a great future in Westport, George. A great future. Killala and Ballina are played out. In five years' time that port will be crowded with grain boats for England. Every grain of Connaught corn will be shipped from Westport. There is a great future for Connaught, thanks be to God. We will become England's victuallers. England and Master Buonaparte are going to settle down to a long, long war and the farmers and the landlords of Ireland will find their breeches pockets stuffed with English pound notes."

"Don't rely upon history," Moore said. "A few years ago, when last we talked, Master Buonaparte was a defeated general, stranded in Egypt. Today he is master of France. Things change."

"Never fear," Browne said. "I leave history in your keeping."

"About the jury assessments," Moore said, and drew the papers from his pocket.

It took them but an hour or so to conduct their business. Both men had a head for figures, and an instinct for detail. At last Browne threw his pen onto the desk, and stretched. "You will stay for dinner, will you not, George? Pheasant and baked ham and a gooseberry flan. I brought down the pheasant with my own gun."

"If I leave now," Moore said, "I can reach Moore Hall before night. Another time, perhaps."

"No time like the present," Browne said. "You are here now, and it has been a long time. Years. You will spend the night here, surely."

Why not, Moore thought. What does it matter? It is all over now, long past.

"I have a pleasant surprise for you," Browne said. "My niece is here. Sarah is here. She is staying with me. You knew her in London, did you not?"

Moore remembered her. Slender. Black hair, brown eyes. The special friend of Dick Galmoy. Dishonored. He had not known her well.

"She will be better off here," Browne said. "London is no place for an Irishwoman."

"I have always been fond of London," Moore said. "A civilized city."

"A fine city," Browne said. "I am there for six months of the year now." Dennis Browne, Member of Parliament for Mayo. "It is a man's city. You must know about her. Herself and Galmoy."

"I don't recall—" Moore began, evasively. Browne cut him short.

"She is well rid of him. Well rid. They are a disgrace to Ireland, puppies like Galmoy."

"I did not know him well."

"To meet a decent Irish girl at a Castle ball and lure her off to England with him. It is an utter disgrace that he brought upon her and upon her parents. They are a disgrace to Ireland, men like Galmoy, wasting their money in London and gambling it away. The English laugh at them and why should they not? She is well rid of that fellow."

"I am sorry that I did not know her better," Moore said. "She was a fine, clever girl, as I remember her."

"Clever, is it? Sure all the Brownes are clever, save for poor Sligo, and he has no need for it, thanks be to God. She is as clever as an egg is full of meat. You would swear to look at her that she had left Ireland for a convent. Ach, sure what family is there that does not have its one misfortune? Who would know that better than yourself?"

Moore did not reply. He was embarrassed by the frankness with which Browne spoke of her. How old would she be now? Late twenties perhaps, or thirty. Not a late age in this country, but rumor would have placed a scar upon her. Clever she might be, but it had been folly to run off with Dick Galmoy.

"What are you thinking?" Browne asked sharply.

Moore smiled. "That I admire clever women."

Browne peered at him, the sharpness now in his eyes. "Take care not to admire them too fervently, George. It would be a great pity should anything disturb our friendship."

"Is that what we are?" Moore asked. "Friends?"

Browne left him alone for an hour, before dinner, and he explored the demesne. It was a fine, clear evening, cool, with a faint wind crossing the fields. A ghost of Atlantic salt in the air stirred his memories. A path along the meadow led through to a stream crossed by a brief, humped bridge. Beyond lay a summer house. The stream was at the full and moved noisily beneath his feet as he stood upon the bridge. Perhaps she is in the summer house, he thought. Reading, or remembering London.

She joined them in the small, dowdy dining room, frayed red Turkey carpet beneath their feet, gravy-colored portraits on the wall, sat facing her uncle from an end of the olive-wood table. Moore had not remembered her clearly —slender, certainly, and brown-eyed, but the hair was not black at all but brown, worn unfashionably. Her throat was tall above a prim dress of blue velvet. She said little at dinner, but listened attentively to each man, turning watchful, quiet eyes toward him. She smiled often, a quick, half-smile which came and then vanished. Her teeth were very white but not straight.

With fingers and pointed knife, Browne tore the wing from a pheasant. "This is most pleasant," he said. "A Browne back home in Mayo where she belongs, and a friend to share a meal with us. We never see enough of you, George. No one does. You should take more part in the life of the county."

"Do you not hunt, Mr. Moore?" she asked. A colored voice. Colors streaked with silver.

"I write," Moore said. "And I manage the estate myself. I am kept busy."

"His brother was the lad for the hunt," Browne said. "George is a different fellow entirely."

"What is it that you write?" she asked.

"History," Moore said. "A kind of history. It has not been going well."

Browne spoke through a mouthful of meat. "History was washed up at his door a few years ago. He didn't welcome it."

"I never read histories," she said. "Poetry and novels. More novels than are good for me. But not histories. All those sorrows and dates."

"Mine will be as dry as any of them," Moore said. "If I ever finish it."

She picked up her wineglass. Moore remembered where he had seen her last. At Holland House. She was different then, the voice harsh and eager. It had been a large party. But she was not a woman one would easily forget. Not now.

"You have come home at a sorry time, Miss Browne."

"Sorry?" she repeated. "I am not certain of your meaning."

"The county has been disturbed. There has been much suffering."

"It is safe now," Browne said. "And it will be prosperous soon. I was telling you that, George." He picked up his own glass. "Pay no attention to that, Sarah."

"Pay no attention to an historian? I am certain that he would not like that, would you, Mr. Moore?"

"Your kinsman's knowledge of Mayo is more intimate

than my own," Moore said. "He has made a name for himself in Mayo."

She caught the thread of his irony. "Have you, Dennis? What sort of name have you made?"

"Whatever name is given to me. I have done more than that, and George knows it. I have restored peace here."

"Pacem appellant," Moore said.

"What can that mean, Mr. Moore?" she asked. "I have no Latin. No Latin and no history, I am an ignorant Mayo woman."

" 'They call it peace,' " Moore said.

"Give her the rest of it," Browne said angrily. *"Solitudinem faciunt et pacem appellant.* 'They make a wilderness and they call it peace.' Very well so. But it is a wilderness we can live in."

"Those of us left alive," Moore said.

"I know nothing of this," she said. "All this unhappiness."

"Your pardon," Moore said. "Your kinsmen and I have lived through difficult days. Everyone in Mayo did. We had our differences. It is all past now. As he says, peace has been restored."

"And once at least we were in agreement," Browne said. "Do you remember, George?"

"Yes," Moore said.

Browne smiled at Sarah. "There is nothing suitable for a woman's ears but talk of silk dresses and trinkets from the fair and hawthorn trees in flower."

"You have grown poetical," she said.

"The words are not mine," Browne said. "They are from a song by a Killala schoolmaster. A song in Irish."

"A schoolmaster was hanged in 'ninety-eight," Moore said.

"All this unhappiness," she said again. "There are always poets."

O Dennis Browne,
If I did meet you.
I'd shake your hand,
But not to greet you,
To have you taken
And strung up quaking

601

On a rope of hemp when
I'd run you through.

He awoke next morning with the thought of her filling
his mind, as though she had left behind a perfume, dis-
creet but erotic. Tendrils of memory, the movement of
her arm as she raised the wineglass, the small hand which
held it, the wide, dark eyes which knew more than the
lips spoke. It was an emotion which had caught him un-
aware, and he felt disloyal toward his own melancholy.
The woman Dick Galmoy had taken once to Holland
House, a prize to be exhibited. Dick Galmoy's wild Irish
girl.

He dressed, and then walked again along the meadow
path to the small bridge. He crossed over it and went to
the summer house. As he had expected, he found her
there, and she was not surprised to see him. She put a
slip of paper in the novel she had been reading, and
placed the book on a wicker table by her chair. Then
she rose to meet him.

"You remembered who I was," she said.

"Once," he said. "One evening. You looked different
then."

"I was different then," she said.

They walked together along the path, the narrow,
quick-moving stream beside them.

"Are you pleased to be here again?" he asked. "In
Mayo?"

"Neither pleased nor displeased," she said. "It is where
I am. I was very excited on the boat, but now nothing
seems familiar. I don't like Dennis's house, do you? I like
Westport House."

"It is very grand," he said. "A better house for a
woman. Will you live there?"

"I like the bay," she said. "And the islands. I have a
great fondness for the picturesque."

"And for novels."

"Yes," she said. "I am a foolish woman. Foolish and
headstrong. It will be my downfall, sooner or later."

"You are not foolish at all," he said. "Since last night
I have been puzzled by you. You remind me of someone.
You puzzle me."

"That is a personal remark to make upon slight acquaintance."

"But you are not offended," he said.

"How can you know that?"

"You will stay here now?"

"Where else can I go? I would not find London pleasant this season."

"I prefer London," Moore said, deliberately misunderstanding her. "London or Paris. I remember Spain, as you remembered Mayo when you were in London. But I am settled here. I will not leave."

"You do not have the look of a man who is at home. You look unhappy."

They had come to the plantation. Beyond it, Browne's house stood bare and stumpy.

She stopped, and turned to face him. "Do you know why I came back? Don't ask my brother: he will invent a story for you. Galmoy ran through the money, and then threw me over. He sent me packing. If he had not, I would be with him now."

"You are that attached, then?"

She broke a branch from the tree and studied it. "I despised him," she said. "After the first year. He is a witless creature, all bluster and fine looks. It was a tedious life for a woman situated as I was, with no company save that of men, and other women like myself."

"Like Lady Holland," Moore said.

"Like Lady Holland. Are you making sport of me?"

"Not at all," Moore said. "I will never make sport of you."

"Never? Not when you know me better?"

"Especially then."

"Take care, Mr. Moore. I am not at all what you may have heard of me."

"I know only what you choose to tell me," Moore said. "Tell me nothing, if you like."

"I am a disappointing woman," she said. "I have been told that often."

"We are well suited," Moore said. "You will see."

Four months later, Sarah Browne became Moore's mistress. He did not find her at all a disappointing woman, and he was delighted by her curious manner, which blended candor and reserve. She was not quite in love with him, he came to conclude, but she almost was. As for himself, he was content to be pleased by her, her nature a puzzle which teased his feelings. Her sensuality, and, as he had suspected from that first evening, she was a most sensual woman, was entangled with her wry, self-deprecating intelligence. As he had told her, they were well suited, making no large demands upon one another. They managed their affair with discretion at first, but within a few months it had become common gossip in the county. He had expected that Browne, upon hearing of the affair, would call him out, but instead Browne affected ignorance of it. "Perhaps he really doesn't know of it," he said to her once. "He knows," she said; "we are an unpredictable family."

They married three years after the affair had begun, and their son, who was born eight months later, was named George, after his father and his grandfather. He was baptized and reared as a Catholic. Moore would have insisted upon this, but in fact his wife did not care about such matters. Although they seldom appeared in society, the county believed that the marriage was a successful one, and perhaps it was.

He never completed his history of the Girondist party in the French Revolution. For several years after his marriage he continued to work upon it, but each year he felt less interest in the task, and less confidence in his ability to complete it, or in his ability to understand the mainsprings of politics and history. The first two manuscript volumes survive, the prose polished but perhaps too formal and too stiff, the handwriting an elegant copperplate, the ink brown and faded. Beyond these are drafts of chapters, revised, scratched out, partially rewritten. And notes for other chapters, clumps of names and dates, broken-backed epigrams and faltering generalizations. He had been left at last with a frozen puddle of history, muddy water frozen in the depression of a woodland path, dead leaves and broken twigs dim beneath its filthy surface.

Throughout the nineteenth century, a story persisted among the peasantry that John Moore had not died in Waterford but had escaped to Spain, and, learning that his brother was to marry a kinswoman of Dennis Browne, returned and challenged him to a duel, which was fought .in the wasteland beyond Ballintubber near the ruined abbey. Neither brother drew blood, and John returned to Spain. A doggerel ballad about the duel lingered in the taverns, a wretched song which had John in a rebel uniform of emerald green, like Robert Emmet in a colored engraving. The legend arose from popular hatred of Dennis Browne, and not of George Moore, a remote figure behind the walls of Moore Hall.

When Moore was an old man in the 1820s, although not as old as his father had lived to be, the Ribbon conspiracy erupted in Mayo, as elsewhere in the country, agrarian terrorists banded together to coerce a reduction of rents, much like the old Whiteboy conspiracy. Mickey O'Donnell, a nephew of Ferdy, was brought to trial as one of its ringleaders. Moore paid his legal expenses, entering them scrupulously if curiously in his ledger: "For the defense at Castlebar assizes of M. O'Donnell, one hundred pounds to Daniel O'Connell, barrister-at-law. John Moore, *in memoriam.*" It was money wasted. O'Donnell was transported to the prison colony in Van Diemen's Land.

That night, after he had made the ledger entry, he took his chair onto his father's balcony and sat there quietly for an hour. He tried to remember his father stumping about before the unfinished house, gesturing with his cane. Or John, riding down the avenue on his chestnut mare. Fading portraits, they had vanished almost completely. He could conjure up only an old man, a young man without distinct features. He wished for tears, but his bone-dry eyes were unused to them. At last he grunted, pushed back the chair, and walked into the house, leaning upon his father's cane.

From the Diary of Sean MacKenna, October, 1798

Thursday. I have just now returned from the gaol, where I sat for several hours with my beloved friend Owen MacCarthy, who is to be hanged in the morning early. When next I take up my pen to indite my foolishness in this ledger, he will be no more, but will be in the Presence of the Savior. I will not be outside the gaol in the morning, and neither should any Christian man.

When a man is to be hanged, his name is written out on a sheet of foolscap, together with the name of his crime and the nature of the sentence, and then are set forth the names of the civil and military authorities, Dennis Browne and General Trench. The paper is then nailed up outside the courthouse, with later ones nailed beside it or overlapping it. The rain pelts down upon the papers and smears the ink. In that way, names are proclaimed and then washed away—Donnellan, Nealon, Duggan, Mulkern, Dunne, Clancy, Burke. But the bodies are not washed away, and neither are they buried, but they are coated in tar and hung up again as a show.

"Owen McCarty," they spelled his name, which is close enough, and he was given his proper calling as schoolmaster. It went on to say that he had accepted arms from the French and had fought against the Crown at various times and places, and had held authority among the rebels, this being the crime of treason and punishable by death. This is true enough, surely, although Owen has told me little of what he did in that month, and I have little desire to know. It is a wonder to me that a man and his death can be thus shriveled to a few words on paper.

This evening, as I walked down High Street to the gaol, was clear, with ribs of red cloud stretched low across the horizon and the windless air was warm for the month it is. High Street and Castle Street were crowded with soldiers and militia and yeomen off duty, swaggering about or lounging against the walls of shops, and the taverns are filled with them. It has been this way ever since General Trench entered Mayo and set up his headquarters in Castlebar. There are militiamen from Munster who can speak only Irish, and men from across the sea who speak a kind of English that is beyond my understanding, as though their mouths have been stuffed with hot potatoes. A great folly it was that has brought down upon us in retribution these swarms of scarlet wasps.

I brought Owen a new linen shirt from the shop, that he might make a good appearance upon the morrow. And I brought him also a jug of whiskey and a loaf of bread that Brid had baked for him from the best white flour and the beads which had been my father's, carved from bog oak in the penal days and worn smooth from my father's sweat and mine.

He thanked me for these, and put them beside him on the mattress. The only light in the cell came weakly from a lamp in the corridor outside, and I saw him in shadows. He had a mat of beard, but behind it, his face seemed hollowed out, the cheeks sunken in. Some of his teeth had been knocked out and others were loose, so that he spoke with a lisp. My heart broke within my chest.

"A poor enough kind of death it is," he said. "The kind of death you would give a puppy."

"Ach, Owen," I said. "It is quick enough over. It is of other things you should be thinking now. Has there been a priest to you?"

"There has. This afternoon. I sent that poor fellow out of here with his ears burning."

"He gave you your absolution, though?"

"He did. But I don't think his heart was in it. He would have had to work on me for days to make a decent job of it."

I knew that he spoke lightly in order to build a wall around himself. He was sitting within a cell of his own making, smaller and darker than the squares of damp stones.

"It was kindness itself for you to come here, Sean," he said at last.

"There are many others who would have come gladly," I said. "Poets of Kerry and West Cork."

"Perhaps," he said.

"Perhaps is not in it," I said, "and well you know it. Wherever you have lived you have been highly esteemed."

He laughed. "Have I? By God, some of them had strange ways of showing it."

I could see him more clearly now. "They will be saying your poems for many long years," I said.

"Ach, they will indeed. The poems have nothing to do with me anymore. They will find their own way in the world. It was not the poems which led me to this terrible place, but my own life of folly and wildness."

"Who knows what folly is," I said.

"The priest does," he said. "He would give no absolution to me unless I repented that I went off with the French. I do indeed, I said to him, isn't it getting me hanged? But that wasn't good enough for him, and he had me swear that it was all sinful from beginning to end and a crime against God and man. A boy in his twenties he was, with a high, unpleasant voice. Ach, sure an absolution from him is as good as one from the Pope. After a time I gave over all thoughts of a full confession. I just touched on the high points, else he would still be here. My God, what a terrible life I have led, Sean. It wasn't until after he was gone that I remembered Mary Lavelle, the Ballycastle girl who married Ferdy O'Donnell's hired boy. I had forgotten her entirely. A wild little thing she was, with haunches that a man's two spread hands could just fit around."

"Dear God, Owen. It is not of such things you should be thinking now."

"Ach, sure, what did it all matter? There was a great passion on me for her, when I saw her there that night, in Ferdy's kitchen. But later, in the darkness beyond the gable end, it was the same as making love to Judy, who was home in Killala waiting for me, and I was left wondering why I had gone to all the trouble. When a man is in passion, he takes leave of all common sense. Sure we all know that. The priesteen was shocked by what I could remember. Lust is a wild, raging beast, he said to me, some formula they gave him in the seminary. It is, I said, and most of those times I was blind drunk as well. That is a separate sin, he said. That fellow is going to be a holy terror that you would walk five parishes to avoid. Murphy of Killala was a madman, but he had judgment in some matters."

"They are sins right enough, Owen. Perhaps God makes special allowances for poets, but He hasn't told the Church about it."

"He seems to have made a special point of telling the Church about the wickedness of rebellion against the King. The priesteen was eloquent on the subject. That was the blackest of my sins, to have gone off with the French. Are you truly repentant, he says, that you took arms against your sovereign? Oh, I am, Father, I say, most heartily sorrowful. You are paying a heavy penalty for it, he says. Oh, I am, Father, I say, I would be hard put to think of a worse one. An innocent young fellow, Sean. It isn't many years that that fellow has had to scrape a razor along his jaw."

For that moment, we might have been back in my room above the shop, with a jug between us, and his wild humor dancing on the edge of irreverence. But then he said, "It was a mad folly. There were men dead and dying all around us at Ballinamuck, with their arms torn off and their bellies ripped open. And in the midst of all my fear I could think only of the folly that had led us there, wandering after that banner onto the red bog of death. The bogside hedges were thick with blackberries, and I knew that I would never again walk down a lane with my hand filled with blackberries and my lips stained with them."

There is in Owen a great love of our earthly existence and it is perhaps because of it that he is so fine a poet. What are the worst of his sins, the wild ways and even the girl at the gable end, if not that love speaking out? I truly believe that his love is so strong that he cannot understand his sinfulness. God help him and make allowances for him.

"I went off with them," he said, "and then I ran away from them and then I drifted back to them. If I had stayed clear of them, I would be safe in Munster now, tucked away in a valley, and boasting and lying about what I had done. Oh, Christ, that is another sin."

When I thought that on the next day there would be no life in him, my heart was wrenched in me. Clearly could I see him in a Munster tavern, leaning against the white wall, with a mug of porter in his hand. Now there was but the shadowy bearded face, and tomorrow there will be far less. It is terrible to know what will be the day and hour of a man's death.

I said, "Often and often I think of it as a wave that swept over us from the great sea. Some of them were carried off for this reason and some for that. And some there were that went off for no reasons that I can think of, the poor landless men and the spalpeens. God alone knows why the gentry went off—John Moore and Malcolm Elliott and Randall MacDonnell and their like."

"Commend me to the gentry," he said with harsh contempt. "When have they needed a reason for what they do?"

"It had been building for a century," I said, "and it broke upon us like a wave."

We were silent for long periods, looking toward each other, or at nothing, or at the wan light in the small barred window of the door. I did not know whether he would have me with him or would prefer the silence of his own company. But I believe that he was glad to have me with him. We have been great friends from the first, since first he drifted northward into Mayo.

Once, of a sudden, he asked me, "Did you ever see a man hanged?"

"I did not," I said, "and I will not. It is a terrible thing that people would want to watch."

"I did," he said. "In Macroom. I watched them hang Paddy Lynch."

"He was the Whiteboy Captain," I said.

"He was. He was hanged for that and for two killings, but he had done worse. The Macroom Captain he was called. Sure, he was raiding and killing up and down West Cork in his last year, but he began in Macroom, a man with a few acres of mountainy land and he was called the Macroom Captain. The Macroom gentry had a special hatred for him. They hunted him with packs of hounds as you would hunt a fox. But in the latter end of things, it took the militia. They found him with four of his men in a cave in the Boggeraghs, and they were all brought back to Macroom and hanged in the square."

"I remember that. It was not until the year after that I left Cork City. That week they talked of little else.'"

"Cork City is not Macroom. There is a great castle from the old days, and the entrance gate of it sticks out into the town. The shadow of it falls across the town, a great ugly castle. It is a market town, and there is a great wide square, as they have them in Munster. And that morning it was filled with people, more people than you would find people and cattle there on a market day. And all of them had come to see Paddy Lynch hanged. I was there myself. It was morning, but I had half a jug in me. People drunk and singing. A fine day we had for ourselves in Macroom, the day we hanged Paddy Lynch."

"He was a hard man to have tears for, that Paddy Lynch."

"He was that, by God. Rampaging up and down Ballyvourney and lighting into small farms. He was no better than a rapparee in that latter year, and what else would he be? Hadn't they made him into an animal with their packs of hounds?"

In those hours, we each had three drinks or four from the jug I had brought, but no more than that. Perhaps he wished to go forward sober in the morning, or perhaps he was saving the jug for the long hours of the night when he would be alone. And either way, small blame to him.

"Sure my father was poorer than any Whiteboy," he said, "a spalpeen carrying his spade to the hiring fairs. Did I ever tell you how he died? In a roadside ditch with no food in his belly. When I heard of his death in that manner I ran wild with grief."

610

"It was a fine poem that you gave him," I said. "There is no stone of black or white marble that is so fine as that poem."

"It was not for lack of a poem that he died, but for lack of bread. And myself far off, roistering at my ease, and drinking in taverns, and shoving useless knowledge into the heads of farmers' sons. It was by my father's sweat that I had gone to school myself, with shillings that glistened with his sweat. And I left him behind, a hired boy grown old. What sort of father had you yourself, Sean?"

"A most excellent man," I said, remembering. "He had a small shop in Blarney Street, and my mother was a maidservant in one of the houses there. That is how they met. He was a great man for the reading. The money went for books, and he gave me a taste for them."

Owen reached out suddenly, and took my hand in the two of his and rubbed the palm. "There," he said. "That hand is like mine. Soft as a gentleman's. My father's hand was like cracked leather, like old leather, with great knobby fingers. And it was never clean, he could never get it clean. The dirt was stained into it, and black beneath the nails. I remember the first time he took me to the school, he tried to hide his hands behind his back. Schooling for a spalpeen's son. I remember his hands as clearly as I do his face."

"It is certain that you loved him," I said. "It is in the poem."

"He was a terrible man for the drink," Owen said, "but it was not often that he could afford it. He would drink himself stupid, God help him."

"God grant him rest," I said, but it was for the son that I prayed.

Later, after another long silence and a pull upon the jug, he said, "Do you remember that poem that kept worrying me? The moon and the bright curve of metal. For a time, when the madness came on me in Killala, I thought I had the answer to it, when I saw the curve of some fellow's pike. But that was a part of the madness itself, like the drums and the muskets and the banner of green silk. The image lay there upon the dirt floor of my mind, and nothing would give life to it."

"It will come to you if you give it time," I said without thinking, and then, appalled, I heard my foolish words echo in the small, silent room.

But Owen laughed and said nothing.

Then, a bit later, he said, "I remember when I was small, and my father and some of them were at the plowing on Hassett's land, God torment his soul. At noontime, I brought a bucket of water to them, to wash down the cakes. The father and I sat down together, at the ditch, and shared out our cakes between us, and then he stretched out and lay looking up at the sky. But I sat looking at the turned furrows and the horses and the plow. One of the wooden plows it was, you don't often see them these days, fitted out with an iron sole-shoe. The whole of the March morning was gathered up into that bit of iron."

"Well," I said, "and why not?" thinking that I had read his meaning. "Didn't O'Sullivan write a poem about a spade? Why not a plow?"

But he moved his shoulders impatiently, the heavy shoulders of a plowman.

"The poems are in a box at Judy Conlon's," he said. "I would be obliged to you if you would go down to her one of these days and take away the box. She is a decent woman, but it is better that they should rest with a man of learning."

And of course I promised him that I would do so, and then once again we had nothing to say. So we passed two hours and a bit more. I sat rooted there. I did not know how to take my leave of him. Once the grating of the window flared suddenly into bright lantern-light, and a dark face peered in at us, and then was gone again.

"That poor fellow will be up all night unless we give him a chance to rest," Owen said. "Best now that you get back to Brid and to Timothy."

I stood up then but Owen sat where he was, and I put my two arms around him and kissed him. I felt weak and ill, and my eyes filled with tears. Owen put his hand upon my shoulder and held it tight. "A safe road home," he said to me.

Friday. To write out all that I have down above took me much of last night, but I could not have slept, and I thought it well that there should be a record of the last night upon this earth of the poet Owen MacCarthy. As I read it over now, I see that much has been omitted but what I have set down must suffice.

I kept my shop closed today. By eight in the morning, the crowds were so thick that they filled Castle Street to the place where it joins High Street. Timothy was still asleep, and Brid and I sat facing each other, with cold cups of tea before us, and our right hands joined. Presently the sounds of drums beating came to us from Castle Street. After a bit the crowd fell silent and then, a few minutes later, it gave a great roar. Brid and I did not look at each other. I made the sign of the cross. *Requiescat in pace.*

Tuesday. This day I visited Judy Conlon at her cabin in the Acres of Killala, and she gave to me most readily the box of Owen's poems. She says that she was most careful to keep it well hidden on the day that the Acres was visited by Fraser's Fencibles, who burned several of the cabins, although not hers, and behaved in a rude and un-Christian manner to the inhabitants. She is an agreeable person, and seems a decent one despite the sinful life she has led.

For several miles between Killala and Ballina I had the walls of Lord Glenthorne's estate for company, most handsome walls of stone cut and dressed. The walls are so high that I could scarcely look over them, but I got a glimpse of that celebrated house, like a fairy-tale castle from some distant land that had been lifted up and floated across the world in the skies to settle down here. Well is he called the Big Lord.

It was the proper time of day for me to be seeing it, between daylight and dark, with a blue green sky, and the clouds tinted red to be a delight to sailors. What have we ever had to do with their world, set off from us by their high walls of cut stone, their entrance gates guarded by mythological animals cut in stone and marble, hippogriffs, eagles, lions, monkeys, Barbary apes, dragons? Their carriages pass us in the roads, laquered wood polished to catch the sun. Their horsemen and huntsmen crash across our fields in the russet autumn, a thrilling and frightening spectacle, the lords and gentlemen in their scarlet coats, and the ladies in habits of black velvet and green velvet. They pause at country inns for cups of sherry or of whiskey or claret, leaning back on their mounts, their dogs yelping impatiently, the men with red faces and high, arched noses, and voices that bay like their hounds. The huntsman's horn echoes from hill to hill, and their cries have the mystery of ritual, from a view to a kill.

But no man living in this land has ever seen the Big Lord, a name to frighten children.

Epilogue

Winter, 1798

The Unpublished Reflections of Arthur Vincent Broome, Author of *An Impartial Narrative of What Passed at Killala in the Summer of 1798*

"Does man learn from History?" I once asked a scholarly and sagacious friend. Rather than dismissing the question with the scorn which doubtless it merited, he reflected upon the matter, and said at last, "No, I believe that we do not. But it is possible to learn from historians." I have upon occasion given thought to this; when, for instance, reading the capacious works of Hume and Gibbon, and the most that I can make of it is this:

Gibbon gives to us the breadth of the classical world, from the Hellespont to the pillars of Hercules, a vast temple with colonnades and recesses, glowing white marble beneath a blazing Mediterranean sun, and displays to us then its hideous and shameful destruction. How firm a sense do we derive of all its constituent parts, of their intricate relationships! How certain is its destruction, with alien creeds subverting its powers and alien races wearing away its far-flung frontiers. Each cause and reason is locked securely into place. And over all the mighty drama presides the awesome authority of Gibbon's splendid language, his unimpassioned rationality. Here, we think, is the chief civil drama of human history, in which tens and hundreds of thousands played their parts, but a drama compelled by the human mind to yield up its uttermost secrets. Great was Rome and catastrophic was its fall, but great too is the energy of the historian's mind, the cool deliberation of his judgment.

But then! We put the volume upon the table, and go out for a stroll in the garden or to visit a sick parishioner or perhaps only to pare our nails, and doubt seeps in, a Gothic tribe at the frontier. Perhaps it had not been like that at all. Perhaps all had been chaos, chance, ill-luck, perhaps even Providence, perhaps the ancients were indeed punished for their sins, as was once believed. Perhaps Gibbon is but a master magician, a sorcerer of language, a Simon Magus of stately paragraphs. Perhaps it is not Rome that we have seen, but Gibbon's imagination bestowed capriciously upon the past rather than upon mountaintop or sunset or ruined abbey or other Romantic flummery. And the past remains therefore unknowable, shrouded in shadow, an appalling sprawl of buildings, dead men, battles, unconnected, mute, half recorded. Perhaps we learn nothing from history, and the historian teaches us only that we are ignorant.

I know myself to be vain and affected when I bring Gibbon to mind as I turn the pages of my own poor narrative. Against the enormous fall of a mighty empire, I set a squabble in a remote province, a ragbag army of peasants, files of yeomen and militia, plowboys hanged from crossroads gallows. And the chronicler is but my poor self, a confused clergyman with an indifferent education, a lover of comfort and civility and buttered toast. How confident and false now sounds to me my opening chapter, where I would be the Gibbon of Mayo, setting forth the contending parties upon the eve of conflict, the several social classes, the topography, the weathers. How false have I not been even to my own partial and fragmentary recollections! Truth was ever my beacon in my task of composition, and I sought to present to my reader a description of all that was done, without fallacious coloring, together with an account of my own feelings, both at the time and in retrospect. Yet now my words lie dead upon the page, like blackened hulls upon the sands.

Now, in memory, I see Ferdy O'Donnell sitting in my kitchen. He stares at me. He is unshaven, and his eyes, from lack of sleep, are sunk in their sockets. His hand rests upon the table, a square, broad hand with thick knuckles. Close to it, a cup half filled with tea. It is late evening, the light is thin, the far corners of the room are in shadow. Neither of us speaks. Men are shouting in the street outside. At last he raises his hand, then drops it again to the table. I have a vivid recollection of the scene, and yet it lacks significance, a random memory. But what if the mysterious truth is locked within such moments? Memory urges them upon us, implores us to ponder them. A hopeless message.

The hour that O'Donnell and I sat there together has been scrubbed away. The rising itself has been washed from town and fields by a hundred rains. But each day I pass in the street men who held me prisoner. Once I watched them from study window, lounging against rain-streaked walls. Memories as vivid as mine must be locked within their skulls, torches flaring across black corridors of time. We greet each other civilly. Perhaps in their cabins they talk of the fighting, and younger men listen, as though to tales of heroic battle. Certainly the rebellion has not been forgotten in the houses of the gentry. They will over the years construct their twin mythologies, compounded of facts and fables and pride. In my own narrative, I sought to set down only the truth. Perhaps the greatest vanity was mine. Memory challenges and mocks me.

In the weeks and months after our deliverance from captivity, I was made aware of how deep had been the distress of my beloved Eliza. In our months of danger and anxiety, she was my certain source of strength, the firm rock of my existence. I have perhaps been remiss not to have incorporated into my narrative instances of her many acts of kindness, the example of Christian fortitude which she placed before those who shared our imprisonment. She has no gift for memorable phrase, has much humor but little of what the world terms wit. And yet, the dangers past, she communicated to me her troubled spirit, not in words, but by a manner too subdued, a distracted air. More than once I came upon her at the drawing-room windows, seated, looking fixedly upon the narrow, empty street. And I would know that she was remembering that street filled with shouting men, remembering that men had died most horribly beneath those windows.

Accordingly, I resolved, with a swiftness seldom granted to me, that we should spend the Christmas season in Derbyshire, at the home of my brother Nicholas. We had spent in that house the first Christmas of our life together, and she holds it in much affection. I knew also the power of an English Christmas as a restorative. Some there are who affect to mock it, calling it a pagan winter festival but ill disguised, yet it has always seemed to me deeply Christian, an affirmation of the warmth of love and sympathy in the very chill of December. Eliza agreed most readily, as, to be sure, she does with all my plans and projects. I cannot recall that she has ever opposed me in anything which I have ever proposed, or disobeyed any just order which I have given. A most Christian woman.

We took the mail coach from Castlebar to Dublin, and were accompanied for part of the journey by a body of dragoons, handsome, heavy-shouldered men under the command of a young captain with a small-boned, gentle face. The coach was waiting for us outside the courthouse, a drab vehicle, unlike its splendid English counterpart, save for the shining, yellow-painted wheels. As we walked toward it, we had suddenly a glimpse into the yard, so sudden that I had no time to warn Eliza, and she looked for a moment without comprehending, and then buried her face in her hands. Five forms hung from a gibbet, shapeless and black, their overcoats of tar frozen and glistening. Mr. Comfort, the captain of dragoons, helped me place Eliza in the coach, and then turned to face me.

"When they hang men in this country, they make no mistake about it," he said.

"It is horrible," I said. "Horrible. And in a Christian land."

"Some question about that," he said with a grin.

"They are Christian," I said, "and their souls demand the Christian burial of their bones."

"That is Duggan there," he said, pointing toward the form on the left end. "I would hesitate to call that one a proper pagan, much less a Christian. In Killala—"

"I know what he did in Killala," I said quickly.

"Of course, sir. I had forgotten. Another Killala man there, next to him. A schoolmaster. A hulking brute, was he not? Look at the size of him."

Once he stood before me in my library, talking about *Gil Blas* and the roads of Munster. And once his voice drifted in song from the open door of the barn, where he stood among servants, his arm around a maiden's waist. An ugly sack of guts and bones, chained and tarred. I turned and climbed into the coach.

The coach rolled through the wasted county. Below us, the yellow wheels spun merrily. Dogs ran from cabins to yelp at us, and old people stood at their doors. Cattle watched us, motionless in the fields. We passed a row of burned cabins, roofless, doors like rotting mouths. Two

619

crossroads were marked by empty gallows, maimed crosses of smooth wood, raw and weather-stained. But the land itself was wrapped in the soft Irish winter. Blue hills, distant beyond fields, the pale blue sky as wide as eternity, clouds touched with silver, quiet rivers. A world brought to perfection, marred by the violence of man.

Our Derbyshire Christmas was all that I had expected of it and more, and the greatest of my Christmas gifts was the brightness which returned to Eliza's eyes and face. All of that season's cheer was welcome to us—the Yule log, the holly, the waifs who gathered outside the windows to sing, the bowls of hot, spiced wine. It was a snowy Christmas. I took many walks through a countryside which had been familiar to me from childhood—for here I had been born—but now mantled in white. No other countryside could have offered a more vivid contrast to the one which I had left. Our village was a proper village, and our inn a proper inn with its warm, snug, and well-appointed taproom.

And Nicholas is a proper English squire. He could sit for his portrait by artist or novelist, the very type of his excellent species. He has also, alas, a mind circumscribed by the boundary line of his county. If I had returned to him from a mission to Tartary, I could not have seemed a more exotic traveler. And yet he had no desire to learn from me. Rather, he wished to give me instruction, as though all of the British interest in Ireland were vested in my poor person, and he the Voice of England.

"It is intolerable, brother, intolerable that you should permit the populace of that wretched island to conspire and band together in open disloyalty and armed treason. Are there not laws, an army, militia, yeomanry? And yet you permit the island to explode."

"I myself did not, brother," I replied. "I have described my parish to you. I have the care of a few hundred souls, cast away in a remote part of the island, surrounded by untold thousands of miserable wretches."

"Untold thousands? Where? In Mayo? I don't believe you. What is the population of the island?"

"No one knows. Millions, certainly. There is much dispute upon the point."

"Much dispute? Why should it be a matter for dispute? Mayo has its landlords, and each landlord has his tenants.

Let the landlords count up the tenants, add the totals. and there you have the population. Good God!"

"No, no," I said. "There are tenants and subtenants and sub-subtenants and drifting men. There are mountain wastes with hundreds of Gaelic-speaking wretches clinging to the sides, and there are wretches clinging to the sides of bogs. Entire communities. Now, in winter, there are families of beggars upon every road, a pathetic spectacle. I assure you, Nicholas, it is not like England at all."

We were seated in his library, as he chose to call a combination of office and tackroom, with a few dozen books gathering dust upon shelves. We were facing a blazing log fire, and comforting ourselves with madeira and biscuits. Nicholas's broad, sturdy legs were stretched toward the fire. He was not angry, not even very interested. It was his manner.

"Laziness," he said. "Laziness and Popery and treason. The curses of Ireland. The landlords are as bad as the rest of them. I've seen them in London, gambling away their rents. And I have heard them, with brogues that you would need a carving knife to cut. Expect people like that to govern properly? I don't."

"They may not be governing much longer," I said. "In Dublin and London all the talk is of a union of the two kingdoms."

"There is a fine Christmas present," Nicholas said. "An island swarming with beggars dropped into our lap. You were mad to take up your task there. Look at your poor wife, harried out of her wits by savages. And in the end we had to settle things for you, send over good English lads to die in your pestilent bogs. Always the same. Cromwell had to go over, and William after him. There is treason in that air; it is bred into men's bones. What did the rebels want?"

"They could not even speak English, most of them. The King was a word to them, they did not know where England was. They have their own language, music, customs."

"What did they want?"

"I do not believe that they knew. They followed a banner of green silk. They had prophecies and superstitions. There were stories that a hero would come from France to save them. They may have had him confused with the Young Pretender. They were punished most dreadfully. There are gallows from one end of Mayo to the other. They are a leaderless people."

"Let them bide at home, and no harm will come to them. Let them heed their landlords. Let them look to the great houses."

It was no use. I looked out the window at the snow-covered landscape. The village rooftops were visible. I thought of the village inn, curtains at the windows, prints on the wall, rows of pewter tankards. And then I remembered Castlebar High Street, a mean laneway straggling toward courthouse and gaolhouse, toward gibbeted bodies. Memory carried me northward from Castlebar, a vault of sky arching toward blue mountains. I saw the beggars on the road. I remembered a barn at nightfall, the sounds of fiddles, feet on the hard-packed earth. I saw the army of the Gael swarming into Killala, ragged, unshaven, boisterous in an unknown and barbarous tongue. It was no use.

No one, it would appear, knows how many Irish there are, and few care to know. This I discovered with the assistance of William Clifford, the vicar of Nicholas's church, a young man of scholarly bent and of decent family, near-sighted and with a companionable stoop. Several evenings did I spend in his modest but well-appointed house, refreshed by his gentle good spirits and those of his wife. He knew as little of Ireland as did Nicholas, but he possessed a fund of Christian sympathy and a small library. As to the population of Ireland, he believed that I might find what I sought in a book which had been published in that very year of 1798, and he pressed it upon me, commending it as a salutary Christian response to Rousseau and Godwin, reminding us of the inevitably melancholy nature of our earthly existence.

In fact, he lent me that evening two books which had appeared in that fateful year, of which one was a volume of verses, some of which were pretty enough in their way, although strained and artificial in their very effort to appear natural; but there was also a long and ludicrous ballad or "rime," in which a sailor slays a large bird with an arrow, for which apparently heinous offense he is pursued around the world by all the powers of hell and his shipboard companions perish miserably. All this set forth in a wearisome style of false innocence and simplicity.

The chief work which he lent to me was not this flight of fancy, but an *Essay on the Principle of Population*, by an acquaintance of his, a newly ordained clergyman named Malthus. Mr. Malthus began simply enough, by demonstrating that populations will always grow at a rate swifter than that of the food which they require, unless checks be placed upon their growth. These checks he divided between the positive and the negative, of which the former included famines, plagues, and pestilences. What an awful vista his words opened up! I could not force myself to accept the inevitability of his argument, yet try as I would I could not escape from it. It was as though, like some darker Newton, he had hit upon a formula which had for centuries lain hidden just beyond the edges of men's minds. Clear and cold as iced water, it clarified and chilled the brain. And all set forth with an air of unimpassioned calm which contrasted most vividly with his abominable conclusions.

I would have thought that Ireland, with its centuries of recurring famines, was well suited to his thesis, but I sought for it in vain. His first volume ranged over the entire world, and brought before our consideration the naked wretches of Tierra del Fuego and Van Diemen's Land, the yet more wretched savages of the Andaman Islands, the paint-bedaubed warriors of North America, the furry Laplanders, the horsemen of the Asian steppes. But of Ireland, which lay at Mr. Malthus's doorstep, there was not a word, until I came to the very last page, where tersely he informs the reader that the natives are too barbarous to admit of counting up their numbers. And then he adds: "The checks upon the population are of course of the positive kind, and arise from the diseases occasioned by squalid poverty, by damp and wretched cabins, by bad and insufficient clothing, by the filth of their persons, and occasional want. To these positive checks have of late years been added the vice and misery of intestine commotion, of civil war, and of martial law." He says not a word more, and his disdain was painful to contemplate. All that I had witnessed, all that tumult and passion, that confusion and blood, were but checks upon population. The dead in the streets of Killala, the obscene weights upon the Castlebar gibbet, the peasants hunted down in the Belmullet wastes, had contributed their lives to an equation. The Irish, it would appear, were doomed to an endless sequence of spawning and starving, spawning and starving.

"It is a most salutary and Christian work," young Mr.

Clifford assured me. "Mr. Malthus reminds us that man is not a perfectible creature. He strives blindly to propagate his kind, but the very laws of nature press down upon him. There is no salvation within nature or within society. I need not remind you of that."

"As it is now," I said, "even without famine, the poor are reduced each winter to beggary. Oh, Mr. Clifford, if you could but see them! And we sit snug in our warm houses."

He then described to me a tract society, newly founded in London, which proposed to distribute Bibles in the west of Ireland, for which purpose sums of money had been collected and agents hired. I did not know whether to cry or laugh.

"But they cannot read," I said. "They do not speak English. What folly is this, what new folly? It would serve as well to cram pages of the Testament into bottles and cast them on the waters to drift to Africa and the Sandwich Islands. Better still, let them translate Mr. Malthus into Gaelic, and thus instruct the poor that they starve by theorem and die to conclude a syllogism."

He was abashed by this, for as I have said he was a good-hearted young man. But he could only rub his hands together, as though washing them.

"What would you have?" he asked at last. "I know nothing of these matters. Perhaps they are indeed inevitable, as Malthus suggests. We must seek to clothe the naked, to feed the hungry. We must be charitable."

"With great caution," I said satirically. "Malthus warns us that unbridled philanthropy can be perverse or even wicked, interfering with the operations of a system nicely calculated to maintain a population upon the edge of grinding misery."

"You are too hard upon him," he said. "Too hard upon yourself."

Dark musings in a season of Christmas joy: I did not long dwell upon them. And yet nagging memories remained with me of the land which I had left, to which I would again return. Clifford's evasive delicacies, my brother's gruff indifference reminded me that the world did not share my concern. Derbyshire was my warm winter blanket, thicker than the snow, woven of childhood memories, certitudes, good cheer. Here I was not an alien, but moved once again among my own, their accents mine, their habits mine. What need had a Derbyshire squire to know the population of Ireland, or a Derbyshire parson to take upon himself the burdens of a foreign island? Thus, and most comfortably did I reason with myself.

Lord Glenthorne, however, was a different matter, and I still remember, with something akin to horror, my conversation with him. In that hour with him, seated side by side in a quiet London room, lies the meaning of what I experienced, and yet I cannot puzzle it out, an oblique meaning, set at a grotesque angle. I may be mistaken. Truth baffles us. We seek it out in vain, and then it leaps upon us and we are unprepared.

I had resolved that I should visit him on my way back to Ireland, for, as I have said, he had the benefice of my parish. I knew that he would welcome an account of events which so closely touched his interests. He had already received from Dennis Browne an account of the murder of Creighton, his agent, and of the damage wrought upon Glenthorne Castle by the insurgents. But letters are cold instruments, they convey little. Accordingly, I wrote to him of my wish and in due course received a civil reply: "My compliments. I am at home every afternoon. Glenthorne."

On the afternoon of the eighth, therefore, I presented myself at his door. The house was by no means prepossessing, built of pink bricks with bow windows overlooking the park. A servant girl opened the door, simply attired, and with her hair caught beneath a mobcap. She showed me into a small sitting room, sparsely furnished, and dominated by two works of art, an ill-executed oil painting of a Highland stag standing in lonely eminence upon a crag and a large cheap engraving of Abraham and Isaac. I seated myself upon a small upholstered chair, which sent up a puff of dust.

This, then, was the dwelling place of the legendary ruler of Tyrawley, an absolute monarch, the "Big Lord." A simple London house, not footmen but a servant girl in a mobcap, walls decorated in a manner which a Dublin grocer would find coarse. I was not surprised. Friends in London had informed me that he was known there not for his wealth or his power but for his benevolence, being a prime mover in the Society for the Amelioration of the Condition of Chimney Sweeps, and a generous contributor to that most worthy of causes, the Society for the Abolition of Slavery.

625

He did not keep me waiting longer than five minutes, and then entered to greet me with simplicity and cordiality, taking my hands in his two. He was a small, bent man, dressed in a suit the color of snuff, with a long, thin nose and full lips.

"You are most welcome, Mr. Broome," he said. "Most welcome. It is seldom enough that I have a visitor from Ireland. That unhappy land has been much upon my mind these past months, much upon my mind. As you can readily believe."

"Most readily," I assured him.

"Come into my library, Mr. Broome. Into my library. It will be a pleasant place to talk, and we have much to tell each other. Much to tell." His habit of repeating phrases needlessly was a settled one. It was as though he spoke once for my ear, and once for his own, telling himself what he had said. A harmless mannerism.

But at the door he hesitated and turned. "Do you see that fireplace there?" It was small, with a trim white mantel above it. "Do you know that fireplace for what it is, a place and instrument of oppression?"

"Of oppression, Lord Glenthorne?"

"Oppression as foul as any in our time. The chimney sweeps of London would break your heart. Little lads of nine, eight, seven. Angels some of them, for all their filthy clothes and filthy faces, faces streaked black as the pit. Little chaps led from place to place by their masters like trained monkeys, taught to clamber up chimneys so narrow that their poor shoulders and hips are scraped raw. Fires lit below them if they don't make haste, or if their cries are too loud. And then cast out into the world in a few years' time. But some of them never grow too big. They die. The soot gets into their lungs. In time it chokes them to death. Their poor lungs coated with soot. A surgeon of Guy's Hospital has explained the process."

"That is indeed horrible," I said. And so it is, but I could not think what more to say.

"Horrible," he agreed. "It will cease, Mr. Broome. We shall make it cease. Their infamous masters will be brought low. The little boys are raised without God, their speech is abominable. Little girls as well. Little girls have been set to the task. The souls and bodies of children destroyed so that we may sit in comfort at our fires. It is monstrous."

"Monstrous," I said.

"And in Ireland? Is it the same there?"

"In Dublin, perhaps. I cannot say. A man comes round to my palace once a year with his son and his brushes, but the boy does not seem ill used. The small farmers have a simpler method, they use birds. Birds are their chimney sweeps."

He peered at me with large, pale eyes. "That is not a jest? They use birds? Birds for chimney sweeps?" He laughed, a dry cackle. "I would believe anything about Ireland."

"I wish you well in your efforts," I said. "The sweeps are badly used. It is time that thought was given to them."

"It is, Mr. Broome. High time. And we shall succeed. Men of consequence are joining us. Godly men."

He led me to a small, crowded room overlooking a garden. Trees and bushes were leafless and stark. Two walls were lined with books, and a long table, running almost the length of the room, was strewn with papers. Papers were stacked beside the two armchairs which faced each other in front of a cold fireplace. He waved me into one, and then himself sat down and rested his hands on his thin knees. "Your palace, you said, Mr. Broome. Surely you do not live in a palace?"

"Only in a manner of speaking. You may recall that Killala was once an episcopal diocese. My house was then the palace, and it is still called so. But in fact it is a modest residence, though most comfortable." Which I myself was not, for the room was cold and it was with difficulty that I suppressed a shiver.

"I am glad to hear that. That it is comfortable, to be sure, but more especially that it is modest."

"It is more than sufficient for our needs," I said. "Mrs. Broome has made it most pleasant. We have no family."

"That is good," he said. "It is good that you are married. A celibate clergy is one of the curses under which the Papists of Ireland suffer. The Papists of all countries. The priests of the early Christian centuries were married. You know that, of course."

"Yes," I said. "I know that. But the Irish priests are strict in the observance of their vows. There are few of the scandals so common in Mediterranean countries."

"My wife died in childbirth," he said, as if I had not spoken, "and my child with her. It was a boy. I never

627

remarried. We are not a fruitful line. I was an only child."

I could find nothing to say to that.

"Had they lived, my own life might have been different. I might have moved more in the world. I am more effective now by far. The chimney sweeps, the slaves. Human slavery, Mr. Broome. Here, in Africa, in America. Entire African villages herded upon their death ships, crossing the ocean to a life worse than death. Their owners deny them the Scriptures. They live and die as pagans. But they have souls. He died for all men. There are many kinds of slavery. The little London sweep, the black man in the fields of Virginia. Do you smoke?"

"No," I said. "It makes me ill."

"I am pleased. It is the leaf of slavery. Bales of tobacco leaf stacked up on our docks, rank with the sweat of black slavery. God waits for us to act. We have the power to sweep the slaver from the seas."

"It is a monstrous evil," I said. "No Christian should support it."

"They do," he said. "By their silence. By their inactivity. I intend to accomplish good, Mr. Broome. Great good. My father did not. He was a sinful man and a pleasure-loving man. Marbles, paintings, rich foods, women, and sins worse than those with women. Do you follow me? Far worse than those with women. I am not spreading scandal. He was notorious. You have heard of him."

"I have visited Glenthorne Castle," I said. "I was a friend of poor Mr. Creighton. It is lovely, a fairybook palace, like a child's dream of the *Arabian Nights*."

"It was shaped by vanity and voluptuousness. Like his villa in Italy. It was worse in Italy. Bricks the color of sunset, a balcony looking beyond oceans of roses to the distant sea. A village could have been fed upon his clothes alone, silks and broadcloths. He used scent. When he bent down to kiss me, it would smother me in its sweetness. All the filth of the world was carried to me upon my father's kiss."

I could not become accustomed to the room's chill. It could not have been much colder in the bare-branched garden.

"I was greatly disturbed by the news of Mr. Creighton's death," I said. "He was a fair man, a just man."

"Just?" Lord Glenthorne asked, "Which of us is just?

He was a practical man, and middling honest. The agents before him were hopeless, thieves and drunkards. You speak of his death. You mean his murder, of course. I have a letter here from Browne."

He leaped to his feet, agile and monkeylike, and rummaged among the papers on the table with one hand, while with the other he fitted a pair of spectacles. "It is here. An atrocious crime. He was run through with pikes. Over and over again. After he had been killed. Bestial."

"We have endured much in Mayo these past months," I said. "All of us have. Rich and poor alike."

But Glenthorne did not hear me. He was reading the letter, his forefinger moving swiftly over the lines. His lips moved silently.

"You were held prisoner in your own house," he said. "Your palace. A wonder you were not murdered, like Creighton."

"I might easily have been," I said. "I owed my safety to one of the rebel leaders, one of your own tenants. He was killed in the fighting."

"I can form no picture of Mayo in my mind," he said. "I see bogland, mountains, a straggling coastline, mean villages. I do not even know the number of people on my lands. Is that not absurd? Years ago, Creighton made the attempt, but he gave it up. He sent me maps, pretty things."

He led me to the map, hung behind the table, in an oak frame. At first I could recognize nothing, then I made out Killala and Ballina, mountains, bogs, the Moy moving past Ballina toward the sea, pasturelands, plantations, the outline of the Glenthorne demesne, the castle.

"Each of those dots is a cabin." Glenthorne said. "Many of them on two acres or three. But he abandoned the task. There are people squatting upon the barren wastes of the mountains. They can pay no rent. How do they live?"

"In great misery," I said. "For part of each year they go hungry and are driven by want onto the roads. Now. In midwinter."

"Horrible," he said. "Horrible."

"He made a kind of model of the estate," I said, "on a table as large as this one. Papier-mâché mountains and bits of glass for lakes. It was quite lovely, like a toy village built for children." A toy world. I did not add that by common report he had been slain upon that table, forced backward upon it by Duggan's mob, his blood streaming down paper mountains.

"It is a great responsibility," he said. "I have been remiss. I have governed them through agents. I cannot bear to go there. That sinful monument to vanity and lust rising up amidst such misery, feeding upon it. My rents are all Irish rents now, you know. We had several estates here, small ones, but I have sold them off. There is so much that must be done, so much good that must be accomplished. I live simply. You can see that I do."

"They know nothing of you there. Where you live, what you want of them. They never speak of you by name. Only as the Big Lord."

He turned away from the map and peered at me sharply. "Do they? The Big Lord?"

"That would be the English of it. It is a Gaelic word."

"They do not speak English," he said. "He told me that. Gaelic-speaking peasants. Papists, sunk in superstition and idolatry. Something went wrong, centuries ago. I know little about Irish history. They have no written records, no history."

"They have needs," I said. "Needs of soul and of body."

He reached out his hand as though to touch my shoulder, then withdrew it. "I chose well," he said. "It is well that they have in their midst a proper emissary of Christ. God send that I can find a proper agent. It is an exacting responsibility. All this." He swung his hand around toward the map. "I will be remiss no longer. I promise you. Poor Creighton had his plans at first, in the early years. I have them somewhere among my papers. Model villages, schools for the children that they may learn sobriety and English. As you say, they have needs of both body and soul. They must learn proper methods of agriculture and husbandry. He had schemes for the reclamation of the bogs, but I told him that they would be too costly. I have been remiss."

Behind his gold-encircled spectacles, his eyes were large and flat, a blue light as the heavens. I was taken aback by his enthusiasm. He held out his hand again, and this time placed it upon my arm, lightly. I felt it there, soft, like a branch from the garden, bare of leaf.

"There is much that could be done," I said. "Life there must surely be as hard as it is anywhere in the world." His words should have exhilarated me, filled me with a wild hope, but they did not. I felt confused and apprehensive. His mild, shielded eyes stirred a faint fear.

"I will find the proper man," he said. "I would not know how to go about the task." His grip tightened upon me. "Savages clinging to mountain wastes, uncounted, unnumbered, nameless. They must go. The estate must be reduced to its proper population. There must be fewer farms and larger ones. There must be a maximum yield. There are ways of providing for this. If the rents are raised, there will be an incentive for the industrious ones. They are not hopeless, they are the children of God, as you and I are."

"They must go?" I asked. My words fell flat upon my ears. "They must go? What do you mean?"

"Grain and cattle," he said, as if he had not heard me. "Sheep-walks. It has been said that Ireland can become England's granary. There have been books and pamphlets upon the subject. Arthur Young. A man named Edgeworth."

"There is nowhere for them to go," I said. I pulled my arm free. "Why else would they live in hovels? You must surely learn more about the country. It is urgent that you do so. You could place them under a sentence of death."

"There are other mountains," he said. "Other bogs. Let them find them." He rubbed his hand, as though I had bruised it. "They are my lands, you know. I intend to improve them. I bear them no ill will. They rose up in rebellion and they murdered but I bear them no ill will. They are children. Disobedient."

I had a sudden, sharp recollection of the Glenthorne demesne, the endless walls of dressed stone, a vista stretching as far as the eye could see, the Italianate castle, mysterious in its loneliness and its exotic beauty. I saw Creighton bending over his model of the estate, a near-sighted, fussy man. He was shaking his head.

He walked away from me toward the window, and then turned.

"I am certain that you will not misunderstand me, Mr. Broome. You see how I live. My wants are simple. The wealth is drawn off from that unfortunate country by those who live in wanton riotousness, in sinfulness. Misery yields up marbles and brocades. I am not an orthodox Christian, but my will to do good is very powerful. I have spoken to you of the blackened children of London, the slaves chained like animals in ships. There are others. Girls are compelled to sell their bodies upon the streets, in vile cribs. Girls of twelve and thirteen. By their mothers. Little boys, to satisfy unnatural lusts. It is all one, a seamless garment of greed and cruel pleasures. I will use my wealth for good, to free souls from slavery that they may seek salvation."

He stood with his back to the thin sun of a winter afternoon. His pale hair seemed translucent, an aureole.

"Surely, then," I said, "you would not want to bring more misery upon those who depend upon you for their very existence. You do not know them, but they depend upon you utterly." They spoke of him as the Big Lord.

"There are laws," he said. "Laws of supply and demand, of property, of the market-place, laws of commodities. I did not make them. I must have wealth if I am to do good, much wealth if I am to do much good. There will be schoolhouses there, model villages. We shall reclaim the bogs. You will be there to see it. I envy you."

"I pray that I will not see it," I said. "Most earnestly do I pray." And I then said, though more to myself than to him, "They will never know why. They will be swept from their hovels and they will never know why. I could not describe this room to them, they would not understand your words."

"A foolish title," he said. "The Big Lord. Beware vanity."

I took my leave of him, but he did not reply, though he was staring at me. I looked again at the map. From that distance, it seemed a cluster of random lines, straight and curving, clumps of brown ink. I could not see the dots, encoded habitations. He spoke to me as my hand touched the door.

"If you see a sweep, you should give a shilling to him. I keep them in my pocket for the purpose. But you must be sly. If the master sees you, he will take it from him later."

In the hall, the maidservant stopped me, a hand again upon my arm. "Is he excited, sir?" she asked.

"Excited? He is animated. Is that what you mean?"

She was a girl, but strongly built. Her muscular arms pressed against the black fabric of her sleeves. There was the beginning of a double chin above a thick throat, a

632

faint dark down upon her upper lip. Her eyes were alert and intelligent.

"Yes, sir. I think so. Excited."

From behind the closed door his voice carried to us in short, nervous bursts of speech. I could not make out the words.

"Is he often excited?" I asked her.

"He becomes excited," she said, "but after a while he grows quiet and unhappy. He goes to bed then. I keep brandy at his bedside, but he seldom takes it."

And yet none of Glenthorne's ambitious and dreadful plans have been put into practice. Perhaps it was a passing fancy, or perhaps upon reflection he concluded that the task was too formidable, or perhaps other, weightier matters pressed themselves upon his attention. To the peasants he remains the Big Lord, remote, unimaginable, motiveless. Perhaps they are right. In the event, he appointed an agent recommended to him by Dennis Browne, a Limerick man named Chute who had managed an extensive estate near Askeaton. The peasants think of him as grasping and tyrannous, but he seems to me decent enough, a rider to hounds and an occasional churchgoer. He manages the Glenthorne lands skillfully if lazily, and evictions are infrequent. He has made no efforts to reclaim the bogs or to establish schools.

He sends his quarterly reports to Glenthorne, who replies with a series of shrewd questions and remarks upon particulars, and then proceeds to a homily upon the responsibilities of landlords and their agents. Several times, the homily has been extended to many pages of spidery script and has branched out upon other matters, the conditions necessary for salvation and the temptations which great wealth carries in its wake. Chute has pressed me for my impressions of Glenthorne, but I cannot trust myself to do justice to these. "Will he ever visit the estate?" he asks. "No, I am quite certain that he will not. It has melancholy associations." "It is an extraordinary situation," Chute says; "whenever he chooses he may overturn my methods." "Let us pray that he does not," I say.

I believe that Glenthorne is mad, the unobtrusive madness which rubs along agreeably enough with the rest of the world and is accounted eccentricity or even saintliness. And yet the policies which he sketched out for me in his excited manner have also been brought forward by the lucid intelligences of our age, progressive and forward-looking men. Would not Mr. Malthus applaud so vigorous a determination to adjust population to land? Glenthorne is the absent center of our Mayo world and the estate is his tarnished Eden. Like the Lord of Creation, he is everywhere and nowhere, center and circumference. What right have I to think of him as mad? Many men speak to themselves behind closed doors. I have done so myself.

When Nicholas and I were children we received as the Christmas gift of our uncle a hollow glass globe within which rested a village—tiny houses and shops and a steepled church, a river with a bridge across it, a pond. When we shook it, the village would vanish within a snow-storm. White flecks would fill the globe. Then, slowly, the globe would clear, snow would drift down upon houses and pond, and at last there would be only the village, always the same but always looking slightly different, because we had not the wits to keep every part of it firm in our memories. When I held the globe, I felt like Almighty God—sky, village, storm of snow lay within my two cupped hands. But it was imprudent of our uncle to give the one gift to two small boys. One day we fell to quarreling over it, and it slipped between our hands and fell to the floor and shattered. We poked at the bits with our fingers, and our grief ebbed. It had been nothing, a toymaker's trick—bits of mirror for river and pond, pieces of colored wood, a white powder.

So too, perhaps, the map upon Glenthorne's wall, Chute's quarterly reports, the model of the estate which stretched across Creighton's table. Ingenious toys. Mayo is its own world, affirming a reality of tree and stone, river and mountain. I hear its music now, as once, when first I came here, I could not. A footfall upon frozen earth, the belling of hounds upon an autumn morning, the cry of a curlew, the scraping of a fiddle, lowing of cattle, voices beneath my window—when sounds, random but familiar, fall into place within the mind, they become a music. I would be lonely now without that music.

I remain an alien here, and will be so always. Without malice, Mayo excludes me. It is an old land, and hugs its secrets. At evening, if the weather is good, I walk down the street of gray, drab buildings until at last the bay is in sight, its waters sluggish, gunmetal in color, or the color of a tarnished pike. The distant hills are low, crouched like

634

animals. When I pass cowherd or fisherman, we nod, exchange greetings in our different tongues. Their faces are not mine, large-boned, long of lip, coarse, matted hair. Then I will turn and walk back to my residence, where tea will be awaiting me before the fire. Heavy curtains will be drawn, to hold back the limitless silences of the Mayo night. We know parts of a world only, parts of a history, shards, bits of broken pottery.

From the Diary of Sean MacKenna, Summer, 1799

July 2. To Killala yesterday, astride a gentle horse lent to me by Robinson the farrier, to receive bolts of linen from Sligo which were waiting for me at the quay. It was a lovely day, the kind of morning that Owen and the other poets write about, the meadows green and the hedgerows glistening. It wanted but a maiden to walk toward me across the meadows and it would be the proper beginning for a poem, but it is only to poets that maidens come. And to those fellows they come all too often, is my own opinion of the matter, for many of those poems are wearisome things, if the truth be told.

For part of the journey I had the company of a peddler from Athlone, a talkative, harmless fellow with a carbuncle the size of a baby's fist. He had much to tell me about Athlone, but little that was of interest and nothing at all that is worth recording here. In a field beyond a cross we spied a Norman keep, and I decided to take a closer look at it, for I have a great curiosity about such things. At the boreen I parted company with the peddler, without much regret, for his company was not worth the price of his chatter. Athlone was the center of his world, although he was a traveled man and should have known better. Certain towns have that effect upon the mind; Sligo is one such and Ennis is a third.

But close to, there was little to say in the keep's favor. The far side had fallen in. I tried to imagine how it had looked centuries before, but I could not. We are cut off from those ancient days as if divided by the deep ocean. It was but a byre now, and served its purpose. Then I saw that far beyond the keep, hidden from the main road by a plantation, stood a big house. I walked closer, and as I approached the entrance gate I saw that the house had been destroyed by fire. It was but a gutted shell, with the windows staring at me. Above the door was an ornate seal of some sort, scorched black by flames. Through the doorway I could see an entrance hall burned bare of wood and plaster, its brick and stone blackened. It was an ugly, crippled giant, its shame shielded by the plantation.

When I got back onto the main road I met a drover, and asked him what place it was. "Fountain Hall," he said. "It is a shocking wreck," I said. "It is," he said, "but there is good stone in it." "How was it burned?" I asked him. "It was burned last year," he said, "in the time of the French." "Was it the French burned it?" "I wouldn't know," he said, "most likely it was." "Go to God," I said, "you have been living all your life in the shadow of that thing, but you don't know what happened to it last year." He beat the switch he was carrying against his leg and studied me. At last he said, "There are some who say that it was burned by the local people. There was terrible destruction between here and Killala. There was a man called General Duggan." General Duggan, indeed; in a few years' time they will all have been generals. "Whose house was it?" I asked him. "They are a family called Morrison. They fled off to Sligo and from there to England or to Dublin. 'Tis said that they will never come back. They are terrible tyrants."

He was a young man and heavyset, with sloping shoulders and long arms like Owen's. I wondered what he had himself been busy at in the summer of 'ninety-eight.

"If you have an interest in such matters," he said, "they will show you the strand where the French landed. Kilcummin strand, it is called. There were three great ships with masts so tall that you could not see the tops of them and on the tallest mast of all was an eagle called King Lewis. That eagle went all the way with them into the midlands, but on the night before the battle the eagle flew off and the battle was lost."

"That eagle was a wise bird," I said. He stared at me for a moment and then grinned. "By God, it was," he said. "And for all the good it did," I said, "it might never have happened. The French and the ships and all the rest of it." "I would not say that," he said; "they burned Fountain Hall. They drove out the Morrisons." It is an ill wind, as the proverb in English has it.

Killala is a most uncouth village, and listless as well,

with none of the bustle you will find in Castlebar and no fine buildings. Mean shops are clustered about the estuary, and beyond the sea is gray. I attended to my business and then for Owen's sake had two tumblers of whiskey at the Wolf Dog, of which he had often spoken to me. It is not a proper tavern at all, of the sort that may be found in Castlebar, but a cabin where laborers and fishermen drink, and yet he had told me that it was a place for a quiet and pleasant evening. He was a laborer's son when all is said, for all the splendor of his fancy and the radiant embellishment of his verses. He could be at ease in such company, with never a thought for his art or for his standing as a man of learning.

It was late in the afternoon that I left Killala, passing as I rode up the street Mr. Broome, the Protestant clergyman, a small plump man of middle years, with well-made clothes worn carelessly, his neckbands askew, and a shovel hat perched awkwardly upon an old-fashioned wig. He walked rapidly with a light step, almost a skip, and with his hands clasped behind his back. Although he does not know me, he said "Good evening" most readily. I was tempted to begin a conversation with him, but did not know if he would welcome it. It is a lonely enough life of it he must have, with most of his parishioners living upon estates distant from the town.

Nothing worthy of record during my return to Castlebar, which I reached at nightfall. The soldiers have for months been gone from Mayo, save for the garrison here in the town, and they are but memories now, like the French. As I rode past Stoballs Hill in the darkness, I attempted to imagine what the great battle there had been like, the drums and bright banners and cannon shot and shouting. I could not. I told myself that the battle already lay with the Norman keep upon the far shore of that sea which separates past from present. But that is not true, there is no such sea, it is but a trick of speech. All are bound together under God, mountain, and bog, the shattered fortress and the grassy pasturelands of death, the drover's eagle that took wing upon the eve of battle, memory, history, and fable. A trick of speech and of the blackness of night, when we are separated from one another and from the visible world. It is in the brightness of the morning air, as the poets tell us, that hope and memory walk toward us across meadows, radiant as a girl in her first beauty.

July 3. The linen which I brought back with me from Killala is badly bleached, and I will think carefully before I have further dealings with Johnston of Sligo.

FINIS

Principal Characters

The Narrators

Broome, Arthur Vincent. Clergyman of the Established Church in Killala, County Mayo.

Elliott, Judith. Wife to Malcolm.

Elliott, Malcolm. Master of "The Moat," Ballina, County Mayo. Solicitor. Member of the Society of United Irishmen.

MacKenna, Sean. Schoolmaster and draper in Castlebar, County Mayo.

Wyndham, Harold. Aide to Lord Cornwallis.

The Characters

Barrett, Patrick. An officer of the rebel forces in Killala.

Broome, Eliza. Wife to Arthur Vincent.

Broome, Nicholas. Gentleman of Derbyshire. Brother to Arthur Vincent.

Browne, Dennis. Master of "Woodlands," Newport, County Mayo. Member of Parliament for Mayo. High Sheriff of Mayo. Brother to Lord Altamont (later the Marquis of Sligo).

Browne, Sarah. Niece to Dennis.

Conlon, Judy. Farmer's widow in Killala. Woman to Owen MacCarthy.

639

Cooper, Kate. Wife to Samuel. Daughter to Mick Mahony, grazier.

Cooper, Captain Samuel. Master of "Mount Pleasant," Killala. Commander of the Killala Yeomanry.

Cornwallis, Charles, Marquis. Viceroy of Ireland. Commander in chief of British forces in Ireland.

Crauford, Colonel John. British commander of dragoons.

Creighton, Andrew. Agent to Lord Glenthorne, Marquis of Tyrawley.

Cumiskey. Physician in Carrick, County Leitrim. Prisoner after battle of Ballinamuck.

Dennistoun, Hans. Gentleman-farmer of Granard, County Longford. Member of the Society of United Irishmen. Commander of rebel forces in the midlands.

Duignan, Anthony. A "prophecy man" wandering through County Mayo in September.

Duggan, Malachi. Farmer in Killala. Chief of the "Whiteboys of Killala."

Edgeworth, Maria. Daughter to Richard Lovell. Future author of *Castle Rockrent* and *Ormand.*

Edgeworth, Richard Lovell. Master of "Edgeworthstown House," County Longford. Member of Parliament for Longford.

Falkiner, George. Master of "Rosenalis House," Killala.

Falvey, Hugh. Blacksmith in Drumkeerin, County Sligo.

Fontaine, Colonel Louis Octave. Subordinate to General Humbert.

Halloran, Patrick. Physician. Member of Dublin Executive, Society of United Irishmen.

Hennessey, Donal. Farmer in Killala. An organizer of the "Whiteboys of Killala."

Humbert, General Jean-Joseph. Commander of French expeditionary army to Ireland.

Hussey, Roger. Parish priest at Killala.

Hutchinson, Major General John Hely. Commander of British forces in Connaught.

Kirwan, Ellen. Housekeeper and mistress to Richard Manning.

Lake, General Gerard. Commander of British forces in the field.

Laverty, Martin. Poet. Schoolmaster in Drumshanbo, County Leitrim.

MacCarthy, Owen Ruagh. Poet. Schoolmaster in Killala. Formerly of Tralee, County Kerry, and Macroom, County Cork.

MacDonnell, Grace. Half-sister to Randall.

MacDonnell, Randall. Gentleman farmer and horse breeder of Ballycastle, County Mayo. Officer in the rebel army.

MacKenna, Brid. Wife to Sean.

MacNally, Leonard. Dublin barrister. Member of the Society of United Irishmen. Government informer.

MacTier, Samuel. Linen merchant in town of Sligo. Member of the Society of United Irishmen.

Maguire, Roger. An officer of the Killala rebels. Cousin to Ferdy O'Donnell.

Manning, Richard. Master of "Castle Harmony," Tobercurry, County Sligo.

Matthews, Mark. British consul in Florence. Travel writer and watercolorist.

Millett. Captain of militia serving under General Lake.

Moore, George. Master of "Moore Hall," Ballintubber, County Mayo. Historian and essayist.

Moore, John. Younger brother to George. Member of the Society of United Irishmen.

Murphy, John. Curate to Mr. Hussey in Killala. Later, chaplain to the rebels.

O'Carroll, Phelim. Farmer in Killala. An organizer of the "Whiteboys of Killala."

O'Donnell, Ferdy. Farmer in Kilcummin, County Mayo. Later, commander of rebel forces in Killala.

O'Dowd, Cornelius. Gentleman farmer of Enniscrone, County Sligo. Officer in the rebel army.

O'Kane. "Captain" in the rebel forces at Killala.

Quigley, Matthew. Tavernkeeper in Kilcummin. An organizer of the "Whiteboys of Killala."

Reagan, Francis. Captain in the rebel army of the midlands. Sometime common soldier in the army of King Louis.

Russell, John. Member of the Dublin Executive, Society of United Irishmen. Government informer.

Sarrizen, Colonel Jean. Subordinate to General Humbert.

Saunders, Hilton. Mayo landlord.

Sinclair. Lieutenant in the British forces at Ballinamuck.

Taylor, General Robert. Commander of British forces in Enniskillen.

Teeling, Bartholemew. Member, Society of United Irishmen. Officer on Humbert's staff.

Tompkins, Robert. Sergeant in the Killala Yeomanry.

Tone, Theobald Wolfe. Dublin barrister. Emissary from the Society of United Irishmen to the French Directory.

Treacy, Ellen. Daughter of Thomas.

Treacy, Thomas. Master of "Bridge-end House," Ballycastle.

Trench, General·John. Commander of British forces in Galway.

Tyrawley, Lord Glenthorne, Marquis of. The "Big Lord."

Vesey, Dominick. Master of Carrick House, County Leitrim. Prisoner in Carrick after battle of Ballinamuck.

Waring, Oliver. Member of Dublin Executive, Society of United Irishmen.